The War God's Favorite

By Jenny Fox

Published by IngramSpark.
Made in United Kingdom
2021

First published in 2020.

Copyright © 2020 by Jenny Fox
Cover & Back Cover credit: GermanDesigns
ISBN-13: 978-1-8381097-2-1
ISBN-10: 978-1-8381097-3-8

Author Jenny Fox
Find me on Facebook & Instagram.

Contents

Acknowledgements

It is with the kind support of the AnyStories App Team, represented by my Editors Wynnie and Lacie, that I am able to complete this new book.

I also wish to thank the kind beta-readers & proofreaders who anonymously volunteered to help me prepare this story for its publishing.

I want to thank my friends and family for their unconditional love and support during the writing and publishing of this new story.

Finally, I want to thank you, dear reader, for accompanying me through this journey in the Dragon Empire. Thank you for supporting my stories, with your reading, kind comment and reviews.

To My Readers.

Chapter 1

The First Day of the Red Moon Festival.

The streets of the Capital were crowded with people from all over the country, as they all gathered near the Palace to celebrate. For the Dragon Empire, the Red Moon Festival was one of the biggest celebrations of the year, held to flaunt its power and wealth to the neighboring kingdoms. Every wealthy person in the country waited for this day, so they could display their riches, and those who weren't as prosperous found creative ways to appear to be. Warriors in shiny armor, officials in pretty carriages, women dripping in lavish jewelry, and even children in their best attire. If one had any assets, he was to proudly display them, or else, hide in shame. For in the Dragon Empire, money and possessions meant power and power was everything. In the middle of the crowd were those no one noticed, those no one cared for, following their masters with their eyes glued to the ground. Slaves.

Lines of slaves followed the processions of their masters in pitiful silence. Walking like shadows, the only sounds that could be heard were the clanking of their chains and shackles with each step they took. Among them, one young slave woman's eyes were not downcast like the rest. Hers were fixated on the blinding gold of the Palace roof.

The Palace. Earth's very own piece of Heaven. And while the people of the Capital may have been rich and powerful, there was a higher power above them all; the Emperor. Sovereign to all, the Emperor was the almighty, considered a living deity among mortals. With unrivaled power, he governed the country with an iron fist. No matter what, his word was law.

The Emperor never wanted for anything, as everything in the country was his already. He was loved, and worshiped by his people, but most importantly they knew to fear him. And on this Red Moon Festival, the Holy Gates of the Imperial Palace would be opened to those deemed worthy. A Palace envoy had gone out ten days earlier to deliver the coveted red envelopes; an invitation that any man would kill for.

The slave girl had watched her master hope and pray for this letter to arrive at his door. He was a Senior Minister, but even his seat at the court could not be guaranteed. He was so stressed that he had been treating his household even worse than usual; his concubines, his servants, and especially his slaves. The girl had a fresh lesion on her back, attesting to his restlessness. Even now, she could still feel the stinging burn of the whip.

Finally, the letter had come. So on the first day of the Red Moon Festival, the old Minister was headed to the Palace in an expensive-looking carriage escorted by his entourage. Seven of his favorite concubines followed in their own carriages, accompanied by their attendants, while twenty slaves walked behind them.

The young woman didn't care for all the festivities around her. They walked past delicious smelling food stalls that awoke the painfully empty stomachs of the slaves. Hers was empty too, but it hardly bothered her. She was used to the dull ache of prolonged hunger. She ignored the shops, the food, even the common people admiring their procession, and continued walking. As usual, the Minister was welcomed to the Palace. He casually discussed the upcoming events of the festival with his peers and showed off his young and beautiful concubines. For the commoners who could not enter the Palace, the festival was celebrated with grand parties held at the houses of the wealthy, and street shows and fairs. But for the chosen ones, many spectacular events and shows were to be displayed in the Palace's Grand Arena. The large plaza, built like a Colosseum, was big enough to seat a few thousand people. A portion of it had been cordoned off from the rest; a special box, facing south, was richly and lavishly decorated, waiting to welcome the Emperor, his family, and their attendants.

The slave girl had only heard rumors about what takes place in the large arena. Heavenly dances, chariot races, warrior fights, displays of mythical and bizarre creatures, elite performers... Anything that could not be witnessed by commoners was to be displayed for the Emperor and the most honorable guests of the Palace during the seven days of the festival.

For the first three days, she followed her master, attending to one of his concubines as usual. She didn't witness any of the shows, staying in the chambers to clean and await orders, speaking to no one. On the fourth day, the Minister's concubine suddenly sent her to be locked in a cold cage filled with other slaves. They were simply told that they had been taken from their masters to be given as offerings to the Emperor. The young woman stayed there for three more days, with no idea what was coming next. On the morning of the seventh day, all of the guests waited with bated breath. The last day of the festival was the only day where, along with the Emperor, all six Dragon Princes had to be present. For anyone attending the event, this was the sole opportunity each year to witness the whole Imperial Family together, as not all of the Princes lived in the Palace the rest of the year.

No one knew which one of these young men would succeed the Emperor. He was rumored to have his favorites, but had yet to name an official heir. From the firstborn to the youngest, any one of the Princes could one day rule the Empire. Choosing which Prince to support and please was the most difficult decision for the aristocracy to make. Fear of backing the wrong Prince and losing their position was always present.

The seventh day held great importance, for it was also the only day of the festival where the guests could see all of the Imperial dragons. The sacred beasts were feared by all, the very epitome of the power held by the Dragon Empire. Though the Emperor's Golden Dragon could be seen occasionally in the Palace, every guest was waiting for the astonishing sight of all the Imperial Dragons gathered in one place.

They started arriving, one by one, in the Grand Arena, each Prince was accompanied by his dragon. Three of them came from the sky, flying their magnificent beasts. The remaining Princes entered the arena by foot, their dragons following close behind them. The sight of the enormous, scaled creatures frightened most of the crowd, yet they could not bear to take their eyes off of them. Each dragon was at least eight times the size of a man, up to twelve or thirteen times for the largest of them. Two of the dragons were brought in cages, while the others were chained or muzzled.

For each of these dragons, three to ten servants came to guard them, but the last dragon was led completely free and unattended. He wore only a chain collar around his neck and he followed his master closely like an obedient dog. Leaving them in the center of the arena, the Princes, one after another, took their seats, all aligned on a broad platform beneath the Emperor's throne.

As the crowd chatted about the six beautiful creatures displayed in the arena, some of the Emperor's sons joined the conversations as well. The Fifth Prince was bragging about how he had fallen for a minister's concubine the previous day, and had eventually beheaded the old man so he could have them all.

"How many did you get in the end, brother?" asked the Second Prince with a sneer.

"Seven. But I don't need that many... I will only take the most beautiful of them!"

"How generous of you..." muttered the Fourth Prince, looking bored.

"How about you leave some beauties for our third brother?" the Second Prince jested. "He has yet to take any women in."

"Not all of us need that much company, brother," grumbled the youngest Prince in defence of his brother.

They all waited to hear their third brother's response, but were greeted with silence. He was the one who had arrived upon the unrestrained dragon. The enormous beast obediently stood still and the Prince's obsidian eyes were set on the arena, ignoring his siblings completely. His brothers stopped chatting and followed his gaze.

A hundred feet beneath them, a young man was introducing the upcoming show, the first of the day: an offering to the Imperial Dragons. Behind him, a large group of people were waiting to be sacrificed, surrounded by armed men. Any time one of them dared to cry out, the guards would lash out and whip them, cutting deep into their flesh. So the group remained silent. They were all condemned to death. Criminals, war prisoners, and slaves - each of them were condemned to die that day. Some of the slaves present formerly belonged to an old Minister. As their master had died, the people of the Palace had just decided to get rid of them, along with the other slaves that had been offered as tributes.

Among them was the young slave girl with emerald-green eyes. She had just turned seventeen this past winter, but had the manner and charms of a woman. She was a diamond amongst charcoal, beautiful despite the dust and grime covering her. Under the layer of dirt, she had very pale skin and was so thin that her bones were clearly defined and protruding beneath her dress. Her long, disheveled hair fell from her shoulders to her hips, like a waterfall. Her face was beautiful, diamond-shaped with a small nose and thin cheeks. Her lips had taken on a light pink shade due to the cold, which had also left her shivering. Her temple was sporting a cut crusted with dried blood and surrounded by fresh bruising. A remnant from a guard who had struck her earlier while pushing them into the arena. Her name was Cassandra.

Amongst the terrified crowd, Cassandra alone remained completely calm and silent. Everyone else around her was trembling with fear, trying to avoid the gazes of the enormous dragons. The six beasts surrounding them were obviously intrigued by the large group, and two of them were already ferociously growling.

It was a common and eagerly anticipated spectacle called "The Offering". The public waited enthusiastically to see the gruesome display as the six dragons would maul and kill people. None of them were even given a weapon to defend themselves because the beasts were considered as sacred as their masters. They were here to die in the most horrendous way possible, and solely for the entertainment of the Dragon Empire's finest subjects.

They all knew it. Some had tried to escape their fate and were killed on the spot. Those who remained were terrified, but they had no choice. How could they hope to survive this? The arena was fully enclosed and the lowest stairs still stood about thirty feet above them. Any second now, six winged monsters would hunt them down, even though one alone would have been enough to wipe them all out.

Someone from the Palace was announcing the upcoming entertainment, showering the Imperial Princes and their beasts with praise, pausing from time-to-time to let the crowd applaud and cheer loudly.

Yet, Cassandra could not hear a word he spoke. Too many people around her were crying or desperately praying. Most had their eyes on the dragons, wondering if they had any chance of escape. Some girls were even glancing up in the Princes' direction, hoping one might be enticed by their looks and save them.

In contrast to the hopeless despair around her, Cassandra was looking calmly towards the vast sky. It was a sunny morning with few clouds, but it was extremely cold. All she wore was an old shredded dress and chains showcasing her enslavement, but she didn't really care. Wasn't she about to die soon, anyway? Who would care about comfort or clothes now? Death was standing less than ten feet away, watching with six pairs of hungry eyes. All Cassandra wanted was for this massacre to end quickly.

Years of servitude had left her with no room for hope in her heart. The Minister was a cruel and violent man, and she had seen and suffered much worse before him too. Cassandra had been a slave for half of her life, witnessing more cruelty, hardship, and death than a girl her age should. Even now, the tight cuffs around her wrists were leaving her in pain. She envied the dead who were free from all the torment and suffering. Thankfully, soon, she would join them.

Her eyes came down to contemplate one of the beasts. The large, unchained dragon was the calmest of them all. As she was not scared, Cassandra couldn't help but think that it was truly a beautiful creature. This one had completely jet black scales that shone like diamonds, and crimson-colored eyes. Unlike its restless peers, this beast stood still, nonchalantly looking around. It did not care about the scared humans close by or the loud audience. The magnificent dragon seemed to sense her gaze, because he turned his huge head towards the group, and his eyes wandered until they found hers.

They both calmly studied each other, mesmerized by one another. She, a weak human, and it, a powerful beast that was meant to take her life.

The exchange caught the attention of someone else. From his seat, the Third Prince took a while to find what his dragon was observing so intensely. After a few minutes, he finally found the skinny figure among the crowd, and watched her too, intrigued. The young woman appeared to be very frail, pale, and scrawny. She wore a ragged dress, her long hair a tangled mess, and chains binding her neck and wrists. His fingers started slowly caressing the pommel of his sword. There was something intriguing about this woman that made it impossible for him to take his eyes off her, though he couldn't name what it was. It would be foolish of him anyways. That slave was about to die. So he averted his eyes and let go of any further thoughts of the woman.

Soon, the speech came to an end and the speaker left the arena. Some of the slaves started screaming in fear as the guards left them too. The dragons' cages were opened, though three of them were still chained and their movements restrained. Hell was unleashed in the arena, and the crowd went wild. The massacre had started. Slaves started running, trying to avoid the predators. But, one by one, they were pinned to the ground by gigantic claws or torn apart by enormous fangs. The dragons were not even bothering to eat the humans. They just played with them, chasing the living and fighting over the bodies. Blood and screams flew through the air as five of the gigantic beasts massacred their prey. The carnage went on for a few more minutes before anyone noticed that something was amiss. One of the dragons wasn't acting like its peers.

The darkest beast was walking very calmly towards a lone slave. That woman, too, was acting peculiar. Unlike the other slaves, she wasn't screaming, running around, or showing any signs of fear. No, the young woman was standing very still on the sand, her eyes focused on the large dragon that was slowly approaching. But the beast showed no hostility towards her, nor did it seem eager to attack.

With few remaining slaves still alive, the other dragons started to settle down or bicker between themselves. Thus, most of the crowd's attention was drawn to the strange duo. Whispers started to grow in the arena. How was that woman still alive? Why wouldn't the dragons attack and kill her like the other slaves? Everyone in the arena held their breath, waiting to see what the Black Dragon would do.

A hundred feet above, the six Princes were also watching the scene unfold with great interest. Their reactions to this unprecedented event varied. The Fifth and Sixth Princes were wondering how this woman escaped the beasts' wrath. The Second Prince was annoyed.

"Why won't they kill her?! Stop playing and finish that woman! Brother, have your dragon kill her!"

The Third Prince ignored him, his eyes fixed on his beast. He was staring intensely, waiting to see what his dragon would do.

The reason the others didn't attack was evident to him. That woman showed no fear, no sign of panic. To the dragons, she wasn't some prey to kill, maybe just a guard that had been left there. After all, this 'hunt' was just a game, why would they pursue a human that didn't play? There was no reason for them to care about that woman.

Only the Black Dragon showed any interest in the slave girl. Almost everyone in the audience thought it would finally kill her as it slowly approached, but once it was close to the young woman, it became obvious that they were mistaken. Far from attacking her, the dragon was visibly curious and stretched its head out to sniff her. The young woman barely reacted, she just continued to observe him as well.

What was going on? People were waiting, eager to see if this slave was going to be killed or not. The prior massacre had been completely forgotten; what was happening now was far more interesting. After a few more minutes, the dragon suddenly laid down, curling up around the woman like an obedient pet. The stunned crowd started whispering, a wave of shocked voices growing louder within seconds. Surprise at the exchange was evident among all the Princes. The Second Prince was, more than anything, infuriated.

"That woman is a witch! Let's kill her right now!" he yelled.

"How interesting... I have never seen anyone survive The Offering before,

14

but to think this frail woman would be able to stand next to the dragons..." said the First Prince.

"Enough! Brother! Order your dragon to-"

Before he could finish his sentence, he was left frozen by the Third Prince's ice-cold glare. The dark eyes scared him so much that he almost choked on his own words and quickly averted his eyes. The youngest prince chuckled.

"How bold of you, Brother Vrehan! Assuming you could actually give orders to the War God..."

He was absolutely right, but that only made the Second Prince flush red with anger. It was a well-known fact throughout the entire empire that out of the six Princes, the third-born was the best dragon-tamer.

Third Prince Kairen, whose perfect partnership with his black beast had allowed him to win many victories in the East for the Emperor as a General, and had earned himself the title of War God. There was no man stronger in the entire Dragon Empire, and certainly no man that could give him orders. Even the Emperor favored him greatly as the prodigal son. That was not the case for the Second Prince, and so he chose to remain silent. The First Prince Sephir, ignoring the short-lived dispute, was still observing the strange duo below.

"A witch...hmm... Whoever she is, brother, it appears your dragon is indeed under her spell. How interesting..."

He turned to observe his brother's reaction, but much to his surprise, the War God's eyes were already back to the arena. Kairen was contemplating over the woman who had subdued his dragon so easily. His fingers were still dancing on his sword. The Fifth Prince, Lephys, noticed it too.

"Brother Kairen, it seems like the dragon isn't the only one entranced. Could it be that the woman has also captured your attention? Judging from here, she isn't too ugly for a slave, is she?"

"Isn't this the first time our brother is showing any interest in a woman?" the youngest brother, Prince Anour, asked excitedly.

"Correct, Anour. Brother Kairen barely acknowledged any of the women he has been sent in the past. Well...other than to kill them," whispered Prince Lephys.

"What do you say, Kairen? Should we ask Father to spare this slave?" asked the First Prince, Sephir.

The Third Prince didn't answer. Instead, he stood up, his eyes still fixed on the arena. He was a very tall man, with tan skin, and large shoulders. A number of people in the audience looked his way, noticing that one of the Princes was standing. But he didn't care. The Black Dragon, still curled up around the woman, reacted to its master's stare. Suddenly raising its chin in his direction, the beast growled loudly and stood up. Reacting to it, the other five dragons started growling too, but none of them dared to approach.

Cassandra, standing next to him, wondered what was going on. Was its master ordering the dragon to hurry up and kill her? She had no idea how they communicated, but it was evident that the dragon and its master were having a wordless conversation. All of sudden, the dragon turned to her and spread its black wings. In a split second, its large maw suddenly plunged in her direction, taking the chains that bound her into its mouth. Cassandra gasped in surprise. The dragon suddenly took off towards the skies, carrying her by her chains, rising higher from the ground and forcing her body to contort into a painful position from the pressure on her neck and wrists.

Thankfully, it only lasted a few seconds. She saw the arena move under her as she was quickly brought to a large stone platform. Some people in the audience screamed in horror, but the beast simply placed Cassandra there, releasing her gently to her knees.

The young woman painfully caught her breath before realizing where she was. The Imperial Family's platform! Still feeling the Black Dragon's hot breath close behind her, she conscientiously raised her head, only to discover a man was standing directly in front of her.

He was tall, and his bare torso was covered by a large, black fur cloak. He was obviously a warrior. Two large swords were attached to his belt, and out of all the Princes, he was the only one wearing barely any jewelry, and the least expensive fabrics. Instead, he simply wore black leather pants, large boots, and dragon scale bracers on his forearms.

At this man's feet, Cassandra appeared extremely vulnerable. Realizing that he was a member of the Imperial Family, she immediately averted her eyes. Why was she brought there? Would he kill her himself? Had she somehow offended the Royal Family?

"She is indeed quite pretty..." whispered one of the Princes.

"Brother, what do you want to do? Shall we get rid of her?"

"Just keep her, Kairen. You could use a few more slaves anyway."

She shivered. Prince Kairen, as in the Third Prince, the Empire's War God? Of all people, it had to be the most terrifying Prince! She bowed even lower, ready for a blade to slice her at any moment. But what were the Princes talking about?

A long and scary silence ensued. She waited, becoming more confused with each passing second, but it didn't seem like anyone was planning to kill her. What was going on?

"Alright, enough. Let's move on with the next performance before I get bored. Brother, you'll do whatever you want with her later. Who cares about a slave anyway."

The First Prince clapped his hands, and down in the arena, servants rushed to clean the bloodied sand on the grounds and prepare for the next show.

Cassandra was still frozen, kneeling at the Prince's feet. She knew she absolutely must not raise her head in front of the Imperial Family, but the Third Prince still hadn't moved. All of a sudden, a loud growl took her by surprise, and she turned her head, just slightly, to see the Black Dragon still behind her. It was close enough to envelop her in huffs of hot breath and for her to see its large fangs.

Suddenly, she heard the hiss of a blade. Before she could even move, the sword plunged towards her, and she prepared for the worst, closing her eyes. The manacles fell with a clang and her wrists no longer felt so heavy. He had severed the chain from her back! Cassandra slowly moved to look at her wrists. The iron bands were still around her neck and wrists, but they were no longer held painfully together from her back. Her arms were now free to move as she pleased.

Her relief was short-lived though as he suddenly grabbed her collar, pulling her to his side. She didn't have time to struggle, as he roughly dragged her to his seat. Cassandra was shocked to be placed against his golden chair, but even more surprised to see him simply sit without adding a word. She was on her knees at his feet, her shoulder against the throne, but the Prince didn't even look at her, focusing back on the arena again.

What was all that? He had placed her facing the arena so she couldn't even sneak a glance up at him. She was completely shocked and at a loss. Looking around, she realized she was the only slave on the platform. Aside from the Princes, only some palace attendants stood behind the seats, like statues, with no one paying her any more attention.

Cassandra was breathing erratically, and trying to understand her current situation. Suddenly, she felt warmth covering her shoulders. Surprised, she glanced to the side, only to realize that it was a part of the Prince's large coat! Did he purposely move it so that it would cover her, too? Or was it mere luck? Her bare shoulders were now covered by the thick fur, shielding her from the wind and bitter cold.

"What is coming next?" One of the Princes suddenly asked.

"Dancers! I heard this group came from across the North Sea!"

It seemed like they had all forgotten the macabre show that had occurred just mere minutes ago. Cassandra kept her head low, silently praying they would ignore her for the rest of the day. As she knelt, frozen in place, she felt a hand caress her hair without warning. It took her a few seconds to realize, as the fingers that gently played with her long waves were so light she barely felt them. For a minute, she was dumbstruck, wondering if she was dreaming. No one but the Third Prince was close enough to be able to reach and touch her. His large hand slowly stroked her hair, almost touching her back. She could feel his warm skin flirting with hers.

Was the War God really petting her like this? She could barely breathe under his touch. She didn't dare to move a muscle. On the arena floor beneath them, a splendid dance performance was taking place with dozens of performers, yet all she could focus on was the faint brushing of his fingertips on her slender nape. Did anyone else notice the Prince's actions under the cloak?

When Cassandra finally dared a glance to the side, it didn't seem like it. The other Princes seated to their left were solely focused on the performances down in the arena, not paying any attention to her or her new master. Because this was her situation now, right? Within minutes she had become property of the Third Prince. It was almost as if he had collected a stone from the sidewalk. But instead of a stone, he had picked up a slave.

All that Cassandra knew of him had come from rumors. When it came to the Third Prince, the gossip mill ran deep. The Emperor's favorite son, he was said to be a dark, cruel, and merciless man. The Empire's War God. Was he really the one who, against all odds, had spared the life of a slave? Did he just decide to do so because of the actions of his willful dragon?

The beast was now peacefully resting a few feet away on a lower step. It seemed bored, laying down while its peers had been brought back to their cages, or chained and seated at the sides of the arena. Cassandra observed the magnificent dragon again, mesmerized by the obsidian scales. She found it more distracting than any performance, especially since she couldn't look at the owner of the hand that was playing with her hair.

Would the Prince order the dragon to kill her if she asked him to let her go? Cassandra didn't even dare to look at him or move. She was submitting to his hand, and the caresses in her long hair. A few times she shivered, not because of the cold, since she was now under the cloak, but from the contact of the Prince's hot hand against her skin. Moreover, his hand was venturing further and further down her nape, onto her shoulders. He wasn't touching only her hair anymore. His fingers were now moving further down, and she felt embarrassed.

She had never been touched like this by a man before. Slaves were not concubines, nor were they worthy to even be seen as women. They were often dirty and poorly dressed. Unlike the noblewomen who went to extreme lengths to have the prettiest dresses, jewelry, and the most expensive make-up available. Cassandra never had any of those luxuries, but she possessed a natural beauty that even years of enslavement and abuse could not take from her.

Like a flower in a bed of weeds, she had managed to stay beautiful. She was tall and thin, with pale skin that had been permanently scarred by a whip in several places. Her breasts were not large, but still round and full enough to make her look feminine. Had she been fed properly, she would have had a beautiful silhouette. But despite the years of malnourishment, the graceful beauty of her face was undeniable. She had large green eyes, a small nose, and thin but full lips. A pure, fragile beauty - like a water lily.

As the afternoon passed, Cassandra gradually grew accustomed to the Prince's touch. She couldn't ignore it, but she didn't shiver or overthink it anymore. After a dozen performances, the Prince suddenly stood up.

"Brother?" asked the youngest prince.

But Kairen didn't bother to answer. Instead, he simply left his seat. Cassandra, wondering for a second if she should follow, decided it would be better than to stay with the other five Princes on the platform she had no reason being on to begin with.

Leaving the balcony, the Third Prince walked through the many corridors so fast that she could barely keep up. To her surprise, the War God's quarters were located in the farthest wing of the Palace. By the time they arrived, she was exhausted.

He opened the double doors, revealing a very simple room, by a Prince's standards, that is. But to Cassandra, that place was still unbelievably large and luxurious with a canopy bed, large enough to welcome four people, and adorned in silk sheets. There were also two chairs and a table made of redwood, one of the most expensive and valuable materials, an empty desk, a wardrobe containing a warrior's armor, and a bath. Cassandra was shocked by how bare the room was. Had it just been prepared to welcome him during his stay during the festival? She had heard each Prince lived in his own Palace after all.

Kairen left his large fur cloak on one of the chairs and massaged his neck. Cassandra suddenly realized that she was his only attendant! Did he come without any slaves or servants?

The War God sighed.

"I want to take a bath."

These were the first words he had spoken to her. Despite her surprise, Cassandra's years in slavery had her obeying right away. Leaving the room, she found the first palace servant she could and asked them for hot water to be prepared for the Third Prince, as well as several herbs for the water. The servant, not knowing the slave girl, was inclined to whip her and send her back where she belonged, but her words of "Third Prince" had the impulse stuck in his throat. If there was one man no one wanted to anger, it was the Third Prince. So, after a doubtful second, he nodded with disdain and turned on his heels.

A few minutes later, Cassandra was busy pouring the hot water into the bath along with a few herbs she had ordered.

"What are those?"

The young woman looked at him, meaning to answer, only to realize her master was undressing right in front of her! She only had a glance at the warrior's impressive musculature before she shyly looked down, yet the image was surely engraved in her mind. A War God, indeed! She blushed while answering.

"Those are medicinal herbs to... to relieve fatigue and muscle pain, my Lord."

Kairen frowned. How did this woman know of his strained muscles? He never showed any weakness. Is it because of the way he had stretched once they had entered the privacy of his quarters? As he pondered this, he realized his slave was looking down again with a flush of red in her cheeks. He snickered while entering the bath. Had she never seen a naked man before?

"Do you need more water, my Lord?"

"Come here."

Hesitantly, Cassandra walked the few steps back towards the tub, trying hard to refrain from taking a peek at him. Indeed, having served only women before, she was totally disarmed while facing a grown man's body. Kairen's body wasn't merely handsome. He was more like a dangerous alpha male, strong and imposing.

Watching her struggle to look away, he knew he was right.

"Massage me."

"...My Lord?"

He didn't bother ordering again. A bit surprised, Cassandra obediently stood behind him and started massaging his broad shoulders. Her fingers were trembling. She was touching a Prince! While trying to contain her inner turmoil, she focused on her movements. She knew what kind of being he was. In a split second, he could decide to end her life. For the young slave, this was infinitely more terrifying than standing in front of wild, scaled beasts.

As she kept massaging, she felt his muscles finally begin to relax, filling her with satisfaction. She moved on to his left arm, using her prior knowledge of healing to properly massage every muscle. When she finally looked back at his face, she realized he had closed his eyes as if he was asleep, allowing her to breathe a little easier.

Cassandra moved on to his other arm, skillfully kneading the bicep of the War God. She felt some pride to see that the medicinal bath she had prepared was so effective. Was the water still warm enough? She glanced down at the water and that's when she saw it.

Her Prince's member, fully erect.

Chapter 2

Cassandra gasped. Her fingers stopped moving, as she realized her master's cock was completely erect and standing tall under the water.

"Don't stop."

She jumped in surprise, as her master opened his eyes and caught her staring. She blushed and resumed massaging, but her hands were not as steady as before. The embarrassing silence and Kairen's staring were completely disarming her. No matter how much she tried, it was impossible to ignore both his dark eyes and his erection.

Cassandra kept her head down and tried to concentrate on her hands, but touching him didn't have the same meaning as before. The massage had become totally indecent no matter how you looked at it! She tried to stop and step back, but Kairen's voice caught her.

"Stay where you are."

She had no choice but to obey as she blushed and tried to steady her trembling fingers. He was obviously doing this on purpose. The fire in his eyes could have consumed an entire forest. He didn't even smile or speak, he just kept his eyes focused on her, the young slave girl who was uncomfortably embarrassed.

Without warning, he moved his hand under her dress, causing her to yelp in surprise.

"Ma... Master," she protested, trying to pull her hips away.

"Don't move."

She opened her mouth in shock, but didn't know how to respond. The Prince's fingers ventured farther, reaching past her panties. From under her dirty dress, he forced his way to her slit, caressing the innocent slave with no trace of shame on his face. Surprised by the warm, intrusive hand between her thighs, she gasped, unable to hold her tongue.

"My... My Lord..."

She meant to ask him to stop, but the words wouldn't come out. Her stomach was filled with something intense as his fingers caressed against her opening. Cassandra had no idea how to react. She was completely inexperienced, and he was just playing with her!

"P...Please..."

"Are you a virgin?"

Already dying of shame, she couldn't even bring herself to answer. But her red cheeks and flustered expression were enough of an answer.

The Prince tilted his head, his face still completely unreadable. It was as if he was merely testing her, yet his fingers left her unable to answer. She tried hard to suppress her moans, but his large hand was pressing and rubbing against her most sensitive spot, driving her crazy. She knew he could feel her getting wet and she wanted to die of shame. She was standing on her toes now, her hands on his wrists, trying to discreetly move away.

Cassandra was panting when he suddenly pushed one finger inside her. Taken by surprise, she let out a startled moan. She tried to muffle her voice with her hand, but it was useless as he started moving and stirring his finger both inside and out. His thumb pressed on her clitoris as his middle finger repeatedly penetrated her, causing her to cry out. The worst part was that he seemed completely casual while he was subjecting her to this! She desperately wanted to step away, but he held her close to the tub with his hand confidently moving between her thighs and leaving her no chance of escape.

"Do you like this?"

His composed voice had her feeling like a little pet he was toying with. She had never even been touched by a man before, and now he had her fluids running down her thighs. Why was her body reacting to this man's touch after seventeen years of innocence?!

Cassandra couldn't contain her moans, and he was enjoying it. He found her desperate state, and vain attempts to hide it, extremely tempting and sexy. She was dripping wet, and obviously enjoying his finger, so why was she trying so hard to hide what her body seemed to enjoy so thoroughly? He wanted to see her cheeks flush with color, the sweat pool on her skin, and her legs tremble under his skillful touch. He inserted a second finger, making her cry out. She was definitely a virgin...

How had she remained untouched until now? She was young, beautiful, and very alluring. He kept going, pushing his fingers to make her moan even more. She was covering her mouth, trying to stay quiet. He pressed his thumb on her little button, teasing her to get a reaction. Under her dirty, once white, thin, and ragged dress, her nipples had started standing out. Did she have any idea how alluring she was at that moment? Her hands gripped tightly onto the bathtub, as she could barely stand on her own anymore.

Accelerating his fingers in and out of her, he pushed her further to the edge. Cassandra's thighs quivered as she whimpered.

"Ma... Master, p... please..."

Her eyes were teary, she couldn't take any more of this torture and embarrassment. She wanted to beg for him to stop, but her voice was no longer under her control. Instead, she was moaning and panting heavily. She felt a fire raging from her intimate parts to her stomach, overwhelming her with new sensations she couldn't handle anymore.

"My Prince?"

A servant had knocked on the door, waiting for permission to enter. Kairen let her go, much to his annoyance, his fingers wet with her juices, and Cassandra immediately fell to her knees. She was dazed and trembling, her entrance throbbing as if she could still feel the Prince's fingers inside her. The wetness between her legs was impossible to ignore as she tried to compose herself and move her dress back into place.

"Come in."

Completely ignoring her embarrassment, Kairen called the man in. The servant didn't seem to realize she was there on the other side of the bath, still reeling from what had just happened.

"The buffet is about to begin, my Lord. The Emperor looks forward to your presence."

"I'll get ready. Leave."

"Yes, my Lord."

The servant left promptly, leaving the two of them alone again. Cassandra had no idea how to react, but Kairen left the bath as if nothing had happened. He grabbed a towel and started drying himself, and she wondered if his... member had gone back to normal, but didn't dare to look. Instead, she pulled herself together and grabbed his clothes to help him dress. Though she remained silent as she assisted him, her mind was in overdrive, trying to comprehend what had just happened.

"Stay here...and clean yourself, too."

Those were his only words before he left for the banquet. As soon as she was alone, Cassandra let out a breath she hadn't realized she was holding.

What had just happened? She knew some men kept their slaves to have sex with, but... that was not quite the same, was it? The War God had surprised her, almost as if he had done it completely on a whim. But for her virgin self, this had been the most impossible experience. Within only a few hours, her status had changed from that of a sacrificial nobody to a Prince's slave!

She pushed her hair out of her face, trying to gather her thoughts. Until now, the Imperial Family had never been something that she would have dreamed of seeing, even from afar. Yet somehow, she found herself sitting on the floor of the Third Prince's chambers, trying to recover from his little playtime with her most intimate parts.

She looked around. Why did the Third Prince not have any attendants? He seemed to be the only one without anyone to serve him. Did he come alone and just leave them all at his own Palace?

The room wasn't messy though, proof that the Palace servants were still doing some chores in here. What was she supposed to do now? The banquet would most likely last a few hours. Cassandra suddenly remembered his order to clean herself. Her eyes fell immediately on the tub. Would it be alright for her to use it? No one would punish her for using the Prince's bath, right?

Cassandra undid her dress and quickly submerged herself in the water. The thought of washing in the same water he had bathed in left her cheeks flushing a vivid crimson. She could still feel the lingering sensation of his fingers inside her. No one had ever touched her there before! The concubines were always too jealous to let the noblemen even look at the female slaves. Cassandra had been whipped many times by her previous mistress just for crossing the Minister's path. She had learned to stay away from men. But there was no way to refuse or ignore this Prince who had claimed her as his own.

Afraid someone would come, she bathed quickly, washing the blood from her back as best as she could and drying her long hair. After hesitating a bit, she decided to wash her dress too. As old and ragged as it was, it was her only piece of clothing. Despite Cassandra's best efforts to take care of it over the years, it was impossible to make it look like anything more than what it was; an unflattering piece of linen, shredded and left brown and grey from years of wear. Once Cassandra was done cleaning it, some of the dust had come off and only a bit of dried blood still remained. She sighed helplessly.

"You! What are you doing in the Prince's chambers?!"

Cassandra jumped. Two Palace servants had entered the room just as she finished dressing. Before she even had a chance to explain herself, one of them violently grabbed her by the hair and dragged her to the ground.

"You wench! Who is your master? Speak!"

"Lord... Lord... the Th...Thi...Third Prince..." she stuttered, despite the pain.

"You liar! Do you take us for fools? The Third Prince didn't bring any attendants with him, you lying whore! Show us your identification!"

The first man ruthlessly slapped her face, before jerking her up by the collar around her throat. Cassandra cried out in pain as she was strangled by the iron while he read the inscriptions engraved on it.

"Lady Lyria of the Green Narcissus Family... Isn't that one of the Fifth Prince's new concubines?"

"It is. She belonged to that old Minister who was beheaded three days ago. I've seen her wearing the red dress. She's quite a looker."

"You little wench, did you really think you could escape your mistress while you were in the Palace?"

They slapped Cassandra again, continuing their insults as they dragged her out. Holding her between them, they ignored her fearful pleading as they forced her through the corridors of the Palace, slapping her mercilessly to stop her gasping sobs and feeble pleas. She tried hard to hold back her tears despite the pain and agony she was in. They had no pity for a runaway slave.

After being brutally hauled through countless corridors, she was suddenly thrust out into the Imperial Garden, where a few concubines not attending the Imperial Banquet were drinking and partying together. Tables were set up for a moon-viewing, and a handful of servants were pouring wine for the ladies present. The concubines all wore elegant dresses paired with expensive and glittering jewels, each determined to outdo the other. As they ate and sipped wine together, they showered each other with backhanded compliments behind beautiful, fake smiles.

The servants violently hurled Cassandra to the ground, at Lady Lyria's feet.

Cassandra was petrified. Lyria had been her mistress for five long and torturous years, since the day she had entered the Minister's House. Though that woman was stunningly beautiful, behind the alluring face she was a cruel and malicious bitch. She never hesitated to whip her slaves, even without a reason. She threw tantrums whenever she didn't get attention, and cried fake tears to manipulate any situation to her benefit.

The Minister had fallen for her graceful beauty when she was only fifteen, raising her from the modest position of her birth, to that of noble status, and she had been ridiculously arrogant ever since. She was truly as ugly on the inside as she was beautiful on the outside. Cassandra knew her wickedness had no limits, recalling how she poisoned one of her rivals merely because she was jealous, and how that same jealousy had led her to physically disfigure another.

Being brought back into the presence of Lyria was a nightmare for Cassandra. The concubine glared down at her with disgust and turned to the servants.

"What is this?"

"We found her in a Prince's chambers, my Lady. She lied to try and escape us, but we saw her identification collar and brought her straight back to..."

"Why would I care about that bitch?! She should be dead! I was tired of her, so I gave her as a tribute to His Highness! How the hell is she still alive?! Where was she?"

The two dumbfounded servants looked at each other, both left feeling ill by the concubine's unexpected reaction. Lyria, on the other hand, was absolutely infuriated to have been disturbed while she was gloating about her new status to the lower-ranked concubines. Seeing Cassandra alive fueled her anger. She had hated the slave from the very beginning, and had sent her to her death to finally be rid of her once and for all.

"She... she was in the Third Prince's chambers..."

Cassandra was trembling in both fear and pain. Lyria's unpredictable anger was something that scared her more than anything.

Her fear was justified when, without warning, the concubine suddenly hurled her full glass of wine at Cassandra's head. One of the concubines screamed as the glass shattered on the ground. A shard reopened the bruised gash on Cassandra's temple, courtesy of one of the Palace guards earlier that morning.

"You slut! How dare you! How did you even survive The Offering?! And then, to hide in one of the Prince's chambers! You unworthy little leach! I will finish you myself. You won't escape death again! You..."

She fisted a handful of Cassandra's hair and started jerking her head violently, as she screamed at her. But she suddenly froze. Everyone in the garden had heard it too.

A dragon's angry growl, right above their heads. Everyone present turned their heads towards the north wall and held their breath in fear.

Standing there was a large, furious dragon. Glaring at them with its red, reptilian eyes, while one large paw was grasping the muraled wall, the other scratching the stone one. The black beast growled menacingly again in their direction; no one dared to move an inch. But Cassandra raised her head, despite Lyria's grip, to look up at the dragon.

"The... the Th-Third's Prince's...dragon," stuttered one of the terrified concubines.

None of the other servants or concubines said a word, petrified into silence. The Black Dragon couldn't possibly be mistaken as any other. It was the biggest among its peers and the only one of its color, with its obsidian scales and blood red eyes. It moved, stepping effortlessly over the wall and stalking towards them. Garden statues and lush plants were crushed under its huge feet as it continued forward, growling angrily.

A few concubines and half a dozen servants ran off, screaming in fear. Those who remained were frozen in their spots.

All except one.

"Ha! See! His own dragon has come to finish you off! Why would the Third Prince have any interest in a worthless slave like you?!"

Lyria was so sure of herself, she brutally shoved Cassandra into the arms of a nearby servant.

"You! Give her to the beast!" she ordered, as if she knew what was going on.

The servant, who knew very little about the dragons, nodded obediently and yanked Cassandra's arm, forcing her closer to the beast. Terrified, Cassandra tried in vain to free herself. Tears slid silently down her face, as the pain from her fresh injuries made themselves known. After all the violent manhandling from Lyria and the servants, within the past fifteen minutes, she didn't even have the strength to break free. Within seconds she was face to face with the Black Dragon for the second time that day.

The servant kicked her in the side, forcing her down to the dragon's feet. As they had been working or resting in the Palace, none of them had witnessed the earlier scene in the arena. He genuinely believed Lyria was right and was doing what the dragon wanted.

He didn't even get the chance to gasp before a giant claw brutally pierced through his chest. In one movement, he found himself pinned to the ground in a pool of his own blood.

People began to scream in panic at the sight of the limp body, pierced by the gigantic claw. Cassandra, also shocked, brought her hand to her mouth in disgust.

"What is going on here?"

His voice thundered out, silencing the screams. Still in front of the dragon, Cassandra turned her head toward him.

The Third Prince Kairen had just stepped into the courtyard. His arrival had almost the same effect as that of his beast. However, some of the concubines were also flustered, too. He was a warrior indeed, and a well-sculpted one at that. Wearing only his large fur coat, part of his muscular chest was left exposed, just enough to leave many women blushing.

As he stepped forward, Lyria, as arrogant as ever, turned towards him. She knew perfectly well who he was, but her new status as one of the other Princes' concubines clearly gave her enough confidence to address the War God.

"My Lord! Please excuse the ruckus, this shameless slave of mine has angered your beast, I fear."

It was hard to say if she was acting seductively on purpose or not. Her pink dress was very sexy, flattering her voluptuous curves, and her hair and makeup were flawlessly done to enhance her beauty. Anytime she talked, her red lips would pout a little, a quality that made many men succumb to her charms.

Kairen, however, only glared at her.

"Who is this whore?" he asked in his low, cold voice.

"It's one of my slaves, my Lord," mumbled Lyria. "A simple..."

"I was not talking to you."

In a split second, anyone who had not caught on already, realized that he was actually addressing the slave, not the mistress standing between them. While Lyria flushed red in embarrassment and anger, Cassandra lowered her head, stifling her sobs.

"She... she is Lady Lyria, my... mistress..."

Maybe she should have added "former", but that didn't seem necessary at the time. The dragon suddenly growled again, impatient, and moved to approach Cassandra. Its obsidian scales felt warm as it clumsily curved its enormous body around her. It was hard to ignore all the blood on its paw, but Cassandra turned her head towards its face - the red eyes were fixed on her. People around them were completely shocked by the scene that was unfolding. The War God's dragon was acting like a clingy pet towards a worthless slave!

Kairen suddenly drew out his sword.

"I told you to stay in the room."

Afraid that he was mad at her, Cassandra bowed her head. Her cheeks were still wet with tears as she struggled to explain herself with her hoarse voice.

"I... I meant to, but... I was brought here..."

"By whom?" he asked, impatiently.

Before Cassandra even answered, the two men who had dragged her all the way here screeched in panic. The idea of the Prince's wrath directed at them was so terrifying that they had given themselves up without even realizing. Kairen's glare caught them right away, and they started to run away in fear.

The Prince clicked his tongue and raised his head to exchange a glance with his dragon. As if obeying a silent order, the beast moved, crushing one of them under his paw, and chomping down on the other one. It was over within seconds. A rain of blood fell from his maw, spilling on some of the concubines and servants, who screamed again in fear and disgust. Cassandra got some on her shoulder too and she brought her hand over her mouth to hold back the strong nausea that rose in her stomach from the smell; the gruesome sight of the beast chewing on the servant still fresh in her mind.

Lyria, splattered in blood too, screamed. She was finally catching up with the reality of this situation and turned her terrified eyes towards the Third Prince Kairen, who was silently walking towards her, like a deadly shadow.

"Your Highness! This slave was mine! She... she is just an insignificant slave! I am your brother's doted concubine! You can't..."

Her voice died as the sword pierced her chest, right between her perky breasts. Her eyes were still open wide, in surprise, as she fell back like an inanimate doll.

With this final act, the bloodbath had scared the last of the remaining crowd away, with the exception of a few servants who were still frozen in fear. Cassandra was shaking.

She watched Kairen calmly retrieve his sword and wash the blood off in a fountain. The War God was acting as if killing one of his brother's concubines had been a totally normal occurrence. Once his weapon was cleaned and back in his belt, he turned toward Cassandra. As he was walking up to her, her mind turned over, she had no idea how to react. She was scared of this man. Her eyes went from the body of the woman she had feared the most for years, to him, who was now even scarier.

"Are you injured?"

His question took her by surprise. Cassandra stared blankly at him, but the Prince was looking at her dress, which was covered in blood. She quickly came to her senses.

"No. No, my Lord. This blood isn't mine..."

She meant to get up, but while leaning on her wrist, a sharp pain made her cry out. Did she twist it when she fell? Or was it from her earlier struggling? Her thin wrist was painful whenever she moved it, and was a bit blue too. Cassandra held it against her chest trying to ignore the pain, but just as she moved to try to get up again, the Prince kneeled by her side.

"My... my Lord?" she gasped in surprise.

"Silence."

The familiar feel of a warm coat suddenly enveloped her as Kairen's sturdy arms reached around her shoulders and beneath her knees, gently lifting

28

her up as if she were a fragile child. Instantly, Casandra's face flushed a bright crimson. A Prince carrying a slave? And like a Princess, too!

She wanted to protest and tell him that he shouldn't do this, but she didn't dare to speak. Thus, she found herself held against Kairen's hard torso, carried like some precious package, wrapped up in his cloak. Above them, the Black Dragon tilted its head and growled quietly. Kairen clicked his tongue.

"You shut up, too."

Cassandra watched the huge beast sulk a bit while following them slowly. Its gigantic body was too big for the courtyard, destroying anything that got in its path, but neither it nor its master seemed to care. Behind them, what had been a nice little banquet not long ago, now resembled a bloody war zone.

Kairen walked away from the scene, unbothered, carrying Cassandra close to him. When they were almost back to the courtyard door, a group of people suddenly arrived. Embarrassed, she stayed still in his arms, completely at a loss of what to do.

The people who had arrived seemed familiar, too. After a few seconds, she recognized two of the five other Princes that had been on the platform, and became even more scared. But none of them, nor their attendants, paid any attention to her. Instead, the Fifth Prince took a glance over his brother's shoulder to see the mess.

"Brother, didn't you go a bit too far? I had just acquired that concubine! Did you have to kill her right away?! Didn't you see how pretty she was?"

Next to him, the youngest Prince Anour, rolled his eyes.

"Brother Lephys, don't you have enough women already? Who cares? If she displeased our older brother, that woman had to die."

"Still... Oh well, I guess I'll write a letter to her family or something. But brother, isn't that the slave from earlier? I thought you had killed her already."

Cassandra was appalled at how easily they talked about someone's death. Unlike Kairen, the two younger Princes were dressed in ceremonial clothing with colorful silk and gold embroidery. Not to mention the lavish jewelry in which they were both adorned. Each had a crowd of servants following closely behind them with their heads lowered.

Both Princes looked around her age, between fifteen and twenty years at most. But they didn't seem to have much in common with their third brother.

"Enough, Lephys, enough," sighed Prince Anour. "If our brother finds this woman to his taste, who cares? But Brother Kairen, Father was angry that you left the banquet so early. He wanted to introduce two new concubines to you."

Kairen snorted, visibly annoyed.

"Tell that old man he can keep those greedy sluts for himself."

Cassandra frowned. Never mind the concubines, how could he talk about the Emperor like that? Kairen ignored both of his brothers as he walked past them, still carrying her. She was embarrassed beyond words to be transported like this in the Palace's corridors, but did not dare to move. Behind them, she heard the dragon's disappointed growl. The large beast could not follow them inside.

As the Prince climbed some stairs, she realized that they were not going back to his chambers. They were heading a bit further into the Palace, and Cassandra was worried as to where he would take her and why. Not to the Palace's cells, right?

Chapter 3

After a few stairs, he finally stopped and Cassandra read the little sign - The Green Jade Palace. Who was living here? A servant hurried to welcome the Prince, bowing down countless times.

"I will inform my Lady of your arrival, my Lord..."

"No need."

Just like that, Kairen forced himself through, despite the servant's attempts to hold him back, and his continuous pleas to allow him to inform his Lady first. The little man seemed panicked, trailing after the Prince. Cassandra felt a bit sorry for him.

Finally, they arrived at what seemed to be a bedroom door. As soon as they got close she heard some very explicit sounds and Cassandra blushed immediately. Whoever was behind that door was obviously busy! A woman's moans were echoing loudly along with some deeper male ones, however, that didn't stop Kairen. With a kick, he forced the door open and entered the large bedroom.

Cassandra couldn't help but peek. As she expected, it was terribly obscene! On the red silk sheets of the bed were two women and a man. The two women were riding the naked male servant; one was straddling him, her pussy being hammered by his savage and relentless moves. She was moaning and crying, begging for more as their flesh pounded loudly. Facing her, the other woman was on her knees on either side of the man's head, moving her hips as the male servant licked and sucked her pussy. She was caressing and forcefully kissing her female partner, while the man underneath was working hard on pleasuring both women at the same time.

"Who dares to...!" One of the women reacted angrily.

Her expression changed when she saw Kairen standing there holding a blushing Cassandra. She smiled and kissed the other woman who was panting hard and being forcefully penetrated by the man's cock. She seemed younger than her mistress and answered her kiss clumsily. She was having a hard time balancing between her breathing and moaning. Under her, the male servant was pounding vigorously, holding her waist while pleasuring their mistress with his mouth.

"My little brother has come to visit! Are you bringing me a new toy, Kairen?" she asked, her eyes going down to Cassandra.

She couldn't have been more embarrassed. It was impossible to ignore the wild sex displayed in front of her, the servant's cries, or the Princess's lusty eyes on her. However, Kairen was as still as marble in front of the scene.

"Enough of your little game."

The Princess pouted, moving her hips a bit more before finally getting up. She sighed and grabbed a large robe to cover herself before turning to the two servants.

"Keep fucking her. If one of you comes before I return... I'll punish you."

"Yes, mistress," answered the man.

He kept thrusting vigorously and the young woman's cries got louder. Satisfied, she turned around to face her brother. Cassandra figured from their physical resemblance, that she was Kairen's full sister, one who also shared the same mother as him. They had the same black eyes, dark hair, and tanned skin color. Even most of their facial features were shockingly alike as if they could be twins. The only difference was that the Princess had a very feminine body, with voluptuous curves and sexy lips.

"Follow me."

Shareen took them to another room. This one was filled with bookcases and a large desk covered in paper. There was a strange smell and some smoke floating in the air, and with the curtains closed, it wouldn't go away. The whole room was dark despite the few candles the Princess had lit.

Pushing her long black curls behind her shoulders, she crossed her arms, displeased.

"What did you interrupt my good time for? Is it because of this slave? You both reek of blood."

"Give her some clothes."

The Princess clicked her tongue.

"To a slave? I'm not that generous."

"You have spare clothing for your whores."

"My servants, Kairen. Even if I play with them, they are still proper servants. What would I get in exchange?"

Impatient, the Prince glared at his sister without answering. But to Cassandra's surprise, his sister didn't seem to take offense. Instead, she suddenly smiled like a feline and walked over to a wardrobe. She took her time before picking a silky emerald dress. It wasn't as fancy as the clothing made for the royal family, but still much better than the rags slaves would usually wear. She held it up to Kairen.

"How is this? I'll give it to you if you have her change here."

"Fine."

Kairen had answered before Cassandra even understood what the Princess had asked for. He put her down letting her stand by herself while still holding on to the fur cloak. Cassandra blushed as the Princess handed her the dress with a mischievous grin. She was already feeling shy for some reason and so she was hesitant to let go of the cloak to take it.

However, she couldn't let the Princess stay like this forever. The fur cloak fell to her feet revealing her bloodied rags, and she took the dress while bowing. Thankfully, most of the blood was on her rags and not herself. The Princess clicked her tongue while taking a seat in one of the leather armchairs.

"I guess Krai made a mess again..."

Cassandra took a few seconds to realize she was talking about the Black Dragon. So it was named Krai? That piece of information, however, was soon overshadowed by her current situation. She didn't know when Kairen had taken a seat next to his sister, but both Imperial Siblings were now staring at her. She became even more red knowing what they were expecting. She looked down.

"My... My Lord, can I change outside?"

"You can undress here," his sister answered with an imperious tone. "See? There's some water for you to wash up with too."

She pointed her finger towards a little basin of water to the side, while she was obviously enjoying the sight of Cassandra's blushing cheeks. Seeing the Prince ignore her query, she felt helpless. Those two really wanted to watch her undress here! She hesitated for a few seconds, but their forceful stares were pressuring her. Slowly, Cassandra reached for the laces on her back, undoing them one by one.

In front of her, Kairen was as still as a statue, but his stare was hot and intense. She felt like he was undressing her from his seat. With trembling fingers, she finally undid the last knot, and the dress was now only held up by her hand. With the injury to her other wrist, she was struggling to keep it together and hide behind the rags.

In front of her, the Princess bit her lip and turned to her brother.

"A virgin?"

He didn't bother to answer, but she knew that she was right. She turned her feline eyes towards Cassandra again.

"Interesting... Keep going," she ordered.

Cassandra would have given anything to hide, but there was no way, not with those two in the room, waiting for her to undress. She had no choice but to let go of the sullied clothing, leaving her in her panties in front of them. She tried covering her breasts with her arm while looking away. With her free hand she reached over to the basin of water, grabbing a little sponge to try and wash quickly, but she saw the Princess stand up and walk her way. Cassandra took a step back but within seconds the woman was standing in front of her, her black eyes sparkling.

"So adorable... Look at these cute breasts, Kairen."

Without warning, she stood behind Cassandra and pushed her arm away to grab one. Surprised, the young slave let out a whimper under her touch.

"Hands off, Shareen," growled Kairen.

Ignoring him, his sister kept going. She took the little sponge from her hand and started caressing Cassandra's chest with it while gauging her brother's reactions. The cold water was dripping down her pink nipples. Wandering over her pale skin, caressing her stomach, Shareen's fingers finally reached out for Cassandra's last piece of clothing.

"M... My Lady..." murmured Cassandra.

"What is it, sweetie? Are you embarrassed? Don't be, it's just your master here... Come on, show him. Let's get you all nice and clean for him to enjoy."

Without listening to her plea, Shareen got rid of the sponge and kept going, fondling the white breasts and sliding her fingers down to her underwear. Cassandra was trying to escape her futilely, her unhurt hand on the Princess's wrist, but she couldn't possibly risk angering a member of the Imperial Family. Moreover, the difference in strength was obvious between them. Instead, she looked to Kairen for help, her eyes pleading to him.

"My Lord...Ah!"

Without warning, Shareen had started kissing the skin of her neck, sending shivers all the way down her spine. Her entire body felt electrified. Cassandra tried to catch her breath, but Shareen had no intention of letting her rest. The Princess's fingers found her little button of pleasure over her panties.

"Uh... Oh! Hm... My... Lady, please stop..."

"Oh my, you're so cute and innocent... Won't you give her to me, Kairen? You're such a stiff! Since you haven't fucked her yet, I have so many ideas for her."

The Third Prince didn't seem amused at all, but that didn't stop Shareen from teasing and caressing Cassandra relentlessly. Plunging her fingers deeper, she played with her slit over the fabric, making her squirm. The Princess pushed a little further each time, forcing her to spread her legs further apart. Cassandra couldn't take it any longer; something hot and unbearable was brewing in her stomach, making her legs tremble and her skin shiver. Her eyes were tearing up as she tried to hold back her voice. With the Princess behind her, she was exposed to her master, almost naked, standing only a few steps from him. He could see everything. Her pointy nipples, her trembling legs, her panties getting wet under Shareen's treatment - it was unbearable.

"Shareen!" he suddenly called out.

His tone was undoubtedly angry this time. The Princess, annoyed, clicked her tongue and stopped her movements.

"So selfish! I am just trying to help out my stiff little brother, Kairen. Do you even know how to play? I was just starting to have fun, too. Look, a bit more and I would have made her come."

Shareen, still holding her by the waist, displayed her wet fingers to Kairen.

34

Cassandra, almost unable to stand on her own two feet, was dying of shame. However, she slowly regained her senses and grabbed the green dress to hurriedly put it on. It was a bit loose on her, but it was definitely the prettiest piece of clothing she had ever worn before. Meanwhile, Shareen was still annoyed at her brother and walked over to his seat. Putting her knee down between his legs, she leaned over Kairen with that feline smile of hers.

"You're such a bore, Kairen. You know, we could have fun together sometimes. I have a couple of girls I would love to watch you fuck... with that."

She was hinting at her brother's obvious hard-on under his pants. Cassandra was completely red just from hearing her. The Princess was so... so shameless! Were all the members of the Imperial Family so loose in morals? Even if they were all-powerful, this was too much! And her new master was obviously excited too, even if he ignored most of his sister's theatrics.

But once again, Kairen stayed cold and silent. Eventually, Shareen sighed.

"Oh, well. You still owe me for that dress, I won't let you forget it. Can you try not to kill this one, at least? I like her."

Cassandra frowned. Not kill her? What did that mean? Why was she expecting the Prince to kill her at some point? But she didn't get any answers as Shareen finally stood to the side to let her brother stand up. Kairen walked over and Cassandra suddenly felt completely embarrassed. She had been standing there just a few seconds ago, naked and being fingered by his own sister!

Once he was in front of her, Cassandra looked everywhere but in his direction. She was so ashamed of the scene from just moments ago! How could he let his sister toy with her like some object! While avoiding her new master's eyes, she missed the moment he grabbed her again, lifting her like she didn't weigh a thing. Wrapping a new fur cloak around her, Kairen carried her out of the room, closely followed by Shareen.

"Did you really leave the banquet early?" she asked.

"You didn't even go," her brother growled back.

The Princess shrugged and walked ahead to open the doors to her bedroom. Cassandra had almost forgotten about the two servants having wild sex in there. They had now changed position and the man was savagely taking the young servant from behind, keeping her bent over the mattress. His movements were fast and relentless, yet the woman couldn't even cry out, her screams muffled by his hand. Her eyes were closed and her hair was a mess on her shoulders. She opened her eyes again upon hearing her mistress coming back and began to moan louder while staring at Shareen with a pleading look.

The Princess ignored her and turned to Kairen.

"Why would I go? I'm having so much fun here. My favorite brother even brought me a little toy to entertain myself with. Well, if you'd actually leave her here..."

She said all that while looking down at Cassandra, with her feline eyes. Inside Kairen's arms, Cassandra tried to avoid the Princess's stare, already deeply embarrassed.

"You've had enough," Kairen replied coldly.

"Never! If you..."

But before Shareen could finish her sentence, several people were heard outside. Judging by the weight and metallic sounds in their steps, there were soldiers among them and when they stopped right outside, Shareen crossed her arms, visibly annoyed.

"His Highness Prince Kairen, Her Highness Princess Shareen, this lowly Imperial servant is here to inform you that your presence is requested by the Imperial Dragon."

Shareen rolled her eyes, not hiding her displeasure.

"He had to send his Imperial pains in the..."

"Your Highnesses, the Imperial Dragon insisted!" exclaimed the servant.

Shareen growled and turned around. She snapped her fingers and both servants ran out of the bedroom while another young lady came in to help her change. Very quickly she was dressed in a magnificent outfit, wearing the Imperial purple silk of her family, a large gold belt, and lots of fine jewelry. Even her black hair was now swept up into an impressive bun by two gold hairpins adorned with several gemstones.

Cassandra thought about how even her former mistress would never be able to wear such delicate and expensive items. Lyria was one of the Minister's favorites, yet even for her, he could never get his hands on these kinds of priceless treasures. The Imperial Family was on a totally different level indeed, and Shareen was wearing those like they were mere trinkets.

Cassandra suddenly remembered that the emerald dress she was wearing herself was far above her own status. What if someone else saw her like this? Her iron collar and clothes were so mismatched, what if she was called a thief again? Thinking about this, her stomach twisted in pain from worry.

However, Kairen didn't seem to care about any of this. He walked out of his sister's chambers, first to meet with the group of servants and soldiers that were waiting outside. The one leading them, a humble man with the blue attire of a Palace servant, opened his eyes wide upon seeing Cassandra in the Prince's arms.

"You... Your Highness, who is this slave?"

He was obviously at a loss for words, but Kairen dismissed it in an instant.

"Didn't my father want to see me?"

"Certainly, Your Highness, but..."

Cassandra knew exactly what the attendant was thinking. A slave like her shouldn't even step into the Imperial Court! The Emperor should never face slaves or lowly servants. Of those that were not nobility, only those who worked in the Imperial Palace were permitted to be in the same room as the Imperial dragon, and even for them, it was considered the greatest honor to be able to bow in his presence.

Yet, here she was, a lowly slave being carried in by a member of the

36

Imperial Family! Cassandra had no idea how to act, but she fruitlessly tried to release herself from Kairen's arms.

"Master, I shouldn't come with you..."

"Why not?" growled Kairen.

"It is not...permitted."

Shareen finally came out of her chambers followed by three ladies in waiting, all wearing similar dresses to Cassandra's, the only difference being that she had the slave collar.

The Imperial servant was almost choking. How could a slave possibly argue with one of the Princes like that? She shouldn't even have been able to be so near him, let alone open her mouth with such defiance!

Shareen walked past them impatiently.

"We decide what is permitted or not. If my brother wants to come with a slave or thirty, it would serve you well to shut up," she said to the Imperial servant, with an imperious tone.

Immediately, everyone else bowed lowly.

"Y...yes, Your Highness. Please, this way."

Cassandra was baffled. How could it happen as easily as that? As they kept walking through the corridors, they saw many servants' faces. All those who bowed a second late and saw her, couldn't hide their shock, but of course, it was likely she was the only slave to ever be spotted inside the Inner Palace!

As they approached the Imperial Rooms, Cassandra was so worried that she couldn't handle it anymore. She turned to Kairen again, whispering with a pleading voice.

"Please, Master, can't I at least walk by myself? Please..."

"Last time I left you alone, you ran away."

Cassandra was taken aback. He was still angry about that? It wasn't even her choice to leave his chambers! She shook her head.

"No, Master, I swear I did not mean to. Please! I promise, I won't go anywhere. Please..."

Kairen clicked his tongue, but after a few more steps he finally stopped to let her down. Cassandra seized the occasion to swiftly put the fur cloak back onto his shoulders, getting it away from her before anyone else saw her with it.

The Third Prince gave her a skeptical look, but she made sure to stand right behind him, as close as she could without touching him. Shareen, watching the little scene unfold between the two, chuckled.

"Look, Kairen, your new pet isn't going anywhere, and you can always have Krai chase her down if she tries anyway."

He took a long moment before taking his eyes off Cassandra and walking with his sister again. Cassandra let out a deep sigh right after, feeling a bit relieved, and started walking behind him with her head low until someone next to her gently tapped her elbow.

One of Shareen's ladies-in-waiting had subtly taken a few extra steps behind her mistress to be right next to Cassandra and gave her a gentle smile.

"No need to bow so low. Just do it like me," she whispered with a smile.

Cassandra realized she was indeed bowing too low. She had naturally taken her slave posture, but it wasn't appropriate with what she was wearing now. Was it alright to mimic the ladies-in-waiting? She still had her collar on, so her current status was probably closer to a servant than anything else.

But the young lady gave her an encouraging smile, making her feel a little more at ease, so Cassandra did as she suggested. This way, she wouldn't stand out as much, and she was already hoping people would ignore her.

They finally reached a large door. Even without the gold adorning the redwood, Cassandra would have concluded it was their final destination by the loud growls coming from behind it - dragon growls.

"Emperor, this lowly servant has successfully come back with Their Highnesses Prince Kairen and Princess Shareen."

The large doors had opened and Cassandra, without lifting her head, felt a breeze, hinting that they were heading into an open area - a very, very large one. She followed Kairen while hearing a lot of people present around them. As she stole peeks to her left and right, she realized several members of the Imperial Family were there, all accompanied by their respective courts. From the myriad of voices and sounds, she could tell at least fifty people were present.

"Finally! Kairen, what do I have to do for you to stay at my banquets? Are they too boring for you, my Son?"

Cassandra couldn't believe she was hearing the Emperor's voice! She was surprised; he sounded more like a doting father than an all-mighty ruler too!

"What about me, Father? Do I not get a proper welcome just because my dear little brother is here?" asked Shareen with a sulk.

"What are you talking about? You know you are the most precious gem in my eyes, Shareen! Come here, my daughter!"

The group suddenly split, with Shareen and her attendants going straight to the golden throne, while Kairen took a left. He walked to a large seat and took his place, spreading his fur coat on it. Cassandra, observing how the other servants were positioned, took a small spot a few feet behind him and knelt on the floor.

She was now partially in the shadow of his seat and had the freedom to observe the room. It was an immense, circular hall with several golden chairs, each sitting atop several steps. Like this, the Royal Family could clearly see the center of the room, where dancers were currently performing a piece no one seemed to care about. Behind each seat, servants were busy attending to their masters, handing them cups of wine or plates of food. Only the concubines were sitting down on the stairs in front of them, with a good view of the show, but no seat of their own.

"You, take this."

A male servant handed Cassandra a glass of wine and a large plate with fruits and meat. She quickly realized she was the only one there to attend to

38

Kairen. She took it, ignoring the pain in her wrist. Her fingers were trembling under the extra weight on her injury, but she took a couple of steps forward and handed the cup to Kairen while he ignored the food.

When she descended back to her position, the male servant was looking at her with furious eyes.

"You idiot, slave! You were supposed to try the wine before your Master! What if there is poison in the cup?"

Cassandra had no idea. She looked at the man, speechless, and went back to Kairen wondering if she could take the cup back. Thankfully, he hadn't drunk from it yet, but as she was about to ask, he put the cup down and showed no interest in it. She swiftly grabbed it, took a quick sip, and put it back where it was before returning again. The male servant sighed.

"Useless slave..."

"I am very sorry," she whispered.

"Save your apology for your Master! What if he died because of an idiot slave like you? Tsk..."

While cursing her, he stepped away. Cassandra sighed. How could she possibly have known? She had never had any training on attending to the Imperial Family.

After reflecting on her mistake, she went back to listening to what was going on. As expected, only the Imperial Family spoke while the concubines whispered amongst themselves, but none seemed very happy to be there.

"Kairen, my son. Can I never keep you entertained enough that you would share a bit of your time with your father?" asked the Emperor.

"Our brother would rather spend his time with his slave," snickered the Second Prince.

A loud growl suddenly resonated throughout the hall, and Cassandra finally understood why the servants and concubines didn't feel at ease. Next to the Second Prince's throne, what she had mistaken for a statue was actually a very alive Red Dragon. She took a quick look around; aside from the red one, two other dragons were sitting next to their masters. While one of those was caged, the other two were merely muzzled and chained, but they were still at the Imperial Family's level, and close enough to scare anyone around.

It took all of Cassandra's willpower to not stare at the dragons, to keep looking down and wait behind Kairen. They were like his majestic Black Dragon, but smaller ones and differently colored. She remembered the slaughter they had inflicted just hours earlier in the arena and shivered. They weren't calm. Even while standing right next to their masters, one could tell that only the chains were really holding them. They were agitated, glaring at the people around them, and pulling on their restraints. The purple one in the cage kept growling for no reason, frightening the Fifth Prince's concubines each time.

"That's right, Kairen. I heard you were enchanted by a slave from today's games?"

Cassandra jumped. She had almost forgotten the "slave" in question was herself! What would the Emperor say? She didn't dare move from her spot, waiting to see how Kairen would respond. But instead, the Second Prince clicked his tongue.

"To think, after presenting him with countless concubines, our brother's interest would be a slave...You really do have odd tastes, Kairen."

"Brother, is that true?" A young, feminine voice suddenly asked, "A slave?"

Cassandra hadn't realized Princesses, other than Shareen, were there too. From what she recalled, there were six Princes and at least twice as many Princesses, but she only counted five women present, each with their own golden seat like Shareen's. The one who had spoken appeared to be among the youngest. Kairen ignored her, but another Princess, this time in a seat closer to him, raised her voice.

"This is inappropriate. How can we allow lowly, filthy slaves in our presence? Brother, you are far too lenient. That kind of dirt belongs to the lower classes. You should have proper concubines and proper servants."

From where she sat, Cassandra could see the Princess's black hair and as she turned her head, Cassandra looked down just in time. She hadn't been caught staring, but nevertheless, she felt the cold glare of the Princess.

"As high and mighty as ever, Phetra..." sneered Shareen, while taking a seat close to the Emperor.

"You and Kairen should be ashamed of yourselves. Meddling with lowly servants and, worse, slaves!"

But Shareen snickered at her angry sister.

"Someone needs to stop talking out of her ass..." she muttered.

She had said it just loud enough for most people to hear. A few concubines and servants chuckled. But what happened next silenced them all.

In a sudden and swift movement, Phetra took out a whip and lashed it in the direction of one of the servants. She caught a man by the throat and his laugh died right away, leaving only an expression of pure terror on his face. Phetra snapped her whip and threw him right into the cage of one of the colored dragons. The Purple dragon inside jumped on the man, instantly ripping his body in half. All the concubines nearby were splattered with blood.

An ice-cold silence befell the room, apart from the dragon's loud chewing. Cassandra was frozen in complete shock. She only dared a glance towards Kairen and Shareen. While her master hadn't moved an inch, both he and his sister were glaring at Phetra.

But the Princess looked satisfied with herself as she pulled back her whip. The Emperor sighed.

"Phetra, not while we're eating."

"Sorry, Father."

She didn't look apologetic at all though, only giving her siblings a prideful smirk. Meanwhile, Cassandra was still terrified. This family was far too scary. They killed without a shred of remorse or restraint, and for such ridiculous reasons too. Moreover, she felt like Phetra had only done this to infuriate Shareen, whom she couldn't confront directly.

Princess Shareen was glaring at Phetra, not hiding her annoyance very well. Cassandra had a feeling that the hatred between all the siblings had deeper roots than a mere confrontation about servants and slaves. She observed them more carefully now. Phetra had a lot of common traits with the Second Prince. Just like Kairen and Shareen, could those two be siblings from the same mother?

"Enough killing already, all of you. Let's see the next dancers. And Phetra, do not kill your siblings' servants. I'm fed up with your little squabbles."

"Yeah, how about you just kill your own servants instead!" protested the Fifth Prince, clearly annoyed.

Cassandra looked around. Despite staying silent, the other Princesses seemed either shocked or annoyed at Phetra's display. It wasn't just Shareen. It didn't seem like that Princess was particularly popular amongst her siblings at all.

"Mine know their place, Brother. But Kairen seems to need help teaching his," stated Phetra, before turning to Kairen. "Do you need help, Brother?"

Cassandra immediately felt the Princess's venomous glare and wicked intent. Even if she was only a disposable slave, that woman's bloodlust was definitely not normal! But Kairen just glared back.

"Mind your own business, Phetra."

"I only mean to help. Maybe, Kairen..."

A growl suddenly resonated through the hall. Cassandra looked up by reflex as the sky was suddenly covered by a dark shadow. Around her, several people gasped or shrieked. The Black Dragon landed right behind its master, next to Cassandra, and growled furiously at Phetra as if it was echoing its master's anger.

"Try me again," threatened Kairen.

But this time Phetra stayed silent. Her proud attitude from earlier had disappeared as soon as she had fixed her eyes on the Black Dragon. The Princess gulped and stopped boasting, her head and shoulders dropped down as the dragon continued to growl at her.

Shareen snickered.

"That's my son!" exclaimed the Emperor, visibly proud. "Kairen, why didn't you summon him earlier?"

"I didn't have a reason to..." Kairen hissed, still glaring at Phetra.

Shareen and the Emperor were the only ones happy with the Black Dragon's arrival. Everyone else seemed uneasy or scared and for good reason. Its size was far more imposing than the other beasts, as were its claws and fangs. The other dragons became agitated seeing their peer. Cassandra wondered if they naturally feared it.

"How impressive... She really isn't scared at all."

Cassandra suddenly realized one of the Princesses was talking about her. She felt several eyes on her and looked down hard, feeling anxious. Indeed, the large dragon was standing with its head right next to her, its huge body so close that she could feel the heat. Its presence wasn't scary for Cassandra. She was more frightened by the human beings in the room than the beast who had its red eyes on her - eyes filled with the same curiosity as before.

"That's an interesting one you have there, Kairen," said the Fifth Prince. "To be able to stay so close to your beast and not be scared at all."

Cassandra again felt several stares on her, wishing she could hide, when a low growl suddenly got her attention. Curling himself up around her, Krai, the Black Dragon, gently pushed her with its head and rubbed its warm scales against her arm. How could she ignore the beast? She dared a glance towards Kairen but he was ignoring her, his eyes focused on his siblings. For once, she wished her master would spare a glance her way, giving her some clue as to what she was supposed to do.

Krai nudged her arm again and, with a discreet movement, she gently caressed its scales. He growled, a very deep sound that was an obvious display of satisfaction. Cassandra blushed slightly, surprised to have a dragon almost purring from her touch!

"Look at this! The woman is obviously a sorceress! To charm an Imperial dragon like so! Let's just behead her now and put an end to this..."

"Silence..."

Before the Second Prince could finish his sentence, Kairen's words cut him off.

"Or would you like to try and take her from my dragon?"

Hearing this, Krai growled threateningly. Several women cried in fear and the whole place dissolved into chaos with the other dragons growling back and the servants trying to calm everyone down. Still, they all avoided the black beast. Krai was getting agitated, standing guard over Cassandra, and growling at the Second Prince.

The Black Dragon was so large that it didn't even realize it was shoving Cassandra around. Forced to the ground, she suddenly feared it would stomp on her like a mere ant under its claws. The scales over her were moving so frantically, she couldn't tell what was going on.

Suddenly, a large hand grabbed her out of the chaos, pulling her from under the dragon. It took her a second to realize Kairen had brought her to safety, holding her against his chest. Behind them, the Black Dragon was still growling and stomping around, but she barely noticed it now. All she could hear was her own heart, beating too fast in her ears.

Chapter 4

Cassandra slowly opened her eyes.

Where was she? It took her a few seconds to recognize the room and remember the prior events. The Prince's chambers! It was still dark though. What happened at the banquet? She could only remember up to the point where the dragon was going wild.

She realized she was laying in a real bed and feeling... warm. She couldn't remember the last time she had felt so content or slept in real sheets.

However, she couldn't move an inch. Something hot was pressed against her body and Cassandra gasped - it was a man's arm! Moreover, she recognized the scaled braces! She froze, almost unable to breathe. She wasn't just in the Prince's bed, he was in it too!

"...How are you feeling?" the deep voice next to her ear surprised her.

How did he even know she had woken up? He was holding her from behind, his strong body right against her skin. As Cassandra attempted to move she realized someone had bandaged her injured wrist and it smelled of herbal medicine, too.

"My Lord, what happened?" she inquired in a whisper.

"You collapsed at the banquet."

She tried to remember, but the void seemed to confirm what he was saying. It wasn't that surprising. She hadn't eaten in two days, and she wasn't in great condition to begin with, and then to have had so many emotions in one day. It was a lot to deal with.

"You didn't answer."

"I'm better, my Lord," she replied right away, afraid he might become angry.

"...I see."

He stayed silent after that and Cassandra wondered if he had gone back to sleep; she definitely couldn't! This situation was just unbelievable.

She should have died as a nameless slave mere hours ago. So why was it that now she was comfortably laying in a Prince's bed, sheltered from the cold and the whip? She even had brand new clothes, something a slave couldn't ever dream about in a hundred years! What kind of Prince showed interest in a slave, and acted as no one else would? Was it only because of his dragon's interest in her?

What would happen next? She was perfectly aware of her impossible situation. Someone would kill her sooner or later for overstepping her place. The Third Prince Kairen was indeed a stubborn and strong man, but he wouldn't care for her forever.

Presuming her death sentence had only been delayed, Cassandra shivered. Was this what it was like experiencing heaven before you die?

She slowly tried to wiggle away, to leave the bed before something happened. She should definitely not be here. For a slave like herself, even the floor of this bedroom was too good. She had to leave, to sleep in the kitchens or anywhere else, but definitely not in her new master's bed!

"Where are you going?"

Kairen had sensed her moving and held on to her even tighter. Cassandra shook her head, trying to free herself.

"I cannot be here, my Lord, I..."

"Enough."

He suddenly pushed her down into the mattress and positioned himself over her, looking down with angry, obsidian eyes.

"Why is it that you're constantly trying to run away from me?"

Cassandra stared at him blankly, completely taken by surprise by the same question again and their sudden change of position. Having him linger over her was way too intimidating. And why did he always have to be half-naked? She tried to ignore it, to remember his question.

"I'm not trying to run away..."

"Are you not trying to leave right now?"

"I shouldn't be here! This is your bedroom, a slave is not supposed to be here. If someone sees me..."

"Who?"

His cold and imposing voice suddenly scared her, as if she was brutally reminded of who she was arguing with. It was hard to ignore his black eyes on her, but she tried to look away anyway, intimidated.

"I don't know," stuttered Cassandra. "The guards, the Imperial Servants..."

"Do you see anyone but us here right now?"

Strangely, they were indeed all alone. The Imperial Family members usually had a lot of attendants. They had people to take care of their meals, to take care of their clothes, people for everything they would need. Their servants even had higher statuses than common people, and certainly far higher than slaves.

Only Kairen didn't seem to have any attendants. Since she had been around him, Cassandra had seen absolutely no one but the Imperial Palace attendants. Unlike his other siblings, who were never alone, the Third Prince was never followed by anyone but her now...

"...They will know," she murmured, afraid.

She was sure, even though there was no one there to witness, people would talk about the shameless slave following her master to his chambers. Too many people had already seen them. Kairen clicked his tongue, annoyed.

"And? So what if they know?"

Cassandra was helpless. Why did she have to explain everything? This man was either way too confident or way too unaware of the world they lived in! Gathering some courage, she answered him truthfully, her emerald eyes still relaying her fear.

"I might get killed, or worse..."

"Worse?" he repeated with a frown.

"Beaten, tortured... Raped..."

Kairen's expression grew darker with each possible outcome she mentioned, so she stopped, biting her lip nervously. Cassandra was still unable to figure out how he thought. He always seemed either indifferent or angry.

Right now, he was pinning her onto the bed, holding her wrists, exposing her and looking at her like no one else ever had, it was too overwhelming. His eyes were sweeping down her body, ignoring the dress, but taking in the numerous scars it left exposed. His expression grew even darker.

"Who did this?"

"My...previous masters..."

Why was he interested in her scars all of a sudden? She had gotten so many over the years; the worst were the freshest ones. Lyria was horrible to people she didn't like and never spared her efforts in punishing her slaves. The dramatic, red lines still ran over Cassandra's limbs, threatening to tear open again at any moment. She could still vividly remember the feeling of the lashes of the whip where it had cut the deepest.

She had experienced way too much pain to not be scared of punishments again. It was much more terrifying than death...

"...What is your name?"

His question caught her off guard. Why would he be interested in her name? Most masters didn't even care enough to know if she had one! She was only called "you" or "slave" in her past years of servitude. Blushing a bit, she spoke it, that name she hadn't uttered in years.

"...Cassandra."

"Cassandra. Look at me."

It wasn't an order she could disobey. Gathering her courage, she looked up at his two obsidian eyes, like two voids she might get lost in.

"From now on, you are mine. If someone touches you, I'll kill them."

His expression was so serious she didn't know how to respond. Was that a promise? Or a threat?

But somehow, something in her heart mended from hearing those words. Could she trust this man? He was twice as scary as anyone else, yet she felt something indescribable when looking at him. Something that felt like... safety. She hesitated for a moment, then slowly nodded, still looking at him.

"Say it," he ordered, his eyes dark.

"I'm... Yours," she whispered.

His expression changed slightly, his mouth opening with heavy breaths. She could feel the arousal build on his dark skin.

"Say it again," he ordered, his voice getting deeper.

"I'm yours..."

The last word got buried under Kairen's lips connecting with hers.

Completely unnerved, Cassandra felt his rough kiss before she could even react. What was going on? The Prince's hot mouth on hers was forceful, unpredictable, and ruthless. She tried to breathe as his tongue entangled with hers. She could feel his body pressing on her, overpowering her effortlessly.

When he finally retreated from her lips and descended to her breasts, she caught her breath.

"Ma... Master..."

She was entirely unable to think straight. His large, warm hands on her skin were exploring and invading everything. Like a wave, his strength was crashing over her, holding her under him while she was subjected to his caresses.

Cassandra had never experienced anything like this before. Her seventeen years of inexperience were cruelly showing, as she had no clue how to respond. Kairen was in total control of her body, his hands firmly holding her. All of a sudden, he tore her dress, exposing her bare chest to his gaze.

"My Lord! The dress..."

They had just borrowed it, too! Cassandra was mortified, thinking about what she had to do in order to get this dress and how it was now torn to shreds... But Kairen obviously didn't care. Without warning, he sucked on one of her nipples, and she couldn't hold back a surprised moan. She felt her body reacting, her stomach tingling with an odd sensation. Unable to think straight, she reached out for him, running her hands through his black hair, shivering under his tongue's movements. He had grabbed her other breast now, playing with both at the same time.

"Hmm... My Lord..."

Cassandra couldn't hold back her moans as much as she tried. The hotness of his mouth on her pink extremities was unbearable. Though she didn't look, she could feel his tongue and his teeth grazing and sucking, biting softly. Moreover, he was pressing his entire body against her, and Cassandra could feel his hips compelling her legs to open into a new, awkward position for her. She could feel everything; the rustling of the sheets, their clothing, his mouth on her skin, and her own embarrassing voice, echoing in the room.

Without warning, Kairen put his hand between her legs.

"Ah! N...No..."

He frowned, his dark eyes on her made Cassandra blush. His hands weren't stopping, but his gaze was fixated on her, making her crazy with embarrassment.

"No?" he repeated.

She blushed and bit her lip. Was she really so unable to control her own body? How embarrassing! She was breathing and moaning louder as Kairen continued caressing her. His fingers found their way to her slit, stroking it until they slid through to rub her entrance. Cassandra gasped, a seductive sensation spreading through her whole body. His movements were fast and insisting, going in and out, rubbing and pressing further into her.

Her legs were trembling, and she was struggling to breathe correctly. The fire raging inside was driving her crazy, and she wanted more. Without realizing, Cassandra had grabbed her master's shoulder with her free hand to brace herself.

"Hm... Ma... Oh! Mas...Master... hn..."

"What is it?"

Kairen's eyes were focused on her, considering each of her reactions to his touch. Occasionally, he leaned down to suck and lick her breasts again, but more than that, he was hypnotized by her cries and moans. Playing with her pussy, he was moving his fingers into her, subjecting her to new pleasures. He felt her juices moisten his hand, while his own body was already reacting to her.

She was his. He had thought this the minute his dragon had put her at his feet - when he had seen her from up close. He wanted this woman, no matter who she was. He wanted all of her.

"Say it again."

"Hm... Wh...What?"

His fingers slowed down their movements, giving her a minute of respite so she could understand and answer.

Catching her breath, Cassandra looked at him, his face so close she could see every small detail. This man was her new master. An odd, unforgiving, and ruthless Prince. A Dragon Lord and War God.

"I'm... I'm yours..." she whispered to him, with a breathy voice.

"Again."

His hands undid his buckle to remove his pants, and she heard the clothes falling to the floor. She trembled, a bit unsure and scared.

"I'm yours," she repeated the words, to also reassure herself.

"Again."

She repeated them again and again, while he positioned himself between her spread legs. As the blood rushed to her cheeks and ears, she felt his member against her entrance, and kept repeating those words, like a prayer.

"I'm yours, I'm yours... I'm... Ah!"

Cassandra whimpered in pain, feeling his cock pushing in. Kairen stopped, his hot breath against her ear.

"Breathe," he said to her soothingly.

She tried, wondering if it was supposed to be this painful. Once he thought she was getting used to it, the Prince pushed further in and she cried out again. His movements were slow, but she was so unused to the sensation, and he was also large. She tried to breathe, listening to his voice as he was groaning.

"You're... tight..."

She held onto him tighter, pulling him in a little and catching his eyes.

"Slower," she simply said.

Her voice came out clear like a demand, the first one she had formulated in years. Almost an order, at this unexpected time. Kairen, a bit surprised, obeyed without thinking. Gaging her reactions, he went at a slower pace, his back and forth matching Cassandra's labored breathing.

She tried to get more comfortable with his hard member inside her, focusing on the better sensations and pushing the pain away. She was used to pain, she could handle it. But behind it now, something much more pleasurable was waiting, and she wanted to reach it. Kairen moved inside her, and she found herself slowly gyrating her hips to follow his rhythm, trying to share the control of their movements.

Cassandra felt him accelerate, his cock rubbing faster inside her, stirring her up. She wasn't even trying to hold her voice back anymore. She was flooded with too many sensations to concern herself with that.

"A...Aaah! Hm...Hm, hm..."

Her cries melded with Kairen's groans. It was painful, but it was good too. And she could tell he was not stopping anyway. The War God was on her, inside her, unleashing himself and moving wildly. Cassandra's moans grew louder as he went faster, holding her under him, his cock pounding...

With a final thrust, he stopped deep inside her, groaning hard. Something warm filled her insides and she moaned again, the sensation driving her crazy.

She trembled as she slowly regained her senses. She felt his lips press against hers and answered the kiss without thinking, too tired to consider anything else.

When she woke up the next morning, Cassandra's whole body felt completely sore. Blushing at the memory of the intense sex with her master, she pulled the bedsheet over her naked body.

But, looking around, she realized that she was alone in the large bedroom. Did her master leave early? She got up, keeping the bed sheet around her. The Prince had torn her only dress, so she felt a bit helpless, naked, and alone in the Prince's room, with no clue what to do. She didn't even know how late in the day it was.

Suddenly, there was a little knock at the door. As a servant entered, Cassandra recognized the young woman as one of Princess Shareen's, the one who had advised her the previous day.

She was carrying a little parcel which she promptly unwrapped before Cassandra.

"Good Morning. His Highness requested a new dress for you."

"Oh, thank you," said Cassandra.

It was a new, dark red one this time. Cassandra frowned upon seeing the color. Didn't servants in the Palace commonly wear green?

"That color..."

"It is the color worn by low-ranking concubines. You'll be wearing this from now on"

Cassandra blushed. So they would all now be aware that she had slept with the Third Prince! It seemed unreal that this information was already known as soon as the very next morning. Were they seen? Or was it because she had slept in the Prince's bedroom all night?

"But this..."

She raised a hand to the slavery collar still hanging around her neck. Could a slave really be a concubine? She didn't think it was possible! The young servant girl gently smiled at her and shook her head.

"Do not worry, it's not like there hasn't been any precedents set for Princes and Emperors taking slaves as concubines. Your life will most likely get a bit easier if you wear this, even if you are still a slave. But you cannot be treated the same as high-ranking concubines or taken as the official wife."

Cassandra nodded. Even to be taken as a low-ranking concubine was too much for her, she couldn't imagine anything more! She looked at the dress again, wondering if her master had known this would happen.

"What is your name?" she asked the young servant.

"Dahlia."

"Thank you for the dress, Dahlia..."

The young woman bowed with a smile and swiftly left the room, leaving Cassandra feeling odd. It was the first time someone had ever bowed to her.

Still a bit hesitant about what to do next, she started by washing herself at the little water basin. She thought of last night again, making her blush once more. The Prince had been so... fierce! She hadn't expected that having sex required so much stamina. She had some mild bruising on her arms where he had held her a bit too tightly. Thankfully her wrist wasn't as painful as before, so she didn't have any trouble putting the dress on - the deep red dress... Cassandra didn't know much about the Imperial Palace's protocols, but she recalled seeing the concubines in various shades of red and pink. Was pink the color reserved for the high-ranked concubines then?

The Prince suddenly came back into the room, his eyes immediately finding her.

"You're up."

"Yes, Your Highness..."

He looked over and Cassandra followed his gaze to a little table, where she hadn't noticed a large tray of food. There were fruits, meats, cheeses and wine. The Prince frowned,

"Why haven't you eaten?"

"I hadn't noticed..."

"Aren't you hungry?"

"Yes."

How could she not be? The last time she ate was more than two days ago! She might have been starving but she was used to the painful sensation of hunger. Upon seeing those delicious looking plates, however, she couldn't repress the hungry growl emitted by her stomach.

"Let's eat then."

He walked over and sat in a large armchair while Cassandra followed and, like she would have done with her previous masters, knelt on the floor next to him, but Kairen frowned.

"What are you doing?"

He grabbed her arm and pulled her up onto his lap without warning. Cassandra was suddenly straddling his leg, facing him, dangerously close. The swift action brought her attention to his bare chest, causing her to blush!

"Master, I can't!"

But he ignored her and took a slice of meat from the table. His other hand was still firmly holding Cassandra in place, and she had to put her hand on his shoulder to keep herself steady. What kind of embarrassing position was this? She hoped he would let her go, but Kairen just kept eating, ignoring her pleading eyes.

"Eat. We have a long journey ahead."

"A long journey?" she asked, a bit lost.

"Going home. The Festival is over."

She suddenly realized it was the eighth day! The Festival had ended this morning and the Princes were now free to go back to their respective lands. So he was bringing her back to his castle then? She wondered what kind of place it was.

Kairen brought a grape to her lips and Cassandra had no choice but to take it. She was a bit embarrassed, but was distracted by the amazingly sweet taste! She remembered eating dried or rotted grapes, but never fresh ones. She took her time eating the little fruit while he watched her with a slight grin. She blushed again; it was her first time receiving something close to a smile from him.

She finally reached out her hand to take another grape and started eating with delight. This was so great, to be able to eat without worry. Before, she had to eat quickly and hidden from her masters, so that she wouldn't be beaten for slacking off. And slaves could only eat what servants wouldn't even want, leftovers and rotten food. Once in a while, she would be lucky enough to get some rice or dried fruits, but never fresh fruit, cheese or meat. This was all a first for her!

Kairen was silently watching her eat, one arm on the armchair and his other around her waist. He took some meat from time to time, but he was mostly busy observing each of his new concubine's movements. Cassandra continued eating small bites like a little bird. It was obvious she was avoiding his gaze, blushing and looking down.

50

As she placed a little cube of cheese in her mouth, Kairen suddenly took her chin between his fingers and pulled her in for a kiss. Playing with her tongue, he stole the little cube, eating it before her stunned eyes.

"M...Master!"

How could he do that?! Cassandra was so surprised by his childish game she hadn't even been able to react. Kairen tilted his head towards the food.

"Give me some meat."

Grabbing a greasy piece of beef, she handed it to him, wondering why he was suddenly acting lazy. But Kairen just looked at her, ignoring the food. She didn't really understand his strange behavior until...! That's when she understood - he wanted her to do it again. It was so embarrassing!

"Cassandra."

His forceful tone made her even more uneasy. She knew she couldn't refuse him, and it was just feeding him, right? She took the meat between her lips and approached him. This time, Kairen leaned in, grabbing it from her mouth while kissing her. The meat's juice dripped from their lips while their tongues entangled. Soon enough, the Prince had eaten the little piece but kept their deep kiss going. Not letting go of her, Kairen kept her close, preventing Cassandra from backing away.

Their kiss was so intense she could barely keep up with his lips. The taste of the meat lingered there, something sweet and sour. When he finally relaxed his embrace, Cassandra leaned back to catch her breath, a bit light-headed.

Without anything more, Kairen grabbed a new bite himself this time, eating the meat as if nothing had happened.

Cassandra was completely lost by his sudden change of demeanor. Still, she grabbed more food, hoping he would let her eat in peace this time. Kairen had apparently decided to oblige her unspoken wish as they ate in silence, Cassandra enjoying a bit of each food that was there. Her master was still holding her by the waist, only occasionally caressing her with his thumb, and only asked for food to be delivered by kissing a couple more times. Cassandra complied, but was just as embarrassed as the first time and was relieved when he finally stopped eating before her.

Even with his close presence and the embarrassing position, she found it impossible to ignore the delicious food and ate her fill for the first time in a very long while. Once she was pleasantly full and feeling much better than before, she awkwardly kept her stare on the plate of remaining food, not sure of what to do next.

Kairen leaned in to kiss her neck without warning, pulling her to face him completely.

"Are you done?" he asked.

"Yes..." she whispered.

Without adding anything else, Kairen got up and pulled Cassandra to follow behind him. He grabbed two fur coats, handing one to her as they headed outside. Cassandra was a bit surprised; a fur coat again? When Kairen opened the door of his chambers, two Palace servants suddenly rushed over and Cassandra instinctively hid behind him. She still remembered how she had been brutally dragged out the previous day.

"What is it?"

Kairen frowned at her strange behavior but she shook her head, only staying close behind him. The two servants didn't even bother to look at her as they bowed in front of the Prince. Those men weren't the same ones as before, and the Prince was there, but they still made her nervous.

"His Highness the Imperial Dragon sent us to remind Your Highness that your presence is requested in three months for the Spring Festival and he sends his congratulations on your new concubine. Gifts will be sent for the Lady to Your Highness's palace."

Cassandra was speechless! Were they talking about her? Was the King truly happy his son had taken her for a concubine? And to send gifts too! She couldn't even begin to process what was happening, but Kairen just ignored the men and walked on.

She followed him closely, wondering where they were headed. If he wanted to leave, shouldn't he have headed for the stables? But instead, he was headed to the large gardens of the Imperial Palace, ignoring all the servants who were bowing along the way.

It was only when they finally reached the end of a large, vined garden that Cassandra understood. A mountain of black scales was heading their way with excited eyes. They weren't going by horse or carriage, they were going to fly!

Excited, the Black Dragon scampered their way, lowering its gigantic head to their level and keeping its red eyes on them. Cassandra had almost forgotten that it was allowed to wander around freely. No one wanted to mess with the dragon and Kairen didn't need to restrain it either.

Despite its impressive size and the limited space in the courtyard, the dragon once again tried to reach out to Cassandra, growling softly in her direction. She still couldn't understand what it wanted, but she was happy to see it so interested in her.

"Get on."

Surprised, Cassandra turned to Kairen. How was she supposed to mount the dragon? Those scales looked way too sharp and uneven! Krai was waiting and watching with big, red, curious eyes. Was it really alright for her to mount it? An Imperial dragon! Most people would feel blessed just getting a chance to see them once in their life, let alone touch one. And not only had she been able to touch it, but the Prince also wanted her to ride it!

"So slow," grumbled Kairen.

Without warning, he suddenly lifted Cassandra up onto his shoulder, making her squeal in surprise.

"My Lord!"

Despite her protests, Kairen climbed on to his dragon in only a few movements, keeping Cassandra over his shoulder until he was securely seated. When he finally put her down, she was sitting right in front of him, close to his warm torso. They were so far from the ground and the dragon hadn't even taken off yet! Cassandra felt a bit scared by the height and held on tightly, gripping his fur cloak in her hands. Kairen clicked his tongue and, beneath them, Krai let out a long, loud growl.

"Let's go," he said, grabbing the dragon's collar.

As soon as the words left his lips, Krai extended his wings. The dragon flapped them a couple of times, as if to stretch, and then took off. Cassandra, surprised by the sudden movements, grabbed Kairen even tighter as she repressed a scream. This was really too scary!

The Prince wrapped his arm around her waist and held her firmly as Krai ascended. She stayed like that for a while, hidden against his chest, holding on as tightly as she possibly could. And while she was too scared to look, she could still feel the huge dragon's movements.

"Cassandra."

She moved just a little so she could look at the Prince's face, as he pointed his chin to the side.

"Look."

Trying to forget her fear, she gathered up the courage to look. They were so high already! Kairen pointed down towards the ground. Cassandra was seeing the Capital like she had never seen it before - from the skies. She could recognize the main streets, the large Market Place, and the biggest buildings. It was like seeing a huge, detailed map of the City she had always known, as it came alive right under her eyes.

Despite her fear, she couldn't stop looking. She recognized so many things, despite the distance!

"Oh..."

"What?"

"That is the residence of my former master."

Kairen looked down, where Cassandra had her eyes set on a large manor, and his eyes became even darker.

"...We can burn it down."

"What? No, no!" exclaimed Cassandra.

He couldn't possibly burn a whole building down like that! Kairen was visibly angry and frowned while still glaring at the Manor.

"My Lord, you can't just set it on fire! What if the fire expands? There are innocent people down there, too."

She thought about the other slaves that were probably still working there, far from her new situation. While he still seemed unhappy, Kairen finally turned his head, the Manor leaving his sight. Cassandra couldn't help but roll her eyes. Her master was really too blunt and reckless at times.

Once that was more or less resolved, Cassandra finally felt better about the ride. Kairen was holding her firmly and Krai had stopped rising and was now keeping a steady altitude. He was very fast though, as she soon lost sight of the Capital. They were headed north-east, further than she had ever been in her entire life.

The flight took them away from the cities and through vast, uninhabited lands. It was a breathtaking sight. From where they were, Cassandra could see the range of mountains in the north and the Eastern Sea. But the farther they went, the more she wondered what her Prince's lands were like... All the Emperor's children had many assets they were endowed with at birth. As one of the potential heirs to the Golden Throne, Kairen probably had plenty of riches too. She remembered he also had an army. Would there be a military camp?

"Cassandra."

Not even realizing she had fallen asleep, Cassandra slowly woke upon hearing her name. The sudden sensation of the descent surprised her so she was now wide awake. Krai was heading down, aiming towards a very large, dark castle. The landscape had changed a lot too since the City. She could no longer see vast plains, but rather a large dry area with a few nearby buildings. It was a much darker atmosphere than the Capital, and more solemn too.

"Are those... the Shadelands?" she asked.

Kairen slowly nodded.

The Shadelands were infamous, like an old legend among the people. Long ago, those territories had been the grounds for terrible wars between the clans. The fights had lasted so long and burned so much of the vegetation, that it was said nothing could grow there anymore. The soil was burned too deeply to even attempt planting anything. Among the desolation there was erected a tall, isolated Castle.

Krai landed slowly in the inner court with a loud growl. Cassandra wondered if the trip had been too long or if it was just happy to be home. Kairen helped her down and as soon as her feet hit the ground, she was suddenly aware of the numbness in her back. Dragon riding was more physical than she had thought... She kept the fur cloak wrapped around her as it was definitely much colder here than in the Capital.

As the Prince dismounted too, she suddenly noticed people walking towards them.

"Welcome back, my Lord!"

An old woman and a middle-aged man, both well dressed, bowed in front of Kairen. He practically ignored them as he walked up to Krai's head.

"Go."

Instead of going, Krai growled softly and turned to Cassandra, pushing her with its snout. She could feel the dragon's hot breath, as it kept playfully pushing her around, its big tail swaying dangerously.

The two people who had come were looking at the scene, completely at a loss. Kairen growled a bit.

"Krai."

The dragon feigned deafness, and continued giving little head-bumps to Cassandra's side. She had no idea if she was supposed to go along with the dragon or ignore it, but it was hard to ignore the mountain of scales that kept nudging her. The Prince glared at the big beast who was intent on playing with Cassandra.

"My Lord, what do you want us to do with, uh..." asked the man, a bit hesitant.

Kairen clicked his tongue, visibly irritated, but turned around.

"Nevermind."

He walked inside the Castle, leaving Cassandra alone with Krai. The middle-aged man, who was so short and broad he was almost a square, followed him on his stubby legs, giving one last glance to Cassandra.

She was left with the large dragon and the old woman, who didn't look amicable at all. The old lady had grey hair and wore a simple, well-maintained dress and a stubborn look on her face.

"Slave, where did the Master get you?"

Cassandra had almost forgotten about her collar. With the fur cloak around her, the lady couldn't see her dress color. She wondered if she should let her know she was also a concubine even though she was obviously still a slave too?

"At the Palace, madam."

"Tsk. Come work in the kitchens once you're done entertaining the Master's dragon!"

"Y...yes."

Cassandra wasn't sure. Was she supposed to work? Kairen hadn't mentioned anything before bringing her to the Castle, but she couldn't possibly laze around and do nothing either.

As soon as the old woman was gone, Krai suddenly rubbed its head against her, lowly growling with its big eyes on her. Cassandra chuckled. Why was this dragon more cat-like than ferocious with her? She gently caressed its black scales. They were indeed incredibly sharp, but they were also smooth, like glass. She could easily cut herself if she didn't pay attention. Some parts were more tender, like snake skin, especially under his maw. Cassandra noticed that Krai seemed to like it a lot when she scratched that spot, hence she kept attending to it, making the dragon growl softly.

"Oh! Em... Ehm... Excuse me..."

A young girl had come into the inner courtyard, pulling a large cart. She froze upon seeing the Black Dragon and Cassandra, obviously impressed, but also rightfully frightened. She looked very young, around thirteen or fourteen, and didn't dare to move.

"I... I have to..."

She was so stressed by Krai's presence, she kept stuttering, unable to take her eyes off the dragon. But the Black Dragon didn't care at all, its head not leaving Cassandra's side.

"Do you need to walk through?" asked Cassandra gently.

The girl nodded frantically.

"Alright... Wait a second."

Cassandra turned around, catching Krai's attention. She walked a little ways away and the dragon immediately followed her, leaving the middle of the inner court empty for the young servant to pass through.

"Ah! Thank you."

While still sending worried glances towards the dragon, the young girl took a wide path to cross the inner court to her destination, pulling her cart quickly. Cassandra made sure to keep distracting Krai until she was gone.

She sighed when they were alone.

"You do look scary," she whispered to the dragon.

Krai growled a bit and spread its wings, suddenly turning its head in another direction. Had it smelled something? The dragon was watching something beyond the wall, only its height enabling it to see so far away. Cassandra wondered if it usually fed itself as it was obviously distracted by something more interesting.

Headed in the direction it was looking, the dragon suddenly took off towards the source of its focus. Cassandra guessed that it was probably hunting time.

"Slave! Are you done tending to the Master's dragon yet?"

The old woman had returned and stalked up to her.

"I am the head of the servants here, Patrina. You will call me Madam, understand?"

"Y...yes, Madam."

"Good. What can you do?"

"Hem... Cooking, cleaning, washing clothes, field work, knitting and writing..."

Patrina frowned.

"Writing? You know how to read and write?"

"Yes, Madam."

It was very unusual for a slave, but that's because most slaves were born into slavery and did not have access to any kind of schooling. Cassandra, however, had been taught as a child and practiced secretly by herself. The skill, unique for a slave, had added a bit to her value in front of her previous masters...

"Interesting. Anyway, come with me. Now that the Master is back, we need extra hands in the kitchen. Why do you have this fur cloak? You need to change. Come."

Cassandra followed the old woman, feeling unsure. Kairen had gone off elsewhere without telling her what she was supposed to do in the Castle.

Walking at a quick pace, Patrina took her to a large kitchen where two other women were working. They both turned their heads when they saw her coming, surprised.

"A new head? And a slave, too?" asked a tall woman with long brown hair.

56

"His Highness brought her from the Palace," said Patrina, not stopping.

Cassandra walked right behind her, only glancing briefly at the other women. The tall one didn't seem to care much about her as she shrugged and went back to her chores. The second one, who was sitting on the side cutting fruit, gave her a gentle smile as their eyes met. She was a redhead with freckles all over her face.

"Come in here."

Patrina took her to a little room off to the side of the kitchen. It looked like a storage room, with baskets of vegetables and dried meats lined up along one side. Along the other, there were all kinds of fabrics piled up on a shelf; Patrina headed that way.

"It's a lot hotter in the Capital than it is here, you'll want to change into something warmer. You..."

She suddenly went quiet. Cassandra had started taking the fur coat off her shoulders. Patrina, surprised, stared at the red dress for a few seconds before regaining her composure.

"You are... the Master's concubine?"

"Yes," admitted Cassandra, blushing a bit.

Patrina sighed.

"And a slave... You should have told me sooner! Really, what was the Master thinking? I don't know if I have anything proper to dress you!"

"Anything is fine!" said Cassandra suddenly. "I really don't mind the dress."

"No, no. There are rules. A slave concubine...I don't even know what I can give you that would be appropriate. Why hasn't this come off yet?"

She was hinting at Cassandra's slave collar; but those collars didn't come off easily. Cassandra shook her head, feeling a bit helpless.

"His Highness doesn't have my slave contract..."

Patrina sighed.

"I see. It can't be helped then. Oh whatever, I guess we'll have to work with it. Let me think... I can't have you doing any hard labor..."

Cassandra felt really odd about the whole situation. Slaves were usually made to do the worst and hardest jobs but, because of her dual status as the Prince's concubine, she couldn't do anything that might injure herself. She also couldn't do anything that would get her too dirty or be too close to male servants. But doing nothing while other servants around her worked wouldn't be appropriate either since she was still a slave too. It really was quite complicated!

"Let's do this. You will work inside the Castle only, and serve His Highness whenever necessary. We will find where you can help eventually, it's not like we ever run out of things to do. Let's see what he decides about your bedroom later. Oh here, try putting this one on."

Patrina had taken out a long, thick wool tunic. The white, sleeveless frock fit over her red dress, ensuring her concubine attire would still be visible.

"My bedroom?"

"Yes, I can't have you sleep in the stables and smell like a horse! We have servant rooms too. So, I'll prepare you one just in case, but His Highness might have you sleep in one of the empty rooms upstairs."

Cassandra remembered the shape of the Castle from her arrival, like a mountain of towers and grey stone; it did, indeed, seem very large. But despite its size, Cassandra had only seen a handful of workers so far. With all those rooms and so few workers... She suddenly wondered how many concubines Kairen actually had here and felt a little pinch in her heart. Could this be jealousy or sadness at the thought that he might have had other favorites? How silly...

"You're so skinny, all bones! Put this belt on, too, maybe you'll look like something. There we go."

Indeed, the thin leather belt added some structure to her ensemble, showing off her thin waist. Cassandra felt more properly dressed in this, something better suited for the cold weather. She quickly did her long braid over and arranged it in a bun so that she could work without it getting in the way.

Patrina nodded, looking satisfied.

"Looks good. I suppose we can always make you other outfits later, if need be."

Cassandra felt this was more than enough already. She had worn the same overused slave dress for years. Just being able to change into something new and clean felt like a blessing! The silk and wool felt great on her skin, too and warmed her up.

Patrina grabbed a basket of fruits on her way out as Cassandra followed.

"We'll give you a tour later. For now, the Master just came back, so we have to cook his dinner. You'll help us."

"What should I do?"

"You can wash those vegetables first."

Cassandra nodded as they returned to the kitchen. The two servant women raised their heads upon seeing them.

"Madam, we are running out of... What is that?!"

Completely speechless, the taller woman pointed at Cassandra's dress, unable to hide her shock. Patrina rolled her eyes and walked over to the large counter.

"That's how it is."

"She can't be a concubine!"

This time around, the woman didn't hide her anger and disgust. She didn't even look at Cassandra, only at the red dress, her eyes burning with obvious jealousy. Patrina clicked her tongue and slapped her hand on the table.

"Enough! Nebora, stop shouting and get back to work!"

Cassandra didn't dare move with that woman still glaring at her. The other servant, who looked a bit younger than Nebora, walked over and took her hand.

"Here, I'll show you the water system."

Cassandra was only too happy to ignore Nebora's seething anger. Ignoring her colleague, the redhead guided her to a large sink and acted as if nothing was out of the ordinary.

"You just have to roll this over a few times, and the water will flow. Careful though, it's very cold. We need to make sure to use it several times a day so it doesn't freeze."

"Thank you. I think I've used this type before."

"Really? Good then! I was wondering if the Palace's systems might be more advanced. Anyway, you can just wash these off for now and I'll cut them. alright?"

Cassandra nodded.

"Thank you very much," she whispered.

The young woman smiled.

"You're welcome, we don't get to see new faces often, so... I'm Marian, by the way."

"Cassandra."

"Oh, you have a name? And it's pretty, too! Alright Cassandra, you can start with those then. Let's hurry up, Patrina gets grumpy when we are slow."

Compared to Nebora's attitude, Marian was more outgoing, she at least smiled at Cassandra, too, which made her feel better. It would be hard if she couldn't get along with anyone here... The redhead turned out to be quite clumsy. She almost cut herself several times while handling the vegetables, mostly because she kept chatting at the same time. Cassandra felt anxious every time she watched her use the knife. So much so, she was careful to only give her one vegetable at a time and keep an eye on her movements. Patrina too, kept telling Marian to focus, despite being busy herself with baking bread.

As the chores went on, Cassandra was surprised to only see a handful of servants walking around. Why was no one else busy at this time of day? The four women worked until the meal for the Prince was ready, but that was pretty much it.

Patrina put the silver tray into Cassandra's hands.

"Here. You can take it upstairs to the Prince's chambers."

"That's my job!" Nebora yelled suddenly.

Cassandra was exhausted by the woman's attitude. Since she had been there, Nebora had continuously shown annoyance towards her. She glared and complained the entire time. What kind of childishness was this?

"Enough, Nebora," Patrina sighed. "Cassandra will give the Master his meal. She is his concubine and therefore has more rights than you..."

"More rights? She is just a damn slave! Have you seen her collar? She shouldn't even be touching his food! I am the one who brings meals to His Highness!"

As offended as she felt by the comment, Cassandra was more annoyed by Nebora's yelling and childish attitude. Even if she was jealous or had something against slaves, her whole charade was too much!

Cassandra pushed the tray of food into Nebora's hands without warning. Surprised, the woman grabbed it just in time for it not to fall.

"Go ahead, take it."

"Cassandra..." started Patrina, but she shook her head.

"She can take it up to His Highness if she wants to so much. I don't want to argue over something so silly."

Cassandra's tempered tone greatly contrasted with Nebora's attitude, making her sound twice as petty, especially now that she actually had the tray in her hands. But that didn't calm her down. Annoyed by Cassandra's display, Nebora threw the tray on the table with a bang. One of the plates fell, shattering loudly and tossing some of the bread on the floor. She started yelling, not even looking at the food.

"Who the hell do you think you are?! You are not to make deci..."

Before she could end the sentence, Cassandra slapped her.

A heavy silence fell over the kitchen as three pairs of eyes looked at her in total shock. Even Patrina had no idea how to react. Nebora put a hand on her burning cheek, trying hard to process what just happened. She was looking at Cassandra as if she was some kind of monster.

"I don't care if you don't have any respect for me," Cassandra stated. "But at the very least, you should learn to have some respect for the food, and the people who spent time preparing it, for His Highness!"

Walking past her shocked colleague, Cassandra crouched down to pick up the bread and put it back on the counter, cutting off the parts that had touched the floor. Nebora looked shaken by her words. Her anger had somewhat disappeared and was replaced by a visible red hue on her cheeks.

"It... It... It's just some bread..."

"It's His Highness' bread," corrected Cassandra. "I have seen people whipped and killed for a lot less than dropping their Master's food."

Once again, she spoke very calmly, while Nebora finally seemed embarrassed by her actions. As she continued picking up the broken pieces of plate, she suddenly cut her finger on one of the shards. Marian hurried to help her pick the rest up. When they were done, Cassandra handed it all to Marian and picked up the tray again. She headed for the stairs, but stopped in front of Nebora, who was in her way.

"Some people are starving and would do anything to get some bread," she said to Nebora. "Patrina spent a long time making this, too. So, if you want to bring this to His Highness, you are responsible for it the entire way. Do you want to take it or not?"

Taken aback by her question, Nebora looked at Cassandra and saw that she was asking seriously, without a hint of anger or hatred towards her. That made her feel even worse, and she shook her head while looking down, completely remorseful and embarrassed.

"Alright. Then you can lead the way for me, I don't know where to go."

Again, Nebora was rendered speechless. After the scene from earlier, was Cassandra still completely willing to let her come along? Unable to utter a word, she nodded awkwardly and turned around leading the way to the stairs as Cassandra followed behind her with the tray.

Still standing in the kitchen, Patrina and Marian were speechless.

Chapter 5

Climbing the stairs in front of her, Nebora didn't dare raise her head. She could still feel the burn of Cassandra's slap on her cheek, but the most painful thing was her wounded ego. Now that she had calmed down, she indeed realized that her actions from earlier were too childish.

She stole glances at Cassandra as they went up the stairs, intrigued by the young woman. They were probably around the same age, but Cassandra's body was marked from her years as a slave. She had scars all over her pale skin. The oldest ones had turned white and faded with time, but Nebora could see there were also more recent ones that were still red and fresh.

That and her skinny body aside though, Cassandra was obviously very pretty. She had gorgeous green eyes and long brown hair, with a reddish tint. Nebora, on the other hand, was quite average; she had brown hair, dark eyes with sun tanned skin, and was too tall. Her only assets were her ample breasts and curvy hips. For a long time, she had hoped these would help her get a husband and a comfortable life as a housewife. However, no one had gotten serious with her and she became bitter as the years passed.

She had thought herself lucky when she was picked to be a servant to the Castle, two years ago, and appointed to deliver the Prince's meals. What woman wouldn't want to be close to a Prince! With every tray she had carried, she had held on to that little hope inside her that maybe, just maybe, the Third Prince would finally see her.

When they finally reached one of the higher floors of the Castle, the walls subtly started to change. Cassandra hadn't noticed before, but the Castle's walls were black, not white or grey like those of the Palace. They emitted a unique smell, too; something acrid and smoky, like charcoal.

As the two women kept climbing, the matte black suddenly turned into a shiny, smooth texture. The area felt colder, too. If her hands weren't busy carrying the tray, Cassandra would have touched it. She could almost see her own reflection in the millions of little facets!

"What is this...?" she asked in a whisper.

"Onyx stones. According to legend, this Castle must always be black, tainted by the ashes of battlefields, the home of the War God... It was built on a sleeping volcano, the previous owners added those black gemstones when they expanded the Castle," explained Nebora.

"The home of the War God...?"

The servant nodded.

"For generations, only the best fighters and generals in the Empire have lived here. It is said the Castle will collapse, or the volcano underneath will burst in anger if the owner is unworthy. It can even stay empty for years if the Imperial Dragon believes no one merits the title. The Castle was gifted to His Highness four years ago after his victory against the Eastern Republic and the Barbarian Tribes. Before that, the Castle had been empty for nearly sixty years."

Sixty years! No wonder it looked so empty and desolate. With no one to live here, most of the rooms they passed through didn't even have the most basic furniture, or if they did, it was old and covered in dust.

Did that also explain why these lands seemed so... uninhabited? Cassandra remembered the vast empty fields they had flown over. She had been surprised by how few villages and houses she had seen. The weather wasn't the best, but it wasn't bad enough to justify the lack of people. Though without a Lord to watch over the area, and govern and regulate it, no wonder the locals had been forgotten about and left on their own.

"These are the Prince's apartments."

The two women stopped in front of a set of large doors. Nebora hesitated a bit, but Cassandra's hands were obviously busy with carrying the large tray, so she stepped forward to push open the large doors.

It wasn't what Cassandra had expected at all. It was a vast tower, with a roof so high nobody could reach it. There were only two windows, but each was so large that the light was radiating into the room. This chamber was also the one with the most furniture by far. Quickly taking a look at her surroundings, Cassandra noticed a desk, several chairs, two tables, a chaise covered with Kairen's fur cloak, a large canopy bed, a couple of bookshelves, and at least three or four chests.

When the women walked in, Kairen was sitting on the bed and raised his head. From his messy hair, Cassandra wondered if he had just been resting until then. Or, was he reading? There were scrolls and documents scattered on the bedside table.

"Where were you?" he asked abruptly.

"In the kitchen, helping, my Lord"

Nebora frowned slightly. Cassandra's calm tone and slight blush while answering their Master was totally unexpected. She gazed at the Prince, but it was obvious he was only addressing Cassandra and wasn't sparing her a single glance. Once again, jealousy pinched at her heart and she looked down, angry. Cassandra's actions earlier had made a strong impression on her and now she was only left with her bitterness.

The Third Prince was an impressive, strong and muscular man. His face was rather handsome as well, but stern with his dark eyes. It was like looking at a tiger - dangerous and beautiful. Despite his coldness, Nebora couldn't help but find him attractive, but he was not a man she could just approach when she wanted. All those times before, she had brought every tray, every bottle, with the slightest hope he might look at her.... He never did.

Yet, that untouchable man was looking at Cassandra, talking to her and listening to her as if it were the most natural thing in the world. Nebora had a hard time understanding why this was happening. The only thought she was left with was that Cassandra was on a whole other level than her.

Stepping forward, Cassandra silently put the tray down on the table closest to Kairen. As she was doing that, the Prince suddenly grabbed her wrist, pulling her to him without even acknowledging the food.

She was brought between his knees, still standing while he was sitting, his face level with her breasts.

"My Lord, your food..."

"Later," he growled.

Indeed, he didn't even look at it and instead placed his hands on Cassandra's hips, drawing her even closer to him. She gasped in surprise at his sudden movement. She recognized the same glimmer of lust in his eyes as before. As he gazed intensely at her, his hand moved down her leg to the end of her skirt, before sliding back up underneath, caressing her skin. Cassandra trembled. It was still the middle of the day, yet he was already intent on touching her!

His torso was bare, and she had no choice but to put a hand on his shoulder when his hot hand suddenly made her shiver.

"Are you cold?" he asked, in his raspy voice.

"A bit..."

Indeed, the room, being the highest in the Castle, was quite cold. Cassandra's milky skin could barely handle it, but it may have also been the contrast with Kairen's seductive hands that made it even worse. He smirked and suddenly pulled her on the bed and into the folds of a thick fur blanket. With Cassandra lying across the bed, he leaned over her, placing his hands on either side of her head.

She started blushing uncontrollably, with his face so close and the memories of the previous night coming back to her.

"My... My Lord... It's still early..." she stuttered.

Kairen obviously didn't care at all. He started kissing her, licking and biting her lips, while his hands were pulling her skirt up. He kissed lower on her jaw, down from the high part of her neck, but frowned when he met the cold metal of her slavery collar.

"Get this damn thing off," he growled.

"W...what?"

"Your collar, take it off."

But Cassandra shook her head.

"My Lord, I can't."

"You refuse?"

"No, I really can't. Look..."

She turned it a little, showing the complex lock that was keeping it closed. There were some very small words and numbers engraved under it...

"These collars can only be taken off by our masters, with a special key... It cannot be simply opened like a clasp."

Kairen was unhappy upon hearing that. She had to keep the damn thing on? From the looks of it, it couldn't be forced without injuring her. It was too thick, too large and too close to her throat. Annoyed, he glared at the collar.

Under his arm, Cassandra saw Nebora timidly gesture something at her before leaving and closing the doors behind her. She sighed, feeling a bit less shy now that they were alone. Yet, she couldn't endure Kairen's anger about her collar. Was it really so upsetting for the Prince? Did he even realize what taking off that collar would mean for her?

He probably didn't care... He just wanted it off, simple as that. Had he ever cared that she was a slave, anyway? Cassandra felt her heart warm a little at that thought. This man was truly too hard to understand. He was a part of those who ruled this world, this land, yet he was oblivious of its most basic rules. Slave or not, he didn't seem to give a damn... And she couldn't help but like him for that.

Slowly, Cassandra put a hand on his cheek and approached his lips to kiss him softly. The surprised look on Kairen's face was a first. He finally forgot the collar and looked at her, obviously baffled by her gesture. But it was over in a second as he kissed her back right away. He pushed it further, using his tongue and kissing her deeply and forcefully like he always did. His hands, too, became more pressing as he struggled to lift her skirt up. When he finally reached her undergarments, he swiftly got rid of them.

His fingers on her clit made Cassandra gasp. He immediately started caressing her, his fingers looking for her entrance and enticing her. The sensations unleashed hot waves inside her and she couldn't hold her moans as Kairen's skillful hand gave her shivers of pleasure. How could she like this so much already? She bit her lip, trying to hold it in as she grabbed the fur around her, but his fingers penetrated her, going in and out, faster and faster, and had her wet and excited immediately. She closed her eyes, too embarrassed to look at him any longer.

She hadn't thought it would make things more intense, but she could now focus only on this devilish rubbing inside her. Cassandra couldn't hold her voice back anymore. Her moaning was echoing in the room and she just couldn't stop it. When his fingers finally stopped and slid out, she could barely catch her breath. Her pussy was still trembling and soaking as the sensation lingered.

Kairen leaned over her again, and she felt him suddenly pushing inside her. She whimpered briefly, as it took a few seconds for her to get used to him, so thick and hard inside her, filling her to her core. Unable to wait, Kairen started moving, thrusting his hot member at a steady pace. His large hands were firmly caging Cassandra in place, submitting her completely to his rhythm. He slid in and out, without slowing down, taking so much pleasure in it already.

She was perfectly hot and wet, yet just tight enough to squeeze him and he loved it. The way she felt and her moaning voice crying out with each thrust, knowing that she was feeling it intensely too, was almost as satisfying as the sensations around his cock. He could thrust fast, hard, and deep, making Cassandra's voice resonate in unison with his own movements.

He straightened and wrapped her legs around his sides, grabbing her hips more firmly as he increased the speed of his thrusts, unable to stop. She was wailing loudly, her eyes closed and her mouth open, her thighs shaking. The bed started creaking under his wild moves and Cassandra suddenly grabbed his shoulder to hold onto, her other hand trying to cover her mouth.

He didn't let go of her, and kept going, showing no sign of slowing down. Cassandra was going crazy, unable to hold her voice or stop her hips from shaking against his. She could tell her pussy was soaking, hearing the carnal sounds of his penetration. Her body was hot, so impossibly hot. She could feel her extremities going numb and her stomach going wild. She began to moan even louder, as she felt her climax coming on. She liked it, she liked it so much she just couldn't believe it.

In a raspy voice, she started begging, unable to control it anymore.

"Yes, yes... Please... Yes..."

She didn't even realize what she was saying as the words continued to flow, feeling her orgasm coming. Suddenly, it exploded inside of her. Her whole body quivered as she felt stars bursting in her head and stomach.

She involuntarily tensed her legs around Kairen's waist, and he slowed down, kissing her without pulling out. His slow rhythm made the sensation linger even longer. Cassandra had a hard time coming back to her senses and catching her breath as he kissed along her jawline.

"Did you come?" he asked in a whisper.

It was a rhetorical question, meant to be a bit of a jest, but she blushed. He chuckled as he kept moving slowly, stirring her up inside again.

"M...Master..."

"I'm not done yet," he whispered.

She bit her lip, helpless. They had been going at it for so long already. When was he going to finish?!

"Cassandra?"

She slowly awoke to the sound of Nebora's voice. The servant was crouching down next to her by the bedside.

"It's past dinner time. Do you want to eat something?"

Cassandra frowned and slowly sat up, holding the bed sheets to cover her naked body. She looked around, the fur cloak was neatly folded and laid at the foot of the bed and several candles were lit, illuminating the room in the pitch black evening. He was gone.

"Is it very late?"

"No, but the night falls early here. His Highness left two hours ago," said Nebora.

"Where to?"

"Probably to see the Army of The East. He usually goes to see his men as soon as he gets here."

Cassandra blushed, she was obviously the reason he hadn't gone right away this time. Nebora cleared her throat, a bit embarrassed for a few seconds. Looking down, her cheeks were already red, and she whispered.

"I...I wanted to apologize. You know, about...earlier. I was a bitch to you. A jealous bitch, and I... realized I... Well, that it was stupid. I'm sorry."

It was obvious she was sincere and embarrassed. Cassandra smiled gently.

"Apology accepted. To be fair, I can't really blame you. I am a slave, and also in a... weird position."

A slave who wore a red dress. Thinking about it, Cassandra was still naked. She looked around for her dress, but it was nowhere to be seen. When she looked under the sheets, Nebora understood and handed her a new, white dress.

"Your dress was... um, soiled, so we took it to clean, sorry. I don't think we have any other red dresses. You can wear that nightgown for now, I guess. It's mine."

"Oh...thanks."

Cassandra felt a bit flustered. How many times had she changed clothes today? She took the nightgown from Nebora. The knee length dress was simple and white, knitted in a thicker fabric than what she was used to, but it was agreeably warm considering the cold here.

"You're welcome. But you should really ask His Highness for more clothes. You can't have only one outfit, it'll be a pain to wash every day."

"I don't know if I'm in a position to..."

Nebora rolled her eyes and got up, speaking before Cassandra finished her sentence.

"You're a concubine. Trust me, even the servants here have around ten outfits to change into. Don't bring up the slave thing, he obviously doesn't give a damn about that. His Highness is very rich, so just ask for it!"

Cassandra nodded as she thought about it. Indeed, she couldn't walk around naked or borrow Nebora's clothes all the time. As she started to braid her messy hair, Nebora took a step back, showing her a little plate full of food.

"Oh, are you hungry? I brought this up just in case. Everyone else already ate, but I figured you might have been too...busy to get a bite. His Highness ate before leaving, but you were still asleep."

"Thanks..."

Indeed, after all that intense activity, she was hungry. It was still so new to her, to be able to eat without begging or having to hide. Instead, she could enjoy plates full of fresh food, just for her. Cassandra started eating some of the little pieces of cheese and fruit as Nebora joined her, sitting on the floor next to the bed.

"How many servants are there?"

"There's six of us in the Castle, plus two more for the stables."

"That's it?" asked Cassandra, surprised.

From the size of the Castle, she had thought there would be at least a hundred people here! Nebora shrugged.

"Well, you've seen how it is. Everything is pretty much empty, and there is only the Prince to take care of, so..."

"What? What about his entourage or other concubines?"

Nebora almost choked on the cube of cheese she was eating, and turned to Cassandra with surprised eyes.

"What are you talking about? You're the only one!"

Cassandra was speechless. The only one? She had figured a Prince like him would have at least a dozen concubines! Maybe even a wife... After all, wasn't one of the Princes infamous for having a harem of over two hundred? But, to think a man like the War God actually had none...

"Well, to be honest, it's not like you're the first one."

"What do you mean?"

Nebora smirked.

"The Emperor and two of his brothers have tried offering him concubines before. But His Highness didn't like them. He killed them. Well, to be precise, he killed three and his dragon killed the others."

Cassandra stood, completely speechless. He actually dared to kill someone sent by the Emperor himself? What kind of man would do that! Was she just lucky to have survived until now? She wasn't sent by anyone from the Imperial Family though. Cassandra suddenly remembered Shareen's words to keep herself alive. Did that mean she actually suspected Kairen could kill her as well? That was really too frightening to think about.

"Don't worry," said Nebora. "I don't think you're anything like those women, you know. Actually, two of them even tried to kill him."

"What?"

"Well, some say they went crazy, but a lot of people think they had orders to kill the War God. It's not like the Imperial Family is a very warm household, you know. Everyone knows some of the Princes are just dying to take the Golden Throne."

Cassandra had noticed that too, at the banquet and the arena. It was obvious the siblings, Princes and Princesses, didn't like each other much. Some didn't even bother to hide their hatred for one another. The rivalry had been just barely contained, probably because of the Emperor's presence...

"Anyways, all that is quite far from us. If anything happens, it will most likely be at the Capital. Nothing happens around here," sighed Nebora.

"Would you give me a tour?"

Cassandra's sudden question seemed to surprise her. She hesitated, eating some grapes while Cassandra grabbed the fur cloak.

"Now?"

"His Highness won't be back for the night, will he?"

"No, he usually leaves for a few days when he goes to see his men... I'm just saying, it's pretty boring out here."

"I just feel like seeing more of the Castle, and I've slept too much already."

She wasn't really lying, but Cassandra's real reason was that she actually felt pretty uncomfortable and alone in the gigantic bed. Nebora sitting on the floor next to her made her feel a bit awkward, too.

Standing up, she noticed how cold this room actually was, and wrapped the fur cloak around her shoulders. Nebora, too, was wearing a large wool shawl that went all the way down to her thighs. She stood up at the same time as Cassandra, but frowned, and pointed at her chest that wasn't covered.

"You may want to hide that a bit."

Cassandra looked down, wondering if the cleavage of the dress may have been too much. Her dress wasn't the problem though. Instead, she noticed a dozen deep, red marks scattered on her neck and between her breasts. She blushed deeply and covered them instantly. They were obviously hickeys! How could the Prince have left so many without her even noticing? It was too embarrassing!

Nebora chuckled at her.

"Well, at least it seems His Highness had a good time..."

"Stop it!" exclaimed Cassandra, embarrassed to death. "Can we just go, please?"

Nebora took a second to stop laughing, and grabbed a few more cheese cubes and grapes for them to nibble along the way.

"Alright, alright, let's go."

The two women left the bedroom, each carrying a candle to light the way. It was a very quiet and cold night. Cassandra thought this Castle would have been a bit frightening to explore by herself.

As Nebora had said, despite its size, most of the Onyx Castle was empty and desolate. A few rooms had old furniture covered in completely empty. There were also some that the two wor couldn't open. In total, they walked down six floors to get different floors were separated by quite a lot of height, to scattered and far apart, that when they finally returned t of hours later, they had only managed to see half of the

"His Highness only uses the top floor, and some

used for guests, but that's not very common. Aside from that, everyone lives on the first floor. We only really see him for meal times, and when he comes and goes."

Nebora went to grab cups to make some hot tea to warm themselves.

"How long have you lived here?"

"I moved to the village near the Castle when I was fourteen. I grew up in the countryside, but I hated field work. There wasn't anything else to do, so one of my brothers and I eventually left to find work elsewhere. Patrina recruited me around the same time as my brother got into His Highness' army."

"I've heard a lot about the Army of The East."

Nebora smiled.

"Of course, they are the best army in the Empire; thanks to the War God. They became notorious after defeating the Eastern Republic and the Barbarian Tribes a few years ago. My brother was lucky to be a part of it then."

Cassandra noticed how happy she seemed when talking about her brother. She couldn't help but smile too. Nebora took a sip of her tea.

"Do you have siblings too?"

Her eyes immediately became a bit sad as she looked down at her cup.

"I had a younger sister... But she was sold too, years ago. I tried to look for her, but I couldn't find anything about what happened to her or who she was sold to."

"So you...weren't born a slave?"

Cassandra shook her head.

"I was born in the south, in the Rain Tribe."

"Never heard of it."

"You probably wouldn't have. The name disappeared many years ago. Every last one of us was hunted down."

Nebora was shocked.

"What do you mean?"

"My tribe lived to the south of this Empire , near the Riverlands. We were one of many tribes who coexisted there together, in a territory between the Dragon Empire and the Eastern Republic. We knew a war was going on between them, but we were living in a very difficult area. It was mostly dominated by swamps and heavy rain. We never thought we would get involved in the conflict."

Nebora frowned.

"What happened?"

"I was only nine years old back then so I don't know all the details, but at some point, someone suspected the tribes were smuggling weapons and information to the other side. Our Chief was captured and tortured...He ouldn't say what he didn't know, and was killed. After that, they decided it d be better to just wipe us all out. To them, we were a nameless tribe of a risk they didn't want to take. It was over in one night."

ra was speechless. It was disheartening to think a whole population had been killed over a conflict they hadn't had any part in. Yet, Cassandra was quite calm as she spoke. It was as if she was just telling a tale. But it wasn't a tale; it was her story.

She sighed and took another sip.

"How did you survive?"

"They didn't actually kill everyone...They killed all of the adults and most of the boys. The rest of the boys, and the young girls under twelve, were sold to slave merchants. I was brought to this Empire and sold to my first Master a few days after."

She didn't ask anything else. Nebora was reflecting on how she had acted earlier, that childish tantrum of hers. About her being a slave? If she had been unlucky, she could have ended up like Cassandra. Losing her whole family and then being sold like merchandise. Yet, she had been the immature one, while a young woman who had already experienced so much tragedy was so calm and collected in front of her. How could she be so reckless and immature given the harsh world they live in?

Suddenly, a scream resonated through the kitchen as a young girl in a nightgown came running in, straight into Nebora's arms.

"A spider! There is a spider in my room again!"

"Again? Did you clean your room this week, Bina?"

"I did, I definitely did!"

The girl, who looked no older than fourteen or fifteen, was almost crying, completely panicked. She hid her face in Nebora's chest, tightly gripping onto her arm like a safety blanket.

"She is very scared of spiders," explained Nebora with a sigh. "We always get a few around this time of year..."

"Where is her room?" Cassandra asked while getting up.

Nebora frowned as she watched Cassandra look through the trash from that morning.

"The first one on the left... What are you doing?"

Cassandra had gathered some fruit peels, and showed them to Nebora. They were all citrus peels.

"Spiders hate these. If you rub it against your doors and windows they won't come in."

"Really?"

Bina had turned her head, hearing a new person, and looked at Cassandra. She was stunned by the young girl's eyes. One was brown, the other was blue, but the girl was only focused on the citrus peels in Cassandra's hands.

"Yes. I use this trick all the time so I never get any spiders. You can keep some chestnuts in your room too; that also works well."

"Alright, let's go test that theory and chase out that eight-legged monster while we're at it," sighed Nebora, getting up. "And after that, everyone to bed. I'm tired!"

Chapter 6

That night, Cassandra slept in one of the servants' rooms. There were several available, so it was no inconvenience for her to take one. Even if Nebora insisted she sleep upstairs, being all alone in the Prince's chambers was too intimidating for Cassandra. Moreover, the bedroom she was given was quite decent. It was simple, with wood furniture, like a bed and a desk, just enough for someone to sleep in comfortably. From what she had seen in Nebora and Bina's rooms, they were free to decorate as they wished, too.

She slept well, but because she had already slept so long the day before, Cassandra was up early. Quickly getting dressed, she went to the kitchen, not thinking she'd see anyone at this early hour. But Bina was there along with another girl and a boy, all standing around chatting. They all looked younger than herself, around fourteen or fifteen years old. Upon seeing her come in, Bina stood up.

"Cassie!"

She walked up to her and turned to the others.

"This is Cassandra, who I just told you about! She's the one with the fruit peels!"

Cassandra recognized the other girl as well. She was the one who was scared of the dragon the previous day in the inner court with her cart.

"Hi... I'm Prunie." She nodded shyly.

"I'm Helmond," said the boy.

"Prunie is a servant like me, Helm works at the stables!" said Bina, joyously.

"Nice to meet you both."

"Hey, Cassandra, do you know how to make breakfast? We're so hungry, but none of us can cook..."

"Would you show me where we keep the food?"

"Sure!"

For the next half hour, Cassandra made breakfast for everyone while she listened to them gossip. Those three, being the youngest, were quite chatty and lively. She quickly learned that Prunie and Bina had been recruited around the same time this year, while Helmond was Patrina's nephew. By the time Cassandra was done making breakfast, Nebora had appeared too, her black curls all tangled.

"The kids made you make breakfast?" she asked while yawning.

"It's fine, I like cooking. There's enough for everyone."

"Great. I'll make some tea..."

Soon enough, all five of them sat around the table to eat, everyone complimenting Cassandra's cooking. Curious, Helm and Bina asked Cassandra lots of questions about the Capital, as they had never been before. She politely answered their endless questions for a while, as the others ate silently.

Suddenly, the roof over their heads made a terrifying noise, like it was about to cave in. Everyone froze as the walls trembled, too. Nebora was petrified.

"What was that?"

"There aren't any earthquakes here, right?" asked Bina, scared.

Cassandra got up as the roof shook again, like some storm was over their heads. When she heard a loud growl, she finally understood and walked outside.

Indeed, Krai's gigantic front paws were on the roof of the building, and the Black Dragon was growling, its claws scratching the walls. Krai didn't even seem to realize the whole building was about to collapse from the extra weight. Cassandra walked all the way to the inner court until she could see the dragon's head. Behind her, all the other servants who had left the kitchen to follow her were petrified.

"It's the Master's dragon!" Bina whispered.

Prunie kept looking at Cassandra as Nebora grabbed her arm, trying to hold her back.

"Don't approach, Cassandra. His Highness' dragon will kill you!"

However, she kept walking until the dragon finally turned its head and spotted her. Immediately, it jumped down from the building and trotted towards her with a loud growl. She heard the screams of fear behind her, but didn't turn around. Instead, Cassandra stayed very still until Krai stopped in front of her, sniffing and tilting its head to the side. She took a peek at its empty back.

"Did you come back alone? What about your Master?" Cassandra asked the dragon, while scratching its head.

If Krai had understood her, it didn't bother to give her an answer. Instead, it was just growling quietly and turning its head from one side to the other, begging for more scratches. Behind her, she heard Nebora speak.

"I can't believe you..."

"He's quite nice," said Cassandra.

"Nice? I saw that dragon eat ten men at once! It didn't even chew! And you're petting it like some cat... What kind of woman are you?"

Cassandra couldn't help but chuckle. Indeed, she had seen Krai kill people, quite gruesomely, in fact. But, for now, the Black Dragon just laid down in the inner court, closing its eyes and letting her scratch its head.

"I wonder why His Highness didn't come back as well?" Cassandra asked.

"They are not always together. That dragon pretty much does whatever it pleases most of the time," said Nebora. "Our Lord is probably still at the Military Camp. "

"Is it far from here?" asked Cassandra.

"By foot, it would take a few days. On the dragon's back, maybe an hour or so. The Military Camp is quite large, almost like a city itself, and right at the Empire's border too. Around two hundred thousand men."

That was a rather large number considering this Castle appeared quite… empty. For such a large beast, that number of soldiers probably didn't even compare, though, as Krai could probably protect the castle on its own. Cassandra looked down at the dragon that was about to doze off under her pets.

No wonder this Empire was so powerful compared to the others. With seven dragons, they could probably take over any country on a whim.

"I don't know how you can stay so close to it. It could eat you in one bite and use your bones as toothpicks!"

Nebora was still being very brave, standing a few paces away while all three of the others had literally run away. Cassandra, however, wasn't scared at all. Despite its gigantic size, the hot breath, and sharp fangs, she didn't feel any animosity coming from the dragon. She waited until it seemed like Krai was asleep and snoring in the middle of the inner court, to walk back to Nebora, who had her arms crossed.

"I don't know if you're insane or lucky."

"I could be both? Come on, we should get to work," chuckled Cassandra.

The two women went back to the kitchen, cleaning the dishes, and talking. Compared to the cold shoulder she had given her the previous day, Nebora's attitude had completely changed. She was still very blunt and a bit rude at times, but as she showed Cassandra everything they did in the Castle, all hints of hatred were disappearing. Instead, she seemed to treat the young woman like a peer and explained to her how everything was handled patiently.

"There aren't many rooms to take care of," Nebora explained as they were bringing clean sheets upstairs. "But there are only a few of us and Patrina is always making sure everything is spotless. She will even have us clean a room three times a day if she sees a little speck of dust."

"Has she always worked for His Highness?"

"No, she used to work for His Highness's mother at the Palace. Her daughter was murdered in one of the jealous schemes between the concubines. After that, she asked to be sent away from the Palace and ended up here."

Cassandra was shocked to hear such a story. Seeing a woman as resilient as Patrina, she had no idea.

"You're lucky to have been brought here," continued Nebora. "You would have been killed within a week back at the Palace. It's famous for being a nest of snakes."

She nodded slowly as they placed new sheets on the Prince's bed. She had already seen it herself. The violence, the death... Not only for the slaves. Even a concubine like Lyria, who was untouchable in the Capital, had been killed on the spot only a week after entering the Palace. It was truly a scary place.

"So, no one comes here?"

Nebora seemed to think for a bit, while folding a fur cloak.

"Aside from his sister, not really."

"Princess Shareen?"

"You know her?"

"I've...met her."

Cassandra couldn't help blushing as she remembered the incident. That Princess Shareen was truly one of a kind! Thankfully, Nebora didn't notice her cheeks going red as she was taking care of the dust on the curtains. Meanwhile, Cassandra changed the candles and added a batch of herbs in a basket.

"Those two are close, from what I've seen. Even if she is a total weirdo... Don't get close to that woman, she's really dangerous. There are some crazy rumors about her, and I wouldn't be surprised if half of them are true. But that's pretty much it for visitors. Our Lord isn't the social type...What is that?"

She was pointing at the basket of dried herbs Cassandra was putting next to the window.

"Just so the room will smell good. I'll open the window a bit, too, so it'll smell even better."

"Oh, I see. I'll open the other one then. Do you need to... Ah!!!"

Nebora's scream resonated throughout the room, making Cassandra almost drop her basket. She turned around to see what was wrong, only to discover that the big window Nebora had tried to open, now had a wall of scales blocking it, with a red eye moving around in the middle.

Cassandra rushed to Nebora's side, making sure she was alright, but it was hard not to laugh. Krai's big muzzle was trying to get inside, and the dragon was making odd growls; its eyes looking around.

"No, no, you're too big!" she scolded. "What are you doing...?"

She could only imagine what it was like from the outside. Had it tried to climb up the Castle to get to the tower? Its head was still too big for the window, though it kept trying to maneuver around to fit through. Cassandra felt helpless.

"You're too big! Oh, come on..."

She tried to push its muzzle away, until it was completely out. It kept looking at her though, with a disappointed look. Next to her, Nebora was still trying to stop her legs from trembling and get back up. Cassandra helped her, trying to ignore the loud growls.

"I can't believe that dragon! It scared the shit out of me!"

"Do you think the whole tower could collapse...?"

"It should be fine, it's not the first dragon to live here. None of them tried to actually get inside though! Let's just hope its Master will call it back soon. I don't think I can work if it keeps popping up at every window!"

"Can he call from so far?"

"What? Oh, yes. Dragon tamers have some special bond with their dragon. Even if our Lord was all the way back at the Palace, this one would fly to him anytime he needs him."

Cassandra was completely astonished at that fact. She had never heard about any of this before. The dragons were considered deities here. It was already very rare for anyone to be able to spot one, as they always stayed with their Masters.

Ignoring the annoyed growls, she closed the window where Krai was lurking.

"I had no idea..."

"That's normal, they don't leak much information about the Palace to the outside. Here, Our Lord doesn't really care, I guess. Come on, let's finish quickly here, that big red eye is creeping me out..."

Krai eventually got bored and went away long before they were done cleaning the room. The dragon had probably gone to hunt somewhere. When they got back downstairs, it was nowhere to be seen.

The two women went to the kitchen, where Prunie and Marian were sorting out vegetables. Cassandra walked up to them, taking what looked like a carrot from the basket.

"Is it fresh enough?"

"Not really," said Marian with a sigh. "But it's hard to get fresh ones around here. The closest farmer is still quite far away."

"Why is no one cultivating the soils around the Castle?" asked Cassandra.

She had wondered this while flying over the land, too. Aside from scattered houses, the whole area around the Castle was pretty much deserted. She kept looking at the vegetables, but no matter how she looked at them, they just weren't very good. Especially not when compared to what she had seen in the Capital.

"They say the soil is not good for cultivating here."

Cassandra frowned. Her native land was much worse than this, yet they still had always been able to provide for themselves. The vegetables gathered in the baskets were definitely ones that fit warmer climates though, like the Capital, not what they should have been growing here.

"What about the pastures? The livestock?"

Next to her, Nebora sighed.

"Cassandra, the livestock were not too happy to be here, they left ages ago. Did you forget? We have the biggest predator flying around the area!"

Cassandra was still thinking about the farming problem that night as she cooked with Patrina and Nebora. The food they were slicing and mashing wasn't so bad, but it wasn't particularly fresh either. With no proper farmers around to tend the land and provide food, no wonder the whole area was deserted.

"What about trading then?"

"You're thinking about that again?" sighed Nebora. "Trading is what we do. Usually we can only buy at the nearest village, but it's two hours from here using the horses."

"Is the village big? Could we go there?"

"Certainly not now!" said Patrina, frowning. "Just focus on your task and stop chatting so much!"

Having said that, she left the kitchen to go to the storage room. As soon as she was gone, Nebora moved closer to Cassandra and whispered.

"She's not wrong, you know. You may not know this because you came from the Capital, but this area is terribly unsafe at night. As soon as the sun sets, a lot of dangerous beasts start to roam around. You would get killed and eaten in minutes."

Cassandra had no idea. Indeed, the Capital was a large and highly guarded City, as most of the Empire's officials were located there. Only the Governors had residences on their designated territories, though some high-ranked nobles had built secondary residences outside of the Capital walls. She also knew of a few other big cities that existed and were doing quite well on their own, but from the day she had been sold to her first master, she had never taken a step out of the Capital.

"I'm also not sure when His Highness will come back, but if I were you, I would stay close to the castle."

Cassandra couldn't help but blush a bit when she heard those words. She wondered when he would be back too.

Krai also hadn't come back. Wherever the Black Dragon had gone, it must have been pretty far, because it was nowhere to be seen; not even from the Prince's tower. The two women kept chatting until Patrina came back with a grumpy look on her face.

"We have to make an extra portion."

Nebora frowned.

"What? That pig is eating here again?"

Patrina just nodded, and went outside again to call Prunie and Marian. Cassandra finished cutting her vegetables and turned to Nebora.

"Who are we talking about?"

Nebora rolled her eyes.

"The Governor, Grovah. The man is a fucking pig. He acts as he pleases here, and if His Highness is gone, he likes to order us around. He has his own manor but this is where he spends most of his time. He even took a room here!"

"Why does he stick around?"

"Because he is so full of himself and likes the Castle better. And because he gets to act like a fucking pervert with the servants here, too. I heard he touched all of his servant girls back at his manor, despite having a wife and five concubines!"

Cassandra almost dropped the pot she was carrying.

"What? Even here?"

She thought of the young girls like Bina and Prunie, who were only fourteen and fifteen years old. Sadly, it was not uncommon for officials to abuse their powers and have their "fun" with the servants, but this was the Prince's Palace!

"Don't worry, he wouldn't dare touch you. You belong to His Highness, and the dirtbag is way too scared of him."

Cassandra was certainly not satisfied by that. She wasn't thinking about herself. She worried for the servant girls here, being subjected to that kind of treatment.

"Does this happen often?"

"Don't think too much about it, Cassie. He just messes around with us when we bring him his food, or when he sees us in the corridors, that's all."

"Are you talking about the pig?"

Marian, Prunie, and Bina had all just entered the kitchen to help, with their hands full. Cassandra and Nebora immediately stood up to go and help them. Marian frowned.

"That man is such a pig! He is so fat and ugly, and..."

"That's not the point here, Marian," sighed Nebora.

"I hate him," murmured Prunie. "He always tries to touch my butt..."

"He does that with me too," added Bina. "He's really horrible. He always talks about how he has sex with his servants when I'm in the room giving him his food, and he says I'm wearing too many clothes for a girl."

Cassandra felt so utterly disgusted hearing all this, she suddenly slammed the pot on the table, making everyone jump.

"I will do it."

"Do what?"

"Bring him his food."

Nebora looked at her as if she was stupid.

"Cassandra, no. He may be a pervert, but the man is a Governor, and you're a slave. If you do anything he doesn't like, he can have you imprisoned, and His Highness is not even here to protect you!"

"He cannot rape or kill me, Nebora. No matter what, I don't have as many risks as you, and honestly, I don't really care about being imprisoned. Regardless, I'm not letting any of you approach him."

"Cassie..." muttered Bina, worried.

"What if he tortures you?" sighed Nebora. "If he gets reckless and His Highness is not here..."

Cassandra shook her head.

"He won't. Don't worry about me. Now, let's just cook as usual."

The girls listened to her, but they still tried to talk her out of it. Even if they seemed scared, Bina and Prunie said they could take it themselves, but Cassandra refused. When the tray was ready, she asked where she was supposed to go, and headed to the Governor's self-designated chambers.

A man's voice ordered her to enter. Cassandra noticed the room was probably the most furnished and richly decorated in the whole Castle. It really was as if the Governor owned the place, except that this was only the third floor. A big dog suddenly barked at her, and Cassandra stood to the side. Thankfully, the dog was chained and couldn't reach her. It just kept growling and barking, loudly.

"Who are you? Where are the usual girls?!" the man suddenly yelled.

Cassandra frowned. He wasn't even properly dressed, wearing only some sort of bathrobe that looked ridiculously tight on him. It was the man whom she had seen run after the Prince upon her arrival at the Castle. He was short, fat, and even a bit bald. As she came closer, Cassandra couldn't help but be repulsed by him and his greasy skin. She dropped the tray on the table, a bit loudly.

"The girls are eating, Sir. Here is your meal."

"I want the little one to bring it! With the soft skin."

"She is eating, and your meal is already here."

He pointed a finger at Cassandra, his eyes gleaming with anger.

"You insolent little whore! You think you can talk back to me? You may be His Highness' favorite, but you're still just a slave! Just wait until I whip the hell out of you!"

The Governor got up and seized a whip that was on his bedside table and quickly walked up to her.

"Go ahead."

He suddenly stopped, surprised by Cassandra's calm tone. His fingers were trembling on the whip. He had never seen a slave unafraid to talk back to him, let alone stand tall and look directly at him like this woman was!

"W... What did you say?"

"I said go ahead. You can whip me."

The Governor was utterly confused. The woman had way too much confidence! What was she hiding? Was she waiting for him to whip her so she could complain to the Prince? With the wounds as proof? He stared at her for a while, hesitating. Cassandra wasn't moving at all, or betraying any fear. After a long pause, the Governor lowered his hand with the whip.

"You arrogant whore... You think you are higher than me? You'll see! Guards!"

Immediately, two of the Palace guards, whom Cassandra had not interacted with yet, ran into the chambers.

"Take her to the dungeon! Have this wench stay there for three days and three nights! You'll see what it costs to be arrogant to a Lord like me! His Highness will understand!"

And just like that, Cassandra was taken away to the Castle's dungeon, showing no resistance.

The guards brought her underground to the cells, all aligned down a long hall, and put her in the farthest one. It only had a bed made of straw and a very small window at the very top of the wall that allowed in a very small amount of natural light. The guards weren't rude, but they also didn't say a single word to her. Instead, they just left.

Cassandra sighed. She had been in worse situations, but still... Her own stubbornness had landed her in the dungeons. She checked her cell for any rats or stagnant water, and arranged the straw to sit on. She sighed again. No doubt the Prince would be mad about this upon his return.

"Cassie!"

She had only started dozing off when she heard Nebora. She raised her head, and saw her new friend standing on the other side of the bars as she walked up to her.

"What are you doing here?"

"I should be the one asking you that, you stubborn woman! I told you this would happen! Don't you have any instinct of self-preservation? You would be dead if you weren't His Highness' concubine!"

"Did he do anything else after he put me in here?"

Nebora sighed deeply.

"No... I think you scared him a bit. He chased everyone out. I told the girls to ignore him for now, but... Girl, you have to spend a long time in here!"

"I've been in worse places. What is this?" she asked, pointing to the little basket Nebora had brought.

"It's for you. I brought you some food, and a blanket too. It gets cold here at night..."

She handed her everything through the bars, under Cassandra's surprised eyes.

"How were you allowed to...?"

"It was easy, the guards aren't bad guys. They let me through without arguing when I said you were His Highness' concubine. Well, that, and I promised them each a kiss."

Cassandra chuckled. She was truly grateful, and thanked Nebora for all she had done to make her imprisonment better.

"Just wait until His Highness gets back... I hope his dragon will chew that damn Governor slowly!"

"I just hope he leaves you alone for a while..."

"Don't worry, we are used to it. And Patrina is pissed you got thrown in the dungeon, she isn't going to let him act as he pleases."

"Nebora! Five minutes!" yelled one of the guards from down the hall.

She sighed.

"I have to go, girl. Take care of yourself, alright? I'll be back tomorrow, I promise."

She left quickly, leaving Cassandra completely alone again.

The night was extremely cold. If it wasn't for the blanket Nebora had brought her, she would probably have gotten sick, but at least there weren't any rats. Cassandra fell asleep remembering the warm embrace of the Prince, and the soft feel of a fur cloak...

"Where is she?"

A cold voice suddenly woke her up. She heard a scream, and a dragon's furious growl. Cassandra stood, keeping her blanket around her, totally confused. It was still the middle of the night, but countless lights were lit up outside.

She heard several people walking quickly through the dungeon towards her cell. A bit wary, she took a couple of steps back into a corner.

The Prince suddenly appeared in front of her.

"My Lord..."

He drew his sword and, without warning, brutally shattered the hinges holding her cell's door, breaking through them as if they were as flimsy as a sheet of paper. He was clearly furious when he walked up to her.

"What are you doing in here?"

Without letting her answer, he suddenly swooped Cassandra off her feet, carrying her like a princess, as usual. They left the cell, followed by two panicked soldiers. She hadn't even spent one night there!

The Prince took her out to the inner court which was brightly lit despite the late hour. Krai was there, growling furiously. All the servants, and a few guards, were gathered with worried expressions. Nebora and the others seemed relieved to see her when she appeared though.

"Your... Your Highness!"

Cassandra suddenly realized the Governor was there too, only he was being crushed under Krai's gigantic paw. The man's mouth was covered in blood, like someone had beaten him.

"S...see! She's fine! I just put her there to teach her a...a lesson!"

But Kairen didn't bother to look at him or even stop. He kept walking back to the main area of the Castle without a single glance behind him.

"My... My Lord!"

Krai growled even louder at the whimpering man and the next second, the disgusting sound of flesh and bones being crushed was heard, before a new scream resonated.

Cassandra didn't even see the Governor's last moments. Carried by Kairen against his chest, she only heard and that was enough. Very quickly, she was whisked all the way to his bedroom and thrown on the bed.

"My Lord... I didn't think you'd be back so quickly."

"What the fuck were you doing in his chambers?"

She was surprised by his question. Kairen started undoing the thick armor he was wearing, the cold metal loudly falling to the floor. Cassandra was searching for words, trying to gather her thoughts while sitting there.

"I brought him his dinner..."

Kairen looked furious. Wearing only his pants now, he threw his shirt across the room and crawled on the bed until he was facing her. He grabbed Cassandra's waist, pulling her against him, and kissed her forcefully without warning. She didn't even have time to breathe. With his tongue on hers, she awkwardly held on to his shoulder to keep her balance. She was sitting a bit on top of him, and he grabbed her hair, keeping her close to him.

When he finally let her go, Cassandra's lips were numb from the intense kissing. She tried to catch her breath.

"Your lips are cold," groaned Kairen.

"The dungeon was cold..."

He clicked his tongue, annoyed, and kissed her again, even more intensely. Cassandra was completely unprepared. It was only moments ago that she was still alone in that cold prison cell. Now she was on his bed, in his chambers, illuminated and warmed up by candles and a roaring fire. She did her best to answer his kiss, still getting used to his savage intensity. The way he played with her tongue was restless. Cassandra could feel her skin warming up, the change so fast she shivered under his fingers and the sensation of his hot palms caressing her body.

Kairen's lips weren't stopping. He kissed her lips, her cheeks, her jawline, her neck, moving lower and lower. Cassandra struggled to undo her dress, taking off the laces and getting rid of it before he would rip it apart again. It was an embarrassing position for her to be in, straddling her master, her arms behind his back while he was caressing and kissing her breasts. She caressed his short black hair, closing her eyes as he kept kissing her breasts, sucking her little pink extremities.

"My... Lord..." She gasped.

Her cheeks were red, and she was flush from excitement, a fire burning within her. Kairen, his hands on her hips, finally raised his head up to kiss her again, a bit gentler this time, as if he had been appeased. Cassandra answered his kiss, almost guiding it as she was on top, and able to keep up. One of his hands climbed up to hold her neck's nape, while the other went down, caressing her entrance slowly.

She shivered at the sensation of his fingers between her legs, rubbing against her sacred parts. He caressed her slit thoroughly, reaching out for her entrance in slow motions. Cassandra moaned faintly, her desire flowing as soon as his fingers penetrated her. She held onto his back, biting her lower lip as the feeling grew stronger. She could feel the bulge in his pants against her thigh, and that only made her more excited. Was she really already used to these sensations? A bit ashamed, she couldn't help but react and move against his fingers. Kairen smiled faintly.

He undid his pants, freeing his dick, and positioned it against Cassandra's entrance. Guiding her, he slowly pushed in, enjoying her long moan. She held onto his shoulders, breathing hard and adjusting to the sensation, the fullness....

"Move," he suddenly whispered into her ear.

Cassandra felt the blood rushing to her cheeks and ears. He wanted her to move? On him? She could barely endure it already... But Kairen waited, only moving slightly under her, and that was far from enough. She bit her lip again, and progressively, moved her hips on him. She could feel his cock rubbing inside her, and panted heavily from the sensation. She liked it, and she wanted more.

Forgetting her embarrassment, she kept moving, finding her rhythm, guided by his hands on her hips. Kairen matched his movements to hers, grinding his pelvis fiercely each time, Cassandra moaning with each collision.

He kissed her neck after each thrust. She was crying out so loudly from their passionate love making. Cassandra felt like this was surreal. She could feel him under her, responding to her movements, filling her up as he held her firmly yet gently. She gasped and moaned, widening her legs over him, feeling the pleasure grow and her rationality wane.

As she started to lose some energy, Kairen took over in full force, forcing his hips up, thrusting faster, leaving her no room for rest. She couldn't control it. Cassandra felt that urge, that explosion coming, and moaned harder with each of his thrusts. He held her by the waist so she wouldn't get away. She clenched around his thick cock. she exploded, her orgasm overtaking her in a huge wave of pleasure. She cried out, long and loud.

A couple of hours later, she was laying on her side, exhausted, her head on the Prince's shoulder. Her lower body was completely numb after their passionate sex. Of course, just once hadn't been enough. She blushed thinking about all the positions she had taken to satisfy her Master.

Kairen had his eyes closed, but his fingers were lazily caressing her shoulder.

"Don't ever go to another man's chambers again," he suddenly said.

Cassandra looked at him, confused.

"My Lord, could it be you're..."

But before she could end that sentence, Kairen suddenly leaned to face her, looking angry.

"You are mine. All of you. I told you, if another man touches you, I'll kill him."

Right after that sentence, he leaned over to kiss her, pinning her to the mattress. She couldn't help but answer his kiss, like a conditioned response. Cassandra was starting to like his forceful ways. She felt warm in his embrace, and safe...

She fell asleep shortly after as Kairen held her tightly against his chest. Cassandra almost didn't need the blanket, as the Prince's body was hot enough naturally.

When she woke the next morning, Kairen was already up. Grabbing the fur cloak to cover her bare chest, Cassandra slowly sat up, feeling some back pain. The Prince was putting on his pants, and noticed she was awake.

"You can sleep more."

"I'm fine... Are you going back to the Military Camp?"

"Yes. You're coming too."

Cassandra took a few seconds to process what he had just said.

"With you? My Lord, I can't go to a military camp!"

"Why not?"

"It's not a place for... women..."

She had wanted to say concubines at first, but that term was still too new for her to use it for herself. Indeed, it was truly unheard of for a woman to visit a military camp! It was a place for men only, soldiers. Women were never allowed to be warriors or to be inside military camps.

"If I leave you here, who knows which man's chambers I'll find you in next..."

"My Lord! I wouldn't..."

"I don't care. You're coming with me."

His sentence was clearly an order, and Cassandra didn't dare argue any further. She couldn't believe he was so jealous and distrusting after that stupid incident. A bit unhappy, Cassandra grabbed her dress and put it back on. While doing so, she suddenly remembered Nebora's words about asking for some clothes.

"My Lord... Madam Patrina mentioned I would need more clothes if I stay here. There's only this one dress."

For a moment, Kairen hadn't seemed to have listened to her, as he was putting his boots back on. However, the Prince got up and walked to the other side of the room, opening one of the big chests.

"Just take whatever you need."

Cassandra left the bed and walked over to the chest thinking she may find an extra dress or two, but to her surprise, the chest wasn't filled with clothes but with... gold bars! She was speechless as she looked down at dozens of perfect gold bars, lined up in several rows. She had never seen so much money in her entire life! One gold coin alone could buy several meals for a family - exactly how much money was there? Just a single gold bar could buy hundreds of dresses!

"My Lord, this is far too much!"

"Then just take one and buy what you need."

She looked at him, truly shocked. Did he really think she would need more than one in the first place? Cassandra didn't even know what to say. She knew the Imperial Family was richer than most, but this was truly too unbelievable. She tried not to think about the two other chests in the room, and just quickly grabbed one of the bars. Even its weight was impressive. Would she even be able to use that in a normal shop? She probably could ask Patrina later.

She quickly closed the chest, wondering why he had such a thing in his room, when someone knocked at the door.

"Your breakfast, Your Highness."

Marian walked in, carrying a large tray of food. A bit embarrassed to have the young girl serve her, Cassandra walked over to help her. Her friend faintly smiled as Cassandra handed her the gold bar. Marian had exactly the same expression as her, eyes wide open and fixed on the shining bar before her. She glanced at the Prince, worried, but Kairen was putting his shirt back on, not even looking in their direction.

"Marian, can you give this to Patrina and tell her it's for buying new clothes for everyone?"

"F...For everyone? But..."

"Just ask her to handle it until I come back, all right?"

"Y...Yes..."

Marian held the gold bar with the tip of her fingers, as if she was afraid it would explode in her hands. Then, she ran off. Cassandra wasn't only doing this because it was too much money just for her. She didn't feel right being the only one to receive new clothes when she had noticed the other servants had some that were a bit too used, or in the case of Bina and Prunie, too short. She trusted Patrina would know how to allocate the money fairly.

Cassandra turned to Kairen, hoping he wouldn't be mad at her for sharing the gold bar, but the Prince didn't seem to care at all about the conversation. He had just finished dressing as he went to sit on one of the armchairs in front of the food.

"Aren't you hungry?" he asked as she stood there.

"Ah, yes..."

She walked over and took the seat next to his so she could start eating. After a few minutes of silence between them, she suddenly remembered something she had been meaning to ask for a while.

"My Lord, how come you came back so soon? Nebora said you usually stay longer at the Military Camp."

Kairen frowned a bit.

"It was boring. And Krai was annoying, too."

"He came back before you did..."

"That stupid dragon flew back here on his own. He was too bored at the camp and kept looking for you."

Cassandra couldn't help but smile at that, thinking about how Krai had missed her. She bit her lip, hesitating slightly before asking.

"Did you miss me as well?"

Kairen suddenly stopped eating, and turned to her. His black eyes on her were making her blush. Oh, how he was scrutinizing her! Cassandra, too embarrassed to endure his gaze any longer, looked down. That's when Kairen grabbed her wrist and brought her onto his knees, so abruptly she didn't have time to resist. Her face was suddenly very close to his, and she blushed even more, unable to avoid his stare.

"Why do you think I'm taking you with me this time?" he suddenly whispered.

Grabbing her hair, he brought her closer and Cassandra, overwhelmed, put her arms around his neck, slowly kissing his lips.

"So, His Highness is taking you there? To the Camp?" asked Nebora.

She was helping Cassandra fold some clothes to pack for the journey.

They had no idea how long she would be gone, so Nebora had decided to lend her some of her clothes again. Cassandra hesitated, looking at one of the dresses.

"Yes... Nebora, are you sure I can take these?"

"Yes! Patrina will get us new clothes in no time with all that gold you gave her, so don't worry about it. It's a pity we only have one red dress, though. Maybe you could try to preserve it?"

Cassandra shook her head.

"It's fine either way. I'll just get new ones when I get back."

"True...Oh, what about jewelry? Do you want us to buy you some?"

"I'm going to the Military Camp, not a party!" sighed Cassandra.

What would jewelry be good for? She was already wearing the slavery collar anyway. Plus, it would only make things heavier and harder to carry. It would probably look weird too. A slave wearing jewelry, that would probably be a first!

Nebora pouted. "Oh, fine. We'll dress you up once you're back. Make sure you take some warm cloaks though, it's freezing up there. You make sure not to get wet, and if it snows, stay inside, all right? And make sure to keep the wood dry. It's a pain to light up otherwise."

Cassandra listened to Nebora's advice carefully, as she had never been so far north before. She was a bit excited at the prospect of seeing snowfall for the first time in her life, but a bit worried about the cold as well. She didn't even know what a military camp was going to be like.

"Do you need anything else? Patrina packed up some food too, but the trip there will be short with His Highness' dragon..."

"No, this should be fine. Thank you, Nebora."

Her friend smiled as they both got up, Cassandra holding her little bag. She only had her dresses, a pair of shoes and a few balms and soaps that Nebora had insisted on her taking. As they left the room, Nebora followed her closely, giving her more advice about the cold.

"And eat more meat," she said as they reached the inner court. "It can't be bad for you, skinny girl."

Cassandra chuckled.

"I got it, Nebora, don't worry."

"Why wouldn't I worry? You're way too nice and clueless. Oh, and watch out for the men! I mean, they should behave with His Highness around, but..."

"Nebora, I will be fine," said Cassandra with an amused smile.

To think she was so hostile to her only a couple of days ago. Now Nebora was acting like a worried, older sister. It was a first for Cassandra, but she truly appreciated it. When they walked back into the kitchen, Marian, Prunie and Bina were waiting for her. The three younger girls said goodbye to her, and Cassandra felt her heart tighten a little, seeing that Prunie and Bina had already gotten so attached to her and were sad to see her leave.

"Do you know how long you will stay there?" asked Bina.

"No, His Highness hasn't said anything."

86

"Stop whining, she will probably be back next week," said Nebora.

"We will pick up some pretty dresses for you!" said Prunie, with a big smile.

"Thank you, Prunie."

Cassandra gave each of the girls a hug before she went out to the inner court again, all three of them following behind her. The Prince was there, putting a large saddle on Krai's back. The dragon was waiting patiently, its head turning to Cassandra when she arrived. It had big bags on its back as well, though they still looked like nothing compared to its actual size. Krai let out a loud growl, looking excited. Except for Cassandra and Nebora, all the other girls froze and stepped back from hearing that. They were still terrified by the mere sight of the gigantic Black Beast, and didn't dare approach. Nebora wasn't looking so good either, but she didn't look as afraid, and still managed to follow Cassandra a few steps closer.

"A toothpick..." she grumbled.

"It's fine, Nebora," said Cassandra with a little laugh. "I'll see you later, all right?"

Nebora sighed and stopped staring at Krai to look at Cassandra. Her heart warmed a bit when she looked at the young woman. She was too proud to admit it out loud, but her heart had done a one-eighty about Cassandra, and though she knew why she had hated her at first, she now thought it was silly. Cassandra was loving and lovable, unlike her own prideful personality. She sighed and stepped forward to hug her.

"Be careful, alright?"

"I will," said Cassandra, hugging her back a bit shyly.

The two girls separated, and Cassandra walked over to Kairen. The Prince immediately took her bag from her hands to put it among the others on Krai's back and without a word, helped her climb up over the dragon's sharp scales. He sat behind her, Cassandra right against his chest, and covered her with one of his familiar fur cloaks. It was a bit too warm and stuffy, but Cassandra knew she would need it for later. Kairen didn't wear anything other than his usual armor, though. Without a glance towards the servants watching them from the ground, he gave a silent signal to Krai, and the dragon took off immediately.

Cassandra watched the others below, but just like before, she was just too frightened and as they got higher, she ended up closing her eyes. Her lips started to feel cold, and she wrapped herself even tighter in the cloak. Would this really be enough in the North frontier? Kairen held her tighter, too. Cassandra was amazed by the warmth of his skin. Did he ever get cold?

Under her, Krai's scales went from lukewarm to cold, too. Despite it's natural temperature, the icy wind was even having a cooling effect on the dragon. Cassandra was happy to have the fur and the saddle between her bottom and the dragon's back, unlike last time.

"How long will it take, My Lord?" she asked when she felt safe enough to open her eyes again.

"Not long," Kairen replied simply.

Cassandra didn't ask anything further. Instead, she decided to rest against his chest, and watch the incredible scenery. She was still lacking a few hours of sleep, but she fought against the tiredness to take in the view. It was a breathtaking sight, just like before. She could already see the range of mountains they were headed to, which were much higher than the mountain the Onyx Castle was built on.

Behind them, it was an ocean of green, a forest so vast Cassandra already couldn't see the castle anymore. And to the east, the Great Sea. Cassandra couldn't help but remember her long lost childhood when she saw that dark blue sea. Would she ever be reunited with her younger sister? She was only two years younger... Was she still alive? What did she look like now? Cassandra had tried to search for her for a while back in the Capital, but as a slave, it was just too difficult. Maybe she would be luckier now... Deep in thought, she sighed and caught Kairen's attention.

"Are you too cold?"

"No, my Lord, I was only lost in my thoughts."

"What thoughts?"

Cassandra hesitated for a bit. The Prince's concerns were probably far from her own. Seeing how he was frowning and waiting for her answer, she decided to be honest. Nebora had advised her to be a bit more selfish afterall.

"I wondered if it was possible to look for someone? If we go back to the Capital?"

"Who are you looking for?"

"My younger sister... I lost track of her many years ago."

Kairen stayed silent for a while, and Cassandra wondered what he was thinking. Did he find this annoying? But she had that little glimmer of hope in her heart, and now, she knew it wouldn't disappear anytime soon.

"Maybe," he eventually said.

However, he didn't add anything else to that enigmatic answer. Cassandra only nodded slowly. She wasn't expecting much, but she felt a bit disappointed. She probably wouldn't be able to hear about her younger sister's whereabouts anytime soon... It probably wasn't a good time, either. She had just been brought to the North and most likely wouldn't be back at the Capital again for a while.

"Cassandra."

She looked at the Prince wondering what he wanted, and without a word, he silently kissed her. Cassandra was completely taken by surprise. Kairen's lips were warm and passionate, as he plunged his tongue between hers. She moaned, trying to catch her breath while responding to him. It was so sudden, if he wasn't holding her so tight she might have fallen off.

Yet, the kiss felt somewhat different, a little sweeter than their usual ones. Cassandra felt his warmth, and her heart felt a bit lighter while answering him. Cassandra was surprised by his sudden display of tenderness. Was he trying to comfort her?

After a while, their lips parted, Cassandra blushing. She was expecting him to say something after that, but he didn't, and only looked forward. She was trying to figure out what it meant when Krai suddenly let out a loud growl.

Cassandra looked down. Far below them, she could see a long building. It took her a while to realize it was actually a very, very large wall, affixed between two mountains. As Krai started descending, she noticed a myriad of tents of various sizes lined up a few kilometers behind the wall, with a few buildings throughout. The Military Camp!

The Black Dragon's growl caught the attention of the army below. As they got further down, all the soldiers lined up in perfect rank, their armor shining under the sun. Cassandra was astonished by the sheer number. How many men were there? A few thousand? She couldn't even try to come up with a number as there were just too many! She even saw flags in front of some ranks, probably to separate them into groups. As Krai was about to land on a large platform, she could hear the men yelling orders.

"Get in order for His Highness' arrival! Faster!"

The Black Dragon finally reached the ground with a loud growl and a few flaps of its wings that sent mini gusts of wind about. Cassandra saw five men in front, all standing perfectly at attention. They were doing a salute and standing tall, waiting for Kairen. The Prince got off the dragon first, climbing and stepping down effortlessly.

"Welcome back, Your Highness. How was your..."

Before the man finished his sentence, he noticed Kairen was already busy helping Cassandra down, ignoring him. The old man, who seemed to be in his fifties, was completely speechless. His eyes were set firmly on Cassandra, wondering if his eyes were deceiving him, before going back to the Prince.

"Your Highness, this woman..."

"She is mine," simply stated Kairen, as if that was enough of an explanation.

Of course, it clearly wasn't! Cassandra felt a bit sorry for the soldiers, and bowed politely, facing them with grace.

"I am Cassandra, My Lord."

Anyone with a military grade high enough to address the Prince was worth calling a Lord, so she decided to use that designation until she could learn their proper names and titles. Hearing such a pretty young woman introduce herself, the old man couldn't avoid introducing himself too, and did so a tad awkwardly.

"Wel... Welcome." That was the best he could do in this strange situation. Who was she? What was she doing with their Commander? Her collar clearly indicated that she was a slave, but the Prince's attitude was nowhere near what it should have been toward a simple slave woman! None of the lieutenants, waiting to salute him, could hide their confusion either.

But Kairen gave them no explanation. He walked away, headed for the camp with Cassandra following close behind him, and Krai right behind her. Even among the soldiers, a large chattering was rising until the old man yelled at them to shut up in front of their Lord.

Cassandra was a bit intimidated following Kairen into this unknown place, but she had already introduced herself and couldn't do anything else about it. With the Prince walking in front, the old man and the other lieutenants had to speed to catch up with him.

They walked past several tents that all seemed to be deserted, but Cassandra figured it was because everyone had come out to welcome the War God back. It was an impressive camp. There were many fire pits, tents, and training grounds. They had clearly been established here for a while and from seeing the perfect cleanliness and order of the place, one could tell this army was trained flawlessly. Not only were the weapons perfectly stored, but the horses were housed quite well, and there were still plenty more spaces available.

Kairen led her to the biggest of all the tents; large and red. Once she entered, Cassandra was impressed by how big and luxurious it was. It could have been a very decent place to live all year round. There was a bed, a large chair that almost seemed like a throne, and a table full of maps and books. In a corner, there was a wardrobe with weapons stored right next to it. Kairen headed for the table to look at the map while Cassandra stood to the side.

She heard some noise outside, and figured it was probably Krai laying its heavy body down next to the tent. For once, it was not fussing about not being able to see her. Maybe the trip had exhausted it enough to need a nap.

"Your Highness!"

The high-ranked soldiers from earlier barged in, and Cassandra stepped further away, retreating closer to the bed. Several of them were looking at her, some even glaring. The old general then spoke up for everyone.

"Your Highness, could you explain this situation? You left without warning and came back with a... a slave woman?"

"My concubine," rectified Kairen.

The shock was even bigger than before. It was just getting more awkward for Cassandra.

"Your... Congratulations, Your Highness, but I don't believe this woman should..."

With one glare from Kairen, he suddenly shut up. Whatever he was about to say stuck in his throat from the Prince's black eyes. The warning was clear.

"Do you have something to say?" Kairen hissed.

After a few seconds of reflection, the old general sighed.

"Can I do...anything for the Lady's comfort, My Lord?"

Chapter 7

While listening to Kairen and the General, Cassandra couldn't ignore all the eyes on her. The camp only had men, thousands of them. They all wore the very same black armor, like Kairen's. The only difference was that the higher-ranked ones, like the men in front of her, had extra decorations, like gold braces or belts. The Prince, however, was the only one wearing dragon scales on his armor and braces. But aside from that, there wasn't any display of wealth.

With so many eyes on her, Cassandra was glad to be covered with the fur cloak. Being the only woman was sort of intimidating, even with the Prince standing right in front of her. Kairen was talking with the old General about conditions at the camp. He had only been gone since the previous day, but many of his men were trying to hold his attention. She could only stay still behind him and wait.

Most of the conversation was about tactics, training, and new recruits. Cassandra listened, but she wasn't knowledgeable about any of those things.

"We also have to consider food rationing, My Lord. We have doubled the hunting teams, but it's getting harder for everyone. The men are starting to talk..." said one of the Generals, awkwardly.

"I have brought more," Kairen said simply.

"Thank you, My Lord."

The man was about to say something else, but another of the lieutenants spoke ahead of him, so he stayed quiet. Despite his beard, Cassandra noticed he appeared to be younger than the others. He would frown every time another of the high-ranked officers spoke, clearly paying close attention to each word that was said. Then, the oldest General, who appeared to be Kairen's second, invited him for a tour outside of the training grounds. He briefly turned to Cassandra.

"Stay here."

"Yes, My Lord."

Kairen left the tent first and all of the men quickly followed after, though some couldn't stop themselves from looking back at Cassandra before leaving. She didn't avoid their stares. Instead, she tried to remember each of them. There were about twenty in total, and once they left, the room felt strangely empty.

Cassandra was now all alone in the large tent. Holding the fur cloak tight around her, she got up and wandered around. Not touching anything, she observed each item in the room, a little curious about her Prince's life at the camp. The table was mostly filled with military books and maps. Cassandra knew how to read, and it wasn't her first time seeing maps, but she couldn't help but smile a little when she spotted one where her homeland appeared. The Rain Lands were so small on the maps compared to the Dragon Empire... The territory had been annexed by the Eastern Republic, so the map was probably old. Her finger slowly traced the route that, as far as she can remember, had probably been taken all the way to the Capital. With being bought and sold over and over again, she had seen a few places, but the majority of her life had been spent in the Capital.

She didn't have any regrets about leaving those places, though. She never made friends there, or had anything of value. Slaves couldn't own anything anyway, not even their clothes. Cassandra sighed and brought her fingers up to her slavery collar. It was heavy and, most of the time, painful too. She had touched the locking mechanism so often she knew it by heart. Only a slave trader possessed the key to open one of these. And even if she got rid of it by chance some day, it would take years for the red marks it had carved into her flesh to disappear. Slavery was something that was never forgotten.

Taking her eyes off the many maps, Cassandra headed to the wardrobe. As expected, the Prince didn't have many outfits, and close to no jewelry, except for a few gold chains and rings that she didn't dare touch.

The furniture was probably the fanciest thing in the tent. Most of it was expensive wood, surely carved by a specialist. There was even gold in some parts, in the throne-like chair or the head of the bed. It wasn't as low-key as the Prince's room in the Castle. Was it because he spent most of his time here?

"Excuse me?"

Surprised, Cassandra turned around. She didn't think someone would come here while Kairen was away. It was a rather young man carrying a large basket. He looked even younger than she was, and seemed quite shy too. He bowed a bit clumsily to her.

"I was told to bring this here for His Highness, Ma'am. Is it fine if..."

Cassandra was surprised he was waiting for her approval to put his basket down. She nodded.

"Uhm, sure, please do."

"Thanks, Ma'am."

He walked to one of the corners of the room and put down his basket, taking out some armor.

"It was done while our Lord was away by our blacksmith, with reinforced iron and dragon scales," he explained with a strong northern accent.

"Is it from Krai... I mean, His Highness' dragon?"

"Yes, ma'am. We collect them when the Black Dragon sheds its scales so our blacksmith can break them and reshape them for His Highness' armors. It's beautiful, isn't it?"

"It is..."

Cassandra walked closer to look at the armor and indeed, it was gorgeous. The black of Krai's scales was shining and perfectly molded into the Prince's armor. The blacksmith had even been very precise while re-carving the scales' shape, making it look like the original pattern. As if she had praised him, the young soldier smiled.

"My teacher is very good! He is one of the best in the Empire."

"Are you an apprentice?"

"Yes, Ma'am. I came here a year ago to follow my master and complete my apprenticeship."

Cassandra realized some of the youngest soldiers she had spotted were probably apprentices, just like him. Indeed, an army required many types of expertise, like the blacksmith master he was so proud of. Embarrassed by her eyes on him, he blushed a little and bowed again.

"I'm Orwan, Ma'am. I'm part of the first blacksmith team."

"Nice to meet you, Orwan. I'm Cassandra."

"Uhm... Nice to meet you, Ma'am... I mean, Lady Cassandra."

Once again, it felt odd to be addressed like that, but she didn't say anything. Actually, she noticed a bad burn on his hand, and frowned.

"Are you all right?"

"Oh, this? It's fine, I get burns like this all the time... It will heal."

"No, it looks like it's infected. Have you not tried to get it healed?"

Orwan frowned, looking a bit embarrassed.

"No, Ma'am..."

"Don't you have healers here?"

"We do, but...there are only a few, and mostly for high-ranked officers."

"What if someone else is injured?"

"We usually put water on it, and our lieutenant will give us a few days of rest."

"What if it's bad? This could seriously lead to losing your hand!"

"Hem... There is the Red Room, but..."

"The Red Room?"

Orwan nodded.

"That's where they take the people who get badly injured, Ma'am. But no one really wants to go there, it's rumored to be a place where... well, where people go to die."

Cassandra was confused. Why would they allow people to simply die...

"Where is the Red Room?"

"In the third East building, Ma'am. But it's not a place for a Lady like you, I have to say..."

"I understand. Thank you, Orwan."

He nodded, a bit embarrassed. Had he said too much to the Prince's concubine? Orwan took a couple more weapons out of his basket to display along with the armor, and left after a quick bow.

Cassandra was left alone once again. She was bored, but she didn't want to disobey Kairen and venture outside. However, there wasn't much to do in the room, except read military books, and she had no interest in those. She went to the other cupboard and, after hesitating, opened it. It was only food storage - dried meat, a couple of wine bottles, and some bread. It seemed someone had brought it recently, though. She closed it and turned around. That was it for the Third Prince's tent. Cassandra spent a little more time looking at the armor and weapons but really, she had no idea what to do. If only she could at least step outside to see Krai and pet him. But Kairen's orders kept her from it. She didn't want to ignore it, as he could easily get angry anytime she did something he didn't approve of.

Without many options, she decided to just lay on the bed, keeping the fur cloak around her, and listen. The atmosphere was very different from the deserted Onyx Castle. The camp was so lively that she could hear a lot of things going on all the time. Horses throttling, men chatting, metal striking metal...It somehow reminded her of the Capital. Back then, whenever she closed her eyes, she would hear the life in the City outside her walls. The tent was even thinner though, so sometimes it felt as if people were standing only a few steps away. Cassandra could even pick up some of the conversations, mostly about the Prince's return or the food shortage.

She woke up from a light kiss on her bare shoulder. The Prince's smell, now familiar to her, took her away from her slumber as she opened her eyes. Cassandra couldn't remember when she had fallen asleep. Kairen was standing over her, with his bare chest and an undecipherable expression.

"Your Highness..."

The Prince didn't answer, and instead leaned in to kiss her. As always, his lips were warm and skilled enough to wake Cassandra completely. He got under the cloak with her, caressing her hips and neck with his large hands. For once, the Prince actually took the time to take her dress off properly, pulling the laces of her corset one by one, kissing the skin revealed underneath. Each time his lips flirted with her skin, Cassandra felt her own temperature rising. She was so accustomed to Kairen's touch now, how could she still be so reactive? Unable to resist, she would shiver, gasp, and wriggle under his hands. It wasn't so scary anymore, except for that hint of shame every time she responded to him.

His lips suddenly ventured to her thighs, and she gasped brutally. Where was he...! But before she could even think, his tongue was licking her there, and she moaned out of surprise. The Prince was actually going down on her, kissing her pussy! Cassandra was completely overwhelmed by the surprise and the embarrassment. Yet, Kairen's skillful mouth soon pushed those feelings from her mind.

"Your Highness!" she almost screamed in panic.

He was mad! A Prince licking his slave, there...! Cassandra had no idea how to respond, except with panic, and... pleasure. It was hard to ignore. She was so wet, and his tongue was driving her crazy, going in circles, diving in and licking again. She was gasping and moaning loudly, unable to stop. She couldn't even think straight, as she felt the sensations deep within her stomach. The hotness between her thighs should be impossible! Her hands feeble, she tried to push him away, awkwardly reaching for his hair. But Kairen ignored her, and kept going with his impossible torture.

"Oh God, Your... Highness..." Cassandra panted.

As her moans got louder, she suddenly realized they were in a tent with thin walls! In a flash of lucidity, she covered her mouth with her hand, trying to hold back her muffled moans that kept coming.

"What are you doing?"

As he had stopped, Cassandra shook her head, she just couldn't endure this! But Kairen grabbed her wrists, trapping both of them in his hands alongside her hips, and immediately went back to pleasuring her. Cassandra was dying of shame. She couldn't repress her moans. It was way too good, as the Prince only focused on her most sensitive area, his mouth, tongue, and lips, attacking her relentlessly.

"Pl... Please... Oh please, stop..." she cried, trying to fight her pleasure and urges.

But he did not stop. Kairen sucked her clitoris, driving her to the edge of pleasure and craziness, making her moan louder. She had never experienced this. Her entire brain was focused on her intimate area, as she closed her eyes, like a fire burning. She couldn't endure anymore. Cassandra suddenly felt it, like a spark, something that suddenly burst inside her and made her cry out in pleasure. A long, intense and almost painful orgasm, came so hard that her whole body spasmed for a few seconds.

She was out of breath when she finally came down. Kairen released her wrists, and she covered her eyes, unable to believe it. Her Master had pleasured her without relieving himself at all!

She was still catching her breath when Kairen laid down next to her, pulling the covers back on them and kissing her temple.

"You can't do that..." Cassandra whispered.

"Do what?"

"Pleasure...me."

The Prince clicked his tongue and looked at her with his dark eyes.

"Didn't you like it?"

Cassandra immediately blushed from embarrassment.

"It's not..."

"Did you like it or not?"

His tone of voice made it clear she wouldn't get out of this without giving him a proper answer. Cassandra made sure to look anywhere but his direction.

"I did, but..."

"Better than what Shareen did?"

"Your Highness!"

She couldn't believe he would dare to ask such a thing. How jealous could he be to actually say that! The worst part was that serious look he had on his face while he asked! Cassandra was so exhausted by his persistence!

"I did not appreciate what... happened with your sister. But it's not the same, Her Highness Princess Shareen was just making fun of me, while you..."

"While I what?"

Cassandra gulped, trying to find the right words, to make him understand while trying not to die of embarrassment.

"You... willingly pleasured me. I'm only a sl...concubine, My Lord. I am the one who is supposed to pleasure you, not the other way around."

Kairen stayed silent for a while, staring at her with his enigmatic look. Cassandra hoped he had understood, but his obsidian eyes were impossible to decipher. So she waited for him to say something, anything. After a few minutes had passed, the War God still hadn't said a thing, but underneath the cloak, his hand suddenly went down to her still wet pussy, taking her completely by surprise. Cassandra gasped loudly and gripped down on his wrist.

"Your..."

"What if I like it?"

Cassandra looked at him, lost. But Kairen kissed her slowly, while his hot and firm hand continued to caress her. She couldn't believe it was her own taste on his tongue...

"What if I like your reactions?"

He sucked and nibbled on the skin of her neck, and kissed it, making her gasp again. She loved the sensation of his lips right there...

"What if I like the way your white skin gets hot and red?"

His lips went down on her bare breast, and his available hand played with the other, fondling them and caressing them while Cassandra flushed.

"What if I like the way your breasts fill my hands?"

She knew what he was doing, and closed her eyes, unable to look at him and his amused yet somewhat serious expression. On top of everything else, the way he looked at her was driving her insane. The way he looked at her...

"What if I like the way you get all embarrassed when I touch you?"

He kept going. His hands were caressing her, gentle and hot on her body. With her eyes closed, Cassandra couldn't predict where they would go next, and that somehow made it even worse. She shivered. He was going over her breasts... her hips...her thighs...her neck...her stomach....

"Your Highness!" she moaned when his fingers harassed her pussy again. He was clearly playing with her, observing each of her reactions, but he was so good at it, she was helpless.

Cassandra was once again at his mercy, breathing loudly and trying to repress her moans. His fingers were rubbing intensely, and she could feel herself throbbing in response. As a reflex, she slowly spread her legs wider, feeling the heat that was coming back.

"I like the way you become wet when I touch you..." whispered Kairen in her ear.

Cassandra bit her lip. She was so responsive to his touch! Her own body was ahead of her, pulsing and wanting more. Didn't she come just a moment ago? But it wasn't enough, not yet. She felt it, and hated that she couldn't control it. Instead, she was willingly spreading her legs, offering herself to his skilled fingers, and wanting more.

Just as she was in this internal war between desire and reason, Kairen leaned in to give her a deep, forceful kiss. Despite her lack of breath, Cassandra answered. It was as if the fire between her thighs had made her even thirstier for the Prince's mouth. It was a savage, willful, and exciting kiss. So exhilarating, it made her moan out loud as she also grew wetter. She felt his other hand grip her hair in a possessive gesture to keep her close.

"Your Highness..." she whispered when they finally interrupted their kiss, both of them out of breath.

"Tell me what you want."

"W... what?"

The question was so direct yet vague, Cassandra was almost afraid she had understood it wrong. Kairen was serious, his black eyes burning with desire.

"Tell me what you want. Now. I want to hear it."

Cassandra immediately shook her head, but he was still holding on to her, so she couldn't look away or ignore him.

"No, no, no, I can't..." she muttered, almost panicked.

"You can. Cassandra, I want to hear it. Now, tell me what you want."

Hearing her name from his mouth again shook her a little. Somehow, it was even more embarrassing than anything else, something she could barely handle. She felt his fingers continuously rubbing against her entrance, playing with her pussy, but Kairen had purposely slowed down, waiting for her answer.

Cassandra couldn't endure it. It was like torture, feeling those slow motions against her wetness, when she just...

"T...take me, please..." she whispered, unable to stand it anymore.

Kairen smiled and leaned in to kiss her, another one of those intense kisses they had gotten addicted to. Just then, as his hot body got closer to hers, she immediately felt his swollen, hard dick against her leg, and shivered. What had she become? She was still a virgin a few days ago, and now she desired this man so intensely.

Cassandra forgot all those thoughts as soon as Kairen pulled her to him, and had her lay on her flank, right against him. His warm torso against her back, he wrapped an arm around her and used his other hand to spread her legs. So close against each other, Cassandra was abruptly left looking the other way when behind her, Kairen penetrated her. She moaned loudly at the sensation of his thick member inside her. The position was unusual as she couldn't even see Kairen's face.

When he started moving, Cassandra immediately began moaning with each thrust. Since she couldn't see him, her main focus was the wild, deep, and intense movements inside her. She was entirely at his mercy, unable to predict when each thrust would come. Kairen used their position to make things even wilder with one hand on her breasts and the other on her pussy. He continued caressing her at the same time he was thrusting, making Cassandra cry out in pleasure. He knew she liked it. Cassandra was moaning loudly, focusing on the Prince's thick member, and how he repeatedly hammered her with it. She was crying out, not in pain, but to this impossible pleasure she was being given.

Their position had a unique, intimate feeling. She could feel Kairen's hot breath on her neck right behind her ear. He was groaning with pleasure too, and occasionally kissed her skin. With one hand on her breast and the other between her thighs, he was driving her crazy with so many sensations.

Cassandra knew she wouldn't last long. She was already in way too deep, and just wanted to dive into the wave of pleasure. His powerful dick left her no time to think. It was intense, so much so, she gripped tightly on the sheets and Kairen's wrists as she moaned louder. She felt like she could lose her mind to this, all reason was completely gone while only her body, in this whirlwind of sensations, would stay and endure it.

Soon enough, she felt her orgasm starting, and began to tremble. Her head leaned back and she gasped suddenly, as she felt it grow inside her until it burst. She froze for a few seconds, and Kairen too, reacted to her and groaned in her ear.

A long silence followed as neither of them moved, still trying to catch their breath and emerge out of the daze. Cassandra felt exhausted, but somehow relieved. She couldn't explain it, but their passionate love-making had calmed her worries. Behind her, Kairen slowly pulled out as he kissed her shoulder and wrapped his arms around her.

"Tell me when you want something. I hate having to guess…"

Cassandra chuckled softly. She could certainly tell. Her Prince was a very straightforward man of few words. She didn't dislike that as he was honest anytime he spoke. She snuggled in his arms, surprising him a bit. For the first time, maybe she could be alright with being a little bold and going along with her feelings. But at that very moment, she felt content in his warm arms, even if it might be for only a short while. Kairen tightened his grip around her and once again kissed her skin.

"My Lord…"

"What is it?"

"Can I leave the tent tomorrow? I…I don't think I'll be able to endure being confined here for long. I'm only hoping to look around, not to bother

98

anyone."

Kairen stayed silent for a while. Even without seeing his face, Cassandra could almost hear him internally debating. She wondered what the real reason was for him being so against it. Was it because she would get in the way of the men? Or distract them? Was it alright for a slave to walk around the Military Camp?

"Fine. I'll find someone to accompany you."

"Oh, no, I can..."

"No. The camp is too large. You will stay with someone."

Cassandra felt bad about monopolizing one of Kairen's men for a day, but she didn't dare add anything else in case he changed his mind. At least now she would be able to leave the tent, walk around, and get some fresh air.

As neither of them wanted to leave their position, they ended up napping like this for another hour, in silence. After a while, however, some sort of loud horn took them away from their slumber. Cassandra sat up, intrigued, but Kairen simply got up to put his cloak back on.

"It's the dinner call... Everyone's gathering at the fire pit. Come."

Cassandra put her clothes back on and, like Kairen, wrapped herself in a thick fur coat before walking out with him. As soon as they got outside, a wall of black scales immediately fell right in front of her. Before Cassandra could react, Krai's big head snuggled up against her, growling erratically. She smiled and scratched its head, despite the cold on her hands.

"I missed you, too," she whispered to the dragon.

Maybe it was because he hadn't seen her for a while that Krai acted exceptionally clingy and demanding; growling every time Cassandra stopped scratching it. Eventually, Kairen had to intervene, calling for the dragon to stop and allow them to walk.

Night-time was already falling. Cassandra had no idea when the sun was supposed to set in the mountains, but the purple waves in the sky indicated it wasn't very late yet. Careful not to slip on the thin layer of snow, she followed Kairen closely. Perhaps due to Krai's presence, or because the Prince's tent was so isolated, there weren't many soldiers in the area. After a few minutes, however, they crossed paths with many soldiers who were heading in the same direction. A lot of them gave Cassandra a look. But as Krai was following closely behind her, nobody could afford to stare without getting growled at.

They progressed along, past the soldiers, but somehow, everyone was careful to stay away from the trio. Kairen didn't pay any attention to the soldiers, only slowing down to wait for Cassandra, who was walking slowly so as not to fall. She was curious to know where they were headed. The Prince had mentioned a fire pit, did it mean everyone actually ate outside?

Cassandra saw the flames long before they arrived. The fire was so high, she wondered how she did not notice it sooner. In the middle of the camp, a very large space had been organized with long wooden tables and hundreds of men gathered around them, making it loud and lively.

Kairen actually walked to what seemed like a special area, where a square of wood had been arranged with a throne, some fur over it, and a table with gold cutlery. It even had a marquee to protect him from the wind and snow. Cassandra felt a bit relieved that she would be able to sit on a warm floor, because some fur carpets were covering the wooden planks. However, once Kairen sat down, he grabbed her to sit on his lap. Cassandra's cheeks immediately flushed.

"My Lord!" she protested.

She could handle this kind of thing when they were alone in his room, but they were currently in front of hundreds of his men! And many of them were staring, too!

But as always, Kairen ignored her pleas and insisted that she settle on his lap. Cassandra was frustrated. She looked at him with an annoyed pout. Was there no end to his shamelessness!

"Good evening, My Lord," said a man who was standing a few steps away, along with two younger servants.

He was probably supposed to assist Kairen during his meal, like was normal for the Imperial Family, but of course, the Prince had no need for that. However, to Cassandra's surprise, he made a little gesture for the young man to approach.

"You. You'll assist Cassandra from now on."

"Cassandra?" repeated the man, confused.

Only then did he make the connection with the young slave on their master's lap. That slave actually had a name! Regaining his composure, the man bowed lower.

"Understood, My Lord. How does the Lady need assistance?"

"Just do whatever she asks, and go with her whenever she leaves my tent."

If the man was surprised by those orders, he made sure not to show it this time. Cassandra thought this man was obviously a trained Imperial Servant, not a soldier. He was too thin and too polite for that. He simply bowed.

"Understood, My Lord. This lowly servant will do so."

Then, he stepped back a bit and stood there, waiting. The two young men behind him glanced at Cassandra, but when they realized she had seen them they immediately looked down again.

"Tonight's dinner, My Lord."

A large selection was provided, all presented on a large gold tray. Once again, Kairen had the best meat pieces, fish, fruits and bread. Cassandra felt her stomach tighten just by the sight of all the food. She felt like she hadn't eaten in ages! Kairen caught her stare and chuckled softly, making her blush. He really never let an occasion to embarrass her go. Behind them, Krai growled loudly and laid down in the snow, circling their space with its huge body. Cassandra frowned.

"Isn't Krai eating?"

"He went to hunt already," replied Kairen. "Leave us alone."

The servants bowed and left the place, leaving them, but they weren't far enough from the soldiers to truly feel alone. The closest tables were only a few paces away, and Cassandra could see every man's face. Kairen started eating, and so did she. She was starving and actually took a bit of the grilled fish on a stick. After eating for a while and watching the loud chattering, she remembered something.

"Nebora mentioned a food shortage. Are the soldiers alright?"

On the tables, as she looked around she couldn't help but notice that indeed there wasn't much meat, mostly vegetables that didn't look too good either.

"The cold is chasing the biggest prey away. It's hard to hunt enough for everyone."

Cassandra slowly nodded. She didn't know much about hunting. All the food she had ever gotten was either bought, stolen, or found.

As they kept eating, she noticed a few stares on her, but overall, most were too cautious of the Prince and his dragon's presence to say anything. Though, Krai was only focused on Cassandra. The Black Beast watched every move she made with curiosity, tilting its head from time to time. She wondered if the dragon had anything to do while its master was at the camp. Maybe Krai would accompany her the next day?

"Cassandra."

Kairen handed her a cup. Cassandra took it, but right before she brought it to her lips, she realized it wasn't tea or water, but wine! It smelled strangely sweet and good, and felt warm in her hands.

"What is it?" asked Kairen after she had been staring at it for a bit too long.

"I've never had wine before."

He smiled and drank his in one go. Cassandra was a bit more hesitant, and tasted just a small bit with her tongue. It was good! She had imagined it would be more sour, not actually sweet. She drank again, under Kairen's amused eyes.

"You like it?"

She nodded, her cheeks a bit pink. She drank again, feeling the hot drink go down from her throat to her stomach, bringing her some warmth. After a while, Kairen frowned and took it away from her.

"Enough. You'll get drunk."

"I'm fine, My Lord," she protested.

Kairen ignored her and drank the rest of her cup himself, then ordered for the wine to be taken away. Cassandra was a bit disappointed, but she didn't dare to ask again, and shifted her interest to the cheese instead.

Suddenly, a big ruckus took place at one of the nearby tables. For a reason she hadn't caught on, two men were now fist fighting and insulting each other. Cassandra was shocked.

"Shouldn't someone stop them?" she asked.

However, no one around them appeared to want to stop the fight. Actually, the men around were laughing and cheering, telling them to hit harder and get the other. Cassandra was shocked to see such violence, as well as so many people happy to witness it. Eventually, one of the men was thrown down and admitted his defeat. The men around laughed, and to Cassandra's surprise, his opponent helped him up with a laugh.

"What...?"

"It's fine. The soldiers like to fight."

"But, it could have ended so badly!"

Kairen grabbed some meat and shook his head.

"There are rules. They are not allowed to fight their comrades with any weapon, disable them, or kill them."

"Everyone respects the rules?"

"Krai gets an extra meal from time to time..."

Cassandra looked at the dragon. She had almost forgotten about Nebora's warning. Krai was so cute to her all the time, she had a hard time remembering that the dragon was actually a man-killer too. Seeing she was staring, the dragon raised its head, curious, but Cassandra only sighed and turned her eyes to the men again. The two that had fought before were now laughing together and showing off their injuries to each other. Men were truly too complicated to understand!

They kept eating in silence. From time to time, one of the generals or lieutenants came up to pay their respects to the Prince and give him a report, but none of them reacted to Cassandra's presence at all. She didn't mind, as she didn't want to attract extra attention to herself.

About an hour later, they were done with their meal, and Cassandra was starting to feel cold. With the night, an icy wind had come along and was biting her exposed skin. The men too, came to eat and left as quickly as they could, to shield themselves from the wind in their tents. She shivered.

"Are you cold?" asked Kairen, putting his hand on her back.

She nodded. How did he never get cold? No matter what, she had never seen him shiver or get goosebumps, despite being less clothed than she was!

Kairen stood up, and they left the table, without a word for the servants waiting close. But instead of heading for his tent, the Prince actually pulled Cassandra towards his dragon, and Krai raised his head.

"My Lord?" she asked.

Without an explanation, he whistled at Krai, and the dragon stood up. But instead of mounting him, Kairen only held on to an area behind Krai's head, with his hand. The other held firmly around Cassandra's waist, she frowned. She had a bad feeling about this.

When Krai suddenly took off, she couldn't even find the air in her lungs to scream. The Black Dragon had gone up so quickly, she felt the wind whip her skin, and hid her face in Kairen's fur coat by mere reflex. However, she didn't have any more time to be scared. Before she realized it, her feet were touching the ground again, with Kairen's arm around her.

"Are you alright?"

She wanted to say no, but could only shiver and stay still instead. Kairen caressed her neck until her nausea was gone.

"Wha... Where..."

Her throat couldn't formulate any sentences, so she raised her head to look around. It was only at that moment that she realized they had totally moved locations, and were surrounded by a warm fog. Cassandra was completely lost. Where were they? But in front of her, Kairen suddenly started undressing, making her blush again. Couldn't he at least warn her before getting naked right in front of her!

"Cassandra."

She dared to look at him again, as he stepped into what seemed like a natural pool. That's when it finally hit her. Hot springs! They were at a natural hot spring!

Cassandra was amazed. It was a completely wild area, where dozens of cavities were filled with natural hot water. She had only seen man-made hot springs so far! Kairen held his hand out to her, and she undressed swiftly before joining him. The water was strangely blurry, and she couldn't even see her feet. She held onto the Prince's arm the entire time, too uneasy to let go. The ground under them was uneven and only Kairen was moving around without worry.

The Prince sat up in one of the hole's corners, while Cassandra was still glancing sideways.

"This is incredible," she whispered.

She just couldn't get the smile off her face, and observed the fog as it melted under her fingers. Meanwhile, Kairen couldn't take his eyes off her. Naked, with her long hair falling over her shoulders, Cassandra was truly a beautiful sight to witness. He moved her to sit on his lap, facing him, making her blush again.

"Kiss me."

She softly smiled and obeyed his order right away, putting her lips on his. For once, she wasn't hesitating, and Kairen liked that. They kissed, slowly and deeply. Cassandra's body was finally warming up in the water, and Kairen caressed her legs below the surface. She shivered, but it wasn't because of the cold this time.

Cassandra put her arms around her Master's neck, kissing him more, and caressing the base of his hairline where it was shorter. She liked to brush it. Meanwhile, the Prince was busy exploring her body. His hands were slowly going up her legs, caressing her thighs , before stroking her little bush. Cassandra couldn't help but gradually react to his hands, and gasped as soon as his fingers reached her slit.

Kairen kissed her neck, breathing in her scent and exploring her skin with his lips. He hated that damn collar that kept him from entirely touching her. He would take care of it, sooner or later. He loathed the idea of anyone else having any kind of claim to her. She was his, entirely his. Angered, he penetrated her with his finger without warning, making her cry out in surprise.

"Ah! You...Your Highness..." she gasped.

But Kairen was too pissed to listen. He kept rubbing her clit with his thumb, while his fingers were going in and out of her, fast. Cassandra was lost by his sudden reaction, and could only clench her hips and bite her lip, undergoing this sudden treatment. She didn't want to come just with his fingers!

"My Lord!" she cried out, hoping he'd hear and at least slow down before she went crazy.

This time, however, he stopped and she caught her breath, her pussy still throbbing from this sudden torture she had endured. But the Prince was still angry, and hungry for her. Cassandra's voice had him excited, his member rose below the surface. He suddenly stood up, and guided her to stand on another side, in front of him, bent over the spring's edge.

"Spread your legs."

She obeyed, yet having her butt exposed outside of the water was definitely the most embarrassing position ever. This was the last thought she had before Kairen abruptly penetrated her, filling her without warning. Cassandra moaned loudly from his brutal incoming, unprepared. With the Prince behind her, she couldn't see his movements, and only felt his strong hands holding her hips, while he started taking her fast and hard. She couldn't withstand his rhythm, think, or react. She could only let him do it, using her hands to hold on and cry out everytime he went in and out. It was brutal, erratic, savage, and she heard his hips slamming into her butt repeatedly, the sounds of their intercourse echoing in the springs.

"My... My L... Ah! Please... Ah! Slow...Uhm...Down..." she begged in a hoarse voice.

She felt like she was about to explode every time he filled her to the brim. Her legs were shaking and her pussy was on fire. But, Kairen's frenzy wasn't showing any sign of slowing down. He just kept going, making her cry out.

Cassandra had no idea why he was suddenly so rough and insatiable, but among the mist, she couldn't respond. His hard member inside her was making her burn, with the frantic rubbing driving her crazy. She was surrounded by her own voice, crying out with pleasure in her ears. She had become another woman, one who took pleasure in her Master's brutal fucking.

Kairen kept going, and she kept moaning, her legs going weak. It was never ending, and she closed her eyes, feeling his hardness inside her. Her thighs were unconsciously clenching and her pussy throbbing as he hammered into her again, and she felt his pleasure coming as hers was near too. His penetrations slowed down, and he gave two last deep, brutal, poundings with a groan of relief. Cassandra, shaking, moaned faintly in response. Out of breath, with her insides reeling from the sudden change, she contemplated the sensations of the weaker orgasm that filled her pussy at the same time as the Prince relieved himself.

She was too tired and her legs suddenly gave up from under her. Kairen, holding her by the waist, took a couple steps back and had her sit on him, as they both came back to reality, in a daze.

Exhausted, Cassandra was still feeling numb even while lying on the Prince's lap. Her mind in a daze, she still felt her hot insides from their wild sex just a few seconds ago. She couldn't believe it. Kairen kissed her shoulder, caressing her hair. His recovery was faster than Cassandra's, and he observed her, as her eyes were still closed, resting her head on his shoulder.

"Cassandra?" he called, softly.

"I'm fine... I just...wonder if you've been holding back all this time."

He chuckled against her shoulder, and helped her to sit better on his lap, her arm around his shoulder. Looking at each other, they naturally exchanged a long, softer kiss. Cassandra wasn't afraid anymore to caress his face while they were kissing, and Kairen liked her soft fingers on his cheek. It lasted a while, as they sat still against each other, softly kissing and caressing each other. They were completely alone in the hot springs, under the night sky. It was a beautiful, eerie sight. Surrounded by the steam, the only noises were those of water, or night creatures coming out to hunt in the nearby forest.

The sky was clear, the moon was throwing a white light on them, making Cassandra's skin even paler than usual. The contrast with Kairen's dark skin was striking. The two were opposites, but they found the other even more beautiful because of that. Kairen was mesmerized by Cassandra's beauty in this setting. Her long brown hair was wet and falling like a cascade on her shoulders, floating around her when she moved around in the water. Her green eyes were shining bright, too.

"What is it?" she asked, blushing a bit from his intense stare.

"Are you unhappy? That I brought you here?" he asked.

Cassandra was a bit surprised. Was the Prince worried she was against coming here? Sometimes, his questions about what she thought or felt were so sudden and disarming... She shook her head.

"No...I'm glad you didn't leave me alone."

She couldn't have endured so many nights in an empty bed, not after she had gotten used to the War God's warmth. The only thing she regretted a bit was to be the only woman here. She missed Nebora and the others somehow. But if she said anything about that, she feared the Prince would actually go back and bring her friend here by force.

Cassandra and the Prince cuddled and enjoyed the hot springs a bit longer, not talking much in the meantime. Cassandra loved the difference between the hot water and the icy air outside, and wondered if she would ever feel like leaving. Especially when she was like this, held firmly against Kairen's chest.

"Your skin is always so warm," she whispered.

She had noticed before, but no matter the temperature, Kairen's body never seemed to suffer from the cold. Even when they rode Krai, his heat was enough to keep her warm for the whole trip.

"It's the dragon's heat."

He grabbed her hand and put it up against his chest, where his heart was, and Cassandra realized that spot was even warmer than the rest. She frowned, a bit confused and surprised. She could almost feel a core, like a fire burning inside his chest.

"Is it because of your dragon? Because of Krai?" she asked.

"We are connected...in some ways."

As if it had known what his Master was saying, at that same moment, the large black dragon came back, landing on a big rock nearby. The dragon crawled down, walking towards them until its large body circled half of the spring Kairen and Cassandra were bathing in. Krai's big head leaned towards her, and Cassandra scratched the dragon's favorite area briefly. She had noticed how the Prince and his dragon didn't even seem to interact or look at each other.

"Can he read your thoughts?" she asked.

It was a bit odd to ask such a thing, but Cassandra had always felt Krai's actions were linked to Kairen's temper somehow. His dragon growled when he was unhappy, got mad when he was upset... And they both yearned for her, too.

"No. Dragons don't think like humans. But he feels...the things I feel. Some say our dragons are our instincts, some say they know our inner thoughts. Sometimes they know what we want before we do."

While saying that, Kairen was intensely looking at Cassandra, and she knew he was talking about their first encounter. Krai had been instantly captivated by her, before even Kairen himself had spotted her in the crowd. Cassandra suddenly blushed, realizing what he meant. She turned to the dragon to avoid looking at her Master, trying to hide her embarrassment.

Krai, only too happy to get more scratches and cuddles from her, leaned in closer, growling softly. But Kairen wrapped his arm around Cassandra's waist and brought her closer to him again. The dragon growled at its Master, a bit unhappy, but Kairen ignored him. Cassandra was still amused anytime those two got jealous.

"It seems like he has his own will though," she whispered.

"He does. Dragons are not pets. He's just connected to me."

"Are you connected in other ways? Like your warmth?"

Kairen showed his arm to her, making her caress his skin.

"I have dragon-tamer skin. It's thicker than humans. My vision is better too, and I can see you in the dark."

Cassandra had noticed that too. Whenever they had sex in the dark, Kairen always knew her moves and expressions. He kissed her shoulder softly, while she was still observing the dragon. Krai had apparently given up on the scratches, and was just lying lazily next to them.

"He's stronger than others, isn't he?"

"How do you know?"

"I noticed it in the arena. The other dragons stayed away from him, and they never turned their backs on him either. Is it because he's your dragon?"

Kairen looked up at his dragon, exchanging a look with the red-eyed beast.

"My brothers' dragons are not well-controlled. They are too weak to have their dragons listen to them."

Cassandra wondered if it was really only about their willpower. She felt like Krai's strength and behavior were linked to Kairen's personality, not his strength. Those were only her thoughts, though. She felt a bit sleepy, staying so long in the baths, and she leaned her head onto Kairen's shoulder.

"We should go back," said the Prince, noticing her fatigue.

They dressed quickly, and once again, Krai transported them back to the camp. Without them noticing, it had gotten pretty late. When the dragon landed in front of the red tent, there were only a few soldiers patrolling around. Once again, Cassandra did her best to ignore them, following Kairen in his tent.

Someone had made up the bed and had brought some more food to snack on, but Cassandra was still full and tired. She hesitated for a second, but Kairen brought her to lay with him under the covers, pulling the large fur blanket over them. She was still sore from the brutal sex earlier, and felt glad when the War God only laid beside her. He put his arm under her head and had her sleep over his chest, where it was the warmest. Her cheek against his skin and his fingers caressing her hair, Cassandra fell asleep in a matter of seconds.

When she woke up the next morning, she could tell it was already pretty late just from all the noises outside. It was still cold though, and she was alone in bed. She sat up, covering herself with the fur, and looked around. A dress was waiting for her on one of the chairs. Had he brought it with him when they had come here?

Cassandra dressed herself up quickly, and did her best to tie her hair up too. Long hair wasn't too great in such chilly weather, though she didn't feel like cutting it either, since Kairen liked it long. Some breakfast was waiting for her, too. On a little gold tray, there was the usual fruit and cheese, as well as milk. Cassandra ate it slowly, wondering if Kairen had eaten here before going, while she was still asleep. She didn't drink the milk, and just grabbed one of the large fur cloaks in the room to cover herself up before going outside.

To her surprise, it seemed a bit late in the morning, as the men were already very busy. A few of them looked surprised to see her as soon as she stepped out of the tent, but no one dared to talk to her.

"Good morning, Madam."

Cassandra had forgotten about the Imperial Servant from last night. However, the man was waiting for her right outside the tent, standing straight and ready. She felt embarrassed to have an Imperial Servant wait on her.

"Good morning."

The man didn't add anything after that, and it was a bit awkward. Cassandra had a hunch that he would simply follow her everywhere she went, but it would definitely be uncomfortable if he just tailed her like a shadow, in that awkward silence all day.

"Can I ask your name?" she said, a bit unsure.

"My name is Evin, Madam. You do not need to ask my permission to ask things, Madam."

"All right. Can you show me around the camp then?"

"Yes, Madam."

Evin was a very cold, serious, and stone-faced man. Cassandra listened to him as he walked around, explaining to her how the camp, and it's two hundred thousand men, worked, day and night. Most men were there voluntarily, but the higher ranking men all came from wealthy or noble families, as it was hard to rise through the ranks. Military service was mandatory for any man in the Dragon Empire, but not everyone could join the War God's Army. Hence, the soldiers in this camp were all considered the best, and were proud to be there. Aside from the regular soldiers, there were also many other professions in the camp. Like the blacksmiths, servants, dressers and farriers for the horses, accountants, and there were even architects and strategists.

"The men are divided between three main units. The Cavalry, the Infantry, and the Artillery. Each is under the command of one of the Generals, and above them are two Assistant Commanders and then our Commander-in-Chief."

Cassandra already knew that Kairen was, of course, the Commander-in-Chief, the highest ranked man in the camp. She wondered if she had already met the Assistant Commanders.

As they kept walking around, Cassandra was conscious of all the stares she was getting. Some leaders scolded their soldiers for staring, but it was hard for the men not to notice a woman like Cassandra. Even covered in the fur coat, they could tell she was very pretty, with her emerald eyes wandering around. Her pale skin and slender figure attracted all the men's eyes to her. It was a bit oppressive, but she did her best to ignore them and act normal.

After walking a while, she realized she had come to a large forge, where several blacksmiths operated. It was probably one of the hottest places in the camp, and also one of the most interesting to watch.

"Madam!"

Orwan had spotted her, and came to meet Cassandra right outside of the forge, his face dark from the smoke and ashes.

"Did you come to watch?"

"I just meant to observe for a bit, I was curious. I hope I didn't hinder your work," said Cassandra.

"Not at all!"

Orwan seemed a bit happy to have a visitor, and proposed to show her around the forge. Most of the time, they had to stay at a good distance from the blacksmiths working, but Cassandra was still very happy with what she got to see. Orwan was proud to tell her all about how their group contributed to the Prince's Army, and showed her several weapons they had already made that day.

"How is your arm, by the way?" asked Cassandra.

"Oh, it's...fine!"

He hid his arm from her though, and Cassandra frowned.

"Can I see it?"

Orwan hesitated, and after a while, agreed to show it. It didn't look any better. The flesh had turned a bit dark, and Cassandra shook her head.

"You need to get it healed properly."

"I'm really fine. I don't need to go to the Red Room."

"Why are you so against it?"

"We don't heal there! It's not somewhere the injured want to go, Madam."

Cassandra was not content to hear that. She turned to Evin, but he was already shaking his head.

"This is not a place for a concubine to go."

That answer wasn't good enough. Cassandra was wondering if she could insist when one of the nearby men clicked his tongue.

"A concubine's place ain't in a forge either! How about you go to His Highness' bedroom? Or do you need someone else to warm you up, beautiful?" he said with a disgusting tongue noise.

Cassandra frowned. She didn't want to get in any trouble, but Orwan got mad at the man.

"Show some respect! She is His Highness' concubine! Our Commander-in-Chief!"

"She's just a bedroom toy!" said the man. "What does he care if we play with her a bit too?"

Chapter 8

Cassandra stared at the man, a bit lost as to how to react. She was no stranger to men's unwanted and dirty sollicitations. As a slave, she had gotten her fair share. She even got touched a couple of times, though she would rather forget those. She even found herself lucky to have preserved her virginity until she met the Prince.

"Isn't she just a slave? We know our Commander-in-Chief doesn't care about his concubines anyway! I bet he doesn't care if we get a taste of this one either."

"You idiot, didn't you attend last night's dinner? His Highness acted differently with this one," said another of the blacksmiths. "Go ahead, Moar, but don't blame us if you lose your head for that!"

Hearing this, the man seemed to hesitate. Actually, Cassandra also noticed the other men seemed torn as well. Those who had been leering at her were now reconsidering the question, looking at her in a new light. Some apparently felt the question wasn't worth losing their life over, and got back to work, ignoring her. The man named Moar, however, clicked his tongue, annoyed from not getting any more support from his fellow peers.

"That little pussy. You better not wander off alone, Missy, or you'll get a taste of me."

Cassandra didn't like the threat, but she did not respond. She felt that man wasn't worth it, and anyway, she didn't want to stay here any longer. He probably wouldn't dare to do anything in plain sight, and with so many witnesses. Ignoring him, she turned around and left, her heart beating a bit faster than usual. She knew the kind of man that Moar was, and she really hoped she wouldn't see him again.

"Should we go back to His Highness' tent, perhaps?" suggested Evin.

Cassandra didn't really feel like it yet. She had visited only a small portion of the camp, and she felt like she would be losing to that horrid man if she went back to hide in the Prince's tent. She hesitated for a second wondering what would be the right thing to do.

"Madam!"

They turned around. Orwan had left the Forge to come to them, running, and out of breath. He shook his head, a bit fidgety.

"I'm very sorry about that, Moar is...a jerk, Madam. I'm very sorry, I wish I could have shown you around some more."

Cassandra didn't hold Orwan responsible at all. She didn't really care about the incident because it was only words and she was fine. Instead, she just gave him a gentle smile.

"It's alright, Orwan. Actually..."

"Yes?"

"Could you show me to the Red Room?"

He shook his head even faster, very embarrassed.

"I can't, Madam. It really isn't a place you should go."

"I'm curious about it, please?"

Orwan exchanged a look with the servant, but as usual, Evin didn't betray a single emotion, staying quiet and still the whole time. It was hard to say what he thought about Cassandra's request, even if he had voiced his opinion against it earlier. However, he didn't say anything now. He probably had to respect Cassandra's choices anyway. Eventually, Orwan sighed.

"All right, but...please, don't make His Highness mad at me for showing you this."

"I promise."

She followed the young man across the camp, ignoring more stares on the way. She wondered where the Prince was. Probably busy with some high ranked general. Krai was nowhere to be seen, too, so she assumed the dragon might have been napping or hunting somewhere. Finally, they reached a building that had actually been carved into the mountain, with a narrow entrance guarded by two soldiers. They only gave a glance at Cassandra's red dress, but let them through without questions. Inside, Cassandra was surprised to find several rooms that had been dug deep into the rocks, most of them were for storage of food or weapons. A lot of people were also working there, and seemed busy enough not to pay attention to the trio.

But Orwan took her to a further, isolated room, where he stood at the entrance. Unlike what they had seen so far, there was no one around that place. The apprentice frowned and stood at the entrance, turning to her.

"The injured are brought...here, Madam."

"Here...?"

Cassandra took a step inside the room, and was immediately horrified. This was no place for people to rest and recover! The whole floor had been tainted with blood, a sad explanation for this place's name. She walked in, still a bit disgusted, but she couldn't ignore the dozens of men laying there, right on the ground. A lot of them were in a really, really bad state. Cassandra had seen a lot in her life, but the fresh wounds, cut limbs, and disfigured faces still gave her nausea, especially since nothing was being done for them. She even suspected there were some dead bodies lying among them.

"What about doctors?" she asked Evin, who was following her with his mouth covered.

"We don't have enough at the camp. They usually take care of the most important soldiers first, which means the higher-ranked ones."

Cassandra frowned. This was horrible. So many of those men didn't even get the most basic treatment and were just left here to suffer! She looked around, but this place definitely wasn't a place to heal. Orwan was right. This was a place to die. It was obvious that no one cared. There were a few men working around, but they only seemed to check on the injured, take out the corpses, and excrements. It was a horrid place, and that only made Cassandra madder. She kept walking inside, surprising Evin.

"Madam, don't you want to leave? This place is..."

"These people need help," Cassandra interrupted him. "This place doesn't even have windows, or water."

"Wh...why would they need windows?"

"The air needs to circulate! A stagnant place like this will only help the sickness spread around."

"They will spread it if we take them out!"

"I doubt it. It's way too cold outside, and the tents are spread far from one another. The cold would kill the viruses and they aren't spread easily anyway. Not when it's from these types of infections"

The servant was speechless. How could a mere slave know so much! Even for a concubine, this was truly hard to hear. Moreover, Cassandra didn't seem to mind the horrid smell, or sight of the injured men, at all. Instead, she kept going from one bed to another, observing the injuries, and checking around as if she was looking for something, or counting.

"Who is working here?"

"Only volunteers...or people who got punished, Madam."

Cassandra turned to one of the men present, who had been observing her in awe. She addressed him, to his surprise.

"Excuse me, are you working here?"

"I came to check on my friend, Madam. He was injured last week."

"Do you come every day?"

"Yes, Madam. I come in my free time, but..."

He didn't end his sentence, but shrugged and sighed helplessly. Cassandra nodded, and started to interrogate the other healthy men that were present. Three of them came of their own will to check on their peers, the six others were sent here as a punishment from their superiors. They didn't seem to have any precise orders though. The Prince's concubine listened to every one of them, making them all the more curious to know what made a woman of her status so interested in this cursed place. When they were done, Cassandra turned to Evin.

112

"Is anyone in charge here?"

"Not that I know of, Madam, this is for the full army."

"So, it's fine if I work here, right?"

The servant almost choked.

"If you what? You can't be serious! You can't stay here!"

"It's fine, I have to keep myself busy, and these men need help."

"Madam, I strongly oppose this. Those men are not for you to take care of! I doubt Our Lord will agree to this either!"

But Cassandra decided to ignore him. She looked down, and tore a bit of her dress, using the fabric to cover her nose and mouth. Then, she turned to the men present.

"Can you help me create a list of how many men are in here and their condition? There should be about...one or two hundred, right?"

The men exchanged looks. Were they supposed to listen to the Commander-in-Chief's concubine? Her request was so odd and sudden. However, one of the men, who was there voluntarily, took a breath in and stepped forward.

"Yes, Madam. Last week, there were about a hundred and fifty-seven men, but more were brought in than were taken away, in the meantime. Can I ask how much you want us to write?"

Cassandra smiled, a bit happier now that at least one of the men was willing to help her. She took her fur cloak off, which Evin immediately held for her, and readjusted her hair up in a large bun while talking.

"I would like their names and ages, and the details of their injuries, everything you can see. Also, if you can find out how long they have been here for, or when they were brought here, that would be great. I guess it would be best to mark them with numbers also."

As she kept exchanging with that man, Cassandra noticed the other men were listening too, and nodding from time to time. Even the men who had been sent here against their will actually paid attention, and once they started counting, even helped too. Evin stayed silent, but he was deeply impressed. She hadn't used her power at all or had forced those men to obey her. She had just asked for help. It was her own behavior, and her will to help those men that had convinced the others to follow a woman's direction.

He had wondered if she was just acting on a whim, but to his surprise, Cassandra kept taking care of the injured for several hours. With those nine men, plus Orwan, helping, her list was done in no time, and she read it over.

"Most slaves don't know how to read or write," said Evin.

"I know," simply answered Cassandra, before writing something.

Then, she kept writing, under the men's surprised eyes. They had no idea what to do in the meantime. Only when she was done, did she show them her list. There was actually quite a lot written down.

"It's unfortunate we couldn't get everyone's information, but at least we know where to start. First, we need to split them."

"Split them?" asked one of the men.

"Yes. I saw several empty rooms on my way in here, it's fine to use them, right? So, we should first separate the men with diseases and infections from those who only have wounds, before they get infected, too. Also, some of them are already in a terminal state, and sadly they won't make it, no matter what we do. It's better to give them a calm place, separated from the others."

"Madam, do you mean there is...hope for the others?"

"Of course," said Cassandra with a nod. "From what I saw so far, I think at least half...no, two-thirds of the men here can be treated and sent back to camp."

The men were left speechless. They had thought everyone here was bound to die! How come this slave concubine said otherwise, and with such confidence, too? They had been here a lot and knew how bad some of the injuries were. No matter what though, the concubine's words seemed hard to believe. But Cassandra kept writing again and frowning a lot, looking concerned.

"Actually, I don't know much about the resources you have here. Do you get any medicine?"

The men looked at each other, totally clueless on the matter. Cassandra wasn't surprised, however. The Dragon Empire wasn't very advanced in healing techniques, herbology, or medicines. The very few doctors they had weren't affordable for most people, who only went to their local apothecary for basic treatments and natural remedies. The common folks didn't have even the most basic knowledge on how to properly tend a wound or treat a common cold. She sighed and turned to Evin.

"Do you know anything about that?"

The servant sighed. He had initially thought his job would simply be to follow a whiny, airhead concubine on her wanderings around the camp, making sure she doesn't break her nail, or hinder other people's work. Turns out he had it all wrong.

"We have some dedicated accountants who make sure of the stocks provided and trade weekly with merchants. If there is anything that is needed urgently, we put a request in for some of the cavaliers to go and fetch it from the nearest village. Also, any trip the Prince makes is supposed to be to bring more provisions."

Cassandra nodded.

"I guess we could gather herbs around the camp, but it would be better if Krai could fly me to the nearest village to buy the first necessities."

All the men around looked at her as if this woman was completely crazy. Did she just suggest she would borrow an Imperial dragon?

As if it was too impossible to think, the men present didn't even dare to comment on Cassandra's suggestion. How would a mere concubine borrow a Prince's dragon anyway? Wasn't she just a delusional woman? They all decided to just ignore it. That slave was already weird enough to willingly take care of all those sick or injured soldiers, so why wouldn't she think she could actually use the Prince's dragon. Maybe the Commander-in-Chief just had a thing for crazy ones.

"Evin, could you tell me where I can find those accountants? I want to speak to them, and see if we can get some necessities."

"I don't think that is a good idea, Madam. It is quite late already. His Highness might be looking for you."

Cassandra suddenly realized she had spent a considerable amount of time there. The Red Room didn't have any windows, and was only lit up by candlelight, so there was no way to even know if it was day or night outside. She had been so caught up in her task and notes, she had completely lost track of time.

"I'll...I'll go back. Is it very late?" she asked, a bit worried.

The Prince didn't even know where she was! There was no way he would look for her all the way here, was there? She had to go back soon, or he might really be mad this time.

"We're a couple hours away from dinner, Madam."

Cassandra felt guilty. She still had some time, but she should definitely head back. She nodded and turned to the men, who assured her they would carry on without her, making good use of her notes. At least she could go feeling like she had done some good around here, but Cassandra still wanted to do more for the injured.

She said goodbye to the men present, and left, escorted by Evin. Orwan had gone back to the forge earlier, and the trip back with the Imperial Servant was a bit awkward without the young man present. Cassandra could feel Evin was against her actions, but he didn't voice it outloud, which made it worse somehow.

Once outside again, she noticed the sun was going down already. The days were short here, which meant it was even later than she thought. Cassandra walked quickly to try and make her way back to the Prince's camp, but a sudden loud growl stopped her. The familiar sound had everyone around her freeze and look up. In the sky, the large silhouette of a dragon was throwing its shadow over them. Krai growled again, and suddenly flew down towards Cassandra. She knew she shouldn't move, but it was hard to repress that urge to run when a giant, black-scaled beast was flying towards her. Many of the closest soldiers did run away in a fright, impressed by the dragon's size and speed.

However, Krai landed a few steps away from Cassandra, its huge paws splattering the snow around.

"Hi," said Cassandra with a smile. "Were you looking for me?"

The dragon emitted a long growl, and rubbed its huge snout against her. Cassandra scratched Krai's favorite spot a bit before moving around the dragon's head to climb up. Without the Prince's help, it took her a few extra seconds until she sat up properly. She actually didn't even know where to hold onto, so she grabbed what seemed to be Krai's horns, hoping the dragon wouldn't hate it. Actually, the dragon didn't seem to mind at all, agitating its long reptilian tail around, splurging waves of snow on the closest men and tents. Krai kept moving his head around, as if trying to look at Cassandra, a bit annoyed.

"Come on, let's go see him," said Cassandra.

On the ground, Evin was still standing, as tall and quiet as before, but his face had turned a bit blue. He looked at the dragon taking off with the Prince's concubine on its back, standing still as ever. Once the dragon was a few meters high though, he couldn't hold it anymore. His legs gave way under him, and the poor man collapsed.

Meanwhile, Cassandra, who had no idea, was focusing hard on holding on and hoping Krai was indeed taking her to the Prince. She was flying on her own, and she was still very scared. She was a hundred and ten pound woman on a several-tons beast's back! She didn't even dare to look down, and only focused on holding on to both the dragon and her cloak.

Thankfully, it was a very short flight, only a couple of minutes, until Krai started going down. She recognized the large area from the previous day, where the dinner had been served, except that the dragon was landing on another end, in front of a very large tent. Cassandra waited until Krai was very still and stable, then slowly climbed down, her legs still a bit weak.

The soldiers guarding the tent's entrance were totally speechless, looking at the frail woman who had arrived using the Commander-in-Chief's dragon. Cassandra was giving Krai some thank-you scratches as if it had been a well behaved dog. The men exchanged looks, completely lost at what to say or do. But Cassandra just walked up to them, looking as frail and innocent as usual.

"Is His Highness inside?"

"Y...Yes, Madam," stuttered one of them.

"Thanks," she said with her disarming smile.

The soldier blushed to his ears, and they quickly stepped aside to let her in. The men stayed a bit red and lost for a few seconds, but Krai's sudden stare had them go from red to white in seconds.

Cassandra stepped inside the tent, a bit unsure. To her surprise, there were quite a few people inside. Eight men were lined up in front of Kairen, who was sitting on his throne with a bored expression. One of the older ones was giving him what was apparently a detailed report about their latest weapons improvements. Staying quiet in the corner, Cassandra wondered if he was a superior of Orwan.

After a few seconds, Kairen spotted her and held out his hand for Cassandra to join him. She couldn't help but smile a bit, and sneaked to the side, to join him while the older man was still talking. Most of the lieutenants saw the young concubine walk in silence to the Prince, but they didn't say a thing.

Kairen pulled Cassandra to sit on his lap, wrapping an arm around her waist.

"...with a higher precision, My Lord. That's it for today's report on my faction, Commander-in-Chief."

"You're all dismissed," said Kairen.

One of the men hesitated, with a frown on his face.

"But, My Lord, I still haven't..."

One glare from Kairen made it clear there would be no more reporting today. The man gave an annoyed glare towards Cassandra before stepping out. The rest of the men also left, leaving them alone.

As soon as they were gone, the Prince turned to kiss her longingly.

"Where have you been?" he asked, while taking the cloak off of her.

"Just...exploring...the camp..."

She had a hard time answering his questions, his kisses, and breathing at the same time. He pushed her hair behind her shoulder, and kissed the depth between her breasts, putting Cassandra in front of him, in that riding position that embarrassed her so much.

"What parts?"

"The Forge, and...the Red Room..."

Kairen stopped. He frowned, and sat straight again, facing Cassandra with a confused expression.

"What Red Room?"

"The one where they take the injured or sick soldiers. At the back of the camp, in the South Mountain."

"What the fuck were you doing there?"

She became white in an instant. She had no idea he would be so mad about it, and she didn't even know how to respond. Kairen had never been furious at her before... She tried to step away, by mere instinct, but the Prince firmly held onto her wrist.

"I just...I was curious about it..."

"Why would you go there?!"

She didn't even understand why he was so furious! She breathed in, really insecure for the first time in a while, and shook her head.

"I didn't mean to...I just...wanted to see..."

"I forbid you to go there again!"

Kairen's yelling made her shiver. She tried to step away again, but the Prince's grasp on her wrist was too strong.

"I only meant to help...the sick! I...please, you're hurting me!"

Her scream was like an electric shock to Kairen. He suddenly let go, and Cassandra, who had been struggling all this time, lost her balance, stumbling backwards. Before he could do anything, she fell on her right side, brutally hitting the floor.

"Cassandra!"

He meant to help her, but Cassandra avoided his hands when he got close, getting away from him. She was shivering, holding her painful arm with teary eyes.

"Don't...please..."

He had never seen her so wary of him before. She looked at him with uncertainty, like a cornered animal, as if she didn't recognize him. But his anger was still subsiding, and he was breathing loudly, trying to contain it and not do something else that he might regret. He clenched both his fists, and addressed her with a cold voice.

"To my tent. Now."

Cassandra obeyed in silence, grabbing her cloak to put back on, and exiting the tent. With Kairen right behind her, she didn't even dare to look at Krai, who followed them, curious, unaware of the situation. She just walked as fast as she could to the Prince's tent, ignoring the sharp pain in her wrist and elbow.

It was an awkward but short walk back. Once she got there, she left the cloak on the bed, turning to Kairen, waiting to see if he was still as furious as before.

Indeed, he was.

"You are not going back there," he hissed.

"What? But I need to go back! I still have a lot to do, I..."

"I said, no!"

With that, he threw his armor across the tent, crashing into something behind her. Cassandra closed her eyes, trying to stay calm. She held her tears in, and looked at him.

"Why not? Explain it to me, please."

Turning away from her, Kairen stayed silent. She could tell he was trying hard to contain his anger, from his shivering fists and the thumping vein on his temple.

"My Lord, please, just..."

"Enough."

He suddenly turned around, and walked over to kiss her. This time, Cassandra felt his strength and his anger in his kiss. It wasn't blissful at all, it wasn't like their usual kisses. She started trying to push him away, resisting his kiss.

"No, no!"

"Cassandra, enough!"

But she kept resisting, and opposing his hands which were looking for her body. Kairen was obviously much stronger, but Cassandra kept opposing him, trying to elude his kisses and make him realize she didn't want to do this.

"Cassandra!"

As he yelled her name again, she suddenly stopped resisting, and stood completely still, not moving anymore. Kairen was completely at a loss. He tried to kiss her some more, but her body was so frigid, he had to stop.

"What are you doing?"

"You wanted me to stop resisting."

"Why are you doing that?"

He didn't even know how to be angry with her when she was acting like this.

"I can force you, Cassandra."

118

"I know that. I'm not resisting you."

She wasn't resisting, but Cassandra was still showing her opposition very strongly. She was inanimate as a doll, and that was it. Somehow, that made him even more furious. He suddenly punched the mattress right next to her, scaring her a little.

"Fuck!"

Right after that, he stormed out of the tent without another word. Cassandra let out a long sigh. She had been holding her breath for a while and felt dizzy. It was the first time she had seriously opposed him. She had never seen him so furious, either. Her legs were actually still shivering when she sat up, pulling her dress back down.

No matter what, she was still a slave and a woman. She knew being alive and so well treated was all thanks to Kairen's attachment to her. This could change anytime. He could kill her or rape her, and no one would say a word about it. That's the kind of world she lived in.

Cassandra stayed there for a long time, her arm wrapped around her knees, thinking long and hard on the edge of the bed. Her eyes were in a daze. She was tired, cold, and hungry, but she didn't feel like moving a muscle.

She felt sad about what had happened. She didn't think that would happen. Cassandra kept thinking about the dispute, all of their conversation, replaying it in her head, over and over. Seeing Kairen's anger, again and again.

"Madam."

Cassandra was surprised to see Evin come in, carrying a tray of food.

"Evin. How...?"

"His Highness was quite angry, and is training with his men. Since I didn't see you at the dinner, I figured you might be...hungry."

Cassandra felt a bit comforted by the man's kindness.

"Thank you, Evin."

Indeed, she had been ignoring her growling stomach all this time. Before, she could go days without food. But since she had been with the Prince, her stomach got used to getting good and consistent meals. She sighed. She was hungry, but her head was too heavy to feel like eating either. It was a strange feeling.

"You look tired, Madam. Have a good sleep."

Evin left the room without adding anything else, leaving her alone again. From how he calmly left the tent, she supposed Krai had left, too. She truly was on her own.

Cassandra grabbed the fur cloak to cover her shoulders, and got up to eat a bit on the couch. She ate little bites, mindlessly, wondering when the Prince would come back. But even after she was done eating, he still hadn't returned. She thought about going to look for him, but their argument still lingered in her mind. He probably wasn't calm enough to return yet.

She laid on the bed, realizing how cold the sheets were without Kairen there. She missed him, his warmth, and the way he held on to her when they slept together. Strange how the body catches onto new habits so easily.

Much later in the night, she woke up to someone's presence in the bed with her. Worried for only a second, she quickly recognized Kairen's familiar smell and warmth. Without a word, he laid next to her, his back facing Cassandra. Was he still angry?

She didn't dare to move too much, and just turned around to his side after a while, the closest she could without touching him. It was heartbreaking not to see his face. She stayed like this for a long time, in the dark, conscious neither of them was sleeping. Cassandra wondered if she should say something, apologize or bid him good night, but the more she hesitated, the more awkward it became. She opened her mouth several times, but with no sound coming out.

Eventually, she slowly moved her arm, and, timidly, her fingers reached for his back. She was barely touching him, but she felt his reaction, his breathing halting for a second. It was a short moment, in which she wondered if he would say something. But even after a while, Kairen stayed silent.

For the first time in a while, Cassandra really felt like crying. Was he really ignoring her? Was he still mad? Would this keep going on for a long time? Or was he going to get rid of her at dawn? She closed her eyes, trying to chase away all those dark thoughts, and not to cry.

That's when Kairen silently moved. Before she could react, the Prince turned around, his eyes still closed, and put his arm around her.

Cassandra opened her eyes, confused, and felt a wave of warmth and relief. A single tear escaped her eye, and she finally fell asleep, snuggling against his chest.

She was awake for a while, but unwilling to move. Cassandra just didn't want to come to the moment when they would have to face last night's issue again. She was still at a loss about the Prince's violent reaction. Why was he so against it? He hadn't given any reason for his sudden anger from the previous night. Cassandra was afraid it would be the same all over again that morning, and didn't dare to say a word.

"How's your arm?"

His deep, low voice surprised her. Cassandra looked up, finally meeting the Prince's eyes. The black irises seemed free from all anger, making her feel a bit better.

"I'm fine."

"You have bruises."

How did he know? Cassandra was still covered by the fur cloak, and held against him. Had he peeked while she was still asleep? And if so, how long had he been awake?

Cassandra shook her head slowly, and leaned a bit closer to his chest.

"It's nothing. I'm fine."

She meant it. Cassandra had experienced injuries that were much worse than bruises, and she couldn't even feel them at the moment. She knew it probably looked worse than it really was because of her pale skin.

Yet, Kairen seemed unhappy. He sat up and left the bed without a word, apparently just to get himself something to drink. Cassandra sat up as well, covering her chest with the fur blanket, concerned. She observed him for a while, but the Prince stayed silent, avoiding her gaze until she couldn't take it anymore.

"My Lord, can we talk?"

"What?"

"About last night. Please."

Kairen sighed, suddenly putting his cup down.

"I didn't mean to."

"What?" asked Cassandra, confused.

"I didn't mean to hurt you. It wasn't my intention."

She stared at him, completely caught off guard. Is that why he was so silent? Sometimes the Prince had such a strange way of thinking, she just couldn't guess what was going on. His silence wasn't from anger, but guilt? But it was just an accident! She had fallen as a result of him being a bit too rough, but... She didn't think he was responsible for that. Plus, she was still a slave, and him a Prince! Even if he had slapped her, any other Prince wouldn't have felt anything about that.

"I know. I'm not upset about that," she said in a soft voice.

"Aren't you afraid of me?"

"No! Sometimes you scare me a little, that's true, but not now, not when we are talking calmly like this."

She watched him release a sigh, and felt her heart warm up a little. Is that what he was truly concerned about? That she would be really scared of him? Cassandra felt her heart melting a bit more for her strange War God, who could act like a normal man at times.

Kairen slowly walked back to the bed, sitting next to her, and Cassandra made the first move by giving him a little kiss. He grabbed her hair very gently and kissed her some more. For a while, it seemed like all the frustration and uneasiness from their dispute was washed away in that instant, with that long kiss.

They parted slowly, still sitting close to each other. Cassandra hesitated a while, but she wanted to ask him while things were still calm between them.

"What were you so angry about? Last night?"

"Because you won't listen."

"The Red Room. Why don't you want me to go there?"

Kairen frowned and turned to her, with a silent anger.

"Why would I want you there? Why do you want to go?"

"I only mean to help your men. The sick, the injured. I can't stand doing nothing, My Lord. This isn't how I'm used to living."

"You're my concubine."

"I'm a slave, also. I've worked all my life, I'm not used to lazing around all day, and spending money, or giving orders."

"Then do something else."

"Why not the Red Room?"

"Cassandra," he said with an angry tone. "I'm not letting you go. Do you know how many diseases are there? All the men there carry those diseases. If you go there, you'll get infected and sick too."

She was stunned. She hadn't even thought of that, she hadn't thought of... herself. But Kairen had. He had seen what normal people would think, why everyone was so surprised to see a concubine among the sick and injured.

Normal people would prioritize their own health, but Cassandra never learned to think like that. Like any slave, she wasn't used to putting her security first. From her own character, she just thought of helping others.

"You were worried...for me," she muttered.

"I don't want you there. If you get white fever or something..."

Cassandra pulled the blanket, and suddenly showed the little scars that were on her hip. There were eight little cuts, perfectly aligned, and were all the same size and shape. Kairen frowned, wondering what kind of weapon could do this.

"White fever, yellow fever, grey skin plague, the nine days disease, swamps sickness, black tongue plague, Samsah, and infection of Krah," she enumerated, showing each of the little scars. "I got all of those when I was a child."

Kairen frowned. Those were very common and deadly diseases that common people could die from, except the two last ones he had never even heard of.

"What do you mean, you got them all?"

"Back in the village where I came from, all the children are infected with each of those diseases when we reach a certain age. It's a dangerous technique our healers practiced, with a one in three chance of survival. But if we do survive, we never get any of those diseases again as an adult."

The Prince looked at her scars again, speechless. This was such a strange technique! To have the children pass this kind of deathly test, with that low rate of survival. But the diseases Cassandra had mentioned were the most common ones, and the main causes of natural death in the Dragon Empire.

He often forgot that Cassandra wasn't born there in the first place.

"In your...village?"

"Yes, my Lord. The Rain Tribe I was born in had...advanced healing techniques, compared to here, I think."

Kairen stayed silent for a while. Cassandra had mentioned her long lost younger sister, but aside from the fact that she wasn't born in the Dragon Empire, he knew very few things about her. To be precise, he didn't care. All of her past as a slave was something that made him angry, if anything.

She covered her hip again, hoping this little explanation would have made him more inclined to let her take care of others, but Kairen was still frowning.

"But you can still get infections, and other diseases."

"I can take care of myself. I promise, I'll be careful."

Truthfully, Cassandra knew perfectly well she was still in great danger by doing this. The germs contained in the Red Room were probably different from the common diseases. She wasn't totally invulnerable, and her body wasn't even used to cold environments in the first place. It was still unknown how she would resist things like a common cold or fever.

However, she was still stubborn about doing this. She would have done it even if she hadn't been vaccinated by her Tribe, but that's nothing the Prince needed to know.

Seeing Kairen was still frowning and silent, Cassandra bit her lip, and leaned a bit closer.

"My Lord, please. I can't help you with matters of war, and I will go crazy with nothing to do all day."

"You can accompany me."

"I will only hinder you and be useless. It's the same..."

She was really hoping he would agree, but he could be so stubborn at times. After a while, she saw him stare at her collar, lost in his thoughts. What was he thinking now? Cassandra waited in silence, as she couldn't think of any other ideas to persuade him.

After a while, Kairen sighed and got up.

"I want you back before sunset. And you stay with the Imperial Servant at all times."

Cassandra's face lit up, and she immediately got up as well.

"Really?"

Kairen nodded. He was a bit unhappy, but he didn't add anything after that, confirming Cassandra's hopes.

"Thank you, My Lord."

"Kairen."

She suddenly stopped moving, speechless. The Prince turned to her, walking in her direction again, and put his arms around her. Cassandra couldn't react, still taken back by what she thought he meant.

"M...My lord?"

"Kairen. No more My Lord or My Prince. Call me by my name when we are alone."

Cassandra turned red then white immediately, completely shook. Oh, could she call him by his first name? He was an Imperial Prince, not even his own siblings were all allowed to call him simply by his name! Yet, he wanted her, a mere concubine and slave, to call him that! That felt even more intimate than anything they had done before!

"I...I can't possibly...just..."

"Kairen. Say it."

She shook her head, torn between confusion and surprise. She didn't even understand that strange feeling of fear in her stomach, like it was something deeply forbidden. Cassandra felt like the sky would open and kill her on the spot if she dared to say his name. She had always been the one with a deep, solid vision of the walls between them; between an Imperial Prince and a slave. She shouldn't even have been able to look him in the eye, or stand in his presence, if things had been normal between them!

But Kairen kept ignoring everything his own Empire had established as normal. He took a slave as his concubine, let her express her thoughts and desires, respected her choices, and now, he even wanted her to use his first name!

"Cassandra."

"I...I can't!"

She was almost more scared of that than anything else. As if the Imperial Guards would come in at any moment and kill her if she dared to cross that line. It was like the most unthinkable thing for a slave to call her master by his first name! She was so overwhelmed, her hands were shaking.

She kept shaking her head.

"I can't do that, I can't. It's not... You're my master."

"I don't care."

"I care! I'm not... You can't have me call you that, like I'm an equal to you. I'm not!"

That's what she had been told for the last ten years. She was a slave, a nobody who stood at the bottom of society. She didn't deserve comfort, warmth, nothing. She was treated worse than livestock, like a shadow who lived to do her chores and suffer in silence.

She had almost forgotten that, in the bliss she had experienced with the Prince.

Kairen had made her forget what it meant to be a slave. But Cassandra couldn't completely forget, and now, it was all coming back to her. She felt her throat become sore, and her eyes teary, from just remembering. Before, she could endure it, because it was normal for her, because she was used to ignoring her own pain. She had learned to close her eyes, let her body become numb and endure it.

However, things changed when she was allowed comfort again. Kairen had given her all that, so much and so fast that she had barely taken the time to adapt. The warm blankets, the tasty food, the gentleness. It had replaced the cold ground, scraps, and pain, so fast. But it was still there, like a scary voice, a monster lurking at the back of her mind. Like the scars on her skin, the collar on her neck. It was heavy and painful.

Kairen, seeing her distress, silently embraced her in his arms, waiting for Cassandra to calm down. He couldn't understand what she had gone through, but he saw what it did to her. She had never panicked like that before.

"Fine... I'll wait."

With those words, like she had been given a bit of rest, Cassandra nodded and calmed down in a few minutes. Meanwhile, Kairen was glaring at her collar.

That damn thing had to come off, and soon!

Chapter 9

The Prince's words from that morning still followed Cassandra's steps as she made her way across the camp. Evin followed her, but both were silent. At times, she wondered if she was just living in a dream. In her dream, everything would suddenly end when she opened her eyes and found herself sleeping in a cold cell of the Emperor's Arena again, or back in Lyria's slave room. However, the cold on her cheeks was real, and so was the snow under her footsteps. Cassandra didn't want to think too much about it. She missed having a friend to talk to, and Evin probably wasn't a good replacement.

It had been only two days since she came to the Camp, but she felt the lack of another feminine presence. Cassandra often thought of the other girls from the Castle, wondering how they were doing, if their life had gotten better without the Governor there. She didn't really dare to ask the Prince when they would be going back. He had already made an extra trip to bring her here.

That was another reason why she wanted to keep herself busy.

Cassandra wasn't totally unhappy in the camp. She was discovering many things she had never seen before, and was basically free to go anywhere she wanted. Her red dress, and the imperial servant following her, were enough of an explanation for the men who had never seen her before, and even a few high-ranked soldiers took time to salute her politely when she crossed their paths. It was clear that no one really knew how to interact with her, though. For the Third Prince to actually have a Concubine was already surprising enough; no one really wanted to ask more. The rumors about the Palace concubines' legendary attitudes and willfulness was enough to keep most men at bay.

Cassandra was actually able to enjoy her walk all the way to the mountain, as soon as she had stopped thinking about the Prince's request that morning.

Once she got to the Red Room, however, quite a surprise was waiting for her. About three times more men than the previous day were all helping around the room, and there was obviously a lot going on, with people moving

126

the injured in or out of the room. She stayed at the entrance, a bit surprised, when four of them rushed to her.

"Good Morning, Madam!"

"Good Morning...Excuse me, but... how come so many people are... volunteering today?" she asked, a bit unsure, while Evin took off her fur cloak.

One of the men stepped forward. Cassandra recognized him as one of those who were present the previous day.

"Actually, once we got back to our units, we talked with some others about what we had done, madam, and many wanted to come and help. The word kind of spread quickly, and even the men who had punishments asked to be sent here."

"I see..."

Cassandra was at bit of a loss. She didn't expect so many people to show up after only one day!

"Madam, we are almost at the end of your notes, and we have counted everyone and reported their status, as you said," the man announced proudly. "We already asked for permission to use the closest rooms and started moving some people, following your notes. Do you want to check?"

"Yes, uh..."

It took a few minutes for Cassandra to get a hold of the situation and move forward, while the men were apparently waiting for her directions. Taking a deep breath, she took a look at the full list that they had done their best at completing while she was gone.

"All right, I will... Wait, everyone stop what you're doing!"

Every man in the room looked at her, surprised. Cassandra, remembering this morning's conversation with the Prince, couldn't leave things as they were.

"I want everyone to get out of the room and go wash your hands and faces with clean water. Only come back once you have some tissue on your face, like I did yesterday."

They all exchanged glances, surprised by her strange request. As Cassandra suspected, these men didn't know the basics of hygiene and self-protection while handling the wounded or sick people. And unlike her, they had received no form of protection against diseases. If things went on like this, she would do more harm than good, as the volunteers would soon fall sick too.

Hence, the first part of that matinee was focused on Cassandra showing them how to properly wash their hands and wear fabrics over their mouth and noses to protect themselves. She also checked their hands before they walked back in.

"What are you looking for, Madam?" asked one of the men.

"Little cuts, open skin...Any kind of opening can let the disease into your own body, I want to avoid that. Thankfully, most of you have thick skin thanks to combat training, but..."

If she had any kind of doubt, Cassandra asked the men to do something that wouldn't involve touching the injured people, like gathering clothes or herbs for her. The others kept moving people to the different rooms following her notes.

By noon, all the people had been moved to different rooms, and following Cassandra's request, the men had gathered a lot of herbs in various baskets that she intended to keep in a storage room. Two of the men looked at the now empty red room in disgust.

"I can't believe almost two hundred men were here. Damn, there are even insects!"

"That's why we need to clean it."

They both turned to Cassandra, shocked. She wanted to clean that? The blood had stained the ground, some remnants were clearly from human defecations, and it had smelled so bad for months! But as the Prince's concubine began bringing in clear water and brooms, it was apparently decided.

"Are you sure, Madam? This place is really…"

"Disgusting? Yes, but this is the largest room here, and we will need it. Nothing here is uncleanable, and we need to make use of any resource we can."

Actually, no one was really enthusiastic about cleaning that room. Saying it was awfully dirty and disgusting was still an understatement. However, as soon as Cassandra started cleaning, three of the men rushed to take it all out of her hands.

"Madam, do you want us to lose our dignity as men? We can't let the Commander-in-Chief's woman dirty her hands while we watch!"

"We would lose our heads for sure!"

Cassandra chuckled a bit, but before she could protest, she was gently pushed out of the room and the men started cleaning despite the horrid task. She sighed.

"I feel a bit bad leaving them to do this…"

"Don't be. They were right about probably losing their heads," said Evin, very calmly.

The Imperial Servant was the only one who hadn't helped at all. Actually, he had spent all day following Cassandra like a shadow, making sure she didn't injure herself or got her dress dirty. It was too much for her at times, but neither her attempts to have him stop or the glares from the men could stop Evin.

"Madam, you should have lunch now. His Highness won't like it if you skip meals."

"Yes, yes…"

"Madam, come and eat with us!"

Several of the men now started bickering about which unit she should have lunch with, surprising Cassandra. When had things become like this? She thought they were merely following her directions, not that she had gained popularity!

"Which is the closest?" She asked, hoping to put an end to the argument before it turned into a fight.

It was then decided that she would eat with the nearby third unit of charioteers. To her surprise, Evin had someone bring lunch for her, with the usual cheese, fruits and meat. It was different from the vegetables and meat the men were having, though. None of them seemed too bothered, which surprised Cassandra at first. But thinking about it, she was having a meal befitting a member of the Imperial Entourage, while those men were soldiers, and supposed to eat what they were given by the army. Eating such luxury foods next to them was making her a bit uncomfortable.

"My Lady, how long will you stay with us?" asked one of the men as they were all sitting in a circle.

"I don't know. My Lord hasn't said anything about my stay here."

"Probably only a few days. The Commander-in-Chief comes and goes back pretty often. You won't like it, Madam. As soon as the barbarian's attack, it can be up to a week of fighting and it gets nasty!"

"Do you still get attacks?" Cassandra asked, worried.

The men shrugged.

"It happens. We don't really know where they come from because no matter how many times we push them back into the mountain, they eventually come back."

"When it's been quiet like this for a few weeks, the next strike is usually stronger. Nothing to worry about, though."

Cassandra nodded. She was a bit surprised how calm the men were about this. But it did appear true. There were very few injuries actually, compared to the size of the Camp. The men, thinking she was impressed, went on to talk about their accomplishments within the camps or in battle, and Cassandra listened for the rest of the lunch.

She kept it short, however, as she wanted to get as much as she could done before sunset. Hence, they all returned to the mountain soon after. Now that the injured and sick were properly sorted, and she had men cleaning the bigger room, Cassandra started sorting the herbs she had at her disposal. It was no use treating people if she didn't have the resources. Six men helped her count the quantities, but they were still confused.

"Are you sure, Madam? Most of those are just wild herbs and weeds."

"No plant is useless. We just don't know all their properties yet."

To be precise, the Dragon Empire's people didn't. They had gathered everything they could, but the men were totally clueless about what those weeds were good for. Yet, the Prince's Concubine started sorting them under their eyes and showed them how to wash the plants without wasting any of them. Soon, they started repeating her moves, sorting, and cleaning all of the green mess.

"Can we get more?" asked Cassandra.

"We need to ask the accountants to buy more, or have more men gather them from the nearby mountains... Don't you have enough, Madam?"

She sighed.

"Certainly not, if I hope to treat as many as I can...can I let you handle these? I'll be back soon."

"Yes, Madam!"

With that, Cassandra left the premises, still followed by Evin, who looked unhappy.

"They won't appreciate it."

"I just need to ask for herbs."

"They won't like it. More herbs means more work, more men mobilized. The accountants do not like buying and giving anything away without getting something back. They will require a high rank official's approval. You're not a high rank official, Madam."

Cassandra sighed. It wouldn't hurt to ask. Evin guided her through the Camp, on which it had started snowing. The sun was slowly starting its descent, meaning Cassandra only had about an hour or so left before she had to go back to the Prince's tent. She wondered if she could expect another dragon ride, or if she should think about the walk back.

Finally, the duo arrived in front of another tent, as Evin guided her.

"The Head Accountant's office...well, tent."

As soon as she stepped in, Cassandra knew this wasn't going to be easy. Because the Head Accountant turned out to be the man whose report had been interrupted by her arrival the previous evening.

"Well, if it isn't Her Mightiness," sighed the man.

The accountant was a tall but thin man, with a thin mustache and a crooked nose. From his attitude, Cassandra could tell he already didn't think much of her.

"Good afternoon, Sir. May I take some of your time?"

"What would the Commander-in-Chief's Concubine need me for?"

"I wanted to ask for some resources."

"Shouldn't you just ask the Commander-in-Chief for that? Isn't that how a concubine is supposed to do things?"

Cassandra exchanged a look with Evin. Though he was still polite, the Head Accountant was clearly set on giving her a hard time.

"What I need isn't for my personal needs. I wanted to ask for some herbal medicine."

The man frowned, apparently surprised.

"What is that for?"

"For the men who were in the red...I mean, in the mountain's rooms. I want to gather some herbs and make medicine out of it to help them, but with what has been gathered I won't have enough."

The man put down the papers in his hands and crossed his arms, visibly doubtful.

"Make medicine? You?"

"Yes. I know of some techniques that can-"

130

"Why would I waste resources on a concubine and sick men? I have no proof that you can do anything you say, and I have no intention to waste anything on dying men."

"These men are your fellow soldiers! How can you-"

"They're a deficit of money. I see numbers all day, woman, and these men are nothing but a waste of resources and energy on my papers. If they die, I hope they die soon and stop wasting extra food and time. We already have doctors who tend to the people we really need here."

He had said those words while frowning at Cassandra, clearly giving into his contempt.

She was so angry, her fists were shaking. How could a man be so cruel and merciless! They were talking about humans, not mere numbers!

Evin took a glance in her direction, wondering what she would do. From what he had seen, Cassandra already had plenty of power in her hand, if only she dared to make use of the Third Prince's Dragon that seemed so smitten with her. However, he also learned that she had a strange temper.

"How many do you need?" she suddenly asked.

"Excuse me?"

"How many men do you want me to heal and send back to their units to prove that it is worth using money, and that my medicine works?"

The head accountant looked at her, speechless for the first time. What was this crazy woman thinking now?!

Cassandra was perfectly calm and composed.

She didn't act arrogant or conceited, despite the Head Accountant's expectations. Just like Evin before him, the man was starting to understand she didn't belong to any of the usual types of Concubine. He had already been quite surprised that the Commander-in-Chief actually brought a woman here, but now, she was going around the camp trying to take care of the men? What was wrong with this woman?

He had noted that she was a slave from her collar, but that only made him think she was uneducated and stupid. So why was he now caught in some negotiation with her?

"What kind of slave knows about medicine?" he asked, frowning.

Medicine was a very precious and rare teaching in the Dragon Empire. There were no medical schools, and very few documents to pass the ancient techniques along. Most of the time, doctors would take a handful of apprentices and select the best, to learn from them. Even so, the techniques of each doctor were kept a secret most of the time, as they were afraid it would spread to commoners and make the prices of common medicine drop. Hence, being a doctor in the Empire was seen as one of the top and highest paid professions-certainly not something within a slave's reach.

"I know enough. But the Dragon Empire's medical techniques are rudimentary, barbaric, and old. Your healing techniques don't travel enough to be improved on, even in a few years' time, and those are not the ones I know of."

Evin was, once again, surprised and impressed. Cassandra had a point. Because the doctors of this Empire were so set on keeping their techniques to themselves, it was rather known that the same methods were used for centuries, and any kind of innovation was seen as a break-through.

The head accountant frowned. He was a very educated and wise man, despite his lack of natural empathy. From hearing Cassandra, he had to admit she wasn't talking like an ignorant slave or a willful concubine.

"Where did you...supposedly, learn medicine?" he asked.

"The Rain Tribe."

The Head Accountant stayed silent for a while, but he was thinking. The name itself was unheard of, but he clearly remembered having studied about some south barbarians, people living in tribes beyond the border of the Dragon Empire. The scholars didn't have much knowledge of those people, considered like any barbaric populations who didn't have material wealth: uninteresting. However, their information clearly mentioned those people's strangely high life expectancies, despite them actually living in swamps, and in dire conditions. Could this woman's words be of some truth?

The Head Accountant thought long and hard, but no matter what, he couldn't really refuse nor give into her request. Those injured soldiers were still a problem among his reports, and if something could be done about them... If anything arose, he could always blame it on this woman. The Commander-in-Chief probably wouldn't scold his own woman, and even if he did, it wouldn't be the accountant's problem.

"Fine. A hundred men. Once you send a hundred men back on the field, I will..."

"Fifty."

"Excuse me?"

"I can send back fifty men within ten days, with my current stock of herbs. But a hundred would be too much, I don't have enough medicine or volunteers yet."

The Head Accountant nodded, pretending to think. He had actually intended to give her a full month's time. Could she really do what she said within ten days? He was still doubtful, but it was worth letting her try. Those men would die anyway. If she made things worse, she would at least save them a few days' worth of food for his reports.

"If I manage to heal and send back fifty men within ten days, will you listen to my request?" asked Cassandra, looking to confirm his words.

The man nodded.

"You have my word. As long as you keep your end of the deal, I'll allow a budget for those medical herbs. But I want proof of those men being actually injured or sick, and sent back to their units..."

"You will," said Cassandra.

Once again, her self confidence impressed him a bit, though he wouldn't let it show on his face. He actually had the means to get the reports on the injured coming in and out of the Red Room, but he wanted to make sure she wouldn't try to cheat her way out of this.

"All right, then, I guess this deal is done. Do you need anything else? If not, I will resume my activities and ask you to leave; I'm quite busy."

Cassandra indeed left promptly, followed by Evin. Once outside, she couldn't help but to let out a big sigh. She didn't think it would be so nerve-wrecking.

"Why didn't you use the Third Prince's authority?" suddenly asked Evin.

Cassandra turned to him surprised.

"What do you mean? I am not His Highness."

"You are his concubine. A few words and you would have been able to use His Highness, the Third Prince's authority to make him comply with your demand. Making that bet was unnecessary, and added to your plate."

She shook her head. They were already headed back to the mountain, as Cassandra wanted to check on a few things and leave some notes before she went back.

"I didn't add anything, I would have been able to send back fifty men anyway. I only delayed the Head Accountant's help by ten days. I don't want to use His Highness' authority. If I did, that man would respect me even less and think I cannot do anything without the Third Prince, and would probably try to give me less than I need. If I can prove what I'm saying, he will trust me and help us more. Or so I hope."

"There are only one hundred and seventy men there at the moment. Do you really think you can send fifty of them back? You sent thirty of them to a separate room, saying those could not be cured..."

They entered the mountain again, passing several of the rooms where the men had been sorted.

"Actually, I'm hoping we will get more men in the meantime. A lot of soldiers like Orwan didn't dare to come here in the first place, remember? But what if I can show them I can heal them properly?"

"More men will come..."

Cassandra nodded, and entered one of the rooms to talk with the men still sorting her medicinal herbs. Behind her, Evin was once again speechless. She had thought that far ahead during her conversation with the Head Accountant? That her changes to the Red Room would convince more and more men to come get healed, and naturally help her win her bet?

"Alright, can you split them as we said?" asked Cassandra. "We will need to count how much we have and then dry or boil it. I'll see later."

"Yes, Madam," answered the men.

Then, she went to the next room, talking to the men who were busy there.

"Please, remember to wash your hands often and keep your masks on. We need to wash the sick men's clothes and sheets often too, and ventilate the room as much as we can. I'll see the people who came in today now."

For the next hour, Cassandra checked each of the men that had come in, inspecting their overall state or injury, and sorting them into separate rooms.

She had spread the men into a total of eight rooms: one for those who hadn't been diagnosed yet, one for small wounds and cuts, one for the bigger injuries, one for the people with light symptoms like a cold, another one for dangerous or infectious diseases, one for the patients with special needs, and the last one she called for "short stay", for soldiers who were suffering from stomach pains or headaches. The eighth room was called the "silent room", where people who wouldn't survive were put to rest.

However, despite that sorting, it was clear there was still way too much work for one woman to do alone. Evin said it out loud as they were leaving the mountain for the day, and Cassandra nodded.

"I know... That's my main problem. I can teach some men, but they are supposed to come and go, and eventually, I will need people to do the exact same thing as I do, like apprentices. But where to find apprentices in a military camp? Do the doctors here have some? You mentioned there were doctors, right?"

"There are currently seven doctors working here, and each military doctor is allowed three apprentices in the Camp."

"That's twenty-eight people. It's not enough for a camp of thousands of soldiers!"

Evin was about to say something about her knowing how to calculate, but didn't. This woman was really too much.

"Actually, most of them only have one or two. I can ask if you want."

"Please do. What are they thinking, with so few apprentices to help..."

Cassandra was still astonished. How could such a large Empire still be so uneducated about medicine and common hygiene? All day, the soldiers had watched each of her moves as if they were learning something, questioning why she did this and that non-stop.

It wasn't like they were unwilling to learn. The main problem was that from the crib until they reached adulthood, every man and woman in this Empire was focused on one career. First sons would take over their father's job, shop, or farm. Second sons trained to be scholars. From the third one on, they would be raised as warriors. Women very rarely had careers, but those who did would become shopkeepers, embroiderers, cooks, mostly positions that were related to the household, and not too tiring.

It was a patriarchal society, with its pros and cons.

"I need to find apprentices," Cassandra muttered to herself.

"Do you want me to ask?"

"For apprentices?" she asked, a bit surprised.

"Some people might be interested. It's a very vast camp, with lots of different people. I can try to ask around, if you wish."

Cassandra nodded. Could it be possible? Would some of those men agree? What about their current positions? Well, it couldn't hurt to ask, possibly...

"Madam."

She turned to him, but Evin was looking up at the dark form that had appeared in the sky. Cassandra smiled. Her ride had arrived.

Krai landed with a loud growl, immediately looking for Cassandra. Wiggling up to her, the dragon waved its tail around with anticipation. As usual, she waited until Krai stopped a step away from her to move.

"Hi, Krai. Is this going to become a routine?" she asked softly, giving a few scratches.

"He is a pain when he misses you..." suddenly said a voice from above.

"My Lord!" exclaimed Cassandra.

Kairen held out his hand, and helped her climb on the dragon's back, making her sit in front of him. She was obviously glad to see him, her cheeks a bit red, and a smile on her face. The Prince immediately pulled her closer for a long, deep kiss. His tongue enticed her, and Cassandra realized that they hadn't had sex since the hot springs.

The black dragon interrupted their kiss while taking off, and Cassandra felt a bit disappointed. She held onto Kairen's cloak, as close to him as she could. It was not dinner time yet, could it be he had come to get her sooner on purpose?

However, as they flew over the Camp, Cassandra soon realized they weren't going to the Prince's tent. Where to then? The hot springs maybe? She had liked it a lot, and hoped they would go back.

To her surprise, Krai landed in front of the forges. Why there? Cassandra wanted to ask, but Kairen helped her down and walked in one of the tents before she could. He pushed her gently in front of an old man.

"Here. Undo this thing."

Cassandra was a bit surprised, until she understood he meant her collar! She turned to him, a bit concerned.

"My Lord, I..."

"Cassandra, sit here."

He had her sit on a little chair, but after a few seconds, she realized the abnormal silence around them. What was wrong? All the men present were either looking at her or the Prince in awe. Could it be...because he had called her by her name?

"What are you waiting for? Take this damn collar off her!"

The Prince's sudden anger made everyone step back, fear and surprise on every face. Then, one of the older men stepped up, standing in front of Cassandra.

"Young Lady, if I may..."

He leaned in to observe the collar, and Cassandra held her long hair out of the way. She could feel the old blacksmith's hands examining the collar, checking the system and metal. After a while, he stood up and turned to the

Prince.

"It won't be easy, My Lord. The cuffs can be removed easily, but collars meant for slaves have really precise systems."

"Can you do it or not?"

"We can try, but...this type of lock isn't made to simply be undone, Commander."

He turned to one of his colleagues, who nodded and examined Cassandra's collar too, but this time he used some tools. She could hear the mechanism at work, and her heart suddenly beat faster. Could they really do it? Could they take it off? Finally?

Kairen stood by her side without moving, his eyes fixated on her collar, not missing any of the blacksmiths' movements. For a long while, Cassandra sat with her head bent, wondering if this could really happen. But the longer it took, the more she doubted it. Those mechanisms were made so that slaves would not be able to escape. Many had tried to get rid of them already, but it was so complex.

Just as she started to feel discouraged, a large hand caressed her cheek. She smiled softly and closed her eyes, relying on the Prince's warmth. Cassandra slowly calmed down. She would be fine. Even if the collar didn't come off, she had him.

Suddenly, the sound of metal breaking was heard, and something scratched her. Cassandra frowned from the little pain, trying to touch the injury by reflex. The blacksmiths stepped back, looking terrified. The Prince was glaring at them.

"You useless..."

"We're so very sorry, Your Highness! This lock can't be undone simply by forcing it! The Dragon Empire would lose its slaves daily if we could."

As the man kept apologizing and explaining, Cassandra glanced at her shoulder to finally see what had happened. Her collar was still there, but one of the blacksmiths' instruments, something that looked like a thin little spindle, was half stuck in it, its other half broken on the floor. It had probably broken when trying to force open the collar's mechanism, and scratched her shoulder by accident.

Cassandra saw the Prince's hand going for the sword at his belt, but she immediately stood up in front of him, putting her hands on his torso, trying to get his attention on her.

"My Lord! It's fine, I expected so..."

"If those men were more competent..." he hissed, but Cassandra shook her head.

"No. They are right. It is this Empire's will that slaves shouldn't be freed so easily."

Cassandra's words finally got to him, as he looked down at her.

It was his Empire, his father, and the slavery system that had put this collar on her neck from the beginning. Those blacksmiths were right. It was no easy matter, and not a simple collar. There was a lot more weight behind it, and Cassandra's sentence.

This did not cool down the Prince's anger one bit. He glared furiously at the men present, despite Cassandra's attempt to have him calm down. Clenching his fists, he resisted the urge to break or throw something across the tent with all his might.

"Let's go, please? My Lord?" she asked in a soft voice.

Kairen's jaw was still clenching, yet he grabbed Cassandra's waist and suddenly carried her, holding her on one arm as if she weighed nothing. They left the tent as she put her arms around his shoulders, while the men behind them let out a big sigh of relief.

There wasn't a word exchanged until they reached the Prince's tent. Cassandra only held on and focused on the cold breeze. Was the evening colder than usual? Or was it the Prince's silent anger only giving her that impression? She held on a bit tighter as they reached the tent, before he let her down.

Kairen was still frowning and visibly unhappy about what had happened. Cassandra took a deep breath in, and stepped closer to him, putting her hands on his torso again.

"My Lord, it's fine. I knew it wouldn't work. I've seen many try to force those locks for hours without it ever coming off."

He stayed silent, looking at her with those dark, black eyes of his. It was hard for Cassandra to guess what he was thinking at that moment. Was he disappointed? Or just angry things weren't going as he wanted?

After a long while, though, the frown on his face seemed to dissipate, and he put his large hands on her waist, looking at her with a calm expression. Cassandra was expecting him to say something, but instead he leaned in to kiss her, a soft very gentle kiss. She didn't know what to do, so she answered naturally to his lips, feeling comfort in it.

The collar was still there, heavy and uncomfortable, but as long as she was by the Prince's side, Cassandra felt safe. She didn't want to leave his side anymore. She enjoyed this kiss, and for once, claimed more with her tongue. One of Kairen's hands went up, twirling his fingers in her long hair like he liked to do.

Gathering her courage, Cassandra gently pushed him towards the bed, blushing from her own boldness. Of course, her strength was barely enough to make the War God move, but as soon as he understood her intent, Kairen complied and stepped back, until he could sit on the bed. As he did, he held Cassandra across his lap, not interrupting their tender kiss. She was starting to feel a bit hot. How long had it been since their last...intimate moment? In that short while, she already missed his hot skin, his large hands, and musky smell.

"Cassandra..." he muttered against her ear as their lips parted, making her blush.

She loved the way he pronounced her name, too. There was this intense mix of sensuality and tenderness in his deep voice.

With her fidgety hands, she took the cloak off his shoulders, exposing the muscular, naked torso she now knew by heart. Kairen had already taken her cloak off, but for once, he let her do most of the undressing, only kissing her shoulder, collarbone, and finally her breasts as soon as she exposed them.

Sucking and stroking them, he made her blush in a matter of seconds. Cassandra had always felt her breasts were on the smaller side, but that didn't seem to bother him... The War God kept playing with them, arousing her, and making it more difficult for Cassandra to focus on taking her dress off. Once she finally had it off though, he smiled and pulled on her hips to have her closer, sitting on top of his prominent bump. She shivered a bit, both excited and cold, as her inner temperature didn't match the one inside the tent.

Kairen's glance, as he let go of her rosy breasts, went to her collar. Cassandra was afraid this might anger him again for a bit, but the Prince suddenly smirked.

"Once we get this thing off, let's have you wear something that really fits you...gold or silver...gems..."

"Like a necklace?" she whispered, a bit surprised.

"Anything you want," he nodded. "Gold, gems, jewelry... We'll get it all. I want to see you wear it..."

Cassandra thought about disagreeing, but eventually, she only blushed and kissed him. She knew how strange and whimsical he could be sometimes. She didn't want to talk him out of it until they got to it. He complained so often about her appearance as a slave, she had to be a bit more careful about it.

Kairen slowly laid down, Cassandra still on top of him, and they both used their hands to help him get out of his pants. She wondered for a second if they should change positions, but the Prince pulled her arms, having her ride him.

Rubbing against each other, she felt their equal arousals. He didn't even touch her, yet she was already wet from their kissing only... Feeling his pride standing tall and hard against her thigh was a torture she couldn't endure any longer. Cassandra bit her lip, her hands in his, and slowly sat down, feeling him fill her with a long exhale.

They both took a minute to enjoy this, the feeling of their bodies connected, filling each other, looking at each other's eyes. Then, Cassandra slowly started moving, to her own rhythm, enjoying it. He was big inside her; any move made her tremble and blush in pleasure. In just a couple of days, she had missed this so much.

Underneath, lying still with the eyes of an excited lion, Kairen watched his concubine move and breathe loudly. Cassandra was even more beautiful when she was exalted. Her body moved like a wave on him, her breasts jiggling around. She closed her eyes when she was too embarrassed or excited, and exhaled even louder, until it became ecstasied moans, her hips moving faster on him. The War God just ogled her, feeling his own excitement rise along with her moves, and that delicious feeling of her body pressing down on him, taking him in, rubbing and hammering.

When he grabbed her hips and thrust without warning, she let out a surprised moan. His hammering was much more intense and bestial. Cassandra forgot completely about moving against him, and held on to his hands, moaning loudly to meet his thrusts. Despite being underneath, Kairen took control in an instant, holding her hips firmly and thrusting repeatedly, lifting his waist, making Cassandra bounce on him. It was fast, erratic, and overwhelming. He couldn't hold it in. He wanted to put his mark on her and make her cry in pleasure.

That intense, savage, hot sex had Cassandra completely lost in her senses. The Prince's burning black eyes made her crazy. The sounds of their bodies colliding, the slaps of their skin and moist sounds made it even more lustful, if possible. Her insides were burning hot, the sensation overpowering her, making her shake and scream out her pleasure.

The bed was embarrassingly squeaking, but that was nothing compared to their exalted voices. As Cassandra was crying out, the Prince was groaning, feeling his pleasure grow inside, reach heavenly levels.

Cassandra orgasmed loudly, one second before his final groan. Both spasmed intensely, his rod deep inside her, exulting and relishing. She breathed loudly, falling on her side, exhausted. It was short but...intense. Her thighs were still trembling and burning, and she felt a bit dirty, shamefully dirty.

Kairen sighed, putting a hand in his hair, feeling the cold air and satisfaction of their intercourse. Cassandra's breathing was still loud by his side, and he caressed her hip silently, waiting for her to recover.

He had thought about it before, but he silently hoped she would soon bear him a child... An heir. He could already see what kind of mother she would be. It had never been a wish of his before, but now, he wanted to see that image become real. If she became an Imperial Dragon's mother, Cassandra would be in a much better place. She could become a Princess...far from her status as a slave.

Out of the six Princes, three already had children. But Kairen was the only one without a concubine, until now. He turned his head to the woman laying beside him, and caressed her hair. If Cassandra got pregnant, she would become a target.

He had never cared for the Imperial Throne before. He would live his life with war and blood, as a Commander. He was bored with the women of the court, and hated the treacherous creatures coveting his wealth or imperial title. Kairen was born in a world where he was considered like a God, deciding the life or death of others, untouchable. Yet, he had seen many of his siblings killed by envy and jealousy at the Imperial Palace. His mother, a concubine among many others, had been smart and cunning enough to have him and Shareen reach adulthood despite her rivals. She probably had to dirty her hands many times for that to happen.

Cassandra was nothing like those women, nor his mother. She was smart, but caring, brave, and selfless. She wasn't afraid to die, or to face a dragon. She could pet a creature a thousand times her size, which would eat her own kind, and even feel empathy for it. She wasn't afraid to look him in the eyes, yet she blushed when he touched her. So innocent, yet so fierce.

Kairen leaned over her, resting on his arm while scrutinizing her.

"My...Prince?"

But Kairen pushed her legs open, and in a swift movement, positioned himself to penetrate her again, making Cassandra moan in surprise. Her insides were still burning, wet and hot from their wild sex just a few minutes ago. She couldn't help but tense her legs upon his sudden entrance, closing her eyes and putting her head back.

"Oh, Lord...gen...gently, please..." she begged, breathing erratically.

He started moving slowly, listening to her pleas and moans, but he wanted more, so much more of this woman.

Chapter 10

The man was grimacing, trying to hold it in. Half a dozen people were watching, as Cassandra was slowly stitching, explaining each movement and proceeding carefully.

"Here. If you make it as even as possible, the scar will be neat and healed in just a couple of weeks. No need to bandage it as long as you make sure it stays clean like I showed you."

The soldiers nodded, some even taking notes, but all of them were impressed. She turned to her patient, who was observing the stitches on his arm with a frown.

"Thank you, Lady Cassandra...I hope my fiancée won't mind this."

"I promise, the scar will be thin and neat. If she's marrying a soldier, this should be fine, right?" said Cassandra with a soft smile.

The man blushed a bit and nodded. Lady Cassandra was becoming prettier and prettier as the days went by. She had already won the hearts of many soldiers with her gentleness and hard work.

No one feared the Mountain Hospital anymore, as it had been renamed recently. The Red Room was forgotten and now people willingly came over to get treated or volunteered in their free time. Seven of the rooms were constantly busy, though a lot of changes had been made in just a few days.

More and more soldiers now knew the first aid gestures or basic treatments for small wounds, and to Cassandra's surprise, it had spread naturally among the troops. Fewer and fewer people came to get treated, unless they were at a loss on what to do, or seriously injured. The soldiers who had volunteered a few times had become knowledgeable in their own units, and helped their peers learn about hygiene or tended to them before they needed to go to the hospital. The number of volunteers was steadily growing. As word spread about the changes in the Mountain Hospital, more men came to help, and much to Cassandra's surprise, some of the unit Captains even sent men who had forced labor punishments to her. But the most impressive difference was how much the attitudes of the men around Cassandra had changed tremendously in such a short time.

Before, she was only seen as the only woman in the camp, a nameless slave that the Commander-in-Chief had brought for his own entertainment. Nowadays, things are very different. Anywhere she went, Cassandra was saluted and welcomed, as the men had started calling her "the Lady of the Mountain". They talked to her with respect, and her reputation grew fast among the ranks, as the new female doctor of the Camp. If a man dared to leer at her or disrespect her in some way, he was soon scolded by his peers. She was untouchable as the Commander-in-Chief's woman, but she was also seen as a respectable Lady.

"Lady Cassandra?" called a man who had walked in while she was tending to someone's cut. "The Head Accountant is here to see you, Madam."

"Oh, thanks, I will come soon."

Cassandra finished tending the wound, which had signs of early infection, and got up. As usual, she was closely followed by Evin, silent as a shadow but very efficient. He always had her cloak ready, made sure she ate her meals no matter how busy she was, and scolded the soldiers who got too familiar with her.

"It hasn't been ten days already Evin, has it?" she asked, a bit worried about this sudden visit.

"No, Madam. We still have two days to go before the deadline."

"I hope he hasn't changed his mind," she sighed.

As they walked through the mountain's tunnels, Cassandra was saluted many times by the men who hadn't seen her yet this morning, and some of them also stopped her to ask questions about which herbs to use for this infection, or how to address a large burn. It took her longer than she thought to finally reach the mountain's entrance, and meet with the Head Accountant. It was starting to snow rather heavily outside, and the man already had a white layer on his shoulders and hood. Despite that, he didn't seem to mind. In fact, he was waiting with a younger accountant, and two large closed bags at his feet.

"Good Morning, Head Accountant," she said while Evin was busy adjusting her cloak and the hood on her hair.

"Greetings, Madam."

"Is everything all right?" asked Cassandra, unable to hide her nervousness.

Even if she still had two days and worked hard, her stock in herbal medicine was getting dangerously low. Cassandra was afraid the Head Accountant had found a way to cancel their bet and leave her to deal with it on her own.

The man seemed quite displeased too, and let out a big sigh.

"Truthfully, I hate making mistakes, Lady Cassandra. However, I am not sure if this can be called one."

"I'm sorry, what is this about?"

"Our bet. I had an interesting talk with the three Generals this morning. Since you took over the Mountain Hospital, it appears thirty-three men were sent back to the Cavalry Unit, twenty-six to the Infantry Unit, and seventeen to the Artillery Unit, and only nineteen men in total from all the units died. You obviously won."

Cassandra was speechless. She had worked hard for the past few days, she hadn't even realized how much she had done. Moreover, with so many volunteers, she didn't even see everything that was going on in the Hospital, and how many men were sent back healed.

"Congratulations. It appears I misjudged your abilities. I also got scolded by the Generals for, and I quote, 'being a scoundrel and a stingy rat'."

The young Accountant behind him almost chuckled, trying hard to repress a laugh. Cassandra repressed one too. To hear the stern and stubborn Head Accountant had been scolded like that was quite funny to imagine.

The man showed the two bags.

"Here is all the herbal medicine we can provide at the moment. You may see my assistant for more. I will listen to your request and decide on a monthly budget after hearing it. The Generals also suggested they can provide money from their own budgets to help, if you send a request for them to do so."

Cassandra was astonished.

"Really? But..."

"They were extremely satisfied with their soldiers being sent back in full health and the recent significant reduction in leaves for sickness or injury, Madam. Hence, they said that the Mountain Hospital was worth investing in."

This was truly quite an achievement. Not only at the Hospital, but the changes were also starting to be visible in the camp. The men could now take care of any small injury by themselves, and look out for diseases and infections. The morale in the camp had been boosted by this new teaching and talk was spreading as the men were sent back to their units.

"Thank you for this..." said Cassandra, her eyes on the bags.

The Head Accountant nodded, and after a little silence, turned his eyes to the bags too.

"To be quite honest, Madam, soldiers like the ones in this army are not found easily. I am also in charge of recruiting more, and counting the deaths. Each loss is significant for this Army. Your work has been...a great relief, if I may say so. I may not understand your abilities, but I see the results. Those medicinal herbs should be used by people who can value them properly. Though, I suspect this may also bring you more trouble."

Cassandra had already thought about that. Her unique ways of healing would soon reach the Army doctors' ears, even faster if she was given actual goods and a budget to pursue. This would probably bring some disputes with them.

"Thank you for your appreciation, Head Accountant."

He bowed respectfully, and gestured for his assistant to go to her side. The young man nodded and carried the two bags over.

"I will now take my leave, Madam. In the future, feel free to reach out to me or ask my assistants if you need anything. I won't make the mistake of underestimating you again."

Cassandra watched him turn around and leave, a little smile on her lips.

"Didn't it sound like an apology to you, Evin?"

"I think that is the best you will get from him, Madam."

She chuckled.

"You're probably right. Come on, let's bring those inside and check what we got so we can order more as soon as possible."

"Yes, Madam."

With the assistant accountant's help, Cassandra and Evin dragged the two bags all the way inside, to the stockroom which had been rapidly depleted in a few days. Two men who were boiling herbs immediately hurried to take over and sort them into the different pots and baskets on the shelves, while Cassandra discussed with the assistant accountant about more stocks.

Suddenly, a loud ruckus was heard at the entrance, making everyone in the room turn heads. A young man came running in.

"Lady Cassandra, could you come? There's a bit of a dispute outside."

Cassandra sighed and followed after him. What now? She didn't even have time to undo her coat and she was going back outside again. With such weather, she would rather stay inside.

It turned out that said dispute was actually taking place right at the entrance, by a large snow-covered hill where a dozen men were assembled. Cassandra had already got a hold of what was going on, before she got there, from all the yelling.

"I am not going, you damn skunks! Let me down right now!"

"But Captain, you cannot stay like this! You will lose your leg if it goes on."

"Lady Cassandra is very skilled! She can definitely help!"

"I do not care!" yelled the man on a stretcher. "I'd rather lose a leg than be healed by a woman!"

"We can arrange that," said Cassandra.

The men turned to her, two of them running to her as soon as they recognized her under her hood.

"Lady Cassandra! Please help the Captain! His leg was injured days ago!"

"It's getting bad!"

"All of you shut up! Bring me back! I do not care for that witch's methods! A woman healing is absurd! Women should be confined to the household and stay quiet!"

A bit annoyed, Cassandra crossed her arms, both from the cold and her impatience.

"I have many patients waiting for my help and not so many beds available. If you are yet to make a decision, do it quietly, please. Some of them need silence."

The Captain glared at her, even more pissed.

"Shut up, woman! I shall not take orders from you! And do not look me in the eye, impudent little..."

144

"I suggest you watch your words in the presence of His Highness' Concubine..." started Evin, but the man interrupted him.

"I will not allow a low woman to talk to me! And a slave, at that! The Commander-in-Chief may have been seduced by this wench, but I... I..."

The man suddenly lost his words, as he had caught a movement behind Cassandra. The snow-covered hill suddenly started moving and growing under his eyes, which opened wide in shock and fear. The snow fell in large chunks, revealing black scales and two glowing red eyes. Evin sighed.

"As I was saying, in the presence of His Highness' Concubine and Dragon."

As the large black dragon was eyeing the group, it lowered its head to Cassandra's side, where she gently scratched under its chin.

Krai was obviously glaring at the man, though. Could a dragon have understood his words? Was he upset about the words used toward the Commander-in-Chief's concubine just now? It couldn't be, right? The Captain swallowed slowly.

"If you do not wish to be healed, I suggest you see another doctor in the camp. But please don't be so noisy in front of the hospital or I'll have you removed."

"Re...removed?" said the Captain, though he had lost most of his voice.

Cassandra nodded, still scratching Krai's maw. The dragon was chewing some snow, some of its back still white. The men around the Captain, despite being impressed, tried to convince him again.

"The Lady of the Mountain is very skilled, Captain! She stitched the Lieutenant's arm and now he is fine! Please, Captain, at least let her examine you. "

As the Captain was still frowning and glaring at Cassandra, one of his men walked to her, pleading.

"Please, Lady Cassandra, our Captain is very stubborn, but he is a great soldier and like a father to most of us! If he loses his leg, he will be sent back!"

"What happened?" finally asked Cassandra.

"He twisted his leg while training a while ago. We thought it might get better, but now it's been two weeks now, he can't even walk, and the area is all black and blue!"

She sighed. This was probably only a muscle contusion, but if that man was this stubborn, he probably hadn't taken any rest for his leg to heal. Two of the men pulled up one of their Captain's pant legs to show her the large bruise that had spread up his thigh. The Captain immediately became red.

"You little scums! How dare you undress me like that! You're all going to regret this!"

"How is it, Lady of the Mountain? Is it bad?"

"Don't you touch me you vicious...!"

But before he could end his sentence, a loud, angry dragon growled at him. The men ran in all directions, just before Krai's paw landed on the Captain, pinning him on the ground. He lost all air in his lungs in a funny expression, the beast crushing him to the ground.

"Hey, Krai, no. No, no, get your paw off. Here."

Krai was still growling, but Cassandra's calls managed to distract the dragon enough. She kept making gestures until the red eyes looked her way instead of the Captain's. Her voice was as gentle and calm as usual, yet every man was shocked to see the dragon attracted to her like a moth to a flame. Krai kept growling, unhappy, and the Captain was still being crushed under his humongous weight.

"Let go, come on. Come here," said Cassandra, stepping away so the dragon would follow.

Eventually, Krai turned around, its paw finally lifting from the man's body, who painfully tried to breathe again.

"Good dragon," said Cassandra. "Come here."

While she was scratching and petting Krai, Evin rolled his eyes and walked to the soldiers, helping their Captain up.

"You idiot. Insulting the Concubine in front of His Highness' Dragon."

"The dragon listens to the Lady of the Mountain!" said one of the men, impressed.

Evin clicked his tongue.

"His Highness' Dragon listens to His Highness only. He just likes to act as Lady Cassandra's bodyguard...and pet, apparently."

Even so, all the men were watching the scene of the young woman, standing in the snow to cuddle and pet a dragon that was about a thousand times her size. Krai seemed to have already forgotten about them, only focused on Cassandra.

At some point, she had the dragon walk away, though they had missed how she did that. Had she thrown something away to play catch? That death machine just acted like a dog around this woman...

"You should have him rest and apply fresh snow on his injury. It will most likely heal by itself as long as he doesn't overdo it," she said to the men.

"Thank you, Lady Cassandra!" said some of the men in unison.

"You better take him out of here, though. Next time, I can't guarantee His Highness' Dragon won't bite him on the first try."

The men left swiftly, taking away the Captain who was still acting grumpy. Evin turned to Cassandra.

"You did a good job preventing His Highness' Dragon from eating him."

"Did I?"

"Yes. Even dragons can get sick from rotten meat."

Cassandra laughed. Sometimes, Evin really surprised her. Was he ironic or really trying to crack a joke? Either way, it was amazing to see how his facial expression never changed one bit.

"The weather is getting worse. I suggest you go back now, Madam," said Evin, looking at the sky.

"All right. Let me give some instructions to the men in the hospital and

146

then we can go."

Indeed, a few instructions were sufficient for the men to know what to do even if she was absent. Cassandra had been surprised with how fast some of the younger soldiers were able to learn from her. Many were very proactive and curious too, always asking questions and coming up with suggestions.

They obviously held her in high esteem, as she was always called "Lady Cassandra" or "Lady of the Mountain" by the men. Some were coming daily, even for a few hours, just to learn more from her and spread the knowledge about first aid around. She didn't feel too bad about leaving the mountain a bit earlier than usual that day, knowing she was leaving it in good hands.

Since the wind was too strong, Krai stayed on the ground, walking beside her, its huge body actually shielding Cassandra from the snow during the whole trip back.

"This is going to be a storm," said Evin.

"Are the storms bad here?"

"They can be, but the men only need to stay confined in their tents. If it lasts several days though, it can be problematic."

Cassandra nodded, and looked up. It was all grey and white in the sky. How long would this last? Evin was probably right, as the snowfall was getting heavier. Snow was piling up on Krai's back. As they progressed in the camp, many men warned her to take cover, too. Cassandra was looking for the Prince though, and was directed to one of the training grounds. Despite the name, it was in one of the buildings.

A very large room, like an interior stadium, was conceived for men to train and attend meetings inside. It could easily contain thousands of men and their steeds. There weren't any horses when Cassandra got there though, actually most of it was empty. On one side a group of men were practising movements all together and on the other some were doing physical exercises. The center was the busiest, twenty soldiers in full armor were all fighting against one man, Kairen, alone with two swords. Immediately, Cassandra couldn't help but worry about the obvious difference.

"Is this okay?"

"Probably not. I hope His Highness remembers it's a pain to replace soldiers."

Cassandra frowned. Was the Prince still at an advantage, despite the numbers? He didn't even have his armor on!

Yet, after a few minutes of observing the battle, she had no choice but to admit Evin was right. The Prince had no need for armor. With his two swords, he effortlessly dismissed any attempt the soldiers made to get to him. He didn't even seem to get tired, or put any effort in. Each movement was perfect and precise. Despite his broad frame, he moved with the agility and speed of a tiger. His muscles' hard at work were showing with each gesture, under his tan skin.

Cassandra couldn't help but slowly start blushing after a while. The lines of his body were just dancing perfectly, the Prince's perfect form revealed. Cassandra felt a slight fever coming up inside. She could have used some more of the snow.

She was just watching from the side, but Cassandra was hypnotized by the fight, as if it had been some dance. Her heart fluttering with each of the Prince's moves, she reacted to every action, fearing for him when a soldier seemed to stand a chance, relieved when he pushed them back, excited when he attacked himself.

As Cassandra didn't bother him and stood silently, Kairen hadn't noticed her entrance. Yet, the fight was over after only a few minutes. Each of the twenty soldiers, no matter how good they were, ended up butt or face in the sand, full of aches and muscle pains. Kairen was unscathered.

"How impressive," whispered Cassandra.

"Of course. His Highness wasn't named this Empire's War God for nothing," said Evin.

She couldn't even hear Evin, her green eyes still stuck on her Prince. Kairen's skin was barely sweating despite all this exercise, but it was shiny and lustrous, making her blush even more. She could vividly remember the feel of his skin under her fingers.

"Shall we go get His Highness?"

Just as Evin suggested that, Kairen's eyes suddenly turned to them. Cassandra immediately blushed even more from having his eyes on her. Just as the Prince turned to walk up to her, Cassandra saw one of the soldiers aiming a knife at him.

"My Lord!" she yelled, a bit too late.

Though Kairen's shoulder movement to dodge was near perfect, it was a second too late. The blade scratched his shoulder, before falling on the ground. A vivid red line appeared on Kairen's skin, before he turned to the man who had done this. Cassandra's heart was worried for a moment. Was he going to kill the soldier? Or get mad for attacking from behind? And injuring a member of the Imperial Family? But contrary to all her thoughts, Kairen talked to the man, calmly, something she couldn't hear. They exchanged words briefly.

"What's going on?" she asked Evin, confused.

"That man managed to injure the War God. His Highness is asking for his name and unit, for him to be rewarded."

"Rewarded? Isn't wounding the Imperial Family something to be punished?"

"Things are different on a training ground."

Cassandra nodded. So it did seem. The Prince's talk with the soldier was short, though. As soon as he was done, he turned around and walked to Cassandra. She found herself unable to stop blushing again as he came closer.

Once he faced her, as she was on some stairs that put her at the same height as him, he put his arm around her waist and leaned in for a kiss. Despite Evin being there, Cassandra couldn't resist him, putting her hands on his chest

148

to respond. His smell was even stronger after training, enticing her. Their kiss lasted a while, as Kairen kept playing with her tongue, caressing her hair and holding her close.

When they parted, Cassandra had to catch her breath a bit.

"Why are you so red?" he asked his concubine with a frown.

"I was...watching you," she admitted, unable to answer any further.

"It made you like this?" he asked with a little smirk, his hand noticeably going down her back.

Cassandra felt ashamed that his hands were exciting her even more, and in the presence of Evin, too! She was about to burn away if things kept going.

"My Prince, a winter storm is coming... Can we go back to our tent?" she asked shyly.

Kairen frowned a bit, turning to Evin, who nodded. Then, without adding a word, Kairen lifted Cassandra, carrying her effortlessly against his shoulder. Since she knew there was no use in protesting against this, Cassandra held on to him until Kairen brought her back to the tent, inside which Evin didn't follow.

Once inside, Kairen put her down, and she put her fur coat aside.

"My Lord, let me look at your injury, it..."

"It's fine."

Cassandra didn't listen and got on her toes to take a look at it. Immediately, she wondered if her eyes were going crazy. Instead of the injury from earlier, on the Prince's shoulder she could see a line of... little black scales?

She had never seen anything like it before. Not on a man's skin...What were those? Little black scales appeared on the injury, covering it. She could only see a darker shade where the blood was visible before. Hypnotized, Cassandra slowly caressed the scales. They had a similar feel to Krai's, she thought.

"What is this?" she asked softly.

"The Dragon's Blood. Our blood reacts anytime we are injured and does this."

A trait of the Imperial Family...No wonder they were seen as gods. To have this kind of heavenly capability was unimaginable for common folk. Yet, from just a scratch, Kairen had little scales immediately blooming to cover it up. The scales were a dusky black color, was it because his dragon was black, too? Did his brothers have similar abilities? This was so fascinating.

As she kept brushing the scales with her fingers, Kairen grabbed her hand, bringing her attention back to him. They were finally together and alone after a long day. And with a winter storm raging outside, they would surely be alone for a while longer.

He grasped her lips, kissing her slowly, enjoying her sweet taste. Cassandra's lips were always soft and a light, delicious pink. He played with them, his tongue imposing a rhythm she was now used to.

Even if the Prince's kiss got a bit more forceful, Cassandra liked it and knew how to respond. Actually, she was maybe liking his forcefulness a bit too much. The strength of his hands, even as he caressed her gently, warmed her up. She put her hands around his neck, closed her eyes, and let herself go in his arms. Kairen, too, was growing hungry for her. His hands got lower, caressing her hips, pulling her dress up. That day she was wearing a white dress, he thought this color looked better than red on her.

As soon as she was left bare-chested and in her panties in front of him, he grabbed her and lifted her up, holding her a bit higher than him without interrupting their kiss. His bare torso against her skin was warming Cassandra up alarmingly fast. She loved the feel of his warm skin and the strong masculine scent that came from it. With Kairen's hands holding her butt Cassandra held on to his neck, kissing him some more, feeling her arousal as much as his. She wasn't even doubting her own desires anymore. She wanted him. She wanted this man to make her his.

Cassandra whispered those words into the Prince's ear, and after a second of silence, he landed her back on the bed, exposed with her legs split open in front of him. As she blushed, Cassandra watched him quickly undo his belt, getting rid of her last piece of clothing, and she closed her eyes just as the Prince penetrated her. She let out a long sigh of relief as he slowly went farther, feeding her with his warmth and hard rod. They both had no patience this time. He started moving immediately, in and out, rubbing her insides and feeling her around his cock. Cassandra was reacting to each move, crying out, moaning, letting go and taking pleasure in his assaults. She liked his forceful, strong strokes that made the mattress jump and the bed squeak. The way it made her hot and gasping, the burn that spread between her legs. Cassandra held on to his shoulder and the bed sheets, feeling his thrusts become faster and deeper, making her all hot and fuzzy.

Kairen wasn't anywhere close to stopping either. He wanted more, always more. His hip movements became faster, loudly slapping against Cassandra's skin. Her white skin was getting more flushed as he kept going, and her exposed breasts were pointing up too. He grabbed one, fondling it without slowing down his thrusts. She was the perfect size for him, and soft under his fingers. He loved playing with them and seeing her react. Indeed, Cassandra was moaning louder, her head thrown back, her legs trembling under his forceful strokes. Her hand grabbed his wrist, but he barely felt the pressure.

"More?" he asked in a raspy voice.

"More, please, please..." she whispered, her eyes still closed.

Holding her thigh, Kairen kept going, tirelessly. His rod filled her to the brim, faster and faster, the sound of their flesh slapping together filled the air. She was tight around him, pressing against him, deliciously holding him in. He felt like he could keep going forever inside her, their bodies feeling insanely good together.

Cassandra was close to coming though. He could tell from her red cheeks, her erratic moans, and her quivering pussy. He wouldn't slow down. She would feel his cock again and again, going at it without rest. She had no way to stop her climax. Like a hot bomb exploding, she suddenly spasmed, her whole body trembling after one more push.

Kairen slowed down, watching her as she exhaled loudly, bending to kiss her breasts.

"You came..." he whispered.

She couldn't blush anymore, but the embarrassment was the same. Cassandra wished she could hide but no, she was completely exposed in front of her Prince. Gasping for air, she undid her hair trying to gather her senses. Kairen didn't pull out though, and she couldn't ignore his hot, and still rock-hard rod inside her. It was hard to calm down in those conditions. She inhaled deeply, closing her eyes, trying to evade her post-orgasm haze.

"I'm not done."

His words took her by surprise.

Grabbing her by the hips, Kairen suddenly pulled out and had her turn over. She was butt naked in front of him, unable to see him. The Prince took her legs down, having her feet touch the floor, as she was bent over the mattress. Cassandra remembered this position from the hot springs and gasped.

Kairen's hardness was at her entrance, pressing again, and she exhaled loudly as he penetrated her once more. She was still plenty wet and he didn't hold himself back. The sensations were different, but the heat was the same. Cassandra couldn't withhold her moans as the War God took her savagely from behind, without rest. He was holding her by the hips, imposing his rhythm, pinning her down on the mattress. His cock filling her, ramming inside, Cassandra kept crying out, completely out of her mind. Her legs, still weak from the previous orgasm, were tensing and shaking.

She couldn't see, but she could hear Kairen's hot breath and his hips slamming against her backside repeatedly. The squishy sounds remained, as he kept going, and her own voice, hoarse and exhausted, yet still loud and out of control. She couldn't control anything. Cassandra was just taking him in, crying out from the pleasure, feeling his back and forth, unable to predict his rod's assaults.

"Huh... Ah! Pl... Please... Slow... Ah! Hn, hn...down..." she begged.

If Kairen heard her, he didn't make it known. He didn't slow down, instead, he intensified his assaults, thrusting harder. Cassandra couldn't say how long it lasted, or how her body held up. She bit her lip and kept moaning whilst still trying to breathe, feeling the burn between her legs, the waves of pleasure still tortured her restlessly.

At some point, finally, she heard his breathing get huskier. His movements suddenly became more erratic, brutal and deeper thrusts inside her, making her cry out again. The Prince unleashed his pleasure inside her with a groan, spasming and cumming profusely.

Cassandra had no more strength. Her legs completely numb, she lay there resting a bit on the mattress while the Prince slowly pulled out. This time, she was sweating too. How long had this been? Minutes or hours, she couldn't tell.

Kairen's lips flirted with her back, caressing her rosy skin, gently.

"Cassandra?" he called to her softly, pulling her to him.

She definitely couldn't stand, so she sat in front of him still in a bit of a daze. Kairen lifted her up though, and to her surprise, brought her to the large water basin that was in a corner of the room. She hadn't even noticed it.

He got in and sat Cassandra between his legs. The water that may have been hot earlier, was now lukewarm. If she wasn't resting against the Prince's torso, Cassandra might even have found it cold. The water felt good on her burning skin though. She closed her eyes, resting her head on Kairen's shoulder, feeling it calm her down. Her insides were still hot and a bit uncomfortable from so much sex, so she focused on something else, laying her legs in front of her and taking deep breaths.

Kairen gently put an arm around her in silence, kissing her shoulder. They could hear the snow storm, the wind blowing outside and the little fire crackling in the chimney pit. Only the War God could have enough warmth with such a little fire though. Cassandra knew she would have been much colder without him.

She shivered a bit as he gently wet her hair. The water running down her, she felt the Prince sliding the soap across her skin, gently washing her. Cassandra sighed silently. He was probably the only Prince to wash his slave. She couldn't refuse him though. Instead she made sure to do the same for him, washing the dust and sweat off him with lots of soap.

"I remember the first time you washed me," he suddenly whispered with a smirk.

Cassandra could remember it too.

"You were a bit too nasty," she replied with a little pout.

Kairen still felt playful. He caressed her hip in a gentle but enticing way. Cassandra was too exhausted for more sex, but she didn't push him away. She enjoyed his touch, the water around her, and this peaceful atmosphere around them.

"Let's go back."

"Back?" she asked, a bit surprised. "To the Onyx Castle?"

He nodded.

"Once the storm is over. Let's fly back there for a few days. You need more stuff."

More stuff? What was e thinking about? Clothes, probably? But Cassandra had another matter in mind.

"What about the hospital? I cannot abandon all the patients..."

Kairen frowned, a bit unhappy.

"They'll do fine without you."

"How long will we stay at the Onyx Castle?"

"We'll see," replied Kairen, visibly unwilling to say anymore.

Cassandra left her questions aside, thinking a bit. She would be happy to go back, see the girls again. They had only been gone for just over a week, but the Onyx Castle felt so far away. She felt a bit happy to go back. She wondered if she should think of anything to do while they were there.

Outside, the storm was raging. How long could a winter storm last? Actually, Kairen was probably right about the hospital. And she didn't mind waiting in this tent for a couple more days. It would be just the two of them in the tent, after all.

Chapter 11

The winter storm lasted two nights and two days. During that time, Cassandra and Kairen spent all their time together in their tent. It was cold, but their bodies were enough to warm each other up. Evin and a couple of other Imperial Servants showed up from time to time to bring in food, and disappeared just as quickly as they appeared.

It was like they were in their own cocoon, far from the troubles their difference in status brought, far from any concerns about the camp or the Capital.

Though as soon as the storm calmed down, they were both ready to resume their duties. After a long kiss goodbye, Kairen and Cassandra parted. The Prince left to see his men, and Cassandra walked back to the hospital. She had some company on the way.

"Good Morning, Madam."

"Morning, Evin. Are you okay?"

"We are used to storms such as this, Madam."

As usual, the Imperial Servant was a man of few words. The black dragon following her every step was more noisy though. Maybe because it had been alone outside for a while, Krai was literally beside her every step, and growling a bit whenever Cassandra ignored it for too long. However, she was glad Krai walked next to her, as she had to hold on to the dragon to make her way through the snow. It was soft like powder, but so high sometimes she would stumble or have a hard time stepping into it. Thankfully, Krai's hot body made most of the snow around them melt under its steps, though it soaked Cassandra's dress. It took a long time for them to reach the hospital and Cassandra was a bit anxious. Were the men alright? How many of them would have suffered during the storm?

As soon as she stepped in though, it seemed like everything had been fine, despite her absence. The volunteers present were doing great following the instructions she had left on some papers and actually didn't notice her before she stepped into one of the rooms.

"Lady of the Mountain! Welcome back!"

"Lady Cassandra!"

A few men ran to her, asking many questions at the same time until Evin ordered everyone to calm down. Cassandra was mostly needed to instruct how to treat complex injuries, which disease they were dealing with, and how to make new ointments and serums. It didn't take long though. Sadly, as she had feared, the cold brought by the winter storm had killed the men who were already sick. Some who had been injured by falling trees or other accidents had come in too, but nothing major. Cassandra did her best in a few hours, but she was supposed to depart with the Prince before nighttime.

Hence, she left after giving some more instructions to the volunteers present. She was still hoping to find real apprentices, but for now those men were doing great on their own.

To her surprise, when Cassandra walked out of the hospital the Prince was already there putting some bags on his dragon's back. Krai was calmly resting in his presence, though its eyes followed Cassandra.

"Are you ready?" he asked.

"Yes, My Lord. Are we leaving now?"

"Get on," he said with a nod.

Cassandra could now climb Krai by herself, but Kairen still helped her. Evin watched the two take their places on the dragon's back. The black beast probably already sensed what was happening since it stretched his wings and got up. Kairen held Cassandra, as the dragon moving around caused her to lose her balance.

Then as usual, the dragon took off, shortly flying high in the grey sky. It was colder than the previous time, and Cassandra felt the bitter wind despite her thick cloak and the Prince holding her. Her cheeks were red and she covered her mouth as her throat started to ache a bit from breathing the cold air. Kairen looked fine, as usual, although he did put on a winter cloak as well this time.

The black dragon had to make double the effort to fly due to the strong wind and the snow. It wasn't as bad as during the winter storm, but Cassandra couldn't see any of the landscape below or far away. She even wondered how Krai knew where to go when they couldn't even see the ground. However, the dragon didn't seem to mind. It was flying confidently, not even bothered by the snowfall, or the winds challenging its wings.

Yet, it took a bit longer for them to reach the castle, or so Cassandra thought. Maybe it was because of the cold, but she was glad when Krai finally landed on the white coat in the Onyx Castle grounds. Just like before, Patrina hurried out to welcome them, followed by the other servants. Though they did not dare to say a word in front of the Prince, the young girls' eyes were shining bright in Cassandra's direction. She could tell they were holding back from running to her.

Patrina stepped forward, bowing to the Prince.

"Welcome back, My Lord. I hope you had a pleasant trip. Several deliveries from the palace have been made."

"Where is it?"

"It was put in your room, as ordered, My Lord."

Kairen nodded and walked into the castle. Cassandra thought he didn't need her, but just when she was parting ways with him to go greet the girls, the Prince turned around.

"Cassandra. Come."

A bit surprised, she followed after him. Did he need her to unpack or something? She wished she could have greeted the others before going upstairs. The Prince seemed impatient though. He climbed the stairs up to his room so fast she could barely follow in his footsteps. When they finally arrived, five large chests were in the room, as Patrina had said. Kairen walked up to the closest one and opened it.

"Cassandra."

She walked up to him to look at the contents. She found herself speechless. Jewelry! So many emeralds, diamonds, other gems, and gold she could have gone blind. What was all this? This was worth so much! Kairen frowned upon seeing her shocked expression.

"You don't like those?"

"What? My Lord, this is..."

"From my father. They said you would be rewarded, didn't they? It came late."

Cassandra suddenly remembered the very short moment when two servants had indeed mentioned a reward, back at the Palace, for becoming the War God's Concubine. However, she only expected a few gold coins, not five big chests full of treasures!

A bit unable to process what she was seeing, she slowly took out a few of the items present, one by one. There were so many, she could barely believe her eyes. She had a long necklace with emeralds in one hand and something like a gold tiara in the other. She tried to count, but the numbers and the thought of the overall price made her dizzy. There was every type of jewelry one could think of. From bracelets, necklaces, earrings, rings, even toe rings, to tiaras, and hairpins. She had never seen so much in one place. And all of these were meant for her?

Cassandra got up and opened another one of the chests. Unlike the first that she found full of jewelry, this one was filled with dresses. Luxurious, warm, and deep red dresses, all aligned there. She got on her knees and took one out, too curious. This dress had nothing in common with her current attire. They were both red dresses, but the one Cassandra was currently wearing looked very shabby and dull in comparison. The dress she had taken out of the chest was a deep, beautiful red, and was very detailed too. There were embroideries and thin little gems in it, making it shine subtly whenever it moved.

"It's beautiful..." she whispered to herself, impressed with the craftsmanship.

"They are all yours. No more dirty dresses."

He opened the last two chests for her to see. The fourth one was filled with dresses as well, in every shade of red that existed. Apparently, she wouldn't have to wear any white anymore. The last chest contained little boxes and bottles, mostly perfumes, creams, and makeup. The kind her previous mistress had by the hundreds, and abused everyday to keep herself pretty. Cassandra wasn't too fond of those, however. Some of the products in the Empire were expensive and not so useful, sometimes having very strong smells but not much benefit to the skin. Maybe she could try to make her own, now that she could access the herbs she wanted.

Kairen walked up to her, crouching down to her level.

"You don't like those?"

"I... love them. They are very beautiful. Thank you, My Lord."

A faint smile appeared on Kairen's face, as he caressed her hair gently.

"They are from my father. No more dirt."

Cassandra knew he was talking about the horrid state of the white dress she wore on their first encounter. The young concubine could still vividly remember the terrible color the water turned when she washed it. These dresses had nothing to do with the cheap white linen she had known for most of her life. Cassandra couldn't even recognize all the fabrics in there. She knew some master creators held the secret to fabrics like the celestial silk or the heavenly wool.

She was completely impressed with how fast these had been delivered here, and in such quantity too. There was plenty enough for one woman! She didn't even know where she could put these. Was she supposed to keep all those in the chests?

"Don't you want to change?" asked Kairen, a bit impatient.

She nodded, yes. Those dresses were probably more befitting of the winter weather anyways. Was that kept in mind when they sent those to her? She took a few minutes picking one, and noticed there were both winter and summer dresses in there. She had so many choices! On a rough estimate, there were about thirty dresses. She finally chose one that looked warm enough and not overly luxurious to put on.

It was long and a darker red with extra layers to keep her warm, only showing off her shoulders and collar line. There were embroideries and little gems around her chest, on the arms, and on the fur around the skirt and wrists.

As Cassandra tried it on, it was obvious the dress was a perfect fit on her. Was it tailored? Moreover, it was her first time wearing such a fine-quality item. The fabric was very soft on her skin, and the color was beautiful. She really liked it, though she felt a bit shy wearing such an expensive dress. She turned around to show it to Kairen.

But the Prince was frowning a bit. Cassandra felt a bit sad that he wasn't too enthusiastic about her outfit. She had wished that he would find her prettier in those.

"What is it, Your Highness? Don't you like it?"

"This color. It doesn't suit you."

Cassandra looked down. Did he not like red? She couldn't change though. All the dresses were red, different shades of red, but still red. She looked at herself in the large mirror in the room. She could see what he meant. With pale skin, green eyes, and brown hair, cold colours suited her more. This deep red was a bit too much.

There wasn't anything they could do about it though. The Empire was very color-coded when it came to the official outfits. In the Empire, slaves wore white, common people wore colors from yellow to dark brown, servants wore blue or green depending on their masters and statuses, and the Officials wore grey or black according to their ranks. The Concubines could only wear two colors: red or pink. Cassandra was only a low-ranked concubine, thus red was her colour. Pink would have complemented her better, but it wasn't something she could access for now.

There were several ways to become a High-ranking Concubine: be of noble birth, do something that would benefit the Empire and the Emperor could reward her for it, or bear Kairen a child. While the first one was impossible for her, she couldn't access the last two for now either.

"Would you rather me keep wearing white, My Lord?"

This only made Kairen frown more. He shook his head, holding out his hand for her to take. She joined him.

"It's fine for now. We'll work on making you a high-ranking Concubine later. "

"Goodness... Don't you have enough now?"

Nebora was frowning while looking at everything Cassandra had bought. Three full baskets of medicinal herbs on the little chariot behind them. The concubine was still looking at the stalls, smelling more herbs and observing the products. Cassandra chuckled.

"Not yet. This is my first time seeing a market in the North, and we rode two hours to get here. I should make sure I don't miss anything before we go, shouldn't I?"

"You're a really strange woman. You have five chests full of riches, yet all you care about are spices and herbs."

Cassandra had never really cared for those things. The young girls at the castle however, had been excited to check out her new dresses and jewelry, and even played with it when the Prince wasn't around. She had fun reuniting with the other girls and answering their endless questions about the military camp and soldiers. It was like she had gotten a lot of younger sisters all at once.

Nebora, however, was two years older and more composed. She was a bit interested in the jewelry, but didn't dare touch it. She only helped Cassandra tie her hair up with golden hairpins and suggested a couple of bracelets for her to wear.

When the young concubine had insisted on going to the nearest village, she had been the only one allowed to go with her. The other servant girls had much work to do with the Prince back, and Patrina had made sure to keep them busy. After Kairen agreed, Cassandra and Nebora had left with only a chariot and a horse they borrowed from the castle.

"I'm still curious on how you got His Highness to let you go alone," said Nebora.

"It's only a couple of hours by foot. He can be there in ten minutes if he flies. And I doubt anything will happen here."

She moved on to the next stall where the man greeted her with a polite smile despite his eyes being riveted on her red dress.

"Well, with the Army so close, no bandits are stupid enough to come to this area, but we still have wild beasts, you know."

"You said they only come out at night."

"That's why we better be back before nightfall."

"Yes, yes..."

Cassandra grabbed a batch of herbs, which were dry, and caressed it between her fingers. It was from the smallest basket on the stall, and he only had half a dozen of those. She slowly smelled it. She addressed the man selling it.

"Lavender?"

"Yes, My Lady. My Lady knows well!"

"You don't grow that here, do you?"

"My sister grows those a bit further south, My Lady. We cannot grow much here, but those travel a long time..."

"Is it still good if it's dry?" asked Nebora with a frown.

"Lavender is great," replied Cassandra, handing her the little batch. "Any flower can be dried and used like that."

"Can you eat it?"

"It's mostly used to perfume things. You can make beauty products, incense, and perfumes. Lavender is good for calming the nerves and relaxing the body, in small amounts."

The merchant whistled after listening to Cassandra's explanation.

"My Lady, you're very knowledgeable! Most folks in this area wouldn't even know what this is called! Give me a second!"

He looked at the back of his stall for something while Cassandra gathered money to pay for her purchase. Fortunately, Patrina had already converted the gold bar into money and given her a good amount of it. There was so much though, that despite everything they had bought that day she hadn't even used a third of it yet.

"Here it is! My Lady, do you know this?"

The man handed her what seemed like a batch of black paper. Cassandra's eyes opened wide in surprise when she took it.

"Is that...dry seaweed?"

"It is! I knew you'd recognize it!"

"Dry seaweed?" asked Nebora, completely lost.

"It's plants from the sea you let dry and you can eat."

"Eat? You want to eat this black stuff?"

Cassandra chuckled and tore a little bit to eat. It was salty but as good as the one she had known in her childhood. Better even. Nebora was baffled, but the merchant smiled from ear to ear.

"It was imported from very, very far in the South, but it stays dry and edible! I bought it a while ago, but it's hard to sell to the people around here. They are wary of what they don't know."

"How much do you have?" asked Cassandra.

"Here we go again," sighed Nebora.

"You know, it's good for keeping the body young," said the young concubine.

"Young?"

Nebora frowned, but took one of the sheets, observing it with curiosity. She hesitated a bit before tasting it, but seemed confused.

"What an odd taste..."

"I'll cook it, you'll see."

Cassandra took a while discussing it with the merchant, who was happy to see someone so knowledgeable. The young concubine was ecstatic too. Nebora knew Cassandra was holding herself back from buying too many herbs, but she didn't understand why. It wasn't like the Prince was going to be anywhere near poor even if she bought the whole market! Besides, most of the purchases weren't even for herself, but for cooking for everyone or creating new medicine. She really was an odd one.

Suddenly, a shadow flew over the sky. Everyone at the market raised their heads.

"Isn't that His Highness' Dragon?"

"It is..."

The merchants, afraid, ran to take cover. Neither of the two women moved, their eyes cast upwards. The black dragon didn't stop, however. It was headed further, and didn't even look down their way. Cassandra frowned.

"Is he going to hunt? So far?"

"That was the direction of the palace," said Cassandra, intrigued as well.

She couldn't see if Kairen was on his dragon's back from that distance. Yet she had an odd feeling about this. They watched the beast's silhouette until it was too far, then she turned to Nebora.

"Let's go back."

"Okay. It's getting late anyway, we better go now if we want to arrive before night time."

They quickly finished purchasing what they needed, filled their chariot, and got on their way back. It wasn't an easy path back to the castle as it wasn't used often, but it was wide enough and their horse knew its way.

However, as Nebora had feared, the sun went down fast behind the mountains. They were still far away from the castle when the temperatures fell and both women tightened their coats around them. Nebora had the horse speed up, though the night was clear and a thin coat of snow was surrounding them. Thanks to that and the moonlight, they saw clearly ahead of them, but the castle was still far behind the winter trees.

Nebora was looking more and more worried, continuing to glance around while hurrying the horse.

"What kind of beasts are there?" asked Cassandra, worried as well.

"We'll be lucky if it's only wolves."

What could there be out there worse than wolves? Cassandra looked around too, looking for any animal that could be lurking from behind the trees, from the deep darkness in the forest. Cassandra couldn't tell how far they were from the castle, but Nebora's worried look spoke volumes. Not close enough.

Suddenly, she noticed a growl on their left, somewhere behind them. Cassandra turned around, only spotting a couple of eyes in the dark, but not the beast they belonged to.

"What's that!"

"Something looking for fresh meat," sighed Nebora. "They won't attack yet, but they are following. They're hungry. Come on, hurry up!"

She had the horse accelerate, but with their weight the poor thing was already doing its best. Cassandra heard more creatures coming after them, rushing in the snow, growling hungrily. Could they outrun them and get to the castle in time?

"Nebora! Watch out!"

One of the beasts jumped at them, all claws out, but Nebora dodged right in time and it hit the chariot instead. Cassandra saw it though and it wasn't a wolf at all.

"Snow leopards! Damn it!"

The snow leopards were white with dark brown spots, explaining how Cassandra struggled to spot them among the snow and trees. Their fur was a perfect camouflage in this landscape. Except for their glowing eyes, they weren't hard to see at all. But they were much scarier than wolves!

"Those damn things are faster than wolves or horses," said Nebora. "They must be hungry, they don't usually come down from the mountain this time of the year."

Cassandra tried to think of something to distract them, but they hadn't gotten much food from the market and surely nothing that would look more appetizing than a horse and two humans!

"Let's abandon the chariot!"

"What?"

Cassandra grabbed the knife under her skirt and used it to cut the ropes, only letting Nebora handle the reins.

"Jump on the horse!"

Her friend hesitated for a second before obeying, unsure. She landed safely and looked back, holding her hand out for Cassandra to take. She hurriedly joined her on the horse's back, as the chariot was abandoned in the snow behind them.

"Crap..." said Nebora, looking at all their purchases scattered around.

At least this mess, and the chariot falling back disturbed the felines enough for the horse to get some distance. She was faster with only two women on her back, both of them not too heavy either.

As the servant had said, it wasn't long until the snow leopards caught up to them though. Cassandra heard their growls only a few seconds after they had parted with the chariot, and looked back.

Three of them were chasing behind in a triangle formation waiting for the right moment. Cassandra was at the back, if the leopards attacked they would either get her or the horse.

"Cassandra! Look!"

To her surprise, Nebora was pointing forward. After a few seconds Cassandra saw it. A large human figure standing in the middle of the road ahead of them. She couldn't see his features, but she still knew instantly.

"His Highness."

Kairen stood there waiting, two swords in his hands. When the two women and their horse crossed his path he didn't flinch, his black eyes fixated on the creatures behind them.

The snow leopards didn't miss the new target in front of them. The large human standing still was such easy prey. However, as they approached, some of the felines slowed down by mere instinct. Two young ones didn't though. They jumped at the same time.

Blood stained the snow and the felines dropped dead at the Prince's feet. Their peers growled, angry. Some were still lurking around, but were either too smart or listening to their instincts. They didn't dare approach within reach of the Prince's swords.

Cassandra wasn't sure if they were supposed to wait for him, but Nebora didn't stop. She watched the silhouette as they rode away. Once they arrived at the castle a few minutes later, Patrina and the girls ran to them.

"Lady Cassandra! Nebora! How could you come back so late?! Are you both alright?"

"We're fine, Patrina," sighed Nebora. "Just had a big fright."

"His Highness stayed behind," said Cassandra, worried.

"Don't worry about him," replied the old woman. "Come on, come inside and drink some hot tea, both of you. You're freezing..."

"I'm damn sweating!" groaned Nebora. "That was the most hellish ride of my life. I need a bath. And Olive deserves a treat too."

Cassandra patted the poor horse. It had been very brave to bring them both back safely. Marian and Helmond hurried to take care of the horse, taking it back to the stables, while Bina and Prunie accompanied the women to the kitchen. Patrina made some hot wine for both of them to drink after Nebora insisted. Cassandra, however, couldn't swallow anything. She was too worried for her Prince.

"Don't worry, Lady Cassandra, His Highness is too strong!" said Bina.

"She's right, you know," added Nebora. "He won't be taken down by a few big cats. He'll be back perfectly fine in a couple of hours, you'll see."

However, Kairen wasn't back two hours later. Cassandra, who had finally drank some wine and was exhausted, even fell asleep in the kitchen waiting for him. Nebora helped her up to the bedroom since she was half-asleep.

"Don't worry, sleep. He'll be fine."

Cassandra couldn't find a peaceful sleep. Why wasn't he back yet? And where had Krai gone, so far from its owner...?

The next morning Cassandra woke up early, around sunrise. Someone was slowly caressing her hair and bare skin. Remembering the events of the previous day, she opened her eyes and checked around, worried.

"My Lord!"

Kairen was indeed there, on the side of the bed, sitting there while watching her. She jumped, her arms wrapping around his neck to hold him, letting out all her worries from the previous night. Cassandra was so worried, she even checked his torso for injuries, but he only had a couple of thin black scale lines on his arms, already healing themselves. She let out a long sigh of relief and the Prince put his hand around her neck.

"I was so worried."

"You're fine now."

Didn't he understand that she was worried about him at all? He only kept looking at her for a long time, like he was trying to capture her face in his mind, until Cassandra blushed. Kairen seemed a bit odd this morning.

"Is there something wrong, My Lord?"

"No."

He got up and brought her one of the usual gold trays, with fruits, meat, and cheese. Cassandra was a bit lost though and ignored the food. She tried to think of what could be wrong.

"When did you get back, My Lord? I meant to wait for you, but I fell asleep..."

"Late in the night."

"Did you get any sleep at all?" she asked, worried.

"I did."

She frowned. She couldn't even tell if he had slept beside her, she was too exhausted herself. Suddenly, she thought of something else.

"Is your dragon back yet?"

Kairen immediately frowned slightly.

"Not yet...He will be here soon."

Was the problem with Krai then? Cassandra couldn't help but worry about its absence. It didn't seem usual for the dragon to leave, and go so far away and for so long, without its master. Did that explain Kairen's odd behavior this morning?

Probably no one else but Cassandra would have noticed anything was different with the Prince, but she was sure. He even seemed a bit...uneasy. She grabbed a bit of food, eating in silence, lost in her thoughts. Kairen didn't say a word either, watching her eat, sometimes taking some meat as well.

After a while, a little knock was heard on the door.

"Your Highness? May I come in?"

Nebora walked in as soon as Kairen gave permission, bringing in hot water and soap for Cassandra. Kairen got up and left without a word, leaving his concubine even more confused than before. She turned to Nebora.

"Nebora! Do you know what's going on?"

"What do you mean?"

"I don't know. His Highness is acting...odd."

Her friend frowned, turning her head towards where the Prince had just left.

"Odd? How so? Come, I'll help you bathe."

It was weird to have her own friend help her take a bath, but Cassandra didn't say no. She had gone to bed quite dirty last night and this was more than welcome. She got into the bath, where Nebora poured the hot water, and started washing herself.

"I don't know, he seems uneasy."

"I don't know what you're talking about Cassie. His Highness isn't like usual? I couldn't tell the difference. But the dragon isn't back yet. Maybe it has to do with that. We saw it leave in the direction of the palace, didn't we? Perhaps something happened there? I guess we won't know until it comes back. Oh, I'll wash your hair too, give me that."

She let Nebora tend to her and help her wash her long brown hair, trying to relax a bit. Maybe she was just worrying too much and it was nothing. Yet she couldn't shake off this feeling that something big was about to happen.

"He retrieved our stuff, by the way."

"His Highness?"

"Yeah. He came back late last night with the chariot and everything in it! I already took your herbs to the storage, as we had discussed. Oh, and he even killed some snow leopards! It's awesome, do you know how expensive their fur is? We can make you some great coats with that!"

Cassandra didn't feel much about getting a snow leopard coat, but she was impressed by her Prince once more. He had managed to kill several of those beasts all by himself and carry their cart back home? The War God was truly worthy of his title!

Once she was done bathing, Nebora picked a new red dress for her and insisted that Cassandra wear some jewelry. After a bit of arguing, she was made to wear some little ruby earrings and a gold hairpin. Nebora even helped her apply a bit of lip balm and scented cream on her neck.

Cassandra felt a bit odd wearing so much, but she was prettier than ever. When she and Nebora got down to the castle's open area, Marian and Prunie ran to them, all sparkles in their eyes.

"Cassandra, you look so pretty!"

"Are those real rubies?"

"Hands off!" said Nebora. "Don't forget, Cassandra is our friend, but she's also His Highness' Concubine. Don't touch her stuff with your dirty hands!"

"Nebora, you meanie!"

Cassandra chuckled at the girls' bickering. She had missed all of them, and insisted on making some tea for them. They walked to the kitchen, meeting the rest of the castle's staff there. Cassandra brought out some of her new herbs to make tea, all the younger girls watching her with expectation.

"It smells so good!" said Bina, humming.

"It's citrus and mint tea," explained Cassandra before serving them.

"A Concubine shouldn't be pouring tea for servants," said Patrina with a frown.

Nebora rolled her eyes at her.

"Who cares, it's just tea and we are the only ones here."

"Do you know where Krai or His Highness are?" asked Cassandra to Patrina.

"His Highness just went to the dragon's field. His dragon might be coming back soon."

"The dragon's field?"

"More like his playground," explained Nebora. "It's the black dragon's favorite spot, it usually lands there instead of directly inside the castle like last time."

Cassandra immediately put down her teapot and grabbed her coat again, hurrying outside. Did this mean Krai was about to come back? Nebora and Prunie ran after her, but she was walking too fast. Nebora helped her find her a way outside to a little hill, where indeed, her Prince was standing still, a hand on his sword. He was looking at the sky when Cassandra walked up to him.

"My Lord?" she softly called him.

"Cassandra. What are you doing outside?"

It wasn't so cold though and she walked easily through the thin coat of snow to get to him. He grabbed her as soon as she was in his reach, pulling her against him.

"Are you waiting for Krai to come back, My Lord?"

"Look."

She turned her head up to where he was hinting at, a little dark shape appeared a couple of seconds later in the sky. Krai! It was obviously a dark dragon and she recognized its large size and way of agitating its tail even from such a distance. How high was it? It was slowly going down to them, getting closer with each flap of its wings. Cassandra felt her heart warm up a little as the dragon was coming down.

Something felt wrong, however. Krai was more agitated than usual. What was going on? It took her a while to realize a silhouette was standing on its back. Did the black dragon usually let someone ride it? Who was that?

With Krai coming closer, preparing to land, she finally recognized the feminine silhouette, totally surprised.

"...Princess Shareen?"

A minute later, there was no more place for doubt. Krai landed swiftly, though it immediately ran to Cassandra, disregarding its rider.

Imperial Princess Shareen didn't seem to be unbalanced, however. She got down with a little jump, landing perfectly on the snow. She was wearing a sexy purple dress and a little fur cape on her shoulders. She smirked upon seeing Cassandra, and Kairen next to her.

"Sister."

"Hello, handsome. Happy to see your older sister?"

"Shut it. How did it go?"

Shareen stopped smiling, crossing her arms.

"Not as we expected, unfortunately. Someone took it before us."

Kairen's anger on his face scared even Cassandra, who had no idea what was going on. She slowly stepped aside, as Krai kept nudging her with its head, growling softly, repeatedly asking for her attention.

"Who?" asked her Prince, not hiding his anger.

"Not one of our siblings. Vrehan was furious and Sephir had no idea. Anour even tried to help me retrieve it, but someone else got into the vault first. They left a clue though."

She stepped to him and gave him a little diamond. Kairen's anger seemed to calm down, as Shareen smiled.

"Bitchy as ever, isn't she?"

"Better her than anyone else."

Cassandra, who couldn't take it anymore, stepped forward again, glancing at the little diamond in Kairen's hand.

"My Lord, could you tell me what's going on? Something was stolen? From the Emperor's vault?"

"It doesn't belong to our father, but to you, sweetie."

"To me?"

Cassandra was confused. Why would something of hers ever be in the Emperor's vault in the first place? She had no idea what was going on. Shareen smirked and stepped closer to her with a cunning expression.

"You don't know, do you, sweetie? What's in our Imperial Father's vault?"

Cassandra shook her head, a bit lost. Behind her, Krai growled at Shareen, annoyed, but the Princess ignored it, playing with a strand of Cassandra's hair

166

around her finger.

"Our Imperial Father keeps everything in a very secret place, especially everything about dragons. That vault is kept by Glahad, our father's dragon, because it's connected to the Dragon's Nest."

"A nest?"

"This Empire's most precious things are Imperial Dragons," continued Shareen, "and their eggs. When a dragon is ready to have its egg, it goes to the nest, lays its egg, and protects it. So our father always knows when another dragon will be born."

Cassandra was completely astonished. She had no idea. She turned to Krai, putting the pieces together.

"You're saying... Krai went back to the Palace to ..."

"Lay an egg," said Kairen.

She was starting to understand, looking at the black dragon. But, dragons were linked to Imperial Family members? So, Krai laying an egg meant...

"Congrats," said Shareen with that little smirk of hers. "You're having my brother's brat."

Cassandra was floored. She was pregnant? With her Prince's baby? And Krai having an egg was proof of that? She turned to the dragon, which was still acting all clingy, asking for scratches from her. Kairen was still frowning though.

"But...What happened to Krai's egg, then?" she asked, worried.

"Somebody stole it before I got there," explained Shareen. "Once an egg appears, it becomes a race to see who will get to it first."

"Why would someone steal an egg?" asked Cassandra, confused.

"To try and destroy it," explained Kairen. "If our son's dragon is killed, he won't be acknowledged as an heir to the throne."

"No one wants Kairen to have an heir. Everyone knows Father would pick him as the next Emperor right away," sighed Shareen. "So, as soon as Krai had it, it was obvious everyone would try to get that egg. Someone got there before me though."

Cassandra glanced at the diamond. Who then? And what did they want with it?

"Who did..."

"Our mother," growled Kairen. "That old witch stole it."

Chapter 12

Cassandra was going a bit whiter than usual. She was pregnant with an Imperial Baby! Kairen's baby, and a little Prince, too, since only sons were born with a dragon... She couldn't believe it. They had been together for only a few weeks! And someone had already stolen the baby's dragon egg?

"Cassandra."

Her Prince's voice barely reached her. Everything was going too fast, too confusing. She slowly started going down, but Kairen caught her before her legs gave way completely. Krai was agitated around them, too. Going in circles around her, growling a bit. The War God carried her, turning to the castle to walk back.

Nebora was worried about her, biting her lips and frowning, yet she didn't dare to suggest anything on the way back. All four of them got back to Kairen's bedroom, where he helped Cassandra sit on his bed, Nebora immediately kneeling at her side. She put her arms around her stomach, frowning a bit.

"So I really am...pregnant? With His Highness' child?"

Shareen rolled her eyes.

"Unless he fucked someone else around here, yes, sweetie. An egg means a pregnancy and it was definitely Krai's. Hence, the brat is his Master's. And our mother wouldn't have bothered with it if it was anyone else's."

"Why would your mother take it?" asked Cassandra. "Shouldn't it stay with the dragon who...had it?"

"If you want it dead within three days, yes. Our father's vault is open to any Imperial Family Member, since it's guarded by Glahad. And his dragon will let any of his children in. That's six Princes and about twenty Princesses, mind you. And I wouldn't trust any of them near a dragon egg."

So any of their siblings could be after her baby...and his egg. Since she was living so far away, protected in the Onyx Castle, Cassandra had almost forgotten what a scary and dangerous place the Imperial Palace could be. She felt something cold inside her heart, a wave of fear surrounding her. This baby was only a few days old! What else would she have to face from now on? Could it be born safely?

Just when she was overwhelmed by those thoughts, Kairen surrounded her with his large thick fur cloak, covering her shoulders. She looked up at him, but her Prince had this dark look in his eyes. A War God expression. Cassandra took a deep breath in. She wasn't alone.

"Father wasn't too happy either," said Princess Shareen. "I bet Mother did it behind his back. His other concubines must be pissed, but at least they won't dare act against her."

"That damn woman," growled Kairen.

"It's still better with her than at the Palace," argued his sister.

"Can't we retrieve it?" asked Cassandra.

The siblings turned their eyes to her. Shareen crossed her arms with a smirk.

"Our mother is a stubborn bitch. She probably didn't take that egg just to have it as a decoration. Kairen never visits her."

That last sentence was actually directed at her brother, who was still frowning. Seeing as he wasn't responding, Shareen shrugged and laid on the bed next to Cassandra, her hands behind her head.

"Anyway, I've done my share. I think I'll stay here for a while. I'm bored of the Palace and your flying lizard is probably not taking me back anytime soon. Do you have any pretty girls? Other than this one."

She said that, pointing at Nebora, who promptly looked away. Cassandra decided to ignore Shareen's antics and turned to Kairen. She didn't really grasp what was truly at stake, but this egg was her child's future dragon. She hated not being able to confirm it was safe. Cassandra stood up and took a couple of steps to reach Kairen's side, taking the Prince's hand between hers.

"My Lord, please...can we at least make sure the egg is safe?"

For a while the Prince remained silent, his eyes stuck somewhere else. Then he turned to her.

"Are you content?"

His question took her by surprise. She had expected anything but that. What was he asking about? She couldn't understand until Kairen silently put his large hand on her stomach. She blushed. He meant her pregnancy! Cassandra hadn't even had time to think about this. What were her feelings on this matter? She was pregnant, expecting a child at seventeen! And an Imperial Baby, no less. Just a few weeks ago, Kairen had taken her virginity, but she hadn't even had time to picture herself bearing his children. She knew men of power needed heirs, but she wasn't even yet accustomed to the idea of being his concubine!

Yet...Cassandra was clear on how lucky she was. Of all people, Kairen was a strong and powerful man, yet he acted unexpectedly nice and gentle to her. After years of slavery, she had risen to the concubine status in just a few days. Moreover, she wasn't with a cruel or brutal man, but with him.

No, having his children wasn't anything bad. On the contrary, her feelings toward him had already blossomed, like tiny, shy flowers hidden in her heart. Bearing her Prince's child was a surprise and a blessing.

Cassandra slowly nodded, showing a gentle, serene smile. Kairen seemed relieved for a second, and kissed her gently.

"How boring," said his sister's annoyed voice behind them. "Are you going to see Mother then? I can't handle much more mushy stuff unless you move on to my favorite part. You know, the hot part."

Kairen glared at his sister.

"You are coming, too."

"Oh hell no, Brother. I think I'll stay here and enjoy my time with your..."

"Shareen."

His sister glared at him, but Kairen's voice did not allow another refusal from her. Cassandra felt a bit awkward, stuck between the Imperial Siblings. Nebora rolled her eyes, hoping they would just make a decision soon. Eventually, Shareen got up with a growl, her hands on her hips.

"Fine!"

She walked out, unhappy, the diamonds on her purple dress glittering as she left the room. Was she immune to the cold as well? Anyway, Cassandra was left alone with Kairen and Nebora in the room after the Princess' unhappy departure. Her servant friend got up and selected another coat for her from the closet, a large brown one.

"My mother lives an hour away," said Kairen.

"Not in the Palace?"

"Only when she feels like it."

What kind of woman could their mother be? Cassandra put on the coat, realizing it was a bit thinner than the previous one, as they were probably heading back to the South. Once she was ready, Kairen accompanied her downstairs, where Shareen was already waiting with a pout.

Next to her, Krai almost jumped to Cassandra as soon as it saw her. She smiled, caressing the huge snout. Was it acting more clingy than usual because of the baby?

Kairen cut short the dragon petting, helping her climb up its back and positioning himself behind her. Shareen, still on the ground, was unhappy.

"Damn it..."

She eventually climbed up too, behind her brother. Krai took off swiftly, Kairen firmly holding on to her, as Cassandra tried not to be as afraid as usual by the flight. She was always impressed by the height, but had learned to watch the horizon instead of the ground, and take deep breaths.

"Imperial Princesses aren't born with...dragons?" she asked Kairen.

"No."

"We have other talents, rather than taming flying lizards," answered Shareen from behind him.

She didn't bother to say what though. Did girls have something to

170

compensate for not being born with dragons? She had heard some of the Imperial Family had heavenly powers. Was it magic? So far, Cassandra had thought Shareen was like any woman, besides her birth status in the Imperial Family, obviously.

Resting against Kairen's chest and lost in her thoughts, she barely realized the trip was already coming to an end. Krai was flying low, over what seemed like a large village. In their line of sight, another castle was waiting. More like a palace, it was a light grey color with gold on its roof and lots of ivy everywhere. It was unlike anything Cassandra had seen before. It wasn't as hot as the Capital, or as cold as the Onyx Castle's location, hence the scenery was very green, filled with trees and plants. Cassandra immediately felt drawn to it.

The black dragon landed outside the castle, in what was apparently a large courtyard. Kairen helped Cassandra down, and she realized it was indeed a bit warmer here, though she still needed her coat. The air was filled with nice floral scents too. It was nothing like the stuffed and overwhelming Capital streets, or the desertic area around the Onyx Castle.

An old woman ran to them, followed by a handful of lower ranked maids.

"Welcome, Imperial Prince Kairen, Imperial Princess Shareen. The Imperial Concubine Mother is waiting for you."

Only then did she notice Cassandra, who had been standing behind Kairen. The old woman immediately bowed again.

"Welcome, Imperial Concubine."

This title felt very strange to Cassandra's ears. However, she didn't have to answer, the siblings confidently walked into the castle and Cassandra followed, a bit impressed.

This palace was very different. First, there weren't many enclosed areas. Every room had large openings and ivy running freely through the walls. It seemed as if most of those rooms had been abandoned and left to nature's goodwill until they reached the higher areas. Climbing a few stairs, they entered a spacious room with a balcony and a large table in the middle. It took a second for Cassandra to realize that the table was shining, the wood covered with thousands of little diamonds.

But most impressive, behind that table, on a large purple sofa, was sitting a tall woman. She had dark skin, her long hair was dyed a dark red shade and pulled up in a very artistic and complex hairdo, and wore a dark pink dress. Her thin lips were dark red, and her eyes were glaring at her children.

"Imperial Concubine Kareen, this is..."

"You think I wouldn't recognize my own children? No matter how unwilling they are to be here, they are still mine."

Her cold voice had the old woman and maids bow even lower. Her glare was still directed at Shareen and Kairen though.

"So? Nothing to say to your mother, after ignoring her for two years?"

"Where is the egg?" asked Kairen coldly.

His mother crossed her arms.

"That's it, Son of mine? Nothing else to say? You even went ahead and had the guts to get a concubine without my consent. You weren't so daring before. And you, Shareen? How many times have you ignored me?"

"I would see you more often if you came to the Palace, dear Mother," sighed the Princess.

"How impudent. I am the parent. I gave birth to both of you, shouldn't you show some respect and at least visit me, instead of having me go all the way there?"

"Father misses you," added Shareen with a smirk.

Her mother's grey eyes got even darker.

"See if I care about that old man!"

Cassandra was almost hiding behind Kairen, impressed by their fiery mother. This woman had such a temper! No one in this country would dare to say a bad word about the Emperor, yet she was throwing a fit so openly. Kairen and Shareen seemed used to it though, as neither of them reacted.

The Imperial Concubine took a deep breath, then her eyes fell on Cassandra.

"Is that her? Your young concubine they mentioned?"

Cassandra had no idea how to react. Who was "they"? She slowly stepped forward, seeing as no one was stopping her. Kairen was still close though, thus she felt a bit more confident. His mother wasn't too satisfied though.

"Come here, child. Let me see you from up close."

The Imperial Concubine's tone didn't leave Cassandra with much of a choice. Seeing how her Prince didn't react, the young Concubine walked closer to his mother, wondering what was expected of her.

"Let's see."

As soon as she was close enough, Concubine Kareen stood up to face her, and Cassandra realized how tall the woman really was. She looked a lot like her children too, with her tanned skin, straight nose, and angular jaw.

"She is too thin. Even for a slave. And your skin is very white. Are you from the south, child?"

"Yes, Imperial Concubine," said Cassandra, bowing slightly.

"Do not bow so low! You are an Imperial Concubine. Hold your rank. You look like anyone could trample all over you."

Cassandra blushed and straightened her back. The Imperial Concubine slowly walked around her, scrutinizing everything for what seemed like hours.

"These hips are so narrow. And you need to eat more. But, at least you're pretty."

Concubine Kareen let out a sigh and turned to her son.

"So? What is your excuse for not introducing her to your mother sooner, Kairen?"

But the Prince remained silent, only walking up to Cassandra to put an arm around her. His mother pursed her lips as she turned to Shareen.

"What about you, Daughter? Do you think I don't know how you behave

172

in the Palace?"

Shareen stayed silent like a child caught misbehaving, crossing her arms and looking everywhere else but at her mother.

"Mother. The egg."

Kairen's cold voice got his mother's attention. She turned to him with her hands on her hips.

"Is that all you came for? Well, I'm not going to just hand it over that easily. You'll all stay and have lunch with me for once. The one time you come to see your mother. "

She clapped her hands and a bunch of servants came in bowing.

"Actually, let's have lunch now. In the Courtyard."

Immediately, most of the servants rushed out to prepare their meal, only a few of them remained by the Imperial Concubine's side. She let out a dramatic sigh and turned to her children again.

"You two better behave. I am too old to scold you."

Cassandra couldn't help but wonder how old she actually was. She didn't look much older than her children! As Shareen and Kairen were probably in their mid-twenties, their mother could be about forty. Her make-up was lighter than what Cassandra had witnessed on other women of that age, too. She was a natural and overwhelming beauty.

"Come, let's go outside where it's warm. You must be cold all the time, living in that dark place."

Cassandra realized she was talking about the Onyx Castle. She followed after the Imperial Concubine, who was nonchalantly walking through the corridors to a large open area. As they walked, Cassandra noticed Kareen wasn't wearing shoes under her long pink dress, but her bare feet didn't seem to mind the uneven floor where the stone was sometimes crossed with patches of wild grass.

"Here, have a seat."

The Imperial Concubine's outdoor garden was a beautiful space. It had walls and pillars around it, but no roof. A few branches covered just enough of the sky to provide some shade and relief from the direct sun. It was like something out of a fairytale. The floor was only flowers and grass, and every surrounding inch had some green on it.

It seemed like the place had been abandoned for centuries to the wild, as the stones had weathered and ivy had taken over. Cassandra instantly loved it. Though she was feeling a bit shy and stuck close to Kairen, she couldn't help but glance at every little wild flower there.

"Sit here, child. What is your name?"

Concubine Kareen gestured to the seat right next to her, startling Cassandra a bit. As she took the seat, Kairen sat across from her to his mother's left. It was a round stone table of a decent size, not too big, but just cozy enough.

"Cassandra, Imperial Concubine," she answered.

"Cassandra. You'll call me Concubine Mother from now on."

"Yes, Concubine Mother."

Around them, the servants enthusiastically brought as much food as the table could hold. There was the usual cheese, meat, and fresh fruits, along with some dried fruits, vegetables, brown rice, and cakes. Just as Shareen was about to take some, a glare from her mother had her pull her hand back.

"Let's drink first."

Without delay, a glass of wine was placed into Cassandra's hands.

"Mother, do not force her to drink," said Kairen with a frown.

"It's fine. I had a cup once in a while when I was pregnant with you. This one isn't strong anyway, it's mostly juice. She can have some tea next."

Cassandra brought the smallest bit of wine to her lips and indeed, she did not taste the alcohol at all, only the sweet grape.

"Where are you from?" Concubine Kareen asked, as she took a sip of her own drink.

"From the Rain Tribe in the south. I was born there and was...brought to the Capital when I was a child, Concubine Mother."

"A Southern Tribe? How interesting. Your people were known for wonders in medicine and agriculture. How shameful that such bright people disappeared over those barbaric wars. Had you achieved any proficiency before that?"

"I did. I use my medical knowledge at the Military Camp, Concubine Mother."

Immediately, Imperial Concubine Kareen glared at her son.

"You took your concubine to the camp? Among so many men? I thought you knew better, Kairen!"

"She is my concubine. None of my men would dare to..."

"Of course not! But a military camp is still no place for a concubine! How selfish of you. You may be strong, but you underestimate others. Don't you know how easy it is to die? You are being naive, my son. Your concubine doesn't have the Dragon's blood!"

Cassandra looked down. The Concubine Mother seemed acutely aware of the struggle to survive that common people face. She was visibly irritated with her son and kept glaring at him, though Kairen didn't seem affected.

"Anyway. Your concubine shall stay here from now on."

"No."

Cassandra was caught between a new exchange of glares between mother and son, and they were totally overwhelming her. The Concubine Mother wanted her to stay here? Why? And for how long? Realizing her son wasn't going to give in, Kareen turned on him.

"You have grown up far too sheltered by your Father, Kairen. Do you know how hard it is to keep a child alive in this Empire? Your brothers will be after her like dogs after a bone! If she returns to the Palace, she will be killed within a day! If she stays at the Onyx Castle, I would give it a week before one of them sends an assassin after her. And the military camp? Even worse! They

174

could bribe any one of your men to do the job for them!"

Cassandra felt her heart grow cold at the thought. The Imperial Concubine Mother was telling the truth. Sooner or later, this pregnancy would put her in grave danger; she turned her eyes to Kairen, who was looking at her too.

"I'll protect her."

"Kairen, I raised two children to adulthood, despite all your father's other concubines. Do you think I don't know what kind of world this is? I lost three of your siblings to those wenches!"

Three? Imperial Concubine Kareen had lost three children? The Concubine seemed to be a strong and powerful woman! But if she couldn't even protect all of her offspring... Cassandra was even more worried.

Cassandra turned to her, trying to control her fear.

"Concubine Mother, please. I'm... I really want to protect this child. Someone has already tried to steal Krai's egg, and..."

"Did they?" asked Kareen, looking at her daughter.

Shareen had a smirk.

"Of course they did. Vrehan was furious."

"Then thank the Imperial Dragon, I got there before them."

"How did you know, Mother?" asked Kairen.

She rolled her eyes at him.

"Do you think I was born yesterday, my son? I know you. You never showed interest in any of the previous concubines your father gave you. Now you pick a slave, of all people, out of the blue? I knew it wouldn't be long until I had a grandchild on the way."

For the first time, Kareen directed what could have been a little smile Cassandra's way.

"Do not worry. I know the ways of the Palace, and those wenches won't get near you or my grandson. You'll be safe here, in the Diamond Palace."

"She is not..."

"She will stay here, Kairen. For her safety, and the safety of your child."

Cassandra was hesitant, but eventually she turned to the Concubine Mother.

"Concubine Mother, I am not sure. I still have many things I would like to do at the Onyx Castle and the military camp."

"And what might those be?" asked Concubine Kareen, unhappy.

Cassandra took a deep breath and told her about the hospital in the mountain and the farming issues at the Onyx Castle. She spoke about everything she had done and everything she wanted to do in the next few months. It was a lot for even her to think she could do so much with her current situation, but Cassandra had taken things to heart.

The Concubine Mother remained silent, listening to her. Shareen was mindlessly eating in the background, but Kairen was listening to Cassandra too.

"I see. Well, you certainly aren't a typical slave."

Cassandra blushed a bit, wondering if this was meant to be a compliment.

Kareen stayed silent for a while, looking at her with an enigmatic expression. Her dark eyes were harder to decipher than those of her children, Cassandra thought. After her silent contemplation, Kareen turned to Kairen.

"You picked well, Son. She has ambition, and the mind of an Empress."

She then turned to Cassandra again without waiting for him to respond.

"Yet, that is a dangerous way to think. You are protected by this Empire's War God and that is your only strength. Otherwise, this knowledge would get you killed. You know that, don't you?"

Cassandra nodded.

Yes. Her knowledge and past were all too dangerous to expose in this Empire. Even with Kairen, who protected her, she had been hesitant to reveal the truth. The Imperial Concubine sighed.

"Fine. Bring it in!" She ordered a servant.

A few minutes later, the elderly woman from earlier brought in a large case, and put it at their feet. Cassandra suddenly sensed a tremendous presence over them at the same time Krai's curious head popped over the wall, watching closely. Was the dragon interested in its egg?

The servant left and Concubine Kareen stood up and raised her hands to her head, plucking one of her hair pins out. Cassandra realized it was actually a very intricate key. Had she kept it there for safety? She opened the chest and Cassandra soon forgot her questions.

"There it is."

The egg was simply laid on some soft leather, but it looked hard enough that it wouldn't easily break. It was much larger than Cassandra had expected too! Bigger than any other animal's egg, and about the length of her forearm. It was not black like she had imagined, but a shiny grey, almost silver-like. She had thought a dragon's egg would be smooth, but it seemed to be covered in some strange substance, like a lustrous oily coating.

Cassandra couldn't resist the desire to touch it and, to her surprise, it actually reacted! Like a magnetic pull, something inside briefly moved at the slight touch of her finger tips. She was in total awe.

"Amazing, isn't it?" whispered Kareen. "Dragon Eggs are among the greatest wonders of this world..."

"When will it hatch?" asked Cassandra.

"When you give birth...if you do. Dragons are linked to their Masters. If the child dies before birth, the egg will use this coating to self-destruct."

"What if the baby dies...after?"

Kareen's eyes darkened.

"Let's not have such somber talk. For now, we just need to make sure that your child sees the light of day in a few months' time. That is, if my son comes to his senses and allows you to remain here instead of behaving like a headstrong teenager..."

Kairen was glaring at his mother, visibly annoyed by her words. Cassandra, however, was hesitating. She was reluctant to part from Kairen, but for the sake

176

of their baby, wouldn't it be better for her to stay here? How was the Concubine Mother so sure she would be safer in the Diamond Palace instead of the Onyx Castle?

Seeing her uncertainty, Kareen rolled her eyes.

"Enough! I haven't seen my children in a while. All three of you will stay here for a few days and I am not asking! Krai too."

Hearing its name, the dragon turned its head to the Concubine Mother and purred softly in her direction as she smiled.

"That's right, I missed you too, little one."

Cassandra wondered if Krai's attitude towards her meant Kairen loved his mother more than he let on. The Imperial Concubine turned to Cassandra again, frowning as she looked at her slave collar. She pointed it out with her finger, displeased.

"This! We need to get rid of this as well when we go to the Imperial Palace for the New Year celebration."

Hearing this, Shareen almost choked on her wine. Kairen seemed shocked too.

"Mother, you will be going back? To see Father?"

"Who said anything about seeing that old man? I am going there to attend the celebrations, and to show off my future grandchild to all those whores at the Imperial Palace."

"As if," said Shareen. "If you show up without going to see Father, he'd send the entire army to fetch you!"

Her mother shrugged, not phased at all. Cassandra was speechless! Their mother was so strong-willed, she would even dare to ignore the Emperor himself! She then instructed them to eat, essentially closing the topic. While eating her little bites, Cassandra tried to remember how much longer until the New Year celebrations. She felt like her time at the camp had been months, longer than the couple of weeks it actually was. As she took the time to count exactly how many days had passed, she realized the celebrations would be held only two months from now. How big would her baby be in two months? And the dragon's egg? Cassandra wondered if the Baby Dragon would look like a miniature Krai.

As they ate silently, Cassandra felt a bit more at ease. The Concubine Mother was a very strong-willed woman, scolding her children for bad posture, and was cold towards the servants. She was nice to Cassandra though, as if she respected her from the start, and ignored her slave status completely. She urged Cassandra to eat more though; insisting she consume more of the dry fruits as they were, according to Kareen, very nutritious for babies.

"Don't Southerners eat meat?" she asked, noticing Cassandra had barely touched it.

"No, Concubine Mother. I'm more used to eating fish...In small quantities, though."

"Hmpf. That explains your good skin, thin build, and character. It is said eating fish helps with all those. Too much meat makes children stubborn. Just look at these two."

Right as she said that, both Kairen and Shareen, who happened to have meat in their hand or mouth, sent glares back to their mother.

Kareen sighed. "Anyhow, just let me know what you want to eat, I'll have servants go fetch it for you."

"Actually...could I go buy it myself?" asked Cassandra, a bit embarrassed.

The Concubine Mother looked at her, confused.

"Why?"

"I just...I like going to the markets. Looking at the stalls, and all."

After a few seconds of contemplation, Kareen chuckled.

"You really are a new kind of concubine, aren't you? Fine, we'll go later. A little outing will do me some good as well. But first, dessert!"

Cassandra wondered exactly how much she was expected to eat! More delicious food was brought out - so many fruits, nuts and cakes that she had to drink some tea to help it all go down. She would definitely get plump if she spent her pregnancy in the Diamond Castle!

After she was done eating, Concubine Kareen stood up, elegantly wiped her lips, and turned to her children.

"I'm going to take a walk in my garden. Don't any of you even think of leaving. And anyway, I'll be taking Krai with me."

Under Cassandra's surprised eyes, Kareen walked over to Krai's head, caressing its snout. The dragon closed its eyes, growling softly like it usually did with Cassandra. It really seemed to like the Concubine Mother. She walked out of the Garden, using an opening between the stones to meet with the Dragon behind the wall. Though she couldn't see Kareen anymore, Cassandra watched Krai as it bounded down from the wall, its big back turning around to follow her.

"This place is so boring," sighed Shareen. "I'm going to take a nap in my room until Mother comes back."

They watched as Shareen retired, leaving Cassandra alone with her Prince. So they couldn't take the egg and leave while she was away, Kareen had locked it in the chest and had the servants take it back inside while they were dining.

Cassandra walked up to Kairen, who pulled her down to sit on his leg.

"We will get it back soon," said the Prince, holding her by her waist.

"It's okay. As long as it's safe with Concubine Mother."

Kairen nodded, caressing her long hair down her back.

"Do you want to stay here?" he asked softly.

"I'm not sure. I want to stay here, for our baby's safety, but... I also want to take care of the hospital, and I know I'll miss the girls at the Onyx Castle."

He didn't reply to that and instead gently kissed her shoulder, lost in his own thoughts. Since his mother had insisted that they stay a while, they could always decide later. She wouldn't be able to keep Kairen here much longer and Cassandra would have to make her decision before then.

They stayed like this for a while, gently caressing and holding each other, lost in their own little world. Kairen seemed gentler and more caring since her pregnancy had been announced, and Cassandra was feeling a bit more confident too. She even wondered if she could find people to teach medicine to here.

"Were you here often?" she asked, looking at the garden around them.

"When I was younger... My father gifted it to my mother after my birth. "

"This castle?"

"This city. It's the place where she was born."

The Imperial Family's standards were truly too extravagant for her to grasp! Cassandra was once again speechless. So not just a castle, but a whole city was their mother's? Shareen and Kairen had probably spent most of their childhoods here in that case.

"How did your mother become a concubine?"

"She worked as a servant for one of my father's counselors. He noticed her. She was smarter than most, and not afraid to voice her opinion. She actually became his counselor for a while, before becoming his concubine."

Cassandra nodded. The story suited his mother's impressive character and also explained why she didn't care much about Cassandra's slave status, since she had been a servant herself. She truly was an admirable woman.

"Can we take a walk? I'd like to see the rest of the Castle."

Kairen silently agreed and stood up, still holding her around her waist. Cassandra ventured back into the Castle, noticing two female servants silently following them from a few steps back. Had Kareen given instructions for the pair to attend to them? They strolled around for a while and the more Cassandra saw, the more she liked it. She had thought upon their arrival that it felt like this place had been abandoned for years and left to the wild. Few rooms were entirely enclosed and most had spaces where stones in the walls were missing or parts of the roof were open so that they were bright and airy. Ivy ran through the walls freely and trees grew up against the walls, their branches replacing missing sections of roof to provide some shade. Unlike the Imperial Palace, there weren't many signs of wealth, except for a few richly decorated rooms. There was nothing else on display and even the furniture was very basic, made of just wood and comfortable fabrics.

To Cassandra's surprise, Kairen pushed a large door open and they walked in.

"This is my room."

It was rather empty despite all the available space, but had a large bath carved out in a corner with a fountain that had dried up. Kairen's old bed was very much like the one at the Onyx Castle, large and with furs on it.

In another corner was what looked like a very large nest that was well worn out and tattered, and Cassandra guessed that this might have been Krai's bed when he was younger...and smaller. Aside from those, there was only a wardrobe and a chest on a carpet in the other corner. It was even emptier than his bedroom in the Onyx Castle.

Cassandra ventured further inside, still more curious, while Kairen stayed a few steps back, watching her.

"So this is...where you grew up?"

"I liked it better than the Palace."

"Why?" she asked inquisitively.

"Less people. Only Mother and us."

She could easily picture how different from the Imperial Palace this place was. Less people also meant less danger for the Imperial Children.

Cassandra turned around and walked back to the War God. He put his hands on her shoulders, feeling her skin was a bit colder than usual.

"Don't get sick."

"I won't."

Kairen pulled her into his embrace, warming her up instantly. Cassandra laid her head against him, closing her eyes and tenderly holding on to her Prince.

"I wish our child could come into this world safely," she sighed.

Unknown to her, Kairen frowned. Cassandra rarely opened up about her insecurities like this, but if she was already concerned about their child coming into the world... He held her a bit tighter. He would definitely make sure both of them were all right.

As promised, the Imperial Concubine took Cassandra to walk around the markets accompanied by an army of servants and her children. While Shareen didn't hide her boredom, Kairen simply followed Cassandra like a shadow, touching her sometimes as if to reassure her that he was there. The little group observed the many stalls with interest and, to Cassandra's surprise, the townspeople didn't seem alarmed to see the Imperial Concubine wandering among them.

They kneeled as they were supposed to in front of the Imperial Family members, but it was obvious that they were used to dealing with Concubine Kareen. She was familiar with some of the merchants too, and many people personally greeted her when they saw her. She was very respected around here.

Cassandra was starting to grow fond of her and her unique character too. She could easily see how Kairen and Shareen had grown into the personalities they had, so different from those of their siblings. Their mother was very cynical, down-to-earth, and forthright.

Cassandra also appreciated that she spoke to her as if they were equals, showing great interest in her knowledge about plants and spices.

"For the skin?" she said doubtfully, as Cassandra was showing her some yellow spice.

"Yes. Turmeric is good for cooking, but it also helps with skin inflammation and redness, and you can drink it as tea."

"Interesting. Let's buy some, I want to try it. I'm old enough to start showing some wrinkles soon."

She was far from looking old though. Concubine Kareen was one of the most beautiful women Cassandra had ever seen, even among the court ladies.

She had a cold, natural beauty, with unique traits. Her hair was colored with that enigmatic deep red color, without an ounce of white to be seen.

They walked up to the next stall where some jewelry was laid out. The merchant immediately started showing his goods to the Concubines, but neither of them were really interested.

Suddenly, a ruckus started behind them. Cassandra, afraid, turned around but the commotion was over in an instant. She heard a snap followed by a man being pinned to the ground, Kairen's foot on his back and Shareen's whip around his throat.

Not impressed at all, Kareen turned around and looked at the man. The knife he had held in his hand had fallen at her feet. She picked it up, observed it, then swung it around.

"Who sent you?"

The man stayed silent. The Imperial Concubine exchanged a glance with her daughter and Shareen smirked before tightening the whip. The man's face started turning blue as he began to suffocate.

"Talk. I won't have any guilt killing you slowly and very painfully, and whoever paid you knew that."

"I...I don't..."

Kareen sighed as the man struggled to talk.

"I...don't...kn...know..."

"How useless. Who was your target, then?"

The man tried to stay silent once more, struggling to breathe, but his eyes betrayed him. In a split second, he had glanced at Cassandra, but immediately avoided her returning stare.

She stepped back, shocked. She had only been there for a couple of hours! How could an assassin already have come to kill her?

"What shall we do with him, Mother?" asked Shareen.

"Whatever you want. Let's go back before another one comes out though."

Kareen turned back towards the Palace and started walking. Cassandra, still in shock, had her eyes riveted on the man. However, Kairen stepped between them, gently pushing her to follow in his mother's tracks. After a few steps, she heard a whip slashing through the air and people screaming. Kairen kept her from looking back though, blocking her view and holding her by her waist so that they continued forward.

Back at the Castle, it was as if nothing had happened, but Cassandra couldn't stop worrying.

"How do they already know?" she asked. "Why would they attack so soon?"

"Those people have rats everywhere, especially where their rivals are concerned. They know this is my city and since I took the egg, they knew Kairen would come, and you with him."

Cassandra felt a chill run through her. To think people were already hunting her down... hunting her unborn child! She knew the rivalry between the

Imperial Family was terrible, but experiencing it firsthand was something else.

In fact, the reason the Emperor had so many more daughters than sons was because the boys were hunted from birth. The six Princes that were alive today had all been through a lot to make it to adulthood, as had their mothers. The Emperor had many concubines, but no Empress, so in the race to the Golden Throne, all six brothers were almost equal. However, having heirs definitely gave them an advantage.

And she was carrying one of the Emperor's grandsons. It wouldn't just be during her pregnancy, Cassandra would be targeted for the rest of her life for being a Prince's Concubine. No wonder it was such a dangerous position.

She had been replaying these thoughts in her head until they had got back to the Diamond Castle and Kareen insisted on her taking a nap.

"Just go and rest in my son's room. A mother-to-be shouldn't experience too many emotions in a day, and with this afternoon's fight, you must be tired. I'll have a bath drawn for you before dinner."

Cassandra silently nodded, and Kairen escorted her back to his room.

She sat on his bed, still frowning, worried and confused. To her surprise, her Prince kneeled down in front of her.

"My Lord, don't kneel!"

"We're alone," he said, ignoring her plea. "Tell me what's wrong."

Cassandra only hesitated a second before giving in.

"That man... He wanted to hurt our baby."

"Yes."

"How many more will come to try and hurt him?"

"Aren't you afraid for yourself?"

She shook her head, putting a hand on her belly.

"I've never been scared for myself. Before today, I... No, before meeting you, I was never afraid of death. But, now that I'm carrying this child, everything is so different. I'm really afraid something bad will happen to your son."

The Prince sighed and wrapped his arms around her waist. With her thin build, he easily trapped her in his embrace, yet he was nothing but gentle with her.

"I'll protect you... and our son. Mother will, too."

Cassandra smiled gently at him, but it was a smile that held some pain in it too. She caressed his cheek, her heart feeling a bit lighter, just from the feeling of his skin under her finger tips.

"I know...but...this is a cruel world. I'm afraid that this baby will suffer. I just wish he could be born safely, grow up healthy and without worry."

Cassandra shook her head. This was really too hard. Now, it wasn't only her own safety at stake, but that of her baby as well. Even if she was having a hard time accepting it, she was pregnant with her Prince's child. A potential future heir to the whole Empire, yet he was still nothing but a defenseless baby right now.

Kairen suddenly stood up and reached for her, enveloping her in his arms without warning. Cassandra was taken by surprise by his big hands holding her, but she was used to it and let herself go, allowing him to comfort her. When she could finally retreat a bit, she observed him, blushing a bit from being so close.

"I'll protect you," he assured her again. "Cassandra. You're mine... and this child is ours. I won't let anything happen to our son. Do you think I would let anything happen to you?"

She realized he was expecting a response, asking how much she trusted him at that moment. Somehow, it made her feel better and she finally relaxed a bit.

"No. I know you will protect our baby."

"I'll protect both of you...forever. I only need you. And our child. And any other children you'll give me."

Cassandra blushed uncontrollably. Not just this one, but her Prince wanted more children with her! She nodded with a smile. She did trust him. Trusted the War God, the one man who had protected her all this time.

She leaned in to kiss him, a long, sweet and sensual kiss. Of course he responded, caressing her. Slowly, Kairen pushed her on the bed, holding her tightly and grazing every inch of her body. Each of his moves were so gentle, yet passionate. She felt her body getting warmer.

"Stay here," he whispered.

"What?"

"Stay here. At the Diamond Palace with my mother and Shareen. They'll protect you, too."

"You think I'll be safer here?"

He shook his head, still holding her and caressing her hips.

"Just...for now. I will come back for you in a few days. I need to see my father."

"Why?"

Kairen shook his head. Whatever he wanted to tell his father, he wasn't ready to tell Cassandra yet. She wondered what it was, but didn't dare pry. She only nodded, closing her eyes and resting her head on his shoulder, where she could feel his warmth and inhale his scent. Cassandra felt much better now that they had talked and she never felt as comfortable and secure as when she was in the Prince's arms. Kairen, gently pulling his fingers through her hair, helped her fall asleep, but the Prince wasn't ready for a nap himself. He kept his eyes open, dark as shadows, thinking of what to do next.

When she woke up a couple hours later, Cassandra was surprised to find Kairen gone. The Prince had left during her rest, according to the servant who woke her up.

His mother, however, was waiting for her at dinner with Shareen. Both women seemed aware that Kairen was gone, making Cassandra feel a bit better about it, though she wished he had said goodbye before going.

"You will stay here for now," announced Kareen, as the three women finished eating. "As discussed, I will keep you safe and make sure your child grows healthily. Outside threats won't get into this Palace."

"Excuse me, Concubine Mother, but...how are you so sure? This man, back at the market, he attacked us so easily."

"The market is the market. This Palace is my domain. No one comes in or out without my permission, and I have the highest security."

Just as Cassandra was about to ask a question, a large shadow suddenly appeared above them. She almost jumped, taken by surprise. It wasn't Krai. The dragon stared at them from above the stone wall looking grumpy. This dragon was much smaller, about the size of three large dogs, dark purple, and with yellow eyes like a cat. Cassandra felt strange. How did the Concubine Mother have a dragon?

"This is Sraï. He is the guardian of this Palace...and an avid eater of intruders."

As she said that, the dragon softly growled and Shareen smirked.

"I wondered if he was still stuck to you, Mother. He is so tiny, but he makes a good watchdog, I guess."

Her mother responded with a glare.

"You too, Shareen. You will stay here and make sure Cassandra stays safe."

"Me? I am not a concubine's bodyguard!"

"Unless I say so," warned her mother. "Do you want to upset me, Daughter?"

The two exchanged glares for several long, unsettling seconds. Cassandra felt badly, caught between the two of them, but didn't dare to say a word before one of them.

"Ugh... Fine!" Shareen finally conceded.

Chapter 13

A few weeks later, Kairen still hadn't returned.

Cassandra was growing lonely, sitting by herself in the Imperial Concubine's garden. No matter how many times she had been told not to worry, she couldn't help but stare at the horizon, beyond the City's high walls.

She had changed over the past few weeks. Under her new guardian's insistence, she had started taking better care of herself. She was now used to wearing the beautiful red gowns and jewelry. Every morning, servants would help her dress, put a bit of pink balm on her lips, and brush her hair, suggesting a few hair pins or bracelets, until Cassandra couldn't take it anymore and ushered them out to finish her preparations alone. She had finally put on a few pounds too. How could she not have? Kareen made sure she ate plenty at each meal and brought her snacks at all times of day. Cassandra had only recently found a way to stop her overbearing actions by faking some nausea.

Truthfully though, she really was nauseous at times, especially in the morning. Her tummy had developed a little bump as proof of her pregnancy, making this child feel a bit more real each day.

Cassandra was caressing her belly, lost in her thoughts when Kareen walked in.

"Concubine Mother."

"Good Morning. What are you doing out so early without a shawl?"

Though she was asking Cassandra, her glare found a servant, who immediately ran inside to get one. But the young concubine shook her head.

"I am fine, really. It's much warmer here than it was at the Onyx Castle."

Cassandra missed it. She wondered everyday about Nebora and the others, and the Military Camp. How did they function without the Prince there? Perhaps he had visited during these weeks and didn't stop by the Diamond Palace?

"So stubborn," sighed the Concubine Mother.

She was about to add something else, but at that same moment, Srai jumped from over the balcony. The Purple Dragon struggled for a few seconds to come in, balancing strangely on the ledge. With his torn wing and uneven weight, the dragon never seemed particularly agile. It eventually managed to get on its feet, and walked to sit by Kareen's side.

Cassandra felt uneasy anytime she watched that dragon. It didn't like her and, up until now, had only interacted with her through warning growls and defiant glares. Even as the Imperial Concubine caressed it, it seemed restless.

"Good boy," said Kareen.

"The dragon...Srai cannot fly, can it?" asked Cassandra.

She had doubts as she certainly had never seen it actually use its wings and Srai never hunted either, only wandered around the Palace letting servants feed him huge portions of meat.

"That is correct. He lost the ability, his wings are too damaged now to support his weight. The child cannot hunt."

"Concubine Mother, is he..."

"He was my first born, Suiren's, dragon. He died at six years old."

Cassandra was struck by those revelations. Six years old? So young! How could a Prince die at such a young age? Kareen, as if she had guessed her silent question, sighed.

"He was killed! Someone threw my child from a balcony like this one."

Cassandra looked at the balcony Kareen was gesturing to. It wasn't something a child could climb over by himself! How could someone be so cruel as to murder a child so brutally?

"My second one... She was a girl. She was killed two days after she was born. Someone got into my room and suffocated her with a pillow."

A pillow? Cassandra felt nauseous. Who would...? To a newborn! She felt sick just thinking about it.

"After Shareen, I was pregnant with another son. I was beyond paranoid about protecting my children, but it wasn't enough. He was poisoned at two years old. His dragon died instantly with him."

How horrible! Cassandra wondered what Kairen's childhood could have been like in such dangerous conditions.

Strangely, however, Kareen didn't seem affected while revealing all of this. Instead, pure anger was painted across her face. Cassandra glanced at the small dragon sitting by her feet. Krai's older sibling was so small compared to him.

"Who dares to..."

Both women glared at the incoming shadow in the sky. Cassandra instantly knew it wasn't Krai, as its tail shape was different. When he got closer, she realized it was a Green Dragon, one that she had seen in the Arena.

"Anour?" wondered a voice behind them.

Shareen had just come out, squinting at the incoming Dragon. It landed outside of the Palace, but neither woman went to him. Instead, Kareen went to wait in a large room by the entrance. Settling into a large wooden chair, Kareen ordered Cassandra to sit next to her while Shareen stood to the side.

"Concubine Mother! Sister Shareen!"

Prince Anour was the youngest of the Imperial Princes and barely resembled Kairen. He had a nice smile and a thin build like his Green Dragon, which looked more like a lizard.

"Anour! What about your manners?"

"Don't be mean, Concubine Mother. I came to give you news about my brother."

"Is he alright?" Cassandra immediately asked, visibly worried.

Anour, surprised that she dared to address him, gave her a glance of disgust.

"Who is that?"

"Have you gone blind brother, or is it that little boys can't see red?" said Shareen.

"Oh, is this brother's concubine? I didn't recognize her! So she is the pregnant one?"

"Anour, enough. Where is my son, you impertinent child?"

"Father got angry with him. He sentenced him to be hung in the dungeons for fifty days, with Imperial Servants whipping him ten times every hour."

"HOW DARE HE!?" roared Kareen.

Meanwhile, Cassandra was on the verge of tears. Whipped? Her Prince had been detained and whipped relentlessly since then? Only Shareen didn't seem affected, stifling her laughter in the corner.

"Looks like Father is really desperate for your attention, Mother."

"He shall see! That old fool will pay for touching my son!"

Her anger echoed within the walls, and she stood up to her full height causing Anour to shrink a little.

"Concubine Mother, this is a bit..."

"Silence! Don't you dare say a word to defend him! Roun!"

To Cassandra's surprise, a wall of green scales appeared on the other side of the door, the Imperial Concubine rushing to it.

"She can command any of the dragons?" Cassandra asked Shareen.

"Of course not. Only those she raised listen to her. Anour's mother was murdered when he was an infant. Our mother took care of him and Roun in her stead, as she and his mother were close."

Cassandra realized Anour's mother had probably been killed in the race to the throne as well.

Kareen was determined as she stood before the large Green Dragon. Cassandra hesitated a bit before eventually following, seeing that Shareen was also accompanying her mother.

It was smaller than Krai, probably because it was younger, but still quite sizable, with a leaner face, and its wings and tail had a different shape. The little dragon turned its head to Kareen, intrigued, swishing its tail left and right.

"Concubine Mother!" called Anour.

"Let's go. We shall see if that damn Emperor dares to injure my precious son again!"

She was obviously dead set on flying to the Imperial Palace. Before the young Prince could even protest, she had taken her place on the dragon's back, and Shareen was helping Cassandra on too.

He sighed, and climbed up. Four people was still nothing for the dragon, who took off right away, visibly excited. Cassandra couldn't help but feel nauseous as it was her first flight in a while and on a different beast, too. Moreover, she was concerned about Kairen. It wasn't until Shareen stroked her back that she was pulled from her thoughts.

"Are you okay? You're paler than usual."

"I'm just...worried about him."

"What are you worried for? Our father is just using him to get Mother's attention, but he won't go overboard. My brother is absolutely fine."

But Cassandra couldn't be comforted, even as they landed at the Imperial Palace. She hadn't been back there in a while and didn't hold many good memories about it. She followed the Imperial Concubine and her children who hurried inside.

A few Imperial Servants tried to stop Kareen.

"Imperial Concubine, you can't walk in unannounced like this.The Imperial Emperor is busy..."

"He is busy? If he is so busy he should have let my son be! How dare he abuse my child!"

Her yelling had every Imperial Servant running away in fear. Kareen stormed through the Palace with no one daring to stop her. Cassandra even witnessed several concubines turning around with terrified expressions as soon as they saw her.

Shortly, they arrived at the Grand Hall's main gates. Cassandra's heart beat louder, filled with worry.

"You old Dragon!" roared Kareen while throwing the gates wide open.

It was quite a unique sight to behold.

The Emperor, sitting on his golden throne, spat out his wine upon hearing her. It was the first time Cassandra was able to really take a good look at him. Previously, she had to keep her eyes down because of her slave status, but now that she was wearing a red dress and accompanied by Imperial Concubine Kareen, she wasn't as afraid to look.

She was surprised. She had expected a much older man, maybe around sixty or seventy, especially since he already had so many children. However, the man didn't look a day over fifty! She was speechless. How could that be? He had children older than Kairen!

"K...K...Kareen?"

Seeing him stuttering like that, he looked like a teenager caught doing something wrong. At his feet, a handful of young women, who were holding plates of fruits or instruments, went completely white at the sight of the Imperial Concubine. They all stood up and retreated, as if some dangerous beast had come into the room. Cassandra, however, had her eyes set behind them. Krai!

The Black Dragon had already turned to her, growling and struggling to come closer. Despite the attempts, Krai was unable to budge, a much larger beast actually trapping it on the ground - the Imperial Golden Dragon, Glahad.

Cassandra was shocked! Krai was big, very big, but Glahad was massive. The golden dragon was the size of a large building and covered in gold scales. Its ruby eyes were the most beautiful thing she had ever seen and also the most terrifying. She was used to Krai, and had learned not to fear the Black Dragon, but Glahad was another level of scary. It was a mythical creature, a God who could decide between life and death in a single bite. When it turned its head towards them, she couldn't help but stumble a few steps back.

"Kareen! You...you're back, my dearest!" exclaimed the Emperor, visibly overjoyed.

He didn't even seem to see his Concubine's angry face as he stood up, smiling wide from ear to ear.

"You should have told me. I would have gathered a few presents, or ordered a celebration..."

"A celebration? A celebration for what?! How you're abusing my dearest son? Hmm? You cold hearted, selfish old man!"

As she kept yelling, Glahad, from his perch upon Krai, abruptly spotted her. The dragon's eyes immediately changed, opening wide while staring. Shareen grabbed Cassandra's arm and had her step even further back, her eyes fixed on her father's Dragon.

The next second, Glahad jumped, almost running to Kareen with a long growl. Though it was scary to see a Dragon of this size run at them, Cassandra immediately recognized the behavior. It was the same impulsive affection Krai often displayed towards her. The Golden Dragon ran until Kareen suddenly turned her head towards it, glaring fiercely.

"Don't you dare, you rascal!"

Instantly, Glahad dug its paws and claws into the perfect wooden floors, grinding to a halt a few meters away from Kareen. The dragon was frozen in an awkward pose, with its body turned towards her, but its collar and head turned away, like a guilty dog. It kept trying to sneak glances at her, but had to turn its red gaze away every time, as the Concubine was glaring. Behind Glahad, Krai furtively took this opportunity to throttle towards Cassandra, wrapping its body around the Concubine as she scratched and caressed its head, happy to reunite with her Prince's Dragon. Meanwhile, Glahad softly growled, jealous, but Kareen had already turned back to the Emperor.

"Where is my son?!"

The Emperor looked baffled, surprised even. He clearly wasn't expecting his Concubine's anger and stared at her with a confused expression.

"Kareen, dearest, I..."

"Answer me!"

Cassandra couldn't help but think about how exceptionally bold Kareen was. Was she some Hell Goddess reincarnated? To be talking to the Emperor like this, you needed to have a few extra lives!

The man sighed.

"Kareen, don't be like this. You know I don't want to be mean, hmm? But how else could I get your attention? And see! Even mad, you're so pretty!"

"Oh, you want to see me mad? Come closer and I'll yank your hair out! Now, give me my son back, you deceitful snake!"

"I get it, dearest, but please stop screaming, you'll hurt your pretty little voice. If we want to be able to have a nice chat later, we should..."

"A nice chat? You force me to come all the way here to retrieve my son and you expect me to sit down and idly chat with you? How dare you!"

"Oh, come now, I'll have your favorite garden prepared. How about that? With your favorite tea, too! Do you want a massage? I have a young lady who can do wonders..."

"Ha! Now you want to brag about your new concubines to me? That's just a bit too much! You think I'll die of jealousy? Huh?"

Meanwhile to the side, Krai was happily growling and rubbing against Cassandra's hands, and sending glances towards Kareen too, gently pushing her with its snout. Glahad, however, was still sitting a few steps away from the Imperial Concubine Mother and was glaring at it with jealousy. The Imperial Golden Dragon growled several times, but Krai ignored it, too absorbed by Cassandra.

When Glahad had finally had enough, it reached out a paw, aiming its claws at Krai's rear, but the Black Dragon growled back. The two started bickering, making an awful lot of noise in the room and no matter how angry Kareen and the Emperor were, two adults yelling couldn't possibly be heard over the ruckus.

That's when the Emperor, suddenly taking on a very annoyed expression, turned to them.

"Enough!"

Both dragons froze, but Krai was still childishly growling, curling its body around Kareen and Cassandra with a defiant look. Glahad walked back behind the throne with a sullen expression, but stayed silent. The Emperor sighed, turning to Shareen.

"My daughter, go get your brother before your mother really gets angry at me."

One could have argued the Imperial Concubine was already angry enough, but Shareen simply left the room, Cassandra following closely behind her. The Princess seemed to know exactly where to go, heading down several staircases and crossing corridors in record time.

They arrived at the dungeons a short while later. It was cold and sinister down there. Shareen gave some orders to the Imperial Servants and they guided

190

her to a large cell.

"My Lord!" yelled Cassandra.

As soon as the door was opened, she ran inside. Kairen was there, hanging by his wrists from the ceiling. He seemed unconscious, but Cassandra was more worried about the number of dark scale lines on his skin. How many times had he been whipped?

She started crying while Shareen looked on, dumbfounded.

"What is wrong with you? Stop crying, he's fine!"

Fine? How was he fine? But Shareen rolled her eyes and walked over, taking her own whip out. Before Cassandra could react, Shareen violently slashed her brother's arm. A few seconds later, the red mark was already covered in black scales.

"What are you doing?! He's already unconscious from..."

"What? Unconscious?" retorted Shareen, satirically. "The idiot is asleep!"

Asleep...? Cassandra stepped closer to Kairen. His eyes were closed, he was breathing slowly and almost...snoring. Snoring! How could he be sleeping in these conditions? His sister rolled her eyes again and slapped his biceps a few times.

"Kairen, you idiot! Wake up, your precious woman is here crying because of you!"

It took a few seconds, but the Prince finally opened his eyes to Cassandra's relief. He frowned, surprised to see her there.

"Cassandra....?"

"My Lord! My Lord, are you alright? Does it hurt?"

"Stop with the pity party, you two, it's annoying," said Shareen. "And you, Brother, what were you thinking? Why would you let yourself be whipped?"

Kairen was focused on Cassandra, ignoring his sister. Seeing her tears flowing, he became angry and confused.

"Cassandra, why are you crying? Who did this to you?"

He struggled a bit with the shackles holding him and then all of a sudden, they snapped with a loud metallic crack, shocking her. Freed, the Prince landed on his feet in front of her, immediately brushing his hands on her cheeks.

"You...you could free yourself?" asked Cassandra in surprise.

"Of course. You think those shackles could restrain a Dragon Master?" sighed Shareen. "So silly. Anyway, I'll be on my way now."

His sister left the cell and headed back into the Imperial Palace, but neither of them paid her any attention. Cassandra was still speechless, looking at him confused, while Kairen caressed her cheeks, trying to understand the cause of her tears.

"Are you injured? Who made you cry?" he kept asking unrelentingly.

All of a sudden, Cassandra pushed his hands away, angry.

"I was worried about you! I thought you were actually hurt! And...and I was waiting and worried! How could you stay here when you could have just freed yourself?"

All she could think about was how the Imperial Family was too much. Who lets themself be whipped and trapped without complaint? And not even try to get free for weeks! How could Kairen be so heartless and not even think of her feelings? Cassandra turned her back to him, both angry and embarrassed. His Highness had gone too far!

"Cassandra..."

Seeing her enraged was a first for Kairen. He was now feeling a bit guilty and had no idea how to make up for it. He put his arms around her, resting his hands on her little baby bump.

"Sorry... Father really wanted to see Mother..."

Cassandra turned around, scowling.

"Don't tell me... All of this was only to have the Concubine Mother come here?"

Kairen nodded.

"It was the only way my father could think of to compel her to come."

"Why did you agree to it?"

"Because he said if I helped him, he would agree to my demands. Come."

Worried about her staying too long in the cold dungeons, Kairen gently ushered Cassandra out and guided her back into the Castle. They walked for a few minutes, until they reached what looked like a little reading nook or tea salon, with two women in red dresses inside.

"Get out," growled Kairen.

They left in a hurry, keeping their eyes on the floor. The Prince then gently guided Cassandra to sit in the middle of a little pile of brightly colored cushions. Taking to his knees in front of her, he grabbed her hands and started tenderly kissing them. Frowning a bit, Cassandra pushed him away.

"I'm still upset, My Lord. How could you have agreed to that? I was worried for weeks!"

But Kairen only smirked, caressing her hair.

"Did you miss me?"

"It's not funny!" Cassandra pouted, throwing one of the little cushions at him. "I was really worried..."

"I get it...I'm sorry. I apologize."

Cassandra looked away from him, her cheeks flushed from a mix of anger and attempts to repress her tears of relief. She didn't want to forgive him so soon for abandoning her for weeks. Weeks! He had simply stayed here without warning her, and not thinking about her feelings at all!

"Cassandra... I'm sorry..."

Kairen softly kissed her skin, leaving a trail of kisses from her wrist, up her arm, and finally landing on her shoulder. Cassandra shivered. A wave of warmth overcame her, along with her Prince's familiar smell.

"My Lord..."

"Kairen," he corrected.

She shook her head, biting her lip and trying to breathe. His hand was slowly caressing her leg, pushing the fabric of her red dress higher above her knee. Cassandra was blushing as she thought about the last time they'd had this kind of contact, how it had been far too long. Kairen's lips were now on her chest, on that little spot of skin her dress wasn't covering. She grabbed his shoulder, feeling the sensation of his hot skin under her fingers. The black scales that tracked over his body were rougher, but she liked their unusual texture.

Kairen shifted her back, having her lay in the middle of the cushions. He reached for her hairpins, taking each of them out and freeing her long curls. He brushed his fingers through, caressing each strand, before firmly grabbing a handful of her luscious locks.

Meanwhile, his other hand was sliding down along her waist to her thigh, playing with the inner layers of her dress. Cassandra was already too flustered to breathe steadily. The blood under her skin was sizzling, flushing it to an excited pink. She grabbed his face in her hands, and pulled him up for a long, deep kiss. Finally allowed to kiss her, Kairen didn't wait to respond fiercely, crashing his tongue and lips against hers, brushing her skin and hair with his fingers.

He finally reached the last layers of her clothes, grabbing her underwear to pull down her legs. Cassandra felt it, and her senses went into overdrive, feeling them slide down until they were gone. His fingers were caressing her, heating things up between her legs, rubbing her thighs, and at her entrance. The slow motions were torture... a very sweet and exciting torture, causing a rush of adrenaline. She was moaning under the movements of his hands, unable to free her lips from his passionate kiss. Kairen wouldn't let go of her, pressing his body against hers, he was ruthless with his mouth and his hands all over her.

Cassandra could barely catch her breath between his lips, while his fingers ventured further, grinding against her insides and making her legs tremble. She wanted to cry out, beg for mercy, but he was barely letting her make any sound, nothing but erratic moans.

How could this be appropriate? They were inside the Imperial Palace, anyone could barge in!

But, of course, he didn't care. Kairen kept going, too engrossed in their sexual arousal and savoring the wetness on his fingers. They hadn't been together in so long... His desire was growing exponentially, as he quickly undid his belt. Cassandra was finally able to breathe when his lips plunged to her breasts, undoing the top of her dress to caress and tease them. She gasped, feeling him pressing between her legs.

"My Lord."

He sucked on her skin, leaving red marks above her breasts and all over her white skin. Cassandra's body overflowed with sensation, holding on to his shoulders, to the soft cushions around her.. She continued trembling in pleasure, but she was wet and getting impatient. Her fidgety hands reached for his member, caressing it. Kairen growled a bit, surprised. He let her do so though, and went back to her lips, deeply kissing her again. He wanted this woman so much... How could he have kept them apart for weeks?

With a swift shift of his hips, the War God slowly penetrated her, causing his Concubine to cry out in pleasure. Feeling him fill her to the brim was the hottest sensation she ever had. Cassandra took deep breaths as they slowly started moving their hips together, but Kairen wasn't that patient. He accelerated, thrusting long and fast inside her, driving her crazy with his perfectly timed momentum. He kept going, in and out, breathing loudly. Cassandra felt her lower body burning, her legs and hips a slave to his wild movements. It was so good... so, so good. And they hadn't done it in so long. She just didn't want this to stop.

Obliging her need, Kairen kept going, only slowing down to change positions a couple of times. Cassandra found she was starting to really like those colored cushions... She was on her flank, his arms around her, going voraciously at it from behind. Kairen kissed her shoulder, caressed her breasts, and rubbed her little button between her legs, making her go insane. His double rubbing on her most intimate parts were bringing her to the verge of explosion, but she was trying hard to hold it back. She didn't want to cum first again.

Cassandra tried breathing deep and hard, but her Prince was relentless, not giving her a moment's respite. Suddenly, she heard him groan as he accelerated further, and she couldn't take it anymore. In a long cry of absolute bliss, she spasmed around him, unleashing. Kairen joined her at the same time, in a long release.

He sighed against her skin.

"It was high time you came..."

As they were putting their clothes back on, Kairen couldn't help but thoroughly behold his Concubine. Why did she seem prettier than he remembered? His mother's influence could be seen on her. Cassandra had always been naturally graceful and gentle-mannered, but now, she was moving with the attitude of a Queen. Or maybe it was just the jewelry enhancing her natural beauty.

"How is our son?" asked Kairen, caressing her tummy.

"He's fine. I can feel him a little now. And the egg has grown bigger, too."

Kairen nodded in approval and took her hand, pulling her out of the room. Cassandra was completely lost in the maze of the Palace, but the Prince guided her confidently. In a few minutes, they were back in the Main Room where the Emperor's golden throne was. Shareen was still there, her arms crossed.

"Kairen!" Kareen sighed out in relief.

"See, he's fine, dar..."

"Fine? Then what are those?!"

The Imperial Concubine was inspecting the scaled scars on her son, looking furious.

"Who dared to injure my son? I want their heads!"

"Fine, yes, whatever you want. Would you move back to the Palace now, please?" asked the Emperor, visibly annoyed.

"Move back to this nest of snakes? Among all those two-faced whores? The little sluts that skulk around here?"

"You...you're being a bit too much, darling."

"Over my dead body!" yelled Kareen. "And know that if anything happens to my children or grandchildren, this will be the last time you'll see me!"

And with that, she turned on her heels and left the room, not hiding her anger.

"Kareen! Ka... Oh, that woman!" sighed the Emperor.

He sat back on his throne looking sullen. Behind him, Glahad looked a bit disappointed too, laying down with a long face. Kairen walked up the first few stairs towards the throne.

"Father, my request."

"Your request? What request? Your mother didn't even listen!"

"You only asked that she would come here," growled Kairen.

"Come and listen to me! All she did was yell at me! Did I deserve that? I feel so pathetic! She won't even look at me anymore! What good is it being the Emperor if you can't even control your own women?!"

"Father!"

"Ah, enough! I've had enough yelling for one day! We'll talk about it later. Just go to your rooms, and... Won't you and your concubine please attend the New Year Celebrations?"

Kairen's fists tightened. This stubborn father of his was really getting on his last nerve, but before he could add anything, Cassandra grabbed his hand gently.

"Let's go," she whispered to him.

He didn't say anything further, listening to her instead and stepping down, before leaving the room altogether. All that time, Cassandra hadn't glanced at the Emperor once. For some reason, she felt very awkward just being in the same room as him...

They kept walking in silence through the corridors, passing by several rooms.

"My Lord, what did you ask of your father? In exchange for all this..."

"To be taken out..."

"Taken out?"

"Of his possible successors."

"What?"

Cassandra stopped, speechless. He had asked for what? As she had stopped walking, Kairen had no choice but to stop and turn back to her.

"You asked for what?"

"For my father not to consider me as one of his successors. To be taken out of the running for future Emperor."

"W...why would you do that?" Cassandra asked, still in shock.

"To protect you," Kairen shrugged.

"That is not a valid reason!"

He didn't even respond to that. Cassandra couldn't understand what was going on. Was it because of what she had said? How scared she was for their child's safety? Did he think everything would be solved if he was ruled out as a potential successor?

Cassandra's mind was working at full speed. This was too much, even if it was for her sake!

"My Prince, you can't..."

"Later."

Kairen started walking again, and Cassandra followed, realizing that they were headed outside of the Imperial Palace. As it was much warmer there, a bit too hot for her. Cassandra tried to stay in his shadow to shield herself from the sun.

As soon as they reached the outer gardens, a bunch of young women suddenly approached them. They all had green dresses on and harbored fake smiles.

"Your Highness! Are you going outside? Do you need help?"

"We can accompany you, if you'd like!"

Cassandra was outraged by the women's smutty intentions. What was this? Didn't they usually fear the War God? And they were all blatantly ignoring her in their efforts to seduce him! Had they no shame at all? However, Kairen resolutely ignored them. Maybe for the first time though, Cassandra felt utterly annoyed. Had they become servants of the Imperial Palace just to try and seduce one of the Princes? Didn't they fear for their lives?

"Your Highness! Wouldn't you like another woman to warm your bed?"

Suddenly, Kairen stopped and turned to the young woman who had spoken. She was pretty with shiny hair and big lustful eyes, but Kairen's eyes reflected back nothing but annoyance.

She didn't realize this and assumed a seductive posture, showing off her curves. Cassandra looked elsewhere as she couldn't bear to watch this kind of scheming.

"...Out of our way."

"Eh?"

"I said, get out of our way."

The woman looked a bit shocked, but kept insisting, trying to use her physical charms.

"B...but don't you think I'm pretty? And I'm very experienced, too..."

Before she could add anything else, Kairen shoved her to the side with enough force to send her tumbling to the floor, falling flat on her ass. None of the other women moved to help her, they were all petrified by the Prince's deathly glare.

Kairen resumed walking, not even bothering to look at them any longer. Cassandra followed in his steps silently. The servants didn't dare to add a word either, especially after a dark shadow suddenly flew over them. Krai landed behind Cassandra, toddling to her until its head could be by the Concubine's side. The dragon's arrival had scared away all the nearby servants, but it made Cassandra smile. Krai softly growled while waddling by her side, following them outside the Imperial Palace's domain.

The Palace itself was so vast that it took quite a while to leave it. Once they walked past the large walls though, the City sprawled out in front of them.

Cassandra took a deep breath. It had been so long since she had been in the City! Not much had changed over the last few months, of course, as she recognized most of the streets and shops. What was different was the way people looked at her though. This was the first time she could walk with her head held high. Before, she would get looks of disgust, people chasing her away like vermin. Now, the women were covetous of her, while the men lusted over her. All of them were careful to look down if the Prince or his Dragon came near though and Krai growled often, warning people not to come too close, forcing a clear path to open up in front of them, obviously disliking crowds. Now, those people were the ones averting their eyes and being careful. It was a vastly different experience.

"Where are we going, My Lord?"

"To the Slave Market."

Cassandra was speechless. Really? Now? But indeed, after a few more steps, she started to recognize the direction they were headed. Was he really going to take care of her slave status, now?

"How do you know where it is, My Lord?"

"I used to run away from the Palace and come to the City."

"Really?"

Was he a mischievous child growing up? Cassandra couldn't keep herself from smiling, imagining a young Kairen playfully running through the streets.

"C...Cassie?"

Cassandra turned around. Hidden in the crowd, a pair of young slaves were looking at her with shocked eyes. She recognized them instantly.

"Ethen? Mira?" she called out to them.

They nodded, and the people around the slaves stepped back. The two were younger than Cassandra. Ethen was fourteen years old, and Mira was just eleven. After a brief hesitation, they walked up to her and Cassandra hugged them as soon as they were within reach.

"Ethen, your...hand..."

She looked at the bandage on his wrist, where his hand used to be. He still had it when she had left their master's house.

"Ah... It's okay, Cassie, I'm fine. The... Master was very angry at that time, so he..."

"Cassie, I thought you were dead!" Mira interrupted, tears in her eyes. "The Master said that you were given as an offering to the...the..."

She didn't finish her sentence, but her eyes were clearly on Krai, afraid. The dragon was looking at her with curiosity though.

"Cassandra. Who are they?" asked Kairen.

"We...worked for the same Master."

"The Old Master is dead, Cassie. Now his son is our Master."

Cassandra felt like screaming. She remembered him. He was about her age, but the Old Minister's son was a horrible, spoiled child. He had laid his hands on the young female slaves several times and was even worse to the men. Ethen's hand was only a glimpse of his cruelty.

She shook her head. She couldn't possibly let them go back. Cassandra turned her head to Kairen, hesitating for a moment. Could she ask for a favor like this? Maybe just this once? Feeling her hesitation, her Prince turned to her.

"Say it."

"I... Can they come with us? Please..."

She didn't even have to ask a second time. Kairen nodded, and resumed walking. The two young slaves were confused, but Cassandra took their hands.

"Come with me."

"B... But...The Master..."

"Don't worry about him."

Still fearing the huge dragon, they started walking next to her, chatting about what had happened since the Arena. Cassandra detailed her story and then asked them the same. The two young slaves didn't have any good news. The Old Minister was a cruel man, but his son managed to be even worse. He had taken some of his father's remaining concubines as his own, and chased away or killed the rest.

"What a pig..." said Cassandra.

"Cassie... We'll really be punished if we don't go back..." cried Mira.

"No, no, don't worry."

The more she thought about it, the more Cassandra didn't want to let them go back, or let anyone go back there. She abruptly stopped, and thought about it for a few seconds, before turning to Kairen.

"Let's go there."

He didn't say anything, but she took a deep breath to explain herself.

"I can't...I can't leave them. All the slaves there were like me, they were all my friends. Some are even younger than Mira. I... His son only inherited his father's wealth and properties, but he doesn't have a title. I can...I can do this, right?"

Kairen smirked. Of course she could. When would she stop doubting herself so much? Cassandra only seemed to realize her own strength and status when she needed it to help others...

"Where is it?" he asked.

Cassandra led the way. It was an odd feeling going back to her Old Master's house. She probably would have been terrified if she hadn't been accompanied by a Dragon and its master. One was a killing machine, and the other could eat several grown men in one bite. And both were smitten with her.

They arrived a few minutes later. Cassandra took a few seconds at the entrance to calm herself. As she stood there, all of the memories resurfaced, as clear as if it were only yesterday. The yelling, the slaps, and the bite of the whip. All that suffering that had marked her skin forever. She could never get rid of the scars, physical or emotional. The worst thing about it was the hunger though. Most people thought the physical punishments were more painful, but only someone who had lived through it knew that there was nothing worse than hunger; it drove you crazy.

She took a deep breath. She wasn't hungry, cold, or scared anymore. Those scars were now just reminders of injuries that had been healed.

"Who dares to...!" the man yelled, furious.

Cassandra had just walked into the room, wearing her red dress, staring at him with disgust. The young man was barely older than her, by a couple of years. He was half-naked in his bedroom, wearing just a bathrobe, and two young women by his side. Cassandra talked to them first.

"Leave us, please."

Her calm and composed tone contrasted strangely with the group of slaves behind her. After some hesitation, the women were about to leave, but their Master suddenly grabbed them by the hair, making them both cry out in pain.

"Where do you think you're going?! You wenches! Who is your Master?!"

"Let them go!"

"Why?" he asked. "Why should I obey you, slave? Huh? Where did you steal that dress! You little slut, do you think I don't recognize you? You were one of my father's slaves! I'll whip you a hundred times for running away!"

"I said, let them go!"

Right after she yelled, a large growl was heard from above. Except for Cassandra, everyone in the room was suddenly terrified, looking up at the roof.

"W...w...what was that?"

Too surprised, the young Master had let go of one of the women, who ran out of the room screeching. His grip was still tight on the other woman's hair, though, and the woman was quietly weeping, obviously scared.

Since it seemed quiet upstairs for a moment, the man, trying to appear more confident, stood up to face Cassandra with a disgusted look painted on his face.

"How dare you walk in here and give me orders, you damn slut! You think you can tell me what to do? How about this?!"

Before Cassandra could do anything, he threw the woman on the floor. He brutally kicked her in the stomach several times. Her screams and the violence of the scene made everyone take a step back; everyone except Cassandra. Despite her own disgust at the man, she suddenly grabbed her shoe and threw it at him.

She wasn't aiming to hurt him, but to divert him so he would stop. Her shoe violently hit his temple making him stumble back away from his victim.

The woman was crying loudly, holding her waist in pain. Cassandra walked up to her, checking on her, genuinely worried. She didn't recognize this young woman, but she was also a slave.

"Are you okay?"

"The...the Master..." cried the girl, but her words didn't make any sense.

"How dare you injure your Master! I'll have you whipped, burned, and killed!"

Cassandra had enough. Ignoring him, she helped the girl get up.

"Where do you think you're...!"

Just when the man was about to hit them both, Cassandra took one of her hairpins out, and held it like a weapon, aimed right at him. She didn't attack, but with her stance and the speed of his hand, the man impaled himself right on it.

Shocked, he saw blood dripping, the needle in the middle of his hand, and took a few seconds to understand what had just happened. Cassandra let go of the hairpin, as he started screaming in pain.

"It huuuuuuurts! It huuuuuuuurts!" he kept screeching.

Cassandra felt no sympathy for him. After what he had done to so many slaves, for all those years, she didn't have it in her heart to give him any pity. He certainly didn't deserve any.

She was about to escort the woman outside, when another loud growl was heard. Understanding it came from above them, half of the slaves present ran out. Cassandra sighed, taking cover on the side. A few seconds later, the room's roof was completely torn away. With its gigantic claws fighting to get rid of the wood, Krai kept eyeing her from the hole just created, impatient.

"Krai, stop it! I said to wait!" She sighed

Whether it didn't want to listen or didn't understand, the dragon kept digging, making a big mess of what had just been a room seconds before. Cassandra had to sidestep to avoid the falling debris. A few feet away from her, the man had completely forgotten about his pain, staring at the huge black Dragon, in utter shock.

"Th... The... Thir... Third Pr... Prince's..."

"His name is Krai," said Cassandra. "And if you move or scream again, you will be his lunch."

With that threat, she finally left the room, unharmed, helping the terrorized slave who was clinging to her, mumbling.

"The ma... Master will kill me... He'll whip me..."

"Don't worry, he won't do anything to you."

Cassandra walked her to the inner court, where the other slaves ran to take care of the young woman, giving her some clothes and checking her injury. Behind Cassandra, Krai noticed she was out, and stepped down to follow her, completely forgetting all about the building it had just destroyed. The slaves were still frightened by the dragon, but watching it happily growl at Cassandra and rub its snout against her arm, was definitely a unique sight.

"How many slaves are there?"

"About sixty," said Ethen. "And about as many servants."

Cassandra sighed a bit. She had hoped it'd be less. She was about to turn to walk out and ask for Kairen's permission, when she stopped. She remembered his words, right before she walked in here. She should do this on her own this time. No more asking for permission. Taking a deep breath, she turned again, facing the crowd in the outer garden.

"I'm on my way to the Slave Market, to get this thing off my neck. I...I am an Imperial Concubine, now. If you want to follow me, I can do the same for you."

"Where will we go next?" asked one of the middle-aged women.

"I can offer you jobs...but not to everyone. Some will have to find work on their own. I only need about twenty people to accompany me back to the Onyx Castle."

A lot of people were hesitating. It was disheartening to Cassandra, but she easily understood them. Most of these people had spent their whole lives working in this place. In the outside world, they had no idea of what they'd become. Even if it was a different person holding it, they would always fear the whip of another Master.

Suddenly, someone banged on the door behind her.

"You wench! You shall die by the-!"

chomp

Cassandra turned to look at what the odd sound was. Behind her, Krai froze like a dog caught doing something wrong. The dragon turned its red eyes to the side, obviously to avoid hers. The inert leg hanging out from its maw was a dead give-away, though.

"Krai..."

The Black Dragon turned its head away, pretending not to hear. Behind her, all the slaves were silently horrified. Did that dragon just...? Someone in the group loudly threw up, while Krai was trying to chew slowly, as if Cassandra couldn't see it. There was only one shoe left on the ground.

She sighed. She didn't think the dragon would really eat him...

"Did your dragon eat the Master?" Innocently asked Mira.

"We're all dead," whispered one of the men. "They won't forgive this... The family... They will kill her and kill us for this..."

Cassandra turned to him, annoyed.

"This is an Imperial Dragon! No one will do anything to you anymore, I promise!"

"You'll just sell us to the next Master! What do you care, now that you're one of them?"

"Cassie won't do that!" yelled Mira, running to her side. "She is our friend!"

Most of the young people nodded in agreement. To them, Cassandra had been like an older sister, silent and helpful most of the time. Even if she had been gone for months, they remembered her gentleness that no one else had shown them after she had left. Ethen, along with a few young slaves, confidently walked over to her side as well.

"Nowhere can be worse than here anyway," growled the woman from before, joining them.

After that woman spoke, a few others came along. Cassandra knew most of them, but they had barely interacted before. That woman was known as Yasora, one of the slaves that worked in the kitchens. The ones staying behind were all staring at her with defiant looks, either doubtful or scared of the Dragon.

Cassandra sighed.

"Fine. We can..."

"Cassandra."

She turned around. Kairen, impatiently, had arrived inside. As he came to her side, a few people stepped away, too afraid of an Imperial Family member. Though he didn't wear any purple clothing, they could tell who he was just by the scales left on his skin, his armor, and his behavior.

He wrapped his arm around her waist, glancing at the people present.

"Are you done yet?" he asked in a cold voice.

"Yes but...some cannot leave."

Kairen stayed silent for a while. His eyes were looking over at the residence, its buildings and all. He stopped where Krai had made a mess, glaring at his Dragon, but the black beast once again looked away.

"Just keep it," he eventually said.

"Keep it? You mean this place?"

Kairen nodded.

"You hate the Imperial Palace anyway."

Is that what he meant for her to keep...this whole residence? Indeed, its last owner had died, but...this was way too big for her to keep! She hesitated, looking at the slaves and servants who had all gathered.

One of the old maids stepped forward, bowing lowly.

"We will take care of it for you, Lady Cassandra. If...if you can do as promised, we will happily work for you. This residence will welcome you anytime."

It was an odd feeling, having her former colleagues be at her service now. Cassandra sighed. She wasn't really happy with this situation, but indeed, it would be much better for them this way. With an Imperial Family member's protection, they didn't risk anything. No one would dare to raise questions about the place's ownership either, the Black Dragon that had wrecked some of it would be enough of an explanation.

"Are we done now?" asked Kairen, visibly bored.

Cassandra nodded, feeling a bit better. She wanted to hurry to the Slave Market. A lot of people were coming with them too. Though it was probably the place she hated the most, it was also where she could hope to find a clue about what had happened to her younger sister.

Chapter 14

"You... You....Your Highness!"

The man couldn't believe his own eyes. A member of the Imperial Family, in the Slave Market? What had gotten into him! He glanced at the concubine next to him, and the obvious collar on her neck. What was that? He probably wanted his new toy's collar off, but... What was the deal with the dozens of slaves behind him?!

"Take that damn thing off."

Kairen's angry voice had everyone sweating in fear. One of the older men took a step forward, looking at Cassandra's slavery collar with a suspicious look.

"It's not that simple, Your Highness. Every slave has a binding contract and a debt to pay in order to buy their freedom back."

"A debt?" repeated Cassandra, shocked. "Are you implying I owe you money?"

Kairen raised an eyebrow, not because of the slave trader, but in surprise at her sudden stance. It wasn't often that he saw her really angry at someone.

Cassandra was shocked and furious. She stepped forward, glaring at the man like she never had before.

"You stole me like some merchandise from my tribe when I was a child! You ransacked every house, killed every man you couldn't sell. You locked women and girls in cages, like we were animals! If any money has to be taken into account, you owe me more than a hundred whole lives could repay, for everything you've done! You owe me everything you took from me, my family, my life, my people!"

The man was shocked that the young Concubine had dared to yell at him. He glanced at the Prince, but seeing that he wasn't taking part in the conversation, he crossed his arms and made an offended look.

"Young Lady, how is it my fault if your tribe, or whatever, fell because of some war or bandits? It's not like people run here for slavery contracts!

That's how the business is. We get the slaves and find them places to work. You should consider yourself lucky. You were provided a roof and food after what happened to your people!"

"Lucky?" repeated Cassandra in astonishment. "You think slaves...are lucky?"

Some of the people following them started yelling at the slave trader, making him step back. The crowd behind him wasn't too happy, either. In the Slave Market, which was basically a huge tent for buyers and sellers to meet and trade the slaves, there were about thirty to fifty slaves per trader. While their wrists, ankles, and neck were all bound by chains, they were free to glare and yell. Seeing the situation wasn't good, some buyers promptly left. No one wanted to get caught between a slave-trader and an Imperial Concubine wearing a slavery collar...especially when she is backed-up by her Prince and his Dragon.

Krai was standing outside of the tent, growling regularly. Plus, with its size, no one could ignore the little mountain of black scales that stood visible behind all of the crowd.

"I've spent almost half my life as a slave, and I should be grateful for it?" said Cassandra, outraged. "I should be grateful for all the times I've been whipped, beaten, and starved? For eating scraps and drinking dirty water? For risking my life every day? Thank you for the scars and nightmares?"

The slave trader rolled his eyes, obviously annoyed at her.

"What are you complaining about, huh? You got yourself an Imperial Prince, didn't you? You, of all people, should be damn grateful you weren't killed!"

For the first time in her life, Cassandra felt utter hatred for someone. She took the little dagger at her hip, and without warning, slashed the man's arm. Not too deep, just enough for blood to appear, making him yell in pain.

"You...you swine!"

"What? Aren't you grateful? Isn't this nothing?!" Cassandra yelled back angrily, with tears in her eyes. "Slaves get injuries like this every day! The only person I'm grateful to is My Lord, for not killing the abused goods that I am! For taking a liking to me, despite all the scars I carry!"

"Cassandra, enough," said Kairen, taking the dagger from her shaking hand.

Gently, he put his hand around her, comforting her and kissing her wet cheek. Cassandra had never been so angry before. She couldn't even express it correctly.

"It's...Those men are..."

"Calm down," he whispered.

He didn't mind her getting mad at someone. He wouldn't have blinked if she killed him, but he didn't want to see her too worked up, not when she was pregnant. She was crying in anger and shaking. He turned to the man, glaring at him with a deadly look in his black eyes.

"The collar. Now."

The man hesitated. Even if this Concubine was upset or whatever, the Prince was a member of the Imperial Family, someone with money to no end. Maybe he could get some more before freeing that slave for him.

"I can do it, but the binding contract, and the fee..."

This time, Kairen had enough. Without warning, Kairen grabbed the man by his collar and pulled him back to the entrance. The man screamed like a pig, terrified. He didn't expect the Prince would get mad over a slave, or even a Concubine. Kairen's apparent calm and composure had misled him to think Cassandra was the only one who was angry.

"Let me go! I'll free her! I'll free her right away! We have a key! A key that works for..."

Before he could end his sentence, Kairen threw him like a sack toward Krai. The Dragon, like a dog catching a ball, crunched him half-way. It didn't even chew, just gulped the man down, ending his life in seconds. After that, it burped loudly, to everyone's disgust. When Kairen walked back to his Concubine, Cassandra was frowning.

"Can Dragons get sick?" she asked.

"What would he get sick with?"

"Rotten meat," she said with disgust. "It's the second one today."

Kairen smirked.

"His stomach can handle fire."

He then turned to the other slave traders present, all of their faces had gone completely white with fear. Before any of them wondered how many humans a dragon could eat in a day, they all ran to Cassandra, each bringing some very odd key. Kairen kicked one that had come too close, warning the others not to overstep that range.

He grabbed one of the keys and gently turned Cassandra around. Her head was spinning a bit. Really, now? Was it...really happening? She noticed her own breathing was getting louder, her heartbeat ringing in her ears.

With a loud clicking, the two half-rings of metal fell at her feet. Cassandra looked down at the rings for a few seconds, stunned. It was more than just those pieces of metal, it was her neck, and the sensation of lightness, that struck her.

There would be no more constant heaviness around her neck, no more pain. She slowly brought her fingers up, touching her skin. It was gone, really gone. It wasn't just the collar that was removed; it was like a hundred pounds of sorrow, fear, and pain had been lifted off her shoulders.

Cassandra silently started crying, hiding her face in Kairen's shoulder. Her Prince held her close, caressing her back and neck, waiting for her to calm down.

With her cheeks still wet, she suddenly grabbed his face and kissed him without warning. The War God wasn't expecting this. Never before had Cassandra been so passionate, demanding, and commanding. Yet, it felt so incredibly good. He answered her kiss, completely forgetting the world around them. It was like another woman had taken over her body, claiming him, hungry and restless. She caressed his cheek, his nape, keeping him to herself. Kairen was pleasantly surprised, his arms around her waist, hugging her until they parted, both of them out of breath.

For a while, they stayed silent, their faces close to each other, in a slight daze.

"Thank you," whispered Cassandra.

Kairen didn't answer, only wiping her tears and kissing her gently again, while Cassandra stood against his chest, her eyes closed. She was still trembling a bit, but he continued to hold her and turned to the slave traders.

"The others. Now."

The slave traders looked at the large group, a bit hesitant, but all of them had seen or heard the sound of a man being eaten alive by a Dragon. No one wanted to be the main dish. They rushed toward the other slaves, each carrying one of the keys, and the collars fell one by one. People started crying, screaming, and laughing in joy. Some even hugged their siblings or friends, overwhelmed with relief. Cassandra only listened. She still had her eyes closed, leaning on Kairen's chest; her Prince's hands holding her tightly.

When they were done with the group, the slave traders returned, visibly pissed by what had just happened. Freeing fifty or so slaves in a day wasn't a part of their plans at all. Kairen's deadly glare on them wasn't stopping, making them feel as if something was wrong.

"S...Sir, we are done..."

"I said, free the others."

For a few seconds, they didn't understand. They had obviously freed all of the group, so why... Then, their faces turned white, one by one. He couldn't possibly mean all of the slaves? Yet, the Imperial Prince's glare was obvious. The men stepped back.

"Your Highness, this... this is our trading business. This is how we...we make our living."

"If we free all our merchandise, we..."

Kairen's unwavering expression was extremely scary and disturbing. Three of the slave traders turned back and ran to free their slaves, with shaking hands. The men left were hesitant. He couldn't be... serious, could he?

All of a sudden, a loud growl was heard. Krai began to bite and tear the tent away. Even though the tent was dozens of meters long and wide, the dragon pulled it like a child would have played with a handkerchief.

Kairen stayed silent again, but Cassandra stepped closer, talking to the closest trader.

"The man who sold me, sold my younger sister too. His name was Nubar."

"Nu...Nubar died years ago, Madam."

"How can I find my sister?" she insisted, still visibly upset.

The man hesitated, but someone from behind him spoke first.

"How...how old was she, Madam?"

"She was seven."

"Then...she was probably sold to a brothel."

Cassandra felt her heart sink.

"To a brothel? I just said she was seven years old!"

"They take the young girls when they are very young, so they can train them and ensure their virginity. If they are very pretty, they can be sold at very high prices to wealthy nobles, but most of them are kept as prostitutes."

Cassandra almost fainted. A brothel... Her sister had really been taken to some brothel? She felt like crying again, and throwing up. Those people were less than human. She turned to Kairen, shaking her head, feeling sick.

"I want to leave," she cried. "I want to leave this place. I never want to step foot here, ever again."

Kairen slowly nodded, and carried her outside, Cassandra's arms around his neck. When he reached Krai, the dragon was growling in the direction of the slave traders, its eyes darkening.

"Stuff yourself," the War God whispered.

Cassandra didn't hear the carnage behind them, and she didn't want to. She cried silently against Kairen's neck. She couldn't endure any more emotions for the day. She was angry, sad, and exhausted. Her Prince carried her without a word, back to the Palace. No one dared to bother them. She didn't look up again until they reached the gates.

Kairen brought her to his apartment and gently placed her on the bed. She wasn't crying anymore, but her eyes were red. He hated seeing her like this.

"I'll send people to look for your sister."

Cassandra sighed.

"Back then, when I had just been sold to my first Master...I looked for her every chance I had. I asked so many people... I was caught and punished several times for venturing outside when I wasn't allowed to. I just wanted to find her so badly. She always looked so much like me, I knew someone would recognize her right away if they saw me."

"What's her name?"

"Missandra."

Kairen nodded, and rubbed her back.

"We'll find her."

"She may not be in the Capital anymore, it's been so long," cried Cassandra.

Before she could add anything else, Kairen gently kissed her, and pulled her into the middle of the bed. He kept kissing her, until she finally began to slowly respond to his kiss.

Her sister had been lost for almost ten years. Even if the news that she may have been sold to a brothel was hard, Cassandra still had hope. If she was alive, with the Prince's help, they would find her.

Right now, there was something important to celebrate. Kairen was going down to her jawline, onto her neck, down to her collarbone. Her skin was now all his to touch, caress, and kiss, as much as he wanted. Even on Cassandra's pale skin, one could see the thin tan line from her slavery days. Eight years... For eight years her neck and shoulders had carried the weight of that heavy, rusted metal.

"I want to bathe," she suddenly said.

"Now?"

Cassandra nodded, and Kairen quickly kissed her before leaving the bed, allowing her to sit up. He had gone to give orders to the servants in waiting. After a few minutes, they had her bath ready, lukewarm water with flowers and oils, right in the middle of the room. They dismissed the servants that were waiting with towels in order to be alone.

Cassandra undressed, revealing the little belly under her dress. Her breasts, too, had gotten a bit fuller and more firm during those last weeks. Kairen helped her step inside the bathtub, sitting behind her as she liked.

She could finally relax a bit inside the water, with the Prince's warm torso against her back. Kairen brushed her hair back, kissing her neck and shoulder.

"We should celebrate," he whispered.

"That I'm no longer a slave?"

"That and... this," he said, caressing her tummy.

Cassandra nodded, smiling a bit for the first time in a while. She put her hand over his, feeling a lot better just from his touch.

"How do you celebrate?" she asked.

"Probably a feast... Gifts... I want to get you something."

She chuckled. She would never have guessed the War God was into gifts. So far, all he had given her was gold bars! He was so rich he didn't need to buy anything for himself, as was all of the Imperial Family.

"More dresses?" She asked.

"No...a necklace."

Cassandra was a bit surprised. A necklace? What kind of necklace was he thinking about?

"I understand my brothers better now."

"What do you mean?" she asked, a bit confused.

"You'll see tonight."

He was probably talking about the Feast. Since they were in the Imperial Palace, they would probably have to attend. Last time, Cassandra had been there as a slave. Now she was a free woman. That feeling was still too new to her. Despite the weight being taken off her neck, she had yet to get used to not being a slave anymore. Her status had risen considerably in just a few seconds. She was a low-rank Concubine, now, which meant she had gone from the lowest status in this country to one of the highest.

"Why did you ask your father to... take you out of the running as his heir?" she asked, suddenly remembering that issue.

Kairen glanced at her pregnant belly, his dark eyes bearing a solemn expression.

"To protect you...and our son. As long as I can inherit the throne, you'll both be in danger. Constantly."

"But...it's such an important matter."

He sighed, and pulled her closer, pouring water on her back, washing her gently.

"I don't care about being an Emperor. I don't want you to be scared or unhappy."

Cassandra shook her head. "You can't make this kind of decision like that. No wonder the Emperor was so unhappy about it."

Wasn't he the most favored of the six sons? The Emperor may act childish when his favorite Concubine was around, but Cassandra knew how smart he really was. He wouldn't act that way towards Kairen if he wasn't a good Heir. Moreover, he was the best Dragon-tamer, that fact alone spoke volumes about him too.

Kairen frowned, confused by her reaction. "You don't like that?"

"It's not just about me. There are so many more people than just me in this country. What if whoever becomes the Emperor is bad or an incompetent person? Hundreds, or even thousands, of people could die."

She gently brushed his hair, looking at him. He was such a powerful and respected man, yet all he could see was her? Cassandra leaned closer to kiss him, enjoying this sweet taste between them. At first, she was so scared of him, but now...now he was her refuge, the one person she wanted to be with, unconditionally.

They kept kissing and caressing each other for a long time in the bath. Kairen had a new and embarrassing game; leaving a trail of hickeys from her neck to her breasts. When she noticed them in the mirror, Cassandra sighed. "I didn't think you would enjoy my collar being gone to this extent."

The Prince smirked behind her, putting his pants back on before calling the servants back. A dozen of them ran in to help them prepare for the banquet. Kairen only had his scaled braces on and stayed shirtless, as he chased and scared anyone who tried to get close to him.

Hence, the servants focused on Cassandra, helping her get ready from head to toe. With her collar gone, it was a whole new attitude they had toward her. They were extremely careful with each movement. They kept bowing and avoiding eye contact until Cassandra begged them to stop.

"It's alright, you'll hurt your back or neck if you keep bowing like that."

They seemed surprised by her attitude. It was probably very different from the usual Concubines. It took a while before they stopped bowing continuously. Yet, they still tried not to look at her directly.

"If the Imperial Concubine has a preference..."

They kept showing her dozens of necklaces, bracelets, earrings, and rings, confusing her. Everything was shining with gold and gems, in all the colors she could think of. How come they had so much jewelry available for her? She had some that she had bought while at the Onyx and Diamond Palaces, but not here!

"The Emperor has insisted, Your Highness. the Third Prince's Imperial

Concubine shall be entitled to own anything she likes."

Cassandra was speechless. Now, even the Emperor was treating her like a Princess! Had The Concubine Mother played a part in this? Kairen didn't seem surprised one bit. He stood up, glancing at the jewelry.

"Father is probably trying to calm Mother through you. And he's happy about the baby, too."

Kairen picked a thin gold one, with emeralds, diamonds, and handed it to her. Cassandra chuckled, putting it on with the help of two maiden servants. They helped her put on the rest of the matching jewelry, which included earrings, hairpins, and an ankle bracelet. After picking a very light, off-shoulder dress that had thin layers and a long skirt, the servants put Cassandra's hair up beautifully. Once she was ready, Kairen took her out of the room.

It would be her first time attending the Imperial Banquet as an official Concubine, as well as meeting the Imperial Siblings and their Concubines. Of course, she was nervous. Half of those people were wishing for her and her baby's death.

As she followed Kairen, Cassandra had a hard time calming down. Everything would be so different from the first time she had walked into the large hall of the Imperial Palace. Most importantly, she could hold her head high, and walk beside the Prince, instead of behind him. The War God had his arm around her waist as they entered, in a clearly protective stance.

"His Highness, Kairen the Third Prince, God of War of the Dragon Empire, and his Concubine," someone announced loudly.

This was very ceremonial; all eyes were clearly on them as they walked in. This time, Cassandra could see all of their faces. First, she realized that the Imperial Concubine Mother wasn't there. Had the Emperor failed to convince her to attend? Shareen, however, was sitting in her golden chair next to her brother's.

Just like Cassandra remembered, each Imperial sibling had their own golden chair. The brothers' were a bit bigger than their sisters. All of the Concubines, in red and pink dresses, were sitting down below them on the stairs in front of their respective Prince. She could guess all the servants were hidden in the shadows behind the golden chairs, but they were completely still and silent.

This time, there were no performers; perhaps they had come too early. In any case, Kairen took her to his golden chair. She sat right in-between his legs, where she could rest her arms and head on his knee. He immediately started stroking her back. She wasn't the only woman touching her Prince, another Concubine had her back resting on the Fifth Prince's leg, acting flirtatiously with him.

The Emperor wasn't there yet, so Cassandra spent time observing the other Imperial Brothers. She had never noticed how similar yet different they all were. All of them had tanned skin and jet-black hair. The First Prince was the only one with long hair and a very quiet attitude. He wore a large purple tunic and only had two Concubines. The Second Prince had his hair very short. He wore a mean expression with his thin features, and he had a total of six Concubines, with half of them wearing red dresses. The fourth seat was empty, but in front of the fifth, there was a crowd. How many Concubines did the Fifth Prince have? She counted at least twenty in front of the young man, but the women kept chatting and moving, so she lost count. Finally, the brother she knew, Prince Anour greeted her with a little nod when their eyes met, and Cassandra did the same in return.

"So, this is your new woman, Brother."

Cassandra recognized that woman. Princess Phetra, who was glaring at her. Didn't she recognize her, though? It didn't seem like she realized Cassandra was the slave she had already insulted a while ago.

All of the ten Princesses present were eyeing her, but Princess Phetra was the only one to speak. Cassandra turned her head to her, staring. She wasn't afraid to look her in the eye anymore. Princess Phetra wasn't the prettiest, but she had a very sexy body and a lot of jewelry to show.

She seemed to wait for an answer, but Kairen didn't give a damn. He kept gently caressing Cassandra's back with his fingers, looking elsewhere with a bored expression.

"Such bad taste..." she said, clicking her tongue.

"Do you have advice to give, Sister?" asked the First Prince.

"Well, one with more curves, to begin with. Aren't you supposed to try and have Heirs? How can you do that with such a scrawny woman?"

"That's rich, coming from a childless slut," said Shareen, with a smirk.

"How dare you!" roared Phetra, turning red.

As usual, Shareen wasn't afraid to bicker with her sibling and turned to her with an obvious satisfied expression.

"What? Aren't you the childless one giving advice to a pregnant woman? Oh, Phetra, really, why weren't you born mute? You're good with your tongue unless it's for talking."

For a second, Cassandra wondered if both women were going to have a catfight. To her surprise, the Second Prince glared at Princess Phetra, making her turn red and look down. Did she fear her own brother more than she feared Kairen?

"The Imperial Dragon Emperor has arrived!" suddenly someone announced.

All bowed to the Emperor's arrival, though it was quick. He walked to his throne, obviously a bit grumpy, and looked around to see who was there.

"Where's this Fourth Son of mine?" he suddenly asked, staring at the empty chair.

"Brother Opheus is sick, Father," said the Eldest Brother.

"Oh, he's always sick of something. Anyway! I'm happy to see you all... all of you who came here. Shareen, daughter, come here to entertain your father.

Bring in the performers!"

Immediately, a group of dancers appeared at the center of the hall, dancing together to a speedy rhythm. Cassandra didn't feel like watching. She felt like a mouse in a nest of resting snakes. The Princes were talking to their Concubines, and the Princesses between themselves, but you can easily see that none of the siblings really got along.

The Second Prince was whispering to his sister, looking angry. Another sister had also taken part in the conversation. She seemed a bit older than them.

Cassandra realized. Anour was still a teenager, but the oldest Princess looked to be in her forties. How old was the Emperor, then? She whispered her question to Kairen.

"He is sixty-two this year."

Sixty-two years old? The Emperor barely looked forty! How could one look so young at that age, when so many of his children were there! Cassandra was confused. Did that mean the Dragon Blood made them age slower? She had heard some of the previous Emperors had died after a hundred years, but... She thought it was all just legends...

"What about you? And your brothers?" she asked Kairen, now too curious.

She had always assumed he was no older than thirty, but...if the Emperor looked like that at over sixty, her Prince could even be forty year old!

"Sephir is thirty-five, Vrehan is thirty-two, Opheus is twenty-four or twenty-three, Lephys is twenty-one and Anour is fifteen. And I'm twenty-eight."

Cassandra blushed uncontrollably. So, they had about a ten-year age difference. She had never thought about it. It wasn't uncommon to see an age gap between men and their Concubines in this Empire, so she wasn't too surprised. The concubine she used to serve was twenty years younger than her Master.

"What are you thinking?" he whispered.

Cassandra just shook her head and rested it on his knee. She was actually feeling quite safe, sitting so close to him. Kairen's hand on her skin chased all of her worries away, even with all the glares she was getting.

The glares were not only from the Second Prince, but from some of the Concubines as well. Were those women jealous? It was an odd feeling, but Cassandra pretended not to see them or care. In the main area, Shareen was laughing with the Emperor, entertaining her father while chatting with him. It was obvious they had a real bond, even without Kareen in the picture.

"Cassandra."

Kairen caught her attention as a servant was presenting them with a gold tray of food. Cassandra took a bite carefully, but all the food here was tested for poison. She could remember back when she was supposed to be the one to test it.

Suddenly, from across the room, a ruckus was heard. One of the Fifth Prince's Concubines, while shifting her position, had mistakenly spilled some of her wine on one of the young Imperial Princess' purple dresses. The Princess screeched like she was burnt to the third degree.

"You idiot! How dare you stain my dress!"

"I...I am so sorry..." stuttered the Concubine, sounding terrified.

"Sorry? You're sorry? Look at what you've done, you idiot!" The Princess kept yelling furiously.

The Fifth Prince Lephys glanced over briefly, frowning.

"It's fine, Kiuna. It is just a wine stain. She'll wash it later."

"It's not fine! I don't want your stupid Concubine to stain my dress! Whip her! She should be punished!"

Everyone had gone silent, conflicted about the situation. It was just a stain... albeit a large one. However, who could say no to an Imperial Princess? The other Concubines were looking down or elsewhere, obviously scared to get involved.

Meanwhile, the young Princess kept screaming, her tantrum growing louder and louder until it caught the Emperor's attention, who simply frowned.

"Kiuna, enough," said her brother, visibly starting to get annoyed.

"I want that idiot Concubine whipped! She'll get whipped a hundred times! No, a thousand times!"

"It is not the same."

Cassandra's calm voice from across the room took everyone by surprise. As they looked at her, the War God's Concubine was strangely calm and unafraid to answer back. The Princess glared at her.

"What did you say?"

"If you whip someone ten times, the skin will be red and sting. If you whip her a hundred times, you'll cut into the flesh, and she will bleed. But if you whip her a thousand times, you'll open the wounds to the bone. There will be no more skin, only exposed, cut flesh, and lots of blood. No one survives after being whipped about five or six hundred times."

Her sudden reality check had everyone silent for a few seconds. Cassandra's cold but serious voice was very different from that of Princess Kiuna's tantrum. She had no idea how to react. With Cassandra's words, it was clear Kiuna had been speaking mindlessly, saying numbers out of anger. The crude depiction of the wound took her back to reality where she was merely toying with someone's life over a wine stain.

It was even more striking that Cassandra knew what she was talking about. She was staring right at Princess Kiuna, unafraid and cold as ice.

"You... You..." said the Princess, out of words.

But who would dare to respond to a woman who was in the War God's shadow? Kiuna was unsure, and all around her, the room's atmosphere had changed. She looked stupid and childish.

"Enough, enough. Sit back, child, and shut up," said the Emperor, frowning. "Aren't you too old to act like this in front of your siblings? Huh? Don't ruin our dinner."

Princess Kiuna sat, looking down, visibly angry and upset. She didn't dare to glare at Cassandra anymore. Kairen hadn't said a word, but the murderous look in his eyes was enough of a warning.

"You. Child. Come here," suddenly said the Emperor.

Cassandra was surprised. Was he calling for her? To come to him, now? But he had barely looked at her before. She hesitated, but Kairen gently helped her up. The young Concubine took a deep breath, and walked to the Golden Throne, hesitant. Behind him, she could clearly see the two ruby eyes, looking at her in the sea of gold scales.

Cassandra barely dared to look at the Emperor as she approached. To her, he was a much scarier being than the humongous golden Dragon behind him. Yet, the old man gently held his hand out until the Concubine placed her hand in his, with a light smile. She could tell there wasn't any animosity in his dark eyes.

"There she is," he said softly. "Aren't you as white as a water lily?"

"So disgusting," whispered someone from behind her, but the Emperor didn't seem to hear it.

"What is your name?"

"Cassandra, Your Majesty."

"And where are you from, child?"

"The Southern Rain Tribe, Your Highness."

"I see. That explains a lot then."

Explains a lot? Cassandra was a bit confused. Next to the Emperor, a servant stepped forward, showing them some letters. What is that? The Emperor didn't look at it, and turned to Cassandra instead.

"I received some very interesting letters earlier today, children. From General Horogan from the East Army."

Wasn't that one of Kairen's Generals? Cassandra had never greeted him in person, but she could remember the imposing man wearing armor with a beard. He had spoken with her Prince several times. Did he complain to the Emperor about a woman being at the camp? Or was there some issue due to the Prince's absence?

"I was curious to hear about how my Son's been doing as Commander-in-Chief," said the Emperor. "Yet all I read were praises for the young woman he had brought with him. According to two of my most trusted Generals, along with seven of their Commanders, this Empire owes the lives of no less than two hundred of its soldiers to a young slave woman."

Cassandra was speechless. The Generals had written to the Emperor about her? She hadn't possibly seen that many men in the Red Room, back at the Camp! Maybe two hundred, but six hundred lives! Did they exaggerate on purpose? Or had something happened while she was gone? The Emperor went on.

"According to them, the Lady of the Mountain has been more efficient in healing and teaching her knowledge to their men than any of the useless, stubborn, and whiny military doctors that had been appointed. The injuries and disease reports have been reduced by nearly half. This is due to the men now being able to take care of themselves. Apparently, they insist on...thoroughly washing their hands, several times a day."

She couldn't help but blush and look down after hearing this. She hadn't been to the Camp in weeks! How could she have known her little stay had allowed so many things to happen back there.

The Emperor smirked.

"It goes on for several pages, with some military matters that would bore most people. The Generals are sending their thanks to my Third Son, for his exceptionally wise taste in women."

He nodded in Kairen's direction, but everyone knew who was really receiving the praise here. Cassandra was in an inner turmoil. She hadn't expected to be singled out by the Emperor in front of the Imperial Family! When the old man turned to her again, she was still too shaken to react.

"After reading so much, this old Emperor couldn't sit still! Who knew so much knowledge could hide in such a young woman? You make this old man very happy, child."

Cassandra had no idea how she was expected to answer, or if she was supposed to answer at all. She wished Kairen was by her side, but the Prince was sitting still in his golden chair, a few steps away. She was standing by herself in front of the Empire's most powerful man.

"As an Emperor, I have to be grateful to the ones who make this Empire prosperous, and its people safe. Your knowledge has been helpful to our valued soldiers. I do hope you will lend us more of it from now on. I had thought of a way to thank you, but it seems my son took a step ahead with your...situation."

Cassandra frowned a bit. He meant her status as a slave, staring at the place where her collar stood just hours prior. The Emperor nodded, looking satisfied.

"Fine, fine. I can just go with my own idea, then. From today on, Cassandra, you will be a Noble Lady and an Imperial Physician."

"Father!" yelled Princess Phetra, her tone sounding more than furious. "You can't give a noble title to a damn slave!"

"Take a good look, Sister, this woman is no longer a slave. Sit and shut up," said an older Princess.

"Still! They can't rise from rags to rubies in a day! She's a slave and a Southerner! What do we look like if just anyone can achieve that!"

"Not anyone, Phetra," said the First Prince. "Lady Cassandra is a skilled doctor, our father's most trusted General attested to that. Can you claim to have any skills as admirable as one that can save lives?"

With her older brother's glare, Princess Phetra was defeated. One could tell her anger hadn't subsided one bit. She sat back loudly, glaring Cassandra's way, clenching her fists. The young Concubine was too shocked herself to react.

A Noble Lady? Imperial Physician? It was all too much for her! Just like Princess Phetra said, it was unbelievable. All of this was happening to her in just one day! Yet, the Emperor was nodding, satisfied.

"It is good, very good. I'm counting on you to meet with my own Imperial Physicians later. You are welcome to study from our Imperial Library, and I bet those old doctors have a few things to learn from you as well!"

"Yes, Your Majesty. Th... Thank you," mumbled Cassandra.

"Good, good! And take good care of yourself, too! I want to see this precious Grandson of mine as soon as possible! Now you can go and enjoy the feast, young Lady."

Understanding this meant their conversation was over, Cassandra hurried back to Kairen's side. As they reunited, her Prince didn't say a thing, he only invited her to gently sit on his knee. Cassandra, feeling a bit embarrassed, refused him, and took back her place in-between his legs. No woman was allowed on any of the Prince's seats. She had already drawn too much attention to herself tonight.

Most of the Imperial Family had their eyes on her for the rest of the evening, including some murderous glares. Cassandra didn't feel as scared as she could have, though. Kairen's warm hand was on her at all times, caressing her arm, shoulder, back, or neck. He was making her confident with his presence right behind her. It was easier to ignore them if she wasn't scared.

As the couple silently ate, watching the performers, Cassandra realized she would now be wearing a pink dress as a high-ranking Concubine. The Emperor's words had made it clear her status had changed again. Did this mean she would be safer or in more trouble? It was hard to predict. As soon as they could, Kairen and Cassandra went back to their room, leaving the Imperial Feast without looking back. Even after returning to the Prince's apartments, Cassandra didn't feel calm or safe at all. She slowly took off her jewelry, frowning a bit.

"Did you ask your father for all this? Or your men?" she asked Kairen, who was waiting for her on the bed.

"No."

So the General really had sent this letter on his own accord. Cassandra couldn't help but wonder if anything had happened back at the Military Camp. It was all going too fast for her.

She sighed a bit, taking off the last piece of her jewelry, and walked to her Prince, who put his arms around her. His fingers gently caressed her skin, making sure to undo her dress in the process.

"Are you tired?" he whispered.

"Just a bit. I didn't expect His Majesty to..."

Cassandra interrupted her sentence, frowning. She was staring down, behind Kairen's back. Something was moving under the bedsheets.

"Cassandra?"

"Don't move."

She slowly took the sword at his side, taking it out in silence. The Prince frowned and was about to turn around when Cassandra screamed.

"Kairen, no!"

216

Just as he moved, Cassandra aimed the blade down, piercing the mattress. A stain of red appeared on the sheets, a few inches away from his hand. She pulled the sheets back, revealing the snake, pinned down by the blade. The Prince took the sword from her hands, glaring furiously at the snake. Cassandra was about to grab the snake, but he got to it first.

"It's not a venomous one," she sighed in relief. "I couldn't tell under the sheet."

To her surprise, Kairen suddenly pulled her in for a kiss. She blushed, pushing him away.

"It is not the time to...!"

"You called me by my name."

Cassandra blushed even more. Yes, she did, without thinking. In the panic of the moment, she had called his name, the one she had in her mind for days.

"We... Someone put a snake in our bed, and..."

"Cassandra."

She turned to him, unable to look him in the eyes. Kairen was smiling, one of his signature minimalistic smiles. He kissed her again, but Cassandra took the dead reptile from his hand and eluded him, too embarrassed to focus.

"It's a Crecca snake..." she whispered. "They are not venomous, but the bite can be painful...and..."

"And what?" asked Kairen.

"It can be dangerous for children or pregnant women."

The War God's eyes darkened as he glanced at the dead snake. This thing... Cassandra didn't seem worried, now that it was dead in her hand.

"These types of snakes do not live in this area. It must have cost a fortune to bring it here. I don't think the person who did this knows anything about snakes. You can find lethal ones or less dangerous ones in the Capital. They are cheaper, too."

"They wanted to hurt you," growled Kairen.

"I think they meant to scare me. Not a lot of people knew about my pregnancy until tonight. Those who did couldn't have bought the snake so fast. Maybe they already had the snake, but it's a peculiar species, so..."

"It doesn't matter. They'll pay."

To his surprise, Cassandra nodded and turned to him.

"If we find out who did this... Can we do something about it? Even if it's one of your siblings?"

"You think I'd let it go?"

"If it's the Imperial Family?"

Kairen shook his head and grabbed her hand.

"Cassandra."

She stared into his black eyes for a while, and after a few seconds, she understood. She came first. Their unborn child came first. Whoever did this... He wouldn't let it go. He was the War God, after all. Not someone who'd stay still after such a vicious threat.

Cassandra nodded.

"I can find out who did this."

She turned around, and carefully put the dead snake into a basket. She washed her hands thoroughly in the little basin. Behind her, Kairen pulled the dirty bedsheets away and laid his fur cloak on the mattress. They didn't need a blanket to sleep anyway, the Capital's humid air was hot enough. Cassandra walked back to him, putting her arms around his neck. Kairen held her close, pulling them both on the bed.

"Are you not afraid?" he asked in a whisper.

"I'm scared for our baby. I just hope he can be born safely. So many people hate me, but here, it's a matter of life and death every single time."

She sighed silently, and before she could add anything else or worry more, Kairen pulled her in for a kiss. Their lips intertwined, and their tongues touched, looking for each other's warmth. Cassandra felt her heartbeat fasten, and climbed on his lap, closer. She was now the one pulling him with her hands, caressing his shoulders and naked torso. Her warmth was rising slowly.

The Prince pulled her dress down to her hips, exposing her bare chest. He began caressing her with his large hands. Yet, a strange desire was rising in Cassandra. Hesitantly, she pushed him down. Kairen didn't resist at all. Instead, he laid beneath her, letting her ride him with a faint smile. For once, Cassandra was being willful and bold, and he didn't hate it at all.

She was breathing harder and louder, undulating her hips, a pearl of sweat running down her body. Cassandra's every breath was so enticing, and those which turned into moans were even worse. The War God couldn't take his eyes off his concubine. With her on top of him, riding him, he wouldn't miss a second of this delightful scene. She was the one guiding him, imposing her rhythm, and it was good, so good, for both of them.

Laying down under her, holding her hips. Kairen was mesmerized by the balancing movement of her hair, the sparkles in her emerald eyes, and her skin, shyly going from white to an adorably excited pink. He could spend hours like this. Unfortunately, his concubine couldn't. Cassandra kept moaning louder, feeling him between her legs and the pleasure that was rising inside like a raging fire.

"My...Lord, I..."

"My name, Cassandra. Call my name."

"Kairen...Kairen..."

She kept repeating it, like a spell. Her eyes closed, she was biting her lips and focusing on their connected bodies. Kairen caressed her little breasts, the pink extremities, making her shiver. She liked it. Cassandra would close her eyes when she couldn't face his dark eyes anymore, and her cheeks were redder than ever. She was close to the edge.

The Prince finally started acting up, moving his hips under her, little assaults that took her by surprise, as Cassandra had to hold on to his shoulders. He wouldn't give her any rest, though. He kept swinging, making her cry in pleasure above him, only slowing down when she truly begged him to, until both of them were tired, pleased, and relieved.

The concubine slowly fell to his side, exhausted. She was still sweating a bit from all that exercise and trying to catch her breath.

Kairen was satisfied too. A warm feeling in his chest, he turned to her, making sure she was okay. He caressed her arm and back gently until Cassandra fell asleep, won over by the exhaustion. Then, he sat up and used the towels in the room to wipe her up a little, and covered her with a thin silk sheet. Only then did he come back to lay next to her, putting an arm around his concubine.

They had come a long way from the time he first met her. His Concubine hadn't revealed any of her secrets back then, her knowledge in medicine, or her admirable willpower. She was just a common woman, among many others, and she had never tried to step above the others or put herself first. She remained pure throughout, the exact same girl that had stood at his feet. Kairen glanced at the basket, where the dead snake was. He wouldn't forgive whoever it was. Not when they had tried to harm her... and their baby. His eyes glanced over her little tummy. How much longer? As long as they are both safe. He'd rather take Cassandra out of this wretched place, but for now, he didn't have much choice. Too many things were happening at once, and with all of his family gathered... Events could unfold drastically at any time now. He hated the idea, though. Their allies within the walls were very few. He didn't trust any of them fully, except maybe his mother.

The next morning, they both got ready in silence. Someone had already delivered a new set of magnificent pink dresses for Cassandra. She picked a pale pink one that complimented her complexion perfectly. Her Prince was also very satisfied while helping her get dressed up. He caressed her hair and the fine gauze of her dress' layers. She could tell he really liked it on her and picked a matching set of pink diamond jewelry. Their time together didn't last long, though. Kairen was soon called to the Emperor's early military council, while Cassandra was invited to Imperial Concubine Kareen's quarters for breakfast. They parted early, but he made sure Cassandra wouldn't be alone. Hence, the young concubine walked through the gardens, along with a very voluntary Krai, the huge dragon happily toddling right next to her.

It was still early in the morning and the temperature was right to Cassandra's taste, along with a little breeze. She took her time, knowing the Imperial Concubine hadn't set an exact time. Cassandra had never really taken time to visit the Imperial Gardens by herself, but despite their beauty, they weren't as wild and free as the ones in the Diamond Palace. She definitely couldn't come to like this Imperial Palace. Something about it always felt wrong to her. Too big, too wide, too luxurious, and...too dangerous.

"Don't make yourself too comfortable."

Behind a pillar, followed by half a dozen servants, Princess Phetra was there, along with her younger half-sibling, Princess Kiuna. Both had very different stances. While Phetra was standing tall and crossing her arms in a proud stance, Kiuna, on the contrary, was looking down and fidgeting with her hands as if she was embarrassed and didn't want to be there, avoiding Cassandra's eyes and her sister's.

The young Concubine took a deep breath and bowed slightly to them. Phetra had been infuriated by her new status and it was still obvious in the way she glared at Cassandra's brand new pale pink dress.

"Good morning, Your Highnesses."

"Where are you off to?" asked the Princess in that imperial tone of hers.

"I was invited to have breakfast with Imperial Concubine Kareen."

"Of course... "

Phetra's words had some deep meaning, but Cassandra couldn't grasp it all. She just knew she didn't want to stay near that woman. Though they obviously didn't like her, the other Princesses didn't look at her in such a murderous, hateful way. Cassandra had felt it early on. Just like the Second Prince hated Kairen to the core, she could tell Phetra was just as dangerous.

Phetra stared at her for a while, from head to toe, with disgust.

"I miss the time when slaves couldn't even step inside the Palace...near us."

Cassandra felt anger rise in her heart. Slaves could only enter the Palace to be massacred in their slaughter games...or if someone from the Imperial Family took them in, just like Kairen had done for her. The young concubine wasn't upset because Phetra was disgusted by her presence, but because of the Princess' obvious revulsion for slaves.

But Cassandra couldn't say anything. Krai was slowly growling behind her, but the dragon probably wouldn't injure a member of the Imperial Family, unless they really tried to harm Cassandra in some way.

"If you'll excuse me, Your Highnesses, I need to get going."

Without waiting for their permission, Cassandra turned her heels and started walking away, trying to repress all of her feelings against that woman. Krai was following from up close, but the dragon's red eyes never left the princesses.

"You were right, you know."

Cassandra stopped, turning to her. What did she possibly mean by that? What was she right about? As she was trying to find the answer, Phetra's icy smirk chilled her to the bone. The Princess was obviously enjoying this, and maybe for the first time in a long while, Cassandra felt truly scared.

"Five hundred and six."

Cassandra was lost. What was she... But after a few seconds, the young concubine understood and all the blood left her face. Princess Kiuna was looking down, with something like shame painted all over her face. But Phetra was thrilled.

"She died after the five hundred and sixth."

Cassandra felt so sick and disgusted, she thought she was going to collapse. That woman was so... wretched! She had...really...

"You know, it was almost exciting. Waiting to see when she would finally die. I took a normal whip, of course, and counted. Each. One. My. Self."

She had said those last words so slowly like she was savoring them. For Cassandra, it was too much. She stepped back, turned, and walked away as fast as she could.

Phetra was evil. Pure evil. How...how could one be so inhumane as to... do that to another human being? And enjoy it? And take the time to count... She almost ran to the Imperial Concubine's quarters, much to Krai's concern. The Dragon was staring at her, curious about her behavior, trying to get her attention with soft growls, but the young concubine wouldn't stop. She kept going, trembling, trying to get there faster. No, the truth was, what she truly wanted was to get away from Phetra.

When she arrived there, trembling and almost out of breath, the Imperial Concubine got up, frowning.

"You little...Why are you running? What is it, child? What would cause you to put my grandchild's safety in danger like this?"

Cassandra tried to catch her breath, shaking her head. She walked up to her, almost falling on her knees at the Imperial Concubine's side. Kareen frowned and caressed her hair, unhappy.

"Tell me, Cassandra."

They were not bonded by blood, but at that very moment, and for the following hour, Kareen acted like a mother to Cassandra. As the young concubine was silently weeping, she caressed her hair gently, waiting for her to calm down.

She couldn't speak for a long while. Her throat felt hoarse. Cassandra had heard too much in those few sentences. Phetra had cruelly reminded her how terrible it could be. That woman had a similar status to hers, that of a concubine, yet Phetra had gotten rid of her so easily. This was the power of an Imperial Princess.

"How did you do it?" she whispered. "How did you survive among them?"

"You mean among those privileged brats and hungry bitches? A lot of willpower and trusting no one but my own blood. Remember my words, Cassandra. No one gets to such a position with clean hands. Even myself."

"I...I know but...."

"Cassandra, look at me. Now."

Her order was clear. The young concubine had no choice but to look up, with tears in her eyes. Kareen's stare was fiercer than ever. She took Cassandra's face between her long fingers.

"Listen to this old woman, pretty flower. I grew up among merchants. Before I was ten, I knew how to lie, bargain, and steal. How to exploit the weak and be on the stronger end of the deal. My mentor took me inside this place when I was twelve. Not because he wanted to teach me, but because he was a snake, a snake who wanted to take advantage of a child that was smarter than he was. I was even smarter than he thought and made sure the Emperor knew, too.

I did not expect that stubborn old man would take a liking to me, but I knew how wretched all of his women were."

"I would have been terrified...if he had other women than me. Even just one."

Cassandra shivered. In a way, she had been lucky to be picked by Kairen. When she was still a slave, she had seen how such jealousy could tear families apart, burn houses, and leave women homeless in the streets, even with their children. The minister she had served had kicked away two of his women to please the newer one, and Cassandra remembered all of the children Kareen had lost.

"Imagine walking in a room full of hungry tigers," whispered Kareen. "Only one master is holding all of their leashes, so you can't help but get a few scratches getting to him."

"You lost children," said Cassandra. "I don't know what I'd do if I lost this baby."

At that moment, the Imperial Concubine's smile got even scarier than Phetra's earlier.

"When that happens, you become something much more dangerous than those tigers, Cassandra. Trust me. You become a two-headed monster that won't ever return to its original self again. I don't forget and I don't forgive. All his women know that. It's exactly why they all fear me more."

"I don't want to become like you."

The woman chuckled, caressing her cheek.

"I know, pretty flower, and I won't let you. I promise. You have this old woman and her son to look after you. I want to see this child's birth, Cassandra. If I have one thing to do before I leave this world, it is to see the face of my grandchildren."

Cassandra slowly nodded.

She had stayed with Kareen only for a few weeks, but she admired that woman greatly, and trusted her. Like Kairen had said, she was probably their greatest and strongest ally in this Palace. Cassandra felt lucky she had come here with them. Despite Phetra's threats or all the jealous concubines, she knew there was at least someone willing to protect her.

Cassandra was not a fighter. She was among those women who had been born with a frail body, but had grown very wise.

"Wipe your tears, Cassandra. Don't show them your weakness, ever. If they think you're weak, they'll enjoy your suffering twice as much. Don't give them that."

"Princess Phetra is..."

"An obnoxious little swine. Just like her brother. They hate me and my children to the core."

"W...why?"

"Their mother made the mistake of trying to defy me. She shouldn't have."

Cassandra frowned. So this was all about some...revenge? Was that

Phetra's case as well? What had happened to their mother? Despite her curiosity, Cassandra knew Kareen enough by now to know that she wouldn't say anything else.

"Well, let's have breakfast now, shall we? I won't let my grandson starve, and his mother is still too thin. Servants!"

Immediately, a horde of Imperial Servants hurried in, bringing endless gold trays of food. It was time for her to dry her tears indeed. The two women ate silently, but Cassandra knew things wouldn't settle like this. She told Kareen about the snake after they finished their meal, but to her surprise, the Imperial Concubine didn't seem worried or surprised in the slightest. She elegantly wiped her lips, nodding as if she had already known about it.

"It wasn't a poisonous one?"

"No, I am sure. Unless they knew I was pregnant and had prepared ahead, but..."

"They're just playing around then."

"Playing?" repeated Cassandra, shocked.

Kareen stood up, walking further inside her apartments to get changed. Cassandra had seen her shamelessly change her clothes in open spaces in the Diamond Palace before, it was nothing surprising. As she had learned over time, the Imperial Family members shared loose morals, especially over nudity. Moreover, only women were allowed in here. Three servants helped her change into a dark pink dress, with purple and golden embroidery in it. Cassandra wondered if this was a gift from the Emperor.

"If they wanted to kill you, they wouldn't have sent such a petty threat. Not into the War God's room. My son won't die of something so insignificant. His Dragon blood wouldn't even have felt the difference. That thing was directed at you, most likely."

"Me? Why would someone want to scare me?"

"You're the new one and the only concubine of the Third Prince. All the concubines around here like to play like children. They fool around like this all the time, testing each other, seeing who's the stronger woman. But you're not a child anymore. You're a mother."

Kareen turned to her, crossing her arms, while the servants were struggling to do her hair.

"It's time you show those women you are not to be toyed around with. Not because you're protected by Kairen, but on your own."

Cassandra shook her head.

"I doubt I'm strong enough to scare them."

"You don't have to be strong, you have to be smart. And we both know how smart you really are, Cassandra. A woman with your past and knowledge is the one they should be most scared of."

She didn't even have anything to reply to that. She took one step back, shaking her head. How? How could she prove to these women they shouldn't mess with her? Her whole life, Cassandra had struggled to stay out of sight, unnoticed, but things were different now. She had no more room to hide and all eyes were on her.

Cassandra knew Kareen had simply voiced the truth, but it terrified her. Not all of those women were like Phetra, but some still were.

Later that same day, Cassandra left Kareen's apartments, holding a basket in her hands. She knew where to go, but she only lacked a bit of courage. It was still early, and she only crossed a few servants on her way out. She was relieved not to meet anyone from the Imperial Family.

She walked all the way to the outer gardens. It was the same place that she had seen her former and last owner face a brutal death: the Gardens. The Concubines' favorite resting place. It was rumored to be the most beautiful place in the Palace, but Cassandra couldn't care for it.

Most of the Concubines were gathered there for their breakfast; those who weren't accompanying their masters, anyway. They giggled and exchanged sweets and pleasantries, seemingly getting along with each other. Cassandra didn't believe any of those interactions were real.

As soon as she entered the Gardens, all the women stopped talking, their eyes on her. Some were showing curiosity, others were defiant or hateful. Cassandra did her best not to betray her emotions and walk to the middle of the place with her basket.

"Did you get lost?" asked one of the concubines with a naughty tone.

"Shall we bow to her?"

"I'd rather drown in the lake than ever bow to a slave!"

Cassandra took a deep breath and put the basket down. Some of the concubines who had remained silent, frowned. What was she planning?

"You...Why are your hands this color?"

One of the young concubines was pointing at Cassandra's blue fingertips and nails. Turning to the young woman, she showed it better, raising her hands to show them.

"This? I got a little infection. A wild snake ventured into my room last night."

Most concubines knew this snake was probably not simply wandering on its own in her bedroom, but of course, they all remained silent. They either thought she was too stupid to realize, or too smart to say it out loud.

"Luckily, His Highness caught it," said Cassandra. "But...this type of snake's skin can be extremely dangerous when it's an impregnated female. The scales contain some of its venom, only in smaller portions. Just touching it can provoke someone's death within a few days."

One of the concubines giggled.

"Are you going to die? With those blue fingers?"

"This? Oh, no. Luckily, since we caught the snake, I managed to make an antidote in time. It made my fingertips blue from crushing the scales to make a broth with some medical herbs. I was lucky, though. While it will kill instantly with a bite, if you touch its skin, most victims would die in their sleep within a few days. The poison spreads slowly through the finger's crevasses, making them more and more tired until they won't wake up."

"This is ridiculous! I've never heard of such a way of dying!" said one of the other women.

"I'm not surprised, this is a rare snake," said Cassandra. "Back where I come from, we call it the sleep thief. Because the victim will feel more and more sleepy until they can't stop sleeping and slowly die in their sleep."

The women started gossiping between themselves, wondering if it was true. Cassandra took the basket back and slowly walked over to one side, washing away her hands in the little river that crossed the garden. She did her best to ignore all the eyes on her. It was a bet, but she knew she could find the culprit this way if everything went according to her plan. She wasn't proud of it, but she knew she had to be a bit like Kareen. Unforgiving.

Chapter 15

When Cassandra felt she had stayed in their sight for long enough, she took her basket back and left without adding a word. Ignoring all the stares on her, she only went a bit further away, into another garden, with a wider sample of vegetation and an artificial lake and fountain. There, she dipped her bare feet in the shallow water, humming calmly.

Her plan was so simple, yet she wondered if it'd work. Most of the concubines had watched when she washed her hands and saw the blue marks that wouldn't go away. Of course, it was on purpose. Cassandra had washed laundry countless times before. She knew what colorants were the hardest to wash away, especially without any kind of soap. If she wanted, she could have gotten rid of it, but this was all part of her plan.

First, have the concubines and Princesses believe her story. Even if they didn't believe her at first, the odd blue colour she couldn't seem to wash off her fingers and nails should have planted a seed of doubt in their minds. That was all she needed. Just a little bit of doubt, ignorance mixed with a bit of fear, and time for it to grow inside a narrow mind.

As she rested on her own by the lake, she was surprised to see three young women come to her side. She frowned a bit. Those women seemed to be sneering between themselves while glancing her way. Two of them had a red dress and only the one walking ahead had a pink one. She had seen those women before. All of them were among the Fifth Prince's concubines. How many did he have exactly?

"Concubine Cassandra, do you mind if we accompany you for a bit?"

Cassandra shook her head. Since those women were on the same level as her, she didn't have to show any extra politeness, but she shouldn't be too rude either. Kareen had already scolded her many times for acting too submissive when she didn't need to, and Cassandra was diligently trying to apply her advice even more now that she was accounted for as a high-ranked concubine.

"We were worried you'd feel unwelcome over there, with such a crowd. It must be suffocating to face so many women at the same time," said the one in a pink dress.

"It's fine," simply replied Cassandra.

She was wary of those women. She had no idea why they would want anything to do with her, the newly brought concubine. If it was merely out of curiosity, it would be fine. All three of them sat within a reasonable distance of her but, judging from the places they took, it was obvious the one with a pink dress was the leader of the trio.

"It is such a blessing to finally see a Concubine to the Third Prince. His Highness must be delighted to have you."

Cassandra couldn't help but wonder if her pregnancy was known to everyone yet. Unlike some of the other women, she wasn't exposing her baby bump. Back in the previous garden, some of the concubines were so proud of their pregnancies, they were showing off their big bellies. On the contrary, Cassandra wasn't exposing as much skin. Her dress was fully covering her stomach, protecting it from the sun and obvious stares. Not all the concubines had been there at the feast last night, but Cassandra knew the chances were high that the news of her bearing the War God's child had probably spread already.

"Thanks."

She didn't want to get too friendly with other concubines. None of them could have been there by mistake. You couldn't stay a Prince's concubine, residing in the Imperial Palace, if you couldn't take care of yourself first. No woman in this place was as innocent as they looked.

For a few minutes, the three women pretended to talk between themselves, about trivial matters such as the weather and their Prince's latest concerns, but Cassandra knew they were observing her. She pretended not to know and soaked her feet, ignoring them.

"Lady Cassandra, what do you think of this?"

Wondering what topic they had finally decided to share with her, she turned her head to them. The woman in a pink dress had a cunning smile Cassandra didn't like.

"My servant made a mistake this morning. I thought I should punish her, but my friends thought I should be nice to her and let it go. She has been a very nice servant of mine for a while but...recently, I've been thinking she's acting too much in front of my dearest Prince. I think maybe the little swine is trying to seduce one's Prince. What do you think?"

Cassandra frowned a bit. It may have seemed like a trivial matter, but her words were heavier than they seemed. Was she hinting at how a servant or a slave, like Cassandra, had dared to seduce a Prince? She obviously had no idea. Cassandra sighed.

"I wonder why you should punish her. Isn't The Fifth Prince the one to have many concubines? If he can split his love so easily, you should be used to His Highness welcoming one more every once in a while, right?"

The concubine's expression turned sour.

Cassandra was clear, though. She wouldn't let this woman imply they were in the same situation or that Cassandra had stolen anyone's property. She couldn't compare her Prince with his womanizer of a brother. Basically anyone could become the Fifth Prince's concubine, with a good body and some sense of seduction. No wonder those women were jealous to death and eager to start fights at any given occasion.

"At least she isn't some slave," said one of those in a red dress, pretending to talk to her peer.

"It has to be difficult, you know. We should even pity her," said the other one. "I mean, the Imperial Family can be so wilful. If it's only a slave or a servant, they can be wiped out without blinking and no one will even remember them."

Cassandra ignored them, a bit annoyed. Were all concubines so petty? So childish? Did they think they could toy with her? She wasn't a slave anymore, so why would she listen to this nonsense? Seeing Cassandra wasn't flinching, the concubine in the pink dress clicked her tongue. She thought she had found easy prey, but this wasn't as fun as she had thought.

"You know, it's been done before. Servants taken as concubines and forgotten the next day. Sent to feed the dragons."

"Really?" said Cassandra, her voice remaining very calm.

Her experience as "dragon food" probably was not the one they had imagined at all. Actually, Cassandra smiled, remembering her first encounter with both Kairen and his dragon. Seeing her like this, the concubine became red, annoyed at her passive response. Wasn't this bitch going to worry at all! The War God wasn't anywhere in sight, so how could she keep acting so mighty! She wasn't even that pretty!

"Well, slaves are meant to be tough after all."

Once again, Cassandra ignored her. She couldn't be affected by such a petty attitude. Actually, she thought this concubine was acting like an annoying flea, trying to bother her with baseless sentences and a mighty attitude.

She couldn't be bothered by that, or she wouldn't be able to withstand one more day here. After dipping her toes in the freshwater some more, turning a blind ear to their nonsense, Cassandra stood up, brushing her hair a bit. To her surprise, the concubine stood up too and stepped closer.

"Now that I see you up close..."

Cassandra did not like this woman being so close. Aside from her Prince and his family, she hadn't gotten used to anyone being so close. She took a step back and the concubine in pink smiled, mistakenly thinking she was afraid.

"If...one was to disappear...mysteriously...I wonder how long it would take one to worry?"

Was this woman an idiot? Or did she think Cassandra was that weak? To be scared by such a childish threat? Cassandra had learned to be afraid of the Imperial Family. Whether it was a Princess or a Prince, she would have definitely been scared. But a concubine was only a woman, like her.

228

"Are you threatening me?" she asked.

Her calm but cold voice was sending a warning. Only the two women in the red dresses understood and carefully stepped back, looking pale and worried. Truth was, Cassandra herself wasn't scary at all, but her calm and confidence in this situation was something their instincts couldn't underestimate.

Unfortunately, the other Concubine missed that warning, smiling like a cat once again. It was as if she had found an easy prey to toy with, and would play until she had enough. Only, Cassandra wasn't in the mood to be playing at all.

"Why would I threaten you, Lady Cassandra? We are both concubines, after all. It would be a shame if anything happened...by accident."

Cassandra hated that word. No accident ever happened in the Imperial Palace. As the other woman kept stepping forward, she kept retreating, closer and closer to the pond, until her heels were touching the water.

"Do you think...I'm scared?"

Cassandra's sudden question, said in a clear voice, finally managed to make her doubt. She frowned. She had been retreating all this time, wasn't she scared?

"Step back," ordered Cassandra.

Her soft and gentle voice didn't match her words. Hence, the concubine didn't move and chuckled.

"Don't you give me orders. You may wear a pink dress, but you're still under me. As any slave. You're under anyone here. Don't think this color will..."

"Step back."

As she said this for the second time, the concubine frowned, annoyed. Who was this bitch to give her orders?! She had been a concubine for over five years here! She wouldn't listen to the orders of a mere...

Before she could add another word, a sudden flap of wings was heard, and she retreated in a hurry. She barely had time to move before a giant claw ripped the grass she had stood on a couple of seconds ago.

If the concubine had been a bit more aware of her surroundings earlier, she would have seen the dark shape that had been growing bigger in the sky, coming their way at a scary speed. Cassandra had seen it coming from far away. Had the dragon gone hunting before looking for her?

Krai growled, wrapping its large body around Cassandra, putting its head right where her hand was, as she gently patted and scratched the dark scales. The dragon was happily growling, glad to be reunited with her, but to the three terrorized women, those sounds were horrifying. Moreover, the woman who stood unaffected at the center of those mountains of scales was still staring at them, completely fearless.

"You got interrupted. Please continue."

"I... I..."

Before she could gather her thoughts, Krai's large tail whipped in the pond, splashing them. All three women got drenched, and yet, they didn't even dare scream.

They tried to retreat, but to their surprise, Cassandra smiled softly.

"I believe you weren't done talking. Please stay."

For the first time, they realized how scary this woman was. Because she could utter those words with the softest voice, the gentlest smile, while a murderous beast was standing right next to her.

Cassandra hadn't really planned on cornering them, but Krai had come at the right time, and in a few minutes, she had decided she shouldn't let such women make easy prey of her. They would be an example, to show others she was no toy to play with. Like Kareen had told her, it would be better to teach them she wasn't going to be someone to take lightly. She would have her hands full dealing with the worst people already.

She had no spare time for the childish games of bored concubines.

After that episode, no other concubine dared to bother Cassandra for the next few days. It was made known within a few hours how scary the gentle-looking woman could be. She had kept all three women alone with her, making them cry, beg, and tremble in fear of being devoured at any given moment, for over an hour. Cassandra had only insisted they told the same stories over and over, but all three concubines didn't dare disobey and anger her or the beast. It could have seemed like a short time, but anyone who had ever been in the presence of one of the Imperial Dragons knew it wasn't.

Truth was, Cassandra had only intended to scare them a bit, and only caressed or scratched Krai during that time, but it had worked beyond wonders. It so happened that the Black Dragon still had fresh blood on its maw, and the concubines saw those ruby eyes shine their way in a scary manner for longer than they could endure. Even if she would never give the order to bite or injure, unless she was in a death-threat situation, that sight was engraved in those women's minds. They had cried for hours after that to anyone who would listen, about how merciless the War God's concubine was, threatening to have the Dragon eat their poor defenseless selves.

After that, even if most concubines still held some doubt about how things really went, the fact that she was often followed by the Black Dragon was enough of a warning, and when Krai wasn't in sight, most feared the beast wasn't too far away.

It was actually a bit of a funny sight.

Krai kept following her like a dog, growling to get her attention, glaring at anyone who came close, and growled even more when she walked inside a building its large body couldn't follow her into. It actually caused a bit of worry to the servants that the Palace's architecture wouldn't be able to withstand the beast's reckless climbing on the roofs to follow her scent.

Cassandra was doing her best to get used to the Imperial Palace, though it was difficult.

Firstly, that place was way too big for her to get used to. She got lost many, many times and would only realize once she asked someone how far she had drifted away from her initial destination.

Secondly, she wasn't with Kairen as often as she had hoped to be. The Emperor called for his son almost every day at dawn, and she helplessly spent breakfast and lunch alone, with the Imperial Concubine Mother, or in the Concubine's gardens, only to be reunited with him right before dinner with all of the Imperial Family.

Lastly, this daily buffet was a torture for her. She hated being confined in a room full of people who glared at each other, no matter how vast that room was. Since she had demonstrated she had the backing of an Imperial Dragon, and when Kairen was in the room, no one dared to defy her too much, but she still hated that atmosphere. The only good part of it was that they would listen together to minister reports and news about what was going on in the country, and after a few days, Cassandra realized those dinners were also a way for the Emperor to test his sons.

While the youngest brothers were usually fooling around with their concubines, enjoying the shows, and were annoyed by those topics, the three oldest Princes were deeply involved.

The oldest Prince, Sephir, was an obvious bookworm and knew every topic by heart. At first, to Cassandra, he seemed to be the smartest of them all. However, after a while, she realized his decision-making was mostly based on past occurrences, and if no similar situations had happened in the past, he was usually at a loss.

The only one who truly rivaled Kairen was the Second Prince, Vrehan. Cassandra didn't like him. He had a face like a rat, tiny eyes, and a mean expression. More importantly, he glared at Kairen anytime he would say anything and seemed like he was about to explode if their father agreed with him. Plus, his sister Phetra supported anything he said unconditionally. Since their last meeting, Cassandra had managed to avoid that woman, but Phetra made sure to glare her way any chance she could over dinner.

"What do you think, White Lily?"

Cassandra was surprised to hear the Emperor suddenly ask her opinion. This nickname he had given her had become sort of a title for her, whenever he addressed her, like she was some precious treasure.

It was the first time he openly asked for her opinion on a matter. Until then, Cassandra had listened and whispered some of her ideas a couple of times to Kairen, but she had never dared to interact with the Imperial Family Members while they had their talks. Also, it didn't seem like any other concubine was ever involved in those talks, as only the Princes and, more seldomly, the Princesses answered. She couldn't hide her surprise, but Kairen soon caressed her back, spreading his warmth to her and making her feel a bit more confident. This topic was about some medical issue she knew about, an epidemic that had risen in the South.

"I support the confinement idea, Your Highness. Until the real cause is found, nothing should leave or enter that village."

"Shouldn't we simply kill all the infected?" hissed Phetra, annoyed that Cassandra was even asked after she had given her own solution.

"Nothing in the reports proves this disease is transmitted by the sick," calmly replied Cassandra. "It could be the food, the water, even the animals. Sending a doctor with medical knowledge, enough drugs to heal those in need, and guarding the area closely, may be enough to prevent the disease from spreading, especially in such a remote place."

The Emperor nodded, looking satisfied.

"As expected of the Imperial Physician! Let's do this! Did you record all that she said?"

While he was checking in with his secretary, Cassandra turned to Kairen, who gently kissed her temple. Those few days, she had been spending a lot of time with some of the other Imperial Physicians present in the Palace, but for now, they had been learning more from her than she had learned from them. Some of Cassandra's knowledge of herbal medicine was revolutionary to them, and despite their annoyance at a female being acknowledged as a doctor at the beginning, the Imperial Physicians had started opening up to her, one by one, teaching her their ways and discussing their knowledge.

Hence, the Emperor knew she was doing well in that aspect and considered Cassandra's opinion.

"Also, make sure to check around, see if it hasn't spread. Now, to the military-"

Before the Emperor ended his sentence, the First Prince suddenly started coughing loudly, unable to stop. His concubines tried to help him, but he needed a few more minutes to catch his breath.

This wasn't the first time. Cassandra had seen Prince Sephir with this kind of issue several times before. Though she had considered a poison, from his pale look and thin figure, she guessed the First Prince had never been healthy to begin with. Probably weak lungs or some respiratory disease. Unfortunately, she couldn't approach another Prince and had to leave it to the Imperial Physician appointed for him. However, as the days went on, she couldn't help but fear for the eldest brother. This man wouldn't live long.

Once Sephir caught his breath and reassured everyone, the Emperor threw the remaining topics away, along with his secretary, and called for more wine. Cassandra, however, was concerned. How would the death of one of the brothers change things?

They only had two days left until the New Year's first celebrations. Once the week-long festivities were over, her Prince had promised to bring her back to the Onyx Castle, at least for the later stages of her pregnancy. Cassandra didn't want to stay in the Imperial Palace longer than necessary. She loathed this place.

"Are you tired?" he whispered in her ear.

"I'm fine..."

"Eat more."

She nodded and took some of the grapefruit he was handing her. She had been craving those lately and emptied almost all the plates of grapefruit at each banquet by herself. Was it because of her baby? Cassandra found herself with some new crazy craving each day. Tonight, it was white fish. The cooks had worked hard to make some more ready for her, and she was enjoying it slowly.

Cassandra wasn't the only pregnant concubine, as two of the Fifth Prince's women and one of the Second Prince's concubines were showing off their round bellies, but she was the only one to be shown so much care. She didn't know if Kairen or the Emperor had given special orders, but the servants seemed particularly careful while serving her and, more surprising, her food was tested before she ate anything.

"Father, how grand will the new year celebrations be this year?" asked one of the Princesses.

"The usual, the usual, Daughter of mine. We invited some neighboring countries, but not too many, and we will reopen the Arena!"

While exclamations rose all around the room, Cassandra got a chill. The Arena.

Memories of a bloody slaughter came back to her mind. Despite her meeting with the Prince, she could never forget that horrid scene, the dragons going after the humans and playing with their corpses. If it wasn't for Krai, she probably wouldn't have survived it either.

Feeling her shiver a bit, Kairen caressed her back. Cassandra usually warmed up from his touch, but this time, her expression was sad and his concubine was obviously lost in some dark thoughts. He frowned.

"Cassandra?"

She shook her head, unwilling to speak.

"Father, can we get fireworks?" asked one of the young Princesses.

"Tigers! I want to see wildcats!"

"And more chariot races! And dancers!"

As the Imperial Princesses started making more and more demands, Shareen, who had been silent on the seat next to Kairen, clicked her tongue.

"Are you going to pay for all this, Sisters? Did you suddenly start working and earning enough to cover your childish, petty whims?"

Her voice had the effect of a whip on them. Cassandra had never noticed, but Shareen was one of the oldest princesses around, and no one really dared to mess with her. Was it because of her being the War God's sister? Or her mother?

However, none of the Princesses dared to talk back to her, all looking down like children caught misbehaving. The Emperor laughed.

"Wise as ever, my Daughter! Well, it is true we won't spend too much this year; we've had a dry year, after all. Let's learn to restrain ourselves a bit, shall we? Fireworks and wildcats are fine, but we'll forget about chariot races. It's only good for spreading dust all around anyway and I'm getting bored seeing the same people every year. Forget it!"

"Father, what about the dragons' sacrifice?"

Everyone in the room immediately went silent and Cassandra frowned. Of course, Phetra had been the one to suggest that, while looking at Cassandra, too. She knew exactly what she was doing, bringing that back up. The Emperor frowned.

"Phetra, we don't make human sacrifices on the New Year!"

"I want to see it, Father. I missed the last show."

Phetra's voice was full of confidence and she was smiling like a snake. Cassandra stood up and, not waiting for the Emperor's answer, walked away. She couldn't speak against an Imperial Princess, but she could show her disagreement. She left the Imperial Banquet without looking back, shivering and angry.

Cassandra walked a few more steps, wondering where to go. She was angry and had no other way to protest than to leave the Imperial Banquet, which upset her. For once, Cassandra felt she was truly too powerless, unable to stop Phetra or oppose the Imperial Princess. This place was really too harsh.

"Imperial Concubine?"

She turned around, realizing someone had followed her. It only took her a couple of seconds to remember the young woman. Weeks and weeks ago, she was the young servant that had given her the first red dress.

"You're...Dahlia, right?"

The young woman smiled.

"I'm glad you remember me, my Lady."

"Please don't... Just call me Cassandra, please."

Dahlia chuckled. She hadn't changed much since Cassandra had seen her. She was still wearing a long green dress, with her dark hair in a braided bun. Bowing slightly, she walked up a bit closer to her.

"Are you alright?"

"I...I needed some fresh air," said Cassandra.

It was partially the truth. She felt stuffed, confined in that room with so many people. Only because her Prince was there could she bear it. Dahlia seemed to understand and nodded slightly.

"Do you want to rest in the Ivy Garden?"

"The Ivy Garden?"

"It's a smaller one, not many people use it," explained Dahlia with a smile. "But it's really pretty at night."

Cassandra nodded and followed her. Dahlia seemed to know her way around the Palace perfectly, even as the sun was slowly setting outside, putting them in the dark before long. After a few minutes, they finally arrived.

As she had said, it was a much smaller one than the fancy garden the concubines usually used, but Cassandra instantly loved it. It only had one bench and a little pond with white fish. The walls around it were covered in ivy and little white flowers she had never seen before. The place seemed incredibly pure and pretty.

While Cassandra walked around, Dahlia lit up a few lanterns, bringing some more light into the space.

The concubine was still observing the place when a long growl was heard. Krai's head popped from behind one of the walls, those big red eyes finding her immediately.

"Come," called Cassandra.

It only took one word. Stepping over the wall, Krai hurried to her side, circling her with its body, head resting next to her. Of course, it was the perfect position for being scratched, and the dragon growled until Cassandra sat and started taking care of its favorite spot.

Dahlia's mouth was open in awe and she didn't dare to step closer. The concubine was sitting right next to the dragon, totally fine, and scratching those scales as if it was just a huge dog! Though she was a brave girl, and the dragon seemed harmless this way, Dahlia sat a few meters away, close to the pond, but remained fascinated by the scene.

"Thank you for bringing me here," said Cassandra after a few minutes. "I needed to relax a bit."

"It's my pleasure, Lady Cassandra. Is it really fine not telling anyone where you are, though? I thought you would have a few servants with you."

Cassandra shook her head.

"It's fine."

As long as Krai was with her, its Master would know and be at ease. That was all Cassandra needed. Kairen had let her leave, but he probably had to stay behind to discuss official matters with his Father. As inexperienced as she was in politics, she understood that much. She also appreciated spending time alone with another woman her age. She missed Nebora a bit, and maybe because of their similar black hair, Dahlia reminded Cassandra of her friend somehow.

"How long have you been working here?" asked Cassandra.

"My whole life or so, I think... One of the Palace's cooks found me on his doorstep and adopted me when I was just a baby. So, I became a servant as soon as I was old enough to be."

Cassandra nodded. Dahlia was among the lucky ones. Most orphans were captured and made slaves. No wonder she knew the Palace so well, despite its size.

"Lady Cassandra, did you go to the Onyx Castle?" suddenly asked Dahlia, blushing slightly, but curious.

Cassandra smiled, and just like that, both women started talking. On one side, Dahlia was loving stories from outside the Palace, while Cassandra was keen to know any detail of this place that Dahlia could tell her.

Having grown up here, Dahlia had seen many, many concubines. That's why she had felt Cassandra was different from the start. She didn't have that mighty attitude of a noble's daughter, or felt entitled in any way. She even spoke to her like an equal.

"Do you want to explore the world, Dahlia?"

The young woman seemed to hesitate for a while, blushing slightly.

"Yes, but...there is also someone I want to stay close to here. So...as long as that person is here, I don't think I'll be able to leave."

"A lover?" asked Cassandra, judging from her reaction.

Dahlia sighed.

"I wish, but...I doubt they even know I exist, so..."

Cassandra felt a bit sorry for Dahlia. She seemed like such a gentle woman, but to fall in love in the Palace was... a sad twist of fate. With so many pretty concubines everywhere, it was probably hard to be noticed by anyone around here.

Cassandra knew how lucky she was that Kairen didn't actually care about such things. If it wasn't for Krai, she would have been nothing but dust by now. Thinking about this, she kept caressing the sleek scales for a while, chatting with Dahlia, actually feeling calmer than she had been in a while.

Much later in the night, the young woman was called back to work, and Cassandra was left alone in the garden. She didn't feel like going back, unsure if the banquet would be over by then, and so she decided to stay a bit longer.

The quiet garden was actually nice. At night, the temperature was much better for Cassandra to endure, with a fresh wind and the warm dragon scales on her back. She rested, watching the stars, until she heard someone step closer.

The Prince slowly walked to her side, putting one knee down.

"So, this is where you were."

Cassandra smiled.

"His Highness, your Father, didn't..."

"He was unhappy you left."

The concubine felt a bit happy about that. It meant he approved of her action, in a way. If he had been against her leaving, she couldn't even have taken one step out of the Banquet Hall. If the Emperor was unhappy, it probably wasn't directed at her, but at the one who had caused her to leave.

Cassandra felt a weight lifted off her shoulders. She wasn't used to being so bold, and every action made her insecure. She could still be killed at any moment, even if she was now wearing a pink dress. Kairen's presence helped her forget about her worries too.

"I like this garden," she said softly.

"You want to stay here?"

Since Cassandra hesitated for a while, he decided to sit next to her, letting her lay against his chest. Surrounded by the Black Dragon, they knew no one would dare to bother them. Resting her head on his shoulder, Cassandra kept staring at the stars, feeling his warm hand caressing her.

"My mom used to tell me about the stars every night. She'd teach me how to read them, their names and their past."

"Their past?"

Cassandra slightly nodded.

"In the tribe I grew up in, we did not believe in dragons and demi-Gods,

236

but in the sacred nature. I was taught that every life is sacred and equally precious. Plants, animals, humans, all equal and living together, each one with a purpose. And the Elders said the stars are little reminders of each life that came and went. My mother said the brighter they were, the purer and shorter a life was."

The Prince frowned a bit. It was so rare for her to talk about her life before meeting him. No wonder she wasn't really afraid of Krai, and couldn't stand another's suffering.

"Did they teach you about medicine?"

"Yes... My Grandfather was the village chief and a good doctor. He knew every plant, every flower, every herb's name, and their properties. He taught me everything. After that, I kept trying to learn what I could when I could access my master's libraries or listen to the apothecary shop owners."

Still, it was impressive. She was captured when she was very young, but had still managed to learn so much in such a short time and kept nurturing her talent by herself. Kairen felt like his woman was more precious than any treasure one could gather in this Palace. He caressed her hair, kissing her fingers gently.

"Your mother..." whispered Cassandra.

"What about her?"

"...Can you tell me what she did to the Second Prince's mother?"

She heard him sigh.

"Their mother tried to poison me when I was young. She hated my mother and didn't want her son to have another rival born from her. But my mother found out and tricked her into drinking it herself. She had a slow and painful death."

Cassandra felt disgusted. How could one do such a thing to a child. Since Imperial Children were so resistant; drinking a poison meant for Kairen must have caused that concubine to be in terrible agony? No matter what, Cassandra couldn't help but think it was a tragic death, even if she had brought it upon herself. Kareen wasn't cruel by nature, but she certainly had to stand up to protect her children.

In the same situation, Cassandra wondered if she would have had the guts to do the same thing and cause someone else's death. She put a hand on her tummy. Yes, maybe. Probably. She already loved her unborn child so much, she couldn't bear the thought of losing him. If she had gone through what Kareen went through, losing several children, she might have gone crazy with despair. She shivered and hugged Kairen closer, in need of his warmth.

"Are you cold?"

"Just hug me, please."

He gently obeyed, surrounding her with his sturdy arms and hot skin. Behind them, Krai softly growled, curling up a bit more around them. They stayed like this a long while until Cassandra fell asleep, and the Prince decided it was getting a bit too cold for his expecting concubine to stay out.

He gently carried her back to their bedroom, only noticing she was awake when laying her on the bed.

No words were exchanged between them for a while. He helped her get rid of her jewelry and dress then laid next to her. Cassandra's emerald eyes were shining with the candlelight between them, as she kept staring at the War God, half-asleep.

"My Prince," she whispered.

Her voice was so soft, he thought he had misheard it.

"My name," he said, getting closer to her, placing one arm around her.

"Kairen... I love you."

The War God remained stunned for a while, unable to say a word. Cassandra chuckled, observing his baffled expression for the first time. Did he really not know? She got a bit closer and put a quick peck on his lips, despite her shyness. Her heart was filled with something warm and sweet, and that secure feeling whenever that man was close.

Kairen didn't stay frozen for long though. The Prince's eyes dropped down to her lips and drew her in for a much more intense, deep kiss. Cassandra helplessly blushed, feeling his lips and tongue claiming her so fiercely. His caresses on her skin were still gentle, but it had a slightly different feel to it.

When they separated, Cassandra couldn't help but smile, a bit out of breath.

"Aren't you going to answer me?" she whispered gently.

Kairen stayed silent, scrutinizing her very seriously. After a while, he took a deep breath, looking stern.

"Marry me, Cassandra."

The young concubine was taken back in surprise, expecting anything but those words. It took her a few seconds to understand what he had just said. To marry him? Her? She was just...and already...her thoughts got lost in a storm. After a few seconds, she laughed nervously.

"Did you just..."

The War God's expression was still just as serious. Cassandra tried to sit up, but he held her wrists in place to keep her lying down.

"You don't want to?" he asked.

The young concubine sighed.

"If you marry me, you won't be able to change your mind."

"I know."

"Even if you meet someone much prettier and younger later," she added.

"I know."

What was he thinking?

Cassandra wished she was inside his head right now, to understand how the War God functioned. Certainly not like most men.

Becoming a high-ranked concubine after spending eight or nine years as a slave was already unheard of, but becoming someone's wife? No normal man would have thought of such a thing. There was a huge gap between the concubines and the official wife. A gap so important, most of the concubines in this Palace would have killed to hear those words. A man's official wife had an unshakable position. The Dragon Empire didn't recognize divorces, and even if one of the partners died, the other would never be able to replace him or her. While concubines could be abandoned or dismissed, an official wife would never need to worry about that. Hence, most men of power made sure to marry a woman from a strong background, with good looks and brains. Cassandra felt like she probably didn't check at least two of those boxes.

"Cassandra," he softly spoke her name, taking her out of her thoughts.

"You wouldn't be able to take another concubine," she said. "I'd never allow it."

That was one of the powers of the official wife. No concubines could be brought in by the husband without her consent. Therefore, most men would rather not pick a wife and have plenty of concubines instead. Or at the very least, make sure their spouse closed their eyes to a new woman.

Cassandra already knew she wouldn't be able to do that. She was already too attached to him, emotionally and physically. She would rather die than share him with another woman.

"It's fine," replied the Prince.

"It isn't fine. I won't be able to do much to help you. I'm not as smart as your mother, or as powerful as your sister."

Cassandra was worried. If something happened between him and his brothers, she would be powerless. She had no backing, nothing to help him. His brothers' women probably had a lot of money, influence and scholars behind them. A merchant or even a minister's daughter would have been a hundred times better than her to be his wife.

However, no matter how much she thought about it, Cassandra knew that man too well. He wouldn't change his mind. He was odd and stubborn about what he wanted and didn't want. Luckily for her, she was among the things he liked most.

She smiled and leaned in closer to him, stealing another kiss. He never refused her kisses and it wouldn't be the case for this one either. Gently brushing his fingers through her hair, he tasted her sweetness, rolling with her on the bed. His young concubine was obviously too tired tonight, her eyes kept closing and her breathing slowed.

The War God was fine with that, she definitely deserved some rest. But...

"You didn't answer me," he remarked as Cassandra was half-asleep on his chest.

She smiled.

"You do that often."

He frowned, wondering what she was talking about. But before he could even begin to figure it out, she had fallen fast asleep. He sighed, putting her small hand to his lips to kiss her pale skin, and wrapped her gently in his embrace. He then closed his eyes, too.

The next morning, Cassandra woke up with a horrible feeling. Something smelled terribly bad. She struggled to sit up. It was so early, it was barely dawn outside and her Prince was still soundly sleeping next to her.

Yet, she couldn't stay in bed. She stood up and glanced at the tray of food someone had brought in while they were asleep. She then stumbled to the washbasin. Her skin was covered in goosebumps and she kept gagging above the basin, her head spinning.

"Cassandra?"

Kairen had woken up the moment she moved, but now she seemed really unwell. He rushed to her side, worried. He had no idea what was going on until Cassandra loudly threw up.

"Cassandra, you're sick? Is it poison?"

"The... food..." she managed to stutter, pointing at the tray.

The Prince frowned before understanding that her sickness was due to her pregnancy, not any sort of poisoning. He grabbed the whole tray and threw it out of the closest open window, before running back to her.

"What can I do to help?" he asked while caressing her hair.

Cassandra shook her head. She was just trying to breathe a little deeper, and she felt too embarrassed to talk after vomiting. She had occasional random morning sickness, but this was the first in his presence and the most embarrassing one. While Kareen knew about the unpleasant consequences of pregnancy, her son was clueless.

Since his concubine couldn't formulate any request, Kairen called out for servants to assist. Dahlia and another young woman rushed in to help Cassandra.

"Lady Cassandra, would you like some water?" whispered Dahlia.

"P...please."

Unhappy, Kairen stood to the side with his arms crossed, watching the two servants take care of his concubine. He hated being unable to help, but this was a woman's matter. If Cassandra was uncomfortable with his help, he'd rather do nothing and let the servants assist her.

After a few minutes, Cassandra was able to sit down and talk. With the Prince by her side rubbing her back, she let Dahlia know the ingredients and smells that usually triggered her nausea or made it worse. The young servant nodded in acknowledgement.

"I will make sure the kitchen knows, Lady Cassandra."

As Dahlia stood up to leave, Kairen watched her and turned to Cassandra.

"You can make her your private servant if you want," he suggested.

To his surprise, Cassandra's eyes widened in mild disbelief.

"Really?"

He had thought she would straight out refuse the idea, but on the contrary, she seemed to love it. He nodded.

"Are you feeling better now?"

"Yes...I might even be a bit hungry, to be honest. This baby is really moody."

Kairen nodded and put a hand on the little bump. His son. That child better be good to his mother once he's born.

After a while, Dahlia reappeared with a different tray and some of the specific food Cassandra had requested. The only thing they could find, though, was a variety of nuts that grew further south, which made the Prince frown. Cassandra, however, was satisfied with what Dahlia had gathered in such a short amount of time. She cleaned herself up a bit, got changed, and decided to eat in the closest open space she could find, as she didn't want to stay in the room where she had just vomited minutes ago.

The Prince followed closely behind her, to everyone's surprise. The Imperial Servants couldn't help but stare at the War God accompanying his concubine like she was a precious treasure he needed to keep within arms reach.

As soon as they sat in the garden, Krai appeared over their heads and even bickered with its Master about who would sit closest to the concubine. Dahlia watched as the scene unfolded before her. With Cassandra chuckling between the dragon and its master, she couldn't help but feel that Cassandra might just be the luckiest concubine around.

"Can we go search around the brothels today?" suddenly asked Cassandra, turning to the Prince.

Kairen frowned.

"You're sick."

"I'm not sick, I'm pregnant. I will be fine. Dahlia can take care of my needs."

The young servant avidly nodded in agreement. Kairen glared at her, immediately causing her to look down in fear.

"No. I wouldn't be able to accompany you."

He probably had more meetings with the Emperor and his military advisors today again, but Cassandra was tired of doing nothing aside from getting lost and sipping tea with his mother. She took a deep breath and insisted again.

"Please. I'll probably be safer there than I am here."

That part was true. With her pink dress and an Imperial Servant following her, no one would dare to lift a finger towards her. In the Palace, however, she could be attacked at any time. The Prince's frown continued, he didn't like having her in a different place. It was fine when she was with his mother in the Diamond Palace, but...

"Go with Shareen," he finally said.

Cassandra smiled widely, unable to hide her satisfaction. She could finally start looking for her younger sister! Moreover, she would definitely be safe with an Imperial Princess. She kissed his scratchy cheek swiftly.

"Thank you," she whispered.

This simple kiss distracted him from frowning. He sighed, surrendering himself to her and kissed her back. Seeing this, Dahlia discreetly left them.

A couple of hours later, Dahlia was surprised to see that the young concubine was still accompanied by the dragon. She had heard from other servants how the beast was infatuated with her. But seeing it like this was a bit different.

Any move Cassandra made, Krai was watching like a curious puppy following its Master. The large dragon struggled to follow her with its huge body, sometimes crawling over the buildings and growling at the servants who appeared too suddenly. When Shareen arrived though, it didn't dare growl at her.

"The Red District? Really?" asked the Princess.

"I am looking for my younger sister," explained Cassandra. "My best opportunity to find her is there."

"I see...very well, that might be a fun outing," said Shareen. "And it gives me an excuse to avoid Mother's nagging about my lifestyle."

Shareen's way to have fun wasn't to her mother's taste. Hence, Kareen usually resorted to a silent protest by visiting her from dawn until dusk, unless the Princess was busy elsewhere that is. Cassandra was surprised to learn Shareen was the most involved Princess in the Empire's politics. She attended most of the meetings along with her brothers and refused to be defeated by any man in the room. She was well-respected in most circles for being a smart, strong woman who didn't need a man to back her up; not even her own father. Like the other members of her family, she had a short temper, however. Bringing her sword to meetings wasn't just for decorative purposes.

As the women left the Palace, Cassandra felt like a big weight had been lifted off her shoulders. She couldn't fully relax in that place without the Prince around.

Though she had never been there personally, Cassandra had lived long enough in the Capital to know where the Red District was. She naturally headed there with Shareen and Dahlia, the black-scaled dragon following behind. It was a truly strange procession that the bystanders witnessed that day. A concubine in a pink dress, along with an Imperial Princess, only one servant with them, and... an Imperial Dragon that struggled to fit inside the busy streets. Many displays fell victim to a wing or tail in its wake, despite the merchants' desperate attempts to push it out of the way. No one wanted to hinder their path, and the trio progressed easily through the streets.

The reputation of the Imperial Family preceded them. Any glance, gesture, or sound could trigger a brutal and violent death, and no one wanted to leave any chance for that to happen. Shareen's purple outfit was like a ghost, making nearly everyone run away. Though she found it sad, Cassandra understood the people's fears and didn't comment on that. There were too many spiteful Princesses back at the Palace, she had witnessed it herself. People were bound to fear them.

As they progressed in the streets, Cassandra was surprised when she realized that Shareen knew the way perfectly.

"Have you been to the Red District before, Your Highness?"

"I already told you to just call me Shareen, didn't I? You're my brother's woman, you need to grow a backbone...and yes, I go there often."

Cassandra didn't mind her rude way of speaking. After living with Shareen for a bit at her mother's Palace, she had grown used to it. Shareen was extremely blunt and literally had no filter on any subject. She spoke that way to anyone, except maybe her own mother.

"Really?" asked Cassandra. "I mean... I didn't think members of the Imperial Family would...venture to such a place."

"Oh, some do. I like to go...shopping."

"For..."

Cassandra then understood her meaning and desperately blushed. A question popped in her head, but she chased it away, as she could never gather the courage to ask. After all, she had experienced herself how playful Shareen was.

Behind them, Dahlia was walking silently, glancing back and forth between the two women. Though she had volunteered to accompany Cassandra, she was just as shy as the concubine about going there. She silently continued peeking at the Imperial Princess, intimidated, but she also kept an eye on the dragon following them. Like common people, Dahlia was naturally afraid of it. If she hadn't seen it being so gentle with Cassandra before, she probably would have been absolutely terrified about coming along.

"So, where do you want to start?" asked the Princess as they reached the district.

During the day, that area was known to be relatively calm. Most people here worked at night, so the brothels were barely just opening their doors to let the caretakers, servants, and slaves inside to do their chores. Cassandra glanced left and right, but she had no real clue.

"I guess we'll just have to ask around?"

"Right. We better do it now before they notice your pet and start screaming and running away."

"Oh."

Cassandra had almost forgotten about the dragon. Indeed, it would be a bit inconvenient to walk Krai around. She smiled and walked up to it, immediately getting all of the dragon's attention. Krai had been following very curiously to where they were going. When the young concubine turned to it, it could barely contain his excitement, crushing two stalls with the swish of its tail.

Cassandra put her hands on the warm snout, scratching it.

"Could you wait for us here, Krai?"

She wasn't sure how much the dragon understood her words, but since the mountain episode, she knew how to make it lay down and wait. She began patting its snout with both hands until it laid its whole body down. Krai closed its eyes, ready for a little nap.

"Good boy," she said with a smile. "Don't eat people!"

Whether it had understood that last part or not, Cassandra wasn't certain. Krai, however, opened one large red eye to watch her walk away with the two other women.

Dahlia was in shock. She thought the young concubine must have the blood of a Goddess to order around a dragon like that. She had it obeying her commands like a pet! The dragon's owner didn't even need to be present! She had previously thought the dragon was pampering her because the Prince was always around, but she had it all wrong! Now, per Cassandra's request, the most dangerous beast in this Empire was taking a nice little nap in the middle of the street!

"Let's start with this one," suggested Shareen, heading to the closest building. "You know what to ask?"

Cassandra nodded, stepping ahead.

Needless to say, anyone who opened their door was completely struck by the sight of the two women. One woman wearing the Imperial Purple and the other was clearly a high-ranked concubine! A couple of the people Cassandra spoke with even wondered internally if this could be some sort of scam, seeing as the strange duo was accompanied by only one servant.

"I'm looking for my younger sister," Cassandra repeated for the eighth time that day. "She would be sixteen years old now, she was captured nine years ago. She probably resembles me."

Back when they were children, Missandra and Cassandra indeed looked a lot alike. They had the same brown hair, the same thin nose, and even the exact same emerald eyes. Even if her sister had matured, Cassandra hoped that their whiter skin would help people remember her.

"Sorry, Imperial Concubine," said the woman. "I don't remember anyone that matches your description. You might want to ask next door though, they usually purchase the girls when they're young. They're well-known for their training."

Cassandra thanked her, but she was starting to feel a bit discouraged. Someone should have been able to remember Missandra by now. Even if many girls came in and out of these establishments, not many would have been from an entirely different origin. Compared to the gold and brown tanned skins around them, Missandra should have stood out.

"So boring..." said Shareen. "We can't even see their girls at this hour."

"We didn't come here to shop, remember?"

"Speak for yourself."

"Do you buy your servants here? Instead of the usual market?" asked Cassandra.

She had noticed how Shareen surrounded herself with beautiful things and attractive people. Most of her servants were gorgeous women and handsome young men. She didn't seem to care much about their personalities though.

Once again, Cassandra repeated the same words to the old woman who ran the next brothel. However, this one wore an odd expression while Cassandra spoke.

"Oh, that's why you seemed so familiar, My Lady! You're Mie's older sister, you look just like her!"

"Mie?"

"Yes, yes, Mie! How could I forget her? That child was a little spitfire! Always running around yelling and stealing food. A little demon, that one!"

Shareen sent a doubtful look to Cassandra.

"You sure that sounds like your sis?"

"She was always more energetic than me," whispered Cassandra before turning back to the woman. "Is she here? Could I see her?"

"Oh, no, no, Imperial Concubine. She left years ago. We sold her to another brothel, one of our top clients couldn't stand her. I think she went to... yes, yes, let me check my notebook, it should be written down somewhere."

The old lady disappeared for a while, leaving those two standing in the entrance. Cassandra's heart was thumping loudly in her chest. Could this really be Missandra? Did she finally find a lead, after all these years?

She returned to give them an address to another brothel a few streets away. As soon as they got there though, Cassandra's heart broke. The place was closed.

"Crap...do you think they will open soon? Maybe we could just wait a bit?" she sighed.

Next to her, Shareen rolled her eyes and took out her sword.

"Seriously, act like your rank, pretty face. You're an Imperial Concubine. You don't fucking wait!"

With those last words, Shareen brutally destroyed the entrance door, sending the panels of wood flying away. She had released her full strength on them, making it even larger than it was supposed to be. Cassandra felt guilty for whoever would have to pay for the damages...but still followed the Princess inside.

A man came running quickly towards them. And while his initial intention was clearly to yell, his mouth snapped shut once he spotted the two women. His mouth curled into an odd grin.

"You...Your Highnesses, can this humble man ask wh...what has caused your anger?" he stammered awkwardly, glancing at the large opening.

"You," said Shareen, visibly out of patience. She steadily pointed her sword at the man's chin. "Tell us if you bought a girl that looked like this concubine, years ago. She may have gone by the name Mie."

The man only took a quick glance at Cassandra, very eager to answer.

"Y...yes, Your Highness! I remember her, but she isn't here! We...we sold that girl three months later, we couldn't keep her! She had bitten the customers and hit the owner."

"Really?" said Shareen, turning to Cassandra with an admiring look. "Damn, Cassie, it sounds like your sis took all the fiery side and didn't leave you any, did she?"

"Where did she go next?" asked Cassandra, ignoring her.

"I...I think the Master sold her to another brothel, a few streets down, but I know that place ended up selling her too. Five weeks later, the same thing happened."

Cassandra sighed. Missandra really didn't make things easy for them... though she was a bit happy that her younger sister had tried to resist her fate. She just hoped she hadn't run into more trouble by doing so.

For the next hour, the same scenarios repeated over and over again. Each time they asked a new brothel, they got similar stories. It appeared Missandra only ever stayed in any of the brothels for a few weeks to a few months. She'd end up injuring a customer or worker, and consequently would be sold again. Even Shareen was impressed.

"I hope she didn't get treated too badly and punished for all of this," said Cassandra as they walked their way to the next brothel.

"Oh, she probably was," replied the Princess. "However, the brothel owners are careful not to scar or permanently injure their merchandise. She probably got cold showers or was starved. Things like that. I'm starting to get very curious though, she must be a real beauty if people kept buying her despite her reputation."

Cassandra had the same feeling. Every brothel that Missandra had been to, no matter how short, clearly remembered her as soon as they saw Cassandra. How much longer would it take to find her? As they were about to enter yet another brothel, Shareen suddenly stopped, her eyes elsewhere with a glare.

"Shareen?"

"Wait, it's..."

The Imperial Princess was staring in another direction, towards two women who were quietly chatting. Cassandra didn't recognize either of them. One of them, judging by her clothes, was a prostitute. While the other woman was distinguishably younger, fourteen or fifteen years old at the most. The most intriguing thing was the green dress the second one was wearing.

To her surprise, Shareen suddenly rushed to those women who hadn't seen her coming and grabbed the younger girl's wrist. She screamed in fright. When Cassandra arrived at the scene, the prostitute woman had fled the scene, but the girl caught by Shareen looked petrified. The Princess, however, looked like a feline who had just caught her prey.

"I wonder what you're doing here, Valeria."

Cassandra wondered if she was an Imperial Servant for Shareen, but that didn't seem to be right. The girl was shivering from head to toe, holding on to a little glass potion in her hand. She was avoiding Shareen's eyes, completely terrified.

"Who is this?" asked Cassandra, feeling lost.

"This? This is one of my younger siblings, Valeria, Twenty-Fifth Imperial Princess. Care to explain what the hell you're doing in this place wearing this outfit, little sister?"

Like a rabbit caught in a trap, the young Valeria didn't dare move a muscle. It was the first time Cassandra witnessed a member of the Imperial Family looking this scared. Was it because of Shareen? She couldn't be one of

Kareen's children, so who was her concubine mother? A girl her age and her rank definitely had no reason to be there, especially alone and in a servant's outfit. It looked like she had snuck out of the Palace in disguise.

"Valeria, talk," insisted Shareen.

However, the young woman stayed completely mute and petrified by fear. Annoyed, Shareen ripped the little bottle out of her hands and passed it to Cassandra.

"Aren't you good with plants and potions? What is that?"

The girl was on the verge of tears.

"Let me go," she begged, trying to pull away from Shareen's tight grip.

Cassandra reluctantly opened the bottle. She didn't like doing this, but if Shareen was asking she had no choice. A quick little sniff made her grimace, nausea jolted to her stomach causing her to almost drop it. Dahlia immediately took it from her. Just like Cassandra, she sniffed it and then applied a bit to her pinky to get a little taste.

"Dahlia don't! It could be poisoned," said Cassandra, worried.

"It is fine, My Lady. I have been trained to identify poisons. This is no such thing. I can taste green orchid, pudding grass, nutmeg, sea squill, twin-leaved gamophilia..."

The more she listed, the paler Cassandra became, understanding what the vial contained. Shareen noticed.

"Cassandra, what is it?"

The young concubine exchanged a look with the servant, who nodded, confirming her thoughts.

"It's an abortifacient. A potion used to...induce a miscarriage."

Instinctively, Cassandra put a hand on her belly and lost all compassion for the young Princess, who was clearly terrified. Her dark eyes went from Cassandra's tummy to Shareen, growing wider and wider.

"No, no, no! Sister Shareen, I swear this wasn't meant for the concubine! I swear! I would never dare to..."

"To try to harm my brother's offspring? Is that it, Valeria?" said Shareen with a menacing tone, raising her wrist higher.

The young girl cried out in pain. Shareen was taller than her, the difference in strength was showcased by the calm and effortless way she hung her younger sister by her wrist.

"Spill it, Valeria. Who is that meant for, you little swine?"

The young Princess obviously couldn't bring herself to say it. Her expression was tortured between pain and frustration, but Shareen was not going to let go until she heard what she wanted.

"I swear...I swear it wasn't for her," she cried repeatedly.

"For who, then? Talk, we don't have all day!"

"Shareen," whispered Cassandra, feeling a bit uncomfortable with the situation. "Maybe we should..."

"No, she will say it, now. Even if she doesn't know who it was destined for, she has to know who asked her for it. Dressing up as a servant, leaving without an escort, and trying to evade me, too. You know how short my patience is Valeria, and I don't think Father would mind much if I lost my temper with you."

The threat was ice cold. Even Cassandra felt a chill. Was Valeria the daughter of a lower concubine of the Emperor? She probably didn't have any of the brothers' backing, from Shareen's words.

However, she was only fifteen and defenseless like this. Cassandra sighed. She truly believed this potion wasn't made for her. Valeria looked like she would have been much more terrified if Shareen had seen through her right away.

"Is it for one of the concubines?" asked Cassandra. "One of the Princes' or perhaps one of His Highness' women?"

Valeria turned her eyes to her, looking a bit surprised by the sudden questioning, but seeing her lack of response, Cassandra was pretty sure neither of those were right. Then there was only one option remaining.

"Is it for one of the Princesses?"

This time, Valeria went from red to white in a matter of seconds. Shareen saw it too, and smirked.

"So that's what it is. One of our dearest sisters ordered you to get this. Now I'm wondering which one of those bitches was dumb enough to get pregnant."

To Cassandra's surprise, she let go of Valeria right after those words. The young Princess didn't wait and ran away in a hurry. Cassandra turned to Shareen, confused.

"Is that it? Aren't you going to ask her which one?"

"There are only a few who could get that child so scared. If it was the daughter of a low-ranked concubine, Valeria would have spilled the beans as soon as I caught her. She is an only child and her mother is of no importance now. Whichever Princess ordered her to get this potion is at least as scary as I am, and there aren't many that can claim that title."

Cassandra finally understood. Though they were all seemingly sisters, not all Princesses had the same status or power. Shareen, for example, was backed up by a favored mother and brother. Phetra also had a rather comfortable position thanks to her Imperial Brother, Vrehan. However, not all Princesses had the same luck. Unless they had a brother or a mother favored by the Emperor, they were probably just pawns for the others to use. Valeria was probably among the unlucky ones, fighting for her own survival just like many others.

Who could be pulling her strings then? Cassandra had an idea, but she wasn't sure.

"Which Princess would want an abortion potion?" she wondered out loud.

"Don't know. But we are not supposed to engage in sexual relations until our father marries us off."

Cassandra turned to Shareen, surprised. She knew it was a rather basic rule for daughters in the Dragon Empire, but somehow, this brought out a completely different side of Shareen she had never thought about.

"Does that mean you are...?"

"Married? Me?" asked Shareen with a snarl. "Oh, hell no."

"But..."

Cassandra still vividly remembered some scenes the Princess was involved in that she would rather forget. She even blushed just thinking about it. Shareen smirked.

"Oh Cassandra, I may be a virgin, but it doesn't mean I can't play, right?"

This sentence would stay for a long time in the young concubine's mind before she put together what it meant, rearranging her whole outlook on Shareen.

She shook her head trying to forget about it for now and turned to Dahlia, pointing at the little potion still in the servant's hands.

"Do you think she only came here for this?"

"I would believe so...no Princess would want to be seen here buying an abortion potion. Father would be furious!"

Cassandra nodded, taking the potion from her. She considered holding on to this until they found the culprit. Maybe she could even find a clue.

"All right," said Shareen. "I've had enough, let's go grab your feisty sister before I really lose my patience."

The three women agreed to go check the next brothel, but once again, Cassandra was left disheartened. Missandra had come and gone from this place as well. This time, however, things appeared to be a bit different, as the young eunuch explained.

"Mie tricked some local thugs into losing a lot of money, and they didn't appreciate that. They came often to harass this brothel, so the owner decided to kick her out. She didn't realize until after that Mie had stolen her money too. I don't know where she is now though, this came to light about eight or nine months ago. She could be anywhere, but I'd be willing to bet she didn't stay in the Red District. Too many people were unhappy with her, and I know there's a group of thugs still actively looking for her. To be honest with you, I wouldn't even be surprised if she left the Capital, Your Highness."

Cassandra repressed the urge to cry. How could her younger sister get into so much trouble? She should only be sixteen by now! Did Missandra grow to be such a mischievous girl from her upbringing in the Red District? The worst part for Cassandra was to think that after all this time, the two women had been in the same city. Though the Capital was extremely vast, they could have crossed paths if Cassandra had ventured closer to this area, or if Missandra had been near one of her old master's properties.

"Well," said Shareen. "I guess that's all for today. At least we know this troublemaker sister of yours was still alive and well a few months ago. She could be literally anywhere now, though."

"I can still ask around...there are a few places Missandra could have tried to go."

Cassandra was already thinking about where to search for her next. After everything she had discovered today, she couldn't give up. She felt closer to Missandra than she had been in years.

"Tomorrow, pretty face," said the Princess with a frown. "The sun is close to setting, and my brother will make a fuss if I don't bring you back before night falls. Especially considering where we spent our day."

Cassandra blushed. Indeed, a lot more establishments were open now, as the brothels and their tenants were preparing to work. More customers were filling the streets too, though they kept a careful distance from the three women. They probably wondered what this odd trio was doing here.

"Come on, let's go."

As they started walking back, Cassandra couldn't help but glance sideways, just in case she might spot Missandra. It was a bit desperate, but she just couldn't stop scanning the people around them. Even though Shareen noticed her slower pace, she didn't bother mentioning it, and continued to walk her back to the entrance.

"You!"

An angry voice came from behind them, but for the first few seconds, neither Shareen or Cassandra realized his shouts were directed at them. When they noticed the people eyeing them however, they turned around.

Charging their way was a large man with a shaved head, and too many tattoos on his face to actually distinguish his traits from other men. He was quite horrendous to look at, but Cassandra had a good guess who the man was anyway. In the Capital, criminals were marked, their wrongdoings tattooed in visible places for others to see. Most people would want to avoid those markings, so they weren't outcast by society. However, local thugs, like this man, displayed them proudly, as if it was proof of their strength. And he surely had a lot!

"You little bitch! Do you think you can hide from us? And use this kind of disguise, too? You'll see!"

Shareen and Cassandra exchanged looks, completely unsure about what was going on. It was Dahlia who understood first and stepped in between the man and the young concubine.

"I think you are mistaken, Sir! My Lady is not the one you seek!"

"Are you kidding me? This bitch is the one I've been looking for! You'd better give me my money back or you'll take a good beating for stealing from me, you bitch!"

Cassandra was speechless. Was that man mistaking her for her sister? Were they really so alike that someone would actually confuse them? A group of men were now gathering behind him, only a few had less tattoos than the first, but all had quite the same horrible faces.

Shareen sighed, swinging her swords hesitantly.

"Cassie, do you mind if I play a bit? I need the exercise and I have some frustration to release."

While Cassandra had a generous soul, she really didn't care much for criminals. That man's crimes were visible all over his skin. She was well aware that this sort of person would demonstrate horrible behaviors towards women like her. Keeping that in mind, she nodded and crossed her arms.

"Alright gentlemen, let's play," declared Shareen enthusiastically.

Cassandra turned around and saw they were only a few steps away from the entrance.

Even while the Princess was happily dueling with all the men present, Cassandra knew she wouldn't be able to handle them all, especially since they were attempting to corner the trio. Dahlia had taken out a little dagger, but it wouldn't do much against the sabers the criminals had.

The young concubine took two fingers to her mouth and whistled. After a few seconds, a large figure shadowed them. The thugs looked up, their faces turning white as a sheet.

"Cassandra! Why are you spoiling my fun?"

"I am tired. And besides, this is not a playground. I want to go back, My Lord will be expecting me."

Krai landed next to her, growling immediately like a big cat would purr. A paw was squishing a man on the ground with a gruesome sound and a long scream, but the dragon didn't seem to hear it. Instead, it was more curious about the men running around in utter fear. Krai gobbled one up, as if trying some new treat out of sheer curiosity. Meanwhile, Cassandra was climbing on its back, leaving Shareen to her little game. Another thug tried to throw his saber at Cassandra, but the dragon sent it flying away with a quick flap of its wing. Unfortunately for the man, his weapon came right back to him, stabbing through him, painfully.

"Fine, you party-wrecker, just go!" Shareen yelled. "But take that damn lizard with you before he eats them all!"

Chapter 16

Krai must have easily been able to sense where its Master was because the dragon flew right back to the Palace without any instruction from Cassandra. She was still a bit afraid of flying, but she was also realizing how nice it was. One thing she'd never get tired of was the view of the Capital from above. She still hoped they'd go back to the north soon, though. She missed the quiet Onyx Castle and her friends. The Capital was too hot and humid.

The dragon landed with a loud growl in one of the big courts of the Palace, a square-shaped area made completely of stone. Kairen was waiting there, his eyes set on the young concubine as they arrived. He held out his arms, and Cassandra slid easily along the dragon's scales until he grabbed her. She smiled and kissed him softly.

Kairen took a step back, still holding her, to pull her off his dragon. He seemed a bit concerned.

"Did you find anything?" he asked.

"A bit, yes, but we still haven't found her," Cassandra sighed.

"You look tired."

She chuckled, putting her arms around his neck.

"My Lord, you keep saying that these days."

"You really do look tired."

"Fine...I'm hungry, actually. We didn't even eat."

Kairen stayed quiet for a little while, with his eyes so intently on her, he had Cassandra a bit confused. What was her Prince thinking about now? After a minute though, he seemed to decide on something and nodded.

"I have something for you. A present."

"A present?" she repeated, intrigued.

Kairen had already gifted her lots of dresses and jewelry. Well, more like his father or mother had, but still. What else could she be getting now? Something for their baby, perhaps? But Cassandra wasn't planning on raising the child here.

He turned around and carried her through the Palace. Even if she had no idea where they were going, Cassandra was patient enough not to ask. She enjoyed the little ride, caressing her Prince's hairline and telling him about everything she and Shareen had learned. He didn't react or say much, even to the part where they had encountered his half-sister, but Cassandra didn't expect him to anyway.

After a bit more walking, he finally let her down in front of a large door she had never seen before, but by the looks of it, it was a brand new one. The redwood stood out from the stone walls, and there weren't many windows nearby. However, they were definitely near Kairen's apartments, making her think it was within his private area of the Palace.

"This is yours from now on," he said.

He was handing her a key, with a complex shape and a unique redwood handle. Cassandra took it with a shy smile, even more intrigued now. She then turned to slowly open the door, her heart rate accelerating.

She didn't expect what was behind the door and was rendered speechless in the doorway.

Green, green everywhere. Green leaves, herbs, and plants as far as her eyes could see. Cassandra took a few steps in, unable to close her mouth. There were four long tables with hundreds of different herbs on them in different colored pots. Under her feet was fresh grass. There were several patches of herbs and flowers growing here and there, in delimited areas. For a second, she had thought it was a greenhouse, but it didn't exactly have a roof. Instead, above her head was a large pergola with ivy and other climbing, trailing plants covering most of the framework. The sun could still pass through, but the whole place was more fresh than what Cassandra usually experienced in the palace. The main reasons were the little fountains and rivers artificially planted that ran from one side to the other, refreshing the whole area. Actually, those fountains even had some flowers in them.

"Waterlilies," she whispered with a smile.

"Do you like it?"

She turned to her Prince, baffled.

"You're giving me a garden?"

Kairen nodded.

"Since you don't care for gold, dresses, or jewelry."

So, he had thought about something that would make her happy and gifted her a whole herbal garden? Cassandra was amazed. She had never thought that Kairen would be able to put up such a thing! And in such a short amount of time! She became teary just thinking about it.

She turned around and walked back to him, throwing herself into his arms.

"I love it...I love you. Thank you!"

Kairen hugged her back and kissed her cheek. He felt like it had been a long time since he had openly displayed a genuine smile like this. Cassandra chuckled and turned her head in search of his lips to kiss him; a long, sweet and grateful kiss. He was relieved to see her happier, after her sour day and how she had been sick earlier.

Cassandra kept her lips going, enjoying the proximity between them, but Kairen pulled away with an annoyed groan.

"What is it?" she asked, a bit surprised.

He sighed.

"If we keep going, I'll want to have sex with you. Here and now."

Cassandra blushed, the red spreading to her ears, so she looked down. Oh, indeed...it was better if they stopped now. She might have been teasing him a bit too much without knowing. She laughed at the Prince's hungry expression and stepped back innocently, turning around to explore her new herbal garden.

She truly loved this place. It was green and cold enough to have her forget the Palace's climate that she couldn't seem to get accustomed to. Everywhere she looked she found new and familiar herbs, dozens of them. Almost every medicinal herb or plant known in this Empire was gathered here for her to play with. She hadn't noticed it right away, but at the very end of that garden was actually a wide desk with parchments about medicine, ink and blank paper for her personal use. Whoever had prepared it had also put dozens of pots, pitchers, mortars, pestles, scales and weights, jars, and show globes. Cassandra could spend hours studying everything here!

While she was still observing everything in awe, Kairen came up from behind, gently hugging her with his hands on her tummy, and kissed her temple.

"So you like it," he simply said.

"I love it, really. Were you trying to cheer me up?"

She hadn't been happy since they came to the Palace, and they both knew that. For the usually aloof man to actually go out of his way and prepare all this for her, it melted her heart.

Cassandra smiled and grabbed his face to kiss him more passionately, making him groan.

"Cassandra, if you keep going..."

"How far are we from your bedroom?"

His brain snapped at her words.

Everything that happened next was too fast for her to focus. She was brought back to his bedroom not even a minute later and laid gently on the bed, her dress quickly lifted above her waist, making her breathe loudly in response.

The Prince didn't lose any time. Cassandra cried out when he slid in, biting her lips and shivering. A hot chill spread through her skin, as he began thrusting, fast and hard. She didn't want to hold back and moaned as loudly as she needed, her heart thumping. Holding on to him, she let him set the pace. Cassandra held on to his neck and closed her eyes, focusing on the sensations. His movements were so wild, he only focused on kissing her skin when it came close to his lips and kept moving, restlessly. The young concubine was running

254

out of breath, crying out louder, struggling to keep up with him.

Kairen couldn't hold back for long however, his rut reaching its edge after a few more minutes, releasing himself, moaning. Cassandra curved her body into him, releasing a long sigh of pleasure.

The young concubine was exhausted after that very short but intense lovemaking session. She kept her eyes shut for a bit longer, as her breathing and heartbeat slowly calmed down. Kairen tenderly sprinkled light kisses all over her smooth skin, allowing her time to recover. They were still embracing one another, and Cassandra didn't want to let go of him, not yet.

"Rest here for a bit."

"I don't want to...it's still early," she protested.

"You're tired."

"I'm fine."

He was about to say something, but all of a sudden, he froze. His reaction had Cassandra on alert too. She sat up, now completely awake, looking for what had caught his attention. She heard it a few seconds later; someone's screams were coming from outside.

Kairen got on his feet and put his pants back on before leaving the room in a hurry. Cassandra followed right after him as soon as she could, worried.

To their surprise, at one end of the corridor Shareen was dragging one of the men from earlier. While she looked fine, her clothes were sullied by a terrifying amount of blood. The man she was dragging was bloodied and soiled as well.

"Ah, there you are!" She exclaimed. "Look, I kept one for you. Ask him."

Cassandra didn't approach, as the smell would definitely make her sick. She stayed a couple of steps behind Kairen.

"Who is that?" Kairen questioned.

"One of the men who tried to attack us earlier," said Shareen. "They mistook your woman for her sister. Apparently, she owes them money."

"You were attacked?" he growled, glaring at the man and taking out his sword.

His sister rolled her eyes.

"I said they tried, brother. Krai took her away and I played a bit, but they weren't much fun. They all died a painful death, except this one. I kept the chief alive for Cassie to interrogate."

Saying she kept him alive was an odd way of putting it. It would have been more believable if the man didn't have a scary trail of blood behind him, an eye missing and several of his fingers cut off. Even for Cassandra who was used to injuries, he was a horrible sight to see. She was getting a bit annoyed at Shareen and her "games".

Cassandra put her irritation aside.

"What do you know about my younger sister, Mie?" she asked.

"That bitch took my money! She...Gaaaah!"

Unfortunately, Cassandra didn't look away fast enough. A couple of fingers flew off, and the man screamed in pain while Shareen clicked her tongue.

"What did I tell you? Watch your language, asshole. Next time I hear you use that word to disrespect any woman, I'm cutting off your eleventh finger, if you know what I mean."

It took a few seconds for the man to calm down and for Cassandra to recompose herself. She knew Shareen was not patient or forgiving, but still.

"My sister," she repeated.

"She...that wo...woman stole our money. We gambled and she cheated us! She took thousands from us! We tried to have her pay it back, but...but she was gone. We only heard about her being in the main street three months ago, but we couldn't find her. So we were looking in the Red District...in case she came back."

Cassandra sighed. At least she knew Mie was still around within the last three months. If she hadn't left before then, she probably had found a way to stay without them finding her. How did she do it, though? The Capital was so vast, if she moved to another part of the city, it would be hard to find her. Did she find a new place with the money she had gotten? If it was Cassandra, she would have hidden from those thugs by relocating to one of the upper areas, where the nobles and rich lived.

"What does she look like?" Inquired Cassandra.

"That woman Mie is... a lot like you...but...prettier and more curvy."

Cassandra couldn't help but roll her eyes. The man's choice of words were really crude.

"Did she ever mention anything? My sister?"

"I don't know! She...she was good with herbs, she always bought a lot. She made potions for the who...the prostitutes. Her...her husband sold a lot too."

Cassandra stilled suddenly.

"What? Her husband?"

"Yeah. She got married last year to a rich merchant's son. He's dead, though."

It didn't make any sense. If Missandra was still working in the Red District then, how did she get married? Cassandra was beyond confused.

"What was his name?"

"I don't know! She said he died of an illness or whatever months ago!"

Cassandra sighed. She wouldn't learn any more from this man. She even doubted if half of what he said was even true. She shook her head when Kairen sent her a questioning gaze, meaning she was done with him.

"Scram," said Shareen.

"W...what?"

"I said beat it before I put my sword up your ass! You're lucky we have a pregnant woman here!"

The man spat blood in Cassandra's way.

"Your wretched sister better pay me back my money, or I'll find her and..."

His head rolled before he finished his sentence. Cassandra turned away,

256

disgusted. Even Shareen sighed.

"Really, brother? I have to pick up the trash after you now. You couldn't have waited for him to go and die outside...Seriously?!"

Cassandra took deep breaths, closing her eyes and focusing on the soothing smell around her. Dahlia gently rubbed her back and helped her relax a bit.

"Does this make you feel better?" asked Kairen, standing off to the side.

She nodded.

With Dahlia's help, Cassandra had concocted a solution of lemon and verbena, and was now inhaling it from a little basin. The vapors were helping to greatly reduce her nausea. She had vomited again after the beheading, it was too much for her eyes and stomach to handle. A group of servants were cleaning the area, while Cassandra had been accompanied back to her herbal garden, where she could bask in some fresh air.

"Damn, I really don't ever want to have children," sighed Shareen, who was watching reluctantly next to her brother. "Shall I call Mother?"

"I'm fine," said Cassandra. "I already feel a lot better."

She may have to keep more of that solution close by from now on. She didn't imagine it would be so effective.

"I will go and buy more lemons later," said Dahlia.

Cassandra nodded, grateful. She could always grow more verbena here, even a whole lemon tree.

"Let's skip the banquet," said Kairen.

"Again? Brother, Father will really throw a fit. And it's the last evening before the New Year Celebrations."

"I don't care."

Shareen didn't add anything as her brother already had his usual glare on. Cassandra also wished the Celebrations were over already, so they could finally leave the Palace. However, she still hadn't forgotten the matter of the snake. She glanced at her fingers, which were mostly clear of any blue tint now.

"No, we should go," she said with determination. "I want to find out who was behind that snake."

"You think you'll know tonight already?" Asked Shareen, interested.

Cassandra nodded and stood up, walking back to Kairen.

"Can we take a bath before we go?"

Of course he quickly agreed, and Shareen decided she would need one too, in her own apartments of course. Dahlia, who had naturally taken the lead of the servants preparing the bath, also made sure to include verbena and a bit of lemon for the water, which helped Cassandra relax even more efficiently. For once, Kairen let her bathe alone, staying by her side once he had dismissed everyone with an efficient glare.

"Those make you feel better?" he asked, looking at the plant of verbena Cassandra had brought from the garden.

She nodded.

"I've always liked this scent. They grew in the south too, but it was probably a different species. The ones I remember were blue and purple, not white like those...I think the smell was stronger, too."

"We can get more if you need them."

Cassandra chuckled. She knew her Prince would gather all the verbena in the country for her if she asked him to. It would be a bit extreme though. She shook her head, getting out of the bath with his help.

"No need," she said while giving him a peck on the lips.

The demonstrations of affection between them were now so natural and regular, Cassandra barely blushed anymore. Kairen always watched her every move, his presence had become something she was used to and she craved it when he wasn't near.

Once again she repeated the usual process of picking out a dress and some jewelry. She even put some flowers in her hair, as she couldn't stand the perfumes brought by the servants. She had never liked those overbearing, heavy scents from the Empire's beauty products to begin with, but now with her pregnancy, her sense of smell was even more hypersensitive. It didn't lessen her beauty at all, though. The white flowers she had picked from her garden suited her adorably, giving her an even purer appearance than usual.

Cassandra got a few whispers when she entered the Imperial Hall from giggling concubines who made fun of her hair decorations, whispering about how her Prince must be unwilling to spoil her. But Cassandra didn't really mind. She probably would stop hearing such things once the news about her herbal garden spread.

Kairen was glaring around, making sure any concubine or Princess that dared to make eye contact would instantly be silenced. Compared to his gentle and innocent concubine, the War God was still as scary and impressive as ever for anyone else. They took their seats, once again, Cassandra on Kairen's lap. No one seemed to react to that anymore, though some concubines were red-faced and green with envy. Shareen sat next to them, sinking comfortably back into her chair.

"So? How do you intend to find her?" she asked.

Cassandra smiled, taking a look around. After carefully observing the various concubines, she only had one suspect.

"The woman in red, the second one from the left, at the Second Prince's feet."

Shareen looked over, lost in thought, trying to remember.

"That's...Vrehan's newest concubine. She's a soldier's daughter, I think. I can't remember her name... Why do you think it's her? Are you sure?"

Cassandra slowly nodded, but remained silent because of the Emperor's entrance. He took his place on the golden throne, looking a bit unhappy. Cassandra wondered if something had happened, but the Emperor simply

258

sat and ordered for the usual festivities to begin. As she was quite hungry, Cassandra began eating while watching the dancers' performance. She wasn't paying attention to them, though. Truth was, her main focus was on the Second Prince's Concubine. After a while, Shareen leaned closer to her.

"Cassie, spill it! How are you so sure?"

"Look at the dark circles under her eyes," whispered Cassandra. "She hasn't been sleeping well, or perhaps, not at all. After hearing what I said that day, anyone who had been in contact with the snake would have been too worried to sleep."

"Because they would believe you?" Shareen questioned doubtfully.

"Even if they didn't, all I needed was to plant a little seed of doubt. With my blue fingers, she probably couldn't help but wonder endlessly if it was real or not; if she could actually die in her sleep. That seed of doubt would make it hard for her to sleep properly. Unable to rest properly, she would feel more and more tired. And in turn, make her wonder even more if the symptoms were all tied together."

Shareen remained speechless. Cassandra's plan was to have the culprit tire herself out and show signs of fatigue? The Princess couldn't help but be a bit sceptical.

"Don't you think that's a bit light?"

"Look at her hands," whispered Cassandra.

Indeed, something looked wrong with the young concubine's hands. They couldn't possibly have turned blue, that was obviously something Cassandra had made up. Actually...they looked red and dry.

"What did that little..."

"She's washed them too much," explained Cassandra. "She saw my blue-tinted hands and her natural reaction was to try and wash off as much as she could, thinking scrubbing would make whatever she had got on them disappear without the need for an antidote."

Shareen was impressed. Just a few words from Cassandra had made such a mess in that woman's mind. Not that their Second Brother's Concubines were considered smart at all, but still.

"You had predicted all that?"

"I didn't think she would ruin the skin on her hands, but I was hoping to see the lack of sleep after a couple of days."

Nevertheless, it was impressive. Cassandra's days of treating patients, and dealing with dumb and entitled concubines had left her with some unexpected skills.

A large part of it was due to the lack of acceptable education available to the people, particularly anything in terms of studying medicine. A strong and educated woman like Kareen was a rarity inside the Palace. The majority of concubines were chosen based on looks, and were not particularly smart to begin with. Cassandra had hoped it would also be the case of the culprit, who had obviously sent the snake in without really thinking of the consequences.

"One of Vrehan's concubines, of course," whispered Shareen.

She was glaring towards the Second Brother, but he didn't even notice. He was completely absorbed in a heated discussion with his sister, Phetra. Cassandra wondered if he was behind this. The feud between those siblings and Kairen wasn't to be taken lightly, not if she wanted to survive.

Her Prince too, had his dark eyes sending daggers their way, all the while holding tightly to Cassandra.

"How are you going to deal with her now?" questioned Shareen with a smirk.

Cassandra had no idea. She would have let her Prince deal with it, but if that woman was only a pawn, she didn't really deserve death.

"I heard Sister Shareen had an interesting outing with Brother Kairen's Concubine today," gossiped Phetra from across the hall.

Immediately, everyone else stopped talking. That woman's voice alone was enough to make Cassandra's skin crawl. What was she up to now? Her eyes were glancing innocently at Shareen. However, the Princess had an amused smirk, like a cat prepared to play with her prey.

"You should watch your concubine more carefully Brother, she seems to carelessly wander outside the Palace."

"What are you talking about, Princess Phetra?" asked one of the concubines.

That woman was a poor actress. She had an obvious smile, and Cassandra could tell she was only too happy to play in Phetra's little games. Cassandra stayed expressionless, but she could feel Kairen's fingers were restless along her back. Despite his solemn expression, she could tell her Prince was annoyed, too.

"You are well informed, Princess Phetra," replied Cassandra. "I wonder why my outings with Princess Shareen are of any importance to you?"

Phetra's face turned sour. One could tell she didn't expect Cassandra to reply back to her, and was pissed about that. Her expression was torn between anger and disgust.

"I suppose you're right, it shouldn't be too surprising to see you two hanging around the whore houses."

The insult was so clear, even the Emperor slammed his hand on his throne.

"Phetra! Watch your words, Daughter! Or else you will really anger me!"

"There is nothing upsetting about this, Dear Father," dismissed Shareen turning to her sister. "After all, you knew that place long before we did...didn't you Phetra? I bet it reminds you of your dear mother."

Cassandra didn't expect this. Their mother was a prostitute? Phetra turned red in anger, standing up suddenly. Next to her, the Second Prince, Vrehan narrowed his eyes on her.

"Phetra, sit."

"What is the meaning of this!" The Emperor roared, clearly pissed. "If you have things to say, Phetra, speak now or shut up!"

"My apologies, Father. But I was upset because of Shareen's misconduct today. Were you aware she abused our younger sister?"

For a few seconds, the Emperor seemed confused.

"Your younger sister?" he repeated.

"Valeria, Father! She mistreated Valeria!"

Shareen laughed loudly, and even Cassandra felt their situation pitiful. The Emperor had so many daughters, he couldn't even grasp who Phetra was talking about right away, even after her name was given. He probably didn't care much for the younger Princesses.

"Oh right, Valeria. What about her?"

Phetra was obviously annoyed that their father didn't care much about the situation. She clicked her tongue, irritated. As if she had been called, Valeria emerged from the shadows behind Phetra. The young Princess was clearly uncomfortable being there, appearing in front of them on the verge of tears. But Phetra pushed her forward anyway without a care.

"See! Shareen grabbed her arm so violently! Is it fine for her to abuse her younger sisters? Don't you hate us fighting, Father?"

Cassandra noticed the bandage on Valeria's arm and shook her head. This was clearly too much of an exaggeration. She had been there, she knew that despite Shareen's tight grip on her sisters' arm, she certainly didn't use enough force to require those ridiculous bandages or even any medicine. Did Phetra have her put it on just for show? This was absurd!

"Aren't you going to say anything in her defense, Father?" insisted Phetra.

"Well..." sighed the Emperor.

"Are you done, Phetra?" growled Shareen, annoyed. "That child isn't even injured!"

"Look at this! Does she seem fine to you?"

Cassandra stood up unexpectedly, all eyes on her. She had enough of Phetra's petty game, trying to make such a performance, even using her younger sister like this.

"Take off her bandage, then."

"Excuse me?"

"Take off her bandage. I am the Imperial Physician, I will be able to tell if she is injured or not."

Phetra was about to protest, but a glare from the Emperor kept her quiet. Cassandra was appointed Imperial Physician by the Emperor himself, she had every right to make use of that title. After a few seconds of hesitation, Phetra put on a smirk.

"I'm sorry, unfortunately she cannot. The Imperial Doctor who already saw her warned that the bandages cannot be removed for two weeks, or else she will scar."

Cassandra sighed. This woman was so stubborn.

One could tell everyone in the Great Hall was waiting to see who would have the last word between the War God's Favorite and an Imperial Princess.

The tension was palpable; some of the women were excited to see how this would turn out. Princess Phetra had a triumphant smile on already. Whereas Cassandra, no matter how favored by the Prince or Emperor she was, couldn't disobey her.

"Is that so?"

Those three simple words from Cassandra took everyone by surprise. Her voice was too calm. While Phetra was still dumbfounded, the young concubine stepped away from her Prince's knee and walked down their way, seemingly unafraid. Everyone watched her cross the Hall without saying a word. Had that woman gone crazy?

However, Cassandra was walking very calmly and without an ounce of fear in her eyes. Maybe her baby was giving her some unexpected strength, but she couldn't stand being afraid of those people anymore. The fire of a dragon was glowing in her eyes.

She arrived in front of Phetra and her younger sister Valeria. While not giving one look at the first, she seemingly bowed to the other. After a few seconds of that strange posture, she got back up, turning to Phetra.

The Princess didn't even bother to hide her annoyance.

"What are you doing! I forbid you from touching her!"

"I do not need to touch her," Cassandra retorted. "This bandage doesn't even smell like medicine. It doesn't smell like anything."

A silence followed her words, and Phetra went paler and paler as everyone present slowly understood.

Medicine in the Dragon Empire always smelled strong, and most of the time, horribly so. It was usually made of greasy and thick balms that would smell even worse, had they been kept under bandages like the one on Valeria's arm. However, from what the young concubine had said, it was obvious. While faking Valeria's injury under such bandages, they hadn't even bothered to apply any kind of balm underneath, and anyone could tell with a sniff. Even the second Prince's dragon behind them, that was usually so moody for nothing, was resting in its cage, unbothered. The creature certainly wouldn't have stayed put with the smell of the medicine so close.

Cassandra stared right into Phetra's dark eyes for a few seconds, not showing an ounce of fear, and turned back before her enemy could even reply.

"You...You...!"

But nothing came out of the Princess' lips, and Cassandra calmly walked back to her Prince. Kairen had a terrifying smirk, much like Shareen's. As his concubine joined him and sat on his lap again, his eyes didn't leave Phetra for one second.

Meanwhile, the Emperor slammed the Golden Throne again, and this time, his Golden Dragon behind him growled loudly, as if to show his Master's anger.

"Phetra, what is this? Valeria, take off that bandage! Right now!"

The Princess was completely white, as was her younger sister. Slowly, trembling hands took off the bandage, revealing a perfectly fine arm. Kairen slowly kissed Cassandra's shoulder, proud of his young concubine. His sister, too, was exulting.

"Look at this, Father. My sisters work so hard at insulting and framing me, don't they?"

"Father, I...I can explain. She...Valeria came to me crying! I only wanted to get justice for..."

Phetra kept trying to justify her lie, miserably. Cassandra frowned. That woman was really too disgusting. She was in such a hurry to throw her younger sister in the death pit when she was obviously the one behind all this. Even worse, the Second Prince completely ignored them, as if this whole situation wasn't his concern. He wasn't any better than Phetra. Cassandra exchanged a look with her Prince, but Kairen remained silent, continuously caressing her back and hair, his dark eyes still fixated on Phetra with a murderous glare.

"Silence!" yelled the Emperor, followed by his dragon's furious growl. "I shall not hear any more! Valeria, you'll be punished by Shareen for framing her and lying. I don't care what it is! And you, Phetra, I will personally deal with you later. Now you better sit down and shut up until this banquet is over! I don't want to see either of you at the New Year's celebrations, either!"

Despite everything said, Cassandra felt unsatisfied. Phetra was obviously devastated, but Cassandra found that the punishment was way too light for her. Seeing her clenched fists, Shareen gestured for her to ignore it.

"She is our Second Brother's favorite sister," she whispered. "Father will never punish her too harshly, unless she really pushes it."

Once again, the importance of the siblings' bonds was showing. Even if he remained silent all along, Phetra's status was protected by her closeness to her brother, the Second Prince Vrehan. Cassandra felt it was very unfair for the poor Valeria.

"At least," said Shareen, "now I will be able to interrogate that little swine."

She had her feline eyes set on Valeria. Cassandra suddenly remembered the issue of the abortion potion was left hanging, too. Was Phetra really behind this? And more importantly, who was pregnant?

"Wouldn't the Emperor know if one of them were pregnant?"

"The Princesses don't have dragon children, only the Princes can transmit the dragon's blood to their children."

"Does the Emperor make it public if an egg appears?"

"Generally, no. Father doesn't check the vault every day. Glahad sometimes guards it, but if another dragon goes in and comes out with an egg, we know something is up. However, not all eggs are taken out."

"Why?"

Shareen sneered.

"Shouldn't you know best? Remember how the dragons know their master's feelings before they even realize them?"

Cassandra took a few minutes to think about that. If what Shareen said was right, then dragons didn't systematically claim their offspring unless they... wanted them. She looked around at all the princes and concubines. Some of the princes probably didn't care much once they had enough concubines and a few sons.

"Which of your brothers have children?" she whispered.

"Sephir, Vrehan, and Lephys," said Kairen.

"Sephir has one son and two daughters," added Shareen. "Vrehan has two sons and six daughters, another on the way. And Lephys...Lephys has four sons and eight or nine daughters. But three of his women are pregnant."

Cassandra sighed. She had forgotten the Fifth Prince was notorious for his many, many concubines. Indeed, he was always surrounded by young and beautiful concubines to fool around with. If the rumor about him having over two hundred concubines was true, it was surprising that he hadn't fathered more children. Despite his many heirs, he didn't seem to have much interest in the golden throne, though.

"What of the Fourth and Sixth Prince?" Cassandra asked.

"Anour is too young; he only has one concubine for now. And Opheus...he has a wife, but she hasn't given him a child yet. I don't think he's very interested, either. His mother is the one pressuring him."

It seemed to be true. The Fifth Prince was happily chatting with one of his women, but the others looked bored and unwilling to be here. In comparison, Vrehan's women seemed desperate for their Prince's attention.

Cassandra felt grateful she wasn't like those women. Kairen only had eyes for her, and Krai had cared for their egg as soon as it appeared, although he had let Kareen take it. She turned to her Prince, lovingly kissing him, and for once, surprising Kairen by doing so. Her boldness in front of so many people was unusual. Many eyes saw the scene, and some concubines were dying of jealousy. There were a few too many glares. Kairen glared right back at them and, as if responding to his master, Krai suddenly appeared a few seconds later, flying down from the open roof with a warning growl. The dragon was at least as persuasive as its master, and soon no one dared to look their way.

The only person to be overjoyed with the dragon's presence was the Emperor, as if there weren't already two of his other sons' dragons there, resting in their cages behind their owners.

"Look at him! This beautiful beast!"

Krai didn't seem to care much for flattery, and as usual, crouched down next to Cassandra, head next to Kairen's knee, making sure to be where the young concubine's fingers could find it.

Once again, they attracted much attention. Some women were sweating to see how many fingers she was going to lose, while the others were even more jealous of her confidence, glaring at the other dragons as if they were untamed wild beasts.

"Pretty White Lily, tell me, did you enjoy your present?" suddenly asked the Emperor.

"Your Highness, you know about it?"

"Of course I know! My son steals one of the Palace's wings and destroys it to have a herbal garden made for his concubine, and I shouldn't know about it?"

Cassandra was speechless. Kairen actually had that garden made from another room, after destroying it, too? In a few days? How did he even manage to have it done in such a short time?

"Anyway, just enjoy it, child! I'll have more herbs or plants and what-not brought for you to play with. So stay a bit longer, hm?"

So that was the Emperor's aim? To have Kairen and her stay longer after the festivities? As she didn't want to refuse him, Cassandra only bowed slightly. After that, the Emperor went on to try and convince Kairen and Shareen to have their mother attend the festivities, but both pretty much ignored his plea, leaving their father to deal with his stubborn concubine.

As it appeared, Kareen was still sulking over him keeping Kairen, and wouldn't even come over, making the Emperor actually visit her instead! Cassandra couldn't help but admire that woman a bit more every day. Meanwhile, her gaze went back to Phetra. The Princess was leaning over to chat with the Fifth Prince, whispering something to him with a forced smile. Cassandra was surprised by the closeness between them, and more worryingly, the couple of glances she had sent her way. What was that snake preparing this time?

Cassandra was waiting for the banquet to come to an end, caressing Krai's head. The dragon had decided to take a nap while curled around Kairen's throne, its hot breath warming up Cassandra's legs.

The Emperor was still discussing the New Year's celebrations, but Cassandra didn't listen to him much. Instead, her eyes were staring right at the woman who had put a snake in her bedroom. She had noticed how that concubine was avoiding looking their way. Actually, that woman's eyes only went from her Prince Vrehan, to the floor, or her fidgety hands. She knew.

The more she thought about it, the more disgusted Cassandra was. That woman had put a snake in her bedroom, and hadn't cared what would happen from that. She obviously didn't know much about the snake's species or its venom, yet she had put Cassandra and her child at risk.

Kairen too was glaring at that woman, making her absolutely terrified. Cassandra could see her lips trembling and her eyes on the verge of tears from where she sat. It became worse when Krai started growling too. Despite its resting posture and Cassandra's caresses, the Black Dragon didn't look calm at all, its ruby eyes were glowing.

It had started slowly, but as the glares at the concubine grew longer and longer, the dragon's growl increased along, to the point where no one could pretend to ignore it anymore.

"Son, what is wrong with you today?" frowned the Emperor. "Your dragon is deafening us!"

"Maybe he is unhappy with snakes attempting to hurt his progeny," coldly replied Kairen.

"His..."

A cold silence spread in the room, as most people paled. The Emperor stood up and threw his cup on the floor.

"Who dares! Who dares to meddle with the Imperial Children! In my Palace!"

The young concubine was still looking down, on the verge of tears, shivering like crazy. Even her Prince didn't spare her a glance, looking completely unaffected. Either he didn't know or was really good at acting ignorant, Cassandra couldn't say.

As absolutely everyone in the Hall remained silent despite the Emperor's anger, Shareen smirked.

"Leave it be, Father. Or do you think my brother won't punish those people accordingly? Who would make an attempt on the War God's child's life and make it out alive?"

"Kairen!" yelled the Emperor. "If you want to settle this alone, make it quick! I won't allow those snakes in the Imperial Palace!"

"Don't worry, Father," hissed Kairen. "I'll take care of the vermin as quickly and painfully as I can."

The concubine was crying silently, her eyes desperately stuck on the ground, but no one around her spared her a glance. She kept trying to get Vrehan's attention, but the Prince resolutely ignored her.

As it seemed she couldn't stand it anymore, she suddenly stood up, trying to leave. Despite her attempt at slipping out discreetly, it was impossible not to notice someone leaving the room when no one else but the performers were moving.

Shareen reacted first, her whip lashing the air and the floor in acute sounds. It made everyone stop moving, and the concubine freeze. Everyone turned their eyes toward her, as she seemed unsure what to do, standing there with shaking limbs.

Gently, Cassandra felt Kairen switch positions with her. She was now sitting by herself on his throne, while the War God stood up, and went down the stairs, walking to the woman. Everyone around held their breath. Despite the four dragons present, the most terrifying being in the room was human, and walked as silently, and as inevitably as death, towards that woman. She gasped, taking one step back, her eyes expressing pure terror.

"I...I didn't...I just... The snake... was... not..."

She couldn't even breathe enough to talk. Even Cassandra's heartbeat was going crazy just from watching the scene, her hands on the throne's arms. In front of her, Krai was growling even more fiercely, arching its back and showing off its fangs, the black tail violently swinging in the air. The dragon wasn't moving away from her, however, as if there was some invisible leash between it and the throne or Cassandra.

The Third Prince, however, was walking to the woman at a stable, scary pace. The woman was the very face of terror itself. She couldn't even cry or beg properly, yet, when he suddenly arrived a couple of steps from her, she gasped again, ugly crying.

"Was it you?"

His question was only three words, but it felt like a death sentence. The entire audience thought the woman would lie. She could deny it, pretend she had nothing to do with it. But with her trembling lips, she only glanced once in Vrehan's direction. He wasn't even looking at her. The utter pain that appeared on her face was heart-wrenching.

After a long, painful silence, she slowly nodded.

"I..."

Whatever she was about to say, the Prince wouldn't hear it. He grabbed her and, without an ounce of compassion, dragged her across the hall. The woman's cries and pleas were unbearable.

"Please! Please! No! I didn't mean to kill her! I didn't! I was just...! Don't kill me, please! Please! I beg you! Your Highness! Save me! Please! I didn't know! I was just jealous! Please! Help me!"

Cassandra did her best not to react, but it was hard. The woman was begging both Kairen and Vrehan to spare her, but neither listened. No matter how much she screamed, no one intervened as she was dragged to the Black Dragon, who was waiting for its prey with a terrible growl. As soon as she was within reach, and without an order from The War God, Krai jumped on the woman, killing her in a matter of seconds. The violent scene excited the other dragons, who all seemed to want to be part of it, growling and opening their maws.

As Kairen reunited with her, Cassandra tried to calm down. No matter how that woman had targeted her, she would never feel content over someone's death. Especially since it felt like that woman had been abandoned by all. The cold in her heart was warmed up as soon as Kairen pulled her in his arms, again.

"What a..." said the Emperor, astonished. "Vrehan! Won't you watch your women better!"

The Second Prince immediately looked irritated. Cassandra couldn't help but feel he deserved that much. How could he act like it was unrelated to him? He clicked his tongue.

"Maybe my brother should keep his woman better, as well, Father. If she stirs up jealousy around her..."

"Didn't you forbid killing during dinner, Father!" claimed Phetra right after him. "How is it fine to let a dragon kill someone now?"

The Emperor looked angry and was about to shout back, but Shareen was faster.

"Rejoice, Sister. Didn't you ask for a sacrifice a few days ago? Don't hesitate, if you or brother Vrehan have more candidates. My brother's dragon is always hungry for deceitful snakes."

Phetra looked as if Shareen's words had bitten her.

All four dragons were still growling, but the most furious ones were Krai and the Second Prince's red dragon, Vhan. They kept growling at each other as if they were about to fight, and their masters were glaring at one another the exact same way.

"Enough, all of you!" thundered the Emperor. "No more fighting and arguing and killing. I have had enough!"

Cassandra noted that despite his generalities, the Emperor's words were mostly said to Vrehan and his sister, and he barely looked Kairen's way. She turned to him, whispering.

"Why didn't you kill her yourself?" Cassandra asked.

"The smell of blood makes you sick," he simply replied.

Cassandra would have found it funny, in other circumstances. Krai eating a human being wasn't a much better sight. But indeed, it was a quick job. There wasn't any trace left of the poor woman.

After what had happened, everyone else was only hoping no one felt murderous anymore, and the conversations were changed to the upcoming celebrations. Neither Cassandra nor Kairen had much interest in those. Phetra and Vrehan remained silent throughout, too, though that didn't stop their murderous glares.

Cassandra ignored them, focusing on her dinner, and chatting with Shareen. Kairen, as usual, didn't talk much, but he was holding her by the waist all the time and caressing her skin, reminding her of his presence every second.

"Can you really make Valeria talk?" she whispered.

Shareen frowned, looking at her younger half-sister, hiding behind Phetra.

"I can. If Phetra lets her live until I get my hands on her, that is. I'll get her right after the banquet, she won't be able to leave. And she is already terrified after Brother's little show anyway. I'll just drag her to my apartments until the little swine speaks. On a side note, do you think you can learn more about the abortion potion?"

"I'll study it," said Cassandra. "The bottle and contents can give some information about whoever made it. But, that will give me another occasion to look for my sister."

"How so?"

"If it was me...If I had a hefty sum of money, my freedom and no more people to work for, I would have tried to set up a way to earn more money. Missandra probably opened some sort of business somewhere. If she did, it has to be with something she knew well, and the only thing I can think of is our knowledge in herbs and plants."

"She could have learned something else in the meantime," argued Shareen. "Or she could work for any shop."

Cassandra chuckled.

"Maybe, but I don't see my sister taking orders if she had a choice. You heard it too; she is as proud as ever. If she acquired as much as that bandit said, then I would bet she also saved some by herself. She would rather remain independent. I am not sure about the business, but medicine in the Dragon Empire is a lucrative business. With her knowledge, she could work it out."

"But you said she was only seven when she was sold."

Cassandra looked around, a bit worried about talking of her childhood in the presence of those people, but with the performers' music and chatter, no one could hear them whisper.

"The Rain Tribe children learn about plants and herbs before we even learn how to write. It is considered the most basic and necessary knowledge. Missandra and I used to follow our mother everywhere, and she was the tribe's doctor. We were the most knowledgeable."

While she talked, both Shareen and Kairen had the same odd feeling. They often forgot that Cassandra had been born and raised in another country, another culture. Her white skin should have been a constant reminder, yet she acted so discreet and quiet most of the time, her past was rarely brought up.

"Fine," said Shareen. "I guess you'll have to look into the herbs businesses."

"You want to go out again?" asked the Prince, with an unhappy frown.

Cassandra smiled at him and gently kissed him.

"I'll be careful again, I promise. With Shareen and Krai, too."

The dragon immediately raised its head, putting its hot snout against Cassandra's thigh.

"I'm curious to meet that mischievous sister of yours," admitted Shareen. "I do have a thing for troublemakers."

Chapter 17

The next morning, everyone in the Palace was so busy with the preparations for the New Year's Festival, Cassandra and her Prince were woken up early by all the outside ruckus. The young concubine, still tired, rolled over to his side, and laid her head on his shoulder.

Despite his closed eyes, she knew Kairen was awake from his fingers gently stroking her hair. The previous night, Shareen had left early after grabbing Valeria and taking her to her apartments. Cassandra trusted her to get as much information as she could out of her younger half-sister, and had left with Kairen to avoid more trouble. The tension was high between the brothers, and she didn't want to stay in Phetra's presence longer than necessary. That woman made her too upset, it was like being in the same room as a venomous, cunning snake.

"Get up, sleepyheads!" suddenly yelled a voice inside the room.

"Your Highness! You can't barge in like that."

Cassandra sighed from recognizing the voices. Kairen sat up and glared at his sister, who was at the end of their bed, fists on her waist.

"Come on, I want us to get out of here before the whole Palace goes crazy."

"It's barely dawn," sighed Cassandra, sitting up, too.

She was glad she had slept in her nightgown instead of naked like most nights. Kairen, very unhappy about the unwanted morning call, was glaring at his sister with an annoyed face. She was good at ignoring him though, and sat on their bed.

"I know, but we have to find what that potion is made of, who made it, and your younger sister. Plus, we have to be back early for tea with Mother before the beginning of the celebrations. And you don't want to be late for tea with my mother."

Cassandra sighed. Indeed, Kareen had limited patience, but what Shareen ignored was that she was most severe about her own daughter's lateness.

Cassandra had never been late, but she could tell the Imperial Concubine would let it go a couple of times.

"Dahlia, could I get some tea, please?"

"Coming right away, My Lady!"

The servant left the room, and much to Kairen's annoyance, Cassandra got up and started getting ready.

"What did you get from her?" he asked with a raspy voice.

All three of them knew who he was talking about. Shareen crossed her arms.

"Phetra ordered her to go get the potion, but she really didn't know who that snake was intending it for. But she said it was before Phetra knew you and Cassie were coming, so... She probably really didn't intend to use it on you in the first place."

"Then, the question is, who is pregnant?" said Cassandra, while grabbing a pink dress out of the closet.

"Someone Phetra would want to lose their child. You would have been first on her list, I guess, but if it isn't you, it has to be one of our brother's concubines. What I don't understand is why she would care since no dragon egg seems to have appeared yet."

While she was relieved it wasn't aimed at her, Cassandra was disgusted that Phetra would try to make someone lose their baby. Kareen had warned her many times about the greedy and jealous women of the Palace, but she could never accept it.

She put a hand on her own belly, which was growing a bit bigger each day. According to Kareen, she still had about three or four months to go before her son would be born. The dragon-tamers always came to the world early, but they would be healthy nonetheless. As long as she could endure one more week in the Palace, Cassandra could leave and have her son at the Diamond or Onyx Castle.

Kairen took her by surprise when he came from behind, putting his arms around her.

"What are you worried about?" he asked.

Cassandra shook her head, giving him a quick kiss.

"It's nothing. I will go to my herb garden and then outside. I'll stay with Shareen and Dahlia."

He nodded, despite his usual frown. If it wasn't for his sister being with her, he wouldn't have let Cassandra anywhere he couldn't see her.

Cassandra finished brushing her hair and picked some accessories with Dahlia's help, before kissing her Prince goodbye. With Shareen right behind her, she walked up to her herbal garden and took the potion from Dahlia's hands. The bottle was green, a bit more expensive than the usual apothecary goods. It had no other indication about any manufacturer, however. Dahlia and Cassandra spent some time studying the potion's content, during which Shareen had to wait. The Princess wasn't too good with patience, however, and started grumbling after only twenty minutes or so.

"Aren't you done yet?" she growled.

"Almost, actually. There's this scent I don't recognize," said Cassandra, frowning.

"I don't smell anything else, My Lady," admitted Dahlia with a sorry expression.

To Cassandra, whose sense of smell was enhanced, there was definitely something else, but she couldn't point it out. Nothing had come out of analyzing the potion's thickness or color. However, whatever it was that she was smelling felt strangely familiar, something that went back to her farthest memories.

"Could it be...petrichor?"

"What the heck is that?"

"It's... the smell of the rain," said Cassandra, still baffled.

Shareen exchanged a look with Dahlia, both a bit doubtful.

"You're telling me rain has a smell?"

"It's more like the smell of the earth after the rain, actually. But the soil's smell after the rain smells exactly like this. I just haven't smelled that in a long time."

It wasn't surprising, considering how rare rainy days were in this country. The Dragon Empire's Capital was hot, humid, and suffocating, except for a short rain season, it was as arid as a desert most of the year. They had to go to further cities, like Kareen's city or the Shadelands, to see something other than dry soil and sand. The Capital relied mostly on the large wells and few rivers that came all the way down from the sea, but the water came from the earth or the sea, not from the sky.

"That potion probably came from outside the Capital," said Cassandra. "If they didn't make it in the Capital, the only reason would be that they must have found a better price having it imported from the outside. Someone must have bought a larger stock."

"It actually makes sense. Valeria bought this potion in the Red District, where they probably use that kind of potion often, for the prostitutes. If Phetra only asked her for an abortion potion, that child probably just went to the first place she thought of getting one."

"So this is a dead-end?" sighed Dahlia.

Both women stayed silent for a while. Cassandra felt like they were missing something, but she couldn't say what. After a few minutes, her eyes fell once again on the green bottle, which she grabbed.

"Not necessarily. Why would they have put this potion in a fancy container like this one?"

"You're right," said Shareen. "If it's from a large stock, the seller wouldn't bother putting it in a green jade container. It's like they knew who they were selling it to."

"The order was placed beforehand," concluded Cassandra. "Valeria was made to retrieve the potion by Phetra, but the seller knew it had been ordered

272

from the Palace."

"So, the seller knew the buyer," said Shareen with a grin. "Now, we just need to find them. I'll send one of my girls to see who sells those in the Red District."

Once Shareen was done giving orders, she and Cassandra agreed it was time they left the Palace to look for Missandra in the upper neighborhood. There was no reason for them to go back to the Red District to investigate the potion, but Cassandra was adamant about looking for her younger sister as soon as possible. Krai was nowhere to be seen, for now, probably hunting somewhere far away from the current ruckus at the Palace.

As they left the Palace, Shareen couldn't help but think about their earlier talk over and over again. Cassandra had taken her by surprise. Though she knew about her brother's concubine's exceptional knowledge in medicine, she was shocked to hear her talk so well about the usual trading habits of the Capital merchants. What kind of life had she lived, exactly? Common slaves didn't get that much knowledge just by some observation. Under her weak and quiet appearance, that woman actually turned out to be even smarter than most of the concubines. No wonder their mother had taken a liking to her.

When they finally reached the neighborhood Cassandra had set out to target first, the young concubine was a bit lost. Where to start? This wasn't like the Red District, where everyone knew pretty much everything that happened next door. She tried to think of what to ask, and as soon as she found a shop, she walked straight up to the merchant.

The old man was speechless upon seeing the three women that had appeared, but Cassandra was now used to this kind of reaction.

"Excuse me, Sir, could I ask you a few questions?"

"Of course, Your Highness! Anything, Your Highness!" said the old man, immediately bowing as low as he could.

"Please get up, Sir. You don't need to bow. I wondered if you had seen any new shops opening in the neighborhood recently? Like an apothecary, or perhaps for southern medicine?"

"No, Your Highness, not that I know of. Many merchants come and go, Madam."

Cassandra sighed, thanked the old man, and then left. Shareen, with her arms crossed, looked bored already.

"Why does it feel like this is going to take forever?"

"This area is considerably larger than the Red District, and my sister doesn't want to be found by anyone, either. I can't even look for someone with her name. She probably found a new alias to hide from the thugs from yesterday."

Cassandra was right. Targeting the middle-class businesses meant they would have to search in a zone that was at least five times bigger than the Red District. Moreover, she had no name to give this time and only a rough idea of her sister's possible whereabouts.

They had left early, but after four hours of walking around and asking as many people as she could, nothing happened. Cassandra had asked dozens of people, without ever getting anything concrete. The few known apothecaries had been established for many years, and no matter how many times she asked, no one seemed to have seen anyone that fit the description Cassandra gave over and over again.

After a while, Cassandra started to feel the fatigue, her feet and back were aching. She had been so adamant about looking for her sister, she had forgotten her pain until she couldn't anymore. Shareen helped her sit in a chair of the closest tea shop, somewhere she could hide from the sun. Even for the first day of spring, it was too hot for Cassandra. She had spent terrible summers in the Capital, with a hard time coping with the heat. She truly wasn't fit for extreme temperatures.

"Go order us something," Shareen said to Dahlia, who walked away after a bow.

The place was crowded, but no one dared to even look at the two women. People were absolutely shocked and terrified at one glance of Shareen's purple dress. After a few minutes, they were truly isolated, as all the nearby tables and chairs had discreetly scooted away from them.

"I can't believe we haven't found anything yet," said Cassandra, disheartened. "I really thought that last apothecary might be hers."

"Well, unless your sister turned into an eighty-year-old granny, it wasn't. You still have one week in the Capital, you'll be able to look for her until then."

Cassandra truly hoped she would find Missandra before then. Dahlia returned with the two cups of tea, and they drank silently. Cassandra was touched that she had thought about ordering a verbena and lemon-flavored one for her, while Shareen had a black tea.

"I'm thinking, maybe I guessed wrong. Maybe Missandra already fled the Capital, or she went to the poorer side."

"Looking for someone inside the Capital is like looking for a needle in a haystack. And like you said, your sister made enough enemies to...to not... want... to..."

"Princess Shareen?" asked Cassandra.

But Shareen's face was quickly turning white, and she was obviously struggling to stay conscious. Her eyes were closing and her words didn't make any sense. She spilled her tea in a clumsy movement and, before Cassandra could react, fell on the ground like a dead weight.

"Shareen!"

Cassandra ran to the Princess' side in utter panic. What was going on? Shareen had fallen off her chair like a lifeless doll! Her first move was to check her pulse and breathing, but in a matter of seconds, she realized the Princess wasn't poisoned but drugged.

"Dahlia!" she called.

"I checked both cups, My Lady, I swear!" replied the young woman, crying in shock. "I swear I drank from both! The tea was fine!"

Cassandra believed Dahlia, but this didn't make any sense! She was completely fine while Shareen was passed out. She grabbed both cups, smelling them. Nothing smelled out of the ordinary, but it could have come from anywhere.

Around them, people were in total panic after seeing an Imperial Family Member pass out. No one wanted to be associated with a crime towards the Imperial Family, and the punishment that would come with it. Everyone around quickly fled the scene screaming, leaving the three women alone. Cassandra desperately tried shaking Shareen, calling her name and hoping to wake her up. Who had done this? Who would be crazy enough to attack the Princess in the middle of the street! And so few people knew about their outing, too!

She brought her fingers to her mouth and whistled loudly, out of despair. She hoped he wasn't too far, because she had no idea what to do!

"Come!" suddenly said a voice, grabbing her wrist.

Before she could protest or resist, Cassandra was dragged away from Shareen. Whoever was running in front of her held her wrist strongly, not letting go.

"Let me go!" yelled Cassandra, despite the shock.

However, her kidnapper didn't stop. She couldn't even see who it was, as they were covered in a dark hood and cloak. They ran across several streets, but Cassandra, with her round belly, was running out of breath.

"Stop! Stop! I can't..."

Whoever it was finally stopped, and took her inside a house. Cassandra was too busy catching her breath to look around, but she could tell it was the one of the most common kind of house for middle-class people, big enough for one or two people to live in. It was pretty dark, however, as the individual left the windows closed.

"It's really you," whispered the woman, still standing a few steps away from her.

"Who are..."

But before she could finish her sentence, Cassandra's eyes finally met the woman's eyes.

There was no mistake possible, no matter how incredible it looked. She had such a strikingly similar face, the same emerald eyes, the same dark brown hair. She only looked a bit younger, and her lips were fuller, her cheeks chubbier.

"Mi...Missandra?" she stuttered.

The young woman nodded slowly, looking like she was having a hard time believing her own eyes, too.

"You're... really Cassandra, aren't you? I can't believe it."

They were both in utter shock. Cassandra fell on the closest seat, her legs unable to support her a minute longer. She observed her younger sister from head to toe, shocked to have found her, but also shocked to see how alike they were, physically. Missandra had grown up to be a strikingly beautiful woman.

Cassandra was pure beauty, but Missandra was a cultivated one. Every detail of her face looked perfect, as if it had come out of a painting. She had some light makeup on, almond-shaped eyes and the bits of her skin visible didn't have a single scar, unlike her older sister, who had marks everywhere. She was indeed a bit curvier than Cassandra, too, showing that she had probably gotten better meals while growing up. Her hair was cut shorter, to her chest, and was a bit more voluminous and curly.

She stepped a bit closer, looking at Cassandra as if she was seeing a ghost. "How did you..."

"I saw you on the terrace of my shop, so I..."

"That was your shop?" asked Cassandra, suddenly realizing what had happened.

Of all places, they had picked her sister's shop! She had thought about an apothecary business but didn't think about a tea shop, although those were increasingly popular in that part of the Capital, as tea was considered a fancy drink.

Missandra nodded, taking off her hood.

"Yes. I couldn't believe my eyes when I saw you, with a Royal, too, but I knew I had to move quickly. So I drugged your drinks and put the antidote in yours. It was easy to know which one. Apparently your tastes haven't changed at all."

So that was why Dahlia hadn't felt anything, like Cassandra she had drunk both the drug and the antidote... Dahlia! Cassandra suddenly realized she had left her at the scene with Shareen. Well, at least the Princess wouldn't be alone when she woke up.

"What the Heavens happened to you?" whispered Missandra, looking at her body and pink dress, detailing her sister from head to toe. "You're so...thin. And...are you really...?"

"Yeah, I'm a concubine, and...pregnant."

Her sister's face immediately seemed on the verge of tears, looking completely sorry for her.

"No, no, Missandra, I am fine! I am really fine, this is not..."

"If only I had found you sooner," she sobbed. "I swear, I looked everywhere for you as soon as I could leave the Red District! But when I finally found your last Master, a few months ago, they said you had been taken to the Imperial Palace as a slave to be sacrificed, I thought...I really thought you were..."

"You thought I died," sighed Cassandra. "No, I was saved unexpectedly. I was looking for you, too! But back then, the Red District was the one place I never went, and when I got there yesterday, they said you had left months ago. Missandra, I am so sorry, you were sold to a brothel."

Missandra shook her head, trying to wipe her tears.

"No, it was probably nothing compared to you, Big Sister. To be taken as a concubine. I am so glad I took you out of there! Don't worry, I can give you some of my clothes, and we can leave the Capital, they won't find us! I have enough money saved away. We can terminate the pregnancy, too, so they..."

"What? Missandra, no!"

Cassandra had screamed without thinking because she was shocked. She hadn't thought her sister would think she needed to be saved, let alone help her get rid of her child! She put her hands on her belly, immediately getting protective of her child.

"No, no, Missandra, you don't understand."

"Big Sister, I know what those red or pink dresses mean! You don't have to be afraid, I will help you! I know it must have been hard to live with those wretched Imperials, but now..."

She was stepping closer to take Cassandra's hand, but the elder sister shook her head resolutely.

"Missandra, listen! I do not need to be saved. You need to listen to me. My Prince loves me, he really takes care of me, and this is our baby, our loved baby. The woman I was with earlier, she's his sister, Princess Shareen. She's here to protect me, too! Actually, we should go back and check on her, Shareen might..."

"No!"

Her sister grabbed her hand, shaking her head, looking completely panicked.

"No, no, you can't go back! I don't know what they told you, but the Imperial Family is cruel, Cassandra! How many other concubines does he have? Those women kill each other every day! And you can get killed anytime, too, as soon as he gets bored! Big Sister, you don't want that life! We can..."

Before Missandra finished her sentence, a loud growl suddenly resonated from above, making them both jump. Cassandra immediately understood what was going on, but her sister's eyes were wide open in utter fear, looking at the roof.

"What is..."

"That's my bodyguard," sighed Cassandra.

The next second, the walls and floor shook strangely, and the roof over their heads was completely blown away in a big gust of wind. Wood and stone fell apart in all directions, small debris falling around them, and Krai's big head appeared above, growling loudly.

Missandra screamed in pure terror and tried to run away, but Cassandra held her hand, preventing her from leaving and trying to have her calm down.

"Missandra, it's fine! It's fine!"

"It will eat us! That beast will eat us! That dragon is..."

"A friend! I promise he won't hurt you," yelled Cassandra, desperately trying to cover the dragon's loud growls. "Krai, hush! I'm fine, calm down, please!"

The dragon, apparently unhappy or confused, kept growling over their heads, its huge claws tearing some of the furniture around them. The red eyes were glowing in anger at Missandra, despite Cassandra's attempt to hide her behind herself.

Right then, the door was blown away from the only wall left standing, and Shareen appeared looking furious, followed by Dahlia.

"What the hell is going on?!"

"Shareen, are you fine?" asked Cassandra.

"Fine? I wake up in the middle of an empty street with you gone, and that big scaled ass making a mess of the place looking for you! What the hell happened? Wait, don't tell me that's really your sister?"

The Princess had finally realized the striking resemblance between Cassandra and the terrified young woman standing next to her. Missandra, after a few seconds of surprise, jumped in front of her sister, taking a little dagger out, glaring at Shareen and obviously getting ready to defend herself and Cassandra, despite her own fear. Cassandra sighed again, totally exhausted by the turn of events.

"Yes, it is. Sorry, she's the one who..."

"I drugged you, how come you're already awake?" asked Missandra with a frown.

Despite glaring at Shareen, she couldn't help but also try to keep an eye on the dragon too, wondering which would be the bigger threat. The Princess rolled her eyes, crossing her arms.

"I have dragon's blood. You think your little sleeping potion can knock me out for so long? I only needed a few minutes for my blood to get rid of it. Don't do that again though, or I'm slicing your pretty little neck next time. And keep that toothpick away. With the way you are holding it, I can tell you'll only manage to injure yourself."

"Hinue, li yunja ya..." whispered Missandra.

"Ya men da paerins da linue," replied Cassandra. "Alshenjei li. Missandra, bato kaichira."

"Kaichira? Hinue, li snaira!"

"Alra, mai li ya hensen. Linue, bato... almere."

What was that? Shareen and Dahlia exchanged a look, completely baffled. They had never thought Cassandra could speak another language! Whatever they were speaking, the sisters' sounds were completely different from the Dragon Empire's language. They couldn't understand a single word they had said.

Whatever those words they exchanged meant, Missandra was still sending doubtful glances at Shareen, refusing to leave her sister's side. Cassandra, though, was obviously trying to have her calm down.

"What the hell was that?" asked Shareen, baffled.

"Alshenjenui, Hinue. Li ghen..."

"Missandra, it's alright. Please. I promise Shareen won't hurt me or you," replied Cassandra, switching back to the Dragon Empire's tongue.

"I still haven't decided on that, actually," said Shareen, clicking her tongue and glaring Missandra's way.

Apparently, she was still not over the drug incident. Cassandra sighed.

Missandra, next to her, couldn't take her eyes off Krai. Upon Shareen's arrival, the dragon had finally stopped growling and was simply looking at them, its red eyes filled with curiosity, with one paw on the last wall that remained standing. The large nose was sniffing Cassandra, as if to check if everything was alright. She gently patted its snout.

"That B... Black Dragon. That's the War God's..."

"His name is Krai," said Cassandra. "He's my friend, and sort of my bodyguard too, as you can see."

"He just destroyed my house!"

"Yeah, he tends to do that when you kidnap his favorite toy," sneered Shareen.

"Kidnap? You're the ones who took my sister away! Snaira!"

Shareen frowned, annoyed, and turned to Cassandra.

"Whatever she is calling me, I do hope that chick knows being your little sister doesn't give her an extra life, Cassandra."

"Missandra, please, calm down. We should go back to the Palace, now. We have caused enough trouble. I don't want His Highness worrying about where I am, either. And we need to talk where we can both be safe, alright? I need you to trust me, just this once."

"Hinue, I don't want you going back there."

For a second, she recognized the eyes of the little Missandra, the little sister she had been separated from many, many years ago. It was heartbreaking to see that scared expression of hers again. Despite everything, Cassandra understood her younger sister's concerns. She had survived all on her own until now. She was scared, just like Cassandra had been, before she had met and learned more about Kairen. Moreover, the terrifying rumors about the Imperial Family that Missandra had probably heard were sadly true, for most of them.

She took Missandra's cheeks between her hands, trying to have her focus on her instead of the Imperial Princess or dragon.

"I promise it will be fine," she said in their native tongue. "I just need you to trust your big sister this time, alright? We just found each other, Missandra, I am not risking losing you again. Come with me to the Imperial Palace, I'll explain everything."

"Are you sure?"

"I am, Linue. Now, come."

As they arrived back at the Imperial Palace, the doors opened wide thanks to Shareen's purple outfit and Cassandra's pink dress, but her younger sister couldn't stop frowning and being wary of everyone they crossed paths with. She stuck right behind Cassandra, checking everything around them as if she was ready to hide, fight, or run away at any moment.

Shareen walked ahead, as usual, to head back to her apartments, not far from her brother's. She was still pissed about getting drugged in the middle of the street, enough that she didn't even want to mention that incident.

Cassandra, however, had other worries in mind. For some reason, she wasn't feeling too good about her sister being in the Palace. Missandra would be an easy target for anyone who wanted to harm her, and she clearly remembered Phetra's evil ways. The cruel Princess couldn't attack Cassandra as long as she wore an Imperial Title and the symbolic pink dress, but Missandra, on the other hand, was a mere commoner. She could be killed without blinking.

As soon as she and Shareen had come back, an Imperial Servant had informed them that the War God was still in a session with the Emperor. Hence, instead of going back to her Prince's apartments, Cassandra decided to go to the one place she thought would be safer.

Her apartments in the Palace had nothing to do with her own Diamond Palace, but Kareen was still ruling over the place like a Goddess over her temple. The servants, used to seeing Cassandra go in and out on a daily basis, didn't even question her. Surprisingly enough, the War God's concubine had less trouble meeting with the Imperial Concubine than the Emperor himself.

"Where are we going?" asked Missandra in a whisper.

"Don't worry, Little Sister, everything is fine."

Behind them, Dahlia was following the sisters closely, still very confused to hear them speak another language. She knew that the Third Prince's concubine had grown up outside of the Empire's borders, but she had never heard about the southern tribes or their culture. It was a very unexpected reminder of the Lady's unique background.

"Cassandra, dearest! What are you doing here?" said Kareen, surprised to see the young woman come in at that time.

Cassandra bowed politely.

"Sorry, Lady Kareen, I hoped I could stay here with my sister until His Highness is back?"

The Imperial Concubine glanced at Missandra after her sentence, not hiding her surprise to see Cassandra's sibling there. She had heard Cassandra mention a younger sister a couple of times, but she had no idea she had been searching for her since she was back in the Capital.

Seeing Cassandra's worried expression, and her younger sister looking terrified behind her, the Imperial Concubine understood quickly what was going on. She gestured for a servant to approach.

"You two must have quite a lot to catch up on. Feel free to use the tea room."

"Thank you, Your Highness."

Just like that, the servant led Cassandra and Missandra into a different room. Kareen watched the women go, well aware of why her grandson's mother had chosen to come here. She immediately gave instructions for Missandra, too, to be monitored closely, and for Kairen to be informed.

Meanwhile, Cassandra and Missandra were finally alone in another room. The younger sister couldn't relax, however. She grabbed Cassandra's

280

hand.

"Big Sister, how come you're here? Who was that woman, and how...how did you become a concubine, of all things?"

Cassandra took a deep breath. She understood Missandra's concerns, but it was time she explained everything. From the first time she was bought and sent to work for her first master, up until her meeting with the Prince, and everything that had happened afterward. Cassandra told her sister everything.

A servant had brought them two cups of tea, but neither of the sisters touched it. They were too absorbed in their conversation, trying to patch together the pieces of their past. When Cassandra finally arrived at the present, Missandra was crying.

"I...I can't believe you've been through all of that. A slave! I...I thought you might have been freed, like me. You're so much smarter, and...educated. I hoped you'd found a good man and married early..."

As she talked, she kept glancing over all of the scars on Cassandra's body, her lips trembling. The concubine was so used to seeing all those scars, she didn't care much about them anymore. They had healed long ago, and even her Prince never reminded her about her damaged body.

However, for Missandra, this was the brutal vision of her sister's hardships. She felt almost ashamed of her own body, spotless and well-nourished.

"Missandra, what happened to you? I told you what we heard, but...I need to know."

The younger sister nodded, trying to wipe her tears away.

"It's mostly as you heard. I was...sold right after you, to a brothel. Until I was thirteen, they simply trained us, groomed us to be beautiful and seduce men. I had my first customer when I was thirteen, but I wasn't tamed. I didn't want to lay and be a toy for them to play with. So whenever I could, I would rebel, cause a ruckus, and make sure I was locked away from the customers for a while. I stole as much money as I could without being noticed. I had intended on buying myself out of slavery, but I didn't think someone would pay my debt for me."

"Was that...the husband they mentioned?"

Missandra nodded.

"A good man, actually. He was a scholar's son. We got along because he was smart, my favorite customer. With the money he borrowed from his family, he convinced my last workplace to sell me to him, and he bought my freedom. Marrying him was part of the deal, but I didn't mind."

"What happened then?"

"His father got mad when he learned what I...that I was a former slave and prostitute. He chased both of us. I wanted us to just go and buy a house, but he kept wanting to go back and convince his family. He went there four times and...the last time, he didn't come back. I thought he had abandoned me, but then I learned one of his father's concubine's sons had killed him. So I never appeared in front of his family again."

"So that's when you decided to open your shop?"

"Exactly. Truth is, I thought many times about leaving the Capital, but... I've been here since I was seven. I wouldn't even know where to go."

Cassandra let out a long sigh, disheartened. She was glad Missandra hadn't suffered too many hardships, but it didn't take anything from her pain as an older sister to hear that she had been made a sex slave.

"I am so glad we are together now," she said.

"I still do not trust those people," replied Missandra with a frown. "They are murderers, big sister! They won't hesitate to murder their own blood!"

"Missandra, I promise he's different."

Her younger sister shook her head in disbelief.

"They take as many concubines as they want, they toy with them, and they throw them away like trash! Do you know how many times I've seen this, in the Red District? Some women are dying to be made concubines, and then a few months later, we find their bodies outside of the gates!"

"I am his only concubine."

"He probably killed the previous ones."

Cassandra stayed silent. Sadly, that was the truth... She had been aware of it since long ago, from her first time at the Onyx Castle. Kairen hated the women thrown at him by his brothers or father and had killed them without thinking twice.

However, she still knew she was different.

"We can leave, Cassandra," insisted her sister. "We can leave and have a normal life, just the two of us. As commoners, away from the Capital!"

Cassandra was about to reply, but rushing steps came from the outside. Dahlia, who had been waiting outside, walked in and opened the door wide for the War God to come in.

Immediately, both sisters stood up, each with a different expression on. Cassandra walked up to him, and Kairen naturally put his arm around her waist, while staring at Missandra. The younger sister had a ferocious look in her eyes, and her hand on her dagger's handle, ready to take it out.

"Your sister?" he asked in a cold voice.

"Yes. This is Missandra."

The two of them didn't say anything, staring at each other with a burning animosity between them. Cassandra wasn't too comfortable about this situation, either. Her heart felt uncomfortable, and she turned to her Prince, trying to repress it.

"Can she stay with us for now?"

"Big sister, I don't want to stay here! You should leave and leave that man!"

"Missandra, I promise you will be fine. But I am not leaving him."

Kairen was surprised to hear the younger sister use another language, and even more surprised to hear Cassandra speak it back, just like Shareen had been. He looked down at Cassandra.

"What is it?"

"Let my sister go!" suddenly said Missandra, not hiding her anger.

Kairen replied with a glare, and his arm holding Cassandra a bit closer to him. He was judging her younger sister, so young but so fierce. Missandra was obviously terrified, but seeing Cassandra close to that man, she refused to back down.

"I don't trust you to protect her; people like you made her a slave!"

"Missandra, my Lord is the one who freed me!"

"I won't hurt her," said Kairen, still glaring at Missandra.

Cassandra couldn't tell if he was unhappy about her sister's tone, or her thinking he would harm her, but his murderous glare was not lessening one bit while saying those words. She was terrified he would kill her if he ran out of patience, and put a hand on his torso, hoping to have him calm down.

"I'll explain to her...Missandra, I promise, you can trust him."

"Trust him?" whispered her sister in disbelief. "Trust him? The last man I ever saw you with, dragged you by your hair across our village to sell you! I am never entrusting my sister to any man again!"

The instant Missandra had let out those words, the War God's eyes darkened, turning to Cassandra, furious.

"Who did that?"

"What?" asked Cassandra, confused.

"Who dragged you by your hair?"

She shook her head, baffled he had been angered by something that had happened to her long before he had even known her.

"I don't remember, it was such a long time ago," she said. "The men who raided our village and sold us. Calm down, please, it is not important right now."

He kept himself from asking again, but Cassandra could tell by the look in his eyes, that the matter was far from over. She turned to her younger sister, who also seemed baffled. The War God's reaction had obviously exceeded her expectations of him, leaving her confused.

"Missandra... stay for a few days at least, please? We have so much to catch up on, and I want to show you how safe and happy I feel with Kairen. Please?"

Though her sister seemed unsure, her eyes on Kairen had changed from a glare to a doubtful look.

"Fine. But I am not leaving your side."

"That's perfectly fine," a voice said from behind them.

Looking as regal as ever, Kareen appeared, accompanied by two servants. Shareen, who was sulking behind her, immediately rolled her eyes.

"Princess Shareen, did you not go back to your apartments?" asked Cassandra.

"That was my plan, however, Mother had her people drag me here to explain what had happened."

So Kareen was already aware of the whole situation? Indeed, she was now observing Missandra, with a little smile upon her face. Cassandra immediately turned to her.

"Lady Kareen, would it be alright for my younger sister to stay here? She'll be far safer with you."

"Of course, my dear," replied the Imperial Concubine. "I would love to get to know your only living family member. For now, she can act as one of my servants to blend in. She can even accompany me to the New Year Celebrations. That Old Dragon will make a fuss if I don't at least make an appearance."

"Older Sister, that's..."

"She's a good woman Missandra, you will be safe with her."

"Why can't I stay with you?"

"I have to be by My Lord's side during the ceremony. Plus, I would rather keep your true identity quiet in the meantime. Others could use you to get to me."

"So there are people who want you dead!"

"Yes, but don't worry, I am fine," insisted Cassandra, taking her hand. "Missandra, please? For me?"

The younger sister glanced at the three people behind her, still unsure. She eventually nodded, tightening her grip on her sister's hand.

"Fine... but it's only because I trust you, Cassandra, not them."

"The feeling's mutual," growled Shareen.

Cassandra smiled and lightly caressed her sister's cheek.

"I'm so glad I finally found you!"

They hesitated a bit before tightly hugging each other. Cassandra was on the verge of tears, though they would have been happy tears. After nine years apart, she had finally found her younger sister; alive and well. She could barely believe it, she had dreamt of this day for so long.

Even as they moved apart, both sisters were reluctant to let go of the other's hand.

"Cassandra, you should go and get ready, dear, or you'll be late," said Kareen. "Don't worry, your younger sister is in good hands. I'll make sure no one notices her."

"Where are you going?" asked Missandra, worried again.

"I'll be right back, I promise."

Cassandra smiled at her sister, before following her Prince outside. She felt anxious to be parting with Missandra, even if it was just for a short while. However, the Imperial Concubine was right, she had to get changed before the start of the ceremony.

The New Year Celebrations were special in the Dragon Empire, inciting joy throughout the entire country.

Upon their return to the Prince's apartments, Cassandra was shocked to discover half a dozen Imperial Servants waiting to help her get ready for the ceremony. Before she could utter a single word, she was swept into a whirlwind of hands, pampering every inch of her skin and hair.

The War God's fearsome aura, as usual, intimidated most of the servants, who all avoided his piercing gaze. He only required the assistance of one to help him put his armor on and so he was ready long before his concubine. As he waited for her to finish, he silently watched her. A small smile gracing his face as he delighted in the sight of Cassandra being pampered and beautified by the servants.

Cassandra's shyness was adorably innocent, she kept blushing at any compliment and each accessory given to her. He knew his father had sent a lot from the Empire's precious treasury. Every piece of jewelry she wore was dazzling on her skin. It was mostly diamonds, gold, and emeralds that accentuated her pale skin and sparkling green eyes, along with her pink dress. The dress itself was exquisite. Little diamonds that were embroidered into the bodice sparkled when they caught the light, while several long layers flowed around her each time she moved. It was seductive enough for a concubine's apparel, yet the pale pink and delicate fabric left a hint of innocence and purity.

Cassandra felt relieved when all of the servants were finally chased out by her Prince. She had never been comfortable with crowds, especially not crowds of Imperial Servants all surrounding her to touch and manipulate her.

She looked at herself in the mirror, fascinated by the stranger gazing back at her. Was that really the woman who was a worthless slave a few months ago? Now, she truly looked like a Princess. Even her hair had been styled beautifully, with little braids and some sparkling gold jewelry in it. She turned to Kairen with a shy smile and walked up to him. She had noticed how much the Prince enjoyed seeing her getting all dressed up, compared to her usual simple looks. Cassandra knew it also satisfied him to see her adorned in pink, leaving no doubt of her current status.

"I want to take you right here and now," he whispered.

"Can we wait until after the celebrations?" Cassandra chuckled. "I think I really like this dress."

He smiled and pulled her in close to him. They exchanged a long, tender kiss. As he was sitting and she was standing, Cassandra wrapped her arms around him to caress his neck and hairline, a gesture she loved doing. After all the events that day, she was happy to be back in his comforting embrace. She was slowly realizing just how much she loved to have him close, and how much she missed him when he wasn't.

"Are you happier now?" he asked.

"I am. I finally found my younger sister...she's grown so much, but she's still a baby in my eyes."

Missandra was sixteen years old now, and Cassandra herself had turned eighteen only a couple of weeks earlier. She was glad they had finally found their way back to each other, despite all the years apart. It was better to have waited eight years than to have never been reunited at all. Cassandra was so grateful for this incredible reunion.

"All is good then," whispered the War God.

"Are you still concerned that I am unhappy here?"

He nodded, putting his forehead against her little baby bump. She noticed he liked touching and caressing her growing tummy.

"As long as you are happy, your sister can come along with us anywhere."

Cassandra couldn't help but smile, a bit moved by his words. She had worried to the point where it felt like a thorn was stabbing into her heart, but Kairen had extinguished that fear without even knowing.

"Truth is...I was a bit worried about you meeting my sister."

He frowned and peered up at her, wondering what she could have been worried about. He never had any intention to harm Cassandra's kin or anyone she loved. He wouldn't even have thought of hurting Missandra, he just didn't care much for her. He couldn't understand her train of thought.

"I wouldn't hurt her," he said.

"Oh, no, I didn't mean it in that way. I was more concerned that you might...like her."

Cassandra flushed red as shame washed over her. She had just found her younger sister, yet that hint of jealousy in her heart wouldn't go away. Since she had been with Kairen, her heart had grown into that of a woman's, and some darker feelings came along with that. She couldn't help it, constantly seeing the other concubines all so pretty and dolled up, striving to get men's attention. Her own jealousy and fear had awoken within her, when those women had tried to seduce her Prince right in front of her.

Despite the joy of finding Missandra, she was also struck with the same horrible envy after seeing her sister's scarless body and natural beauty. Missandra had grown into a beautiful woman with lustful curves and a natural charm. She was sure to be the envy of many women.

"I thought...She looks a lot like me, but...prettier, and more womanly, too. I was afraid you would... become more attracted to her than me."

The Prince remained silent, processing her words, looking at Cassandra with a thoughtful expression. She couldn't tell what he was thinking, which made her nervous. Did she seem self centered, or egotistical? She had never thought of herself as a woman who would need reassurance, but her words may have made her sound so...envious and selfish.

However, when Kairen finally spoke, his words were definitely not what she was expecting.

"She...looks like you?" he asked, looking confused.

Cassandra was speechless. Of course she looked like her, Missandra was obviously her duplicate! How could he not see that at all?

"You didn't notice that Missandra resembled me?" she asked.

"No."

"Really?"

"I don't see the similarities at all."

She couldn't help but laugh after the shock wore off. What kind of man says this? Even Shareen had said their resemblance was uncanny! They had the same green eyes, the same pale skin, practically the same faces! People had even confused them for one another in the Red District, too.

"So you didn't...feel attracted to her?" she asked, trying not to think about

286

how childish that sentence might sound.

"Not at all."

Cassandra didn't expect that at all. Her Prince had never seemed responsive to any other woman besides her, but Missandra was her younger, prettier and curvier sister. And yet, Kairen didn't seem to feel anything or even see the similarities between them!

She couldn't stop laughing, realizing how stupid she had been, and how incredible this man was. The whole thing seemed ridiculously funny now.

Kairen was still baffled by her laughter, but he couldn't stop himself from smiling too. Cassandra rarely looked so genuinely amused, and her musical laughter and sparkling eyes were beautiful.

"Does it make you that happy that I'm not attracted to your sister?"

She shook her head, kissing him softly. Then, she put her hands on his spiky cheeks, unable to stop her smile or the wave of pure love she felt for that man. She stared intently into his dark eyes, her feelings bursting out of her chest.

"I'm happy because you see me for me," she whispered in his ear. "Like I'm the only woman you can see...the only one you want."

He was a Prince. He could have any woman, slave or noble, from anywhere in the world; even the most beautiful ones. Yet, he only had eyes for her. Cassandra the Slave, with her scar-blemished skin, malnourished body, and pale complexion. She was among the least beautiful women in the Palace, in her opinion, but he never seemed to see that.

Kairen agreed that indeed, his eyes only admired Cassandra, but was more stunned that Cassandra hadn't realized this already. Truth was, he had barely ever looked at other women, except to satisfy his sexual desires. He knew what beauty in a woman was, of course, but Cassandra had come and destroyed every standard he had long ago. Ever since he had set his eyes on her, this inexplicable and unmeasurable attraction he had towards her eclipsed everything else. She was the only woman that appealed to him after that, and the more he learned about her, the greater his attraction grew. The numerous scars and her undernourished body that left her feeling so self-conscious were, for him, merely the infuriating reminders of what his woman had gone through. He hadn't even realized how other women no longer appealed to him until she had pointed it out. What he had become aware of, however, was the devouring desire to keep her all to himself, and the bloodthirst for any man who dared to touch or even look at her.

He nodded and stood up, holding her in his arms gently.

"I want to see you in a gold dress."

"A gold dress?" Cassandra asked.

She had never heard about golden dresses before.

"The dress used for Imperial weddings."

She was rendered speechless. So brides in Imperial weddings wore dresses in gold? How fancy! She had assumed they married in purple. Or maybe orange or yellow, like the commoners. She tried to imagine a dress of gold, but it only came through her mind as some strange sculpture.

However, she knew what he had meant by that statement.

"Can we ask your mother's permission first?" she asked.

"My mother? Why?"

"I am not so sure that would be a good idea. I want Lady Kareen's opinion."

"My mother loves you."

"I know, but she is also a very reasonable and smart woman. If I hear her opinion, I will make up my mind faster. Please?"

The Prince frowned. He didn't like the idea of Cassandra needing anyone else's opinion to become his wife. He wanted her to be sure, to say yes here and now, then get married right away. The fact she would want to include anyone else in the matter annoyed him.

However, the Imperial Concubine liked Cassandra a lot. The Prince was certain she would approve and so eventually nodded.

"Thanks," said Cassandra, giving him another quick kiss.

Chapter 18

Cassandra didn't know much about the New Year Celebration in the Imperial Palace. In most modest families, a little dinner was prepared, prayers of thanks were uttered to the Dragon Gods, and families spent the night in their garden or the streets looking at the stars. Street fairs would appear everywhere around the Capital, for people to go out and enjoy the festivities. There were plenty of tents around full of hot food, prayer candles, incense, and decorations. In the rich or noble families, the festivities came to them. They would have their garden set out for a great reception, where they would invite friends and family to watch entertainers and spend the night together. They definitely wouldn't mix with the commoners, though.

Cassandra was pretty sure most of the same festivities would take place within the walls of the Imperial Palace as well. So she wasn't surprised when the Prince took her to a large garden surrounding a beautiful lake. With the night slowly falling, the colors reflecting off the water under the moonlight were absolutely gorgeous. It was a very flowery garden, and the servants had hung hundreds of decorations, paper lamps, and dragon puppets.

All the ladies wore their prettiest gowns. The women lounging around wore thick makeup and flaunted every piece of gold jewelry they owned. Their dresses appeared brand new and extra fancy. A lot of people turned their heads when Cassandra and Kairen walked by. Everyone except the Imperial Family had to bow, and that's when Cassandra realized there weren't many outsiders invited. She recognized a handful of generals, some ministers, and the Emperor's Counselors. Aside from those people and their families, the whole Imperial Family was present. Around a hundred people were there in total, including all the Princesses and concubines.

The servants were working hard, constantly bringing food and drinks to the tables, while serving the whims of everyone and being careful of each guest. For once, there were no dragons in sight, but truthfully, there wouldn't have been much space for anyone to sit if they had attended. The whole garden was filled with people and tables surrounding the large shimmering lake.

Cassandra was stunned by the beautiful scene in front of her. She stayed close to her Prince, holding on to his arm while he guided her towards his mother. Kareen and Shareen were already there, and no one dared to approach the duo. The Emperor's favorite Imperial Concubine had picked a simple dark magenta dress and some gold jewelry for her hair, but that was it. Cassandra knew she didn't want to look like she had put too much effort in for the Imperial Emperor.

Shareen had simply put on one of her purple dresses, and her military belt to keep her sword by her side.

"You two took your sweet time. Did you get lost?" she growled when they arrived.

Cassandra bowed respectfully as she was required, and Kareen gestured for her to come closer and sit next to her. The Imperial Concubine had her own table big enough to seat eight or nine people, but everyone knew that all those seats wouldn't be used. She had probably been given a large table and seated so close to the Emperor out of respect, as she was his favorite and the mother of a favored Prince.

The Emperor hadn't arrived yet, so the four of them were able to drink and chat freely. The conversation was mostly led by Shareen and her mother. Instead of sitting with them, Kairen stood behind Cassandra with his arms crossed, not engaging in the conversation before him.

"What are the usual celebrations for the Imperial New Year like?" asked Cassandra.

"Oh, that old man will give a speech about it. Afterwards, we will get to enjoy a few shows, some of the concubines might sing or dance, then we can eat and drink the rest of the night away, until we are too tired."

Cassandra was surprised to hear that some of the concubines might demonstrate their talents tonight. She hadn't expected that. The women usually watched professional performers along with the Imperial Family, but she had never seen any take the stage. She hoped she would be left alone, though. She hated having any form of attention on her, and would rather go unnoticed, staying by her Prince's side.

"The ministers and generals usually use this occasion to have their daughters or younger sisters noticed by the Emperor or the Princes, too," said Shareen. "You should expect some fighting between the concubines and the greedy newcomers."

Cassandra understood that perfectly. No wonder all the young concubines had gone the extra mile to appear prettier than ever. They were probably hoping to eclipse all their opponents. Indeed, some younger girls by the generals' side were dressed in their best outfits and with lots of jewelry, already sending glances here and there. Cassandra couldn't help but frown, seeing some of them sneakily eyeing her Prince.

"Those little pests," grumbled Shareen. "As if the concubines weren't annoying and petty enough, they give them kittens to play with."

"Do the Princes usually...notice them?"

"You bet," scoffed the Princess. "Our Fifth Brother is a real dog when it comes to beautiful women, he just wants them all."

Indeed, she could see the Fifth Prince already talking to two young ladies, despite the numerous concubines glaring behind him. How could he handle so many women?

She heard one of the servants behind Kareen Psst quietly and looked over to see a woman smiling. Missandra had been given a cloth to cover her hair and most of her face and she wore a large servant's dress. It wasn't uncommon for the young servant women to hide their appearances, to remain unnoticed. She was a bit relieved that her sister was hidden that way, and still able to be close.

"So shameless," she sighed, swiftly going behind Cassandra.

"Try not to be noticed, Missandra, please?" she whispered.

"I will, don't worry, big sister. Who wants to be in those leeches' way!"

"I still think you should have left the girl in your apartments, Mother," Shareen commented disapprovingly. "If she gets killed..."

"The one who got tricked by a sixteen-year-old girl does not get to speak on the matter," retorted Kareen.

Shareen's red and ashamed face was an unusual sight, Cassandra could barely hold her laughter. Even Missandra made a little sound to show she was proud of herself, and thankful to the Imperial Concubine that she mentioned it. Apparently, Kareen had managed to win a bit of her trust in that short lapse of time without Cassandra.

Cassandra could tell her younger sister was silently checking their surroundings and everyone present, but she wordlessly prayed Missandra wouldn't do anything crazy or put herself in danger.

Suddenly, the usual music announced the Imperial Emperor's arrival, and everyone stood to welcome the most powerful man in the Dragon Empire. It was quite strange to see him arrive last, in his purple and gold outfit, and without his dragon or anyone to guard him. He silently stepped forward, everyone lowered their heads as he took his place upon the large Golden Throne. His magnificent throne was perched atop a small hill that allowed him to oversee the entire garden.

"Please rise, dear family and friends. It is my greatest pleasure to welcome you all tonight as we burn the ashes of the past year and open our arms to a new one, full of prosperity for your beloved Empire."

After everyone stood, he began a long speech about the past and difficulties the Dragon Empire had faced that year, but also praising its greatest accomplishments. Cassandra was surprised to hear him mention some uncomfortable topics like war, disease, and poverty in a speech, but also congratulating some great medical discoveries, new markets, and new alliances found with neighboring countries. She had expected a much more shallow speech and found herself entranced by the deep sentimental words he spoke.

"In the light of our past mistakes, it has come to my attention that we shall shift, improve our ways and in doing so, enrich our culture and people. We shall no longer turn a blind eye to the misery and suffering of others. No longer lavishly enjoying the blood sacrificed by others for our own selfish comfort. The sons and daughters of the Dragon Empire shall grow wise, strong and fair. I, the Emperor of this Empire, am Justice. I am the Golden Dragon who rules over this Empire. For the new year, Your Emperor has a new edict to proclaim. Hear my words, my dear children, and obey."

Cassandra was astounded, she wasn't the only one holding her breath either. What changes did the Emperor demand his people to follow?

"From this year forth, let it be known that the Dragon Empire will no longer ignore the misery of its people. Each and every child, woman, and man in the Dragon Empire, are my people. As such, I declare from this day forward, that no man or woman will be labelled the property of anyone but the Dragon Empire and the Golden Dragon! Let it be known that the Golden Dragon will not turn a blind eye any longer to the innocent blood spilled and lives taken."

Like Cassandra, many people around the garden were quite puzzled. Only the scholar and a few of the Princes and Princesses understood enough to be shocked. Cassandra couldn't understand what was going on.

She turned to Kareen who had a knowing smile on her face. Next to her, Shareen was smirking, too.

"Lady Kareen, what do the Emperor's words mean?" whispered Cassandra.

"He's referring to the slaves," replied Kareen. "From now on, no one will be able to own any human being. The slaves will be the property of the Emperor and the Empire only."

"But that..."

"Father wants no one to be able to kill a slave," whispered Shareen. "You cannot kill or harm the belongings of the Empire. Our people will have to request them from the Emperor, which allows close monitoring of the slaves. And he's made it, so no one will have the authority or permission to kill their slaves freely."

Hearing the speech explained left Cassandra stunned. She felt like crying, but she couldn't. It was too much of a shock for her. If she hadn't been seated already, she would have most likely fallen to the ground.

But then she caught the eyes of the Emperor who was staring directly at her.

"This year has been a year of great change in my heart. The Golden Dragon has seen many things and heard even greater things. Because the most beautiful treasures can be hidden away from the bright eye of a dragon. Because the weak, frail demeanor of a simple slave woman can hide great knowledge and the ability to save hundreds of lives. Tonight, this Emperor is most proud of his Third Son! For the Black Dragon was wise enough to discover a raw diamond, even disguised as she was, amongst the coal. Our Nation's God of War has performed spectacularly, both in matters of war and in matters of the heart. All rise in my son's name, Kairen, War God and Third Son of the Golden Dragon."

In a split second, every person present was bowing, not towards the Emperor, but towards Kairen. Cassandra's breathing hitched. Witnessing all those people rise and bow to her Prince was an incredible sight. Aside from his father, everyone else had no choice but to obey and show their respect to the War God.

She felt her heart could not possibly bear any more emotions. As she was about to bow to her prince herself, Kairen placed his hands firmly on her shoulders, holding her in place so she couldn't.

"Let them bow to you, too."

Her heart was overwhelmed with emotions. Cassandra stood speechless, and hesitant. How could all those people bow to her? The most powerful beings of this Empire were all gathered here!

She could understand them bowing to Kairen. He was the Third Prince, the War God with many achievements behind him. It wasn't just about his parents' relationship, he was truly a remarkable man by himself. No matter how much the Emperor loved his concubines, he wouldn't have been so proud of a useless son no matter who his mother was.

Cassandra, however, didn't feel like she had achieved enough to deserve such treatment from the Emperor. Her medical accomplishments had been restricted to only the military camp for a few weeks.

Once the Prince was sure she wouldn't move, he released her shoulders and instead held her hand tightly, gazing at her with that determined look in his eyes. He would not let her bow.

So, though a little frightened, Cassandra didn't bow, despite her trembling hands and that little burst of fear growing in the back of her mind. As she looked around, the only other person not bowing was, of course, the Imperial Emperor himself. To her disbelief, as their eyes met, he gently smiled at her.

That was the most heart-warming, unexpected exchange she had with that man so far. With just one look, he gave her the confidence she needed to keep standing, to wash away the fear that had been engraved into her from the many years she endured as a slave.

"All right, you may all rise," announced the Emperor shortly after.

As everyone stood up, Cassandra only had one thought. She turned toward the Second Prince with his entourage, and sure enough, the whole group gathered there was glaring at them.

Cassandra wasn't clueless about what the Emperor had just done by putting one of his six sons forward. Though he couldn't be named as the official heir yet, Kairen was clearly his favorite, and the fact that Cassandra was bearing his child was bringing the most joy to the Old Emperor. As soon as their son was born in a few months' time, the Third Son would be appointed as the official heir.

She tried to understand the reactions of his brothers. Sure enough, the

Second Son Vrehan had a sullen look on his face that said it all. Anour, as expected, was as happy as usual, speaking to one of their sisters. The Fifth and Fourth Princes didn't seem phased at all, for one was gawking at the young ladies, and the other looked bored to death. The First Prince however, was looking in their direction with a gentle smile.

Cassandra had heard little about the First Prince Sephir, but he was clearly in favor of Kairen being picked. Even during the usual banquet dinner talks, which she tried to listen to a bit, he was often on Kairen's side and supportive of him. She wondered how their relationship was so good.

"Your Highness, this is too much! A lot of nobles won't accept this change," suddenly said one of the ministers, stepping forward. "Slavery is an essential part of our Empire's economy. Besides, we are already doing a great favor to all those war prisoners by giving them jobs, and a chance to stay alive! We should..."

"How many slaves do you personally own, Minister?" asked the Emperor.

"I...I would say roughly thirty, Your Highness, but my wife manages such things in my stead, so..."

"How much do you pay your slaves?"

"I...I am not sure. The usual amount for a lower servant, I guess."

Several people sitting around clicked their tongues. The Emperor sighed.

"My dearest, White Lily, come here please."

After a few seconds, Cassandra realized that the nickname didn't belong to one of the Emperor's concubines, but to her. Kareen gently pushed her forward, and Cassandra shyly walked up to the Emperor, who was holding out his hand. A bit hesitant, she put her hand in his, and he caressed it, like a grandfather would have shown affection to one of his grandchildren.

"Do you see this beautiful young Lady, Minister?"

The man had his mouth open, clearly confused. Despite her gorgeous pink dress, and the jewelry she was wearing, Cassandra's scars were visible. Thin white lines on her pale skin, like the disturbing canvas of the perfect beauty she could have been. He seemed to slowly understand, but didn't dare say a word yet.

"My son took her as his concubine a few months ago, and she is now carrying my grandson."

"C...Congratulations, Your Highness."

"Thank you. But before my wise Son picked this flower, do you know where she was blooming?"

"N...No..."

"Tell him, White Lily."

"I was a slave," said Cassandra.

The guests around had no idea and gasped. Some may have remembered the unusual incident that had taken place during the dragon's offering at the Red Moon Festival, and were able to make the link between the frail slave back then, and the beautiful young lady now standing before the Emperor. Due to her Prince's care and her pregnancy, Cassandra had regained a few pounds, and she was nowhere near the dirty and scrawny girl they had remembered from before.

"Exactly. This young Lady was a slave in the house of the previous Minister, the exact same spot you acquired six months ago."

Cassandra was surprised. So her former Master had been replaced by this young man. He was as shocked as her, and bowed, a bit ashamed.

"I had no idea, Your Highness."

"My White Lily, how much did you earn back then?"

"N...Nothing, Your Highness."

"Not a coin?"

Cassandra shook her head, a bit embarrassed by the memory of those days. Not only did she not get any money for herself, but she also had to beg for scraps from the kitchen, and considered herself extremely lucky on the days she could have a hot meal, or fill her stomach.

"Do you think this young Lady is a war prisoner, Minister?"

"I... I would think it's unlikely, Your Highness," admitted the man.

Indeed. Any scholar present knew who the enemies of the Empire were, and none would include white-skinned people. Aside from that, a young woman like Cassandra would have nothing to do with war prisoners who were enemy soldiers, usually captured on the battlefield. She was proof that the slavery system was unfair, and put innocents in shackles for the sake of the wealthy.

"See," said the Emperor, "a young woman was made a slave. Not because her country lost a war, but because some greedy scum captured young innocents for profit. Then, she was sold to the house of one of my subjects, and made to scrounge for years to survive. No wages, only whips and work."

Cassandra was blushing. She was standing next to the Emperor, the old man holding her hand firmly but gently, hearing him tell her story, with all eyes on her.

On the side, the First Prince coughed a few times, breaking the heavy silence after the Emperor's words before he resumed.

"And yet, did you know that this woman is a doctor? A precious, knowledgeable healer, with new techniques our own doctors are struggling to understand. Instead of resenting this Empire, who treated her worse than livestock and brought her to the very brink of death, she worked along with my Third Son. Despite being a young woman, she willingly went to our Army Camp to heal our soldiers. Our people, Minister! Not just a handful, but hundreds of them were sent back to their units! I still receive her praises, day after day, from men on the front, from our own Generals. Now tell me once again, Minister, I dare you to tell me just how much your slaves are paid!"

Despite the shock, the young Minister seemed reasonable enough to acknowledge his wrongs. He bowed lowly, not only to the Emperor, but to Cassandra as well.

"Not enough, Your Highness. I thank Your Highness and the young Lady for opening my eyes to such unfairness. I promise to pay closer attention to my household's slaves from today on, and will give Your Imperial Majesty my full support on the changes to be made within the slavery system of our beloved Dragon Empire."

Cassandra was surprised. Most people would have been terrified by the Emperor's anger, but despite his obvious fear, that man was also truly acknowledging his mistake. Not only because the Emperor had been angry, but because he seemed shocked by Cassandra's story as well.

Behind him, some other people bowed, stating they would do the same, and bring more support to the Emperor for his reform.

Meanwhile, the young Minister stood and bowed again, clearly to Cassandra alone this time.

"My Lady, please accept the apologies of this blind man for underestimating these issues. I am grateful for this lesson, and hope you haven't been hurt by my ignorant words earlier."

"It...it is all right," said Cassandra, unsure of what she was supposed to say in this situation.

"The Third Prince is truly wise, for picking such a precious jewel," said the Minister.

Behind him, many more people praised Kairen too, and Cassandra realized this was a political move on their part. They wanted to make sure the Third Prince knew he had their full support early on after the Emperor had pointed him out.

"All right, all right!" declared the Emperor. "Please, all of you now enjoy the celebrations. No more politics, we will have plenty of time to discuss those topics later! Enjoy yourselves!"

A wave of applause and praises rose before all the guests went on to chat, drink, and eat. The Emperor, however, still held Cassandra's hand, not letting her go, so she turned to him.

"Are you having fun, White Lily?" he asked her.

"Your Imperial Majesty, thank you for your generosity. That matter is truly important to me," Cassandra replied, trying to hold back her tears of gratitude.

"I know, my dear White Lily. It is for me too. Now, tell me, how is my grandson growing?"

"Just fine, Your Highness," she said with a smile, rubbing her little bump.

"Good, good! I can't wait to meet him. Be sure to rest often and bring him to me as soon as he's born! You make sure to give my son a daughter or two, after that! I want a granddaughter as cute as her mother!"

Cassandra chuckled. Did the Emperor want granddaughters to dote upon instead of Shareen or Kareen? He smiled back at her.

"I have a present for you, my White Lily! Wait just a moment..."

He gestured for a servant to approach, who was carrying a little chest.

"Look at this!"

Looking very proud of himself, the Emperor opened the chest. It contained...a golden tiara.

Cassandra was speechless. The design was thin and intricate. It was beautifully made. Despite the little tiara being so thin, she could tell it was a valuable item. Aside from the gold there were little lilies made of white jade with pink diamonds in their center, making her realize why he had gifted that item for her.

"Your Highness..."

"Do you like it?"

"It's beautiful..."

"Isn't it!? I had one of our best Imperial Artisans craft it especially for you. Now, you must wear it, let's see how it looks!"

She was a bit overwhelmed. Was it alright for her to wear a tiara? That kind of item was usually reserved for the Imperial Family only! Regardless of her uneasy thoughts, she couldn't refuse the Emperor. She lowered herself down to allow him to place the precious tiara upon her head.

Despite looking so thin and delicate, the precious piece of jewelry felt quite heavy on her head. Cassandra stood up, and the Emperor looked proud.

"Perfect, perfect! I knew this one would be perfect for you, my precious White Lily! Now go, enjoy the festivities! That stubborn son of mine will get angry at me if I monopolize too much of your time here. He and his sister never learned how to share!"

Cassandra chuckled politely before thanking him once more and walking away. Sure enough, she felt many, many eyes following her as she made her way back to her Prince, who was indeed waiting. He held out his hand for her but was staring at the item on her head.

"That old man," he sighed.

"You don't like it?"

"I don't like you wearing another man's present."

His jealousy was really something else. Cassandra smiled gently though, and gave him a quick kiss to appease him. It worked, as he helped her sit back with their little group. She heard her younger sister step closer.

"Hmpf. I guess that old man is not completely rotten to the core after all..."

"Are you admitting His Highness might not be a villain?"

"I'm still deciding," replied Missandra.

Cassandra knew just how stubborn her sister could be, so having her revise her judgment, even just a little, was quite an achievement after only one day in the Palace. She smiled at her younger sister, who blushed under her hood.

"Oh...so the wild kitty can be tamed, I guess," joked Shareen, who had watched the whole scene.

Missandra frowned and turned away from Shareen, ignoring her. Meanwhile, everyone had resumed their socializing and drinking. The first performers had arrived, playing songs and singing hymns to the glory of the Dragon Empire.

"What language was that, with your younger sister?" asked Kareen, whispering to her side.

"Our native language, from the southern tribes. All tribes spoke the same language, though each had their own slightly different dialects."

"It's very impressive that you both remember the way of your people after you lost them at such young ages," admitted the Imperial Concubine.

"I used to sing," Missandra suddenly said. "I remembered our mother's prayers and sang them over and over again, so I'd never forget."

"I did the same," whispered Cassandra, surprised her younger sister had the same sentiment that she had.

In their tribe, children learned a lot of the language through songs and prayers. It was an important part of their culture, to show their respect to the Nature Gods, who Cassandra still firmly believed in. Whereas, the songs the musicians were currently performing only sang about men. About the glory of the past warriors, Emperors, and scholars of the Dragon Empire.

Cassandra hadn't sung out loud in years. Her previous master had heard her sing once and beat her half to death for it. She accused Cassandra of cursing her in a savage language, most likely because she had no idea what her song was about.

Cassandra was looking at the performers, and something silent and painful was blooming in her heart. She missed her homeland. Reuniting with Missandra, who had changed so much after all these years apart, had brought back memories she had buried deep in her heart. The familiar sounds of the water, the smell of the seaweed and soaked wood, were still engraved in her. She loved the rivers surrounding her village; the wild streams, fresh winds, and peaceful waterfalls. Playing barefoot in the mud, diving with her sister, and swimming with the fish, learning from their mother about every treasure the Nature Goddess had to offer.

"Are you alright?"

Kairen had put his hand on hers, scrutinizing her with a concerned expression. Cassandra nodded, smiling in reassurance.

"I was just lost in my memories," she admitted.

She was about to add something, but not far from them the First Prince started coughing loudly again, so much so that people were distracted from the performances, and turned to watch him. The closest woman to him that was patting his back, looked genuinely worried.

Cassandra frowned in worry as well. This cough sounded really horrible. She turned to Kairen.

"Do you mind if I...?"

"It's fine, I'll come with you."

Kareen frowned, but she didn't say anything to stop them. They both stood up and walked over to the First Prince, who was having difficulty catching his breath. Cassandra politely bowed to him.

"Are you all right, Your Highness? Do you need any help?"

"Ah... Lady Cassandra. If... if you don't mind?"

"He's been coughing more than usual," explained the lady in pink next to him. "He had a bit of a fever, too..."

Indeed, he looked extremely pale. Kairen pulled a chair up to help his older brother sit, as the First Prince's concubines were gathering around. Kairen's glare kept them at bay though, leaving only the first concubine next to them.

"His Highness was born with weak lungs," she explained. "Usually, he only gets sick once in a while, but..." She trailed off, not needing to finish.

Cassandra was careful, but she had to check him out. She put her fingers on his forehead, confirming his fever, and put a hand on his back and chest as he was coughing again, closing her eyes.

"What are you doing?" asked the concubine, confused.

"I'm trying to sense how his lungs are reacting to his coughing. The sound resonates through his thoracic cage."

As the Prince's cough subsided, Cassandra's expression was becoming gloomier. She knew this kind of chronic disease. It wasn't so rare, but unfortunately, it had to do with his weak respiratory system, and she knew there was no definitive treatment.

She stood up, looking around.

"This kind of environment will make His Highness' symptoms worse. The air is too cold, and the smoke from the food and candles will make him sicker."

"What do you suggest, Lady Cassandra?"

"Put him in a very clean room, with fresh sheets and not one speck of dust. I'll write down a recipe for a herbal tea, make sure he drinks it with a bit of honey and at a warm temperature, not too hot or too cold. Let him rest and sleep, I'll visit tomorrow morning."

"I will do, Lady Cassandra. Thank you so much!"

As soon as she was done writing the recipe down, the worried concubine escorted the First Prince out. Compared to the other young ladies who were reluctant to leave the party and follow them, Cassandra could tell that one following genuinely loved and was worried for her Prince.

A lot of people who weren't watching the First Prince's exit, had their eyes on Cassandra once again. The concubines rarely cared for anyone but their own Prince, yet she had spent several minutes checking over Prince Sephir, and chatting with his favorite concubine, too.

She walked back to Kareen and Shareen, trying to ignore all the eyes on her. There were way too many people around.

"Father!"

All heads turned to Phetra, and Cassandra stilled. Whatever that woman was about to say, she knew she wasn't going to like it.

"Isn't it time for the young ladies present to show off their skills? It would be boring to only have professional entertainment, right? Fifth Brother, didn't you mention some of your ladies just yesterday?"

It wasn't like Phetra to praise anyone else. Shareen and Cassandra exchanged a look, unclear of the Princess's motives.

"Let me guess... This one is as cunning as a snake?" whispered Missandra.

"Dieni. Stay away from her, Lihue."

Missandra nodded. She had already noticed how that woman was often glaring their way. It was indeed a nest filled with venomous serpents.

"Oh, I know!" replied the Fifth Prince, Lephys. "Where is the redhead? Show them!"

Cassandra was absolutely disgusted. He didn't even bother to call her by her name! It was no wonder though, when he had over two hundred. Actually, he had only brought about forty or fifty women along to the party, which still created a huge feminine crowd around him.

Cassandra exhaled, glancing over at Kairen.

"What is it?" he asked.

"Watching your brother reminds me just how lucky I am," she whispered.

Kairen clicked his tongue. He could overlook Cassandra touching Sephir for medical reasons, or getting close to Anour as he was younger, but he wouldn't ever let his concubine near that pervert Lephys. He was notorious for his complete lack of self-control when it came to women. He had even forced himself on two of the Emperor's concubines, who were executed as soon as word got out.

The red-headed concubine stepped forward and bowed lowly, but did not introduce herself or say anything. Cassandra immediately noted how short her red dress was, and that she wasn't wearing any jewelry. She looked very unsure and embarrassed to be there. Nonetheless, she took out two long, red ribbons and started dancing. It was stunning, and the musicians soon began playing to accompany her.

Minutes passed by, and Cassandra realized the concubine's two ribbons had started to burn. She kept dancing, causing the flames to dance through the air. The people present in the garden were having fun watching the show. It was mesmerizing to watch fire snakes dance around the air, threatening to set fire to the grass under her feet or her red hair.

When she was finished, she threw her ribbons into the lake, the flames extinguishing in the water. Everyone around applauded, and the young lady bowed before going back to the Fifth Prince, her head down. Cassandra could tell she had not done this out of her own desire.

"That was a bit boring, Brother," scoffed Phetra.

Even though most people didn't agree with that statement, no one dared to speak against an Imperial Princess. Cassandra felt uneasy. Phetra then had her brother put forth six more of his concubines to dance or sing. One after the other they obliged, but no matter how talented they were, Phetra appeared dissatisfied.

After the seventh one, Lephys was aghast to see her still so unhappy.

"Aren't you too hard to please, Phetra? Why don't you suggest a performer since mine are not to your satisfaction!"

Her victorious smile appeared right away.

"Should I? I mean, I would be curious to see our Third Brother's

300

concubine perform. If she is as talented as everyone praises her for, surely she should have a talent to show us all?"

Cassandra's mouth pulled to a slight frown. So that was what Phetra had intended from the beginning...to have her perform in front of the whole crowd, reminding her she was just a mere concubine. Kairen furiously put a hand on his sword, but Cassandra stopped him.

Next to them, Shareen clicked her tongue.

"If you need a show, I'm very good at throwing knives, Sister. I would love to show you how skilled I am."

The threat was so obvious, no one dared to even breathe too loudly in the immediate area. However, Cassandra stood gracefully.

"If you want a performance, I'll give you one," she announced fiercely.

"Cassandra," said the Prince, holding her back. "You don't have to..."

"Don't worry," she said with a gentle smile. "I'll be quick."

Cassandra didn't care for Phetra's childish ways, but it was high time that woman stopped underestimating her, treating her like some toy she could freely play around with. If she were to hide behind Kairen and ignore her again, Cassandra would forever be seen as a weak concubine who couldn't stand up for herself.

It was time to get rid of that image. For good.

As she walked up to the center of the crowd, every pair of eyes were on her. Most people were eager to learn more about the War God's Concubine, the young lady the Emperor himself was so fond of.

Despite being alone, Cassandra's frail figure looked very proud and confident in that moment. With her elegant dress, sparkling jewelry, and those gorgeous, emerald eyes, no one could deny her beauty. If it wasn't for the scars that she never bothered to hide, no one would have even known she was a former slave.

The young concubine walked up to the lake, but instead of stopping at the edge, she continued on, taking off her shoes and stepping barefoot into the water. The fresh sensation on her little feet was very welcoming.

Cassandra stood still there for a few seconds, making people wonder if she was going to dance. Contrary to their expectations however, she sat down on her knees. All of her lower body was now immersed in the water. She put her palms face down over the top of the water, her hands not breaking the surface, as if to merely get a sense of its untold secrets.

Shareen peered over at Missandra, who was smiling. It was apparent the younger sister already knew what Cassandra was doing. Shareen thought about asking, but then decided against it. She would rather see for herself.

After a few seconds of silence, Cassandra opened her lips and began to sing softly.

No guest could have guessed this. Not only was the language Cassandra sang in completely unknown and very strange to them, but her voice was deeper and much clearer than they had expected. It was entrancing, almost like an echo.

Her silvery voice spread quickly around the garden like a cold wind. There was something sort of eerie and unreal about it, which left the crowd speechless.

As Cassandra continued singing, people exchanged uneasy looks, hardly believing their ears. Was this haunting voice even human? It sent shivers down their spines and left goosebumps appearing on their exposed flesh while their heart beats accelerated. Some people felt strangely drawn to it, while others found it...scary. As if the woman sitting there was singing some forbidden chant...a chant that didn't belong in this world.

As her song continued, something else started happening. One of the concubines saw it first and gasped, pointing it out with her finger without a word.

The water.

Something was happening with the lake. It was flat and calm moments ago, but slowly, little circles were now appearing at random on the surface. At first, it was very subtle, making people think it was just a coincidence until they realized the truth. One by one, little ripples started appearing, and the precision in which they matched Cassandra's voice left no doubt that the young concubine was actually doing this.

With her eyes closed, Cassandra kept on singing, and it was as if the lake was echoing her beautiful song. The circles started growing bigger and bigger, crossing each other, matching every note she sang. No one dared to speak or even move. They were absolutely mesmerized by the foreign lullaby.

When they believed they had seen it all, another guest pointed to something in the water. And sure enough, under the clear rippling surface, another phenomenon was occurring before their eyes.

Small, swift movements were seen atop the water. The hypnotized guests eventually realized those quick movements were fish. As if they were dancing, hundreds of little and middle-sized fish were swimming around the surface but not crossing it. Moving in shoals, the underwater creatures were gliding in circles and curves, so synchronized it was incredible to witness. As unbelievable as it was, they were definitely reacting to Cassandra's song. Most of them were gathering close to her in such large numbers that all of the water around her was filled with fish of various sizes now.

Bigger fish started to appear as Cassandra's voice became deeper, taking the majority of the audience by surprise. Among the arriving fish, a large white carp was dancing around in the middle of the lake, following the currents created by the others. With the song taking a new turn, the ripples increased, smaller ones, but more agitated.

Something was getting a bit creepy about her song now. The clear surface suddenly broke and little waves appeared randomly, chasing the smaller fish back into the lower levels of the lake. The larger fish stayed.

At that very moment, Cassandra opened her eyes, staring directly at Phetra.

The Princess was visibly uncomfortable with that. There was something threatening about this song; the more she heard, the more she wanted to run far away from Cassandra.

She was shivering uncontrollably, feeling frightened and worried. The lake, too, was getting dangerously violent. The little waves grew bigger, like an angered sea ready to swallow its surroundings. The young concubine didn't feel like a frail useless woman anymore. She felt more like a water creature, waiting to trap her victim.

When the song came to a sudden end, it took a few moments for everything and everyone to settle down.

The lake returned to its quiet state, and only a few fish hung around to circle Cassandra. Some little ones were brushing against her legs and feet with curiosity. The crowd stayed speechless for an entire minute. No one dared to break the silence as if the magic would be washed away.

The first claps came from the Imperial Concubine Kareen. The sharp slaps had many people jump as if they had been awoken from a trace. Kareen's applause was joined by her children and the Emperor. Since the most powerful man in the Empire was clapping, the rest followed in his stead.

While everyone was cheering loudly and applauding her, Cassandra rose gracefully, sending one last glance at Phetra before turning around to leave the water.

"Beautiful! Absolutely heavenly!" complemented the Emperor.

Cassandra bowed, before walking back to her Prince. Kairen stood to go and meet her halfway.

In her chair, Shareen let out a long breath.

"What the heck was that? This is divine power!"

"It's called the Mermaid's Chant," explained Missandra. "In our native tribe, every child begins to learn it when they turn seven. Our people have this ability to modify our voice to have it match and change the water's natural rhythm."

"You're telling me this was all a...water trick?"

"That was no trick! It takes years of training to master it! My sister was naturally gifted with a great voice, she learned it in a few short months. Some people practice their whole lives without success. Your people could never even attempt to master it."

"Missandra, please," said Cassandra as she arrived at their side.

"What? It's true! The Rain Tribe is one of the very few tribes who descend from a Mermaid and inherited her voice. People in the Dragon Empire can't imitate that."

"That's only what the legend says," chuckled her sister.

While Cassandra and Missandra kept bickering, Kareen was still utterly amazed. While the Imperial Family had inherited the gift of Dragon Taming, she had never suspected other people could have characteristics to rival it. Underneath her meek appearance, Cassandra had kept quite a precious gift hidden. Today's demonstration was a real shock.

"Well, well!" exclaimed the Emperor. "Phetra, after that, I don't think you could claim you're unimpressed any longer! My White Lily, what a gift you have! You need to come and sing for this old man sometime, I would be delighted to hear that beautiful song again!"

No one around said a thing, but they were clearly shocked. Why did the Emperor make it seem so normal? That woman had just sung something so strange and shook up the whole lake! No one could look at Cassandra with the same presumption as before. That song was heavenly! And whether people had felt fear or bliss while listening, they all shared the same strange feeling of wanting to hear the song again.

The Emperor ordered for more entertainers to come, but after Cassandra's song, everything following her felt quite bland in comparison.

However, there was an unexpected effect from Cassandra's performance. While Shareen went on to chat with the ministers present and Kareen slipped away to converse with another Imperial Concubine, a group of young concubines quickly appeared to greet and compliment Cassandra.

"Lady Cassandra! Your song was marvelous!"

"I didn't realize you had such talent!"

"Your dress is so beautiful, it suits your skin tone perfectly!"

"Is that the Emperor's gift? How lucky!"

While she was taken aback by the sudden wave of praises, Cassandra answered politely, but nothing more. She hadn't forgotten the cold treatment she had received previously from those very women. Cassandra couldn't trust any of them, regardless of their words and smiles. She was actually grateful to Kairen, as the War God's presence next to her discouraged those women from standing too close to her. They didn't dare get within a five foot radius of him. Cassandra was sure they all would have been overwhelming her otherwise.

They didn't even mind her clipped answers much. Most of their chatter was amongst each other, about how beautiful and smart she was, or how surprising it was that she could sing so well, as if Cassandra needed to hear them repeat it a hundred times in order for her to believe their words.

"What a bunch of annoying leeches," sighed Missandra behind her.

"What did that servant say!" yelled one of the concubines who had heard her.

"Nothing that wasn't true," replied Cassandra, standing up. "If you are done, I'd like to eat in peace, ladies."

In other circumstances, the concubines wouldn't have let that remark go. They would have complained to their Princes, maybe got the servant killed and perhaps even Cassandra punished. However, it had been made very clear that the War God's favorite was not someone they could even consider punishing. Hence, they had no choice but to bite their tongues and swallow their pride.

"Where are you going?" asked Kairen.

"Just going to take a stroll. I'll get sleepy if I just stay here, laze around and eat."

"I'll come with you."

Cassandra shook her head, glancing pointedly at the group of men decked out in uniforms. She knew they had been waiting patiently to the side for an opportunity to approach.

"Aren't you going to talk to the ministers at all? It's alright, I'll take Mie and Dahlia with me."

The War God pouted. It was the expression he always made when Cassandra was making a reasonable suggestion he wasn't very fond of. He reluctantly nodded, glaring the poor ministers' way.

"Fine. But be careful, and stay where I can see you."

"I'm not leaving the area," she promised, giving him a quick peck on the lips.

Chapter 19

The area was indeed crowded with people gathering in little groups to chat. Cassandra soon noticed most of the groups consisted of concubines gathered around their man, or men talking amongst themselves.

Much to Cassandra's surprise, many of them paused their conversations to greet her. Whether it was her relationship with Kairen, the Emperor's speech earlier, or her song, something had changed in the way people looked at her. The women started actively trying to befriend her, while the men were a bit... extra. She didn't care for either performance and did her best to avoid the groups. All the young concubine wanted was to take a quiet stroll, but she hadn't thought it would be so complicated.

Missandra played the part of her servant, carrying a small tray of food, and providing excuses to avoid people who were acting too obnoxious. Compared to Missandra, Dahlia was being much quieter and somewhat awkward. Cassandra had realized that the young woman had become a lot more shy since Missandra had appeared, but couldn't figure out why.

As she was talking with both of them, a duo she hadn't expected to encounter walked up to her, followed by a crowd of concubines - The Fifth and Sixth Prince.

"Lady Cassandra! That song was terrific!" exclaimed Anour, polite and smiling as usual. "I had no idea you could sing so well!"

"Indeed," sighed Lephys. "None of my concubines could sing half as well as that, not even the best ones! I'm a bit disappointed. I thought our older brother's tastes were odd, but now I realize he might actually have a good eye for women."

Cassandra didn't like the way he spoke or how he was talking about his concubines. The ladies behind him were all strikingly beautiful, and visibly desperate to win his attention, wearing splendid red outfits and lots of jewelry and makeup. However, no matter how rude she found him, Lephys was the

306

Fifth Imperial Prince, and so she couldn't afford to offend him.

She bowed politely.

"Thank you for the compliments, Your Highnesses, I am glad you both enjoyed it."

"Isn't this your first New Year Celebration at the Palace, Lady Cassandra?" asked Anour. "I need to show you the dragon burning flames! Wait here for a second!"

The young Prince ran off to get something, followed by two servants who were struggling to keep up with his energetic pace. Meanwhile, Lephys smirked as his eyes pervertedly swept over Cassandra's body.

"Actually, now that I can look at you up close, you are quite fine, aren't you? I'll revise what I said earlier, my older brother has an eye for women. After all, sometimes it's not all about the outer appearance!"

"Thanks..." Cassandra said indignantly.

Lephys winked at her, making her feel even more uneasy. She could feel Missandra's disapproving glare from behind her but hoped her younger sister could stay quiet just a few more minutes before causing a scene.

"You know, I'm amazed that such a feeble-looking woman like you was able to seduce my older brother. Your voice probably isn't your only skill though, is it? Do you have other secret talents my brother enjoys? Come on, feel free to tell me, I'm curious! I realize women have many secrets I have yet to..."

"Women do have secrets, your Highness, and sometimes it's best to respect that," replied Cassandra coldly.

She'd had enough of his attitude. Treating his concubines like toys, and implying that she was some cunning whore who only acted innocent to seduce Kairen into sleeping with her was more than she would tolerate. No matter how patriarchal and sexist the Dragon Empire was towards women, there were limits. The Emperor himself treated his concubines better than that.

Lephys, however, didn't seem to take the hint. Whether she was too subtle or he was too sure of himself, he was oblivious to Cassandra's anger.

"There's something about foreigners. Maybe I should try more foreign women? I'm getting awfully bored, always seeing the same faces. I can always... Ouch!"

He suddenly doubled over, grabbing his foot and making a horribly theatrical scene, wailing about being stung. Cassandra knew exactly where to look, but Missandra was playing innocent, pretending to be absorbed in the non-existent details of her dress.

"It hurts! You! Aren't you a doctor? Do something!" he yelled, still gripping his foot.

"Sorry, Your Highness, I'm afraid a woman like me is not skilled enough to treat you," replied Cassandra.

Meanwhile, his concubines crowded around him, asking how they could help and showing pity for him. They were mostly useless and noisy, but in a matter of seconds, the wall of women between Cassandra and the Prince was deep enough for her to walk away without being impolite.

Missandra was laughing behind her, unable to hold back any longer.

"What did you do?" asked Dahlia, at a loss.

"She dropped some stinging nettles onto his foot," chuckled Cassandra. "I didn't see you do it but I recognized the leaves on the ground. They definitely weren't in this garden before."

"I always have some with me, just in case. You have no idea how many men I have needed to use them on... Actually, that guy should consider himself lucky, I don't usually use it on their feet."

Dahlia gasped in shock, while the sisters laughed together.

After that, Cassandra made sure to keep her distance from the Fifth Prince, who continued to complain for the next hour before an Imperial Physician was called to treat him. Anour, however, finally came back to show her the interesting little candles he had gone to retrieve that were shaped like dragons and would burn blue when lit.

Though Anour was twelve years younger than the War God, he still had an air of youthful innocence, despite having been raised by Kareen. Or, she wondered if the Princes had such different personalities because they had actually been born from different mothers.

Cassandra chatted with him for a little while longer, happy that no one dared to interrupt them. The Sixth Prince was still a bit too young to be of much interest to the single ladies. Instead, they all focused their attention on his older brothers.

Although she had seen it before, Cassandra still couldn't believe how desperate some women were to enter the Imperial Harems. Some girls younger than her were making eyes at the Emperor or shamelessly throwing themselves at the Princes' present. The only two who were free to walk without being harassed were the War God and Anour.

Cassandra exchanged a quick glance with the War God from where he was standing and chatting with some ministers and scholars. She had seen him frowning and glaring a lot during her brief exchange with Lephys, but Missandra had solved the problem before he had needed to intervene.

No matter where she stood, Cassandra could feel his warmth shadowing her. The War God was protecting her from a distance. It was the best and made her feel so safe, though she liked it better when he stood where she could actually feel him.

After another round, Cassandra couldn't stand the distance anymore and headed back to her Prince. He was still not done talking with the ministers but welcomed her silently, putting an arm around her and kissing her temple causing her cheeks to flush a shy pink. The men present acted accordingly, nodding politely to the young concubine.

They were speaking about war and matters of the North. Cassandra knew exactly what was being discussed, and listened carefully. Most of the men thought she was standing there simply for decoration, not understanding anything that was being said, but they would be wrong. The few weeks she spent at the camp had taught her everything she needed to know. She didn't say anything, however, as she didn't particularly care what those men thought.

Ironically, those days in the camp were among the best she ever had in her entire life. She couldn't help but blush as she remembered the snowstorm and the long, long hours with Kairen in his tent. Their child had likely been conceived during that storm, too. Cassandra couldn't repress a soft smile while thinking about it.

Lost in her thoughts, Cassandra didn't realize that her dreamy expression had caught the attention of all the men. The young concubine was truly too charming at that moment, with her skin as pink as her beautiful dress.

Unfortunately for the ministers present, the War God had seen it too. He dismissed them with a glare and turned to Cassandra, putting his hands on her hips.

"Don't do that in front of other men."

"Do what?" she asked, confused.

He frowned, but whatever it was, he couldn't express it. Eventually, the War God just sighed and held her closer.

Cassandra chuckled and gave him a quick peck on the lips, brushing his growing beard with her fingers. She didn't care for the curious crowd around them anymore. Actually, she wished they were alone as they had barely spent any time together all day. She sent a glance back and Dahlia understood her completely. She grabbed Missandra's hand and dragged her to Kareen's side, ignoring the younger sister's complaints. Cassandra then turned to her Prince again, giving him a shy smile.

"Is it alright if we... step out for a little while?"

The Prince took a few seconds to understand her request. He was elated as Cassandra's pink cheeks and bright eyes confirmed what he thought she meant. It wasn't like her to be this...forward. Was it because of the pregnancy? Or was it her sister's influence? In any case, there was no way he was going to complain.

Guiding her out of the garden, Kairen walked to the closest corridor and found an isolated and deserted salon where no one was likely to walk in on them. As soon as he closed the door, both lovers turned to each other and kissed. Cassandra was rarely this bold, but she had missed him so much. Her whole body was craving this. Her thoughts became blurry and she could only focus on his lips on hers, the touch of his hands exploring her body, lifting her dress's skirt to caress her legs. She brushed his spiky cheeks, his neck, and every inch of his skin. The simple sensation of him under her hands was spreading an incredible warmth through her entire body. The little flame that had ignited earlier was growing into a wildfire, something she couldn't and didn't want to stop, and it was consuming her flesh with an intense burning desire.

Kairen wasn't able to hold back either. He gently steered her towards the luxurious couch off to the side, unable to stop touching her. He wanted to get drunk on her perfume and lost in her soft skin.

This woman was a mystery, yet he knew her far better than he had known any other woman before. Mermaid or woman, Cassandra opened up her arms to him. He didn't care how many more secrets she had. He loved her and all the mysteries she held close, and all those she had yet to reveal.

He pulled her onto his lap, one of her favorite positions, and gently moved the straps of her dress down her shoulders. The dress continued to slide down past her waist, revealing her perfect breasts. Kairen loved that they had become larger and rounder since Cassandra had become pregnant. He started kissing her, the movements of his tongue making her moan. Every sound she made was like music to his ears and, while he hadn't forgotten her song from earlier, his favorite tune was the sounds she made when she was excited by his touch. No one knew that song but him.

Cassandra shivered, feeling her skin warming up too quickly under his sizzling touch. Her cheeks were red as he played with her breasts, breathing loudly and closing her eyes to fully take in and enjoy the sensations. Could he hear her heartbeat going crazy when he was this close? It felt like it could burst right out of her chest! Cassandra moved her hands from his shoulders and struggled to undo his armor. She desperately wanted to feel his bare chest against hers.

Once the armor finally fell to the floor, Kairen smiled and reached out for her lips again. He teased his fingers through her hair, playing with the free strands and caressing her nape, keeping her close. His other hand playing between her legs, his fingers driving her crazy and making her wet. He knew exactly what to do and obviously took pleasure in watching her tremble and react to his every move. Cassandra felt him growing harder. She wanted him. She wanted him, now.

Kairen was just as impatient as she was. Lowering his pants, he finally sprung free, and slowly positioned her. Feeling his manhood so close to her entrance caused Cassandra's legs to tremble and her core to tighten in anticipation. She was hot, moist, and too excited to bear it anymore. She slowly lowered herself onto him, exhaling loudly with pleasure. It took a few seconds for both of them to adjust, but those seconds were filled with kisses and lustful touching.

It was the best sensation. Him, filling her, spreading his warmth like fire from head to toe. Cassandra had gotten addicted to this sensation. She was panting a bit, but his lips soon found hers again, keeping them busy with another wild kiss. They were both impatient and unable to wait any longer. Kairen started thrusting his hips and Cassandra responded naturally, trying to tame the beast under her. He was wild, savage, and unpredictable. She moaned, gasped for air, and moaned again. The writhing of her body on his had something terribly indecent about it, and yet, she loved it. She wanted more, crying out his name and holding on to his neck. His fierce rod plunging into her was driving her crazy. Something broke free in her, and she couldn't hide her pleasure anymore. Her own voice was becoming hoarse, loud, and feral, but she didn't want to stop it. Kairen didn't give her a second to catch her breath. He just wanted more, so much more of this woman. He'd grab her hips and pull her closer, thrusting in and out of her, guiding her shaking body to relish in this ecstasy. It was carnal, primal sex. The oldest dance in the world, a man and a woman together indulging in the pleasures of the flesh.

Cassandra's skin was flushed and sweaty from the blood rushing to her extremities and her limbs were numb from the exertion. She kept calling his name, like a prayer, her voice so embarrassingly sexy and raw. The War God was like an untamed beast, mating with his queen and unleashing his desire for her. Cassandra felt it coming. She knew his body all too well and immediately recognized when he was about to completely let go - that incredible, final moment of fierce pleasure where he'd accelerate, pant and groan, and deepen his thrusts inside her. Cassandra relished every last second as she moaned even louder, feeling him release deep within her. Her own voice broke into a hoarse moan as they came together, satisfied and exhausted.

The heat began gradually decreasing, but that short session had been intense. Resting her head on her Prince's shoulder, Cassandra took a minute to catch her breath and wait for her heartbeat to slow down. Her body was still quaking a bit, and Kairen's warm hand caressing it was soothing her.

He gently pulled away, making her flinch a little, and kissed her skin gently. Cassandra let out a long satisfied sigh, her desire appeased. They didn't need any words as she kissed him gently, savoring his taste just a bit more.

"Feeling better?" he asked.

"Much..."

It was as if he knew she had needed this. A little break away from the world, just the two of them, indulging in their desires.

They stayed like this a while longer, just caressing and kissing each other, gently and slowly, savoring the moments alone. Neither of them felt like leaving their little bubble and going back yet. After a short minute, though, Cassandra exhaled.

"We have to go back."

Kairen nodded, looking at her with his dark eyes.

"You look content."

"I am," she admitted, still flushed.

She did her best to dress again, making sure nothing looked too out of place. Somehow, she felt like their intimate moment was going to show one way or another on her, and felt a bit bashful. She helped Kairen put his armor back on to keep her hands busy instead of fidgeting, and he adjusted the little diadem on her head with a frown.

"What is it?"

"I don't like it."

"The diadem? It's very pretty though."

It was curious that he didn't like something she was wearing. He usually seemed happy whenever she had an occasion to dress up a bit. However, it seemed that the little diadem actually offended him.

"You really don't like it? But it's from the Emperor."

She couldn't refuse to wear something the Emperor had personally gifted her!

"I don't like you wearing something from another man."

Cassandra was rendered speechless! Again? Did his jealousy know no bounds! How was she supposed to respond to that? From his expression, she could tell he was going to be stubborn about this. After thinking about it though, she shouldn't be surprised, the man bickered with his own dragon after all. And his father had some concubines that were her own age, too.. She sighed.

"I have to wear it tonight, though, His Highness personally gifted it to me."

Kairen's frown deepened. He obviously didn't like it, but the situation was unavoidable. She let out a small exasperated laugh before giving him a quick peck on his lips despite his sour expression.

"I'll leave it in your mother's apartments when we leave, alright? I don't need to wear it outside of the Imperial Palace, it should be kept safe here."

"Fine," he growled petulantly.

Cassandra smiled, happy she had placated his jealousy. She was getting better at handling him. She took his hand, trying to distract him.

"Let's get back," she said with a gentle voice.

They walked back to the big area where the festivities were still going on. There were so many people in attendance, it was unlikely anyone had even noticed that they were gone for those few minutes.

As she walked beside the War God, things were different for Cassandra. People would glance their way, but no one dared to stare or stand too close. A new performance of exotic dancers had also begun which had captured most of the crowd's attention.

Cassandra and Kairen returned to their table. After their little cardio session, she needed to rest a bit. She let out a sigh of relief while sitting down, although her body was still clearly buzzing from the vigorous activity earlier. Sitting next to her, Kairen dared anyone who came too close to her with a threatening glare.

Cassandra couldn't have been more grateful though. She was hungry again and enjoyed being able to eat in peace.

Her favorites had changed once again. The cheese cubes she used to love now made her feel nauseous, and she was now unexpectedly craving...red meat.

She whispered to Kairen about it when she heard a peal of familiar laughter behind her.

"Ah yes, carrying a dragon's child will do that to you," said Kareen while taking her seat back at the next table.

She gestured for a nearby servant to come and ordered them to bring an assortment of cooked meats for Cassandra. The young concubine felt a bit strange letting Kareen take care of things for her, but this was a first. She usually didn't eat red meat. She was more used to a pescatarian-like diet largely dominated by fruits and vegetables.

"Don't eat raw meat though," Kareen instructed. "Your stomach is still human, even if it tells you to eat like a dragon."

"It feels so strange. I feel like a different person."

"You still have a few months to go, dear, you better get used to it. And once your son is born, prepare to feed a carnivore. Kairen could eat almost as much as his dragon when he was a baby and was horribly grumpy when he was hungry."

Cassandra laughed thinking of her Prince's younger days. She wondered what kind of child he was? And if their son would be like him.

She caressed her little baby bump. She couldn't hide it under her dresses anymore and it was only getting more obvious as the days went on. However, she didn't mind. She had developed new curves and started filling out a bit more, her hair was shinier, and her skin was glowing. She was grateful to be so well cared for though. Having to deal with her nausea and growing appetite would have been terrible if she didn't have Kairen or the servants of the Diamond or Imperial Palace.

"Brother!"

Shareen was returning with a frown and her hands on her hips.

"Did you listen to that annoying minister on the War Affairs? Should I have punched him for you, too?"

Indeed, behind her, the poor man was on the floor with half of his face looking very, very painful and purple. No one dared to come to his aid though and all kept a careful distance from him until some servants came to help him up.

"Shareen, I already told you not to make your fights too obvious, didn't I?" chided her mother. "You could have hit him somewhere less obvious, but you just had to go for the face."

"He should walk around like that, Mother, I don't care. That idiot was disparaging brother's army, calling them lazy for maintaining the border and not crossing over!"

"Oh. You should have completely knocked him out then. He looks too fine for me."

Shareen ignored her mother and turned to Kairen, waiting for his answer.

He didn't say anything though, not out loud anyway. Just as Cassandra was wondering what was wrong, she heard the flap of wings.

"Krai!" she shouted, happy to spot the familiar black silhouette.

However, the dragon didn't stop, only briefly turning its head towards her with a light familiar growl. It was obvious Krai wouldn't be able to land in this area, not without crushing a few people. The dragon extended its giant claws, causing people to run away in fear, and flew just low enough to snatch that same minister up from the ground. The man's screech was so high-pitched, people were covering their ears from the pain. Whether they had heard the fight with

Shareen earlier or were too scared to ask, no one dared to comment on the incident, as the dragon flew away with its prey.

Shareen smiled, looking satisfied, and helped herself to some wine.

"Kairen! Son, what was that?" asked the Emperor.

"Taking out the trash, Father."

Several people couldn't help but laugh at the sentiment, though they were smart enough to hide it. Others were more terrified; they avoided Kairen's vicinity at all costs, and their faces were white as a sheet. Meanwhile from his throne, the Emperor sighed in exasperation.

"Make sure your dragons behave, will you? How can the party go on if there are no more guests!"

"Dragons tend to be wilful, Father," said Shareen with a sneer. "Who knows, if they get too hungry they might come looking for snacks again."

"Don't make us laugh, Shareen," the Second Prince suddenly growled. "As if he doesn't control that Black Dragon perfectly..."

Shareen didn't appreciate the Prince speaking out against her and she immediately glared back at him.

"How about you teach us about controlling dragons then, Brother? Call yours out now, let us all see how much of a dragon-tamer you are!"

Right as she finished saying that, a threatening growl echoed from somewhere in the Palace. No matter where it was, the Red Dragon was clearly echoing its master's anger. Cassandra couldn't help but be concerned. What if he really called it all the way here? Wouldn't it get in a fight with Krai or injure people? Every time she had previously seen the Red Dragon, it was securely caged, but what if it was actually freed? The animosity between the brothers would definitely have it target Kairen. She trusted Krai to respond immediately, but...

Just as she was lost in her thoughts and worrying, Kairen gently put his hand on hers. He wasn't looking at her though, he was still glaring Vrehan's way, but his thumb was gently caressing her skin, helping her calm down.

Vrehan paused for a few seconds and then, to her surprise, a disturbing, reptilian-like smirk spread across his face as he glared at Shareen.

"Why would you need me to teach you anything about dragons, Shareen? Women don't need to know about dragon-taming."

The insult was evident, and even Cassandra felt outraged. He clearly looked down on the Princesses, because unlike their brothers, they had no dragons of their own. Shareen became red with anger, but just as she was about to say something, the loudest growls yet were heard.

Though she wasn't surprised to see Krai return, Cassandra had not expected to see the Golden Dragon make an appearance too. Glahad was growling even more furiously and clearly glaring at Vrehan with its ruby eyes. The arrival of the two biggest Imperial Dragons was enough to scare a lot of guests away, many of whom, for some reason, thought the wisest place to hide would be inside the buildings. Cassandra considered differently as the walls

314

looked like they were about to collapse under the weight of the two beasts.

Even Missandra and Dahlia had run back towards her, both of them hiding behind her seat afraid. She couldn't blame them. She probably would have been just as terrified if the War God hadn't been holding her hand all this time. The dragons' angry growls were deafening, in line with their anger.

Shareen was unphased by the chaos going on around them and stood up, furious, while pulling her sword from its hilt.

"I dare you to say that again, Vrehan."

"Enough!"

The Emperor was standing up now and glaring at both of them.

"Enough of your squabbling! This is the New Year Celebrations. I want no fighting in front of our guests! Not tonight, not tomorrow, not for the next few days either! Vrehan, Shareen, enough, you two! Both of you go back to your apartments for the night!"

Shareen was about to protest, but her mother clicked her tongue. The two of them exchanged glances for a second, almost as if they were having a silent conversation until Shareen cried out in frustration. She violently swung her sword through the air in protest then put it back before turning to leave without another word.

Cassandra felt bad for her, and couldn't help but glare in Vrehan's direction. The Prince was watching Shareen go, but hadn't moved himself. He was about to say something, but the War God opened his mouth first.

"Father told you to leave, Vrehan."

The ice and enmity in his voice were so intense, the whole area became as cold as the Onyx Castle for a few seconds. Cassandra wondered if the Second Prince would argue or try to fight Kairen.

After a long scowl, he stood up silently and walked away in a strange silence. The air was thick with tension, so much so that absolutely no guest dared to say a word for several minutes after the Prince was gone. Cassandra, who hadn't realized she was holding her breath, suddenly exhaled. She felt sorry for Shareen, but couldn't help but be grateful that Vrehan was gone too - at least for the night.

Just as the awkwardness and tension began to settle, the Emperor took his seat, looking drained. Glahad and Krai, who were obviously faster to calm down, seemed unwilling to leave now. Both dragons were overlooking the area with curious eyes, their front paws on the roofs of the building. They looked like they were speculating if they could fit into the area if they climbed over. The answer was a resounding no. Even if the area were clear of people, there would still be too many food stalls and tables left everywhere.

The braver of the guests were slowly trickling back in, since the dragons had stopped growling like feral beasts. Cassandra, who had just been delivered a humongous platter of meat, grabbed one of the big chunks by the bone and stood up, walking over to Krai.

"Hinue! What are you doing?" asked Missandra, skeptically following behind her.

She kept glancing back at Kairen hoping he would stop Cassandra, but he wasn't even looking their way. Meanwhile, Cassandra was still walking over towards the building Krai was on, waving the piece of meat through the air as it sniffed out the aromas drifting through the wind with deep interest.

The dragon growled softly and lowered its head as much as possible into the garden so that Cassandra could throw the meat. Krai caught it, happily eating the little snack with a satisfied expression. When it finished licking its lips, she smiled and extended her arm, making Missandra squeak.

"Hinue, are you crazy!? That is a wild creature! He can eat you!"

"He won't," said Cassandra with a confident smile.

Indeed, Krai only touched her hand with its snout, eyes wide open, curious as to what its favorite human was playing at. Cassandra scratched the dark scales a bit before stepping back and grabbing Missandra with her other hand.

"Oh, no, no, no," said Missandra, "I am not going to do this."

"It's alright, he's a good boy."

Missandra did not believe a dragon several times her size could be anything close to a "good boy"! However, she only half-heartedly struggled as Cassandra confidently pushed her in front, talking to the dragon.

"This is my younger sister. Can you try not to eat her? Please?"

Krai was staring at both of them, sniffing with curiosity. Of course, there was no way to know if the dragon understood. It tilted its head to the side and growled a bit, making a curious impression, as if chatting with her. Its claw was scratching against the roof though, so maybe it was just getting a little impatient.

Cassandra smiled, but it was time for the dragon to go before the building really collapsed. She wasn't sure the Imperial Palace was fully dragon-proof.

"See you tomorrow," she said to the dragon, before walking away, still holding Missandra's hand.

Krai apparently didn't understand as the black dragon was still on the roof, growling a bit and trying to grab her attention. Cassandra ignored it and walked back to her seat, where she couldn't see it anymore. Releasing Missandra's hand, she washed her other one that was full of meat juice and whatever dirt Krai had on his scales.

As soon as she let go, the younger sister's legs turned to jelly, and she fell to her knees with a huff of relief. Dahlia crouched down next to her.

"Are you alright?" she asked.

"I am not! That was the most terrifying experience of my life."

The young servant girl chuckled. It was the first time Missandra had lost her fierce and feisty attitude like that. Cassandra laughed too and gave her a few minutes to regain her composure. Missandra kept pouting after that though, stating that her older sister had risked her life with the crazy idea of befriending a dragon.

The last of the guests were slowly coming back now at the Emperor's insistence, and attempting to resume the party as if nothing had happened and two enormous dragon heads weren't still hovering over them. Glahad and Krai soon grew bored though, and after a little while longer, both of them flew away. It was a magnificent sight to watch the Golden Dragon actually spread its wings and fly. Glahad was shining brightly in the moonlight, while Krai was like a black shadow, hard to follow while swiftly soaring through the dark blue sky.

The New Year Celebrations were supposed to last for a full week, all day long and into the nights, but of course, people had to take breaks. At the Emperor's party though, most people tried their best to stay as long as possible so as not to offend the host. And the Emperor seemed to have incredible stamina despite his age, not showing any signs of fatigue.

Kareen, however, was soon bored and decided to leave. She was obviously upset after Shareen was kicked out, and no one could manage to keep her any longer once she had made up her mind - much to the Emperor's disappointment.

It was especially true for Cassandra as her pregnancy was taking a toll on her. Several hours into the night, despite her best attempts at staying entertained, and eating and drinking, Cassandra kept dozing off and could no longer argue with Kairen about leaving. The Prince gently helped her up and took her in his arms, no one commenting on their early departure. Cassandra felt bad for being among the earliest to leave the party, but it couldn't be helped, she was already half-asleep.

Kairen dismissed both Dahlia and Missandra when they reached the room and placed her gently on the bed. Cassandra was completely out of it, she didn't even feel him undressing her and removing her jewelry. She was just relieved to be finally laying in bed. She hadn't even realised her back was hurting so much until then.

Finally, the War God laid down next to her, wrapping her up in his embrace, and once she felt her skin against his, she let go and fell into a deep sleep.

Chapter 20

Cassandra had been utterly exhausted by the whole day. She had a peaceful, dreamless night, surrounded by warmth and the soft scent of the verbena plants that had been put in their room for a good night's rest.

Kairen made sure to position his arms in the most comfortable arrangement for her before falling asleep himself. He was even more cautious than usual, as his concubine was recently struggling to get a good night's sleep, often waking up throughout the night due to her nausea.

Cassandra slept straight through until the morning, no one daring to wake her from the much-needed respite. When she finally awoke, she was feeling well-rested and refreshed. Her body was still a bit sore, but nothing unbearable. She sat up and stretched a little. Feeling the Prince's side of the bed was a bit cold, Cassandra confirmed she had been alone for some time. How long had she slept?

Outside, music from the ongoing festivities flowed through the window and, judging by the accompanying warmth from the sunlight, Cassandra guessed it was quite late in the morning.

She grabbed her robe and walked to the window, glancing down. Indeed, she could see the lake and the garden flooded with people again. Some had probably been there all night, but she was too far away to recognize anyone.

"Lady Cassandra! Did you sleep well?"

Dahlia had just walked in carrying a new dress for her, while two other servant girls entered right behind her with hot water and some oils. They started preparing her a bath, which immediately filled the room with a refreshing citrus smell.

"I did, thank you. I slept late, didn't I?" Cassandra said with some concern in her voice.

"His Highness insisted we let you sleep, my Lady. It's almost midday now, but Imperial Concubine Kareen said she would like to have a late breakfast with

318

you."

"She's been waiting for me?" Cassandra was a bit embarrassed.

"She knows you were sleeping, my Lady. She said she was fine with waiting as long as you got some good rest. His Highness the Third Prince agreed to it too, and insisted we wait on you to wake up."

"My Lord is with his mother?" asked Cassandra while undressing to get into her bath quickly.

"Yes, My Lady, Princess Shareen, and Lady Missandra as well."

Cassandra felt a bit flustered at the thought of everyone waiting for her. Moreover, they weren't even attending the celebrations, but just waiting to have breakfast at Lady Kareen's apartments? She wondered if Shareen was still implicitly banned from them, or if Kareen was the one who refused to go again. Both mother and daughter definitely shared the same fiery blood.

As she didn't want to keep anyone waiting much longer, Cassandra asked the servants to help her get ready after the quick bath. She let Dahlia pick the jewelry for her and put on her diadem before walking out hastily. Only Dahlia followed her, as the two other servants stayed behind to clean up the room.

Cassandra was grateful to be spared of her usual nausea as she hurried to Kareen's apartments, not quite running but still not walking too slowly. She arrived only a few minutes later and walked in as she knew Kareen didn't need her to be announced.

It was a large room with panels on one side that opened onto a large garden for them to admire and allow the sunshine to come in. However, unlike the warm sunlight, the atmosphere was icy inside. She walked up to the large table where Kareen, Shareen, Kairen, and Missandra were all seated and strangely quiet. To her surprise, the young Prince Anour was seated with them too, though he had obviously just arrived as his plate and cup were empty and clean.

They all raised their heads when she entered and Cassandra noticed both Missandra and Kairen were unhappy, while Kareen was pointedly ignoring them, drinking her tea.

Shareen rolled her eyes. "Finally!"

"Good Morning!" said Anour, who was apparently the only one not sulking or upset.

"Sorry, I'm late..." muttered Cassandra, confused by what was going on.

Kareen stood up and walked to her, gently smiling and taking her hand.

"It's fine, my dear, a pregnant woman needs a good night's sleep. I'm glad you rested, you look better than last night. Now, come. You must be hungry."

Indeed, she was. Her baby and his dragon stomach were already starving, and the large display of food on the table made it worse. She sat next to the Imperial Concubine, greeting everyone as she was served some of her favorite lemon tea.

"What's going on?" she finally dared to ask.

"Oh, well," said Shareen. "That dearest brother of mine is fighting with our mother and your just-as-stubborn sister. For the record, I'm on their side as well, but it's been like this for over an hour, so I do hope you can talk some sense into him."

"A fight? About what?" asked Anour, curious.

"Their wedding."

Cassandra was speechless! Their wedding? He had already discussed it with his family and Missandra? She suddenly remembered! She said she wanted his mother's approval. But she hadn't really thought he would go ahead and ask her straight-out, or so soon! It wasn't exactly a breakfast topic. Anour too, had his mouth open, visibly shocked. He was about to say something, but Kareen gestured for him to be quiet and eat, like a child.

Cassandra sighed, putting down her cup.

"I guess you didn't answer the way my Lord wanted?" she asked Kareen.

"Of course not. But you don't seem too surprised by that, dear. You already knew I'd be against it, didn't you?"

Cassandra sighed, glancing at the War God's furious expression. He was quiet and still, but she could tell he was furious. He had a frown, and his dark eyes were glaring at everything nearby. This was going to be a complicated one.

"If something happens to me," Cassandra said, "My Lord won't have any chance for another child."

"Finally, someone with some sense here!" Shareen declared. "Kairen, let her lead your army next time, this one knows how to think!"

Her words were met with another deadly glare from her brother, but of course, she wasn't one to be so easily intimidated by him, crossing her arms with a proud expression.

"Kairen, stop being a child and listen to Cassie," said Kareen.

"I won't marry another woman," he growled.

"We are not asking you to, you stubborn child! Just to wait until you two have several children. Do you need me to remind you of what happened to Anour's mother?"

The Sixth Prince immediately nodded, looking resolute. Indeed, his mother had died in childbirth. If it wasn't for Kareen, he probably wouldn't even have reached his teenage years.

"I'll protect Cassandra."

Seeing his resolute expression, she stood up and walked to him, taking his face in her hands, and forcing him to look at her. She knew he couldn't resist her for long and gently brushed his beard with her fingers.

"It's not that I don't trust you to protect me," she said softly. "But anything could happen in the next four months. So many people are opposed to me having this baby. Even if there weren't any external threats, this is my first child. I could face complications or die while giving birth. Those things happen, even with all the medical knowledge."

"Cassandra is only eighteen," added Kareen. "She's still young and not as durable as us."

Talking about her possible death wasn't exactly comforting for Cassandra, but she needed him to understand. If something went wrong during this pregnancy or after it, she didn't want her Prince to lose his opportunity to become the Emperor because of it.

"Still... I won't want anyone other than you," he growled.

"You can't think like that," Cassandra replied. "You could make a great Emperor... If you have a son."

"I only want the children you'll bear."

She sighed. He was being too stubborn. Shareen let out a long sigh of exasperation.

"Do you two have to be so cheesy and mushy at breakfast, seriously? We are still here!"

"I'm against it, too!"

Everyone turned to Missandra, surprised to hear her speak.

"Can someone please remind me who she is?" asked Anour, confused. "She looks like Lady Cassandra."

"Her younger sister."

"You have a younger sister?" he exclaimed, his eyes wide in surprise. "How come I didn't know? It was you at the celebrations yesterday, right?"

"Anour, it's a secret," said Kareen with a serious expression.

"Yes, but..."

"A secret," Kareen repeated firmly.

He opened his mouth again, but seeing his adoptive mother's glare, he shut it and nodded. Cassandra couldn't help but chuckle at their little interaction. Kareen was obviously a good mother to her children, no matter how strict she could be.

After a few seconds, Missandra crossed her arms.

"I am still against it. And I don't understand your weird practices, anyway. The dragon people are strange. One man can bed as many women as he wants, but women can't? And this whole wife-concubine status thing, too! This is just..."

"Missandra, calm down," said Cassandra.

"Wait, I'm curious," says Shareen. "You girls are from a different country, after all, tell us about it."

"It's not a country," replied Missandra. "We don't own the land or anything on it but ourselves. You people see a square of land and declare it yours. It's ridiculous!"

Cassandra was waiting for Shareen to get mad, but she just looked genuinely surprised. Kareen too was rubbing her chin with her finger, looking interested as she grabbed her tea.

"Tell us more, child. I'm curious too. None of us have ever heard about other cultures or tribes besides the Eastern Republic and the Northern Barbarians."

Missandra seemed surprised to hear her interest and looked around, a bit perplexed. She glanced at Cassandra, unsure, but seeing her older sister give her a little nod, she proceeded to speak, blushing a bit. For once she looked her age and shyer than Cassandra.

"W...well, I was only seven, so I don't remember too many things... But I know we only lived by the swamps, and in our shacks. "

"Shacks? Not real houses?"

"The soil was too uneven for stones like it is here, it would have gotten muddy and moldy in no time," explained Cassandra, who remembered it better. "We used special types of wood, and grew creepers around it.

"Us children played all day in the rivers, catching fish, swimming and diving," Missandra reminisced, smiling.

"You were the best at catching fish," noted Cassandra with the same smile.

"You were the best swimmer! My sister could dive the deepest and stay the longest underwater. All the kids always followed her around and tried to imitate her. I was always so proud to be your sister ."

Missandra blushed a bit after saying that, and Cassandra was touched. Indeed, she remembered the cheeky little Missandra, always following right behind her, playing around and going on adventures in the swamps. She wasn't afraid to get dirty or climb high up into the mangroves.

"You mentioned that your mother taught you about herbs?" Kareen probed.

"Everyone in our tribe knew all about the basic herbs. We cooked with most of them, but we also used some for hygiene, medicine, or cleaning. Most of our knowledge was based on what the Elders passed down to us. They were our main resource."

"Our Grandfather was the Chief of the village, as the eldest of the adults," explained Missandra. "Mother was the best doctor. She taught my sister a lot, and the other children who were old enough, too."

"You kept making everyone eat tingling leaves once you discovered their effect," chuckled Cassandra. "You even put it in Paba's tea when he was nagging you."

The sisters laughed at the memory, making everyone else chuckle too.

"Paba?" repeated Kareen. "I noticed you two can talk in that strange language. What is it?"

"Our mother tongue," explained Cassandra. "It doesn't really have a name. Paba means Grandpa."

"You call each other Linue and Hinue," said Shareen.

"It's 'little sister' and 'big sister' . They can also be used to address other girls, even if they are not from the same family, as long as they are close.

"Interesting."

"How do you say husband?" asked Kairen.

Everyone was surprised to hear him speak. Missandra immediately frowned.

"We don't say it," she said. "And we don't get married to men who take concubines!"

"Missandra," sighed Cassandra.

The little sister pouted, crossing her arms, visibly unhappy. Cassandra turned back to her Prince.

"We don't really have a word for 'husband' since we don't get married like you. We do have a union ceremony, though. Partners call each other Almien."

"Almien?"

"It means 'who is mine'," sighed Missandra. "You can only ever do that with one person though!"

"So lovers do this?"

"It's not just lovers, but people who are promising to unite their lives forever. You cannot change or take another one after!"

"Missandra, I think they understand," said Cassandra. "Anyways, it's..."

"Let's do that."

She turned to Kairen, confused.

"Do what?"

"You and me, let's do that thing from your tribe. Almien."

Cassandra laughed nervously. Though it was meaningful to her, their tribe's union ceremony would have absolutely no legal recognition in the Dragon Empire, it would only be something symbolic. Now he was interested in that too?

"That's... ahem... We did say that getting married is..."

"Actually," interjected Shareen, "you shouldn't get married yet under our country's law, but...I guess a foreign ceremony would be alright. Mother?"

To Cassandra's surprise, Kareen seemed to actually be considering it. Were they serious? The Imperial Concubine took a couple of minutes to reflect on the option before nodding in approval and grabbing a biscuit.

"Mh, Shareen is right. If my son is going to be stubborn about this, I suppose a little ceremony would be fine, as long as it's kept secret! We have yet to hear what this whole ceremony entails though."

Cassandra was speechless! Really? It would be like a secret wedding, but would hold a deeper meaning for them. She turned to her Prince, a bit baffled.

"Do you really want to do this? It would have no legal bearing here."

"It would have meaning to you, right?" asked the Prince.

"Of course. It was one of my tribe's most sacred rituals."

"Then I want to do it."

Would a secret ceremony really be enough for Kairen? While they couldn't get married in the Dragon Empire until her son was born, would this make them feel more secure about their future? For now, there were too many things that could throw off the balance. One of the biggest being that the heir to the throne was still yet to be named and, while he had limited interest in succeeding his father, Kairen was obviously the best fit. Sephir would also be a good choice, but Vrehan would make things go from bad to worse. There needed to be some security in their future before they could plan for it.

So they just couldn't marry legally, for now, Cassandra had to side with

Kareen and Shareen on this one. It was a bit selfish of her, but she would rather stay the War God's favorite than be his wife right now - for her own safety. She didn't want him to have another concubine, but she also couldn't predict what was going to happen with so much uncertainty about the future of the Empire.

"Cassandra dear, don't overthink it too much," said Kareen. "My children are clearly very stubborn. If this is enough for my son to hold on to, until an actual wedding is possible, and if you're fine with it, let's just go ahead with it."

"Mother, you're just thrilled to organize something like this behind Father's back, aren't you?" mused Shareen.

"What are you talking about? I don't need that old man's permission, regardless! And anyway, we are organizing this secret ceremony, aren't we? Cassandra, dear, what does it involve exactly?"

"Hinue!" protested Missandra. "Are you sure?"

Cassandra sighed and stood up.

"Can I have a minute with my sister?" she asked.

Kareen nodded.

"Of course, dear."

Cassandra took her sister by the hand and guided her out to the garden. It was large enough where they could walk to the opposite side and be far enough away so that the other's couldn't eavesdrop, even with their enhanced hearing.

Once she felt they were an acceptable distance, Cassandra gently released Missandra's hand and faced her.

"Missandra, I understand your doubts, but..."

"No, you don't understand. Hinue... We only just found each other. We missed almost ten years together, and now you're...you're almost one of them."

"How so?"

"You act like them, you speak like them. I don't know, I just thought things would be different when we reunited. I dreamed about it so many times! But now, you're carrying a baby and you're talking about getting married to some Prince... to the... the War God. I feel like I'm going to lose my sister all over again. I don't like these people involving you in their schemes and everything."

Cassandra sighed.

She often acted more mature than her age, but Missandra was only sixteen. She had experienced so many hardships since she was seven, being sold to one brothel after another. She didn't have a good childhood or grow up with family, and she probably only made a few friends, if any. Typical girls her age in the Dragon Empire were all about meeting boys and having fun, but no matter how she had grown up, Missandra had always been different.

The only thing she likely held onto was their past, the memories she had from her early childhood with the Rain Tribe. It was probably the best way she had found to deal with all the craziness going on around her. Holding on to the idea that, maybe, she would find a way to get back there again. That idea had probably been ingrained deep inside her, along with the memories of her older sister. Cassandra could tell how much Missandra still missed the Rain Tribe, even after all these years, by the way she held on to a language she had learned when she was so young and hadn't even had anyone to speak it with.

Cassandra sighed and gently took her younger sister's hands.

"Missandra, I am not going to leave you alone again."

Her sister seemed relieved by her words, looking at her with wide eyes. After a few seconds of silence, something in her expression changed and tears slowly appeared. Her little emerald eyes grew awfully red and watery before Missandra broke down into heart-wrenching sobs.

Cassandra drew her into a tender embrace, letting her younger sister cry against her shoulder and gently caressed her hair, soothing and whispering to her. She must have been holding it all in for a long time.

"I promise we won't be separated again. Just because I will become a mother or someone's partner, doesn't mean I won't still love you. I'll be by your side, anytime you need me, I promise Missandra. We'll always be together."

Her sister kept sobbing, showing her weakness for the first time in years, and the flow of tears didn't show any signs of stopping. Eventually, Cassandra drew back and put her hands on her sister's shoulders as she was met with her sister's emotional, green eyes.

"Missandra, I am sorry, but our tribe is gone. What you remember from our childhood... It's fine to hold on to those memories, but you also have to let your anger go. What happened to us was a tragedy, but you can't keep blaming everyone for it. You have to grieve, and let it go. Our mother, Paba, all our friends...they are gone, Missandra. I am really sorry, but Linue, you need to accept it now."

Missandra cried some more, but despite her runny nose and puffy eyes, she nodded, as she tried to calm herself down.

"I know...I know it won't...won't be like before, but..." she stuttered. "I just...hoped...I don't know... I was afraid... You had left it all... And forgotten... and didn't care..."

"I haven't forgotten anything, Linue. I carry them all with me in my heart, and I treasure each fond memory. I have sung our people's old prayers many times in my head. I'm still happy when I feel the water on my body, I still eat as we ate in our childhood. I couldn't forget all of that. But I won't be able to enjoy the present if I still hold onto too much of the past."

Her sister nodded again, clumsily wiping her tears. It was a bit embarrassing for a teenage girl to cry so much, but it was time she let it out. Cassandra gently helped her get rid of her tears and brushed her hair behind her ear.

"We need to look forward to the future. You're no longer a prostitute and I'm no longer a slave... The future won't be all bad. It's alright to remember our past but think about where you want to go from now on. I know I want to have a healthy baby, this baby, and be with the man I love."

Missandra begrudgingly accepted.

"He'd better treat you well."

"Do you think he doesn't?"

Both sisters glanced quickly at the breakfast area. Shareen and Kareen were chatting, but Kairen had his eyes on them, watching them from afar like a hawk. Missandra sighed.

"I'll admit, he's doing fine so far."

Cassandra chuckled. Her younger sister was as stubborn as ever.

"You can keep an eye on him too, alright? But please, try to go a bit easier on him, and his sister and mother, too. They... He saved my life, Missandra. For real. And since I met him, I'm happier than I've been in a very, very long time. I want to keep it that way, and I would be happier if you could be happy with me."

Her younger sister nodded again, grabbing Cassandra's hands with a bit of a sorry expression.

"Hinue, I'm sorry... I should have congratulated you on your baby. But I just was too upset. I really am happy you're pregnant, though. I'm so excited for you to become a mom."

"You'll be an Auntie, too."

Missandra smiled and nodded, excited at the prospect of her new title.

"I'll make sure to protect it. I mean him! It's a boy, you say? How do they even know that?"

Cassandra chuckled and explained the whole situation about Krai's egg as they were making their way back to the breakfast area. Just as they were halfway there, the sun was briefly blotted out as a dragon-sized shadow passed over them.

Krai softly landed right next to them after letting out a loud growl, causing Missandra to scream and hide behind Cassandra, utterly terrified.

"Missandra. He won't do anything..."

"You can't be sure of that!! He eats humans."

"He eats pigs!" yelled Shareen from the table, as they were now close enough.

"I saw him eat a man just yesterday!" Missandra retorted back.

"Isn't that exactly what I said?" Shareen laughed.

Missandra frowned. But to their surprise, Krai kept sniffing and wiggling closer, showing some interest in Missandra. She kept hiding behind Cassandra, making a comedic scene of the dragon and her circling around the young concubine for a while.

"Why does he want to sniff me?!" she cried.

"He's just curious," Cassandra guessed. "Here, scratch him there, he loves it."

"I am not scratching a dragon! My arm would just be a little snack for him!"

"I promise, it won't," said Cassandra, encouraging her younger sister in front of her.

Missandra was trying hard not to scream while Krai's body was encircling her, but the dragon indeed seemed curious about her. It kept sniffing and gently pushing her arm with its snout until Missandra had no choice but to give it a shy scratch in the spot her older sister had pointed out. Immediately, the dragon started acting a little sprightly, growling softly and moving its head so she'd scratch more.

After a minute, Missandra's terrified expression softened a little.

"Oh... alright...I guess you might not be so...dangerous after all," she said.

Cassandra chuckled and left her sister and Krai to get to know each other as she walked back to the breakfast table. Shareen and Kareen were laughing at Missandra's awkward introduction to the dragon, but they undoubtedly hadn't forgotten the previous matter.

"So?" asked Kareen with a knowing smile.

"Alright, we can do a Rain Ceremony," Cassandra conceded. "But we'll need to prepare a few things and it'll have to be a simpler version. It also needs to be done on a rainy day."

"Oh great! The next rainy season isn't due for months here!" growled Shareen.

"Stop fussing," her mother scolded her. "We'll do this at the Diamond Palace, my city has far more rainy days. What else, darling?"

"We will need some Borean ink, purified water, a silk thread..."

"The water flowers, too!" Missandra shouted from where she was still rubbing the scales of a very contented Krai.

"Yes, and we should find green outfits."

"Green? Like servants?"

"It's the color of happiness for our tribe. We usually make traditional wedding clothes with green fabric and embroider them with prayers and symbols with a white thread, but I guess we can skip that..."

"What are you talking about?" protested Kareen. "Even if it's a secret, a ceremony is a ceremony! We will go by the book, so make a list of anything you need for your Rain Ceremony, and I promise this old woman will get it right on time for the next rainy day in the Diamond Palace! You'll see!"

They resumed breakfast after that, Kareen asking Cassandra a lot of questions about the Ceremony, making sure she knew absolutely everything they'd be needing. It was obvious she was only too happy to organize all of this, and Cassandra started to suspect Shareen was right when she said her mother was happy to have something to do behind their Father's back. She repeated several times that it would be her responsibility to gather everything Cassandra had mentioned so they could plan the most perfect ceremony possible once they'd be back in the Diamond Palace. They were still a few days away from that, though.

The New Year Celebrations had to go on. For the next few days, Cassandra felt like there was nothing to do but watch shows, eat, and sleep. She was surprised by how the guests did their best to attend as much as they could, despite being obviously tired. The concubines attended if their man attended, but anyone who had a chance to improve their status made themselves seen. However, there were very few unusual events after that. It seemed like the Second Prince had found his perfect excuse to not attend any more of the celebrations, while Shareen was back.

Cassandra however, had something extra to attend to. As promised, she visited the First Prince's apartments and examined him. If she wasn't an Imperial Physician, it would have been inappropriate for another Prince's concubine to go into another Prince's chambers. It was obvious no one could be suspicious of her for visiting the First Prince, however. His poor health was no secret, and the Emperor had personally approved of Cassandra examining him.

Sadly, she had no good news for him or his worried concubines. Even after chatting quickly with Missandra, who was still hiding her appearance under a veil and cloak, the sisters had reached the same conclusion. She turned to the Prince, who was sitting in his bed, waiting for her to speak.

"His Highness suffers from a chronic respiratory disease called the Sickness of Dust."

"The Sickness of Dust?" repeated the only concubine wearing pink.

"Yes. It's something that makes his lungs extremely sensitive to any sort of dust, smoke, bacteria... Unfortunately, it's a birth condition that can never be fully treated. His Highness needs to be in a very clean environment, dry, and not cold. Also, you should avoid going out in the next few weeks."

"The next few weeks?" asked the First Prince, frowning. "Why?"

"With the New Year Celebrations, a lot of smoke is going to be in the air for a while. Also, the pollen will be back soon, and may make you worse."

"Can't you do anything about it?" asks one of the concubines.

"The tea you had us give him yesterday helped a lot!"

"There are several medicinal herbs that will help improve his lungs condition, I'll write them out for you. If you feel like coughing again, you should put them into a pot and breathe them until you calm down. Just sit down and inhale until it goes away."

The concubines looked disappointed, but the Prince raised his hand before his women could speak.

"Thank you, Lady Cassandra. None of the previous Imperial Doctors were able to give a name to my condition or speak to me honestly about its gravity before you did. At least now I know how to do better."

"You're welcome, Your Highness," said Cassandra, bowing politely. "I will be taking my leave now, but I will definitely come back and visit you before leaving if you'll allow me."

"Of course, of course. Enjoy the celebrations."

With that, Cassandra turned around to leave, Dahlia and Missandra following closely behind her. She let out a little sigh. She felt sorry for the First Prince. There truly was no cure for his condition, none that she knew of. He would have to live with it his whole life. If he took her recommendation seriously, he could at least potentially avoid any life-threatening crisis, but even her medicinal herbs had their limits.

"I wish I could do so much better here," sighed Cassandra as they were about to walk out of the First Prince's Apartments. "There is such limited knowledge about the properties of plants."

"The doctors here are rip-offs," said Missandra. "I sold my unguents to the girls for much cheaper and with better effects."

"Why don't you continue?" asked Cassandra.

"What?"

"You wanted to make a living for yourself, didn't you? Why did you sell tea instead of medicine?"

Missandra sighed, shaking her head with a little smile.

"Hinue, you overestimate me! I don't have your knowledge or your patience. I wouldn't treat people, I would just fight with them continuously. With tea, people can just come, order what they need, and leave. With medicine, people while arguing, tell you you're wrong and women know nothing about it. The only customers I ever had were prostitutes who knew me well. But even when I did start to sell, I had some concurrence, you know. Those jerks of retailers just don't like competition, they made a fuss so I would stop."

Cassandra stopped and turned around, surprising both of the girls behind her who almost ran into her.

"So you...You know the people who sell the abortion potions in the Red District?"

"Of course. I lived there for years! Why that question, though?"

"I..."

"Lady Cassandra!"

To their surprise, two of the first Prince's concubines were trying to catch up to them, walking hurriedly despite their long dresses. Cassandra wondered if anything had happened, but the two girls bowed.

"We wanted to thank you deeply for treating our Lord," said the lady in pink.

"Oh, you're welcome."

The two of them stood straight up.

"I'm Berissa, and this one is Chiara. The two of us were hoping to get closer to you, Lady Cassandra, and if...you'd accept to have some tea with us later on?"

Cassandra was a bit surprised, and it took her a few seconds to understand.

"Yes, of course. Please let me know when you'd like to spend time together."

The two women's faces brightened, and they thanked her profusely before Cassandra insisted she had to leave, after which both went back.

Missandra and Dahlia exchanged glances, both confused by what had just happened.

"Hinue," said Missandra. "Why would these women be interested in having tea with you? They are already concubines with their own Prince."

"I think they were acting on the First Prince's behalf," said Cassandra. "If his concubines are close to me, the War God's pregnant concubine, it could show he is close to his brother, and supports the Third Prince as heir to the throne."

"Maybe they were just looking out for themselves," said Dahlia. "It isn't rare for concubines to befriend concubines with more power than they do, just to increase their chances to survive in the Imperial Palace. With the news about His Highness the First Prince's health being bad, maybe those two thought it would be good for them to get close to you, just in case anything happens."

"What? I don't want them to use my older sister like a stepping tool!"

"It's alright, Missandra," said Cassandra. "I actually hoped to befriend some concubines within the Imperial Palace. So far, the Emperor and First Prince's concubines are the only ones who haven't been mean to me."

It was the truth. Cassandra felt like Kairen and her couldn't have only enemies within that Palace. The differences between all six Princes were obvious, but there were definitely some who were close to one another. While Vrehan and Kairen were clear enemies, she still hoped they could find some support among the other brothers.

"Oh right, Hinue," said Missandra as they were walking back. "What did you want to ask me before? About the abortion portion or something?"

Cassandra realized she was so lost in her thoughts about the First Prince's concubines, she had almost forgotten! She nodded, and talked softly, as they were walking down several corridors and could easily be heard.

"Yes... Someone got one of those, and I wanted to know who they got it for. I thought there would be no way to know."

"Of course you can!"

"What? Really?"

"Sure," said Missandra with a nod. "You know, the people who sell such stuff in the Red District have to keep a strict record, because the establishments' owners want to know if the girls get pregnant, in case the father is someone rich, they can make them pay for it. Also, if someone outside of the Red District orders one of those, they need to know, they want to avoid trouble."

"Trouble?"

"You know, from rich families. If one's daughter or wife orders one of these, the Head of the House has to know. But if the girls don't say a thing, what do they do? They run to the Red District to make a scene and threaten to behead the seller if they don't give a name. Trust me, I've seen this situation happen so many times. Any wise shop owner keeps their buyers' list as tidy as they can!"

Cassandra was speechless. She didn't expect her sister would be able to help them in such a way! However, Missandra seemed sure about what she was saying...

"So, who was it?"

Cassandra explained to her the whole situation as they were going back to her apartments, her younger sister nodding and frowning all this time. Once they reached Cassandra's new private garden, she knew about the whole situation.

"I see. Of course, I could find out! The only problem is I risk my life if I

330

go back there, though."

"Could you go with Princess Shareen?"

Missandra frowned.

"Mh...I don't know if I could endure her for so long."

She sighed.

"Can you let me send a few letters, actually? I still have friends there. They could definitely ask for me, and I wouldn't have to leave the Palace!"

"Of course. I think my Lord has ink and parchments in our bedroom, though he never uses it."

"Alright, I'll go and borrow it then!"

Missandra left the garden like that, leaving Cassandra with Dahlia, who looked a bit upset, watching Missandra go. Cassandra was a bit surprised. What was wrong between Dahlia and her sister? They had barely met.

She took a few leaves she needed for the First Prince's decoction, watching her young female servant.

"Dahlia?"

"Yes, Lady Cassandra?"

"Do you perhaps...not like my sister?"

Dahlia immediately blushed, looking down in embarrassment.

"It's nothing like that, my Lady! I don't... Hold any hard feelings against your younger sister, really. I just... I... I'm a bit jealous of her."

Jealous? Cassandra was perplexed. Was it because she had taken her younger sister as a servant? It seemed like a rather foolish issue for Dahlia to be jealous of, though.

"Jealous of Missandra? Why?"

Dahlia blushed a bit more, looking down on the basket she was holding for the leaves, blushing.

"It's that... P...Princess Shareen seems very interested in Lady Missandra, and... I... I like Princess Shareen very much..."

Cassandra was completely caught off guard. So that's what it was! She had almost forgotten Dahlia said she liked someone in the Imperial Palace. But of all people, it was Lady Shareen!

Cassandra was completely caught off-guard. She hadn't expected that.

"Really?"

"I know it's shameless of me to be thinking about one of the Royal Princesses in such a way! I just... I've always admired her since I was a little servant. Lady Shareen is such a strong-willed woman, and she knows how to fight, too... I swear I am fine with admiring her secretly! It's just... I was a bit surprised by how quickly she seemed to like Lady Missandra."

It was rare for Dahlia to open up with her feelings like this. Cassandra felt a bit bad, as since she had found Missandra, she hadn't paid too much attention to Dahlia. She chuckled and took her hand gently.

"It's fine, Dahlia. I wish you'd be more open with me like this. I'm glad I have you as a friend here."

"A friend... Lady Cassandra, do you really think of a lowly servant like me as a friend?"

Cassandra was taken aback. Not because of Dahlia's reaction, but because her words echoed her own, not too long ago. A lowly servant, or a lowly slave. It was something she would say often about herself, notably when her Prince tried to get his feelings across to her. Now that she was thinking about it, their relationship had been so awkward and unprecedented from the start. Back when she was sitting against that throne, with some of his fur cloak covering her, she would have never guessed the position she would be standing in today.

"Dahlia, don't call yourself that. You are no lowly servant. You are a servant, and my friend, if you'll accept."

The young woman's eyes immediately got filled with tears, and she bowed profusely.

"Thank you, Madam! I'll treasure our friendship!"

Cassandra still felt like this was a bit different from what a friend should say, but she understood Dahlia's long years of service in the Imperial Palace prevented her from saying what she wanted, or changing her habits in a few days. It would most likely be a gradual change. Self-confidence couldn't be built in a few days after years of serving others.

"About Missandra and Shareen," said Cassandra. "You know, I don't think they see each other in a romantic way. My younger sister is a bit stubborn, and I think Princess Shareen just enjoys watching her because she is entertaining. She rarely sees someone of a lower rank rebel like Missandra does. Princess Shareen is someone who enjoys strong characters, but from what I have seen, her lovers are more... submissive types."

Cassandra felt a bit shy talking about Shareen's tastes, but after all, she had seen it first hand. Their first meeting had left quite a strong impression on her, not necessarily in a good way. However, since then, she had learned to understand Shareen a bit better. The Princess was stubborn and hated when someone resisted her. She enjoyed mostly teasing people she liked, like her brothers. And lastly, she had very low standards of decency.

"I see," said Dahlia, blushing a bit more.

"I don't think my younger sister would be interested at all, either," added Cassandra with a sigh. "They bicker nonstop. Plus, though neither of them look like it, Missandra is half Shareen's age."

Indeed, sometimes, Cassandra wished her younger sister wouldn't act so defiant when she was just a sixteen-year-old girl. Missandra had grown too mature and stubborn, but if it wasn't for Cassandra, she wouldn't have survived in the Imperial Palace with such behavior.

"I feel a bit bad for being jealous," said Dahlia. "I'm already well aware that Princess Shareen has taken many lovers. The servants talk, you know. I know she likes to play around, but somehow, since Lady Missandra was different from them all, I just got... a bit worried."

"I guess it can't be helped. We feel jealous when someone gets close to our loved one."

"Is it the same for you, my Lady?"

Cassandra nodded. They were slowly tending to all of her plants, as Cassandra didn't really feel like going to the Celebrations yet. Moreover, her Prince was busy at the moment, and she didn't want to go there without him. So, she was just taking her time, taking care of her garden, and collecting some leaves in the basket Dahlia carried for the First Prince's decoction.

"Yes... I guess one can never feel at ease," she sighed.

"You should! His Highness the Third Prince obviously only has eyes for you!"

Cassandra chuckled, picking another flower.

"Thank you, Dahlia."

However, Cassandra felt somewhat awkward discussing her personal feelings with someone else. It was part of her personality, she was still incredibly shy about her own relationships. She felt like Kairen and her shared something she wouldn't have been able to share with anyone else. Cassandra liked thinking of their bond as something...special.

A little while later, Missandra came back with a little smile.

"Alright, I sent it! I hope they can answer soon."

"I hope so too," said Cassandra. "We planned to leave for the Diamond Palace as soon as the New Year Celebrations are over."

"So soon?"

They turned around. Immediately, Cassandra frowned, pulling her younger sister.

Phetra was standing at the entrance of her indoor garden, with a nasty smirk. She was wearing a very revealing purple dress, and a little golden diadem.

"I believe you have no right to be here, Your Highness," said Cassandra.

"No right? If a slave can be in the Imperial Palace, why can't a Princess be?"

Cassandra tried to remain calm and composed. Phetra wouldn't be stupid enough to do something to her in the Third Prince's apartments, would she? Moreover, was she ever going to let go of the slavery thing? This was really getting old, even for her.

"Ah... I guess my older brother really went the full way for you," she said, glancing all over at Cassandra's garden.

Calmly, she stepped forward and pushed one of the plant pots onto the floor, making it break on the ground. Cassandra clenched her fist. There really was no end to that woman's childishness.

"Have you just come to mess around, Princess Phetra?" she asked.

"Well, I was bored... And hearing that you didn't have your usual pet around... I couldn't help but come and visit."

She stepped forward, breaking yet another two pots.

"Please stop!" yelled Dahlia. "Those plants are important to My Lady!"

"Shut up, servant," retorted Phetra, crashing another pot onto the floor.

"I wonder if his Highness the Second Prince knows of your presence here?" said Cassandra.

Phetra froze. Cassandra had hoped her brother's name would somewhat make her react, and she was right. She had noticed long ago how Vrehan was cold to everyone, including his concubines and sisters. Phetra probably only had a very limited amount of trust and liberty from him, too. Moreover, from what she had witnessed, the Second Prince hated confronting Kairen or Shareen directly. He had abandoned one of his concubines to her death because she had acted on her own with that snake. Though he probably wouldn't want his sister dead, he certainly wouldn't see her actions in a good light either. Any time Phetra had stirred up trouble or fought with Shareen, the Second Prince had stayed out of it, leaving Phetra in her own mess.

"Don't you dare talk about my brother!" growled Phetra.

Cassandra was scared of her, but not to the point she would step back and let Phetra act however she wanted. Not in her garden, and especially since this part of the Palace was part of Kairen's apartments. Half-siblings or not, she knew no Princess or Prince who wasn't Kareen's child was allowed here.

"These are my Prince's apartments and my garden. Please go back," said Cassandra.

"Don't you give me orders, either! You know what? Actually, this gives me an opportunity. I could have your head for acting up and thinking you can order an Imperial Princess around!"

"I am his Highness' The War God's concubine," retorted Cassandra in the coldest voice she could. "Don't think your threats can intimidate me any longer, Princess Phetra. The Emperor..."

"Oh? You want to go and cry to my father now?" said Phetra.

She took the diadem she had on her head and threw it to Cassandra's feet with a smirk.

"See? I have dozens of those. Do you think you're special because my father gifted you one? Don't you realize? concubines like you are replaceable. Do you think wearing a pink dress makes you even remotely close to an Imperial Princess? You're wrong. You're a low-born, good for nothing."

"Good for nothing?" repeated Cassandra. "I think you keep misunderstanding something. I am an Imperial Physician. I contribute to this Empire's well-being. One of those pots you just knocked over contained a plant to heal the First Prince's cough. Shall I tell his Highness Prince Sephir that I can't heal him now? Because Princess Phetra came over to act up in my herbal medicine garden?"

Phetra got red, staring at the mess at her feet, and glancing at Cassandra, unsure.

"You're lying..."

"The first plant was blue limonea, a plant to improve blood flow," suddenly said Missandra. "The second one was demonis helebora, a plant that whitens any fabric, and can be used as makeup. The third one is wild chloriane, its flowers produce a perfume that helps clear the lungs' impurities. You're a Princess and you don't even know this much?"

While Phetra, in awe, looked down at her feet, Cassandra turned to her sister.

"Linue, stay out of this," said Cassandra in their mother tongue.

"As if I'd stay put and watch this snake woman insult my sister!" replied Missandra, annoyed.

"How dare you talk to me, you low servant!" yelled Phetra, sounding very pissed off.

"This low servant is more educated than her Highness," Missandra shouted back. "Next time you can think about that before you come and destroy someone else's precious medicinal herbs on a whim!"

"I want that servant's head!" yelled Phetra, furious. "I will kill you, now!"

She took out a little dagger, furious, and started walking towards them. Cassandra was totally panicked. She was no fighter, and anyway, none of them could injure a member of the Imperial Family without being punished or worse, executed. Krai couldn't enter the garden, and Kairen was busy elsewhere. She pulled Missandra and Dahlia behind her, hoping Phetra wouldn't dare attack her, a pregnant concubine.

As she kept stepping forward, Cassandra reacted by reflex. She took one of the buckets at her feet and threw its content to Phetra's face. It was full of dirty water, one she had prepared with fertilizer for the plants.

As soon as the water hit her face, Phetra stopped and screamed horribly. She tried to wipe the dirt off of her face, and in this short time, Cassandra slapped her hand for her to let go of her dagger. The blade fell, and Missandra immediately took it away, dropping it in one of the fountains.

"You..." hissed Phetra, having managed to wipe some off her face.

She lifted her hand to slap Cassandra, but the young concubine wasn't going to stand still. She was scary when she had a weapon, but without it, Phetra was nothing but a woman who was about Cassandra's size, and certainly didn't have any fighter's reflexes or speed. In a hand movement, Cassandra pushed her hand away. It was still a bit painful as Phetra slapped the back of her hand, but it was better than taking a slap in the face and doing nothing.

As her move had been blocked by Cassandra, the Princess looked even angrier, pointing a finger at her.

"You're dead! You're as good as dead! You won't get away with this!" she screamed as she stormed off.

A few seconds after she was gone, Cassandra let out a long sigh of relief and fell down on her knees. Both Dahlia and Missandra jumped to her side, worried.

"Hinue!"

"My Lady, are you unwell!"

"It's fine... I just got a bit too agitated. I didn't think she'd go away."

"Lady Cassandra... we will be in trouble. Lady Missandra, you shouldn't have gotten involved! What if Lady Cassandra is in danger because of you!"

"In danger? That crazy Princess was here to stir trouble anyway! I wasn't going to stay still and watch her insult my sister calmly! Do you think it gets better if you let them mistreat you? It just gives them an excuse to be worse the next time!"

"Enough, you two," sighed Cassandra. "Help me go to Lady Kareen's apartments. It will be safer there until his Highness comes back."

Chapter 21

All the way to Kareen's apartments, Cassandra couldn't shake off those worried feelings inside her heart. What if she had pushed it too far? What if Phetra took her revenge on Missandra, or even Dahlia? The girls were bickering non-stop behind her, but she just headed right to Lady Kareen's apartments, trying to get there as fast as she could.

"This was foolish and reckless of you, Lady Missandra! What if Lady Cassandra gets blamed for what happened? You went too far!"

"You didn't do anything to help my sister!" Missandra retorted back. "So what, I should have let her be insulted? That woman had no right to come and pick on her! I can't stand bitches and bullies!"

The girls just kept going at it until Cassandra reached Kareen's place. Their argument somewhat made her panic even more, and when she finally spotted the Imperial Concubine, who was taking tea in her garden, Cassandra ran to her, falling at her feet, in tears.

"Cassandra, dear! What happened?"

But Cassandra had given too much of her strength in that little confrontation with Phetra, and for some reason, her nerves couldn't take it. She had been so scared for her sister, for Dahlia, scared for herself and her baby, and she was angry all at once...

"Servants! Get some fresh water!"

"I'll prepare..."

"Don't you two dare move from here!" roared Kareen, furious. "You two girls better not move an inch before telling me what in the world happened!"

Kareen was glaring at both Dahlia and Missandra, making the girls white with fear. The two of them were experiencing the Imperial Concubine's wrath first-hand for the first time.

While several servants helped put Cassandra on a chair and brought her fresh water and dried fruits to help her recover from her emotions, Dahlia and

Missandra told Kareen what had happened, bickering a bit in the process. She seemed to be caring for Cassandra more than listening, but Kareen wasn't losing one word from them.

When they were done, Missandra was angry again, frowning while looking at Cassandra.

"I can't believe that Princess dares to pick on my sister like this! She..."

Before she could end that sentence, Kareen stood and slapped her.

The noise resonated loud and clear in the little garden, making the servants run away like scared mice. Dahlia, too, had her eyes open wide in shock.

"I'm fed up with your reckless attitude!" yelled the Imperial Concubine. "You are not in the Red District anymore! This isn't some girl's fight where you can talk back and get away with some light punishment! You are in the Imperial Palace! When are you going to realize that your childish attitude is putting your sister in danger?"

Missandra was completely speechless. She put a hand on her burning cheek, unable to say one word, staring at Kareen. The Imperial Concubine was absolutely infuriated with her.

"You can't be stupid enough to provoke an Imperial Princess and think you'll get away with it! Your sister has done her best to survive so far, you're here for two days and you piss off an Imperial Princess! Do you think everyone here will let you get away with it, as my children do? Kairen and Shareen are only putting up with your attitude because of their love for Cassandra!"

"But she... that Princess is the one who came..."

"Yes, she did, and you should have left it for Cassandra to handle! If you hadn't provoked her, Phetra wouldn't have dared to pull out a weapon in my son's apartments! Now you put a target on your back, and there is no guarantee we will be able to save you! Do you think it was smart to retort back if you lose your head for it? This isn't a child's game! Stop acting like a brat and thinking you'll always get away with that attitude! Whether you like it or not, this is a Dragon's Den! Our Palace, our rules! Stop trying to apply your logic here, before you get all of us and your sister killed!"

Missandra was on the verge of tears, now, and took a few steps back before running away, crying. Kareen gestured for a few servants to follow her, making sure she didn't leave her apartments. She sighed, sitting back by Cassandra's side.

"I didn't say anything until now, Cassandra, but that sister of yours needed to hear it sooner or later."

"No, I'm the one who should be sorry," sighed Cassandra. "I should have been harsher with her earlier..."

"You just found your long-lost sister. It can't be helped that you didn't want to scold her too much. I hate having to fight with my children, too."

Cassandra still felt sorry for Missandra. Somehow, she regretted forcing her younger sister to come to the Imperial Palace when she wasn't prepared for it.

She couldn't stop worrying. What if Phetra really managed to kill Missandra? She would never forgive herself.

"Do you think... Phetra will...?" she asked, not even able to bring the words to her lips.

"Don't worry, Cassandra. That little bitch won't get away with threatening you and my grandson this time. Just you wait until my son hears of this, he won't sit still. Just because he seems so calm, those people shouldn't forget he is the War God."

Cassandra nodded, despite not feeling much better. However, she knew she needed to calm down. So much worrying was not good for her baby. Truth was, she had such a fright earlier. She tried to relax a bit, drinking the tea brought by the servants, but nothing could chase away the darkness in her heart. Kareen stayed by her side, caressing her arm gently.

To their surprise, Krai arrived first. The big black dragon showed up all of a sudden, popping its head above one of Kareen's walls with a growl.

"Where have you been, boy?" scolded Kareen.

Cassandra would never get used to the Imperial Concubine treating a humongous beast like Krai as she would a mischievous child. The dragon ignored the mother, and scooted to Cassandra's side, sniffing her frantically. She sighed and put her hand on the dragon's warm scales, feeling a bit better by its contact.

"Where is your Master?" she sighed.

Krai growled softly, lying down next to her, though it was big enough for Cassandra to still caress its head. As she was waiting for her Prince to arrive, Cassandra remembered something she had meant to ask Kareen.

"Some of the first Prince's concubines approached me earlier."

"Did they?"

Cassandra explained their brief exchange to Kareen in a few words, looking for her opinion on the two concubines. The Imperial Concubine stayed silent for a few seconds, but she didn't seem too surprised.

"I don't think those two have any ill intentions," she said. "They are aware Sephir is weak, and could die in the upcoming years. If it happens, those women will need someone's protection in the Imperial Palace. They are probably thinking you might be the next Empress, and are taking an early start on befriending you."

"Why would anyone want to attack widows?" asked Cassandra, confused. "No concubine can get on the Empress throne without their Prince becoming Emperor first..."

"They may lose their Prince, but those two have children. When a new Emperor gets on the throne, he often gets rid of the potential competition, as much and as fast as he can. That includes his brothers' male descendants. Those women are probably hoping you'll watch out for their children if anything happens."

Cassandra hadn't thought of things that way. Kairen's nephews were also potential rivals. If she remembered correctly, he had seven of them already. Prince Sephir had one son and two daughters so far, but he could still have more. Those concubines were probably seeking her protection, just in case... However, Cassandra doubted Kairen himself would take any action against the children unless he had a good reason to.

Cassandra realized she had never seen any of the Princes' children. Were they all staying with their mothers, out of harms' way? Maybe in different locations than the Imperial Palace? She knew she wouldn't want her son here unless she had no choice. It was too dangerous for a young heir. Just like her son, Kairen's nephews probably each had young dragons, too.

"How many dragons are there in total?" asked Cassandra.

She had just realized, not only did the young Princes' have dragons, but also, like Srai, some dragons had probably outlived their masters as well!

Kareen seemed hesitant.

"As far as I know, about twenty. There are only seven adult dragons, that I know of for sure, but the old schmuck might be hiding more."

Cassandra realized Kareen was right... The Emperor could have kept some of his dead brothers' dragons, or some of his nephews'. No wonder the Dragon Empire was so strong compared to other countries. Not only do they have dragons, but their enemies couldn't even know how many there really were!

She wondered if all the rumors she had heard about the army of dragons were true. Cassandra couldn't help but think it would be a truly beautiful sight to see all seven flying together.

"Cassandra!"

She sat up at the Prince's call.

Kairen came in like a storm, headed right her way, looking half-worried, half-furious. Shareen was behind him, but Cassandra only got a quick glimpse of her. Her Prince immediately grabbed her in his arms, carrying her like she weighed nothing once again.

"Are you injured?" he asked while scanning her all over.

"No, no I'm fine, I just got a bit of a fright..."

"That sister knows when to get her in trouble," said Kareen.

In a few words, Cassandra tried to explain what had happened, from the moment Phetra had appeared in her garden. At each sentence, the War God's eyes darkened scaringly. Cassandra was worried he would get mad at Missandra, while she thought Kareen had already scolded and scared her enough.

"So?" said Kareen. "What are you going to do now?"

"That bitch Phetra needs a lesson", hissed Shareen. "A real one."

"Wait, Missandra provoked her," said Cassandra. "What if she gets punished?"

"Actually," said Kareen, "your sister could use some punishment."

Right after that, she walked off, leaving the siblings and Cassandra alone in the garden. She was worried.

"I know I shouldn't have let Missandra provoke Phetra," she said. "But I just couldn't stop my sister, and things got out of hand so fast..."

"Don't worry," whispered her Prince. "You don't have to apologize. I shouldn't have left you alone."

Cassandra could have argued she wasn't alone, but in that case, it probably wasn't what he actually meant. Kairen seemed relieved to see her fine, as he kept gently caressing her, refusing to let go of her for one second.

After another minute, Kareen suddenly returned, followed by Dahlia and Missandra. The younger sister looked deeply sorry, looking down and with her eyes all red and puffy. It broke Cassandra's heart to see Missandra in such a state, but she couldn't do anything at that point. She had no choice but to let the Imperial Family deal with it.

"Let's go," said Kairen.

"What? I am not going!" suddenly claimed Missandra. "You said this woman would have me dead!"

"Missandra, enough!"

It was the first time Cassandra got mad at her or even raised her voice. The younger sister was speechless. However, she saw in Cassandra's green, angry eyes that this time, she wouldn't idly sit by and let her act however she wanted. Missandra finally understood. She had gone too far, and she couldn't oppose her sister or anyone there. She nodded, defeated.

To Cassandra's surprise, Kairen carried her out, and even refused to let her walk by herself as they left the Imperial Concubine's apartments.

"I'm fine," she said, trying to convince him.

"Cassandra, you could barely stand earlier," Kareen reminded her.

Cassandra felt embarrassed nevertheless. Thinking about it, she probably hadn't eaten properly earlier. With all the discussion about their secret ceremony, she had barely touched breakfast, and her appetite was unpredictable these days. Plus, with the earlier fright, her nerves had too much for one day.

Kairen was getting more protective of Cassandra any time something happened. His eyes had a murderous glare since Phetra had been mentioned earlier.

Their little group, including Missandra, Dahlia, and some of Kareen's servants, walked quickly through the Palace towards the Imperial Chamber. Seeing Kareen, Kairen, and Shareen altogether was a way to make any servant turn around and leave as quickly as possible.

For a while, Cassandra thought they were going towards the garden where the New Year Celebrations were still being held, but she soon realized she was wrong. Their group was heading to the inner part of the Palace, where the Emperor gathered all the ministers, generals, and scholars to officiate and discuss the Country's future. Despite the ongoing event, the upper ranks probably still had to work and make sure everything in the country was going smoothly.

Once they arrived, Kairen finally put Cassandra down, letting her stand by his side, and brutally opened the large gold doors. Everyone inside the room jumped in shock, and all eyes converged their way. There were at least fifty people inside, all men. All of them looked shocked to see the War God making such a brutal appearance, and their glances went back and forth to the Emperor and his son, trying to figure how bad this situation could turn out to be.

The Emperor probably had his mouth open the widest of them all. His eyes went to Kairen, Shareen, Kareen, Cassandra, and Kairen again, as his son was leading the group.

"Son, what is..."

However, the War God made his way towards the men gathered, and without warning, grabbed one of them by the collar. Cassandra recognized, a bit late, the Second Prince Vrehan, struggling to get away from his younger brother's grip.

The strength difference was painfully obvious. Kairen held him by the collar, at arm's length, well above the floor. Despite his pitiful attempts, Vrehan didn't manage to make him move one bit.

"Where is your damn sister?!" roared Kairen.

Even Cassandra had never seen him that furious. As if to support his Master, Krai made an appearance with a terrible growl, making the whole building shake. The terrified scholars went white, as the black-scaled head appeared above, in the usual open roof.

The Emperor had absolutely no control over the situation. His eyes went from Kareen to her son, again, and he tried to step forward, looking unsure.

"Kairen, son...What is..."

"I said, bring out your damn sister!"

"Let me go," hissed Vrehan.

"Your sister. Now."

He didn't even need to ask precisely which one he was talking about. With an annoyed look, Vrehan gestured for two servants to run out of the room. Meanwhile, Krai was trying to get inside, the growling getting louder and louder. The room wasn't exactly too small for the beast, but the opening definitely wasn't made for a dragon to squeeze through. It could only get one front paw inside and with just that, the closest wall was dangerously scratched.

The Emperor slammed his hand against his throne.

"Kairen, enough! Put your brother down this instant!"

"I'll put that vermin down as soon as I get his sister."

Everyone was shocked. No one ever opposed one of the Emperor's orders, but apparently, that rule did not apply to the War God. Kairen's wrath was blindly aimed at Vrehan and his sister, enough to completely oversee his father's authority.

The Emperor, maybe, didn't seem as surprised or angry as he could have been. Putting his hands on his hips, he turned to Kareen and Shareen, who had been patiently waiting to the side.

"May I know what this ruckus is for? Kareen, dearest, I'm glad to see you, but..."

"Oh, don't worry, you'll soon be very aware of the situation, dear."

Apparently, Kareen's cold smile and use of a pet name were enough to have the Emperor blush and distract him completely from the current situation. Cassandra wondered exactly how much influence the Imperial Concubine could have on him.

A short while later, the servants returned, looking a bit embarrassed and bowing.

"Her Highness Princess Phetra re...refuses to come, your Highness..."

The Emperor rolled his eyes, annoyed. Meanwhile, Kairen's grip on Vrehan's throat, who was already getting red from being held like a ragdoll, got tighter.

"Your sister better change her mind quickly, or I swear you'll pay in her stead."

"Tell Phetra to come here immediately!" yelled the Emperor. "Since when does she dare ignore us!"

The servants left again. Cassandra was speechless. The Emperor had taken things personally, already? He sighed, and waved his hand, dismissing most of the high-ranked officials immediately.

The little crowd was only too happy to leave, as Krai had been raining some grated marble on their heads for a little while already. None of them wanted to stay in the area when the War God was that angry, either.

As the time started to get longer and neither Phetra or the servants were coming, Shareen took her sword out.

"Shall I go get that bitch myself, brother?"

"Shareen, enough! Put that thing away, you know I hate when you use weapons inside! And will someone finally explain what is going on here, by the Great Dragon!"

"It appears, dear, that your seventh daughter thinks she can threaten the War God's Favorite, an Imperial Physician, and get away with it by not coming here," slowly explained Kareen.

The Emperor immediately frowned, his eyes switching from Kareen to Cassandra, who was standing next to her. His face turned red.

"What! What is Phetra thinking?! Someone go get her! Right now!"

Of course, the Second Prince had already sent two servants prior, but two more Imperial Servants swiftly left the room. If Phetra didn't come after all that...

While waiting, Kareen even ordered a chair to be brought for Cassandra, insisting she shouldn't stand for too long. She took one for herself, actually, installing herself like a queen in the middle of the Palace.

"How...How have you been, dearest?" asked the Emperor.

Cassandra was still amazed to see a man his age blush so much when addressing Lady Kareen. The Imperial Concubine nodded and wiped off some invisible dust from her dress.

"I have been fine, aside from the children's endless bickering."

"I know, right? So tiring, so tiring!"

"It would be better if their father monitored them more closely."

After that, the Emperor's mouth closed, looking a bit contrite. Cassandra couldn't help but feel a bit sorry for him. Kareen really didn't cut him any slack.

Finally, the servants returned, but they were followed by Phetra's furious screams. Kairen put Vrehan down, who breathed out, readjusting his clothing with a bitter expression.

The War God's anger had already shifted to Phetra, who barged in screaming.

"Vrehan, Father! Why are you summoning me?! What is..."

She stopped when she saw Kairen's furious glare. Her face went immediately white, her eyes displaying endless terror. She unconsciously took a step back, and Krai's loud growl got her attention, too. Phetra turned around, to try and leave, but the servants immediately stood in her way, and though they were all bowing, it was obvious she wouldn't get through that way.

She turned around again, shaking her head.

"Third Brother was looking for you," said Vrehan, still looking pissed.

Cassandra realized he was angry at his sister as well. He probably didn't like getting involved and having to face Kairen.

However, something felt wrong with Phetra, too. Unlike her revealing dress from earlier, she was covered in a purple shawl, covering her body and even a bit of her face. Cassandra wondered why she had put that thing on?

"I...I only..."

Kairen wasn't going to show any patience with her. He walked the distance that separated them and grabbed her throat, just like he had her brother earlier, making her squeal like a pig. She panicked immediately, trying to free herself and screaming like crazy.

"Let me go! Let me go! You can't hurt me! You can't hurt me!"

"Phetra, will you stop screaming like this, it's extremely disagreeable to my ears," said the Emperor, annoyed. "Kairen claims you threatened his concubine, what happened?"

"Her...her bitch servant insulted me! Father! That dirty servant insulted me, and the slave concubine attacked me!"

"Who attacked who?" said Kareen, frowning. "Phetra, you lying little snake! Didn't you draw a sword in the presence of a dragon's son!"

Phetra ignored her, still screaming, begging to get her Father's attention and for him to take pity on her.

"Father, they disfigured me! Look what that witch did to my body! Father, you must have justice for me!"

Indeed, the shawl had slid down with Kairen holding her in the air, and now, everyone could see the large red rashes on her skin. Kareen sneered, visibly satisfied.

"What...What is that?" said the Emperor, lost.

"An allergic reaction, I believe, your Highness," sighed Cassandra. "I did throw some dirty water on Princess Phetra."

"Why would you do that? Kareen, dearest, what was that about a sword?"

"Princess Phetra came to my Medicinal Garden earlier, your Highness," explained Cassandra, stepping forward. "She acted recklessly, and I got scared. My servant tried to defend me, but Princess Phetra took out a sword to attack me. I reacted and threw... ahem, some water on her, which certainly caused her...current condition."

The Emperor took a minute to take it all in, but meanwhile, Phetra started screaming again.

"Her damn servant attacked me! She insulted me! I want her head, Father! Father, you can't let me be insulted like this! I am an Imperial Princess!"

Krai growled, and it was obvious the dragon was trying to get to her. It only made her panic and scream even more.

"Father! Father! He will kill me! Brother! Brother help me!"

However, Vrehan remained silent, ignoring her as if this situation was completely unrelated to him. Cassandra hated that, he was abandoning his sister in such a situation.

As she kept screaming, Kairen suddenly tightened his grip, choking her a bit. He wasn't suffocating her, but at least she had to stop screaming if she wanted to breathe. Truth was, Cassandra hated seeing a woman mistreated like this, but Phetra had gone over a limit this time.

The Emperor shook his head.

"Kairen, son, enough. I don't want you killing your siblings in the middle of my Imperial Chamber!"

"She insulted and assaulted Cassandra," hissed the War God. "I will not let this go."

"Calm down, calm down, will you! Cassandra is fine, isn't she? She's just..."

"Since when do you know anything about pregnant women, you old man!" roared Kareen, making the Emperor jump. "Fine? Do you know how fragile she is at the moment? What if she had lost her child? What if Phetra had injured her!"

"Calm down, dearie, I will handle this. But first, Kairen, let her go, please, Son."

"Kairen..." said Cassandra, gently.

She was afraid things could go wrong if he ignored the Emperor's orders any longer, and killed Phetra in such a place.

Kairen opened his hand all of a sudden, and Phetra fell to the floor brutally. A *crack* sound was heard, announcing nothing good. She started screaming in pain, again, but now holding her injured ankle. The War God suddenly grabbed her wrist, forcefully dragging her and throwing her to his Father's feet. The Emperor sighed, his hands on his hips.

"Phetra, you unruly child. You never listen, do you? I guess I have been too lenient with you. Attacking a pregnant Imperial Concubine! How could you be such an idiot?!"

"They are the ones you should punish, Father!" she sobbed, trying to act pitiful, pulling on his clothing. "They made me like this! You can't allow a servant to treat me like this!"

"Enough! Enough of you, Phetra! You really need a lesson! Guards!"

Imperial Guards appeared all of a sudden, but none of them actually dared to approach Phetra and the furious War God next to her.

"Take her to the Imperial Prison for her to stay... Mh... Fifty days! The prisoner's treatment! Yes, fifty days sounds like enough time for me to find her a husband."

"A hus...husband?"

"Yes. You've annoyed me enough. Time to send you away, you can marry some scholar or whatever. You'll be stripped of your title as an Imperial Princess, too. I've had enough of you stirring trouble."

"Father! You can't do that! I was born an Imperial Princess, I'll die an Imperial Princess!"

"Looks like you just expired your first life, Phetra," sneered Shareen, satisfied. "Brother, if I remember correctly, the Imperial Prison is... this way."

She was pointing a finger, and a second later, Cassandra understood what she meant. He was going to...

Kairen grabbed Phetra once again and, despite how much she screamed, hysterical, he suddenly threw her out of the window Shareen had shown. Cassandra and her servants were shocked, covering their mouths in horror.

"Don't worry, dear," said Kareen. "It's only two or three floors down until she lands on the building."

Landing wasn't exactly the right word!

Kareen and Shareen were almost smiling as if Phetra's screams had been some pleasant melody. Cassandra couldn't help but feel a bit bad for her on the inside. From the way she was piercing their ears, she must have been in such horrible pain.

The Emperor's mouth was still open, as he was still processing what had just happened, staring at the window. He finally turned to Kairen, angry.

"Kairen, when I ordered for Phetra to be taken to the Imperial Prison, I actually meant for her to be taken there through the door, the damn door!" he exclaimed. "Why is it that you children are always only thinking of fighting and killing each other?!"

His yelling had no effect on his son. Kairen turned around and walked back to Cassandra, looking almost satisfied. At least, the murderous look in his eyes was gone.

"Well, from what we can hear, Father," said Shareen. "She is still pretty much alive."

The Emperor glared her way, not amused by her antics this time. He sighed, massaging his temples and looking truly exhausted by all this ruckus.

"Anyway, someone go grab her from... wherever she is now, and get her an Imperial Physician immediately. She's still going to the Imperial Prison. Now I have to find someone who'll be willing to marry this pest... Ah, what a headache... Those children..."

While the poor Emperor kept rambling, the guards subtly glanced Cassandra's way for a second, but after thinking about it twice, figured it would probably be better to find another Imperial Physician. With the current state of things, the Imperial Concubine probably wouldn't even have agreed to treat the Princess' rashes.

Once the guards had left, Cassandra let out a little sigh of relief. Things weren't over, though. Vrehan turned to their father, looking very serious.

"Father, we still have an issue to solve."

"What? What now?"

When his eyes surreptitiously went Missandra's way, Cassandra's heart sank. She knew this wasn't good. She had thought that man had been too cold, watching his sister being thrown out of a window without saying a thing, but now, it was clear he had been waiting for this moment all along. Not caring about Phetra, just this moment.

"The servant. She still insulted an Imperial Princess."

"She did it to defend me!" said Cassandra, immediately standing in front of her sister in a protective stance.

"The Imperial Law does not care about the reasons for her actions," hissed Vrehan. "No servant, slave, or anyone else outside the Imperial Family can be forgiven for insulting an Imperial Family member. Isn't that right, Father?"

The Emperor sighed, visibly annoyed by the situation. He knew the law, of course, but he could tell that the servant had only acted to protect the young concubine.

"Whatever," he said. "Bring this servant forth."

"Your Highness, please!" claimed Cassandra. "She isn't an Imperial Servant, she is my family!"

It was her last resort. Maybe, if Missandra couldn't be considered as part of the staff in the Imperial Palace, the Emperor would forget about punishing her. However, she could see Kareen frowning, and that didn't announce anything good.

"What is that now? Your Family, my dear White Lily? How so?"

Missandra, trembling, stood forward and took off the veil she had been using to cover her face outside of Kareen or Cassandra's place. Her appearance was revealed, and she bowed lowly, acting docile for once.

"She is my younger sister, Your Highness," explained Cassandra. "We reunited not too long ago."

"I invited her as my guest," added Kareen.

"Oh, is that so..." started the Emperor, but Vrehan interrupted him.

"Guest or not, Father, no one in the Dragon Empire is allowed to defy a dragon's family member. Those who do should be punished, regardless of their rank. Wasn't my sister just punished for insulting the concubine? Why should the concubine's sister get away with insulting my sister then?"

Cassandra was going whiter with each word. No matter what, she didn't want Vrehan anywhere near her sister, or able to do anything to her. She couldn't stand that man, his rat face, and his cunning words. Kairen moved his position, putting himself between Cassandra and Vrehan, and Krai's anger was now directed at the Second Prince.

However, it was clear that the dragon wouldn't be able to injure him in any way from that position, and so, the Second Prince ignored it completely. Vrehan kept his eyes on his father, with an accusatory stance.

"Are you going to let everything go my brother's way, Father? If you are so tired of seeing us fighting, how about showing some equality for once? That favoritism of yours for the concubine has to stop, Father."

The Emperor had no answer to that, and for once, Kareen and Shareen had nothing to retort, either. It only worried Cassandra more. She had to hold on to Kairen's arm so as not to fall, as her heart was going crazy.

After a long while, the Emperor, who seemed hesitant, eventually sighed and nodded.

"That's right... I need to go by the rules. Sorry, my White Lily, but Vrehan is right, I cannot let it go so easily. A punishment seems befitting of the situation."

"May I suggest, Father," said Vrehan.

Whatever he was about to say, Cassandra knew she wasn't going to like it. Something in that horrid face of his told her he was about to come up with something she didn't want to hear.

"I think... Being whipped for... let's say five hundred and six times should do it."

"Five hundred and six? Why would you come with such a ridiculous number!" said the Emperor.

Missandra was appalled, but Cassandra was even worse. She knew what that number was for. It was the number of times Phetra had whipped the concubine she had tried to defend, months ago.

She realized Vrehan was doing all of this on purpose. While pretending he didn't hold it against them, he was clearly getting revenge for his sister. He was just not letting his emotions show at all, so as to not seem revengeful.

"Father! This is too much!" said Shareen, furious.

"Will you stop yelling! I'm thinking!" replied the Emperor, annoyed.

Cassandra's heart was beating like crazy. He couldn't agree to that. If Missandra was whipped five hundred times, she would die for sure! She exchanged worried glances with Kareen, but there wasn't much the Imperial Concubine could do at this point. With Vrehan's words about the favoritism they already benefited from earlier, she couldn't say anything.

After a while, the Emperor nodded.

"Alright, we will do this. The young servant will be whipped a hundred times. That will be enough."

"Your Highness!" screamed Cassandra, on the verge of tears.

She couldn't believe it. Missandra would have to suffer the whip a hundred times! She didn't even want them to touch a hair on her sister's head. She almost collapsed, but Kairen grabbed her before that, holding her.

"Enough, enough," said the Emperor, leaving the room.

As the Emperor left, Vrehan was staring at Cassandra. He didn't seem happy or unhappy, his expression was indecipherable, aside from his eyes as cold as ice.

"A hundred times..." cried Cassandra.

"Hinue, don't worry!" said Missandra, running to her side. "I can stand it. Don't worry, please, please. Don't cry. I...I did this to myself, Cassandra. Lady Kareen was right, I've been getting ahead of myself, this is my punishment. Don't cry, please?"

However, Cassandra's tears wouldn't stop. She felt horribly guilty for all this. Missandra had only tried to defend her, and now she was being punished! Her younger sister had never been whipped in her life!

Kareen came to her side, too, rubbing her back and consoling her.

"Don't worry, dear, it will be alright. His Highness won't allow them to go too hard on her."

Meanwhile, Shareen was still standing, on the side, glaring at Vrehan along with Krai. The dragon was still growling at the Second Prince from earlier, even more frustrated to not be able to attack him.

"Are you satisfied, now?" hissed Shareen. "Go and scrape up whatever is left of your bitch sister!"

Vrehan stayed silent for a while and actually left the room without saying a word. Shareen clicked her tongue, pissed.

As they were left alone in the Imperial Chamber, Kareen insisted that they go back. Cassandra didn't want to return to her apartments, so they headed once again to the Imperial Concubine's apartments. Missandra felt more sorry for her sister than she actually was for herself. She had caused this, and now Cassandra was worried sick for her. She couldn't even stand by herself, her Prince had to carry her all the way back. She understood that she had to go through this, and how light the Emperor's punishment for her really was. Neither Kareen or her children had looked at her since it had been announced.

When they returned to Kareen's garden, Cassandra had stopped crying, but she was still devastated about what her sister would have to go through. Kairen gently put her in the chair, and Missandra immediately sat on the grass next to her, taking her hand.

"Hinue, please, don't worry, okay? You've suffered so much more than me already, I can stand this much, trust me!"

No matter if she could stand it, Cassandra was already sick at the simple thought of her younger sister, her flesh and blood, being injured.

A servant came running, bowing politely.

"Your Highnesses, Imperial Concubine Kareen, Concubine Cassandra, my greetings. His Highness the Emperor has ordered for the servant Lady Missandra to be brought to the punishment cell for her sentence."

Cassandra almost broke down in tears again, but Missandra confidently stood with a resolute look.

"I'm coming," she announced, determined.

"I'm coming with you," said Cassandra.

"Certainly not!" roared Kareen. "You are already sick enough, you are not going to watch that, too!"

"I don't want to leave her alone through this!" she insisted.

"I will go with her, Cassie," sighed Shareen. "Don't worry. They won't dare go too hard on her if I am there. I promise, I will bring her back as soon as it's over. Just stay here with Mother and Kairen."

Cassandra wanted to protest, but no one would side with her. On the side, even Dahlia silently cried too, feeling sorry for Missandra. She internally regretted she hadn't been braver earlier and said something to stop her or the Princess before things escalated.

Cassandra stood and hugged Missandra, holding back her tears.

"Don't grind your teeth, and don't get tense," she said. "It'll only make it worse. T...take deep breaths, and... and... I'll heal you when you come back. I promise."

"I know. My sister is the best healer in the world."

Despite her confident smile, everyone could tell Missandra was just trying hard not to break down and cause her sister more pain. After a while, they let go of each other, and Cassandra stumbled back. Kairen helped her to sit back in the chair.

Missandra gave her a weak smile and turned to the servant and Shareen.

"I'm ready. Let's go."

Chapter 22

As soon as Missandra was gone, Cassandra couldn't help but cry again. Dahlia tried to get some herbal tea prepared for her, but she didn't touch it and only sobbed in the War God's arms for a long time. It was the first time Cassandra had felt so powerless and defeated. She could stand being injured herself, but seeing her loved ones being injured was the worst thing possible for her. She hated having to wait for her sister to come back after her punishment. She wouldn't be able to do anything for her until then.

Kairen didn't say anything. He wasn't good at comforting her, aside from holding her in his arms, and caressing her hair. His physical contact was the only thing seemingly able to comfort Cassandra a bit, as she stayed curled up in his arms for a long time. Even Krai had arrived in the garden, growling so softly it was almost a whistle, putting its head next to Cassandra, looking sorry for her.

Kareen couldn't seem to sit still. The Imperial Concubine paced around, ordering the servants to do useless things. She kept going in and out of the garden, fidgety. Kareen was a proud woman and hated being powerless. The young sisters had grown on her, even the belligerent Missandra. She felt partially responsible for her punishment too. If she hadn't pushed for her to come with them... No, it wouldn't have changed anything anyway. Vrehan had gotten what he really wanted. To harm Cassandra indirectly, he took aim at the only person he could openly attack in Kairen's entourage. She felt even madder thinking about that brat. They needed to be ready in case something else happened, or even better, give him payback. He had probably already got one, though. Though he had been careful not to show it, Phetra was his closest sister, her downfall was probably painful to him as well. Compared to that, the punishment befallen on Missandra felt too light, even.

"I can't sit still," suddenly declared Cassandra.

The young concubine stood up, surprising everyone around.

"Lady Cassandra, we should wait for Lady Missandra," said Dahlia, worried for her.

"No. I'm counting mentally, again and again, if I keep imagining it without doing anything, I'll go crazy. I need to do something. I want to prepare the medicine for when she gets back. I want to go to my garden."

"You are not leaving my apartments!" roared Kareen, wary like a lioness. "Cassandra, you should stay here for now!"

However, Kairen stood next to Cassandra and took her hand.

"I will go with her," he declared.

Despite his apparent calm, Kareen knew her son was probably as frustrated as she was. He hadn't said anything, but seeing Cassandra so sad and miserable probably affected him as well. Krai stood up too, looking curious about the change of situation.

The Imperial Concubine sighed.

"Fine! But you two come back here as soon as that ointment is done! Shareen will bring her back here anyway."

Cassandra nodded, and left, followed closely by the Prince. Kareen sighed and sat in the chair she had just left. Krai, who couldn't follow them, growled too and put its head on the Imperial Concubine's lap. She scratched its snout.

"Those children," she sighed.

Meanwhile, Cassandra was hurrying back to the prince's apartments. She was aiming right for her herbal garden, still holding Kairen's hand. She had nothing else in mind but her sister. She wasn't scared at the moment, just focused.

As soon as she got there, she let go of his hand and started gathering everything she needed in a hurry. In a few minutes, she had gathered enough herbs and water, and started working on it at her little table, a determined expression on face. Her eyes were still red, but she didn't care.

Kairen let her do whatever she wanted. He understood she needed to keep herself busy to forget about all her sadness and frustration. Something else actually caught his attention. One spot of the grass was still humid and muddy, where the girls had fought with Phetra just a couple of hours earlier. He circled the area, and suddenly spotted Phetra's dagger, still lying at the bottom of one of the fountains. With a frown, he took it out, observing it. It was a good weapon, but it hadn't been taken care of properly.

For a while, the garden was relatively silent. Cassandra was focused on making the best ointment possible, crushing her herbs into a mortar, adding water and preparing some kind of green medicinal paste. She then moved on to a second medicine, a pain-killer decoction. At the same time, Kairen was sitting near her, and had begun sanding and sharpening the dagger. He scraped off all the unnecessary decorations that added to its weight, letting the little diamonds and rubies fall on the grass without a care.

After several minutes, Cassandra assembled everything she had prepared in front of her, shaking her head.

"I don't know if this will be enough," she said, looking defeated.

The Prince stood up, and looked at the table. She had made a pitcher full of ointment, and a large glass of medicine, too. It would probably be enough, even for two people.

"Let's go back," he declared.

"Maybe I can make more," she said. "I can find something else to ease the pain, or make it less bitter, or make more of it..."

"Cassandra, it's enough. Let's go back."

"But..."

"Enough."

She bit her lip, and Kairen grabbed her chin to have her finally look at him instead of the medicine. His deep black eyes almost took her by surprise.

"It's been over an hour," he said, gently but firmly. "Let's go. Your sister will be back soon."

"I..."

Forced to confront his eyes, Cassandra suddenly felt like crying again. She shook her head, but the tears came anyway. She covered her eyes.

"I... I had promised our mother I would protect her... I can't believe... I'm such a bad sister... I shouldn't have brought her here."

The Prince sighed, and gently had her let go of her tools. He took her into his strong embrace to try and calm her down. It had been a while since she had cried so much.

Cassandra had only really cried three times since he had met her. The first time was out of fear for him, when he was locked up by his father. The second time, it was out of anger, for the slaves, when the slave traders showed no compassion. Now, she was crying for her younger sister. It seemed like that girl always cried more for others than herself, when she was the one who had been going through so much.

Her own scars, from being whipped so many times, added up to much more than a hundred or two. There wasn't a spot on her skin that didn't have one of those white, thin lines he hated. Given that Cassandra's skin was among the whitest possible, the scars were sometimes harder to see, and sometimes very visible, like little silver threads, but Kairen felt it under his fingers anytime he caressed her. That precious, frail body he adored had been mistreated until it got like this. Her legs, her arms, her back, her chest... There wasn't an area that had been spared. She even had some on the back of her hands, and on her neck, though the spot where she formerly had a collar had been protected by the metal. His blood would boil just thinking about all the pain she had been inflicted.

"What if she dies? Kairen, if something happens to my sister, I..."

"Cassandra, look at me."

She lifted her head. Her eyes, full of tears, were the most dangerous weapon against him. He put his hands around her neck, his fingers in her hair, and gently caressed her cheek with his thumb.

"Your sister will be fine. As soon as she comes out of there, and can travel,

I will send her to the Diamond Palace with my mother. I will get her out of here, and as soon as these damn Celebrations are over, we will, too. It's my promise to you."

Cassandra nodded weakly, but her heart wasn't at peace. She felt like she was going to crumble at any moment.

"Can I be honest for a minute?" she said.

"What is it?"

"I don't want you to be an Emperor."

Kairen wasn't exactly surprised by her words, but it was certainly the first time she said something like that. He frowned, a bit confused.

"I thought you said..."

"I know what I said," sighed Cassandra, pushing him a bit. "I...There's a part of me, a selfish part of me, that wishes we could leave, just the two of us, and our family. Go far from all the Politics, the murders, the plots, and everyone who wants to harm us. I want... If I could live in a dream, it would be anywhere but this Empire. I...don't want to give birth to children and worry about which ones will be killed. I don't want the jewels, the dresses, the fancy banquets... I just want you, our people, and our baby, living in peace. I want to bear your children, and get old with you. I could hop on Krai's back and let your dragon take us anywhere. But..."

She took a deep breath, calming herself down, closing her eyes.

"There is also a part of me that wants you to change this Empire. I hate... I hate this Dragon Empire, Kairen. Everything is wrong with it. I hate how you and your brothers can kill people without remorse. How slaves and servants are treated like disposable livestock. How women are seen as merchandise, even Princesses. How you see the destruction of my people as nothing more than some unfortunate event from the past. I... I was raised with the idea that life and death are sacred, and must be honored. Your people don't care about life, and they don't even respect the dead."

"Cassandra..."

She shook her head, asking him to let her speak a bit longer.

"That day, in the arena... I was ready to die. I didn't care about the Imperial Games. I wasn't scared, I had no more expectations for life. However, of all people, you chose me. The moment when Krai dropped me at your feet, and you put that little piece of your coat on my shoulders, something in me changed a little. Since we met, every day, I have been seeing what a wonderful, loving man you are. You don't care about gender when you interact with people. You respect your siblings based on their skills, not their gender. You kill when you have to, not when you want. You protect those you love... and punish those who deserve to be punished. You are not perfect, but... You are the kind of man that could change this Empire into a country I can love."

The Prince was very still, listening to every word. Cassandra's voice was hoarse because of all of her earlier crying, softer and huskier than usual. She was almost whispering.

"If a man like Vrehan becomes Emperor, this will go on. People will die unfairly, women like Missandra will be treated poorly. Truth is, if I believed any of your brothers could do this better than you, I would root for them to take the Golden Throne. But... I have seen what they can do, and it isn't what you can do. They can't take an abused, damaged woman, forget about her appearance and still be able to see her value. To turn her into an Imperial Physician. They can't respect their sisters like their equals. They can't have empathy for slaves, servants, or for their people. They live in Golden Palaces, while you're fine with eating and sleeping in a camp. You are not like them, my love. This is exactly why you made me fall for you, and why I believe you should be the next Emperor, even if it breaks my heart."

Kairen gently caressed her arm. He understood everything she said, however, there was one thing that was worrying the War God at that moment, and he couldn't not say it.

"I am not leaving you," he said.

Somehow, he felt as if, at one point, all of this was going to be too much for her. That fragile woman, no matter how strong her heart was, would reach her limit, and be unable to follow whichever path he was fated to follow. Kairen didn't want that. Of all the things he had ever desired, since the moment he had laid his eyes on her, there wasn't a single one that didn't include Cassandra.

"I know," Cassandra chuckled. "I won't leave you either. Your fate will be mine, my Prince, I promise. I've come to peace with that already. Don't worry."

He sighed, and once again, hugged her closely. Cassandra felt relieved he had understood what had been hidden in her heart for a while now. Even for her, it had been so hard to deal with the whole situation, and to come to terms with what she truly wanted. However, she knew one thing for sure: she wanted to stay by this man's side.

She stayed in his embrace for as long as it took for her to calm down. Once her tears were dry, and her heart a bit more at peace, she sighed and took a step back with a chuckle.

"I really want to see our son soon."

Kairen nodded, caressing her tummy.

"Let's have many children," he said.

"Why many?"

"You look better when you're pregnant."

Cassandra chuckled, amused. She knew what he meant, but his way with words was really too much. She softly kissed him.

"I won't suddenly go back to being skinny after our son is born, Kairen. But I am fine with having many. I would love a big family."

She took a deep breath, feeling a bit better, and turned to her little table.

"Alright, time to go back."

The Prince nodded and helped her take the medicine back to Kareen's apartments. Kareen and Krai were still in the same position, Dahlia standing a few steps behind, but strangely, Missandra and Shareen hadn't come back yet.

Cassandra put her medicine down on a little table the Imperial Concubine had in the garden, and sat, worried.

It only took a few seconds, though. Suddenly they heard a commotion from the entrance of the garden. The servants went rushing, and Cassandra stood up. Shareen was carrying Missandra on her back. When she gently put her down on the chair, it was obvious the young girl had cried a lot. She looked exhausted, and the back of her dress was ripped open. Cassandra did her best not to cry again.

Her younger sister's hair had been put to the side in a braid, so the first thing Cassandra saw was her back, covered in cuts, some deep and still bleeding fresh blood. As if it kept her from breaking down, Cassandra immediately ordered for her sister to be taken to a bedroom, and made to lay down so she could treat her. Before the servants even had a chance to move, Kairen gently lifted Missandra and carried her himself, followed by the little group.

"Your sister was brave. She didn't even scream or beg. She endured it until it was over."

"I...I'm fine," Missandra said.

Her voice was so weak, she could pass out at any moment. Cassandra gently helped her take little sips of the medicinal water that could ease her pain, and kissed her cheek once she had drunk it all.

"It's okay if you want to close your eyes, Linue. I will treat you," she whispered.

"How did you...endure all that..."

But before she could end her sentence, Missandra's tired eyes closed themselves, and she passed out, exhausted. Cassandra sighed, but it was half of a cry. She grabbed the towel that a servant had just brought, damped it in the clear water and started cleaning her sister's injuries. The servant girl stepped forward, wanting to clean Missandra's injuries instead of letting the concubine dirty herself, but Kairen glared at her.

"Get out."

All of the servants cleared the room in a couple of seconds. Kareen sighed, caressing Missandra's head and hair gently.

"Poor thing..."

Shareen nodded. She had been truly impressed with the younger sister that day. Her resilience to take the pain without complaining had been admirable. Most people would openly scream and beg for mercy, but Missandra had done none of that. She had closed her eyes and muttered things silently, waiting for it to be over with.

Once the injuries were cleaned, Cassandra suddenly took a strand of her sister's hair, and started sewing her deepest and largest cuts, patiently. Kareen frowned.

"With her hair?"

"The body recognizes its own," whispered Cassandra. "It lessens the risks of infection,"

It was a technique she hadn't been able to use in the army, since the men's hair was cut short, but Missandra's hair was long and clean enough to be used to sew her injuries. With determination, Cassandra sewed each injury one by one. She was singing something softly, in their mother tongue, probably to soothe her sister.

"That song... Missandra was mumbling the same thing the whole time," said Shareen.

"It's the Water God's prayer. It's a very sad song."

She kept singing, softly, while applying the ointment on her sister's superficial injuries. At some point, she sang it again, in the Dragon Empire's language this time, for them to understand it too.

Ô God of Water
Will you hear this prayer
Will you hear your children
When they die under the sun

Ô God of Water
Will you hear and remember
The prayer of your daughters
For they cried alone

Ô God of Water
All your people's tears
Shall you ever hear
Please cry for us

Ô God of Water
If your children are gone
Please take them home
For you loved us

Ô God of Water
When I rest in your embrace
Please help me brace
The last river

Ô Father of Water
Let me dive and sleep
Won't you cry and weep
For you loved us

Ô Beloved Father
Please cry for my sisters
Please cry for your daughters
For you loved us
For you loved us.

When she was done, both singing and putting on the medicine, she took a long sigh, watching Missandra's resting figure. Her sister had aged a few years in just a couple of hours.

"It's the saddest shit I've ever heard," said Shareen.

"Our Elders sang it in times of pain and grief. Our legend said it was the last song of the last mermaids, sung before their death. It was a requiem. Our people made it a prayer."

358

"Do you really descend from mermaids?" asked Shareen curiously.

"Who knows. A long part of our history was forgotten, the other comes from tales and legends. It's hard to tell how much is true."

Cassandra didn't care much for their ancestors' secrets at that moment. She kept staring at her sister, hoping she could heal fast, and feel as little pain as possible.

"Anyway, with Missandra punished, that should settle it for Father," said Shareen.

"Your Second Brother won't be satisfied with that," retorted her mother. "This was only a small payback for how we insulted Phetra. He won't stop there. A servant came earlier to tell me the Princess has several bones broken and is suffering hell. He will want to pay that back."

"I'm getting Missandra out of here as soon as possible," said Cassandra. "I don't want my sister anywhere near where she could be hurt again."

"Don't worry, we will make sure she can leave quietly."

Cassandra stood up, shaking her head.

"She needs to rest for now. The journey to the Diamond Castle would be too much to handle for her in this state. Hopefully, she will be fine by the end of the Celebrations, and we can all leave together."

"Only four days to go," said Kareen. "Missandra won't leave my apartments until then, so she can rest and stay safe. I promise nothing can happen to her here."

Cassandra weakly nodded. She didn't feel like going back to the Celebrations for the day, anyway. She didn't care what the Emperor would say, she didn't want to indulge a man who had inflicted that to her younger sister, no matter what.

"Can I dine here tonight?" she asked.

"Of course, Cassie. That old fart won't dare protest if we say you feel unwell. Let's just have you rest here and do a little dinner together, alright?"

For the rest of the afternoon, Cassandra stayed by her sister's side, with Dahlia. She didn't want to leave her side until she woke up, and everyone understood that. Kairen, Shareen, and their mother gave the sisters some space, finding their own occupations in the Palace, though they stayed nearby.

At some point around the end of the afternoon, Cassandra needed to use the bathroom. She had stayed next to Missandra all this time and couldn't take it anymore. She left Dahlia to watch her in her stead, and went to the closest bathroom.

Kareen's apartments were vast, and among the prettiest in the Palace. There were many, many rooms for her to use, though she only seemed to use a few. Cassandra hadn't gotten accustomed to the place yet. She was used to the Diamond Palace, but inside the Palace, a lot of corridors and doors looked the same. Somehow, she got lost on her way back to the room Missandra had been taken to. She might have taken a wrong turn somewhere, because, after a few minutes, she still wasn't back. She knew she was still inside the Imperial

Concubine's apartments, she just had no idea where.

There was something strange in this area. Actually, she had thought about asking a servant for the way back, but this corridor was completely deserted. Cassandra was lost. This part of the Palace looked abandoned, nothing like Kareen's rooms full of plants and life. In here, there was a deadly silence floating around, like a cathedral.

As she was trying to figure the way back, she came across what might have been a dining room, long ago. It was all dusty, and less refined than the one they actually used. Some cutlery had been forgotten in an old buffet, along with spiderwebs and dust.

Cassandra frowned. She didn't understand why Kareen, who loved clean and decorated spaces, would leave a wing of her apartments empty like this. She kept walking until she found another corridor with rooms. All the doors looked alike, but one caught her attention. It was torn down. Not like it had crumbled naturally, but like some beast had attacked it. The room was open, and, pushed by curiosity, she stepped in.

It was a child's room. There was a bed a bit smaller than the norm, some old furniture, and toys. She collected one that looked like a dragon plushie, left on the floor. It was cute, but old. Whose room was this? There was such a nostalgic feeling hanging in the air. Something deeply sad, too. Cassandra glanced around. There were toy blades, three of them, on top of a chest. So it was probably a boy's room. The desk still had some old books piled up, collecting dust. The library next to it as well. A bit further, something like a large couch made of straw was in a corner, a shape still visible in its center. Was it for some pet to sleep in? A dog, or...

"Cassandra."

She jumped and turned around. Kairen was standing a few steps behind her, outside of the room. She sighed in relief after that scare.

"Sorry. I got lost..."

"Come."

"Kairen... Whose room is this?"

The Prince hesitated, looking inside the room. He wasn't stepping in, which intrigued Cassandra even more. His eyes fell on the stuffed toy she was holding.

"It was mine."

Cassandra was surprised, though she was suspecting it already. The straw couch's indent was too large and deep for a regular animal. The size of it would be fitting if it was for a dragon... A young dragon.

"It's your...childhood bedroom?"

He nodded. Was it really? She thought it might have been one of his brothers', but... Cassandra couldn't imagine a Prince's room would have been left like this, even less if Kareen was in charge. Yet it felt completely abandoned, forgotten.

However, the way her Prince was standing outside, instead of coming to her, intrigued her as well. Something in his attitude didn't feel right, like he was wary of the room. He...loathed this place. She could tell just by looking at him. He had the same look as when he was glaring at Vrehan, or the women who had tried to approach him before. Something about that place disgusted him. Why would he hate his childhood bedroom? It looked like it used to be a warm and nice bedroom for a child to be in. She looked at the damaged door again. Something had happened here. As if someone had gone berserk on it.

She turned around and left the room, but she had kept the little dragon toy with her. For some reason, she liked that stuffed toy. It only needed a bit of cleaning and sewing. As soon as she was next to him, Kairen put an arm around her waist and held her close. He was still glaring at the abandoned room.

"Let's go," he said.

He gently kissed her forehead, and Cassandra nodded. Somehow, she felt like she shouldn't ask about that room now. He obviously didn't want to talk about it, and she didn't want to push him to.

They walked back together, the Prince guiding her silently to Missandra's room. Her sister was still asleep when they got there, and Cassandra, worried, checked her temperature. She frowned, her hand on her sister's forehead.

"She has a bit of a fever. I hoped she wouldn't..."

Despite her worry, Kareen had already ordered some fever medicine to be prepared, just in case. Cassandra had nothing to say against it, so she gave it to her sister, once she was sure it had been tested, and let Missandra rest again.

"Son, your dragon is making a fuss in my garden," said Kareen.

The Prince went out to go and handle an impatient Krai. The dragon had been waiting in the garden all afternoon for Cassandra, and was getting impatient and grumpy. The young concubine sighed.

"I'm so thankful to you, Lady Kareen. If it wasn't for your help..."

"Don't say such things. Of course. When an old woman like me can help, she will. There is nothing I wouldn't do to protect my children."

Cassandra blushed a bit, honored to hear the Imperial Concubine speak about her like so. She already knew Kareen was fond of her, regardless of Kairen's relationship with her, but this was the first time she referred to her like she was her own daughter. For an orphan like Cassandra, this was probably the nicest thing Kareen could have told her.

"Lady Kareen, earlier... I got a bit lost and ended up in an... abandoned ell," she whispered, hoping Kareen would understand.

"I know," sighed the Imperial Concubine. "My son has had that upset expression since earlier, and... that toy... Did he say anything?"

Cassandra looked down at the dragon plushie, and shook her head.

"No... I didn't ask either."

Kareen nodded sadly.

"It's good that you didn't, Cassandra. Men are men, they do not like to show their weakness and they do not share their secrets easily. Even the War God... Give him time. He will talk when he is ready."

Cassandra understood. She wasn't curious enough to pry into someone's past. She felt that whatever it was about, it was something Kairen wouldn't share easily, either. Something dark and painful happened to the War God.

The two women discussed Missandra's health a bit longer, but when it became clear that the young woman wouldn't wake up for a while after taking the fever medicine, Cassandra finally agreed to leave her for a bit.

In the garden, the sun was setting, and Kareen's servants had prepared a little space for them to have a cozy dinner outside. The black dragon almost jumped on Cassandra upon seeing her, dangerously wagging its tail around and growling happily. Thankfully, the garden was large enough for the dragon to move around, or else it would have been a disaster.

To her surprise, the dragon seemed curious about the toy, too. Krai kept sniffing it, and Cassandra wondered if he could remember it somehow. She turned to Dahlia.

"Could you get me a washing basin? And a sewing kit, too..."

"I can do it for you, Lady Cassandra!"

"No, thank you, Dahlia, I would like to do it myself."

"I understand. I will go get it then!"

Cassandra thanked her and went to sit nExt to Kareen on the large rug on the grass. There was a whole buffet waiting for them, their own little Celebration. Kairen and his sister joined them right after, too. The War God sat behind Cassandra, wrapping her in his arms, while Shareen laid down.

"So, what's the plan?" asked Shareen, grabbing a cheese cube.

"There is no plan for now," replied her mother. "We will treat Missandra, and as soon as the Celebrations are over, we are flying back to my Palace. I want to see Srai, too."

Cassandra had almost forgotten about the little dragon. He probably missed his mom. Their baby's egg was still in the Diamond Palace, too. Kareen had it safely guarded back there, and Cassandra trusted her fully with it. Cassandra wondered what color the baby dragon would be?

"Oh, I'm bored!" sighed Shareen. "Brother, come and spar with me! Like old times!"

Kairen frowned, but eventually got up. He and his sister drew out their swords and started dueling together. Cassandra wasn't very worried. Those two were on the same level, and wouldn't get too serious in front of their mother.

Meanwhile, Krai saw an opportunity and swiftly trotted to take Kairen's spot behind Cassandra. Its large and long body actually allowed it to be circled around Kareen, too, making the dragon all the happier. It rested its head on Cassandra's lap, while the Imperial Concubine laid her back against its body, used to this behavior.

The two women watched the siblings spar for a while. Dahlia had brought what she had asked for, so Cassandra slowly started working on improving the little dragon plushie's condition while watching the duel. Cassandra was truly impressed at Shareen's strength. Not only was the Princess extraordinarily strong, but she also didn't have any issue fighting on equal terms with her brother, the War God. She was using two swords, and a perfectly balanced style, so elegant it almost seemed like a dance.

"Those two," sighed Kareen. "I should have bought them dolls when they were kids!"

Cassandra chuckled, remembering the many toy swords she had seen. They may have not all belonged to Kairen, after all. Shareen was a bit of a tomboy, it seems.

"What kind of children were they?" Cassandra asked, still focused on her sewing.

"Exactly like now," sighed the Imperial Concubine. "Kairen was silent and grumpy, Shareen was loud and grumpy. Those two little brats had such tempers... I only seldom brought them here. It was such a ruckus every time we came. Not only did they always spar between themselves like this, but they caused fights absolutely everywhere. Krai, too."

"With their siblings?" asked Cassandra, glancing at the dragon who was sleeping, or pretending to.

"With their siblings, with their father's concubines. Shareen once broke all of one of her sister's fingers because she had insulted me. Most Concubines can't scold Imperial Children unless they are their own, but with those two? Ah! I never had to raise my voice once, they'd always take care of any problem before I did!"

Cassandra had never imagined those two were once so protective of their mother. She could still remember how they weren't thrilled about visiting her when she got hold of Krai's Egg. Kareen probably didn't let herself be bullied, either. They definitely inherited a lot of their mother's traits, especially Shareen.

"Lady Kareen, pardon me for asking this, but... Why didn't you marry the Emperor? You've been his favorite since...long ago."

Kareen sighed, sliding her finger on her wine cup.

"That old man... He did propose a few times. However, every time we got close to an engagement, something happened. I almost died or lost one of my children. Jealousy won over everything, I suppose. He already had too many women before me, and I realized that marrying him meant my children would be in more danger than ever. I couldn't forgive that. Especially the idea that I would have to live in the same place as my children's assassins. We didn't find who had done it. So, I decided to isolate myself, and focus on raising those two. That's when he gifted me the Diamond City and Palace. It was an apology for being useless in finding our children's murderer... I was devastated then, and became paranoid over protecting those two. I left the Palace. Since I ignored him, he got other concubines, other children... Time passed."

"I thought... The Diamond Palace was a present for Kairen's birth?"

"That's what I told them. Trust me, a mother will find many lies to hide from her children, exactly how ugly the price for their survival was."

Cassandra felt a bit sorry for Kareen. She had met the Emperor too late, and gotten involved in the cruel games of the Imperial Palace. She put a protective hand on her tummy. Maybe, in other circumstances, she would have made the same choices as her. Now that she was expecting, her instincts were all about this baby's protection. Her refusal to marry Kairen for the time being had to do with that too... Though she was only willing to wait. She still held on to that idea of becoming his one and only woman, when they would be in a safer place.

"Talk about the dragon, and he will show his tail," said Kareen.

Cassandra lifted her head, and so did Krai, who growled immediately. To their surprise, Glahad was flying high above them, making circles in the sky and seeming hesitant to come down. Its golden scales were almost blinding with the sun's reflection in it. The Imperial Concubine clicked her tongue.

"Looks like he didn't appreciate me not coming to his damn Celebrations. Well, suits him. He can send his dragon, I don't care."

Cassandra kept staring at Glahad. Did the Emperor send his dragon to spy on them? She couldn't help but feel a bit sorry for it. The golden dragon probably didn't dare approach, and was only sent to check on their beloved. Krai kept growling in warning, though the black dragon would probably have lost a fight against Glahad.

"Hey!"

Meanwhile, on the grass Shareen had just gotten an injury. Probably unfocused because of Glahad, the sister had just received a large cut on her arm. She frowned, staring at it. To Cassandra's surprise, scales immediately appeared on her dark skin to cover it up, just like Kairen's injuries. Shareen's scales were more of dark indigo than black, though.

"She can do that too?" said Cassandra, surprised.

"Of course! My daughter has dragon blood too, after all!"

Shareen, who had heard them, rolled her eyes.

"Really, Cassie, you underestimate me that much?"

With a little laugh, she suddenly seemed like she was inhaling a lot of air, and, turning towards the area Glahad was flying in, Shareen suddenly exhaled a fireball!

Cassandra jumped in surprise, while the large golden dragon, though it hadn't been hit, growled, annoyed. Shareen's flames had died in the air, way before they reached Glahad, who was flying too high. Yet, it was so impressive! The young concubine was both impressed and frightened.

"I had no idea the Princesses could do such a thing!"

"Not all the Princesses, Sweetie," replied Shareen with an arrogant look. "It takes talent."

"What talent?" retorted her mother. "It's just like how your brother is so good at taming his dragon. It has nothing to do with talent."

"Do you mean it's also about their characters?" asked Cassandra.

She had slowly started to understand the bond between a Prince and his Dragon. The more true they were to themselves, the more their own dragons were tamed. Compared to Kairen, who never hid his emotions and acted as he wished, someone like Vrehan was unable to tame his dragon. His cunning nature and how he always hid his real thoughts were what kept his dragon wild. Had the Red Dragon been able to roam freely, it would have probably gone straight to kill its enemies in a rage.

Krai, however, was free to act. The dragon could kill, growl, and attack who Kairen hated, except for the Imperial Family. It was free to express its love for Cassandra, too, making it easier to tame than any of its peers. Cassandra wondered if the red dragon had no one to show love to.

"Shareen is more gifted than any of her sisters. Only a handful of Princesses can do the dragon's breath, or have the dragon skin."

"I thought it was mostly about blood?"

"It's a bit more complicated than that," said Kareen. "The Princes are born separately from their dragons. The Emperor's daughters, however, are half-dragons themselves. There is a theory that they are too weak for an actual dragon to be born, so instead."

"It... grows in them?"

Cassandra was astonished. Didn't that mean the Princesses' potential was almost unlimited? They may not have dragons, but judging from Shareen's skills, they may not even need to have one! Moreover, her injury was healing even faster than Kairen's. What else was the Princess able to do?

"Doesn't that mean Phetra will be healed soon?" she asked, suddenly remembering about the other matter.

"That... I'm waiting to see," said Kareen with an enigmatic smile.

Cassandra wondered what Kareen had in mind about Phetra. Somehow, she felt like something bigger was at stake.

The siblings resumed their sparring, but Shareen and Kairen were obviously of equal strength. It could take a while, and even Glahad eventually left the skies above them, flying away. Cassandra sighed and caressed Krai's warm scales. The dragon had gone back to its nap as soon as the older dragon was gone.

As they kept dining, some Imperial Servants came twice to invite Kareen and the siblings to the Celebrations, but the Imperial Concubine stubbornly ignored them. When another servant showed up, she frowned.

"Didn't I say no twice already! How many times do I need to get mad for that old dragon to give up!"

"My apologies, Imperial Concubine," said the poor servant. "I am only here to deliver a letter to the Third Prince's Concubine."

Cassandra got up to receive the letter, surprised. It came from the outside, and she suddenly understood. It was the intel Missandra had tried to gather about the abortion potion! She quickly sent the servant away, and opened it to read it quickly. A friend of Missandra from the Red District had apparently asked around, and it turned out, the order was made from the Imperial Palace indeed.

"It says someone from the Red Wind Pavilion made the order," read Cassandra, confused.

Kareen sneered.

"That's Vrehan's dead mother's pavilion. With this, the person who ordered the potion is obvious. It was probably Phetra. She is the one in charge of that place."

"Phetra? Why would Princess Phetra order an abortion potion? If it wasn't to be used against me then who?"

"Maybe that bitch was dumb enough to get pregnant," muttered Shareen.

The siblings walked back to join the dinner, ending their duel after over an hour.

"I don't think that bitch Princess was pregnant..."

They all turned around, surprised to see Missandra. The young woman was standing, looking a bit tired. Cassandra jumped on her feet, almost falling over Krai's large head.

"Missandra! Why aren't you in bed?! I thought you would be sleeping."

"Their fever medicine is crappy. I needed some fresh air, too."

With Dahlia and Cassandra's help, Missandra sat next to them, grimacing with each movement she had to make using her back. Cassandra helped her drink some fresh water, but surprisingly, she seemed fine.

"Ah... The fresh air feels so good."

"Eat, child, you need to regain your strength," said Kareen, putting one of the plates before Missandra. "How would you know if Phetra is pregnant or not?"

"I'm good at that. Back when I was in the Red District, I could tell who got pregnant after only a couple of weeks. All the girls came to me to get my abortion medicine, too, so I got used to finding out who was pregnant. That Princess is definitely not pregnant."

Kareen nodded, though she still looked doubtful.

Kairen and Shareen walked back to their side, too. Kairen, for once, let his dragon keep its spot behind Cassandra, probably so as to not scare Missandra. She was already looking uneasy with the dragon's head only a few steps away from her. Shareen, next to their mother, grabbed some wine and shook her head.

"I don't like that. I wish we knew who that damn potion was for."

"Can it be one of the other concubines?"

"Aside from you, I don't see who it could be. That idiot Lephys has pregnant concubines that we know of, but he's too dumb for our father to ever consider him as an heir. No, my guts telling me it has to be for one of the Princesses."

"I don't think I've seen anyone wearing purple that was pregnant the other night," said Missandra. "But I'm not a hundred percent accurate."

"Not all the Princesses were there anyway," said Kareen. "A lot of them try to be forgotten so that no one will ask the Emperor to marry them. They'd rather remain single than be forced to leave the Palace."

"Will Phetra have to leave if she gets married?" asked Cassandra.

"That's the whole point. Once we get married, Imperial Princesses like me lose most of our status. We can still wear the Imperial Purple, but aside from throwing tantrums and making the idiot husband kneel, it's not that great. Father doesn't care much about anything outside of the Palace. It's less trouble for him if he has less whiny children to handle. Hence, most of the time, our sisters make sure to live their lives quietly. Or they work hard to help their brother get the throne."

Cassandra suddenly understood why Shareen, despite being over thirty years old, was still single and living in the Palace. If she had been married off, it would have been one less ally for Kairen in the race to the Golden Throne. Indirectly, not marrying off Shareen was a way to show the Emperor's favoritism once again. Without Kairen born a few years after her, Shareen would probably have led a very different life.

Once again, Cassandra thought the Princesses were very unlucky. Their destiny was closely tied to having a brother or not, and that brother's actions.

"How many sisters does Vrehan have?" suddenly asked Cassandra, curious.

"Only three from the same mother. The oldest is already married. Phetra is the second sister, and they have a younger one."

"Oh, what was her name again?" asks Shareen, frowning. "We rarely see that child, I almost forgot about her."

"Phemera," replied Kareen. "She must be around Missandra's age now. She rarely goes out though, I think Phetra and Vrehan keep her from attending any banquets."

Cassandra frowned. It seemed strange that they would hide their younger sister. Perhaps it's to protect her? Or to keep her from spilling their secrets?

"Could she be the pregnant one?"

Both Shareen and Kareen stared at her, confused.

"Phemera rarely goes out," repeated Kareen. "That child is so fragile, I heard she has to stay in bed all day. She probably never even gets a chance to see any man!"

Cassandra nodded. So, who then? Another concubine whose pregnancy could have been a threat to Vrehan?

"I wish Phetra was the one pregnant," sneered Shareen. "That would make an excuse for Father to repudiate that vermin."

"He already said he will marry her off! What more do you expect? Also, don't wish for a pregnant woman to be in that state. Even if she's a snake, her child would have nothing to do with it. Watch your words, Shareen. No, actually, eat and shut it!"

After that, the Princess sulked, and it appeared the topic was over. In the end, they still had no idea who the abortion potion could have been destined for. Without any definite answer, the conversation would only keep going in circles.

At least, they were sure of who had ordered it, but the culprit was now locked up in the Imperial Prison with several fractures and no reason to answer them.

Cassandra felt like they were missing something, though. It was odd that Phetra would go out of her way to get that abortion potion. She hated not knowing who the victim should have been. It felt like another threat was hanging above her head with that unsolved question.

Thankfully, Cassandra could soon forget about that matter. As they were having a quiet dinner, Kareen had fun entertaining them with many rumors about the other concubines from back when she was in the Palace and the many stories she had witnessed. Between the feuds amongst the concubines and her own adventures, she had enough stories to write a full book! To Cassandra's surprise, she and Missandra had a lot of fun exchanging about their favorite tricks to piss off their rival concubines or prostitutes. The Imperial Concubine wasn't afraid to talk about some very crude topics, and Cassandra was the one, several times, to blush and try to change the topic a bit, much to Shareen's amusement.

Somehow, it also became obvious that Missandra had taken in the lesson about her attitude with the Imperial Family. Even if it was only the five of them, plus Dahlia chuckling on the side, Missandra was very careful with her words, and absolutely avoided showing any disrespect for the Imperial Family. Cassandra thought it was a topic they would have to discuss sooner or later, but at least, it seemed her younger sister had finally understood that her words, if said at the wrong time and place, could have her killed.

It appeared that the Dragon Empire's fever medicine wasn't so bad, only late to take effect. Missandra started dozing off at the end of their dinner and had to be taken back to her bed, half-asleep, to finally finish her night properly. Cassandra stayed a while looking at her younger sister's tired face, unsure.

Somehow, she wondered if Phetra was like her, trying to protect her younger sister from all of the Palace's schemes.

Sturdy arms appeared from behind to embrace her gently.

"You should go to sleep, too."

"If we skip the Celebrations, we might as well rest early," she nodded.

Kairen gently guided her to their room. For that night, another bedroom had been prepared for them to sleep inside Kareen's apartments. Somehow, Cassandra didn't feel safe going back to their bedroom after what had happened in her garden.

As she laid alongside her Prince, tired, it still took her a long while to fall asleep. Her thoughts kept going in circles over all of the events of that day; the unsolved questions she still had, and the threat of Phetra and Vrehan's vengeance. Somehow, she felt like Phetra's punishment had triggered something much more worrisome.

Cassandra finally fell asleep as the fireworks started outside. The thumps of her Prince's heart against her back echoed with the Celebrations, finally soothing her to sleep.

Chapter 23

"Your Highness! Your Highness!"

Cassandra frowned, waking up from all the ruckus. Next to her, Kairen was just sitting up too, with an annoyed expression. What was going on for them to be woken up so early? She could hear several servants outside, desperate to get their attention.

She had a bad feeling about this. What could it be? They wouldn't have dared to wake up the Prince in the middle of the night if it wasn't urgent. Kairen left the bed, grabbing his sword as a reflex, and Cassandra took her night robe to cover herself up too, following him to the door.

As they opened it, a handful of Imperial Servants bowed.

"Our apologies for waking the Third Prince and his Lady Concubine at such an hour! His Highness the Emperor is requesting your presence immediately!"

"Cassandra too?"

The servants exchanged glances, apparently unsure of what to answer.

"Uh... His Highness the Emperor only asked for you and Her Highness Princess Shareen to come at once, Your Highness."

Shareen too? Kairen frowned and turned to her, as Cassandra was starting to really worry. What could have happened for them both to be called by the Emperor? Did it have to do with Vrehan, or Phetra? Had something big happened during the night?

Kairen clicked his tongue and turned to Cassandra.

"Go back to sleep," he said. "I will be back soon."

"No, it's alright, I want to come with you."

The Prince frowned, putting a hand on her shoulder.

"You need more sleep..."

"I won't be getting any if I don't know what's going on. Instead of staying here and worrying, I would rather come along. Please."

The War God frowned, but indeed, it would be unlikely that his concubine would peacefully go back to sleep after she had heard that. She was awake and looking very concerned already. Cassandra rarely fell back to sleep once she was up. He nodded.

"Fine."

They both followed the Imperial Servants out. They had no more information about what was going on. Shareen met them right outside of her bedroom, in her nightgown as well, looking grumpy with her black hair all over the place.

"I can't believe they dare to wake us up in the middle of the night," she groaned.

Indeed, it was still a couple of hours before dawn, too early for anything else but an emergency of some sort. The siblings didn't exchange another word and followed the Imperial Servants out.

It was a long walk to the Emperor's chambers, but Cassandra was impressed by how busy the Palace already was. Everywhere they walked, Imperial Servants were busy working, silently cleaning rooms and preparing for the day. Everything had to look perfect before the members of the Imperial Family got up.

Once they finally arrived, the Imperial Chamber was still in the dark, only lit by many candlelights. A few people were present. The Emperor, in a gold robe, with dark circles under his eyes, was walking in circles in front of his dragon. The man looked older than usual without his usual fancy outfits and jewelry. By his side, two older men in military suits were standing, along with a man in a minister's official blue outfit, and some Imperial Servants.

"Ah, Kairen, Shareen! Finally!" exclaimed the Emperor upon seeing the trio.

"What is it, Father?" asked Kairen, while his sister yawned loudly next to him.

"Son, news just came from the border. We are under attack! I can't believe those damn Republicans have the guts to throw an attack during the Celebrations"

"The Eastern Republic?" said Shareen. "I thought Brother defeated them already! Where did they find the courage to launch a new attack?!"

"I don't know, I don't care!" sighed the Emperor. "But they are making a ruckus at our border, and I don't like that. We just got the news, they attacked last night. Anyway, while the Northern Barbarian Tribes are contained, Kairen..."

"I shall defend the border," said the War God.

"Yes, yes. I really don't like this! Losing time over this! So annoying, so annoying!"

Cassandra's heart tightened. The Eastern Republic's attack made no sense now! That country was much weaker than the Dragon Empire. However, no one in the room seemed to doubt that this attack could be pushed back

370

without trouble. The Emperor was more worried about his Celebrations being ruined, and for a while, that was all he vented about, while the siblings waited, arms crossed until one of the Generals reminded him about the more pressing topic.

"Oh, whatever! Kairen, you can go and lead the army to crush them! Crush them for good, I'm fed up with those idiots! If it wasn't so much workload I would just conquer them and that would be the end of the story! tsk!"

"Father, what about the Northern Tribes?" asked Shareen. "Even if the barbarians are quiet at the moment, Brother can't just pull out his army like that."

"You can go and replace him, for now. Kairen, you can take the Imperial Army with you, and let Shareen handle the north. One or two Imperial factions should be enough anyway, just go with Krai and handle this quickly!"

Cassandra was speechless about how this matter was handled. The War God only had to take a dragon, a portion of the Imperial Army and that was it? She had known about the strength of the Dragon Empire before, but now, they were talking about the fate of another country as if it was just a small matter to be handled overnight!

"Let Shareen go to the East," suddenly said Kairen.

His sister frowned, turning to him.

"Kairen, I'm not the War Goddess," she said. "What are you..."

Then, Shareen's eyes fell on Cassandra, and she understood. He didn't want to take his concubine to another battlefield. Shareen rolled her eyes and slapped his arm.

"Are you an idiot? We will just leave her with Mother! She was supposed to go back to the Diamond Palace with Mother soon anyway. You can just take Cassie back when you're done with that stupid battle."

"What? Who is going to the Diamond Palace?" suddenly asked the Emperor.

"Mother wants to go back," said Shareen, her hands on her hips.

The Emperor turned white.

"Why! The Celebrations are not even over yet! Why can't that damn woman stay here for more than a few days? She is so mean to me! She never lets me see her, she even ignores the Celebrations! How much more heartless can your mother be?!"

While the Emperor kept rambling and complaining about Imperial Concubine Kareen, Shareen sighed and turned to her brother and Cassandra.

"Seriously, Kairen, don't be an idiot. Cassie will be just fine with mother, and it's only for a few weeks anyway."

"A few weeks?" repeated Cassandra.

From what she had heard until now, it looked like the matter of the Eastern Republic attack would be solved rather quickly, but to think it would last a few weeks? She felt really unsure about being separated from her Prince for so long, a second time. It would be just like the first time, when he was locked up here in the Imperial Palace while she stayed back with Kareen. Shareen sighed.

"It's still about moving an army and pushing the enemy out of our territory, sweetie. The trip itself will take a few days to the East, and even if Brother has his dragon, the Army will need to get there the old way."

Kairen was still frowning. The Third Prince didn't like this situation either. Cassandra was upset, though she did her best not to let it show too much. This was so sudden. She didn't think they would have to separate so quickly!

The two of them exchanged a long glance. Cassandra's heart was breaking, but she was well aware that this was his duty as a Prince. Eventually, she gathered her courage and nodded, gently taking his hand. Kairen put his arm around her and kissed her head before turning to the Emperor.

"Father, give me the command of the Imperial Army. I will leave at dawn."

"Oh, yes, yes," said the Emperor, interrupted in his rant. "Can someone here write this down? Oh, you there, perfect. As of today, yada yada yada, I hereby confer the power to lead the Imperial Army to my son, the Third Prince Kairen, War God of The Dragon Empire, and dala, dala... Just leave it, I'll fill in the blanks later for the paperwork. Copy this, I'll make the official announcement later. Alright, Son, it's done."

Kairen nodded and turned to Cassandra.

"I'll take you and my mother back to the Diamond Palace before I leave," he whispered.

"I understand."

"Father, are we done here?" asked Shareen, impatient.

The Emperor exchanged looks with the two generals, nodding.

"Yes, Daughter of mine, but your mother..."

"Bye, Father!"

Before he could add anything, Kairen and Shareen promptly left, pulling Cassandra with them. She could still hear the Emperor's frustrated yells several corridors away. She sighed.

"I feel a bit sorry for His Highness," she whispered.

"Don't be," retorted Shareen. "Mother is doing this on purpose, anyway. I'm fairly sure her two favorite hobbies are pissing our Father off and ignoring him."

"How are you going to go to the North, Shareen?" asked Cassandra. "Without a dragon..."

"Brother and Krai will drop me off half-way. I can ride a horse from there. The northern border isn't a problem for now anyway."

For a moment, Cassandra wondered if she shouldn't go to the Onyx Castle. However, she had already entered the second trimester of her pregnancy. In any case, she knew she would be safer by Kairen's side, in the Diamond Palace. Moreover, she would be too lonely, waiting in the Onyx Castle without the Prince there.

The siblings and Cassandra walked back to the Imperial Concubine's apartments. Kareen had been woken up by the earlier ruckus and was already waiting for them in her garden. Shareen quickly explained the situation, making the Imperial Concubine frown more and more as she went on.

"And that old man is sending you two? What about me! Doesn't that old man have other children to send to the front? Am I his only woman producing warriors!"

"Mother, stop it. You know Kairen and I are the best fighters. Sephir will just get killed, and Father doesn't want to give Vrehan an opportunity to earn merit. Just let us go without a fuss, you know we love it anyway."

"A fuss? How are you talking to your mother!"

"I will take you and Cassandra back to the Diamond Palace," said Kairen.

The Imperial Concubine was still sulking and turned her anger to him.

"Of course, you agreed to it too! What next? How long will I wait to see my children next time? And Cassandra? You better be back before your son is born, Kairen!"

Her son obediently nodded, putting his arms around Cassandra in a possessive stance. She chuckled, trying to be brave.

"It will be fine, Lady Kareen. I didn't want to stay here any longer, anyway. So this is a good opportunity to leave without angering his Highness."

"Speak for yourself," says Shareen. "He was furious about Mother leaving."

"Why would I stay here if my children are elsewhere?!" shouted the Imperial Concubine. "How dare that old man complain! Let's just have breakfast and leave!"

Cassandra sighed, watching the Imperial Concubine angrily walk away, yelling for the breakfast to be served already.

"Will you be alright?" he whispered.

"Yes. I'm more worried about Missandra. I hope she can handle the journey."

"She will be fine," Shareen replied. "Your sister is probably stronger than she looks, she was already fine last night."

Cassandra nodded. She was a bit dizzy from all the events in the last hour. They had plans to leave as soon as the Celebrations were over anyway, but she didn't think it would all happen in such a rush. Moreover, it meant she would have to say goodbye to Kairen, again and soon.

Shareen sighed and went to go and calm down their mother, who was already storming left and right, making preparations for their departure. Cassandra watched them argue and go back to another room, fighting over the ruckus.

Left alone with Kairen in the garden, she turned around, still wrapped in his arms, to face him.

"When will you leave for real?" she asked.

"I will drop you and mother at the Diamond Palace, and stay until the Imperial Army catches up. Maybe a few days. A week at most."

A week... They had a week left together. Cassandra nodded, but her throat was tight, and her heart was so heavy, she almost felt like crying.

"You won't be in danger, will you?" she asked.

"No."

She chuckled. He was so sure... Of course. The invincible War God of the Dragon Empire. Cassandra hugged him, feeling a bit vulnerable at that moment.

"Kairen... If it rains during this next week... Let's have our Ceremony. Please."

"We will."

Under Kareen's impulse, their departure was put in motion quite promptly. None of them had much to take back to the Diamond Palace anyway, so they took their time, decided to have breakfast and let the servants prepare whatever they needed to pack.

Once again, they had breakfast in the Imperial Concubine's Garden, much to Krai's pleasure, as it could lay next to Cassandra and nap in the rising sunlight. As everyone had been woken up quite abruptly, they somehow agreed to take their time whilst having breakfast. They even waited for Missandra to wake up, and Anour showed up before their departure, too.

As promised, they were ready to depart soon after dawn. To Cassandra's surprise, the First Prince's concubines, who had heard of the news, showed up to bid her goodbye before she left. Cassandra gave them a couple more recommendations about Prince Sephir's health and politely said goodbye.

Krai seemed ready for this flight, stretching its wings and walking around in the garden, a bit impatient. To everyone's surprise, Roun, Anour's Green Dragon, actually showed up too.

"I'll accompany you," said the young Prince. "This way, I can take Shareen straight to the Northern border and save you some time! I want to go help her at the border, too, the Imperial Palace is so boring!"

"Fine," said Kareen, with a pout. "Aren't you two just in a hurry to leave me to go play with swords!"

After that, she got on Krai's back, as if it was her dragon. Cassandra wondered what a young Kareen handling baby Krai would have been like. The Black Dragon always seemed happy to see the Imperial Concubine, growling softly at her the same way it did to Cassandra. She secretly wished her own son's dragon would have a similar attitude with her, even when she would be old.

Missandra and Dahlia both agreed to climb on Roun's back, behind Anour, as the green dragon was smaller and less scary to them than Krai. Shareen climbed on Krai's back after her mother, and both her and Kairen helped Cassandra up.

Just like that, the little group took off without much of a ceremony.

It had been a little while since her last flight, and Cassandra took a deep breath, hoping she wouldn't get nauseous again. Slowly, the Imperial Palace got smaller under them, and she realized once again how big it actually was. She thought about her medicinal garden, and wished she could have brought it back with them. It was a pity she had only been able to use it a couple of times.

As it was still quite early, the sky was colder than usual. Cassandra was wrapped up in one of the fur coats, and was held on to tightly by her Prince, as usual, while Krai was peacefully flying to the Diamond Palace. The dragon knew the way all too well, it was an easy ride. Actually, it even bickered a bit with its younger brother, Roun, fooling around, growling at each other and trying to bite each other's tail playfully. They kept changing spots, one above and one under until Kairen and Anour had them stop before the women on both sides got sick.

To Cassandra's surprise, Roun was slimmer and smaller, but considerably faster than the black dragon. Its personality, for what she had seen so far, seemed to match that of Anour, too, being more cunning and curious than Krai.

The two of them kept playing more quietly for the rest of the ride, but as they arrived above the Diamond City, Krai got more interested in the Diamond Palace. The dragon accelerated a bit, in a hurry to land there. Both dragons knew the place well and didn't need to be told where to go. Another dragon's growls welcomed them as they landed in one of the larger gardens.

"Hello, my darling," said Kareen, getting off first.

Srai, the little dragon, was excited to see her, jumping all around the place and growling loudly. It even bumped into Krai a couple of times without caring. While Kareen caressed it, calming the young dragon a bit, Shareen jumped off Krai's back, and Kairen helped Cassandra down.

On another end of the garden, Anour was helping Dahlia and Missandra down. The two girls were a bit green and white, but they took deep breaths once they were on the grass, relieved.

"I'm never, ever getting on one of those creatures again..." muttered Missandra, still shaking a bit, walking back to Cassandra with a frown.

Dahlia was quiet, but her expression was not good either. Cassandra felt a bit sorry for them. She had ridden on Krai's back over a dozen times, and was still feeling a bit sick at times. Moreover, the dragons had made the girls' first trip a bit rowdy.

Behind them, Krai was a bit impatient. It kept growling and tottling in circles, getting grumpy. The Imperial Concubine sighed.

"Oh, enough, enough... Let's go."

Cassandra, too, was sharing Krai's excitement, just a bit more quietly. They followed the Imperial Concubine into several corridors. Unlike the Imperial Palace, the Diamond Palace was more dragon-friendly, and full of roof-less rooms. Hence, even if the adult-sized dragons couldn't follow in one room, they would find a way to reunite with the little group through another opening. Behind Cassandra, Missandra kept staring around, impressed, just like her sister the first time. Cassandra chuckled once she noticed this. Indeed, the Diamond Palace was much more to their taste, with all of its wild plants growing freely, wide-open spaces, sunny chambers, and the many water fountains and natural rivers crossing here and there.

"Here it is."

For once in the Palace, Kareen had to open a lock for them to have access to another large indoor garden. It could be accessed through the open roof for the dragons, but for humans, it would have been impossible to climb, with such height and the slippery stonewall.

Hence, when she walked in, Cassandra found Krai already circled up around the egg, rubbing its snout against it.

Cassandra couldn't describe the warm feeling that filled her heart upon being reunited with the Dragon Egg. She walked up to it, putting her hands on its warm shell.

"Is that...?" asked Missandra.

"Our future nephew's dragon," explained Shareen.

Quickly, she explained to the younger sister about dragon eggs and their birth, while Cassandra and Krai were happily re-discovering the egg. It had indisputably grown since last time. It was now about as tall as a young child! Once again, it reacted to Cassandra's presence, the shiny light inside glowing where she was putting her hands, or where Krai was sniffing.

"You're telling me the... The Black Dragon is a female?" whispered Missandra, confused.

"Dragons are agender, neither female nor male," explained Kareen. "Dragons are a unique kind of creature, as they don't reproduce like humans or animals."

"They just need to pee and poop."

"Shareen!"

Behind them, Anour laughed, but was soon interrupted by some furious growls. Roun and Srai, curious, had shown up, the first above and the second from the door, and were brutally growled at by Krai.

The black dragon was fiercely defending its egg, warning the two other dragons from coming closer. Actually, Cassandra noticed that, aside from her prince, Kareen, and her, none of the other people present had walked further than the entrance of the garden. Though she could understand about Missandra and Dahlia standing away from the black dragon, as its size was taking up most of the space, she was surprised that Anour and Shareen had also stayed back. She had thought it was because there wasn't much space, but seeing how even Roun and Srai couldn't approach the egg, Cassandra realized Krai would have probably chased them away too.

She gently patted the Black Dragon to calm it down, while the other two gave up and retreated a bit.

"This egg is getting bigger than expected," said Shareen.

"Is it a problem?" asked Cassandra, worried.

"Of course not. Your son will probably be stronger than the norm, but that's not so surprising given his lineage!"

Cassandra smiled. How she wished she could see her baby and his dragon soon! She wanted to guess it's size, it's color, but she truly had no idea. Would he be black like Krai? Or maybe another color? Roun and the other dragons were all of amazing colors as well.

Krai, too, was affectionately rubbing its snout against the egg, growling softly. Had the black dragon missed the egg as well? After a while of watching the dragon's affectionate behavior, Cassandra stood up and walked to Kairen, hugging her Prince. Sometimes, she forgot that Krai was an embodiment of his tamer's emotions.

The War God hugged her, keeping her in his arms, gently caressing her back.

With a gesture from the Imperial Concubine, everyone else but the couple and the black dragon cleared the room in a few seconds to give them some privacy. As they were now alone in the little garden. Cassandra smiled and, with a bit of boldness, stood on her toes to kiss him lovingly.

Of course, Kairen answered her kiss back. For a while, they were alone with his dragon, exchanging tender kisses and hugging. Truth was, Cassandra hadn't been able to relax like this in a while. Not since they had left the Diamond Palace, actually. Now that they were back in Lady Kareen's domain, the young concubine could finally breathe a little, and not be on guard at all times. Missandra was there too, so she didn't have to worry about her younger sister either.

Those feelings transferred into her bold kisses and the hands with which she gently caressed her War God, her man. Kairen was agreeably surprised. He had noticed Cassandra was uneasy during their stay at the Imperial Palace, but he had never thought coming back to the Diamond Palace would free her like that.

For a while, they kept exchanging kisses, hugging and caressing each other. However, they were unwilling to leave this room. As they both ran out of breath, Cassandra chuckled, resting her head on his shoulder, in a way that she could look at the egg and Krai wrapped around it.

"I hope it will rain soon," she whispered. "I don't want to part with you yet."

"I will be back as soon as I can. You can stay here, and rest. Take care of yourself and the baby."

She nodded, putting her arms around his neck. Cassandra wasn't worried about staying behind at the Diamond Palace, but she hated the idea of parting with him. She had such fond memories of her time with him in the North, at the Military Camp.

However, things were different this time; she couldn't follow him into this battle. Cassandra sighed and turned to Kairen.

"We have about a week, right?" she whispered.

"Until the Imperial Army reaches here, yes."

"Let's just stay together as much as we can... please?"

Cassandra's begging voice, when she was pleading like that, was the most desirable thing in the world in the War God's eyes. Kairen softly smiled, and without saying anything else, suddenly lifted her, taking her into a wild kiss, out of the room and to where they could really be alone.

Cassandra had no idea how her Prince had found a bedroom so easily, but at that moment, she didn't care much. He was carrying her effortlessly, her legs around his waist, and their kisses were getting wilder and wilder.

She couldn't stop. The taste of his tongue, his scratchy cheeks, his hot breath. She was melting under his touch. Kairen's hands were as hot, large, and pleasant as ever. Cassandra could feel all the soft fabric ruffled by his fingers, how he played with her skirt, the silk going up and down on her thighs. His hand found its way to her hair, undoing her hairdo, the pieces of metal falling one after the other onto the floor. As the hairpins kept coming out, her long hair came down, letting the Prince play with it as much as he wanted. He would tangle her curls around his fingers, grasp it, hold it tight, and let go again. Cassandra was able to catch her breath when he moved on to kiss her exposed throat, sucking on her bare skin and giving her delicious chills. The touch of his lips drove her crazy anywhere they landed on. He was reckless, restless in covering her with savage kisses. She could hear herself moan and breathe louder, unable to hold it.

His hand found its way under her skirt, caressing her butt, his fingers sliding under the thin fabric of her panties. Cassandra brushed his hair with her fingers, looking to lock her lips on his again. She wanted him so badly already. She could feel the bump beneath his pants, already rubbing against her, and it was terribly exciting. Her body was so responsive already, her inner parts shamelessly throbbing.

Cassandra struggled to get him out of his clothes while kissing him, only interrupting when they had to, but she wanted his skin. She wanted to touch him more, caress his bronze skin, and feel his warmth against hers. She was out of breath, but Kairen pulled the top of her dress down, and suddenly toppled her on the bed.

She chuckled, suddenly finding herself under him, so fast she hadn't seen it coming. Kairen sat back a second, and pulled her dress down to her ankles and out of the way, leaving her with one last little piece of clothing. Cassandra felt embarrassed, exposed like that on the bed, but the sight in front of her was not to be missed either. The muscular, hunky War God's body, shining with a thin layer of sweat as he took off his pants and braces in a few seconds. He was staring at her the whole time, ogling her with those burning, dark irises. Cassandra blushed, feeling her body react to the lust in his eyes. He was detailing every inch of her skin, like a beast looking at its prey with a torrid hunger. Her skin was so hot already, she couldn't take that burning stare. Cassandra bit her lip, and unable to hold back, her hand reached down between her legs. Staring right back at the War God, she caressed herself with her fingertips, but her panties and belly were both in the way.

Now fully naked, the War God was on his knees, sitting at the end of the bed, watching her struggle. His fingers gently caressed her ankles, but he wasn't coming any closer. Kairen was simply staring, a little sneer on his lips while Cassandra was getting frustrated. Her fingers barely had room to move around her little button of pleasure, and it wasn't anywhere near enough. Not when she was already this wet.

"Kairen..." she called him with a begging voice.

"Keep going."

That order pronounced with his deep, commanding voice made her whole body shiver. She accelerated her movements, locking her eyes with his, feeling his intense stare on her naked body. The War God was caressing her leg slowly, his hand gently going up from her ankle, yet nowhere near where she wanted. He was obviously teasing her. When Cassandra started feeling her first waves of pleasure coming, he suddenly pulled her legs up, her ankles on his shoulders, in a horribly tempting position.

Her entrance was now so close to his virility. Yet still a few inches apart. Cassandra bit her lip, horribly frustrated.

"Please..."

"Keep going, Cassandra."

His game was too cruel. Her position made it even harder to focus on what her fingers were doing, when his manhood was so close. His fingers, too, were stroking her legs gently, up and down, going a bit lower each time. Kairen turned his head, kissing her ankle, making her blush even more. How could a simple kiss on her ankle excite her so much? Cassandra wanted to beg, have this torture stop, but she was completely mesmerized by his hot obsidian eyes.

She breathed louder, her fingertips clumsily playing around her dripping entrance, trying to get there. She was so hot already, how could she reach it? Kairen's eyes were driving her crazy. The beast was just there, enjoying the show and torturing her with that hot gaze. Cassandra was melting under his stare...in so many ways. She tried closing her eyes for a second, but it only made it worse. As if his gaze was even more intense on her skin. He suddenly moved on the bed, and as she re-opened her eyes with a surprise, she felt his lips going down her leg. Cassandra gasped. What kind of torture was this. He gently kissed her knee, went back up inside her thigh, and a bit higher...When his tongue found her entrance, she moaned loudly, arching her body. The sudden invasion of his hot breath, tongue, and lips was ruthless, and Cassandra couldn't help but cry out, overwhelmed.

"Oh... uh... hun....Ah!"

She kept trying to hold it back, but it was impossible. Her fingers hooked in his hair, as she kept quivering. His tongue was not giving her any rest, diving and licking in her hottest part, eating her up, filling her with unpredictable attacks. His lips would suck on her little pink button until she was about to come, and stop at the last second to go down and dip his tongue again, driving her nuts. Kairen's hands were firmly holding her hips, she couldn't get away from his hot breath burning her insides. His head between her legs, he was wholly devoted to her pussy, making her tremble and moan. Cassandra kept writhing under this torture, torn between wanting more and not being able to stand it any longer. She wasn't even trying to hold her voice back anymore.

"Kairen, please, please... Please..."

Cassandra's words kept echoing along with her cries, higher and higher, the fire devouring her. Her Prince didn't stop, licking, sucking, digging into her until she squealed, a raging pleasure bursting through her whole body.

For several long seconds, she quivered under him, unable to stop the sparks spreading under her skin. Her limbs filled and emptied with waves of pleasure, and the numbness that followed such an intense storm.

When her body finally calmed down, Cassandra was out of breath, trying to reconcile with reality.

Kairen chuckled, landing gentle, innocent kisses on her skin, caressing her hips and waiting for her to calm down. He moved over her, going up to where their lips could meet. He gently kissed her temple, while Cassandra was still panting.

"You're so... mean," she whispered with a cute pout.

The War God took the compliment silently, caressing her hair. Cassandra sighed and put her hands on his torso, her fingers stroking down the lines of his muscles. She loved his build so much. Every lump was perfectly defined, the silent strength under his skin oozing with his breath. He was truly a War God. No sculpture could have depicted such a perfect drawing more accurately.

Her hands slid down, reaching his inner regions as she kept caressing him. Kairen slightly tensed up, his breath on her neck, when she touched his rod. Cassandra hesitated a second and gently started caressing it, her hands slowly going up and down, watching his reactions. He was still a bit tense, but she could hear his breathing accelerate against her ear. He kissed her neck again, more sensually, and she knew she could keep going. Cassandra felt a bit shy, holding him in her hands, but she wanted to be the one to please him this time around. She gathered her courage, and kissed his shoulder, his neck, going a bit further down one kiss at a time. She gently pushed him, inversing their positions to get on top, and kept her exploration going. Her lips went down on his chest, his abs, his abdomen... but when she was about to reach her goal, Kairen stopped her.

"Kairen...?"

"Don't."

His voice was gentle but firm, and he was holding her arm, preventing her from going any further down despite her hands already there. She frowned, a bit surprised by his abrupt refusal.

"I don't mind..."

"I said no."

Somehow, she felt that little thing in his voice that made her understand. She nodded, and to show him it was alright, went back to his lips, calming him down a little. Their kiss got gradually wilder, more passionate, and the heat increased again between their bodies. Her hands kept their gentle stroking going, but soon, it wasn't enough anymore. Cassandra moaned a bit, as their lips got restless, and positioned herself.

On top of him, she locked her eyes on his, and slowly went down. Cassandra didn't hold her voice back as he slid inside her, pushing her walls and filling her. There was something so satisfying, just to feel him, hard and rocking her throbbing region. She closed her eyes, her hands on his chest, just trying to appreciate those sensations, and move slowly.

Kairen was mesmerized by the vision of the young concubine on him, indulging herself in pleasure. Her white skin would bloom with undertones of pink, and her long hair falling like a waterfall on her shoulders, balancing along with her movements. He held onto her waist, watching her take control and move her body as she wanted. Cassandra's voice was a melody to his ears, getting deliciously sexy when she was indulging in pleasure, and surely she was. He could feel her clamp and grind around his rod, her lips trembling, her voice translating her pleasure into moans. She kept moving her hips, balancing her body in a gentle dance, holding onto him. At some point, Cassandra locked her emerald eyes onto him, breathing a bit louder. Kairen's hands traveled up to her breasts, fondling them and making her react with shivers of pleasure. She felt it tingling, his hands making her even hotter if possible. She rushed her movements a bit, biting her lip. Was he going to let her do it all by herself?

Cassandra bent over, to kiss his lips, softly, playing a bit with her tongue and teasing him. Her fingers brushed his hairline, holding on to his nape. She moved her hips a bit more insistently.

"Kairen, move... Please...?"

The War God smiled, answering her smile and demand. Cassandra yelped when he suddenly started moving brutally under her. She hadn't predicted he would get so excitable! She moaned loudly, the ride getting wilder, leaving her no rest. It was nothing compared to her lascivious movements just a few seconds ago. Kairen was plunging wildly inside her, his hips giving her a hell of a ride. She had to hold on to both of his shoulders, completely overwhelmed by his assault, crying out and unable to focus anymore. The sounds of their love-making were echoing in the room, obscene and terribly lewd. Cassandra could both feel and hear their bodies slapping against each other, with the wetness she was guilty of. She couldn't control her indecent behavior anymore. She just kept moaning at each thrust, her voice getting hoarse. His rod was rubbing her insides, giving her exactly what she had been begging for.

"Ah! Yes... yes... Ah... Ah... more... yes..."

He was not going to stop, just for the sake of hearing her beg for it. Kairen kept thrusting, groaning, moving until she couldn't take it anymore. His savage desire was untamable. He couldn't hold back. He wanted her, all of her, deep and hard. Even when her voice broke from crying out so much, he wouldn't slow down. Not when she was swallowing him deep like that. Every time he pulled back, it made him want to dive back even faster. He got on top somehow, pinning Cassandra where she was completely submitted to his assaults. The beast was unleashed, she had to hold on to his wrist and shoulder to take it.

When she started calling his name, with that worn-out voice, he lost it. The last movements were ruthless and had her crying out, her body spasming, bringing a brutal orgasm as he froze inside, unleashing in a husky groan.

The pleasure was out of this world. Cassandra felt fireworks explode in her head, feeling him fill her, her body quivering. Kairen stayed tensed up, deep inside for a long while, letting the last bits of his pleasure die in her, enjoying those seconds of eternity until it ran out. Their breathing slowly calmed down, both completely exhausted. All strength had left Cassandra's body. She sighed, and her Prince hugged her, holding her in his embrace.

Cassandra rolled to the side, slowly catching her breath. Her body was still slightly shivering from the aftermath of that wild sex. How many times has it been? She vaguely remembered them changing position three or four times, but her mind was still foggy. She sighed. She could feel that pearl of sweat on her nape, and her hair sticking to her temple.

Kairen gently took her in his embrace and pulled one of the familiar fur blankets over her. The young woman was only too happy to lay on his chest.

Somehow, despite her exhaustion, her body was still too excited for her to calm down enough and sleep yet. She kept her eyes open, her finger drawing circles on her Prince's chest. For a long while, they stayed together like this. His hands were gently caressing her back, going up and down her spine. With the silence that had fallen in the room, they could hear the noises coming from the windows. Some exotic birds were chirping. Human voices too, though they were too far and numerous to be understood.

Unlike the Onyx Castle, which was completely isolated, the Diamond Palace was still in the heart of a vast city. There was always something going on inside. Cassandra liked this atmosphere. Just the two of them, cuddling in that bedroom, while the world kept itself busy outside.

After a while, she heard him sigh, and couldn't help but worry a bit.

"Are you alright?" she asked.

"I don't like leaving you here," he said. "I'll be back as soon as I can."

"Don't worry. I'll stay here with Lady Kareen. It will be fine. Just be careful, please."

Kairen took a deep breath, and kissed her forehead. It didn't feel like enough for Cassandra. She got up a bit, lying on his chest, to come and kiss him properly. The War God wrapped his arms around her, hugging her and answering her kiss. This time, it was a slow, tender kiss. He let Cassandra take the lead. Her thin lips on his were like a flower's petal, so smooth and light. She was getting just a little bit bolder every day, too. He could feel the tip of her tongue, teasing him, giving him a little taste of her and making him thirsty for more.

Cassandra smiled, and her lips went left, to kiss his cheek, where his beard was growing. The little spikes she liked to play with were slipping through her fingertips on the other side. Kairen smiled, satisfied, letting her gently cover

382

his face with her shy kisses.

When she stopped, placing her chin on his torso, he brushed her hair with his fingers, a bit amused.

"What are you so amused about?" she whispered.

"You've changed. I remember the shy girl who would blush every time I touched her."

Cassandra blushed again hearing that, with a little pout.

"You were so... You would put your hand under my skirt and say such obscene things."

"Did I?" he said, with a little sneer.

Cassandra softly slapped his chest.

"Yes, you! Putting your hand under my skirt and asking if I was a virgin, too. You just enjoyed teasing me so much."

Kairen smiled, and while she wondered what he was thinking, she suddenly felt his hand sliding between her thighs, making her yelp in surprise. The War God gently caressed her opening, but she was still so wet and sensitive from their wild activity just before, Cassandra was already shivering.

"Was it like this? Or..."

Just as he played, his finger moved between her wet lips, making her moan again. Her legs tensed up, and Cassandra bit her lip, sending him an offended look.

Kairen chuckled, amused, and came to kiss her temple, though it was obvious his concubine was sulking a little bit. She moved slightly, and pushed his hand with a sullen look.

"So mean," she whispered.

"Mh..."

He obviously had no remorse or intention to apologize for his past behavior. Cassandra sighed. She was so scared back then, the Prince suddenly taking an interest in her had been completely unexpected. Thinking about it, her feelings for him had evolved so quickly. She had been caught in a storm and happy to submit.

Kairen gently kissed her temple again, caressing her hair gently. She couldn't ignore him, she just enjoyed his touch so much. Cassandra smiled and wrapped her hands around his neck, locking him into some more kisses. It had been a while since they had been able to rest and snuggle together, without worrying about any event to attend or anyone to accompany.

"Kairen... Why didn't you take any other concubines? Before me?" she asked, feeling a bit curious.

He sighed, frowning a bit. He didn't like that question. They both knew he'd had concubines in the past, but none of those women had made it out alive. They weren't picked by him, either. Cassandra clearly remembered Nebora's words. All the concubines Kairen had been presented with were sent by his brothers or father. From their meeting, she had somehow assumed it was natural for him to take new concubines on a whim, as it was for any Prince. However, she had been proven very wrong as soon as she arrived at the Onyx Castle. Not only did Kairen not have any other concubines, but he also didn't show much interest in any woman besides her.

His glare and disgust towards the women that had tried to seduce him previously had made her realize, he absolutely loathed that kind of behavior. She truly was the only woman he ever showed any arousal or interest towards. He didn't care about any other woman, no matter how young or beautiful she was. As a healthy young man, it was a bit surprising.

"I hate those women," he whispered.

"The concubines?"

"You... Didn't ask about my bedroom. The one in the Imperial Palace."

"No... I figured you didn't want to talk about it... and I didn't want to pry."

The Prince sighed. For a while, Cassandra wondered if he was going to end the topic there. He put an arm over his face, covering his eyes. He didn't look sad, just...bothered. She felt a bit unsure, as she couldn't see his expression. Was it too sensitive to bring up? She hesitated a bit on what to add, biting her lip.

"Kairen?"

"That room... We lived there when I was younger. Shareen, Mother, and I. One night, when I was twelve or thirteen...I woke up, it was very late. I was feeling sick, strange. I didn't know what it was. Then I realized I wasn't alone. A servant woman was there."

"In your bedroom?"

"In my bed. She was on me... Sucking me. I stayed there. I couldn't move. I felt like a monster was trying to eat me. I got mad... Krai got mad, and we killed that woman. I'm not sure exactly what happened. You saw the room."

Cassandra was speechless. She clearly remembered that bedroom. It was as if a beast had gone berserk inside. It was Kairen and Krai's wrath that had been unleashed inside.

The young concubine felt her heart going crazy inside her chest. She was mad and terribly sad. She was sickened by what had happened to her Prince. He was so young! How could that woman do such a thing? For a minute, she had a hard time calming down and holding in her tears. Never had she seen such a vulnerable side of her Prince, or even imagined he had one.

"I'm so sorry," she whispered, her voice almost breaking.

"Don't be. That woman is dead."

"But... why did she..."

"She was probably trying to become a concubine. Some women target the Imperial Family so they can improve their lives this way."

Cassandra felt utterly disgusted. How greedy could a human being be? To go ahead and rape a young boy! She had never been so shocked before. She had always felt like the Imperial Family was absolutely untouchable, always the ones inflicting the pain, the ones in control of other people's fate. Never in a million years would she have imagined they were the target of such monsters.

No wonder the Prince was so disgusted at those lecherous women, after

384

what he had gone through. Then, two of the concubines he had been sent afterward had tried to kill him. How could he still believe in any woman after that? He was seen as prey by those monsters from such a young age. The War God had grown to be the man he was because he had learned to fight the worst kind of monsters from a young age.

"She was the first person I ever killed," he whispered. "Mother found out in the morning. She got rid of the body, and we moved back to the Diamond Palace again. She kept as few servants as possible, but I wasn't afraid. I would just murder anyone if I had a doubt. I kept killing, my father sent me to the front, where I could unleash as much as I wanted. It wasn't the same, but somehow, the sight of blood helped me more than anything else."

"So that's how you became the War God so young."

"I felt like I belonged on the battlefield more than anywhere else. I hated being here, or in the Imperial Palace. I slept better on the ground than in any bed."

Cassandra suddenly remembered how desolated and empty the Onyx Castle always seemed. Any of Kairen's bedrooms, she had always thought they didn't look like anyone lived there...and no one did. The Prince avoided those places, preferring his army tent. Everything made so much sense now.

"When I met you... You were the first woman that didn't care. You showed only fear. Any woman I had met, no matter how scared they were, there was always that...thing in their eyes. That slight hope that I might get interested in them, fuck them, and make them my concubine. That greed, the same greed I had seen in that woman's eyes. I'd rather kill them."

He took his arm out of the way, to come and gently caress her soft cheek.

"You were the only one. You didn't lust for me. You were just scared. When I tried to tease you, see if you'd show your true colors, your lust as a woman, you just turned out to be even more innocent than I had thought. When that woman hurt you..."

"Lyria? My former Master's concubine?"

"Yeah. I saw...the way she looked at me, and the way you looked at her. You were different. Somehow, I understood why Krai liked you. You were just... pure. So pure. You didn't have that greed that was in her eyes, not even the will to save yourself. You were just scared of me."

Cassandra sighed. It was all so... sad.

She hadn't thought much about their first encounter. The War God was so indecipherable back then. She would have never imagined he looked at her that way. That certainly explained a lot.

"Is that why you didn't let me... satisfy you?"

Kairen caressed her lips with his thumb, slightly nodding.

"I don't want to see you like that...I don't need that."

"I understand," she whispered.

They stayed silent for a few seconds, just staring in each other's eyes lovingly. Cassandra could tell, there wasn't anything the War God feared anymore in women. Instead, it had been replaced by this wrath, this bloodthirst. The way he had found to cope had become his way of life. The blood that dirtied his sword, the way he had dirtied his hands to save himself.

She was falling a bit deeper for that man. How was he still able to love her so tenderly, after what he had gone through? Kairen had such a loving side... just for her. She smiled and gently kissed him again. The War God answered her kiss, caressing her hair, her cheek...

Cassandra deepened their kiss, taking the reins. She wanted him to feel her love for him. He wasn't that scared boy anymore. He had grown into a strong, powerful man, who could kill, but still love.

Chapter 24

Despite a long and love-filled afternoon nap, they couldn't possibly stay hidden in that bedroom forever. Notably, because Cassandra found herself starving when she woke up and sighed. Her baby was truly eating like a young dragon. She stretched her sore and painful muscles a bit with a groan, sitting on the side of the bed. Kairen sat behind her, giving her a quick kiss on the neck.

"We have to go..." she whispered. "I'm really hungry. Is it dinner time yet?"

"Who cares."

She chuckled. Her Prince helped her put her dress back on, while he kept his torso bare, only putting his pants on. Cassandra blushed a little. Though his tone was rather dark, one could still see the red marks on his bronze skin. He was slowly pushing her to become bolder and bolder every time they had sex, now she was the one who left him covered in hickeys. Was he exposing them on purpose?

Once she was ready, Cassandra decided to let her hair down, and simply followed her prince out of the bedroom. She hadn't paid much attention when he was taking her there, but this was one of the guest bedrooms. They walked quietly back to Kareen's salon, where they could hear people talking and laughing.

It was another one of those open rooms, with lots of wild plants everywhere, a few furniture pieces with some rugs and colored cushions for them to rest on. Anour was taking care of his dragon, brushing his scales with some sort of big comb, while Shareen and Kareen were talking on the side and having tea. They all turned heads hearing the duo enter.

"Oh, look who it is!"

"Where is Missandra?" she asked, a bit worried.

"I gave her a room for her to rest, your servant girl Dahlia went to watch over her," said Kareen. "I think our dragons chased them away. Anyway, aren't you hungry, Cassandra?"

"I am... is it alright if we have dinner early today?"

The Imperial Concubine immediately ordered for the dinner to be prepared at once, and meanwhile, a full basket of fresh and dried fruits, along with several kinds of nuts, were brought to the young mother-to-be. Cassandra and Kairen sat down on the cushions next to Kareen's chair. The Prince kept his arm around her, and though she was seemingly focused on the green grapes more, Cassandra was resting her back against his torso.

On the side, Shareen had a smirk on, staring at the young couple.

"I don't know how it goes for your people, Cassie, but here, people usually keep the wild sex for the honeymoon after the wedding."

Kairen replied with a glare, while Cassandra frowned.

"Were you eavesdropping again!"

"No, you were loud! You can't blame me, Mother dearest here and Father are always keeping me busy. I need to find entertainment when I can!"

Cassandra sent annoyed glances at Shareen anyway. The Princess was truly too nosy about their sexual life. She would insist on them being a bit more careful from then on. They hadn't shown much restraint, and with all the open roofs here, it was true that a lot of ears could easily hear them.

Kareen clicked her tongue.

"You unruly child! Getting to the North will hopefully cool your wild ideas!"

"Of course, Mother. When you send me to an army full of hunky soldiers..."

Kareen clicked her tongue again and tried to slap her shoulder, but Shareen was quick to move and get away from her reach. Cassandra couldn't help but wonder how the Princess would do at the Camp. She remembered Evin, Orwen, and all the soldiers that had helped her put together the Red Room there. Even her friends at the Onyx Castle. If she hadn't been pregnant, she probably would have gone there instead. However, it was best for her to stay here until her son was born, under Kareen's protection and where she could easily have access to a doctor and servants to tend to her.

"Shareen, could you deliver letters if I give them to you?" asked Cassandra.

"Where to? I'm not a courier!"

"Don't worry, it's for the Onyx Castle and the Army Camp. If you can even just give them to the servants there, they'll know what to do."

"Fine then."

Cassandra felt a bit relieved. She would at least be able to write to Nebora and the girls, and to Evin and Orwen, too. The two men had been such help to her at the camp. She hoped they both were doing well.

The servants started bringing in dinner, as grand as usual, with lots of meats, fish, fruits, and everything Cassandra loved. After living together for a few weeks previously, the Imperial Concubine was well aware of her tastes, and the Diamond Palace was more than ready to satisfy the pregnant lady's appetite. The smell of the cooked meat actually even attracted Krai and Roun, who started bickering again on the side when Kairen threw a big piece at them. The two young dragons obviously had more fun fighting about it than actually eating the meat. Thankfully, the garden in the open room they had dinner in, was wide enough for the two to get wild without risking injuring the humans present.

Missandra and Dahlia appeared a few minutes later, having smelled the delicious food all the way to the bedrooms. As they had all skipped lunch for various reasons, they were all more than happy to start eating early.

Cassandra was amazed a bit more every day about her tremendous appetite. She still had about three months of pregnancy ahead, but her baby had her eat almost as much as her Prince. Of course, it didn't bother anyone around her, and actually, Kareen wasn't surprised at all, and kept encouraging her to eat more.

Missandra too was starting to look a bit better. She was eating, and somehow, Dahlia and she seemed to have gotten closer, chatting about the herbs they could pick for the healing decoction Missandra wanted to try making.

"Lady Kareen, would it be alright for us to go out tonight?" asked Cassandra. "Missandra has never seen the Diamond City, and their Celebrations are still going on in the streets."

"Would it be alright for... people from the Imperial Family to go out?" whispered Missandra, a bit surprised.

"Of course!" said Kareen. "People are used to seeing me. What do they expect, that I stay locked up in my Palace all year long? I may be an Imperial Concubine, but I am a free woman and the owner and ruler of this place. Of course, we shall go. Let's have some fun for once."

Cassandra smiled. She was a bit excited to participate in the Celebrations in the streets like regular folks. It was something she had never been able to do as a slave, and the ones in the Palace were different from all the food stalls in the streets and the livelihood of the ordinary people.

They finished dinner calmly, only interrupted a few times by the two dragons that were trying to steal some meat as a game. Even the shy Srai showed up, and Kareen gave him the most meat, making his younger brothers sulk and try to steal from him next. The little dragon was quick to escape though, as he could crawl into small spaces they couldn't follow.

It was fun for everyone to watch until dinner was over. Even Missandra and Dahlia, amused by their antics, seemed to forget about being scared.

Once everyone was full and ready, they prepared to go out at sunset. As always, Kareen refused to bring many servants, only a few of them. But with Anour, Shareen, and Kairen with them, they didn't need any guards.

As they left the Diamond Palace, a whole new world opened to them. The Palace was elevated compared to the street and wasn't echoing all of the noises properly. Everything was much more busy and chaotic down there, but Cassandra loved it. She was wearing a fur cloak over her pink dress, as the nights were a bit colder than in the Capital. However, Kairen was walking so close to her, she wouldn't have been cold anyway. The young ones were excited to be out. Missandra had never been to the Celebrations of any other city but the Capital, and she obviously loved them. Anour, Dahlia, and her, kept running from one stall to another like children, trying the unique foods and seeing the little street shows here and there. One man was demonstrating some dancing monkeys, and a woman was doing a belly dance with some folklore music played by her children.

Somehow, the streets were actually so crowded that a lot of people didn't notice the Imperial Family right away. The road was cleared in front of them as the passersby recognized the purple outfits and quickly got out of the way, but all of their little group was so cheerful and acting normally that a lot of people didn't pay attention to them. Some small children even ran into Lady Kareen at one point, but she didn't care and gently helped one of them up.

It was nice for Cassandra to be able to have fun with her sister in the streets without worrying. Missandra and her laughed together and tried some new spices, before she took it to Kairen, amused. If he was having any fun, the Prince wasn't showing it, but he stayed close to her, talking with her and touching her when he could. His hand on her shoulder, around her waist, or simply holding hers were small demonstrations of affection she loved most.

For the first time, she was hanging in the streets with her lover, almost like a normal couple. Cassandra wondered what kind of life they would have lived if they had been of normal statuses.

She sighed, and seeing the young ones were having fun at some game stall, while Kareen and Shareen were also watching, she turned to her Prince.

"What is it?" he asked.

Cassandra smiled, getting on her toes to kiss him softly.

"Nothing. I'm just really happy here. Being here with you. I want us to enjoy this as much as we can before you go."

Kairen kissed her forehead gently, wrapping his concubine in his arms.

"I didn't know you liked these kinds of things so much. The Celebrations."

"It's just... I never really got to stand among the people as a free woman or enjoy any of this before. I'm happy when I see my sister acting like the young girl she is. I'm happy when we get to stroll like this, without any threats, any plots, or any rivals."

The atmosphere of the Imperial Palace was so suffocating at times, Cassandra couldn't help but feel such a difference now that she was out. Even if it was for a short time, she just wanted to enjoy this as much as she could.

Kairen kissed her again, caressing her cheek. They were in the middle of the street, in the middle of a crowd, but neither really cared. There were dozens of lovers here, many couples just enjoying the Celebrations. They were just a little bit differently clothed.

"I'll bring you here again for the Celebrations next year," he whispered softly. "And all the years you want after that."

"Is that a promise?" she asked with a smile.

"Yes."

He grabbed her chin and gently sealed their promise with a long kiss. Cassandra smiled against her Prince's lips, enjoying this little minute of intimacy with him. There was something unique about being able to act like this with her lover, in the middle of a busy street. Like she could show her love to the world, without fear of judgment. A few weeks ago, she was always so afraid of what people would say, what people would think. Now, she was able to act however she wanted with him. Somehow, she had become so comforted by Kairen's feelings, she knew nothing could stop her love for him anymore. Cassandra didn't care much if he wasn't vocal about it. He was telling her just enough when she actually needed it.

"Hinue! Look!"

Missandra ran up to them, and ecstatic, put a big flower crown on her older sister's head. She had a wide smile on and had apparently forgotten all her hatred for the Imperial Family. Cassandra was so happy to finally see her act her age. She had one of those big flower crowns on too, and behind her, Dahlia was playing with some flower bracelets.

"Aren't these pretty! Should you get one for the ceremony? Come!"

Missandra pulled her to come to the flower stall, and check all of the flower crowns. It was the first time she showed interest in the Rain Ceremony, so Cassandra was happy to check out the items displayed with her. For once, they felt like a pair of sisters hanging out naturally, having fun with their friends, and chatting happily over trivial matters.

Cassandra was made to try several crowns by Dahlia and Missandra, so many that her hair was covered in petals after a while. The merchant was happy to have caught the girl's attention and was overdoing it with the flattery.

"Those white lilies are so fresh, and suit Your Highness so well! You should try it! Your hair is so beautiful, any of those look perfect on you!"

Cassandra chuckled. White lilies again! She picked the flower crown, made of ivy, white lilies, and pink lisianthus among some filler leaves. Putting it on in her hair, Cassandra checked herself in the mirror, blushing a bit. She rarely felt so pretty. That evening, her hair was down, she was wearing the pale dress that complimented her rosy cheeks so well, and radiating with happiness.

She turned to Kairen, standing behind her, to show it.

"Do you like it?" she asked.

He nodded, but he was clearly looking at her instead of the crown. Cassandra smiled and turned to the merchant.

"Could you pack this up for me?" she gently asked.

"What are you talking about! You should keep it on," said Missandra with a cute pout, Dahlia nodding behind her.

"Your sister is right."

Behind them, Kareen and Shareen walked up to them, both looking at the crowns of flowers. The merchant immediately bowed politely to Lady Kareen. Like many people around them, he recognized the ruler and owner of the City. The Imperial Concubine handed him some money.

"You young ladies should have fun. Have your sister and that servant of yours pick some, too."

Immediately, Missandra and Dahlia's eyes shined in excitement. Those flower crowns were expensive, not something they would have been able to spend their pocket money on. However, the shiny gold coins the Imperial Concubine had handed the merchant were more than enough for them to pick anything they wanted.

They both thanked Kareen profusely, and started picking some flower crowns for themselves, even bullying Anour into trying some too. Shareen chuckled, crossing her arms while watching the scene.

"A Prince being forced to wear a flower crown by two servant girls. This world is really changing faster than I thought! Mother, you can't spend it all on Anour and the girls. What about your actual daughter?"

The Imperial Concubine sneered.

"What about her?"

Shareen frowned, crossing her arms and pouting.

"Aren't you going to buy me anything, Mother? With this heavy purse of yours? When do you ever gift me something?"

"Gift you something?" said Kareen, turning to her with her eyebrow raised. "When does this daughter of mine ever visit her mother? I'm already this old, yet neither of my children pampers me or worries about me. What should I buy you anything for? You heartless children seem to be doing well enough without me!"

Cassandra had the hardest time repressing her laugh while Kareen walked away, looking as proud as ever, and pushing Dahlia and Missandra to come and see some food stalls, probably to spoil them more and anger Shareen.

Meanwhile, the Princess stayed speechless.

"That old witch! Old, her? Who is old! She's going to bury us all!"

Kairen didn't seem much surprised or affected by their mother's rant, but Shareen went on to sulk and complain about Kareen's attitude. Cassandra chuckled. Despite acting like this towards each other, it was obvious they loved their mother. Even more so watching Krai's attitude with the Imperial Concubine.

She grabbed Kairen's hand and pulled him to follow the group, though they walked slowly, keeping a little intimate space around them.

"Why don't you visit your mother more often?" she asked.

"I don't know... I usually spend my time at the Military Camp."

Cassandra nodded. Shareen had mentioned before that their mother was a bit too nosy about her private "activities". And from what Cassandra herself had seen or experienced, she was sure Kareen wouldn't have approved either.

She caressed her little tummy that was sticking out more and more every day.

"What are you thinking?" asked her Prince, seeing her lost in her thoughts.

"I hope our son will visit me often when I'm older. I'd be sad if he didn't."

Kairen frowned a bit, looking concerned about her words. Cassandra wondered if this was making him reflect on his attitude, but didn't ask. They walked a bit longer, in silence, following the little group ahead that was enthusiastically checking the stalls. Apparently, Lady Kareen was only too happy to spoil the younger ones, probably a bit to piss off Shareen too.

"Who will you love more?"

"What?" asked Cassandra, surprised by his sudden question.

"Who will you love more? Between our son and me?"

She was so stunned by his question, she stayed speechless for a while. However, Kairen couldn't have looked more serious, with his usual frown on and dark eyes. Cassandra sighed, trying hard not to laugh.

"My Prince... You can't compare love like that. A mother's love is something unique."

"Does that mean you love him more?"

Cassandra chuckled this time, shaking her head.

"Do you think your mother loves you more than the Emperor?"

"Yes."

Well, maybe that wasn't the best example to use. Cassandra thought for a minute.

"What about Princess Shareen then? Do you think your mother loves her more?"

This time, Kairen looked baffled by her question. He glanced his mother's way, frowning a bit more, and Cassandra waited for him. It was amusing that he would be so baffled by such a simple thing as a mother's love. Sometimes her Prince had this incredibly childish side to him. He could fight and win any battle in this world, but jealousy or matters of the heart were a real problem for him to understand.

Cassandra got on her toes and kissed his cheek, ending his deep thinking with a gentle smile.

"Love doesn't need to be shared or compared. It's unique and endless. I love my baby so much, and I love you too. I love you both, but differently."

The Prince nodded, and replied to her kiss with one on her forehead, then her nose, until he got to her lips. She wasn't sure he had fully understood, but at least, he wasn't frowning anymore, her lips were keeping him busy enough.

Suddenly, Cassandra felt some droplets falling on her. She looked up and, sure enough, rain was starting to fall. She smiled wide, exchanging a glance with her Prince.

"The rain!"

However, the little drops were now starting to come by the hundreds, and the rain was rapidly increasing around them. Kareen and the rest of their group quickly gathered, everyone trying to cover themselves.

"We should head back," said Shareen. "The locals say this isn't just going to be some light rain, there's a storm coming, and they get nasty in this area!"

Everyone agreed and, quickly, they walked back to the Diamond Palace. No one had been expecting that rain. The streets were quickly cleared, as the merchants were closing up their stalls and putting their merchandise into a safe place.

The Palace wasn't far, but by the time they got there, everyone was soaked. The servants ran to hand them some towels to wipe themselves with, but the young Imperial Concubine was a bit upset at her disheveled hair and messy clothes.

"What a mess."

Like the locals had said, it wasn't just a downpour. Above them, the wind picked up, and the claps of thunder and lightning flashes cloaked the sky in no time. This was truly a thunderstorm, not just rain. In the Diamond Palace, so many rooms had open roofs, Cassandra could hear the rain all around them. Of course, the servants had quickly moved the furniture where it needed to be, being used to the rain, but so many rooms were now unusable.

"Well, someone wanted rain," sighed Shareen.

"Should we wait until it calms down, Cassandra dear?" asked Kareen.

The young concubine nodded, looking a bit sad.

"It can't be helped. It would be too dangerous to go out in this weather."

If it wasn't for the wind and lightning, this rain would actually have been perfect for the Ceremony, but Cassandra had to admit, the current conditions weren't good. The wind would have blown things away, and that lightning would be dangerous for anyone outside.

Feeling her disappointment, Kairen suddenly lifted her up.

"Kairen?" she asked, taken by surprise.

Without explaining a thing, the Prince slowly walked out of the room, leaving everyone else behind, and took Cassandra deeper inside the Diamond Palace. She couldn't help but wonder where he was taking her. She could hear Krai climbing the walls around them and following their path from the outside, but those rooms around them were some she had never been to before, she couldn't tell where they were. Kairen was obviously very familiar with the Diamond Palace. He was navigating easily, avoiding the rooms being flooded or taking corridors where they could avoid the downpour from the open roofs.

Finally, he put her down in front of a large door and pushed it open. Cassandra took a minute to understand. It was obviously a bathroom and a very large one at that. Actually, the large basin was overflowing with water. This room didn't have a fully open roof per se, but some openings in the walls were letting the heavy rain through, and it was slowly adding up. However, the most interesting part of that room was that instead of being surrounded by four or six walls like most rooms, this one had only five. One part of the wall had been left open, giving her an incredible view of the city, and access for Krai to sneak its head in. The large basin was actually going all the way to that open part, and the excess water was being poured down below, overflowing the border of the basin.

She was amazed. This was such a strange room, and the tub was almost working as a large natural fountain, being filled by rainwater and flowing on the lower levels. She wanted to get in and go see the full view, but with this windy weather, it was obvious she should stay in the covered part.

To her surprise, Kairen walked in first, taking off his clothes and going into the water. Behind him, Krai growled, and without warning, spat fire.

Cassandra was afraid, seeing Krai do that for the first time, but the dragon wasn't doing it in her direction. Actually, it was burning the water next to Kairen, and shortly after, some vapor was visible. Cassandra chuckled and put her feet in the water. It was warm!

Krai's fire had heated the water, turning this place into a hot pool. She chuckled and took the hand Kairen was offering her to walk in.

Cassandra took his hand, blushing slightly, but followed him into the water. She had only taken off her shoes and newly-bought flower crown. Her dress was already wet after all, and she was a bit too shy to venture in a half-open bath completely naked. Even if her Prince had taken off all of his clothes, he didn't say anything about her not doing the same, and gently pulled her in.

Kairen was carrying Cassandra on his lap, making her chuckle. She had no idea how deep this bath really was, but she could tell her Prince was navigating around easily. He took her as far as he could in this pool before the curtain of rain. She was amazed. Not only was the view of the Diamond City absolutely breathtaking, but the majesty of this infinity pool was truly beautiful. Cassandra felt that if her Prince were to swim a bit too far, they would fall out. She couldn't see the edge, as the rain was actually blurring the real limit of the water and confusing her perception, making it both exciting and scary. They stayed back far enough though, remaining under the roofed part.

The Black Dragon, standing outside but sticking its head in, didn't seem to mind the downpour much. The rain was rolling down the black scales, while its red eyes were focused on the couple. Cassandra, her arms locked around her Prince, couldn't stop smiling. Her whole body was floating in this warm water. It wasn't nearly as hot as the hot springs from the North, but the difference in temperature with the cold rain still made a thin layer of mist float around. It was such a unique scene. Even the room itself was somewhere between eerie and ancient, as if before them, no one had come here in years. Cassandra absolutely loved it.

"This is amazing," she whispered.

"You like it?"

She nodded and turned to her Prince, brushing his hair gently.

"Why did you think to bring me here?"

"You enjoyed the hot springs... and you seemed sad we couldn't hold the Ceremony yet."

Cassandra's heart melted once again. How could this man always surprise her with this extreme gentleness and consideration he was hiding under his armor? She nodded, and gently kissed him.

She loved any form of bath and he knew it. She loved when they took baths together; the simple sensation of her body immersed in water was one of the most comforting feelings in this world to her. Of course, it was even better when her Prince was by her side like this. They kept kissing for a while, tenderly, though their bodies were obviously really close to one another. The layers of her dress were floating around her in the water, while she curled her legs around Kairen's, holding on to him.

A low growl distracted them a bit. They both turned their heads as Krai was putting the lower part of its maw in the water, staring at them. Cassandra couldn't see it as its body was outside, but she was sure the black dragon was wagging its tail. She had learned to recognize that playful look in the ruby eyes.

The dragon couldn't fit more than its shoulders inside, but it was still plenty enough. Cassandra smiled, and detached herself from her Prince to go play with the dragon. Krai growled happily, seeing her approach. She gently rubbed its snout, and to play with the dragon a little she dived underneath the surface. She felt the dragon's snout, looking for her in the water, but Krai wasn't a water creature. When she emerged a few feet away, the dragon turned its head, surprised, making her laugh. Krai growled and put its snout in the water, suddenly throwing a whole wave at her. Cassandra laughed and dived in again.

This little game between them lasted quite a while. However, after a few minutes, while she was in the water, Cassandra felt some human hands grab her.

Kairen lifted her up, pulling her into his embrace again. She chuckled.

"Were you feeling lonely, my Prince?"

"Don't just play with him."

Cassandra laughed and kissed him, focusing on her Prince despite the jealous growls. With the rain in the background, the sounds of the water, and her dripping hair, she almost felt at home. She and her Prince kept kissing lovingly, swimming around in the water as if they were alone.

However, Cassandra suddenly paused their kiss, frowning.

"What is it?"

"I..."

She went silent again, with a confused expression. Did she just imagine it? She grabbed Kairen's hand and pulled it next to hers against her tummy. He touched her right in time and a second later, it was his turn to have a shocked expression. Cassandra chuckled again, ecstatic.

"Did you feel that?" she whispered.

The Prince nodded, keeping his large hand spread out on her stomach. He had felt it. A little bump under her skin, so weak he had almost missed it. He stayed there again, waiting.

"I feel him again," she whispered. "Oh, God... He's moving."

Kairen frowned. He couldn't feel it anymore, or maybe it was too faint. Yet, Cassandra was completely absorbed in the baby's faint movements. She hadn't thought she would be able to feel them so early! However, it wasn't a mistake. This wasn't her stomach, but her son; she could feel some little movements. Sometimes, they were too faint for her to be sure, and other times, she was sure. They stayed like this for a while, but nothing else happened.

It was plenty enough, though. Cassandra couldn't stop smiling from ear to ear. Kairen grabbed her hair and gently pulled her closer to him for another kiss. Somehow, he didn't seem to want to take his hand off of her belly, as if he was still hoping for another little hit.

"You have to come back to see our son," Cassandra whispered, suddenly becoming much more serious.

"Why are you so afraid?"

"I don't know. I have a bad feeling," she confessed. "Maybe it's just my pregnancy making me more worried. I just don't like that you won't be here."

She sighed and snuggled against his neck, closing her eyes, feeling the warmth of his skin. Kairen frowned, caressing her gently. He hadn't realized how much Cassandra needed him more because of her pregnancy. Somehow, she was a bit needier, looking for more of their cuddling than before. He wasn't sure if it was due to their relationship growing or part of the pregnancy, or both.

He kept caressing her, letting her rest against his shoulder. He had thought of bringing her here to comfort her, but truly, comforting a pregnant woman was harder than expected. Would she really be alright staying here with his mother? The Prince was a bit afraid the young concubine would be lonely or feel too bored. He definitely couldn't bring her to the battlefield, though. He wouldn't even have let her anywhere near a military camp, not when she was pregnant.

"I will be back as soon as I can."

"I know...and it's your duty. I know it can't be helped. I just don't like that we will be separated again."

"I'll stay with you as long as you want after the war is over. I'll take you back to the Onyx Castle."

Cassandra chuckled. How did he know she missed that place the most? Somehow, she had grown attached to that lonely, isolated castle in the last few months, she was surprised herself to be missing it so much. She nodded against his skin.

After a while, however, the wind picked up even stronger and Krai flew away, annoyed. Without the dragon to heat it up, the water was going to get cold soon. Cassandra and Kairen got out of the water while they were still feeling warm. Somehow, right behind the doors, the servants had already brought some thick towels. Cassandra abandoned her dress there, knowing someone would come and pick it up, and wrapped herself in one of the very large towels. Once again, the War God, who never seemed to feel the cold, only wrapped it around his hips, letting his natural heat dry him.

He picked Cassandra up off the ground and carried her gently back to their room to change into her nightgown. She was now dry, but the young concubine still took her time brushing her messy hair and put it up into a long braid for the night. The servants had brought a little tray of food, including her favorite green grapes and cheese cubes, with some mulled wine. Surely, Lady Kareen had ordered this.

Cassandra felt a bit guilty for wanting to eat again, but she couldn't help it. She sat on the bed, grabbing the little bowl of grapes, and pouring some of the cheese cubes on top. For some reason, she almost wanted to see the cheese melt on top of it. Kairen laid down next to her, he had already helped himself to some wine and was caressing her back, letting her eat all she wanted.

"It's really impressive. I'm hungrier than I ever was, even when I had been unable to eat for days. Babies are truly something," she whispered.

"Are you tired? Or is your back painful?"

Cassandra stretched her back a bit. It was true her lower back pain was constant those days, but it was a really mild pain, not something she would complain about. At least she was grateful to be over her nausea. She hadn't had any for several days now.

"I'm fine... Just hungry like a dragon."

Kairen chuckled and kept rubbing her back. When Cassandra leaned to take the mulled wine, however, he frowned.

"Cassandra."

"Just a little sip on my tongue," she promised. "For the taste."

Despite his frowning, he let her take a little bit, as promised. He was afraid his mother's bad habits would slowly transfer onto the young concubine somehow. Hence, Kairen was quick to take the glass out of her hands and finish it in one go. Cassandra didn't even protest. Her thoughts were already elsewhere.

"The baby... Maybe we should find him a name already."

"You can pick whatever you want."

"Really?"

Kairen nodded. He didn't really care, and trusted Cassandra fully. The young concubine wasn't surprised or disappointed. She slowly smiled, trying to think. She would have loved to give the baby a name from the Rain Tribe, but this was a future dragon Prince they were talking about. She couldn't risk picking something too odd. What about a Dragon Empire name then? She quite liked them.

"How did your mother pick your name? And Shareen's? Do you know?"

"She just took hers and twisted it. concubines like to give names similar to theirs to their children."

Cassandra could understand. Among the many, many children of the Emperor, this was a way to remind him of themselves through their children. She doubted Kareen had exactly the same idea, though. It was probably her own possessiveness over her children rather than her relationship to the Emperor that had prevailed.

"Kairen?"

"Hm?"

"What about... your siblings? The others? Do you know their names?"

He nodded.

"My mother has them buried here. I saw their names on the stones. Suiren, Shaneen, Kassen."

Cassandra felt her heart pinch a bit at each name. She couldn't forget the painful words of the Imperial Concubine over her children's deaths. There was one question she had been curious about, though.

"How is Srai still alive? I thought a dragon died after his tamer passed, but there are exceptions, aren't there?"

"He was old enough. Newborn dragons are more fragile. Most die with us if we die young."

Cassandra nodded. That explained why Srai had been the only one to survive. According to Kareen, the young Suiren, her firstborn, had died at six. Apparently, it was enough for his dragon to survive, even disabled. But her second and fourth children had died as infants. She put protective hands around her belly. How did the abandoned dragons feel? Missing a part of themselves. She couldn't imagine Krai without Kairen, or the other way around. Would her baby be as close to his dragon? She couldn't wait to meet both of them. Her two babies, the human and the dragon one. Cassandra silently promised herself: with or without Kairen, she would protect their child. She would do anything for him.

"Cassandra."

He gently pulled her into his embrace, taking her away from her deep thinking. Cassandra chuckled, putting her half-emptied bowl to the side, and snuggled against him.

"I'm tired," she said.

"Then sleep. If the rain calms down, we will have our Ceremony tomorrow morning."

"I hope so."

Cassandra had no problem falling asleep that evening. She was soothed by the sounds of the downpour outside, the wind shimmering in the leaves, and the slow breathing of he Prince against her ear. A peaceful sleep after a nice evening outing, and a long, warm bath was just the best.

Chapter 25

When she woke up the next morning, her senses immediately picked up the sound of the downpour, still ongoing outside. She smiled and turned around to face Kairen. However, she was surprised to find her Prince still deep asleep. This was a first! He would usually wake up the second she moved. Yet, Kairen was still obviously sleeping, with his slow, steady breath and serene expression. Cassandra bit her lip, only too happy to secretly witness such a precious moment.

He looked a bit younger when he wasn't frowning or glaring with those dark obsidian eyes of his. She loved being able to scrutinize him from up close. She often forgot their age difference. He was a grown man, while she had just barely gotten to adulthood. She brushed his beard with her fingertips. He hadn't cut it in a few days, but she liked it.

As Cassandra was still caressing his beard as gently as possible, Kairen swiftly moved to wrap his arm around her, his eyes still closed. The young concubine pouted a bit.

"So you were awake after all?"

"Hm."

She chuckled and came a bit closer to gently kiss his lips. Kairen smiled, but for once, didn't give in, letting Cassandra spread her kisses on his lips, on his beard, and on his cheekbones. He could tell she was just having fun teasing him. He let her do that until she got bored and pushed him over to get on top of him. Only then did the War God consent to open his eyes to see the face of his smiling concubine.

"Good morning, my Prince," she whispered.

"Good morning."

"It's still raining," she said with a smile.

"I hear that..."

Cassandra chuckled. She knew his faint answers were part of his character, not a lack of interest. She kissed him once more and got out of the bed. She was

400

a bit more excited about this than she thought. The gentle music of the heavy rain outside was making her happy and the thought that they could finally do the Ceremony.

As always, the servants came in shortly after they had woken up, bringing a new set of clothes, and disappearing as soon as possible. Cassandra wondered how they always knew. She put on the new dress and tried to sort out her messy curls. The rain had done no justice to her chocolate brown hair. She had to spend some extra time taming it and left it untied, knowing it was no use in that humidity.

"Lady Cassandra?"

Dahlia was gently knocking at the door, bringing in another large tray of food for breakfast. The young girl smiled upon entering.

"Lady Kareen sent me to give you your breakfast! Did you sleep well?"

The young servant was apparently only too happy to be back to her old habits of assisting Cassandra. She even helped her arrange her hair a bit and put on the flower crown they had bought the previous day. As they chatted about the previous evening, Kairen was getting up and getting ready behind them. He walked to Cassandra's side to give her a quick kiss and grabbed some of the meat on the tray before leaving.

Dahlia's shoulder relaxed a little as soon as the War God was out of the room, making Cassandra chuckled.

"Are you still scared?" asked Cassandra.

"It cannot be helped, Lady Cassandra. I've been raised to always fear the Imperial Family. I understand that Imperial Concubine Kareen, the Third Prince, and Lady Shareen are different, but still..."

"Old habits die hard."

Cassandra understood that better than anyone else. It had taken her weeks to fully trust Kairen, his sister and his mother, and even now, she was unable to approach any member of the Imperial Family without that fear automatically growing in her stomach.

She had no idea where he had gone, but Cassandra enjoyed the bit of time she had alone with Dahlia. Apparently, she and Missandra had gotten quite close and stayed together late into the night to chat. Her sister was still asleep, but the rest of the inhabitants were all up already. Most couldn't sleep well because of the storm from the previous night. The thunder had only calmed down late in the night, but Cassandra was among those few people it hadn't bothered at all.

"Lady Kareen has been very busy preparing everything for the Rain Ceremony!" explained Dahlia, her hands busily braiding some of Cassandra's hair. "She said she wants to have it done before the rain stops. I don't think it will stop so soon, but..."

Cassandra nodded while eating breakfast. She didn't think so either. She could recognize when a downpour was going to last, and this was definitely one of those. The actual storm was over and the wind had calmed down, leaving only regular sounds of heavy rain.

She closed her eyes, letting Dahlia finish her hairdo while eating in silence, just listening to the rain. This sound was so familiar. She was born during a storm like the one on the previous day. Now that she thought about it, her baby had been conceived during a snowstorm. This was such a cute coincidence. Maybe it would take another of those for him to be born.

"Lady Cassandra? What are you smiling about?" asked Dahlia.

"I was just thinking a little. Are we finished?"

"Just a little bit more! I want to see if I can adjust this..."

"Hinue!"

Missandra showed up at the door looking tired, but tightly wrapped in a big fur cloak. She looked a bit cold, but her cheeks were of a rosy shade. She walked up to them, looking happy.

"I love those flower crowns.Hinue, did you have your breakfast? Do you want more? Prince Anour showed us where to find the kitchens yesterday!"

Cassandra chuckled.

"Aren't you close to Anour now? For him to show you around?"

Missandra pouted.

"Don't start treating me like a child!"

Sulking a bit, she grabbed some of Cassandra's breakfast, biting into one of the cheese cubes hungrily. The older sister chuckled. Actually, she was happy whenever Missandra acted her age. She was obviously a lot more comfortable now that they were in the Diamond Palace, enough to befriend Anour at least. The rain probably raised her younger sister's spirits, too.

After bickering a bit more, all three young women headed out of the room. Cassandra only had to follow Dahlia, who had apparently been woken up early too to prepare for the Ceremony.

Finally, they reached a large room. Cassandra recognized it instantly. It was one of Lady Kareen's favorite salons, one with an open roof and lots of green plants sprouting wildly from all sides. This time though, all the furniture had been taken out as the rain was pouring in. It was alright though; the floor had some crevices where the water would flow in, as dozens of little rivers headed towards the outer parts or the fountain on the side. Cassandra had always wondered how the Diamond Palace could have so many open rooms, but now, it was obvious that most rooms were properly conceived for the water to be expelled one way or another.

This one was actually rather perfect for the Ceremony. It had a square shape, was letting the downpour in, and yet the floor wasn't completely flooded, only a thin layer of water remained under their feet.

"How is it, dear?" asked Kareen, walking up to her in one of her gorgeous magenta dresses.

"It looks perfect, Lady Kareen. But do we have everything?"

The Imperial Concubine clicked her tongue.

"Don't you dare underestimate me, young lady! Dahlia, take her to the other bedroom where we have everything. And someone go wake up that sleepyhead daughter of mine!"

Cassandra was swiftly pushed to another room. She had thought she would get ready in her room, but once she walked inside, she understood why she couldn't. In front of her, a gorgeous green and gold dress was displayed. It was the first time in years she saw what looked like a real ceremonial outfit from her tribe, and tears came to her eyes right away. There was even the veil, and all the golden embroideries had obviously been handmade!

"Do you like it, Hinue?" asked Missandra, excited. "Dahlia and I stayed up late last night to finish it!"

"We had some help from other servants, of course," added Dahlia. "But we all followed Missandra's instructions down to the letter to have it as close to your real ceremonial outfit as possible. Do you like it?"

"It's gorgeous," whispered Cassandra, unable to find any more words to describe it.

Indeed, the dress was divine and just as beautifully made as her usual pink dresses. The gorgeous green silk was of the best quality, shimmering with several shades as she touched it, and the gold threads had been embroidered so well, to retrace the traditional arabesques she remembered all over it. The piece of cloth didn't have a single gem on it, but it was shining and glowing better than any treasure.

The girls had even prepared, with Lady Kareen's help, some jewelry to add to her outfit.

"Hinue, look! We couldn't find borean ink, but I made something similar. I tested it, so your skin should be able to bear it just fine!"

Indeed, the blue ink in the little pot she was handing her looked very similar to proper borean ink. Cassandra put the pot aside, and took the two girls in her arms to hug them.

"Thank you so much... Dahlia, Missandra... Thank you for preparing all this for me."

Both Missandra and Dahlia were surprised by this sudden hug, but happily responded to it. After that, all three of them chuckled, excited, and it was high time they helped Cassandra get ready.

A while later, Kairen was waiting outside, wearing a similar green silk piece of clothing. For the tall warrior, the girls had only made a large cloak, which he was wearing over his shoulders, with some black pants. Kairen wasn't very familiar with anything about the Rain Tribe's ceremony, but when Missandra came up to him, he listened to her.

"Could you just stand there? Right there, please. Alright, and if you can wait a bit, my sister is coming!"

She ran back inside and suddenly, Cassandra appeared. Everyone was completely speechless. The young concubine was more beautiful than she'd ever been. The long green dress was tightly wrapped around her body, showing her curves more than the usual pink dresses. It was only covering her chest, belly, and legs, so her back and arms were nude, only her hair running down. The visible pieces of her skin were actually shining with a strange light, like some thin silver shimmer. Anyone in the room could see that the emerald dress was absolutely gorgeous on her, and with that flower crown and the painting on her skin, she looked like she had just stepped out of a large painting, like a nature Goddess. Several male servants had their mouths wide open in surprise and even the girls were blushing, shocked by how pure yet sensual she looked at that moment.

However, the most stunned of all was Kairen. The War God was looking at his young concubine with such a deep expression on his face. His deep black eyes were mesmerized by the vision before him. He was struck; not shocked by how beautiful she was, but how even more beautiful she could be. For maybe the first time, he wasn't just quiet. He was speechless.

Cassandra had always been a gorgeous young woman, a flower that bloomed in adversity, but that day, for the first time, she was able to shine in all of her glory. The War God, behind his impassible facade, was properly stunned. In terms of natural beauty, Cassandra was indisputably beautiful. All the jewels and attires of the concubines of the Imperial Palace couldn't beat such a natural beauty.

Though they were of different shades, the deep green of her dress was complimenting her eyes perfectly. Her brown hair was falling in natural curls on her shoulders and down on her back and belly, with that crown they had bought together on top. Several of the servants whispered about her looks, but the rain covered any sound, and the War God wouldn't have been able to hear them anyway. All of his senses had gone numb as he could only focus on the holy vision in front of his eyes.

Cassandra gracefully walked up to him, like a nymph, with a gentle smile on her face. He could barely recognize the woman he held in his arms every night. There was something unspeakably different about her, as if she was from another world, another realm. She took his hand.

"Kairen? Are you alright?"

"...You're beautiful," he whispered, as if saying that truth would release him from this trance.

Cassandra blushed, as always, feeling a bit proud. She hadn't thought she would be able to cause such emotion in her usually undecipherable War God. The rain was falling around them, but they didn't care. It was just as if the two of them had been alone. The green clothes were slowly getting wet, but they were still very pretty to observe.

Missandra walked up to them.

"Since I'm the only one aside from Hinue who knows about the Ceremony, I'll tell you two what to do. Dahlia, bring the thread, please!"

While Missandra took the silver thread and started gently wrapping it around both of their wrists, in a complex ensemble of knots, Kairen's eyes were on Cassandra's skin. The shimmering from earlier was actually that strange ink that she had used to paint herself with. From the look of it, those weren't simply lines and strange shapes, but obviously some foreign language he couldn't decipher at all. He frowned.

"What do those say?"

Cassandra blushed a bit, looking down, and her younger sister was the one to answer.

"The partners can paint whatever they want on their bodies as a sign of affection. Hinue put your name and titles with the symbols of protection, health, and strength."

Kairen was surprised. He kept looking at all those strange scriptures on her skin, unable to decipher what was which.

"Do it on me, too."

"What?"

"With that ink. I want to write her name."

Missandra sighed.

"But I'm almost done with the silk thread! Hinue, you didn't tell him earlier about the borean ink?"

"Just bring it to me, please," said Cassandra, with an apologetic look.

While Missandra pouted and kept doing her knots, Dahlia ran over, with an umbrella in one hand and the little bowl of ink and a brush in the other. There wasn't much left of what Missandra had prepared, as Cassandra had painted a lot on herself already. She took the brush with her available hand and pushed the cloak a bit to access his torso.

"What do you want me to write?" she whispered to him.

"Your name."

"Are you sure? Just my name?"

"Yes."

Cassandra chuckled, and proceeded to do as asked. It was so like him. No prayers, just her name. She knew Kairen wasn't a man to believe in prayers or divine will. He only trusted himself and the people he cared about. She wrote her name on his skin, as many times as she could before running out of ink. The ink Missandra had made wasn't as good as the real borean ink and was already starting to drip a bit because of all the rain, but this was good enough. The silver ink shined strangely on the War God's torso and arms. Maybe because of his natural musculature, they looked more like tribal fighting signs than his Favorite's name.

"Alright, I'm done!" said Missandra, looking satisfied.

Dahlia swiftly walked away, going under the little porch to shelter herself from the rain, close to Shareen and Kareen. Mother and Daughter were standing side by side and watching the Ceremony attentively, not saying a word. They were aware that although there wasn't anything official about this, this ceremony was sacred to Cassandra's people. As they knew nothing about this foreign custom, they were silently watching, curious.

Cassandra and Kairen's wrists were now tied together by that silk thread.

The gentle fabric wasn't painful on their skin, but their wrists couldn't move, being tied so tightly together with those complex knots. Cassandra looked at her left wrist and Kairen's right wrist, with a smile. She had never thought she would get to have this ceremony ever, let alone with a Prince, and a man she loved. Kairen chuckled.

"Are you so happy?" he said.

"Yes...I feel a bit like it's a dream."

"Sorry, we can only do this for now."

"No, it's plenty," Cassandra whispered, her cheeks blooming with pink.

"Alright, if you two are done being so mushy," said Missandra. "I'll start... Hinue, should I translate it into our tongue or theirs?"

"Just do it in our tongue and I'll translate in the Dragon Empire's tongue, Missandra."

"Understood. Then..."

Missandra took a deep breath and took a couple of steps back, opening her hands, palms towards the sky, and closed her eyes. She started speaking, and Cassandra repeated in words everyone else could understand. Both sisters talking in the exact same rhythm, one echoing the other.

"Today is the Day of Rain, the Sacred Day. As the Sky God is showering the Earth Goddess with love, their children are born with the rain. We are children of the rain, children of sacred love. O, God of Water, let your rain pour, and hear your children today, for they carry their faith, love, and joy in their heart too. O, God of Water, Son of the Sky and Earth, if love is your eyes, let them see. If love is your tongue, let it speak. If you can hear us, hear your children's pledge of love today, as we share it with you."

Cassandra was talking softly while staring at Kairen, their eyes not leaving each other's a single second.

"O, God of Water, our ancestors taught us love. Help us teach our children too. We'll share that love to all of your children, from all rivers they come, from all seas they come. Let us speak of love, and let our hearts beat together. Let your love flow in our veins and words, for you showed us how to love with your rain. Gather your children together under the rain, gather us, and remind us how to love if we forget. Teach us to be patient, kind, sincere, and truthful. Teach us love, teach us how to cry, and pray. Fill our lives with love, water, and grace. O, God of Water, your children are thankful today, as with love you teach us the way again."

On the side, Kareen shed a little tear, impressed. Even the servants were all feeling sensitive to the words of Cassandra, and the prayer that echoed in the walls despite the rain. Both sisters took a little pause, breathing deeply before reciting again.

"O, God of Water, your children will remember. We will remember your love is patient, kind, sincere, and truthful. We shall not give in to anger, and we shall not give in to evil. We shall not lie, and we shall not betray. Your children promise to remember, each day the rain falls, how love is patient, kind, sincere, and truthful.

O, God of Water, your love has no beginning and no end. Your love is blind and deaf. Your love is infinite."

Missandra's voice suddenly broke into tears. Something in her memories kept her from going on. She kept hanging her hands in front of her, but she was crying, unable to continue. Cassandra understood why it hurt so much for her sister. She took a deep breath, and continued alone, while Kareen walked over to gently hug Missandra's shoulders.

"O, God of Water, your children of the rain shall not lie, and they shall not hurt. I will be blind and deaf if I can't see or hear love.

O, God of Water, your children gather today, in harmony, to love again.

O, God of Water, hear our prayer. Your children will give up their wealth, their bodies, and their mind for love."

Cassandra took a deep breath and gestured for Kairen to take one of the ends of the silk thread, while she took the other.

"Rain has come to us blind and deaf. Rain will witness our love today. I give my wealth, my body, and my mind for this love of mine."

She mimicked with her lips for Kairen to repeat her words.

"I give my wealth, my body, and my mind for this love of mine."

"I will love eternally, in the eyes of my beloved, and in the eyes of the Water God."

"I will love eternally," repeated Kairen, "in the eyes of my beloved, and in the eyes of the Water God."

"I swear to keep my love patient, kind, sincere, and truthful until I die. I swear to honor the Water God in every way, until I return into his arms, side by side with my beloved."

Once again, the War God repeated without flinching.

"O, God of Water, love is infinite. Love is mine. You are mine."

"Love is infinite. Love is mine... Almien."

Cassandra was surprised to hear Kairen had translated the last word by himself. She was shocked and incredibly overwhelmed.

They stayed silent for a little while, staring deeply into each other's eyes. There was no sound around but the rain, falling quietly around them, the downpour slowly turning into a gentle rain. Cassandra smiled and took his other hand, linking her fingers with his. Then, she stepped forward, and they exchanged a long, deep kiss.

Their kiss had a fresh taste of rain and eternity. Despite the cold around them, Cassandra's heart had never felt warmer than at this moment. They exchanged that kiss in a religious atmosphere as if they were sealing their promise. When they gently stepped back, a drop rolled down her cheek, but no one would have been able to tell if it was a tear or the rain. Cassandra was smiling, and it didn't matter much.

Then, they both pulled on the silk thread at the same time, and, to his surprise, it separated perfectly, leaving two little bracelets wrapped around their wrists. The people watching were confused. How did that long thread separate into two so easily, and in such perfect knots, too?

"We're done for today," whispered Cassandra.

"Done? Already?" repeated Shareen, surprised.

The young concubine walked over to her sister, hugging Missandra in her arms to try and calm her down. They went to shelter themselves under the roofed part of the room, where the servants rushed to bring them thick towels.

"Yes. Both partners usually keep this thread around their wrists until the next rain, and it is done."

"I was expecting something much bigger! Do you have any idea what hassle the wedding ceremonies are here? Let alone the ones in the Imperial Family!"

"The Rain Tribe isn't the... showy type. As long as the God of Water has been able to witness it, any kind of ceremony is holy and perfectly valid. We don't need grand ceremonies, decorations, or a lot of people. As long as both parties were sincere, we are now acknowledged as lifetime partners; this is all that matters."

"It was a beautiful ceremony, Cassandra," said Kareen, glaring at her daughter for her to shut up. "Your tribe has a beautiful tradition. I prefer it to the ones here. We are all about the grand celebrations and showing off, while this feels much more intimate and sincere. That prayer was beautiful."

Missandra was still weeping silently. Cassandra kept hugging her and caressing her hair until she calmed down. This may have been a bit too much for her. It brought back painful memories of a time where their friends and family were alive, and they were both living very differently. Missandra had lied, stolen, and hurt other people, and hearing the whole prayer again made her feel ashamed and disgusted in herself.

As the ceremony was over, Kareen ordered for them to move to another room to sit comfortably and rest for a bit while the servants brought large trays of food once again. It was something like brunch probably, as it wasn't really early enough or late enough for a proper meal. To help everyone warm-up, some tea was brought and Missandra insisted on being the one to prepare it and serve it to everyone.

Cassandra sat on a couch with Kairen's arm around her shoulders as she snuggled under a large fur blanket. She hadn't really realized how cold she was until then. However, she also didn't want to change into normal clothes yet. She was happy to wear the traditional green of her tribe, even if all of the fake Borean ink had already been washed away by the rain. If it had been real, it would have lasted several hours at least, but it couldn't be helped. Cassandra kept caressing the little silver thread around her wrist, feeling a bit numb with happiness.

Meanwhile, Shareen was gazing at Missandra, frowning a bit. The young girl's tears had dried, but her eyes were still red and she would sniffle from time to time.

"What were you crying for? Marrying your sister away?" she asked.

Missandra answered with a glare, though she quickly stopped to go back to preparing the tea. Kareen slapped her daughter's thigh, frowning.

"You insensitive Daughter! When did I raise you to be so heartless?"

"Do I have to answer that?"

Shareen got another slap and shut up after that, only making annoyed faces and sulking on the side.

Aside from Shareen, most people in the room actually understood the real reasons behind Missandra's tears, though they wouldn't have been so blunt about it. The prayer they had recited taught about love and being true and selfless. Missandra had lost all of that at a young age and grown into someone far from those ideals. For the first time in a while, she felt sullied by her past as a prostitute, and the thefts she had committed. That ceremony had been too much of a brutal reminder of that.

"Did your parents hold that ceremony too?" asked Lady Kareen, trying to pull the topic away from Missandra as she distributed the tea.

"No... Our father died when our mother was pregnant with Missandra," confessed Cassandra.

"May I ask how?"

"He was in an accident," replied Missandra. "Our mother said he died when they were building houses. There was an accident and our father got badly injured."

"One of the houses they were building became unstable because of a storm. Our father wanted to go and help secure his friend's house, but it collapsed on them," said Cassandra. "Our Uncle was there too, and he saw three men die with him. The house collapsed in the river and just... washed them all away. Our mother got the news once it was all over. Only our uncle returned, but he was severely injured. He passed a few hours later."

"By the Great Dragon," whispered Kareen. "I can't imagine how sad your mother must have been."

Cassandra was about to say something, but a loud growl interrupted her. They all heard Krai land loudly next door, and a few seconds later, Roun too. Its growl was higher-pitched than the Black Dragon's. Then, little Srai showed up in the room, as the only one small enough to sneak in, and went to curl up at Kareen's feet, its eyes watching the wall behind where they could hear its siblings bickering again.

"I don't remember him," said Cassandra. "Our mother told us about him many times, though. He was one of our tribe's best architects and he had built our house too."

"I wish I could see our house again."

"Maybe you could go there again?" asked Shareen.

Cassandra shook her head.

"It would be very dangerous. The swamps we lived in are now under the Eastern Republic's territory. I don't even think there's anything left of it, they probably destroyed it."

Missandra nodded sadly. Even Lady Kareen didn't dare to ask about their old tribe again. She was aware that, despite the fact that their rival had taken over the former tribe's parcel, it was the war between the Dragon Empire and the Eastern Republic that had destroyed these girls' homeland.

Somehow, it was only luck that the Dragon Empire hadn't been the one to destroy the Rain Tribe. If they had, it would have made this conversation even more awkward, and added another gap between Kairen and Cassandra.

This conversation had gone a bit sour after such an intense ceremony. Somehow, the Rain Ceremony had been so solemn, it had brought some deep-buried memories to the surface. The nostalgic feeling that hovered over Cassandra's heart made her feel a bit bittersweet. For a while, everyone focused on eating, and an awkward silence filled the room until Shareen spoke.

"So... After that ceremony, what is changing, exactly? You mentioned something about giving up your mind, body, and all. Is it for real? That sounded a lot like you two were going to commit suicide."

Cassandra chuckled.

"No, not at all. It had a deeper meaning than that. The Water God teaches us to not hold on to material things, not even our body."

"But your mind?"

"It means we have to elevate ourselves from earthly things. We only see through the eyes of those we love. It means we must care about others before ourselves."

"Well, I like to care about myself more," said Shareen. "Others can come after. Your people had a very selfless way, but I still think this is a bit odd."

"I agree," replied Cassandra with a chuckle. "Since I grew up in the Dragon Empire after that, I do see our differences, but I've also grown to love both. I like the dedication of the Rain Tribe to others, but I also like how living in the Dragon Empire is teaching us to care about ourselves. It's a very different environment, after all."

Cassandra had already thought about this before. Somehow, she felt that having met Kairen had allowed her to grow as a person. She wasn't afraid of her own shadow anymore, but she cherished her own life more. She was miles away from the slave girl who had lost all her will to live in that arena. She had grown a lot more in those few months, more than in the previous few years.

After her words, Missandra and Shareen started an argument about the different ways of life between the Dragon Empire's people and the Rain Tribe, but Cassandra was too tired to take part. Somehow, all this rain had made her a bit sleepy, and she just enjoyed this long brunch, her head on Kairen's shoulder. She kept snacking on those cheese cubes and green grapes, but also some slices of dried and smoked meat, which Missandra quickly took notice of.

"Hinue, you're eating meat again?" she said with a frown.

"Sorry, it's...the baby."

Cassandra couldn't see it, but Kairen glared at Missandra, warning her.

410

The War God put a hand around his concubine's belly. Kareen, too, clicked her tongue.

"Let her eat. Your sister is pregnant. She can eat and drink whatever she wants as long as she stays healthy!"

"Is that why you sent that bottle of wine to our room, Mother?" growled Kairen, annoyed.

It wasn't that often that the Third Prince would get mad at his own mother. All the servants in the room froze on the spot, their eyes going to the Imperial Concubine with a bit of worry. He wouldn't do something to his own mother, would he? However, Kareen was not impressed at all. The War God was her own son, after all. His obsidian eyes had no effect on her.

"Why can't I? I know Cassandra is reasonable. You would drink most of it by yourself anyway!"

She wasn't wrong, but Kairen still glared at his mother, a bit annoyed. Cassandra chuckled. Truth was, she really didn't mind that little taste of mulled wine before sleeping. It may have helped her sleep better, even. However, she wouldn't dare to say that in front of the War God.

Moreover, she had noticed, throughout the lunch, Kairen didn't take his hand off of her belly. Even while he was eating, the War God would only use his right hand. It wasn't that surprising that he would easily hold her and cuddle, but Cassandra was starting to wonder if there hadn't been a bit of change since the previous night. Maybe it was only her imagination, but they had slept in a spooning position, and that time, he also had his hand covering her little baby bump. Was it because he had felt the baby kicking? Cassandra silently hoped that the father of her unborn child would slowly grow more attached to this child. Until then, Kairen had shown more care for her than usual since the beginning of the pregnancy, but not much care about the baby at all. Maybe he hadn't realized much before? She was the one carrying their son, so maybe, to Kairen, she still came before a baby that had yet to come to this world.

She secretly wished this large hand spread in a protective way around her tummy was a good sign for their future as a family.

As they finished their lunch, the rain kept falling continuously. It probably wouldn't stop for a while, either. Cassandra secretly hoped all this rain and the storm would slow the Imperial Army as much as possible before they arrived there. Shareen, however, was sulking.

"As soon as that damn rain stops, Anour, we're leaving," she announced.

"Already?" asked the teenage boy, sulking a bit.

"We are not going on a holiday, remember? I want to hurry and go to the camp to whip those damn idiots' asses."

"Aren't you just going there to play?" said Anour.

Kareen chuckled, but Shareen didn't answer that. Of course, the War God's Army was probably doing just fine without her or even their Commander-in-Chief. The real threat would be the East, and Cassandra was in no hurry to have Kairen go there.

Once their lunch was finished, Kairen and his sister had to talk over military matters, so Cassandra went back first to finally change into warmer clothes. She carefully hung her green ceremony clothes where she could see them, as if that would make the dream last a bit longer. She took a bath to clean and warm herself up first, and put on a new pink dress, with a light fur cloak, as the rain was keeping the temperature low. Between the hot and dry weather of the Capital, the humidity of the Diamond Palace, and the cold of the Onyx Castle, Cassandra felt like she could get sick very easily. Hence, she made sure to cover herself, and drank some more warm tea.

She had another intention while going back to her room, and that was writing her letters. She asked for some ink and parchment. She wrote a long letter to Evin first, wondering if the Imperial servant would be happy to hear any news from her. He was the most serious man she had ever met, but she kind of liked him. He had been of great help back when she lived at the camp with Kairen. She was hoping to get some news from the Red Room as well, see if her medical teaching had done some good there. What she had heard from the Emperor in the Capital wasn't enough. Cassandra was hoping to hear more from Evin directly. She also added some more recommendations, about some herbs she remembered seeing there but hadn't taught them to use yet. She ended her letter wishing him well.

After that, her next letters were for Orwen, the blacksmith apprentice, and the servants of the Onyx Castle. She was curious to know how they were all doing. She missed Nebora most, as her first friend there. They had a rocky start, but she truly appreciated her honest nature. Cassandra took her time to let her friend know most of what had happened for her and realized that, once it was put on the paper, it was indeed quite a lot. Finally, Cassandra wrote some shorter letters to the younger servants, and Patrina, the Head Maid there.

"You look busy..."

She smiled, feeling two sturdy arms around her waist as she was writing the last couple of sentences. Kairen put his face into her neck, letting her finish. Once she was done, Cassandra put her letters to the side for the servants to collect and turned to him.

"What about you, my Prince? Did you finish discussing war with your sister?"

Kairen suddenly put on a grumpy front, surprising her a little.

"Don't you have something else to call me now?"

"You mean, Almien?" said Cassandra with a chuckle.

Kairen nodded, and leaned in to kiss her, satisfied.

"That's right, your man."

Kairen's kiss was gentle, slow, and sweet. Cassandra couldn't help but smile against his lips. Now that she was done with her letters, she wrapped her arms around his neck and let him pull her close, standing up and guiding her to their bed. Kairen's hands on her skin were warm, so warm that her skin would get little goosebumps from that delicious warm sensation. She loved the familiar smell of the War God. Her heart sank when Cassandra realized that, in a few days, she would have to say goodbye and wouldn't be able to enjoy this for a few weeks.

Hence, she was even thirstier for his kisses than usual, caressing his neck and brushing his hair. She suddenly stopped, though, looking at it.

"What is it?"

"Would you let me cut your hair?" she asked in a soft voice.

"My hair?"

"Yes...Do you mind?"

Kairen shook his head, and kissed her forehead. Of course, he didn't care at all. The War God never really bothered about his hair. The lustrous black hair was usually pushed back on his shoulders, he never really cared to cut it. His mother would do it for him from time to time, but there was really no particular attachment from him. He didn't care what Cassandra would do with it. Taking off the green cloth from his shoulders, Cassandra hung it next to hers, but as she did, Kairen frowned.

"Wait...I forgot about this," he said.

He stood and walked to one of the bags they had taken back from the Palace, searching for something, and eventually pulled out a little dagger from it, handing it to her. The blade was wrapped in a thick leather cloth, but Cassandra took it out carefully.

"I've seen it before," said Cassandra, observing the weapon with a frown.

"It was Phetra's. I modified it to make it a better weapon, and lighter too. Keep it with you."

Cassandra was surprised to receive the weapon of her enemy. Indeed, the dagger had changed a bit since Phetra had tried to harm her with it. She vaguely remembered Kairen working on it while she was making the decoction for Missandra's injuries, but she hadn't really paid much attention back then, and somehow forgot about it. Now, she could observe it a bit more carefully. The War God had removed all the unnecessary decorations, gems and gold for which neither of them cared, and sharpened it. Cassandra couldn't yield one of Kairen's swords, as they were way too heavy for her thin build, but this little dagger was indeed just the right weight in her hand. She could move it easily, though she hadn't much knowledge about how to use a dagger. She slid her finger on the blade, but avoided the edge. It was obvious this had been sharpened with precision, and she didn't want to cut herself.

"Can I cut your hair with this?"

"You can tame it this way."

Cassandra chuckled. She actually liked the symbolism behind keeping this weapon. The young concubine insisted on washing his hair first. Then, Kairen sat on the floor next to her, as even on a stool he would have been too tall for her. Cassandra was a bit excited to cut her Prince's hair, but she had to think about what she wanted to do first. Kairen's hair had grown long, it fell below his shoulders. She knew that length wasn't comfortable for him to fight with. She combed his hair with her fingers first, pushing it back, and trimmed the ends a bit. Then, she decided to shave the sides. She had seen some men with this haircut at the camp. She proceeded carefully. Indeed, the blade was very sharp... Cassandra had to proceed slowly, as she was agonizing over the idea of cutting him. It took longer than she had thought because of that, but once she was done, the shaved sides pleased her a lot. She carefully kept his freshly cut hair, too, putting it in a little napkin on the side. Then, she put the dagger down on its leather wrapping, and braided the hair left on top of his head, which was still plenty and long enough to fall between his shoulder blades. Then, she decided to tie it with some little gold rings she had in her chest, that she would probably never use. Once she was done, she stepped back a little and looked at the result, satisfied.

"What do you think?" she asked.

"Do my beard, too."

Cassandra laughed. His heavy beard indeed felt a bit too much now that his sides were shaven. She grabbed the dagger again, observing it to think about what she should do.

"I need to think about it..."

"Just shave it."

"I like your beard though."

"Then just shave what you don't like. It's too long."

Cassandra chuckled.

"Aren't you a fussy customer, Prince Kairen?"

"I'll pay you, then."

"How much would you pay me?" asked Cassandra, as she started trimming his beard.

"A gold bar."

She laughed.

"I would be the most overpaid barber in the Empire!"

"It's fine."

Cassandra shook her head, and focused on the trimming. It was his gold anyway. She knew very well he didn't care much about it. The Imperial Family was way too rich to really care. She focused on his beard, cutting it but leaving some, as she loved the spiky feeling of it. Once she was done, she had cut about two-thirds of it, but still leaving about half an inch for herself to play with.

"Alright, we are done," she said with a satisfied smile.

Kairen nodded, checking his newly trimmed beard with his fingers. Cassandra knew he was satisfied as he didn't ask her to cut more. She put her dagger down, and went to gather the hair she had collected in a napkin. Then, she very carefully started wetting it in the little basin and braided it. Kairen frowned a bit, wondering what she was doing now. She even got up several times to look through her little chest full of jewelry she seldom used. Once she was done, Cassandra proudly showed it to him. She had made a bracelet of his cut hair, adding some of her little gold rings to it. Kairen was surprised. She finished knotting the silky black hair around her wrist, around the thread from their ceremony, and it was clear it wouldn't come off unless cut.

"Did you intend to make this from the start?" he asked, stroking the little bracelet.

"Yes... Your hair is very long, and I like it. It will be my memento for when you're gone."

He nodded, a bit curious. Then, his eyes went to her hair, frowning.

"Do you want one from me too?" asked Cassandra, reading his mind easily.

"I don't want you to cut your hair."

She chuckled and grabbed the dagger again. Kairen was frowning, but Cassandra knew very well he loved her long hair, and had no intention to cut it short either. Instead, she grabbed a strand around her nape, where it wouldn't be seen. She cut a good portion of it. Her hair was long enough, and that bunch alone would suffice.

"Will a bracelet fit you?" she asked, a bit unsure.

"Can you braid it into my hair?"

Cassandra immediately loved the idea. She checked the braids she had done in Kairen's hair, and worked around it. The final result was actually surprisingly beautiful. From what she had done before, the black braids on his head were fading into her dark-brown strands, and falling a bit lower down his back. It looked like his hair was naturally fading into hers, and the now rather long braids down his back were quite beautiful and unique. She had a wide smile observing the result. The War God, too, grabbed the braids to look at it, stroking the dark brown strands with his fingers.

"Are you happy with it, dear customer?" Cassandra asked.

"Very," he replied with a nod.

He pulled her in for a kiss, now that they were done with the hair-styling fun. Cassandra was so happy, she wished those few days of peace together could last forever. She felt safe wherever the Prince was, even more so when they were staying at the Diamond Palace. This Rain Ceremony had been a dream come true, so simple yet so beautiful. She didn't know if Kairen grasped the full extent of this vow, how much it meant for her, but she was satisfied enough to have been bonded with him in the ways of her people. She didn't want to take this silk thread or her newly made hair bracelet off, ever. Even if they had to part soon, she knew she'd cherish it and comfort herself with it.

She was just so eager to enjoy all of him while she still could. She kissed him back, so eager and demanding. She would never get tired of this man. Especially since she really liked that new hairdo. Kairen looked even manlier, if possible. He truly looked like a God of War, like this. He wasn't a particularly handsome man, but Cassandra had grown to love his strong jaw, his obsidian eyes, and his features. His muscles, too. She was never into burly men, but Kairen's powerful arms just ignited all of her desire so easily, with those large hands. She would blush every time he caressed her, her body so conditioned to his touch after all of those hours of love making.

There was something about knowing those were their last days together for a while. Somehow, she didn't want to let go of him, not yet. Her whole world had been spinning around this man for several months now. The weeks without him had been hard. Now, how long would she have to wait until the next time they could be together again?

Hence, for once Cassandra wasn't too shy about taking the lead. She pushed him gently on the bed, and of course, her Prince wouldn't reject her. Kairen actually liked to see her act a little bit bolder, to let her take the lead in bed. They had made love so many times, their bodies didn't hold many secrets from each other.

Cassandra sat across his hips, while Kairen pulled them both into the middle of the bed. She felt a bit guilty about having sex after they both just changed, but it was a bit too late to reconsider. Their passionate kissing wasn't giving much room for her to think, and her skin was burning up already. She undid the laces of her dress, and helped her Prince take off his pants. Within a few minutes, they had their skins against each other, and no piece of clothing left. Cassandra kept caressing the long, freshly cut braid on Kairen's back. She really liked his new hairdo, and her fingertips would caress his head, feel the bare parts behind his ears, caress it down to his nape, then find the braid, trace it back to the top, and redo that gesture, over and over again.

"Stop that."

Cassandra frowned, a bit surprised. She tilted her head, but when she tried to pass her fingers behind his ears again, Kairen avoided it. She chuckled.

"Don't tell me...it tickles?"

"Just stop."

Cassandra laughed. Who could have known the War God was ticklish behind his ears!

Chapter 26

Cassandra slowly woke up to some rummaging behind the door. She frowned, wondering what was going on. If she focused enough, she could hear a bit of the conversation...

"But... It's been two days..."

"I told you, they are fine! Just leave it here. They eat it, don't they? Just come and clean it up later. Don't disturb them, they'll come out when they have had enough."

"Oh... I see..."

Cassandra sighed and snuggled inside Kairen's arms. Had it been two days already? They hadn't parted and left the bed except for taking the trays of food inside and back outside. Her last three nights and two days had been filled with love and sex. She felt like they had gone into their own little bubble, away from time. Or maybe just trying to forget about time. She wasn't ready to part with him yet, but she probably never would be.

Kairen's slow breathing above her head made her a bit sad. She didn't want to have to sleep alone, without the sounds of her partner beside her. He had become everything to her. The fact that she knew this was going to come to an end was devastating her, making it so much worse. She didn't know when, she just knew that it was going to happen soon. Cassandra hated the wait. The only way for her to forget was to sleep or have sex with her Prince. Somehow, she hated feeling depressed before he was even gone.

She sat on the bed, sighing and pushing her hair away from her face. Of course, behind her, Kairen immediately reacted, and came to wrap her in his arms.

"What is it?" he whispered against her ear.

"I just... I need to do something. I'm going to go crazy if I just stay here thinking about how you're going to leave soon."

"Are you sad?"

"I don't think I'm sad...yet."

Cassandra turned around, kissing him gently, brushing his beard with her fingers. It had already grown back a little. Then, she took a deep breath and smiled softly.

"I'll be alright. Just focus on the war, and I will focus on our baby."

Kairen nodded, agreeing with her. Cassandra gently kissed him again and left the bed to go and see what clothes she could put on. She didn't want to stay locked in this room anymore. It had been a bit too long already, and she didn't want to be rude to their host, Lady Kareen, or make her sister unhappy. Kairen grabbed the food tray to bring inside while she washed using the little water basin, and they ate together in silence.

When they were both full, dressed, and ready to go, they walked out of the bedroom. The Diamond Palace was actually rather quiet. First, Cassandra wanted to go and check on the Dragon Egg. It was a bit of a funny feeling, but she felt like she had neglected her baby by not going to see the egg for a while. Once they got there, to her surprise, Krai was wrapped around it sleeping. She chuckled.

The Black Dragon woke up, and watched her come close, but did not want to leave its egg, letting Cassandra approach instead. She got on her knees right next to the dragon, and Krai's snout sniffed her belly, rubbing against her dress curiously. She scratched the dark snout a bit, but her hand was busier touching the egg. It was still warm, with this strange light moving inside. It was almost as if something was beating inside. Actually, the egg seemed even warmer than she remembered, almost hot now. How many more weeks until she gave birth? At this rate, it would be burning hot before her baby was born!

Krai softly growled when Kairen approached, and the War God also scratched its head. It was rare for the two to interact directly. Cassandra watched them for a while, but she was more distracted by the egg. She had grown attached to it a lot, and couldn't wait to meet both the baby dragon and her baby. The egg was already so big, she wondered what size a newborn dragon could be? Maybe it was half full of liquid in there, or maybe the baby dragon was already as big as that?

"Oh, look who finally came out of the den!"

They turned around. Kareen was just at the entrance of the garden, followed by some servants carrying meat. She smiled widely and walked up to them. Krai, excited, suddenly got up, smelling the meat.

"Good Morning, Lady Kareen," said Cassandra.

"Good Morning, dear. You look well-rested!"

Cassandra blushed a bit. The Imperial Concubine couldn't ignore that they had just spent two days in bed. Of course, she would be rested, having done nothing but sleep and...the rest.

"How come you are feeding Krai here?" asked Cassandra, a bit curious.

The dragon would usually leave the Diamond Palace, or wherever they were staying, to go and feed by itself. It was a good enough hunter to provide for itself. It only came around to steal some meat from their meals out of gluttony, not hunger.

"That big boy doesn't need me!" laughed Kareen. "This is for Srai. Srai, come here baby."

Suddenly, a Purple Dragon's head popped up from behind Krai. Cassandra hadn't noticed Srai was here! The other dragon was so tiny, Krai's body could easily hide it. Srai climbed over its younger brother, and wiggled all the way to Lady Kareen, though Krai was right behind, the ruby eyes fixed on the meat.

"Don't move, Krai," said Kareen with her motherly voice.

The Black Dragon growled softly, sulking a bit, but stayed where it was, with no choice but to watch its older brother eat the meat. Srai's owner had died at six years old. Would that mean her future baby dragon was going to be even tinier than that? Cassandra couldn't be sure, though. Sephir and Vrehan's dragons were both smaller than Krai. It was really too hard to say, though Lady Kareen had hinted before that their dragon would probably be on the bigger side.

"Stop sulking you big boy, you should go out and hunt if you're hungry!" said Kareen, scolding Krai who was still growling, upset.

"Didn't he go hunting yet today?" asked Cassandra.

"He went this morning, but he's been glued to his egg for as long as you two were locked in that room. He only leaves it to go hunting. I don't know what's wrong with him. Kairen?"

Both women turned to the War God, but Kairen stayed mute, looking at the egg with a little frown. Cassandra, however, was the quickest to understand what was going on.

They didn't want to leave. Just like Kairen had kept her in the bedroom for three nights and two days, Krai didn't want to part with its egg. The dragon probably didn't want to part with Cassandra, either. The pair were dreading this war, unwilling to part with their loved ones. This truth hit Cassandra right in the heart. She hadn't realized before. Because her prince seldom showed his feelings and was always so attached to her anyway, she hadn't even thought about how he could feel about leaving her here in the Diamond Palace. She had focused on her own feelings alone, and only realized now how selfish and self-centered that was of her.

Kairen was the one who had to leave. He was the one who would have to go to war, to fulfill his duty as the Third Prince, the God of War of the Dragon Empire, while she'd stay back. Cassandra would be safe here in the Diamond Palace, while her lover was sent to the frontline. Underneath the armor, the War God was a man. Just a man, who had learned to muffle his feelings his whole life. However, Krai was a mirror of its owner's feelings. It didn't want to leave them.

Cassandra got up and walked up to him, putting her arms around his chest, hugging him gently. Kairen didn't answer much, aside from putting his hand on her lower back, and playing with her hair.

"Oh... I like this new hairstyle, Son," said Kareen, inspecting it from a bit closer. "Perfect for going to war..."

"It better be soon!" yelled someone behind her.

Shareen appeared, stealing some meat from the dragons. Cassandra frowned a bit, as it was raw meat, but obviously, the Princess couldn't care less and was eating it directly off the bone. Lady Kareen clicked her tongue.

"Shareen, your manners!"

"I am starving, Mother. I trained all morning with those useless guards of yours, they better get back in shape before I come back, or I'll have all those idiots replaced. Anyway, is the honeymoon over you two? I hope you do know you can't put another baby in before this one is out, though, right?"

Cassandra decided to ignore her. She was used to Shareen's crude ways by now, and she was almost expecting it at this point.

"Enough, enough. I'm hungry, too. Let's have a late morning brunch, before you end up fighting with my babies," said Kareen, walking back inside.

Cassandra chuckled. Anything was an excuse to have brunch for Lady Kareen, as she liked holding big feasts for breakfast no matter how late or early in the day it was. Hearing her call both dragons her babies was so endearingly cute.

They all walked back inside, but to Cassandra's surprise, though Missandra and Dahlia were here, Anour didn't show up. When she asked about it, Missandra frowned, and Shareen chuckled.

"The young ones had a bit of a fight last night, so he's been sulking. Don't worry, that big baby will show up eventually."

"A fight? What did you fight with Anour about?" asked Cassandra, turning to Missandra.

Her younger sister pouted a bit.

"He kept saying how a woman will always be weaker than a man, and wouldn't change his mind. So, I challenged him."

"You fought with Anour? Missandra!"

"What? I lost anyway!" protested the younger sister.

Shareen laughed loudly.

"You barely lost, and that's what upset Anour. He struggled so much not to hurt you he got a big black eye, so now that idiot is reflecting. Well done, by the way, Missie."

"Stop calling me that," whispered Missandra with a cute pout.

Cassandra couldn't help but smile, thinking about how her younger sister had learned from her mistakes and was finally changing her attitude towards the Imperial Family. Of course, she shouldn't fight, but from what she had heard, this was just normal bickering between teenagers.

They set up for another brunch in one of the gardens, and Cassandra finally felt a bit better than before. Maybe staying in bed for so long had gotten to her. She felt better now, sitting in the garden, breathing in some fresh air, and spending time with everyone.

Suddenly, loud noises were heard from the outside. The ruckus had lots of people cheering, and applauding. A servant came running inside the garden, but they all already knew what was going on.

"The Imperial Army has arrived, Your Highnesses! They are asking to see the Third Prince Kairen, the War God of the Dragon Empire!"

Cassandra's heart sank at those words. The Army had arrived even faster than she thought.

Somehow, Kairen, Anour, and Shareen got ready to leave incredibly fast. A couple of representatives from the army showed up, but there wasn't much time to lose. The news from the Eastern Front wasn't good, they had to go as fast as possible. Hence, there wasn't much ceremony involved, but everything was done in sad silence. Once everything was packed and ready, all dragons and humans gathered at the entrance of the Diamond Palace. Cassandra could even feel Krai's unhappiness, as the dragon was lethargic, its head turned towards the direction of the egg.

The young concubine approached the dragon, scratching its maw gently.

"Don't worry... I'll take care of our babies," she whispered to him.

The dragon growled sadly, rubbing its head against her belly. She stayed there until Kairen had said goodbye to his mother, and finally turned to her.

She sighed, but she couldn't say a word. Her throat was already choked up, despite her best attempt not to cry. The Prince gently took her in his arms. Cassandra hid her face in his shoulder, trying to inhale deeply, to remember his smell and his warmth. She really wasn't ready to let go.

"Stay safe," he whispered to her. "Take care of yourself and the baby. Eat well, sleep well... I'll be back soon."

"I know..."

She wanted to tell him the same, to stay safe and healthy, but the words didn't come. Instead, she started tearing up, and raised her eyes to look at him. She was going to miss him so much, again. Finally, she put her hands on his face, and kissed him longingly. This was going to be their last kiss for a long time. She needed that taste on her lips to linger for as long as possible.

"By the great Golden Dragon, how much cheesier and mushier can you two get? Alright, that's it, I'm out of here," declared Shareen.

The two lovers separated slowly, and Kairen put one last kiss on her forehead.

"I'll be back soon," he repeated.

Cassandra nodded sadly, and took a couple of steps back. Kareen came to her side, putting an arm around her shoulder as they watched Kairen, Shareen, Anour, and the two dragons fly away, leading the Army.

Cassandra broke down in tears a few minutes later. After Kairen's departure, Cassandra was sad for a couple of days. However, she knew she couldn't stay like that forever. Once she was done crying, she tried to spend time with Kareen, Missandra, and Dahlia, and keep herself busy. Somehow, they all cooperated to keep her occupied.

Lady Kareen was used to her children being gone and having to find hobbies for herself. As it turned out, she was rather busy as the City's owner and Mayor already, but she still found time to have other hobbies. She liked painting and tried to talk Cassandra into it. Though the young concubine wasn't fond of it, Missandra was interested, and even proved herself to be a good student. Eventually, Cassandra was used as a model a couple of times, as it allowed her to rest yet spend time chatting with them.

There was something else Lady Kareen did for her, however. Somehow, the Imperial Concubine was well aware of Kairen's present for Cassandra in the Imperial Palace, and decided to give her a little garden in the Diamond Palace, too. This was probably the most successful attempt at cheering Cassandra up.

Once she started taking care of her plants, studying the books she was given about them, or writing herself, Cassandra didn't notice the hours pass by. Missandra would join her often, to learn from her, as well as share her knowledge on the matter. Somehow, the two sisters started working on new hybrid species, trying to grow sprouts that would survive in the Shadelands. This little project was keeping Cassandra busy, and also helping her remember that, sometime soon, she would be able to go back to the Onyx Castle with Kairen. Anything was good to keep herself busy. She'd write, chat with Kareen and Missandra, work on her plants, write about new medicines, go to the local markets, study more books, and find more things to keep herself busy with.

That workaholic behavior of hers started worrying Kareen and Missandra a bit, as it never seemed like the young concubine took a break, despite her belly growing quickly. Cassandra was busy, too busy. She'd spend all day working on one thing and then another, only stopping to eat. The Imperial Concubine was starting to dislike this obsessive behavior and insisted on Missandra and Dahlia watching her more closely.

However, one day, Kareen unexpectedly found her napping in the Dragon Egg's garden. Cassandra was wrapped up in a warm blanket and had fallen asleep with some of her notes, right next to the egg. The discreet Dahlia was watching her from afar, making sure she wouldn't get sick. She silently smiled at Lady Kareen when their eyes met, meaning she already knew about Cassandra's little naps. After that, the Imperial Concubine decided not to be on Cassandra's back so much. When she wasn't constantly watched, Cassandra would eventually take breaks by herself, always agreeing to Dahlia's suggestion for some tea, or a stroll in the gardens.

Unknown to Kareen, however, the hardest times for Cassandra were at night. The young concubine hadn't imagined she would have so much trouble falling asleep by herself. The idea of going back to an empty bed haunted her every day after dusk. She would drag on the time to go back to her bedroom, find excuses to stay up late with Lady Kareen or her notes, and when she had no choice but to go, she'd turn sad and silent. Dahlia had set up a little routine for her, where the young concubine would take a long hot bath in her bedroom, and chat with her about her day. Helping Cassandra bathe, wash her hair, and brush it before bed, somehow helped her get sleepy and fall asleep more easily. The weather was getting a bit colder, so Dahlia brought in little scented candles, finding the ones that supposedly helped with insomnia.

Her pregnancy was also a big help in keeping Cassandra from doing too much and tiring herself out. Somehow, reaching the seventh month made her more tired than ever before, and she started taking naps by herself. Her growing, large belly was incapacitating her in several ways, giving Dahlia and Missandra more excuses to stay around and help her.

Eventually, Cassandra's sadness passed. She wasn't over Kairen's absence, but at least she had reverted back to her old self and didn't look as sad or on the verge of crying anymore. Truth was, Cassandra had spent many nights crying silently, but she couldn't take it anymore. She couldn't stand being a shadow of herself. She was even more worried it would impact her baby negatively. From then on, she started every day with a big breath, something to look forward to, and did her best to live her days eating well and resting well, as she had promised her Prince. When she missed him, she'd caress the little bracelet of hair around her wrist, or go to see the dragon's Egg. Somehow, Cassandra got a bit better by herself, and life went on for everyone at the Diamond Castle.

After a few more weeks, however, Cassandra could tell something was wrong. There was no way Kareen hadn't gotten any news about the Eastern War yet. It had been more than two months already. When she mentioned it to her, the Imperial Concubine always pretended like she was going to ask about it soon, or was waiting to hear from some of her spies. Cassandra couldn't take it anymore. After a while, she had even received answers from the people at the Onyx Castle and the North Army camp by a normal message-carrier service. There was no way Kareen had absolutely no news about the war against the Eastern Republic!

That morning, she insisted once again, and this time persisted until she got the truth, with Missandra's support. After half an hour of arguing, Kareen was exasperated.

"You're so stubborn!"

"I need to know the truth! I know my Prince is out there fighting! I can wait but I can't stand not having any news, and I know you must have some information! That is all I ask, Lady Kareen!"

The Imperial Concubine looked like she was about to throw her cup of tea across the room. Instead, she slammed it on the table, and rolled her eyes.

"Gosh, I didn't think you could be as stubborn as my children! Fine, I will tell you!"

"Really? So you know something?"

"Of course I do! Who do you think I am? There isn't a city in this Empire I don't have a spy in! Anyway, I did get some news half a month ago. While Shareen is perfectly fine in the North, on Kairen's side, the Eastern Army somehow got further into our territory than we thought. The Capital was actually notified very late of the attack, someone there didn't, or couldn't, do their job correctly. By the time Kairen got there, the situation was very messy, and you can't have a dragon simply burn everything down when your enemies are spread in your own city, among our people."

"Oh God, no..." whispered Cassandra, shocked.

She hadn't imagined the situation was that bad! All this time, Shareen and Kairen had made it sound like this would be a simple task that would be solved easily. Cassandra had no idea the frontline was in such a bad situation, even before Kairen had gotten there.

"That's why things are complicated. He has to wipe out the enemy and push them back to the frontier, but those imbecile Republicans have realized that Krai won't attack, or at least fire, while they are still inside the Dragon Empire. So all of their strategies seem to focus on staying in."

"Since when does the Eastern Republic know so much about dragons?" asked Missandra. "Those tactics don't sound like theirs at all."

"I know," sighed Kareen. "That is what worries me. I wouldn't be surprised if a little rat had gone ahead to give them those bad ideas."

"Lady Kareen, do you think... The Second Prince could have..."

However, the Imperial Concubine raised her hand to stop Cassandra.

"Let's be careful and keep what we think to ourselves for now. I already wrote to the Imperial Palace, but that snake Vrehan hasn't left his apartments there since we left. Apparently on the pretense of looking after his sister."

"He definitely has people to do it for him!" said Missandra. "Everyone knows the Imp... I mean, people like him never dirty their hands themselves."

Kareen smiled, but this was more of a scary smile than a heartfelt smile, and nodded.

"That's right, dear. Just like me, he probably has people working for him. Vrehan is much smarter than Phetra. She's the type who will dirty her own hands, if she's pushed over the limit. However, Vrehan learned a lot from his snake mother. He loves to scheme and get rid of people who annoy him without leaving traces. You can never, ever be alone with him or his people. I don't believe he'd stay locked up under the Emperor's nose only for his sister's sake, either. This sounds too much like some trick he'd be pulling off."

"Can't we do anything?" asked Cassandra.

"I have sent people to watch him, but he probably knows that too. In any case, Vrehan won't move until he's sure he can win, and I don't see how he could do that. No matter what, my son is the War God. He won't lose a war just because it started late."

Cassandra slowly nodded, but she didn't feel reassured. Kairen wasn't like Vrehan, someone who'd plot behind people's backs, and use underhanded methods. She tried to think of several scenarios. Somehow, she felt it was unlikely her Prince would die in this war. What could Vrehan do? Send an assassin, or worse, find some way to poison him? Cassandra knew that Dragon

Tamers like Kairen were more resistant to poison, but no matter how strong his body was, there was only so much a man could withstand. Cassandra hated not being able to do anything for him.

She suddenly stood up, surprising both women in the room. Kareen sighed.

"We are not done with brunch, dear."

"I've had enough, Lady Kareen, thank you. Do you think you could have something delivered to the front, if I was to give it to you?"

"Of course, dear. What are you thinking about now?"

Cassandra took a deep breath. The idea had just popped up into her head.

"I'll prepare some first aid kits for the military."

"First aid kits? For the front? Those men in the Imperial Army aren't trained to do any medical procedures, dear."

"It's fine, they won't need training, just common sense. If I taught the men in the North Army Camp, I can have those men at the Eastern Front learn too, even without being there."

Missandra, smiling widely, and got up too, her excitement evident.

"I love that idea, Hinue! I'll help you!"

"Oh, you young ones are so full of energy," sighed Kareen. "Anyway, Cassandra, I assigned your servants to work for you before, didn't I? They have learned how to write and calculate already. Just have those girls come over and help you."

"Thank you, Lady Kareen. Can I entrust you with the transportation part?"

"Of course, dear. As if this old lady would sit on her arse while my children fight here and there!"

Cassandra smiled. At times like this, Kareen would be even nicer than usual, and hint at treating her and Missandra as her own daughters. The two sisters then left the garden they were eating in, though Dahlia packed up some more food for Cassandra to snack on later, and went to the little room next to Cassandra's garden, which had pretty much become her office. Behind her, Missandra was excited.

"Do you already know what we will do?"

"We need to list all kinds of injuries, diseases, and other health issues the soldiers in the front could face, how often, and find a way to resolve and treat any of them in a short amount of time."

"Alright," said Missandra, grabbing what she needed to write down. "We can start by listing all of the most common diseases in that part of the Empire, common infections, and also some basic injury treatments they should use. Should we write some sort of instructions down to put in those kits?"

"It's a battlefield, Missandra, they don't have time to read, and it may be that some of the soldiers don't even know how to read. So we need to make it as simple as possible."

"We can make drawings or use colors. When I worked in brothels, some of the girls weren't literate, but they knew which medicine to take based on their stamping or colors."

"Right, we can use that. Do you still remember them? We need to think about how we can pack them in light, easily transportable ways."

Just like that, both women started working together. Once they were done planning and compiling information, they brought their project to Kareen, who gave her own opinion on it, and called in some of her personal soldiers, military as well, for them to give their input.

Within a week, Cassandra, Missandra, and several more people started working hard on this. Kareen had more than enough money to support their project and ship it to the front in record time. Not only did the young concubine have her hands full with this project, but the whole of the Diamond City became aware of the efforts made at the Diamond Palace, and offered to contribute to show their support to the soldiers in their own ways. An unprecedented event in the Dragon Empire.

It took a couple more weeks for everything to be ready and the first samples to be sent to the frontline. Eventually, Cassandra and Missandra had come up with little boxes in two sizes: one that could fit in a pocket and be carried by any soldier, and a bigger one, for the ones who could store it in their horses' satchels or inside a chariot. Those medical boxes included medicines, to treat the most common issues a soldier could encounter on the battlefield, from fevers to large injuries, with very little explanation.

According to the Captain of Kareen's guards, even the dumbest soldier could use it with confidence. The girls had come up with a compartment system and little images engraved in it, so the soldiers could find what they needed in one glance, even if they opened that box for the first time. The longest part had been to find out how to make everything in a tiny size, but Missandra was the one who found a way to make all the medicine into small and colored pills that wouldn't be crumbled by any rough movements. Cassandra had to come up with the improved medicine, compared to the Empire's old ones, and Missandra took care of finding out how to fit them inside. They also included some bandages and little bottles of alcohol to disinfect, making sure the smell was not the kind that would make the men want to drink it.

The Imperial Concubine Kareen was most helpful in gathering the resources for all that. She spared no expenses to have all the bandages, medicines, or plants Cassandra needed be brought to the Diamond Palace. Even paying for the metal the boxes were shaped in, and every worker who participated in their large-scale production.

Soon enough, news came from the Imperial Palace that the Emperor knew of their project and would shoulder all the costs, which made Kareen laugh. She didn't dismiss the chests of gold bars that arrived in her garden the next morning, though, and even sent a personal letter to thank the Emperor.

Cassandra could easily picture the old man jumping around upon receiving a letter from the usually cold concubine.

Even after everything was finalized, they didn't stop producing more. The first feedback from the front was very positive, but Cassandra read every letter very carefully to see where and how they could improve the kits. She realized they could even send bigger containers, and the army accountants could spread the contents depending on the situation. However, Missandra, Dahlia, and Kareen all stopped her from working on that new project. Cassandra's pregnancy was starting to make it too difficult for her to keep working like she was.

Hence, Cassandra was almost locked away from the next steps of the boxes' preparations and found herself bored again. While Missandra worked hard in her stead, the sweet Dahlia stayed with her, or more exactly, watched her. Cassandra couldn't complain, however. Her belly was big and hindering her in many ways. She felt tired no matter how long she slept, and her back was aching constantly. Kareen gave her some hot balm to calm her pain, but even if Dahlia massaged her, it would only numb the pain for a short while.

The only thing Cassandra was still authorized to do was taking care of her garden, and keeping her correspondence with her friends from the North. All of them answered her quite fast, and she was happy to get some news from Nebora and the girls, and from the camp. Evin was surprisingly diligent in telling her everything that was going on there, including how the Red Room had evolved. They now had a fully dedicated team taking care of it and applying all the instructions she had left in the letter. He would even include some more questions from them, compiling any issue they encountered for Cassandra to take care of from where she was.

Orwen was now a full-time blacksmith and quite busy, but he never missed a chance to tell Cassandra about whatever happened on his side of the camp. The men there still called her the Lady of the Mountain, as if she had been some royalty by herself, instead of just the Third Prince's Concubine. He even let her know about how Shareen's command had changed the camp, and how the young Anour was doing under his older sister's harsh training. It looked like the youngest Prince wasn't particularly cut out for the military.

However, no matter how fast they all tried to send their replies to her, it would take ten to twelve days for the letters to be delivered, and that was a long time for Cassandra to wait. She hadn't realized how the dragon flights had modified her perception of distances, but now, it was cruelly showing.

"Lady Kareen, you called for me?" asked Cassandra one morning.

For once, the Imperial Concubine wasn't interested in her brunch. Instead, she was walking in circles in the room, looking very disturbed. That wasn't like her at all, and Cassandra immediately knew something was wrong. Missandra arrived behind her sister, looking as confused as she was. On the side, a soldier was waiting, his head lowered, probably one of her spies. Finally, Kareen sighed.

"There is some bad news from the Imperial Palace. Prince Sephir died."

"What?" exclaimed Cassandra, astonished. "What happened?"

"Nothing is certain at the moment, the Emperor has closed down the Imperial Palace for an investigation."

"That doesn't sound like something they'd do for a natural death," whispered Missandra.

"No, it isn't. Either the Emperor suspects Sephir was murdered, or he wants to be sure he wasn't. Either way, the Emperor will get to the root of it. I have a bad feeling about this."

"Do you think he could really have been...?" asked Cassandra.

Kareen hesitated a second, looking lost deep in her thoughts. She shrugged.

"The timing is really off. Only two Princes are in the Capital at the moment, two are at the front, and the fifth went back to his own Palace days before that. There is no way Opheus has anything to do with it, that little idiot doesn't give a damn about becoming the Emperor. The main suspects would be Vrehan, someone close to him, or one of the other concubines."

"You really think one of the Imperial Concubines could be behind his death?"

"I am not too sure. They might have thought it was a good time to get rid of him, with Kairen, Shareen, and Anour gone. Sephir doesn't have many allies inside the Imperial Palace. Even Opheus' mother could have acted without her son's knowledge, but those are all assumptions. I think Vrehan is preparing something."

She turned to the soldier who was waiting to the side.

"I want another report as soon as possible about this investigation. And don't lose Vrehan or his sister for one second!"

"Yes, Your Highness."

The soldier rushed outside. Cassandra already knew Kareen had an impressive network of spies, but she truly had no idea how it worked, and she wasn't sure she wanted to know either. Kareen had probably dirtied her hands several times to protect herself and her children, and if she didn't talk about it with Cassandra, it meant she had no intention to.

"Anyway," sighed the Imperial Concubine. "We will know more about this soon. The Imperial Palace will have to make an official statement. This is truly too sad. Sephir wouldn't have become an Emperor, but he was a smart and gentle boy. His mother would have been... Oh, poor Saphia."

"You knew his mother personally?" asked Cassandra.

"She and I got pregnant around the same time, and we both lost children. She was gentler than me, and way too nice. She died in childbirth, sadly."

Cassandra immediately thought about her own baby. She couldn't imagine her child growing up without her around. She had seen it many times, though. The streets of the Capital were filled with orphan children, too young to fend for themselves, resorting to beggary or slavery to survive. Cassandra was well aware that even if no one attempted to kill her, she could die from childbirth, or natural causes. She only hoped that if anything happened, Kairen and his family

428

would take care of her son.

"Have you heard anything from the concubines, Hinue?" asked Missandra. "Didn't you exchange letters with them lately?"

Cassandra nodded.

"The last letter I received was already two weeks ago, but the concubines were saying Prince Sephir was well. My remedies were helping with his Dust Disease, there was nothing alarming about his current state. Maybe something happened since, or he had a bad flare up."

"Or maybe someone pulled some dirty strings," said Kareen. "Anyway, there is no use thinking too much about it, it's all happening in the Capital for now. Let's see in the upcoming weeks what becomes of it. However, be careful, dear. My spy also told me Phetra was getting back on her feet, and able to walk already."

"What! Already?" exclaimed Missandra, shocked.

"She is of dragon blood, just like Shareen. It's not that surprising that she can heal fast. It would have been more of a fuss for Kairen to throw her out the window if she'd died!"

Cassandra didn't know if she should be happy or sad about this. She certainly didn't like the idea of Phetra getting back to her old self. The Princess was definitely waiting to pay them back for what Kairen had done to her. She may be healed, but this kind of pain wouldn't go away so easily.

The young concubine sighed, and after breakfast was promptly eaten, she went back to her room. She needed to be alone for a while, and write to her Prince. She had no idea if Kairen received her letters at the front. She hadn't gotten any answer from all the letters she had sent, but she was hoping he was only too busy to answer. No matter if the Prince received them or not, those letters had become her personal therapy. Writing to Kairen every day, to let him know about what she had done that day, how she felt, how their baby and the dragon egg were growing, about her project of the medicinal box, they all made her feel so much better. It was her only getaway from the Diamond Palace. Anytime Cassandra tried to imagine what her Prince could be doing at that moment, she imagined him on a throne, like the one in his tent in the North Camp, talking military strategies with some old General. She could only pray that he was doing fine, safe, and unharmed, and winning this battle bit by bit.

The news received by Lady Kareen was all leaning that way, too. The Eastern Army was slowly losing ground to the War God's men, and his fierce dragon. Cassandra even heard about it when she'd go to the markets in the Diamond City. The locals all knew who she was and admired her a lot. Cassandra never went alone, and was always in a pink dress, but the merchants liked her very much. They were impressed to see a young concubine so graceful, gentle, and nice to the ordinary people, and would give her some extras at any given chance. Somehow, they had heard about her doings in the North Army Camp, too, and her Lady of the Mountain nickname was now used here as well.

Just like that, Cassandra was building her own reputation around the

Diamond City and she was told some rumors of how the war was going. Some merchants would congratulate her when it was known that the War God had freed another City. Some of the women would tell her to take care of herself and her baby, for when her beloved would come back. Truth was, under Kareen's impulse, the baby's room was already finished and full. The Imperial Concubine was eager for her first grandchild to be born and was overdoing it a bit, in Cassandra's opinion.First, the nursery was way too big, and full of toys for both the baby and the young dragon. It was almost ridiculous. Second, there were no less than three maids already hired to take care of her son, no matter how many times Cassandra argued that she wanted to take care of her son by herself, with maybe Dahlia's help from time to time.

However, as the weeks passed, Cassandra was slowly getting used to the idea that Kairen wouldn't be able to keep his promise. The war would still be raging when her baby would come into this world.

Chapter 27

Cassandra realized something was wrong a few days later, when, at dinner time, Lady Kareen barely ate anything, and looked extremely preoccupied. When she asked about it, the Imperial Concubine sighed.

"I don't like this. I haven't heard from the spy I sent to the Capital yet. He was supposed to be back last night, and he is usually never late. I sent another one to investigate, but I'm afraid Vrehan took this opportunity to purge his surroundings. I haven't received any non-official news from the Imperial Palace in a while, and I don't like it. I don't like it at all."

Missandra and Cassandra exchanged glances, worried. For Kareen to be this upset was not reassuring at all. What if something bad had happened in the Imperial Palace? No matter how she thought about it, Cassandra knew the worst that could possibly happen was the Emperor's death. If the Dragon Emperor passed without having named an official heir yet, the eldest son would have to take over until the ministers elected the right heir. However, no one was blind. With Prince Sephir dead, Vrehan was the next in line, and while Kairen was away, he would definitely secure his position on the Golden Throne before his younger brothers could react. Cassandra was terrified just to think about this possibility.

"Don't worry," said Lady Kareen. "I will go there myself if necessary, but I won't stay still! I already sent news of this to Shareen and Anour, just in case. Kairen is stuck on the battlefront at the moment, but even so, Vrehan won't be stupid enough to try and act if Shareen is around."

"Aren't you afraid he'll try to harm her?"

"He can try! My daughter is not so weak that she would submit to that snake!"

Cassandra sighed. She didn't believe Vrehan would have acted if he wasn't sure of himself. What was the point of killing Sephir now? Was it because Kairen was away? This felt terribly wrong. Things were not in the best state right now, and even at the Diamond Palace, they weren't fully safe. Cassandra put a hand on her belly. She really didn't need any additional stress right now. She took a deep breath. Anyway, the Second Prince wouldn't be able to do much as long as the Emperor was alive and well. Prince Sephir's death was truly sad, but for now, they had yet to confirm the cause. Perhaps they would hear it was a natural cause soon, and Kareen's spy would return with a good explanation.

Despite Kareen doing her best to act normal and not show how uneasy she was, Cassandra knew this was only to keep them from worrying too much. For Lady Kareen to be worried meant something was really wrong, and Cassandra felt it too. She tried to convince herself that there was nothing more she could do, as she walked to the little garden where, as always, the dragon egg was steadily growing.

Her project with the medical boxes was going well too. Cassandra could just oversee it and let Missandra take care of managing the flow of supplies sent, their people, and the stocks coming in and out. There really wasn't much to do for her, aside from taking it easy for the last weeks of her pregnancy and taking care of her plants. Thankfully, the baby was doing well. Kareen had hired a midwife from the City to take care of Cassandra, and be ready for when the day would come, but once again, the young concubine didn't like all the extra attention. She could feel her son, very well, alive and kicking. It was probably what rejoiced her the most these days. Feeling her baby move. Every time he did, Cassandra took a minute to caress her belly. Sometimes, she would even talk to him. So much so that even Kareen, Missandra, and Dahlia had started talking about the baby as if he was here too.

Shareen's answer arrived a few days later in the form of a letter, around dinner. A servant brought it to Kareen, who put her cup down and opened it right away, reading the content quickly.

"Apparently, Shareen is busy in the North, too. The Barbarians heard of the Eastern Republic attacking and thought this would be an opportunity for them. Hpmf! Anyway, Shareen says she will have settled this soon and will arrive here in ten days. Oh, that letter is from four days ago, so less than a week now. Fine!"

Cassandra felt a bit better after hearing this. Even if it wasn't Kairen, Shareen's presence would definitely make her feel more secure. These days, she couldn't shake off the feeling that something bad was going to happen. However, now it would only be a matter of waiting a few more days and...

"My Lady!"

One of Kareen's servants rushed into the garden, out of breath. He almost fell on his knees at her feet, sweating and looking panicked.

"What is it?" asked Kareen, unhappy.

"The... The... His Highness the Second Prince just arrived at the Diamond Palace! He is here to arrest the Lady of the Mountain."

Next to Cassandra, Missandra jumped on her feet like a cat, all her senses alert. All the servants around too exchanged glances, and a couple of them ran inside to go and check.

"What is this nonsense?!" roared Kareen, slamming her cup on the table and getting up too.

"Th... They say she is an accomplice in the First Prince's murder! I... I don't have the details yet, but Madam, the Second Prince will really be here any second!"

"Cassandra, let's go," said Missandra, grabbing her sister's hand.

"But..."

"No, the young one is right, dear," said Kareen, gently pushing her towards the end of the garden. "Follow me!"

While the servants hurried to take the remains of their dinner out of sight, Kareen led the two girls further into the garden, rushing between the trees towards one side. They were almost running. Cassandra's heart was thumping like crazy. What would she be arrested for! An accomplice to Prince Sephir's murder? What had taken place at the Palace for this to happen?

The Imperial Concubine suddenly stopped in front of one of the walls surrounding the garden they were in and pushed some of the ivy covering it like a large curtain. To their surprise, it revealed a long and wide crack in the stonewall. It was tight, but definitely an entrance wide enough for them to sneak into. Missandra and Cassandra exchanged a glance, shocked. They had walked by that wall a thousand times but had never noticed this secret opening! Kareen pushed Missandra in, and they helped Cassandra get inside right behind her.

"Stay hidden here for now," whispered the Imperial Concubine. "This is a secret passage only a handful of my servants know of. If things go wrong, start leaving through there immediately! This will lead to a secret room, I had everything prepared for you there, just in case. This place leads to the back garden. You can..."

Before she could finish that sentence, a ruckus was heard from behind her, and Kareen left quickly to see what was going on, while the two sisters retreated a bit. Missandra grabbed her older sister's shaking hand. For a few seconds, everything was silent in the Palace. Then, soldiers barged into the garden, surrounding the Imperial Concubine. Cassandra retreated further as she could hear men stepping close to their hideout, but she could barely see what was going on behind the thick curtain of ivy. However, the two of them were able to hear very well when Kareen started yelling furiously.

"What is this?! How dare you barge into my Palace!"

"Good evening, Imperial Concubine," replied a cold voice.

Cassandra shivered and retreated another step. That was definitely Vrehan's voice. Next to her, Missandra was livid, her hand covering her mouth. Everything was so calm just a few minutes ago, but now they were kept hidden while the Second Prince had taken control over the Palace!

"We are looking for a criminal, and I have the Emperor's permission to do anything in my power to bring her to the Imperial Palace...safe and unharmed."

From his voice, Cassandra wouldn't even have trusted him for a second. How could the Emperor trust Vrehan with that task?! She knew that, despite the Emperor's best intentions, Vrehan would have no second thoughts in killing her and the baby she was carrying at the first opportunity he'd get, and any witnesses along with her. She could easily imagine him reporting some unfortunate incident to the Emperor. There was no way Cassandra would ever give that man any chance to touch her, no way.

"What does it have to do with me? This is my Diamond Palace! How dare you come and chase some criminal here! On what grounds?!"

Cassandra realized Lady Kareen was trying to play dumb on purpose, to get more information on what was really going on. It may win them some time, too. Behind her, Missandra was gently pulling on her hand, trying to bring Cassandra away from the opening, but she wanted to listen to what was going on.

"The said criminal is none other than Kairen's favorite, Imperial Concubine. I know she is here. Your son wouldn't entrust his woman to anyone else!"

"Oh? And what did she do for you to arrest her?"

"She is suspected of taking part in the First Prince's tragic death. One of his concubines poisoned him with some plants that the slave gave her!"

Cassandra was astonished. The recipes she gave the concubines? Is that what Vrehan was chasing her for? Even if one of the concubines had meddled with the content of the teas, she had nothing to do with it! This was obviously his scheme to capture her! Did he poison Sephir's drink himself? What had happened to his concubines? Were they to be interrogated, too?

"How ridiculous! What would Cassandra poison Prince Sephir for?"

"Well, anyone can be greedy at some point. Who knows what a woman..."

"How dare you speak about greed! If anyone has that kind of dirt in their mind, it would be anyone but my son or his concubine! You, of all people, are the last one who can accuse others of that!"

"Watch your words, Kareen! I am not..."

"It's Imperial Concubine Kareen to you, little runt! Or do you think you can insult the Imperial Dragon's Favorite to her face? Huh?"

A tense silence reigned after her words, but Cassandra could feel Vrehan's anger from here. Lady Kareen's nerves were really made of steel, to confront him like that. Cassandra was fearful for her, but she was well aware the Imperial Concubine would never submit to Vrehan, or do anything other than protect her children.

"Enough, bring that woman here!" yelled Vrehan.

"Have you heard anything about a pregnant woman being here, Vrehan? Did you question the people? Investigate? She isn't here. Kairen took her to the Onyx Castle!"

Cassandra could barely breathe. What if Vrehan's soldiers really interrogated the people of the Diamond City? Would they say the Lady of the Mountain was indeed here? Or had they tried already? She knew the local folks liked her very much, but would they lie to an Imperial Prince?

"You're lying!" suddenly yelled a feminine voice. "I already know you wanted that slut to stay with you until she gave birth, their dragon egg is here!"

Cassandra's heart dropped. Phetra was here too? That woman was already able to travel? Cassandra suddenly froze at the mention of the dragon egg! They could never leave this Palace with it if they had to flee this place!

"Do you see a concubine here, other than me? How dare you bother this old woman without any proof!"

"I will have my proof once I find this damn woman! I know you're hiding her here, in this Palace!"

"Oh? Fine, you can look then. The sooner you find yourself empty-handed, the sooner you leave me alone, you arrogant little boy!"

As soon as the soldiers started running and searching through the whole Diamond Palace, Missandra pulled Cassandra's hand towards the rear of that secret passageway. Even for their small frames, it was hard to go through the whole passage. They had to be as silent as possible to not be noticed by the men searching for them. Cassandra had never been so scared before, but it became even worse when they heard a dragon's screech. Both sisters froze, realizing the situation was more dire than what they had thought.

Missandra gasped, and turned to her.

"That wasn't the black one," she whispered.

"No," whispered Cassandra, shaking her head. "That was... Vrehan's Dragon."

The two girls were absolutely terrified. That crazy Red Dragon was looking for them.

Suddenly, they heard the stones above their heads making an awful noise, and for a second, they froze, fearing that the walls around them were going to collapse on top of them. This would be a horrible way to die, buried alive under meters of rocks! Missandra shivered, but she pulled Cassandra's hand again, to take her out of there. If this dragon was able to smell them or hear them, they had to get out of this secret passage as soon as possible!

Both sisters kept walking, slowly and silently, until it turned completely dark. Missandra, in front, had a better vision, but she had to walk very slowly. Both arms extended in front of her, to make sure they weren't hitting something. She was scared Cassandra would bump into something with her big belly, but thankfully, she soon found the end of the passage. It seemed closed, in front of them, but she recognized a fabric under her fingers, instead of rocks. They were behind some sort of curtain. Missandra waited for a second, hesitating. What if soldiers were already in the room, searching? She took a deep breath and waited a second. With her eyes blinded by the darkness, she could easily focus on her hearing.

After a full minute, she was sure there was no one on the other side. She very carefully pushed the curtain aside and glanced behind it. Then, when she was sure this place was safe, she pulled Cassandra in. This place wasn't exactly a room, more like a large wardrobe, or a tiny storage room. There were dozens of clothes and large fabrics hung here and there, like the one they had come from behind. Missandra's first instinct was to run to the door, making sure it was locked. It was, but she could hear people running on the other side. Was the door hidden on the other side? It seemed like no one was stopping to check it.

"Missandra!" whispered Cassandra.

The older sister had just found a big bag with some clothes, dried food, and a lot of money. This was definitely meant for their escape. Missandra nodded, and walked up to her, away from the door, but they had another issue.

"How are we supposed to leave?" she whispered as well. "They'll catch us the minute we go out of that door! Shall we stay here?"

"There has to be another exit."

Both sisters started checking the whole room, until finally they found it. This one was actually on the floor, hidden under several piles of heavy rugs. Missandra and Cassandra quickly worked together to clear the way to their escape route, both keeping an ear out for what was happening on the other side. They could hear the dragon's growls every now and then, but it seemed further away from their current position. Cassandra wasn't even able to think, at the moment. She just focused on getting to that exit, and silently prayed for Lady Kareen to be alright.

Finally, they cleared the path, but just as they were about to get in, someone slammed on the door.

"Here! There is some secret entrance!"

Cassandra froze. They were just about to get out! Within a split second, she made her decision. She threw the bag at Missandra and pushed her sister towards the opening.

"What? Cassandra!"

"We don't have time to both leave! Take the bag and meet me outside the Palace!"

"But..."

"Missandra, I don't have enough time to get in, and if I do and they forcefully pull me out of there, I'm afraid they'll hurt me and the baby. Don't worry about me, go. You're tiny enough, you can escape and I'll close it behind you."

"Hinue!"

"I promise I'll find a way to leave, but if they catch you, Vrehan can kill you on the spot. He can't kill me inside the Diamond Palace, there are too many witnesses. Linue, I promise I'll find a way to get out of here. Now, go!"

Missandra hesitated, but another violent slam resonated from the door, and no matter what, it was now obviously too late for Cassandra. She bit her lower lip and squeezed through the little opening. As soon as she was in, Cassandra pulled the rugs next to her, making a pile collapse to hide it. If they found her here, with the first entrance exposed, they wouldn't think of looking for someone else through a second exit. She took a deep breath, and retreated to the back of the room, waiting for the door to be broken open.

It only took a few more seconds, then soldiers barged in, yelling and grabbing her forcefully.

"Who were you talking to?"

"Let me go! I was praying, now let me go!"

"Your Highness! We found the criminal!"

Cassandra kept thinking of a way to free herself without struggling too much and risking getting hurt. However, both men were obviously stronger than her, and she couldn't find a solution before Vrehan arrived with his sister a minute later. Lady Kareen was there, too, and she became livid when their eyes met.

"Let go! How dare you brutalize a pregnant woman!" she roared.

"Who cares," hissed Phetra. "She's a criminal!"

"She is a suspect, you damn bitch, and she carries a Dragon Prince, too!" yelled Kareen.

Even if her shouts only angered Phetra more, the Imperial Concubine's stance was enough to terrorize the two guards holding Cassandra, as they realized she was right. Despite their Master being right there, they both eased their grip on her arms, their face a shade paler than before.

Meanwhile, Cassandra was trying to assess the situation as quickly as possible, despite being scared. Because the corridor they were in was rather narrow, there were only a dozen guards, plus Vrehan, Phetra, and Kareen. No large dragon could squeeze in there, and Srai was probably hiding somewhere. Cassandra was not a fighter, but she was sure of one thing: if she left the Diamond Palace with the Second Prince, she wouldn't be able to survive. No matter what, she had to find a way to escape before they brought her out of the Palace and Kareen's protection.

"I wonder why a suspect was hiding," hissed Vrehan.

"Who said I was hiding, Your Highness? This is a storage room, I had come to look for some fabric," replied Cassandra.

She wasn't used to lying through her teeth, but those few weeks with Kareen had taught her a couple of things. The Prince was obviously glaring at her round belly, and Cassandra really felt uncomfortable under his murderous stare.

"You damn, little witch," said Phetra.

"You look like you're doing well, Your Highness," retorted Cassandra.

That was an obvious lie this time. Phetra still had bandages all over, and some large scars on her body. She had obviously been in a lot of pain, but if she angered her, Cassandra was hoping to win some more time, or create an opportunity that would allow her to escape.

However, she didn't expect what happened next. Phetra stepped forward, with a little smile.

"Oh, you think so?"

Then, she slapped Cassandra. The slap wasn't very strong, but if she hadn't been held by the two men, she might have fallen down. Phetra was smiling wide, but behind her, Kareen went mad.

"You crazy little bitch! How dare you injure Cassandra, the War God's Favorite! In my Palace!"

"Injure her? This was merely a little slap!"

With that, Phetra slapped Cassandra a second time before Kareen could react, on the other cheek this time. Cassandra felt the pain resonate from her cheek through her whole body. Even her baby reacted, kicking her stomach. A strange worry crossed her mind. Was her baby feeling her pain? Was he okay? She could handle a few slaps from Phetra, but if anything happened to her baby!

"Phetra, enough! Stop it!" yelled Kareen.

"What? Does it hurt? I think she needs another one!"

However, to her surprise, someone pushed her away from Cassandra, taking the slap a second later. The Princess was so surprised that she stepped back, looking at who she had slapped this time.

"Dahlia!" exclaimed Cassandra.

Her handmaiden was standing in front of her, in a protective stance. Cassandra had no idea where she had come from, but the young maid was obviously resolved in protecting her at any cost.

"Please don't touch her!" she claimed, despite shivering in fear.

However, Phetra was too furious to listen to the young servant at the moment. She glared at her.

"You want to protect her, you little rat? You think you can oppose me?"

A red flash appeared in front of Cassandra's eyes. She didn't understand what had happened. Dahlia collapsed at her feet, her eyes opened wide in surprise, her throat sliced wide open. Cassandra's ears went deaf, and she started feeling numb. She wanted to scream, but no sound came out of her mouth. She couldn't speak, only watch the girl dying at her feet. Somehow, the rational part of her brain knew that this was not an injury anyone could heal from. It was cut wide open, and bleeding way too much, way too fast. The shock got her completely numb, her blood leaving her face, and she didn't even react to what happened next.

It wasn't until Phetra screamed that she looked up. Vrehan had brutally grasped his sister's throat, throwing her to the ground, and it was her scream of pain that made Cassandra come back to her senses.

"I said not to kill anyone yet! Are you so stupid that you can't understand such orders?!" he yelled.

His brutal yelling surprised Cassandra, and she looked their way, still stunned, barely understanding what was going on around her now. Then, Vrehan brutally kicked his sister, who was already on the ground. The incredibly violent situation gave Cassandra another shock, waking her from her slumber. She had never seen Vrehan being violent before, but he kicked his sister's injured leg twice, making her scream in pain.

"Brother, stop it!" she screamed, tears running down her face, terrorized. "Stop it, please! You can't kill me, Brother. I know your secret! You can't kill me!"

"I will kill you if you disobey me again, you useless bitch!"

Cassandra felt like she was dreaming. The two siblings she had always seen as perfect accomplices were fighting, and Phetra was crying on the ground, next to Dahlia's dead body. This was so unreal. This had to be a nightmare, one she was going to wake up from.

This only lasted a minute, however. Vrehan stopped kicking his sister, out of breath and glared at her one last time before taking a deep breath, returning to his normal stance. Cassandra had never seen a scarier attitude than that. He was abusing his own sister just a few seconds ago, but now, he was turning to her, looking perfectly calm and composed. This man was worse than a monster.

"Now, enough of you women, fighting. You're coming with me," he hissed at her.

After that scene, there was no way Cassandra was going with him. She was terrorized, in shock, but her survival instinct was screaming in her head telling her not to go with that man, no matter what happened. She couldn't get the vision of Dahlia's death out of her mind, but now, her eyes were focused on Vrehan's hand, which was coming close to grab her. Cassandra retreated, even pulling the two soldiers who hadn't expected her to resist, with her.

"Don't touch me," she said, with a cold voice.

Her emerald eyes had never been so determined, so defiant. Even the Prince was shocked for a second, but soon enough, Vrehan frowned.

"Don't you dare oppose me, you damn witch."

He tried to extend his arm to grab her again, but just as he reached out, a white shadow brutally jumped from behind Cassandra. It took a quick leap onto her shoulder and pounced on the Prince's arm. Vrehan screamed and stumbled back as horrifying sounds resonated in the room. Blood splattered, the flesh brutally ripped open, and as he pulled back, his hand was covered in blood, some fingers missing or chunks ripped off. Cassandra looked down, but whatever it was had just jumped in a flash onto one of the soldiers holding her, attacking him violently. The small creature was biting the man, and growling furiously. The other soldier let go of her arm, terrified, while Cassandra looked down at it, speechless.

When the man stopped moving, the little dragon turned its head towards Cassandra. Its two big emerald eyes stared at her for a second, and, without warning, it jumped towards her with a cute little squeak. Cassandra barely had time to open her arms and receive it. It was so heavy! However, she was more stunned by the gorgeous, adorable, silver-scaled creature in her arms, rubbing its little head against her chest. The little silver dragon was growling softly, just like Krai would do whenever she was scratching its snout.

"Oh, by the Lord... Don't tell me you're..."

"The Baby Dragon," whispered Lady Kareen, on the verge of tears. "He hatched already! To protect his mother!"

Cassandra was rendered speechless.

Her baby dragon was in her arms! Now! When had it even hatched? Was it because of the slaps earlier? Or, because her baby had felt her fear? She kept staring at the adorable creature in her arms, growling softly and rubbing its head against her chest innocently. In front of them, Vrehan was holding his head, covered in blood, looking at the newborn dragon with a horrified expression.

"No, no! Capture her! Now!"

"Cassandra, go!" yelled Kareen.

The Imperial Concubine's voice was what Cassandra needed to wake up from her inner turmoil of emotions. There were so many things going on, but for now, she stuck to the one thing she had to focus on, escaping Vrehan's grasp, no matter what. She turned around and started running, despite her heavy belly. The Baby Dragon jumped out of her arms to follow her, jumping around, almost looking excited. Cassandra heard Vrehan yell orders somewhere behind her, but she didn't listen. All she needed was a way to leave the Diamond Palace and hide. She had to find Missandra and escape, escape at all costs. Her heart was bleeding for poor Dahlia, but she couldn't stop to mourn her friend now. She trusted Lady Kareen to take care of her.

Moreover, she had other problems now. She could hear the soldiers running after her, and Vrehan's voice still shouting orders. The birth of the baby dragon had apparently made the Second Prince absolutely furious. No wonder. He had been on the verge of killing Kairen's pregnant concubine, but now, she was about to escape and have this baby! That sole thought motivated Cassandra more than anything. The Baby Dragon's birth wasn't a coincidence, her baby was going to come out soon, and she would do anything to protect her child. However, she was still heavily pregnant, and unable to run fast enough to escape anyone. She needed a way out, quickly. She was already deep inside the Palace, where could she escape to now? Cassandra found the solution after recognizing one of the corridors. It was a bit of a crazy idea, but it was the only way out she knew of, and the only way that neither Vrehan nor his soldiers would be crazy enough to follow her.

Just as she recognized the door she was looking for, one of the soldiers grabbed her. Not for long, though. The baby dragon furiously jumped on the man, attacking him ferociously. Cassandra heard the man's screams, but she couldn't look, as she was busy opening the doors. The large room finally appeared in front of her, with her way out.

She had returned to the infinity pool room. The wide pool in front of her, Cassandra walked in quickly. She heard the man hurrying behind her when the water was already up to her waist.

"Baby! Come!"

The Baby Dragon immediately dived in the water, not looking afraid at all, and disappeared under the surface somewhere around her. Cassandra didn't have time to check where it had gone to. The men were starting to follow her into the pool, with their swords, and Vrehan yelling at the entrance of the room.

"Catch her! If you let that crazy bitch die here or escape, I'll kill you!"

Cassandra glared at him, and kept walking and swimming inside the water. Once in her element, she had a big advantage in speed over the soldiers chasing her. None of those men were good swimmers, and with their heavy armors, each step was a struggle. For Cassandra, however, she was faster than on the ground.

"Don't you dare!" yelled Vrehan.

Oh, yes, she would dare to. Cassandra was almost at the wall's end, at the great opening towards the waterfall, when she heard a loud growl. She retreated just in time, as the red dragon's head appeared. Thankfully, she had seen how far Krai was able to reach inside and had evaluated right. The Red Dragon was smaller than the black one, but it encountered the same problem. Only its head could fit in. That saved Cassandra's life.

However, with Vrehan behind her, and his dragon guarding the exit and the waterfall, she was trapped inside the water, with the soldiers closing in on her. Cassandra hesitated. Should she dive in? Krai couldn't find her in the water, but if that dragon decided to attack blindly, her chances to go unnoticed were not that high. She had to make a decision, and quickly. She knew she couldn't go back anyway. She had to try.

"Don't you dare! You..."

Cassandra dove beneath the water before hearing Vrehan's curse. Like her people, she had the peculiar ability to see underwater and keep her eyes open without trouble. Hence, as soon as she dived in, she saw how deep she could go, and where the large claws of the red dragon were resting. However, as she had predicted, he started moving as soon as she disappeared. She could see his fangs and claws attacking blindly, making waves underwater. Cassandra tried to stay away for a while, but she couldn't stay underwater for too long, and her pursuers were still coming.

To her surprise, the baby dragon suddenly appeared next to her. It tilted its head, and she realized, just like her, it had no problem seeing or swimming underwater! Was it because of her? Did the silver dragon get some of her characteristics? Was that possible? Cassandra didn't have much time to wonder, though. While the baby dragon was comfortably swimming around, the bigger, older version was furiously looking for them. Cassandra took her little dagger out. They had to secure their way out, one way or another. If she could get the timing right ... Next to her, the silver baby dragon suddenly stopped swimming around, too, fixated on the red dragon's movements, agitating its butt like a cat about to jump.

That's when Cassandra decided to attack. Judging its position from those large paws, she waited for the next attack, and just when its maw appeared in the water next to her, she jumped with her blade to attack. She got the red dragon right in the eye, and on the other side, the baby dragon jumped too.

Both Vrehan and his dragon screeched in pain. She saw the Red Dragon panic, moving recklessly, and suddenly, one of its claws brutally scratched her arm. Cassandra didn't have time to scream in pain. Taking a deep breath, she dived right back in, and this time swam to the edge. She felt the border and jumped over.

This was the craziest thing she had ever done in her entire life. She felt the water rushing all around her, and for a second, she thought she was jumping to her death. She could literally smash herself on the soil or hit the surface brutally. However, as she arrived towards the end of her fall, she felt something pulling her dress, and her fall was slowed down. She couldn't see, but she heard the baby dragon's flapping wings, and they both dived into the river underneath a second later. Her fall hadn't been nearly as brutal as she had imagined, but it took her a second to find her way up. She broke the surface, and caught a new, deep breath of fresh air, swimming away from the waterfall.

Cassandra hadn't jumped into the unknown. She had visited Diamond City enough to know that the waterfall ended at a river, and that the river was large and big enough. Struggling a bit, she kept swimming, using the strength of the current to spare her strength a little. She had to get out of the water quickly, though. She could hear the dragon still screeching in pain, far above her head. It may have gone blind, but it still had its nose to find her.

After she felt like the river had taken her far enough, and she was out of strength, Cassandra swam to get out of the river. She was exhausted when she finally got on all four on the riverside. She heard the baby dragon jumping to her side, and sure enough, it walked up to her, rubbing its little head against her arm. That sensation made her smile. The Silver Dragon was so tiny, just a newborn, but it had just saved her life multiple times. She caressed its head. It was smaller than she had imagined, just the size of a big cat, plus its long tail. It was a bit leaner than Krai, and its wings were longer compared to its body size, too. Just as she was taking a minute to caress the baby dragon, and catch her breath, she felt a sharp pain between her ribs.

"Oh, God…" she whimpered.

She knew it would come soon, now that the baby dragon had hatched, but she didn't expect it that soon! Cassandra took a deep breath and got up. She still wasn't safe. She was on the outskirts of the Diamond City, but Vrehan would send for a search party soon enough, and she couldn't stay around. Moreover, she had to find Missandra. She had no idea where the secret passage had taken her younger sister! Cassandra tried to think of where Missandra would go. Surely, she wouldn't leave without her, but where could she wait for her?

The two sisters had gone to the Diamond City several times in those last weeks, they both knew this City well. Where could they meet up? As she started walking towards the City, out of strength, the rain started falling heavily. Cassandra was grateful. This would make her harder to find. However, she still had no idea where to go. Missandra had a few favorite shops inside the Diamond City, but there was no way Cassandra was going to find her in time if she had to search through all of them!

Cassandra kept walking until she reached the first houses, and hid against the walls, hoping the roofs could keep her safe from the rain. The Baby Dragon was following her closely, rubbing its back against her ankles so she could feel it being here from time to time.

However, Cassandra was out of strength. She was absolutely exhausted, devastated by Dahlia's death, and desperate to find Missandra. Yet, just when she thought she was going to pass out, she heard a door opening nearby.

"By the Great Dragon! It's really her!"

"What are you waiting for, go help her!"

A man ran to Cassandra's side, and before she could even react, she was taken inside a house. The Baby Dragon followed her from afar, growling at the humans, but not sure if it should attack or not. It watched Cassandra being taken inside a large room and sat on a bed by the man who had taken her inside.

Cassandra was having a hard time understanding what was going on. She was on the verge of collapsing.

"My... Sister... I need to find my sister," she whispered.

"Don't worry, Your Highness, we will look for her! Son, go spread the word!"

Cassandra heard a door open and close, and a young woman gently helped her lie down. She felt a wet towel on her forehead, and someone helped her take her dress off. She had no strength to resist while two women helped her change into some other clothes.

"Mother, she has a fever..."

"My baby..." said Cassandra.

"Don't worry, Your Highness," said one of the young women. "We will take good care of you, and we will find Lady Missandra, too. You're safe with us. Please just rest, you are safe here."

Cassandra nodded. She really was too weak to protest. So many things had happened, she just wanted to lie down. She could feel another contraction, which worried her. She had felt some in the past few days, but never as strong as this one. She knew it was a sign.

"My baby... I felt..."

"Did your water break? Mother! I think she's in labor..."

Cassandra felt someone sit at the end of the bed and examine her. The Baby Dragon jumped next to her, between her shoulder and her face, and growled a bit, as a warning.

"She still has time, she doesn't seem to be having too many contractions for now. You should rest, Your Highness. Try to sleep a little while we look for Lady Missandra. You'll wake up when the labor starts for real."

"Don't worry, Your Highness," repeated the woman next to her, gently caressing her wet hair.

"We will take care of you," said the other, covering her with a blanket.

Just like that, Cassandra couldn't resist anymore and fell asleep.

It was another sharp pain that woke Cassandra up. She frowned and opened her eyes, her hands going unconsciously to her belly. A part of her had to touch it, make sure her baby was still there. She was cold and afraid, but she could feel her belly. However, the first sensation that reassured her was the warm little body curled up against her cheek.

"Hinue! Are you awake?"

Missandra was next to her, holding her hand with a worried expression. Cassandra frowned, confused. It took her a few seconds to remember everything that had happened. She felt like she had slept too profoundly to reconnect with reality, as if she had just had a terrible nightmare, where dreams and reality merged.

However, reality was quick to catch her. She realized it hadn't been a nightmare, but the sad truth, when she saw the unfamiliar surroundings. They were in a common house, with a lot of people moving around. Cassandra, still lying down on some bed, turned her head. A little group was there. Women and men, several adults of all ages, all watching her with worried expressions. Missandra was quick to explain to her.

"Apparently, you arrived here about an hour ago, drenched.Those nice people found you and brought you here. They changed your clothes, too, and you fell asleep right away. You have a fever, but you are fine. We are safe here for now. I was hiding in the market, but all the inhabitants spread the word that you were looking for me, so I was able to come here a few minutes ago. How are you? Is that... the baby dragon is..."

Cassandra nodded, lifting her hand to caress the little one next to her. With Missandra's help, she sat up, still feeling tired. So she had slept only an hour? The baby dragon immediately walked to her side, rubbing its head against her hip. Cassandra caressed the young creature and stared at the people around them.

"You...I don't understand. I remember someone pulling me here."

An old woman nodded and stepped forward.

"We heard something was going on in the Diamond Palace, My Lady. We all know that the relationships are bad between the Diamond Lady and the Second Prince . So, when the word was spread that they had come to arrest the War God's Concubine, we knew something was wrong. We hoped the Diamond Lady could do something, but when my son spotted you, all alone on the City border...We immediately brought you here to hide you."

"The soldiers are searching for you...I mean for us," said Missandra. "That crazy Prince is furious you escaped. What happened?"

"The...waterfall. I escaped through the waterfall."

"You jumped from that height while pregnant? Are you crazy!"

"Missandra, we don't have time for that... ugh!"

Cassandra grimaced, holding her stomach. Her contractions were getting more intense. She took deep breaths, while the young woman brought her some warm tea.

"The baby dragon being here means you're going into labor?" asked Missandra, visibly worried. "Cassandra, the soldiers are searching for us everywhere. If they hear of a woman giving birth..."

Cassandra nodded. This was the worst possible situation. She had made it out of the Diamond Palace, but the Prince would do anything to find her. He was going to search every house in the Diamond City for sure. Cassandra turned to the old woman.

"Thank you for helping us, but we...we can't stay. If they find us here, you will be punished too."

The old woman shook her head.

"Your Highness, we know who we are saving here. You're the Lady of the Mountain! Do you know how many of our sons have gone to the war in the east? You have no idea how everyone felt here when we heard the Lady of the Mountain and the Diamond Lady were sending those survival kits to the front. Concubines caring about soldiers! We already knew our Diamond Lady was one very strong and brave woman, but to hear that the War God's Concubine was a healer, and doing what she could for our families?"

"My brother and my husband were summoned to go to war, Your Highness," added one of the young women behind her. "I'm fearing every day that they won't return, my Lady, but not being able to do anything was the worst! When we heard what you were doing from the Diamond Palace, everyone started working to send what we could to the front!"

"That's right," added another woman. "We prepared packages of food, and started cultivating the same medicinal herbs as you, Your Highness!"

Cassandra was astonished to hear all that. She had no idea so much was going on in the Diamond City recently. She had noticed that people were respecting her a lot when she would go out with Lady Kareen, but she thought that was because of her status as a concubine, not because of her actions. The old woman bowed politely.

"Your Highness, there is no one in this City who isn't ready to protect you. I can tell you that absolutely no one will talk if the soldiers interrogate them. We have our own dignity as the Diamond citizens. You have worked hard to help our sons that were sent to war, Your Highness. Now let us help you."

Cassandra was on the verge of tears, listening to the old woman's words. She couldn't believe it. She had never imagined that the Diamond City's people were aware of her actions, let alone that they respected her that much. Cassandra knew very well how feared the Imperial Family usually was, but now, she was surprised how she had even made such a strong impression on those people without having ever met them. Missandra, too, was blushing a bit and exchanged a look with her sister.

"We are very grateful that you are all willing to help us, but...This Prince is really, really crazy. Even if no one talks, he will search everywhere for my sister. If she is about to give birth here... Even with the rain, the baby's cries will be heard outside."

One of the middle-aged women stepped forward.

"Don't worry, Lady Missandra, we have already come up with a plan. This is our City, we know where we can hide the young concubine where they won't find her, or hear the baby."

"We will also distract them," added one of the young women. "The word is already spreading to keep the soldiers busy in another part of the City. Our neighbors went to signal a woman in a pink dress fleeing on the other side of the City."

"We actually did take your dress to make a decoy, Your Highness, I hope you don't mind."

Cassandra was speechless. She had slept for a mere hour, and so much had happened already? They had sent a decoy with her dress! How many risks were those people willing to take for her? She wanted to protest, but another contraction came, and she had to stay quiet for it to pass.

"Thank you so much," said Missandra in her stead. "So... Where do you think you can hide my sister?"

"We are almost done preparing!"

That's when Cassandra noticed. Aside from the four women, there were two teenagers, twin boys from what she could see, and one older man behind them, getting a whole bunch of things ready on the table. It looked like they were packing things in big bags. There was a bit of food, but mostly blankets and tissues, a couple of bowls and basins, even some baby clothes.

"I will accompany you with my youngest daughter and my niece, Your Highness," said the old woman. "I have been a midwife for forty years, I can help you give birth safely to the little Prince."

"We will take good care of you," promised one of the young women behind her.

"The young ones will just help us carry everything and go back to make sure no one follows us."

"Where are we going?" asked Missandra.

"You'll like it, young Lady," said the old woman with a wink.

Missandra and Cassandra exchanged a look, but after that, there wasn't much time left to wonder. In a few more minutes, the five women and the young twins were ready to leave. Cassandra realized how careful they were. First, in a short time span, there were no less than five young people, from children to teenagers, who came and went to the house to let them know how things were going, where the soldiers and the dragon were focused on.

Cassandra realized how close all of the inhabitants were to be working together like this. They were sending the young ones from one house to another to relay the information, making sure the information traveled through short distances to not catch someone's attention. No soldier would care about young people running around in their own city. They were so busy interrogating the adults that they didn't care for the kids rushing in and out.

Hence, they made sure the soldiers were really busy elsewhere and proceeded to move Cassandra and Missandra quickly from one house to another. The two sisters had changed clothes and left behind any piece of jewelry or piece of clothing they were wearing previously, to hide their smell. Even the Baby Dragon was carefully hidden in a basket, carried by one of the teenage boys as it would have been too heavy for the women. Cassandra, staying next to it, kept tucking the little blanket around it to keep it hidden. The Baby Dragon was very curious and kept trying to pop its head or tail out. Cassandra was most scared that it would make a sound or growl. She didn't know how the red dragon's hearing was, and even with the rain, everyone was very careful to move around silently until they reached another house.

However, the one Cassandra had found herself in was already very close to the border, and to her surprise, she found they were headed right back to the waterfall.

Their little group moved very carefully until they reached the house closest to the waterfall. Then, they left it and went next to the Diamond Palace's wall. Though, instead of going for the entrance, they were headed in the completely opposite direction, towards the forest. They stayed almost against the wall, off-road, everyone checking the sky from time to time with the fear of spotting a dragon's silhouette. Finally, the old woman suddenly turned right, and Missandra was shocked for a second, as it seemed she had disappeared between the rocks. However, it soon appeared that there was an entrance there, to a cave. Missandra was speechless. Only a local could indeed know about this little cave! The Diamond Palace was old, but so were its foundations. Everything had been built on large rocks, and with the waterfall and the river crossing the Diamond Palace, it appeared that some natural caves had appeared underneath.

Cassandra was astonished. This natural cathedral of stones was gorgeous. After walking for a while, the roof was getting higher and higher above them, and they almost couldn't hear any more of the rain. Instead, Cassandra realized that they were walking around the actual waterfall. She would have never imagined there was a large cave hidden behind that waterfall! The floor was actually half little lakes, half rocks. It was rather flat, and completely safe for everyone to move around. Hence, when they reached a large area, the young women and teenagers immediately worked together to unpack everything.

"This is incredible," whispered Cassandra, still in awe of this cavern.

"Isn't it?" replied the Old Woman. "No soldier from the Capital would know of this place, we only show our young ones when they are old enough. It's a secret of the Diamond People. In times of war, people would come and seek refuge here, many, many years ago, when the Dragon Empire didn't yet own the land completely. Nowadays it's just for young ones to bathe in the lakes, and lovers to hide."

Cassandra was indeed amazed. With the waterfall a few meters away, it would definitely cover any sound better than the rain outside. It was noisy even from where she was.

In front of her, the Diamond People were carefully laying several blankets on the ground, boiling some water with what they had brought, and preparing everything for the birth of her son. Cassandra was overwhelmed with emotions. This was nothing like she could ever have imagined. In her imagination, she would have been in one of the Diamond Palace's bedrooms, with her Prince holding her hand. Now, she was hiding several meters underneath, with complete strangers who were doing all they could to help her and her baby.

Another contraction came, and Cassandra had no choice but to lay down, helped by the young women present. Missandra immediately sat by her side, taking a deep breath.

"Everything will be fine, Hinue," she whispered. "You and your baby will be blessed by the Water God, giving birth under a waterfall!"

Cassandra chuckled and nodded.

"You know, my baby was conceived during a snowstorm. And now he will be born under a waterfall. Isn't it amazing?"

The baby dragon suddenly jumped out of the basket with a cute little squeak, catching everyone's attention. It looked around, but its little paws were naturally taking it to Cassandra. It walked up to her and curled up by her side. Cassandra caressed the silver scales, taking a big breath.

"I'm so sorry their father can't be here," she whispered.

Missandra shook her head and grabbed Cassandra's hand.

"Don't worry. With this crazy family of yours, I bet your baby will be big enough to kick his own dad's butt for missing this in no time!"

Cassandra laughed, but just as she did, another contraction came, and she grimaced instead. The teenagers soon left, as they had planned, and they were left with the old woman, her daughter, and her niece, all getting ready to help Cassandra give birth.

"I don't... even know your names," said Cassandra, a bit sorry for not asking earlier.

"This old woman is named Chantra, Your Highness. Those two young beauties are Elianne, my daughter, and Sunel, my niece. Now, let's take deep breaths and focus on this baby. We have a little Prince to take care of."

The cries of the newborn echoed inside the cave's walls.

"The little Prince is born, Your Highness!"

Cassandra was exhausted. She had no idea how long it had been, or how exhausted she truly was, but the cries of the baby were all she needed to hear. It took a few more minutes for them to clean the newborn and Cassandra to catch her breath, but then she could finally relax, and that's when she saw him.

The old lady put the baby in his mother's arms. He was carefully wrapped in a blanket and had already stopped crying. Cassandra was amazed. Her son. Kairen's newborn son. The baby she had carried for months, was finally in her arms. He was so small. Compared to his father, he was so tiny and fragile, just a defenseless newborn. His skin was still a bit pinkish, but she could tell he had gold-colored skin, a perfect mix between hers and the Dragon Empire's tan. He already had a little bit of hair, a dark patch on his tiny head. She couldn't tell his eye color yet. It seemed dark, but her baby was barely opening his eyes, just squirming a little in his blanket.

Next to Cassandra, the Baby Dragon stood up, staring at the baby, and rubbed its head against Cassandra's arm. Was it curious about its other half? Or maybe a bit jealous to not be in Cassandra's arms? She couldn't tell. The bond between those two was so unique.

"He is so tiny," whispered Missandra next to her, staring at the baby in awe.

"He's actually quite big for a newborn, Lady Missandra," said Chantra with a smile. "Are you alright, Your Highness?"

Cassandra nodded, but she was absolutely mesmerized by the sight of her son. She had never thought such a precious existence could even be in her life one day. She had dreamed of having children and a loving husband one day, but nothing could compare to this feeling. It was her baby. This little, precious being she had created, with Kairen's love and hers. She gently kissed the baby's forehead, and he moved a bit, reacting to her touch. Cassandra smiled. She was glad he was finally born safely, the baby dragon as well. Despite the circumstances, it was all that mattered.

While the women were cleaning everything, Missandra stayed by her side, looking at her newborn nephew, amazed.

"He is really cute. Have you thought of a name already? For the baby dragon, too?"

Cassandra nodded.

"I discussed it a bit with Lady Kareen before. I wanted something that resembled his father's name and mine, like the Dragon Empire tradition, and yet was inspired by our Rain tribe. His name is Kassian."

"Oh... You're writing it with their letters, then?"

"Yes. And this little one here..."

The baby dragon squealed when Cassandra caressed its head, growling softly as Krai would.

"This little dragon is Kian."

Missandra chuckled.

"Kian? It's rather cute. It suits him. Actually, it suits them both. Kassian and Kian."

Cassandra chuckled, caressing the baby dragon's head. It was so similar to Krai's build, but a bit thinner, and a magnificent silver color. Its emerald eyes were like big jewels, too, making it cuter than the adult dragons. Cassandra was exhausted after giving birth, but she couldn't forget about their current situation. They had been hidden in this cave for several hours.

The teenage boys had come back twice to give them information about the situation outside. As she had expected, the Second Prince was absolutely furious. His men were raiding the Diamond City, looking everywhere for her, searching every house, and threatening people. As Chantra had promised, none of the villagers would tell them a thing about the young concubine hidden behind the waterfall. However, Cassandra knew it wouldn't be that easy.

While the three women were busy cleaning their hands nearby and chatting about how to go back without being noticed, the two sisters exchanged a look.

"How did you manage to leave?" asked Missandra. "You said you jumped from this crazy waterfall... Is Lady Kareen alright?"

"They caught me right after you left. Princess Phetra was there, too."

"That crazy bitch! ...They didn't hurt you, did they? How did you escape then?"

Cassandra took a deep breath.

"Missandra, I need to tell you something..."

The younger sister frowned.

"What is it?"

"When they caught me, Phetra tried to attack me. Dahlia got between us, and she... Missandra, Dahlia was killed."

Her sister stayed speechless for a moment, completely shocked. Cassandra knew this was a huge toll for her. The two girls had bonded a lot in the last few weeks, and even Cassandra herself still couldn't believe this had happened. Missandra's lower lip trembled.

"W... what?"

"Missandra, I am so sorry. Phetra killed her while she tried to protect me."

"Are you sure she's...?"

Cassandra nodded. There was no way Dahlia had survived. Cassandra even suspected the poor girl was already dead when she had fled the scene.

Missandra took a deep breath in, shaking her head. Cassandra could tell she was trying hard not to break down. A few tears ran down her sister's eyes, as Missandra nodded frenetically.

"I...I see."

"Missandra, I'm sorry."

"Why are you the one being sorry? Dahlia tried to protect you from those monsters, Hinue. Don't be sorry when she died to protect you! You should be sorry those people aren't paying a heavy price for that now! How... How did all of this even happen! Everything was fine just hours ago."

Cassandra still couldn't believe everything that had happened, either. It felt unreal. She couldn't understand why she was a suspect in Prince Sephir's death, or why the Emperor would send Vrehan to get her. The old Emperor definitely knew what was going on between the Second and Third Princes. Why would he send Vrehan, of all people? Something didn't feel right about all of this.

"For once, I wish Lady Shareen or the Prince were here to slaughter them!" growled Missandra. "Those horrible siblings deserve worse than death, even the God of Death ripping their limbs apart would not be enough!"

Cassandra wished Kairen or his sister were there, too. She missed her

Prince more than ever. His baby was brought to this world, and they were already in so much danger. Had Krai felt the egg hatching? Was the Black Dragon on the way back already? The latest news they got from Lady Kareen was not too bad. Her medical kits helped the war efforts a lot, but there was no clue about the War God being able to leave the front. Kairen was probably fighting on the very frontline, not the kind of place one could walk away from just like that. Cassandra didn't even know if any of her letters got to him. Probably some general was collecting them halfway, but there was no way to call him there now.

Either way, the young concubine had to accept the fact that she would have to survive without her Prince's protection for now.

"Where do we go, now?" sighed Missandra. "We can't go back to the Diamond Palace or the Diamond City, this horrible Prince is already everywhere looking for you, and that horrible dragon of his too. Shall we go to the Onyx Castle you had mentioned? You should be safe there, no? We can try to hide while we travel to the North."

"No," replied her older sister, shaking her head. "That will be the first place Vrehan will look for me. He will definitely send men to all the routes to the North, thinking I'll be seeking Shareen's help."

"But Lady Shareen will know of the situation by now, won't she? If we just waited a bit longer."

"Lady Kareen said Shareen would be coming in a few days, but we can't wait that long. The longer we stay here, the more we put these people in danger. Even if these people are very nice, there is no guarantee one of them won't give up and talk about this waterfall. Plus, they will need to do a lot of travelling from here to the City to bring us necessities. What if Vrehan or his dragon find us before Lady Shareen arrives? We can't stay hidden here, and we cannot do nothing either. Plus, I'm worried Lady Shareen might not be able to stop Vrehan and Phetra, even if she comes here, he's a Prince after all."

"What then?"

Missandra was really worried. She understood Cassandra's reasoning, but how far could they go with a newborn baby and her sister who had just given birth? Moreover, a baby dragon wasn't small enough to be hidden so easily!

"We can't stay here. I escaped the Palace from this very waterfall. We are so close, if they think about checking nearby they might find us just like that. Even in Diamond City, they will keep looking through every house to find me. They know Lady Kareen's people would help me. No, I think we should head to the Capital."

"The Capital? Are you crazy! Vrehan already controls everything there!"

"That's exactly why. First, he won't expect us to go there. Secondly, we both have friends who can help us once we reach the capital. Also, my priority, for now, is to see if the Emperor is fine, and find out what happened there. I don't believe the Emperor sent Vrehan to catch me, I think there's something going on. Don't you think it is strange that Princess Phetra is here too?"

"Now that you mention it... Wasn't that crazy bitch supposed to be imprisoned or married?"

"Exactly. Something doesn't feel right about all this. I don't understand why the Emperor would even allow them to be here, and I'm worried something happened in the Capital. I need to check if the Emperor is okay, and also, he's the only one, other than Kairen, who can stop Vrehan!"

"But... Lady Shareen, maybe with Prince Anour..."

"We don't know if Anour will come with her, Missandra, and even if he does, I doubt he can stop Vrehan. He's less than half his age, and certainly not as cunning as Vrehan. Even Lady Kareen wasn't able to oppose him! I really have a bad feeling about everything going on. We can't risk staying here, we don't know exactly when Lady Shareen will be here, if she will be able to stop them from capturing me, and they can find us any minute."

Missandra kept shaking her head, thinking this was a terrible idea. It felt like going straight into the snake's nest instead of running away! However, Cassandra had never looked so determined. Maybe it was because she had just become a mother, with a baby to protect, or because she was pushed to her last resort, but her older sister looked stronger than ever before.

"Listen, Missandra. We need to get out of this territory unnoticed. You and I both know how to survive in the wild, and with a young dragon with us, we won't have to worry about predators."

"You're saying we should travel off-road?"

"Exactly. There are mostly forests from here to the Capital, and it's less than a week's journey if we walk fast, this way. Prince Vrehan won't think two women and a baby will make it without traveling through the usual routes, he will have every road checked. As long as we can get far enough from Diamond City, he won't know how we got away, and we will be able to rest in smaller cities and villages."

Missandra nodded, understanding Cassandra's plan. The two of them kept talking for a while, thinking of how to secure their escape and go unnoticed. Chantra, and her daughter and niece had listened to everything and stepped in.

"Are you sure you will be alright, Your Highness? I wish there was something more we could do for you."

"Actually, you can," said Missandra, determined.

She took out her knife and, without warning, suddenly cut off her long hair, leaving only a very short bob cut. Cassandra was speechless, but just like her, Missandra was determined. She watched the big strand in her hand, still tied in a braid, and nodded before giving it to the woman.

"This is almost the same color as my sister's, they won't be able to tell the difference. Disperse this in the North, in the river or the forest, anywhere as long as they end up finding it and think we went there."

"Missandra..."

"It's just hair," she said, turning to her sister. "I don't care at all. I get your point, Cassandra. but this time, it's my turn to protect you, okay? If there's one thing I'm good at, it's tricking people. I promise I'll get us out of here."

Chapter 28

The large, Black Dragon growled furiously, its claws ripping the soil and killing several soldiers, grasped or crushed underneath. The beast was roaming furiously among the ranks of the enemy, dispersing them. The soldiers of the Eastern Republic kept spreading around it to try and attack. They would do anything they could to get to the black scales, but it was an impenetrable armor. No blades or arrows could pierce the thick-skinned creature. The only thing that worked was the catapults. The heavy rocks thrown at the black dragon would be like stones annoying it, pissing it off even more. The Dragon would focus on destroying those annoying machines, then move on to the next group of soldiers it could find. It was impractical for such a large-sized creature to be fighting in a City.

Krai was left to unleash its fury at the border, using claws and fangs to tear the enemy apart, and its growl to terrorize the enemy. The border to the City of Dagaria had been the theater of this war for three days now.

The War God's arrival had been a huge relief to the Dragon Empire's people. His accomplishments preceded the man. Not only were all the citizens well aware of his past accomplishments, but for several weeks, the Empire's favorite Prince had been freeing one City after another. The Eastern Army had made great progress long before the news reached the Capital. The lack of communication to the Imperial Palace had been a fatal flaw that had given them a considerable advantage. The Eastern Army had taken several cities by surprise. Acting under the cover of night, they knew exactly where to strike; getting rid of officials and messengers, thanks to the secret information they had obtained, and they had secured their new locations one after another. It had been almost too easy for the Army.

This attack had been carefully prepared. After years and years of feeding their hatred against the barbaric Dragon Empire, the Eastern soldiers were almost too eager when the order had finally been given. Following the Commander's plan to the letter, they had made tremendous progress, one city after another. The hired mercenaries and assassins raided the cities, getting rid of the people in charge, and the soldiers arrived next to definitely capture the city or village. It was almost too easy. The army posted there had shown close to no resistance, completely taken by surprise. All the men were captured, some tortured publicly to scare the locals. Women and children who didn't resist were captured and sent to the Eastern Republic to work as prisoners.

The news of the Dragon Empire's War God's arrival had changed things. The Eastern Army had stopped their progression right away, and instead, focused on taking full control of all of the acquired cities, gathering the men, equipment, and resources to stage a siege. They already knew the War God's Dragon wouldn't fire inside of a City, so they thought they could resist the Imperial Army's arrival.

They were wrong. The War God was not someone they should have underestimated, especially not when he was guiding the Dragon Empire's most powerful army. The first City where the two armies had met was the least consolidated, yet the Eastern Army had spent time getting ready for this confrontation. They had barricaded all doors, gathered the men inside the walls, and got ready to aim at the War God mostly.

They had been defeated in two days. The men were already scared from hearing of the War God's arrival, with his terrifying Dragon, but seeing this man in person had been a terrible experience. He had arrived on foot, and upon facing the door that kept him out of the City, he hadn't stopped. They had tried everything. Arrows, blades, even little fireballs. Nothing had stopped him. At best, they had scratched him, only to watch the scar turn black from afar. Someone had screamed he was a scaled beast, but they weren't sure. The real nightmare had occurred when the War God had used his bare hands to tear the door down. That's right, the heavily barricaded door hadn't stood more than ten, long, painful minutes. That human monster had torn the thick wood apart like one would rip a paper sheet. Many men had been absolutely terrorized by those hands' power.

A dragon's strength could be understood by its size, and species. This man, however, didn't belong to the human realm. There was no other explanation but that Prince being a Demi-God. The Eastern Army had understood for the first time the heavy reality of a man nicknamed the War God by its own people. As soon as Kairen was in sight, their fate was sealed.

The Eastern Army would not give up on their position easily, but the mere sight of the black armor of the War God was enough to petrify a lot of men. His dark eyes showed no mercy to his enemies. The men were falling one after another, killed like fleas in his path. One single man was leading the Dragon Empire Army with so much assurance that it took a lot of resolve for the Eastern Army leaders to not surrender. They had orders coming from their own

Capital, but the politicians had no front seat for this massacre!

The only thing saving them was the time they had won ahead. Being able to secure their positions in the Dragon Empire's own City guaranteed a bit of restraint from the enemy soldiers. They didn't want to destroy the houses or harm the locals, unlike the Eastern soldiers who didn't care at all. Even the War God, known to be the most merciless, wouldn't harm any woman or child that got in his way. That was surprising, considering the extreme violence that man displayed to get rid of his enemies.

Kairen was enraged by this war. It was taking too long. He knew the fault didn't reside in the Generals accompanying him or his men. All the military officers agreed that the late start in this war put them at a major disadvantage. Freeing a city was much more complicated than fighting an army on a proper battlefield. The fights were taking place all over the City, and their population was caught in it, often used as hostages as well. It wasn't a situation that could be resolved by brute force alone.

The Generals were doing their best, but it took time to solve each conflict. Anywhere the War God went, things were settled quickly. However, there was only one War God of the Dragon Empire, and the man couldn't be everywhere. The days were inevitably long, and the longer the war went on, the more the men were exhausted.

Though the War God's presence was the main source of comfort for the Imperial Army, who knew they wouldn't lose this battle with such a Commander, the biggest relief came from elsewhere.

Several weeks after the beginning of the war, messengers came from the back of the Army to let the Generals know the Lady of the Mountain and the Diamond Lady were sending medical supplies. The officials were astonished. Since when did women bother about matters of war? However, when the promised medical kits had arrived a few days later, they were speechless. Everything sent was ready to use, and practical. The Generals were totally baffled, except for one of them, who had been dispatched from the North. That old general knew the Lady of the Mountain, the War God's Favorite, the only lady who cared enough about this war to fight with them.

There wasn't much to argue about anyway. Those medical kits had come at a good time to raise the morale of the troops, and the Lady of the Mountain wasn't only a high-ranked Concubine, she was named Imperial Physician by the Emperor himself. It was enough for all the supplies to be sent everywhere on the battlefield.

Kairen only got to see those kits a couple of days later. The War God had barely rested since the beginning of this war. Returning to a battlefield after such a long time was actually refreshing. Kairen stood at the very front of the battle, slaughtering one man after another, sometimes fighting several at a time. He had gotten a few injuries, but nothing his Dragon Blood couldn't heal. Instead, he was actually frustrated at his dragon, getting impatient outside of the City.

Krai was forbidden to fire or enter the Cities, but the dragon was keeping itself busy by clearing the grounds around it. If any Eastern soldier had a bad idea of trying to run from the City, he was greeted right away by a wide-open mouth, and quick death.

However, this wasn't where both the Dragon and the Prince wanted to be at this moment. They were all longing for a different City, a different company. This fact made Krai irritable, and the Dragon was even harder to keep in check. The Prince was well aware of his conflicted feelings, but there was nothing that could be done about it. His duties came first, and only when this war was over could he go back to his beloved Cassandra.

"What is this?" he asked as one of his soldiers had taken out a little box to try and save his injured peer.

"The medicinal kits from the Diamond Palace, Commander! They were distributed last night to all the men at the front!"

While the man was wrapping an injury, Kairen observed the little box. He recognized the familiar smell of medicine and plants. Cassandra's hair always smelled the same after she had spent time in her garden. A little smile appeared on the War God's face, terrorizing the men around. The War God, smiling? What kind of crazy demon was awake now?

The Commander turned around, swinging his swords with a smirk that wouldn't leave his face. So she had decided to do something, as well. It was so like her to refuse to stay put. A proud feeling spreading in his chest, the War God worked even harder at clearing the City, only resting when he absolutely had to. He even made sure to send some men literally flying, where the dragon could catch them in one bite.

However, it wasn't enough. More precisely, something was wrong about this whole war.

He had felt it since the beginning. The information had come too late to the Palace, and the Eastern Army was well too informed. They had known how and where to strike to get a considerable advantage ahead of them. This was not a simple coincidence. Kairen immediately informed his Generals that he wanted them to capture officials, and make them spill about the rat that had sold the information. He wouldn't let them get away with this.

Finally, in the next City they freed, they captured the right man to interrogate.

Truth was, the poor fellow was about to meet a tragic fate. The War God was annoyed. This war had been going on for several weeks, more than he had promised already. He wanted to get things done quickly, and this man was the one who was about to receive his anger.

Kairen walked into one of the houses used as a headquarters of the front. Two Generals to the side, one accountant, and two soldiers holding their prisoner on his knees.

"Talk," said the War God, as cold as ice.

The man may have kept his tongue tied, in other circumstances. If the

War God hadn't been absolutely terrifying, in his black armor and murderous eyes, for example. The man was shivering, already exhausted by the fights, and the struggle he had put into not being captured.

"I know nothing! I..."

One of his legs was loudly broken. The man screamed in pain, but no one else flinched. The men present were all highly trained, and would not offend their Commander with any mistake.

"Last chance," warned Kairen.

"We... We got the information from here! A messenger arrived with a lot of information! Our King agreed to his terms!"

"Who was that?" Asked Kairen.

"I don't know! I really don't know! They only said if we could kill the War God and his army, the new Emperor would give us all the South and North territories, and a hundred chests of gold!"

Kairen glared even more. Some rat had sold out his own Empire for his head.

"Who is that new Emperor they talked about!" roared one of the Generals. "How dare they, when our beloved Imperial Dragon is still healthy as a young dragon!"

"How dare they, indeed," said Kairen.

The Prince took out his sword, and with one blow, sent the prisoner's head flying.

"Your Highness! That man might have had more information."

Kairen didn't answer and left the building without explanation. He didn't care about the prisoner. He already knew this rat would have been way too smart to leave any information behind. The faster way was to send word to his father, and end things quickly here.

He looked down at all the blood dripping off his armor. The black metal had turned a reddish, horrid color over the last few days. Kairen didn't even have time to wash it. He looked around him. The fight was dying. The remaining Eastern Army soldiers were all killed or taken as prisoners by his men.

To his surprise, the city people had even helped a bit, providing food and shelter to the soldiers who needed it. This was a first for the Imperial Army. Aside from the Capital, most cities were terrified by the Emperor's Army. They had never seen the Imperial Military, aside from their own City militia, and the rumors about the Imperial Family held everyone in fear. However, Kairen himself had been surprised to see how things had changed lately. First, the news of him freeing the previous City was enough to have the War God's arrival celebrated whenever they reached another one. Plus, he didn't know how, but the people already knew that, unlike the Eastern Army who did not care, the War God forbade his men from assaulting or injuring any women or children. That was enough to have all the locals support the Imperial Army anywhere they showed up.

Cassandra's shadow was also everywhere. Not only were the soldiers delighted by the medical kits that had already saved many lives, but the story of a former slave turned Concubine and an Imperial Physician was running like a legend in the streets. As soon as they saw the medical kits, the common people treated it like a treasure, looking incredibly grateful when the soldiers used it on the innocent people who had been injured.

Strangely, Kairen was feeling incredibly proud of his Concubine's doings. It was as if Cassandra was there on the battlefield, supporting him with her own strength.

As he walked back to the little building where his army had established themselves during this battle, he witnessed more soldiers using the little kits, now perfectly familiar with all the contents. He had even seen some of his men discussing with the accountants and the men watching the supplies about what they were running out of the fastest, and using the empty compartments to store food.

"Are you alright, Your Highness?" asked one of the Generals as Kairen walked in the building.

Of course, he was alright. He didn't bother to answer and instead, took off his bloodied armor. His bare torso was perfectly fine except for a couple of scratches. Kairen walked upstairs, finding the little room they had prepared quickly for him. The War God could only afford to take short naps, but this was plenty enough for him. He laid on the bed, but instead of trying to sleep, his hand reached for the little box on the bedside table.

Kairen had kept one of those for himself. He probably wouldn't ever need what was inside, but having one of those boxes was meaningful enough for him. He opened it. The supplies hadn't moved, but on top of the compartments, he grabbed the letter he had already read many, many times. Cassandra's handwriting was pretty and delicate. As he was re-reading, he touched her hair tied with his. He could easily imagine her gentle voice saying each word. The War God sighed, imagining his Concubine as she wrote every line, thinking of him. He could fight a hundred wars, but he never would have imagined that being away from her for so long would be so hard. Back at the North Army Camp, he could see her at the end of the day, so he hadn't really stopped to think about even missing her.

Now, this war was getting too annoyingly long, and Cassandra wasn't anywhere near. It was better this way. He didn't want to see the fear he witnessed in the innocent villager women's eyes everyday, in her beautiful emerald-colored irises. She was so sick just from the smell of blood. This place would have been an utter nightmare for her.

He tried sleeping for a bit, just a couple of hours. He had done most of the job in fighting off the Eastern Army, his generals were competent enough to finish whatever was left in his absence. Most of them were smart enough not to disturb the War God's few hours of rest.

When Kairen got up, a full plate of food was ready for him. He ate while listening to several reports, but all in all, this City was now free, and they should move on to the next one. Finally. They were about to reach the last City the Eastern Army had been able to establish a decent siege on. The final fight would occur soon, and then, he was free to go back to his Concubine. Kairen left the building once he was satiated, and his men were done talking. He went outside to join Krai, who was laying in the middle of an abandoned garden of a wealthy villa. That was one of the only spots large enough for the Dragon to sit comfortably, as most of the City had been ravaged by the attacks.

The large black dragon was obviously bored by this war. The Eastern Army had done great by locking themselves inside the City, where it was hard for him to access the narrow streets, and unless Kairen and his men pushed them outside or in areas he could reach, the big dragon literally didn't have much to put its fangs or claws in. Hence, Krai was looking even more depressed and ignored the Prince walking its way.

"Stop sulking, we're almost done."

The answer came as an angry growl. Krai turned its head away, and kept growling, terrorizing the poor soldiers who just happened to be walking by. Kairen sighed and leaned against its big body. Both turned their heads in the same direction, where the Diamond Palace stood, miles and miles away. Kairen promised himself to fly there the minute he would be done with this war. He had already had enough.

Suddenly, Krai moved, pushing the War God and hiding its head under its black wing. Kairen glared at his wilful beast that was now showing him its rear.

"I miss them too, you know."

Another pissed growl came. Kairen couldn't blame him. They were both dying to fly back and meet their babies. His son and the Baby Dragon. Kairen had a feeling that the birth had already happened, from the way Krai was acting. His dragon had acted all agitated, two nights ago, but they were right in the middle of the raging battle. However, his angry dragon's attitude had been even worse since then, and now, Kairen could tell the dragon wasn't only just missing Cassandra.

The War God had enough. After a few more minutes, he angrily walked back to the main building, yelling for the generals to gather. All men assembled in less than a minute.

"We are attacking the next City in two days at dawn," he said. "Warn all the men we are taking no prisoners."

No one dared to protest or even raise a single concern. Two days would be plenty enough for the men to rest, and the next City could be reached in two hours by foot. One would have been crazy to object to the War God when he had this murderous glare on. He was merciless with his enemies, but his men knew Kairen could be as deadly with anyone who disrespected him, too.

Hence, just as the War God had ordered, the Army arrived at the next City exactly before dawn, two days later. Just like the Black Dragon flying above them, the soldiers were actually quite excited. This was the last battle,and victory after victory, they had gotten to the last City needing to be freed. Even if this one would be just as heavily consolidated, the mere thought of ending this war soon was enough to energize the troops. Just like Kairen, many of these men had families or lovers they were all dying to return to.

As Kairen stood forward, lines and lines of soldiers behind him, an Eastern soldier, probably some general, appeared on top of one of the City's walls.

"Imperial Army! You have fought brilliantly until now, but we won't let you win this City! Our great Eastern Republic won't submit to some barbarian country who..."

"Shut the fuck up."

The man stopped talking, shocked by the War God's words. Kairen hadn't yelled, but his voice was powerful enough to be heard all around. Some men snickered behind him, making fun of the poor soldier.

"We... We are not going to s-step down in front of the tyranny, and..."

"I said, shut the fuck up."

Some of the men behind Kairen laughed at the man's baffled expression, but the War God wasn't laughing. Instead, his glare was absolutely terrifying. The poor spokesperson tried to stutter something, but it came more as some pitiful squeak than any word. It was indeed hard to dare open his mouth when being glared at by the most terrifying black eyes in the world. The most spine-chilling beast wasn't in the sky.

"W... We... d... don't..."

Kairen quietly took out his sword, and in a silent deadly movement, sent it flying. The distance should have been hard to conquer, even for an arrow. However, the blade went right into that man's head, perfectly in the middle. He fell backward and out of sight.

The large door stood in front of them, surely barricaded, but this was the twelfth door they were facing in those few weeks. The soldiers knew exactly what to expect. Kairen glanced up, waiting. The dragon kept circling lazily until the War God clicked his tongue.

"The sooner we're done, the sooner we go back," he muttered, still glaring at his dragon.

Just then, Krai finally flew down, apparently headed right into the door, but a few meters before, finally spit its fire. The door melted in seconds against the pressure of the heat. Even the men started sweating under their armors, but they watched the door disappear and got ready to fight.

"All men, ready!" yelled the Generals in unison.

Kairen took out his second sword, and with one swing of his hand, all the soldiers started moving at the exact same moment. The Imperial Army was perfectly trained to do what they had to. The Generals alone were enough to guide the men, while Kairen marched in front. Anyone who got in his way wearing the wrong armor was killed instantly. Many men tried to fight him, as it would be the ultimate honor to be able to kill the Dragon Empire's War God, but they were greeted with death instead.

460

He was like a machine. He didn't stop, didn't flinch, and kept going with nothing to stop him. Krai, too, was flying over the City, looking for any spot where it could attack and bite a few enemies. The dragon was only too happy to have an opportunity to end this war as soon as possible. It even wandered off to chase some men who were trying to flee the City, as the beast had no pity for deserters.

On the ground, Kairen was leading his men silently. They were barging into a building, making sure the inhabitants were safe and the enemy was killed and moved on to the next one. It was harder to progress because the Eastern Army had no remorse in taking hostages. Somehow, they had to find a way around any situation, but after twelve cities of the same scenario, all of his men were trained to act accordingly.

The War God didn't even have to yell any orders, the Imperial Army was the best in the Empire. Instead, Kairen focused on the larger buildings, or the houses where many hostages could be held. One was particularly barricaded, and he kicked the doors open. Something felt strange inside that place.

It was... too silent. No one had progressed that far into the City yet, but he was almost surprised no one had raided such a big mansion. Was this a possible trap? That thought wasn't worrying him one bit. He had faced countless traps and rendered all of them useless. His enemies were smart, but his strength and stamina were hard to overcome. Not only that, but his Dragon Blood made his enemy cry in frustration, for any injury that they barely managed to inflict onto him was absolutely useless.

However, his instincts were telling him something was wrong with this place. The large rooms would have been perfect to store men or weapons, but it seemed empty. The ceiling was strangely high, too, as if one of the floors had been taken out. From the outside, the roof seemed robust, so why...?

The answer came a couple of rooms further in. Kairen's instincts warned him first, and he placed his sword in front of him. Another trap, surely. When he kicked another door open, however. There was quite a surprise behind it.

Two young dragons, facing him with their yellow angry eyes. The two beasts stood still, but they were not restrained in any way. Kairen frowned. The Eastern Army shouldn't have any dragons. Those two were unknown, he had never seen those before. They were young, obviously not adults. He swung his sword around. Finally an interesting battle.

There was no record of a man able to single-handedly kill a dragon. Let alone two dragons. The War God had a smirk on. They had really worked hard at trying to kill him.

One of the dragons suddenly growled, and they both jumped on him. The room was big but just enough for those two to attack. No adult dragon would be able to sneak in there, but those dragons were the size of three or four adult men, not even half of Krai's size. They really had prepared the perfect trap.

Kairen barely dodged one of their claws, and the other dragon furiously growled, jumping next. The War God didn't have time to think. He raised his sword and, at the right moment, stabbed one of their flanks, making the dragon screech in pain. However, right next to him, the other jumped, and tore Kairen's armor off his chest in a loud metallic bang. The pieces of metal fell, with holes from its claws in it. The War God frowned.

He jumped to get on one of the dragon's backs, using it as a stepping stone, and attacked the other, aiming for its jaw this time. He barely missed it, but his sword still opened a large cut on the beast's neck. Both dragons were now injured and furious, and they attacked back. The War God felt a sharp pain, and saw his blood flowing from the injury. He glanced down. How long had it been since he had seen the color of his own blood? The injury was large, and strangely, at that moment he was reminded of Cassandra. Something about the pain, maybe. He looked up, and both dragons got ready to jump again.

* * *

As soon as the Green Dragon landed, three people dismounted. Princess Shareen led the way, furiously charging inside the Diamond Palace and ignoring all the servants that had run out to greet them. After receiving the infuriating news at the Onyx Castle, she was seriously hoping that there was some sort of mistake.

"Mother? Mother!"

The Diamond Palace was awfully quiet, more so than usual. She had noticed little groups of soldiers stationed around the Diamond City on her flight there, but they were in such small numbers that it didn't seem important. However, now that she was actually inside the Diamond Palace, Shareen felt restless. What the hell was going on here? She had only been absent for a few weeks! The journey to the North Camp was almost like a holiday trip for her. After she was done getting Kairen's men back to work and up to her standards, Shareen had been almost bored. Truth was, Kairen's army was well trained - enough to be able to function perfectly well with or without their Commander present. There had been a few attacks from the Northern Barbarians, but it wasn't anything they couldn't handle. Shareen herself had taken part a few times, having more fun fighting alongside them rather than leading the men. She participated in a few debriefings, had listened to their reports, and made a few minor changes here and there, but really she was not particularly worried about the Northern Army.

As it had been reported to the Imperial Palace, the Northern Barbarians had been attacking more frequently than usual, but it wasn't as bad as what had been described. She was even shocked at how easy it had been to get rid of them. After a few days on the battlefield, she'd had enough. The General also made sure to have her visit the Mountain Hospital that had been Cassandra's doing. Shareen wasn't too surprised to hear them praising the Lady of the Mountain endlessly, but she was surely impressed with her legacy there. Her protocols would certainly be worth implementing in all the Dragon Empire's armies in the future.

After all of that, Shareen had decided to return to the Onyx Castle. After having spent so much of her time in the Imperial Palace, she found the place to be incredibly boring. The Onyx Castle felt like a forgotten remnant of their Empire, with nothing to do and nothing to see. Sure, she had found a servant who was fun enough to play with for a while, but her mother's letters had put an end to that fun time.

Imperial Concubine Kareen wasn't one to ask for anyone's help, or the type to worry over small things, which is why Shareen had been truly alarmed by her mother's letters. Once she told Anour, her younger brother had become restless too. The last one she read before leaving had been telling her about her mother's spies going missing one by one, and that no more news was coming in from the Eastern Front.

Although Shareen wouldn't have been too worried about Kairen ignoring their mother under normal circumstances, it was highly unlikely that he would ignore his Concubine. Cassandra was quickly approaching her delivery date, and Shareen had witnessed how much Kairen loved her. If he hadn't come back yet, it meant he wasn't done fighting, and if a war led by her brother, the Empire's War God, still wasn't done, something was indeed wrong.

Hence, Shareen had grabbed Anour and Roun and raced back to the Diamond Palace. She had also decided to bring that uptight old guy with them. The poor Imperial Servant had been left outside to puke after his first flight, but she could worry about him later.

"Mother!"

"Shareen!"

Finally hearing her mother's voice, the Princess let out a long sigh of relief and quickly picked up her pace. The Imperial Concubine was in one of the gardens with her arms crossed tightly over her chest. Sitting like a queen on one of the chairs with a young maid at her feet, she had been still as a stone until her daughter appeared. The little dragon, Srai, was also curled up at her feet, and continuously growling at the unwelcome woman before them.

"You have got to be fucking kidding me," growled Shareen, unsheathing her sword.

Of all the people she had not expected to see, Phetra was at the top of that list. However, the Princess was seated in front of Lady Kareen, flanked by no less than six soldiers. She no longer displayed any of the injuries that Shareen fondly remembered and was strutting around in her purple dress like she owned the place. Meanwhile, the Imperial Concubine was flanked by two soldiers and neither of the men belonged to the Diamond Palace's militia either. Shareen immediately recognized the color of Vrehan's militia with their red armor. From an outsider's perspective, it may have seemed like the two women were hanging out in that garden with heavy security, but the atmosphere was as cold as ice. Phetra seemed to be in control, and had an arrogant sneer on her face.

However, as soon as her eyes fell on Shareen, it disappeared in a flash and she turned white, visibly terrified.

"Y... You... What are you doing here?"

"That's my line, you crazy bitch!" retorted Shareen, heading straight in her direction.

"Do not take another step, Princess Shareen," warned one of the soldiers, taking out his sword and walking up to her. "We have orders to..."

Shareen grabbed him by his hair and brutally slammed the man's face against her knee. It probably wouldn't have made such an atrocious sound if she wasn't wearing metal knee pads, but alas... The man fell at her feet, his face completely wrecked. Upon seeing that, all the others remained in a religious silence, not daring to risk the same fate.

"Finally," said Kareen, standing up. "Why did it take you so long to get here?"

"What the fuck is going on, Mother?" asked Shareen, still glaring at a petrified Phetra.

"Can't you tell? I'm a hostage. In my own Palace, too!"

Shareen raised an eyebrow, turning to her mother. There were a lot of adjectives that could be used to describe Lady Kareen, but not something even remotely close to a victim's status - she would never have thought to hear her mother call herself a hostage, actually. That woman was probably the most influential woman in the Empire, if not the most powerful.

However, glancing towards the horrified Phetra, Shareen already had a rough idea of what was going on.

"Where's Cassandra? And the girls?"

Lady Kareen quickly explained everything as Anour arrived in the room just in time to hear it all as well. The Imperial Concubine detailed Vrehan's arrival in her City, and how he had barged into the Diamond Palace with his men and seized control. Kareen had spent several hours that night agonizing over Cassandra's crazy jump down the waterfall, before one of the servants interrupted to let her know of news from some of her people in the Diamond City. Not only did they confirm that the Concubine and her sister were alive and well, but also that she was being hidden by them and was about to give birth. After that, Vrehan had spent two nights and two days in an absolute rage, looking for Cassandra everywhere and sending his men left and right to interrogate the local people to find her. They had found clues indicating that the young Concubine was headed North and, fearing Shareen's arrival, had left in a hurry, leaving only a few of his men and Phetra there.

Shareen and Anour were both in shock over what had happened in such a short time. Not only had there been no news from the Capital or the Eastern Front in weeks, but Vrehan had come to wreak havoc?

"What the hell was Father thinking?" asked Shareen. "He is surely not stupid enough to send Vrehan here!"

"I don't think so, either" replied her mother, glaring at Phetra. "However,

464

that little rat did come here and claim he was acting on behalf of the Emperor to arrest Cassandra. She had no choice but to flee."

"Damn it! Do you think Sephir is really dead?"

"It seems so... The official news arrived here early the next day and your father placed the entire Empire in mourning for the First Prince."

Shareen shook her head. The official news had been validated by the Palace so this couldn't be Vrehan lying. However, she didn't believe for one second that Cassandra had anything to do with his murder. She turned to Phetra with rage and determination in her eyes.

"Where is that damn little rat now?"

"He left yesterday. His annoying soldiers searched the entire City to find Cassandra, but they couldn't. Apparently, his original plan was to lock down my City and use me as a hostage, but when he found out I had already sent a letter to have you come back before he had managed to kill all my couriers, he panicked and left like the coward he is."

"I see he left some trash behind," growled Shareen.

Phetra was absolutely frozen, and terrified.

"Oh, the little bitch is supposed to be watching the hostage." Kareen jested before rolling her eyes. "Needless to say, it has been incredibly boring."

"Your brother is the most horrendous scum to have ever lived," Shareen sneered, slowly walking towards Phetra. "Not only does that fucker dare to barge in here, to try and harm my brother's Concubine while he's gone, but then you have the fucking audacity to use my mother as a hostage?"

"Don't touch me!" screeched Phetra, retreating in utter fear.

Even the men who were supposed to guard her stepped back in cowardice as Shareen came closer. No one wanted to be next to have their facial bones violently smashed by the furious Princess's knee. Phetra was left alone to face her, and she couldn't even hide her fear.

"Y... You can't touch me! The Emperor ordered you not to kill me!"

"If I remember it correctly, Father's exact words were, 'not while we're eating', and 'not in the middle of the Imperial Chamber'. Too bad for you, this is neither of those times or places," hissed Shareen, slowly raising her sword.

"Stop! Stop! You can't kill me! I...I know Vrehan's secrets! I'll tell you everything!"

Shareen hesitated, tilting her head. The truth was, she had been dying to get rid of this vermin for a while, and even Kairen's cruel punishment of her hadn't been nearly enough in her eyes. It was almost too infuriating to see Phetra already walking again so soon. However, this wasn't a normal situation.

"Mother, what do you say?"

"I say I want my family back!" yelled the Imperial Concubine, exasperated. "This damn duo of siblings got rid of all of my soldiers and chased Cassandra away while locking me in here. If Cassandra, her sister, and my grandson aren't all alive, unharmed, and well when we find them, I swear I'm going to peel every layer of that bitch's skin off and break every single one of her bones myself!"

"Oh, good idea, Mother. We can get started on that right now," said Shareen with a sadistic smile. "You! Break one of her legs."

The soldier she had pointed her sword at became livid. Phetra was his Master's Sister, and when the Second Prince had gone, he told them to protect her or at least make sure she didn't end up dead. The poor man hesitated for too long - Shareen got rid of him with one swift movement of her sword, making Phetra scream in horror. She then turned to another soldier pleadingly.

"I can do this all day," she said with a terrifying smile.

"Why are you doing this?" yelled Phetra. "Just do it yourself, you monster!"

Shareen turned to her.

"Oh, I would gladly do that, Phetra, but each one of those men had the fucking balls to hold my mother here and kill her militia. So, now they are either going to learn to obey who rightfully rules this place, or die like Vrehan's damned dogs."

Behind her, Kareen smiled, obviously proud of her daughter. Though she wasn't a fighter, Kareen praised herself for raising her two children well. Phetra looked at the soldiers, realizing what Shareen was doing. This was simple and cruel torture. Vrehan had left those men behind to protect her, not for them to maim her!

"Mother?" asked Shareen after a short silence.

"Yes, Daughter of mine?"

"How tall is the highest tower in the Diamond Palace?"

"About... seven or eight floors, I think."

"Well, you see Phetra, we do have an option in case all of Vrehan's men remain stupidly obedient to your scum Brother. I mean, it's only a few more floors than before, you might die for real this time, or maybe not."

Phetra was panicked and so scared that she was on the verge of passing out.

"B... Break it!" she screamed at the closest soldier. "Do it! P...Please, hurry!"

Shareen almost let a satisfied smile out watching it. She knew Vrehan had actually done nothing but abandon his sister to her own fate, but she also really didn't care. Phetra had harmed Cassandra, killed Dahlia, and imprisoned their mother here. Shareen was too enraged to let this go.

The sound of her bone breaking and the scream that followed, resonated for a few seconds. Anour couldn't watch, it made him a bit uneasy, even though he knew how merciless his family could be. But until now, there hadn't been many occasions to witness it himself. However, he was also livid about what happened.

"What do you have to say about Vrehan?" he asked, finally stepping forward.

"He... He's... prepared a trap... for... Kairen," whimpered Phetra, holding her broken leg.

466

"What kind of trap?"

"I...I don't..."

"Damn, you really are useless," sighed Shareen.

While her daughter was still glaring at Phetra, Kareen stepped forward, grabbed her sword, and without warning, slashed Phetra's hand. Another scream echoed within the Palace's walls as the severed hand fell to the ground. The Princess held her bleeding stump, her face white and deformed from the pain.

"Try to heal that," hissed the Imperial Concubine.

No one else could bear to watch the scene. Dragon Blood could heal a lot of injuries, but it certainly couldn't regrow a limb. The blood continued to flow and Phetra clumsily tried to wrap it in her clothing, desperate. Meanwhile, Kareen handed the weapon back to her daughter so Shareen could carefully clean it.

"That was for slapping Cassandra and killing my servants and my men," said Kareen. "I strongly advise you, never to use your remaining hand like that, or I'll cut it off too. I am not as merciful as my children, and I have no problem killing a bitch like you."

Though she raised an eyebrow at being called merciful, Shareen didn't say anything.

"So you're not going to kill her now?" asked Anour.

"First, she doesn't deserve a quick death," replied Shareen. "Second, she'll still be useful until I can get my hands on Vrehan. The bitch probably knows more than she lets on."

"How will we find Cassandra and Missandra now?" he asked. "Is there a chance that they're still within the Diamond City?"

"They couldn't be, Vrehan searched everywhere," replied Kareen with a sigh. "He even tortured some of my people and found the hideout under the waterfall. Thank the Gods, the girls were long gone by then, but they left some fake clues that sent those idiots towards the North. Brilliant girls. But no, from what my people have told me, the girls decided to go to the Capital with the babies."

"By the Great Dragon, I can't believe they're born already. Kairen will go crazy when he gets back!"

"I know, and I haven't even seen them since their birth! I'm going to kill them for making me miss that!" growled Kareen, while glaring at Phetra and her guards.

"Is Brother Kairen going to be okay?" asked Anour, worried.

"I'll go and check on him first," volunteered Shareen. "I don't want to be presumptuous, but that rat is smart, and if he planned a trap for my brother, it's probably pretty serious. Everything about this war sounded off from the start."

"What about the girls? Shouldn't we find them first? If they're going to the Capital by themselves with a baby and a Baby Dragon in tow."

"They don't have an adult dragon to fly with, it will take them days to get there. They are smart enough to stay out of sight until they reach the Capital, and if those girls are hiding from Vrehan and his Dragon, it will be hard for us or Roun to find them as well. No, I'd better go save my brother's ass and get him there as soon as possible. Krai should be able to find his baby or Cassandra."

"I'm worried about your father," said Kareen. "I don't think that old man is senile enough to have given that order willingly, not if everything was alright with him. Something must have happened in the Capital, Vrehan would never have dared to act so boldly otherwise."

"How long will it take you to send new spies to the Capital, Mother?"

"I can send people right away, but it will take longer for them to come back than for you to return from the Eastern Front with Kairen! Also, aren't you going to help me clean up around here?" Kareen said, while pointing out all of the soldiers who were still waiting by Phetra's side. The men, suddenly getting nervous about what was going to follow, exchanged glances.

"Seriously, Mother? You want me to take care of them before I go? Don't we have more urgent matters?"

"I've cut enough hands off for today, I'm tired. Plus, are you really going to leave your poor defenseless mother to deal with these men? Do you know how many Vrehan left here? I can't even walk around or take my brunch quietly!"

"What about recruiting them?"

"Are you kidding me? Vrehan's army of little mutts? I wouldn't even allow them to scrape dragon shit off my floors!"

The men were still confused at the situation, and shocked by the women's words, as Shareen rolled her eyes and took out her sword once again. While Anour sighed and had to look elsewhere, sure enough Roun appeared over the walls, willing to help the Princess do the bloody work.

Between Shareen and Roun, every last one of Vrehan's soldiers were killed in less than ten minutes, even the ones who desperately tried to escape. He really hadn't left many behind to protect his sister. After all was said and done, only Phetra was left standing with her half-healed stub, and Roun remained behind in the garden to guard her, even though it seems highly unlikely she'd be able to go anywhere in her current state. She was still white as a sheet, both from the fear and loss of blood.

Then, Shareen accompanied her mother back inside, followed closely by Anour.

"So, Brother really doesn't know what happened here?"

"How could he? Vrehan killed all of my couriers and spies before I had a chance, not even a fly could have gotten out of this place before today! I bet Krai was able to sense his egg hatching though, he's always been very sensitive."

The Imperial Concubine seemed to be back in charge as she was hurrying through her Palace's halls. Shareen knew her mother well enough to know that, despite Vrehan's siege, there was no way Kareen had completely run out of resources. The little dragon still followed her closely, as Kareen walked to where a door was hidden, which opened into another secret hideout. Shareen raised an eyebrow. She had spent half of her childhood in this Palace, but there were apparently still many things she had never seen before. Through the hidden door, they climbed some very narrow stairs all the way to the top of a secret tower.

It was a room filled with birds, including a couple of falcons. Kareen whistled, and one of them flew to her wrist. She rolled up a small note she had taken the time to write while Shareen was getting rid of the soldiers and tied it to the bird's foot. The falcon left the tower with the message, clearly heading towards the Capital.

"Mother, I thought all your spies were dead?"

"Those who were supposed to return! However, I of course do still have many friends in the Palace. That was my fastest bird, we'll get news quicker this way."

"I see... Mother, you never told Cassandra about Dahlia being one of your people, did you?"

"She didn't need to know and now it's irrelevant... Poor girl. Come on, let's go back downstairs. I want to get the production of the medical kits back on track to help your brother, and I need to recruit more people as soon as possible."

"What are you talking about? Medical kits?"

While they walked back down into the Diamond Palace, Kareen quickly explained everything Cassandra and Missandra had been doing to help Kairen's army while staying here. In a few words, she let her know about the production of medical kits and the feedback they had received from the front before Vrehan's arrival. Shareen nodded.

"Oh! I was getting fed up with all those officials praising her all the time back at the Northern Camp as if she was some Messiah, and now the girl has done it again. Kairen really knows how to pick them. Does that woman ever stop?"

"As if. But it's not like everyone can go around playing with a sword to solve their problems!"

Shareen rolled her eyes again, exasperated. Her mother had been very happy to see her and her sword just minutes ago to clear her Palace of all of Vrehan's men, hadn't she?!

"Anyway, we still need to figure out where the girls might go once they reach the Capital," said Kareen. "They probably won't be able to enter the Imperial Palace without us, and we might not get to the Capital before they do, but we can find ways to help them before that. If only I knew exactly where they would go."

"Missandra mentioned an... an ex-husband," said Anour, a little bitter.

"I have one better than that," said Shareen with a smirk. "I had almost forgotten about the guy before you mentioned the medical kits and all of Cassandra's doings, but..."

The Princess walked back to the entrance of the castle, where the man she had arrived with was still looking a bit sick. He was standing very straight, and trying to look anywhere but at the bodies Shareen had left behind during her cleaning episode earlier.

Kareen looked at the man, a bit confused. She had never seen him before, but he was obviously dressed as an Imperial Servant and had the demeanor of a man who had been trained for that role as well. He kneeled respectfully as soon as the Imperial Concubine, Princess and Prince were in sight.

"Greetings, Imperial Concubine Kareen."

"Who is this?"

"Cassie's former babysitter," said Shareen.

"My name is Evin, Your Highness. I was indeed Lady Cassandra's escort and assistant back when she resided in the Northern Camp with his Highness, a few months ago."

"Oh. Why did you bring the man here then?" asked the Imperial Concubine Kareen, still refusing to acknowledge the servant.

"Tell her."

"Yes, Your Highness," said Evin, bowing again. "This humble servant happens to have exchanged a flattering number of letters with Lady Cassandra over the last few weeks. I mentioned our close relationship to her Highness, Princess Shareen, and she politely agreed to bring me here to see the Lady again."

Kareen exchanged a look with Shareen, but the Princess immediately turned to Evin again.

"You know where Cassie would go in the Capital, don't you?"

"Yes, Your Highness. In her latest letters, Lady Cassandra happened to mention a residence she had acquired in the Capital recently, thanks to His Highness the Third Prince. As a suggestion to Her Highness Princess Shareen, I strongly believe Lady Cassandra will be very likely to go there first."

Kareen was baffled for a few seconds.

"A residence? Since when did my son have a residence in the Capital to gift Cassandra? When did he buy it?"

Evin cleared his throat, slightly embarrassed by the next bit of information.

"Well, His Highness didn't exactly... buy said residence. I would classify this as...forcefully retrieved compensation from Lady Cassandra's former... owner."

"Oh, now that makes more sense," said Shareen, nodding. "Anyway, do you know where that residence is?"

"I do not have an exact address, but I certainly have enough of a description of its facade and neighborhood for someone who knows the Capital City well enough to find out, Your Highness."

"Good. Go get one of my servants and have them send a courier in my name to the Capital right away. We can't lose any more time. I'll make sure our Cassie and her sister get everything they need, and some extra protection too. If Vrehan wants to make another attempt on my beloved grandson's life, he's

470

going to have to kill me first!"

Evin bowed once again and left quickly to follow Kareen's orders and send the courier right away, making a clear detour around the bodies still scattered in the Palace garden. Meanwhile, Shareen turned to her mother with suspicious eyes.

"Aren't you going to go there yourself, Mother?" asked Shareen, crossing her arms.

"What are you talking about? I'll go with you and your brother once you've retrieved him from whatever battlefield he is on! Besides, now that Vrehan's little mutts are handled, I need to interrogate his useless sister some more."

"You think you can be more convincing than me?" asked Shareen, placing a hand on her sword.

"Shareen, I am your mother. I was dealing with the Palace's schemes and snakes long before you were born, dear. This isn't my first fight and she isn't the first person I'll be interrogating. If I couldn't make a girl like her talk, I wouldn't be worthy to be called the Emperor's Favorite anymore!"

As Kareen walked back to the garden, Anour grimaced.

"She's really scary sometimes."

"Well, that's my mother. Come on Anour, let's get going before Kairen gets himself killed like an idiot. Mother is capable of burning the Capital down if anything happens to him or her new grandson."

Chapter 29

The little dragon crouched in the grass, its eyes set on the target. Its long, thin tail waved in the air while its little hips swayed a bit, getting ready to jump, and its little snout twitched as those big, green eyes focused on its prey, waiting for the perfect moment.

Suddenly, the little rodent moved and the dragon pounced on it. The little creature squeaked at the sudden attack, but it was too late. The fierce hunter had caught its prey. The little paws had it trapped and it was watching the rat trying to escape from its grasp with wide-eyed wonder. The Baby Dragon was far too hungry to wait any longer though. It was time to eat! It finished his meal in four bites, licking its chops and paws carefully to make sure nothing was missed. Then, it turned around and trotted back, very pleased with itself. What a fierce hunter it was!

"Kian, did you eat again?" asked Cassandra, seeing the little dragon bounding back to them.

The dragon scampered over to her side, rubbing its head against her hip. Cassandra smiled, caressing the young dragon. She was seated against a tree, busy breastfeeding her son. Just like Kian, Kassian had a ferocious appetite. Both never seemed to have enough. Whenever Cassandra saw Kian walk away to go hunting, she knew her newborn was probably hungry as well. Though it was tough caring for the two of them, there were some advantages as well. The only problem they really had was that a hungry dragon could get very fussy and would bite pretty much anything. While Kian would never hurt Cassandra, Missandra had quickly needed to buy a pair of very thick shoes.

"Hinue, I'm back!"

Missandra appeared between the trees, carrying a bag with some recent purchases. They had agreed that she would need to do the shopping alone, as Cassandra was afraid someone would recognize her in town. Moreover, Kian was never far from her, and the little dragon hadn't quite grasped the concept of staying hidden.

The younger sister kept a watchful eye on the little dragon's movements as she approached. Kian had a bad habit of trying to hunt her fingers or toes as a game, but the young dragon hadn't quite caught on that the playful biting was really quite painful. She had several bandages on her little digits to prove that.

"Kian's done eating already," chuckled Cassandra. "They are probably just going to nap next."

Indeed, Kassian wasn't really drinking anymore, and his eyes were starting to close. They were still dark, but Cassandra suspected they might lighten a bit as he got older, and she could see hints of green in them.

"Good," said Missandra. "Because I won't be able to keep walking much longer if that little guy keeps chewing on my toes."

Kian's head raised up, turning to her with knowing eyes as if the dragon could tell what she was talking about.

"Yes, you!"

The Baby Dragon let out a little grumble that resembled a cat's husky meow more than a scary growl. Missandra shook her head. She actually liked the little, mischievous dragon, if only it would hold back on the biting and chewing on her.

"I still don't know how Lady Kareen handled two or three of these," sighed Missandra, opening up her bag.

Despite her complaints, she had of course bought some more dry meat to help fill the little dragon's stomach. Kian had only begun to hunt recently, and was still perfecting it. From what Cassandra had learned from Lady Kareen, a dragon's parent would share its food until their baby could hunt well enough on its own. The thought made her feel a bit sad. If only Krai was there, Kian would have learned how to hunt properly by now.And to bite less too!

"Anything new?" asked Cassandra, watching her sister empty the contents of the bag.

"Well, first I've got more diapers for the little Prince because I can't believe how many times a day we have to wash those, and I've even started feeling sorry for those poor river fish. Also, more food. Oh, and I found your favorite berries. Some dry meat for the little carnivore."

"Do we still have enough money?"

"Yeah, don't worry, Hinue. I'm making sure we get a good deal on everything. Plus, the stuff we sold was worth a lot. I've never carried so much money on myself before, it makes me happy to spend and get rid of some of it. We'll definitely have enough until we reach the Capital, especially if we keep going at this rate."

Cassandra nodded. The girls had left the Diamond Palace almost a week ago now, and they were finally close to the Capital, despite having walked slower than anticipated. It was mostly her fault, though. Even if Missandra helped her carry Kassian, Cassandra was exhausted after giving birth and she couldn't move as fast as she had hoped during those first few days. Moreover, there had been news of soldiers looking for her much sooner than she had counted on. Vrehan had left some of his soldiers in two of the towns he had come through before the Diamond Palace, but thankfully, no one seemed to recognize Missandra. However, this forced them to walk even further away from the towns, and though they tried to see as few as possible, pausing for each of Missandra's supplies runs was just adding further delays to their trip.

"Plus, your little sister is really good at getting discounts," Missandra added with a wink.

Cassandra sighed. The truth was, Missandra was very pretty and she was very good at using her charms, but she still couldn't help but worry about her methods used to get discounts. She knew there was nothing wrong with flirting with the merchants a little, but she was afraid she'd overdo it and have to fend off one of those men by herself.

"Don't get into trouble, Mie…"

"Don't worry, I can handle myself. I'm used to it, remember? Plus, those townsfolk are nothing close to the Imperial Family, I can defend myself just fine. Anyway, it's their mistake for being morons."

Suddenly, Kian's tail started wagging again, its eyes riveted on Missandra's bag. She noticed and sighed.

"Well, he definitely smelled the dry meat. Damn it, I thought I had wrapped it up enough this time! He's worse than a dog, and he's not even tamed yet"

"He's a Baby Dragon," chuckled Cassandra. "I don't think there's any way to tame him."

She put her hand on Kian's back, scratching those silver scales to distract and prevent the little dragon from pouncing on the bag.

"Well, at least he knows how to listen to his mother. Also, Hinue…I heard some weird stuff while I was in town."

Cassandra frowned. Missandra's expression looked somber. What had happened? Could it be about Vrehan? Or the Emperor? Getting news as they travelled through the forest, while avoiding main roads, made getting information much harder even though they tried to ask at each town Missandra stopped in - they just hadn't heard much. The information wasn't travelling into the little towns as fast as it did between the bigger cities, and most townsfolk didn't pay much attention to the news from the Capital either, unless it involved their taxes.

Missandra sat in front of her, her face a bit scrunched, as Cassandra laid Kassian down and put her top back on.

"Some guy at one of the stands was saying that the Capital is getting ready to crown a new Emperor. They said the old one is dying."

Cassandra's heart sank. Dying? The Old Emperor? Kairen's father? What had happened? This was worse than bad news. She had been hoping that the Emperor would grant her refuge inside the castle and protect her from Vrehan, but now, if he was dying? Cassandra bit her lip, unsure of her next steps now and heavy with worry.

"Did they say anything else?" she asked.

"Not really. The guy at the shop heard it from his brother's wife, who heard it from her cousin who knew a soldier's sister, blah blah blah, and so on. You know, the modern way of getting information around here. I don't really know if it's reliable, but it sure sounds fishy."

"It really does," whispered Cassandra.

This was too much to just be gossip. The Emperor was perfectly fine and healthy a few weeks ago, so what could have happened since then? Cassandra couldn't believe this was only some coincidence. Kairen being sent to the battlefront, the First Prince Sephir's unexpected death. This was too much all at once, and a bit too convenient for the Second Prince.

Missandra bit at her fingernail, looking worried as well.

"Are you sure we should keep heading to the Capital? If something really did happen to the Emperor, it changes things, right? You wouldn't be protected at all."

Cassandra was trying hard to decide on which way to go. Indeed, if anything had happened to the Emperor, the Imperial Palace wouldn't be safe for her anymore. She wasn't sure Kairen would get there before she did, and if she arrived just as the Palace had a new owner, she might not survive this time. Cassandra wasn't losing sight of the fact that the Second Prince also had a dragon; his dragon was the third largest in the Empire, after Glahad and Krai. She had escaped him once, but Cassandra wasn't in any hurry to face them again. Her injury from it was carefully wrapped in some bandages, but she wouldn't forget about the pain of it so soon.

"Hinue?" Missandra called out to her gently.

"Let's keep going. For now, we don't have anything confirmed. As you said, those may only be rumors. We can always confirm them once we reach the Capital without going to the Imperial Palace directly."

Missandra frowned, unsure about the plan. She wasn't fond of the idea of going back to the Capital to begin with, but now, this could be more deadly than they had originally thought. She was going to go along with her older sister's decisions in any case, but she couldn't shake the feeling that everything was not going to be as Cassandra hoped.

"The Emperor is definitely still alive," said Cassandra.

"How do you know?"

"Lady Kareen. When Vrehan arrived in the Diamond Palace to kidnap me, she confronted him, and he couldn't seem to answer. If the Emperor was in fact dead, he definitely wouldn't have let her talk to him the way she did. So, Lady Kareen is still the Emperor's favorite Concubine, and thus untouchable. The Second Prince hates her just as much, if not more, than he hates Kairen and Shareen."

"Oh..."

Missandra realized Cassandra was right. It all made sense. But for how much longer would that still be valid? The rumors said that the Emperor was dying, not dead. Which meant that if they were right, this was now going to be a race against the clock.

"Have you heard anything about the war?" Cassandra inquired.

She shook her head.

"No. Which means it's still going on," sighed Missandra

Cassandra nodded with a somber expression. No matter how isolated the little towns were, news of a victory would travel the fastest, most notably because people would spot the Black Dragon in the sky. Plus, if Kairen was searching for her, he would have been to both the Diamond Palace and the Imperial Palace by now, which made Cassandra think something bad had happened. Shareen had hinted that this should be a quick win, but it seemed as if the Princess had been wrong.

"Don't worry, I'm sure he's fine," said Missandra. "Whatever the Eastern Army has going on, Kairen is the War God and the best fighter in the Empire."

Cassandra smiled gently.

"Lady Kareen mentioned this war was probably not a coincidence either. With Prince Vrehan's arrival at the Diamond Palace after Prince Sephir's death, too."

"That rat face is definitely pulling the strings," Missandra interrupted. "I bet his whole plan was to get Kairen far enough away from the Imperial Palace for as long as he could. That way, he could eliminate the competition as quickly as possible, and make his moves quietly.."

"I don't understand. Even if Sephir and the Emperor died, and Vrehan is named Emperor, Kairen could still return at any time," whispered Cassandra. "What is he thinking?"

"Cassandra, your Prince is with the Imperial Army. No matter who the Emperor is, they'll act as he says. Now, imagine you have an evil mind and crazy ambition for a second. I mean, if I were Vrehan, I would try to get rid of all my enemies at once; send the most threatening one to a far-away battlefront to be killed, or at least kept busy, so I could get rid of the other obstacles - my eldest brother, and the Emperor with a shiny dragon. That way, even if the War God isn't killed in battle, I would now be the one who could give orders to have the Imperial Army kill him."

Cassandra sighed.

"Sometimes you're awfully devious, Mie."

"Try growing up in a brothel," scoffed her sister. "You have no idea how petty and wicked people can be in there."

Cassandra tried to imagine other scenarios, but actually, her sister's logic was pretty sound. The only thing that didn't make sense was the timing - it all felt awfully rushed. She couldn't see Vrehan as a man capable of putting such a risky plan into action. As she shared her doubts with Missandra, the younger sister thought out loud.

"Well, you know, there might have been a little detail that forced him to rush things."

Without saying anything else, Missandra nodded towards Kassian.

Cassandra and her sister exchanged worried glances. For a while now, they had been among a massive crowd of people, looking at the long, long line that was waiting to enter the Capital. Dozens of people of all ages were waiting to get in, a lot of them annoyed by the draconian security checks. About ten guards were manning the front, checking all the men, women, and even the children.

The sisters, both hidden in the crowd, were strategizing how they were going to be able to get in, and how risky this could be. The soldiers were scrutinizing every person, not even letting a toddler get through without scanning them over. Cassandra and Missandra had covered themselves under newly bought shawls and were trying to avoid any suspicion. There were actually quite a few habitations and shops outside the walls, so the crowd wasn't that surprising, and they could easily blend in like trees in a forest. Kassian was asleep, strapped to Cassandra's back, but Kian kept popping its head out of Missandra's bag, and thinking she was playing, the young dragon kept trying to bite her fingers each time she pushed it back in.

"They're really checking everyone," whispered Missandra. "This is definitely one of the stupid Prince's moves to prevent you or the War God from getting in."

Indeed, this much security at the wall wasn't normal. Usually, people could come and go as they pleased and the guards at the doors only just inspected to verify they weren't carrying weapons illegally, or to check the merchandise. Cassandra bit her lip. She hadn't foreseen such a problem. With their white skin and green eyes, the sisters would be recognized immediately if they tried to go in like this. She couldn't even sneak just Missandra in, as her sister fit most of the description Vrehan would have given out about her!

"Alright, plan B then I guess," sighed Missandra, suddenly opening the little pocket where she kept their money.

"What plan B?" asked Cassandra, surprised.

Missandra counted how much money they had left and nodded.

"We need someone's help to get us in, and I happen to know someone who can help with that, but not unless we give him lots of money, so...I really hope you still have that residence and people who can at least feed us afterward."

Cassandra hesitated for a moment, then suddenly realized what her sister was planning.

"Mie... You're thinking about the men you owe money to?"

"Yeah. I mean, I owe them a lot, but if your Prince can pay up once this is over, and I tell them they can make even more money if they help us, then they might."

"Missandra, I'm...not sure those people you owe money to are alive anymore?"

Missandra lifted her focus from the bag, frowning.

"How is that?"

"When we were looking for you, Princess Shareen and I ran into a bunch of bandits...with tattoos. She and Krai kind of killed them all."

Missandra seemed surprised for a moment before she looked lost in her thoughts, and then turned to Cassandra again.

"How many people do you think they killed?"

"Maybe about... twenty or thirty in total. I'm not sure."

"Oh, that's fine then. I pissed off way more people than that."

Cassandra was speechless! Missandra laughed at her sister's look of shock as she walked to the closest shop and bought some paper and ink to write a quick note. Then, her younger sister found a boy in the crowd and gave it to him, asking him to deliver it to the Red District in exchange for a bit of gold. The boy nodded and happily took it.

The two sisters watched him walk through the line, but Cassandra was still unsure about this plan.

"Is it fine if he just hands it to anyone in the Red District? Didn't you have a name or something?"

Missandra smirked.

"I really pissed off a lot of people there."

Cassandra nodded as she remembered the quite exhaustive list of establishments that kept a bitter memory of her younger sister, having visited each of them and listened to stories of Missandra's mischief first hand.

"Trust me," Missandra added. "If we don't hear anything in the next hour, it only means that the boy kept the gold. But I can always send another one."

So they waited. To Cassandra's surprise, the answer wasn't long to come. The sisters watched as an older woman stormed out through the gate carrying a bag and glaring intensely into the crowd seemingly looking for someone specific. Of course, Missandra was watching the whole scene from afar with a little smile on.

"Not a bad pick, I guess."

They didn't approach, instead waiting for the woman to spot them. When she finally spotted Missandra, she barreled their way, looking furious. While Cassandra was worried, Missandra was quietly waiting with a caustic smirk and crossed arms.

The woman was about twice their age and unusually muscular, with short black hair and tattoos on her face. She looked like a demon on a mission as she approached.

"You little bitch! I can't believe you have the fucking balls to send me this crap!" she yelled, throwing the note at Missandra's feet.

"Nice to see you again, Verna. I missed you, too."

"Don't give me that arrogant crap, Mie. I only came because you owe me some damn money, a fucking lot of it, and you paid that boy three gold coins! Three! Where is my money?!"

The woman reached for Missandra's bag, but unfortunately for her, it was well guarded. As soon as her hand was within reach of it, Kian furiously tried to

478

bite her, making her scream and quickly retract her hand. Missandra chuckled while the woman stared at the bag, her eyes wide in shock.

"What the fuck was that thing?"

"A personal security system," Missandra laughed. "Now, before I give you anything, did you bring what I asked for?"

The woman scowled and tossed the bag at the girls.

"I did, you damn little... Yes, I do have it, but I want my money, you little brat!"

Ignoring her for a moment, Missandra crouched down to inspect the contents of the bag as Cassandra frowned behind her. To her surprise, her younger sister pulled out some little pots filled with what looked like makeup, two large circles of metal, and two white dresses.

"That's..."

"My plan," said Missandra with an apologetic smile. "I know it's probably not a good memory for you, but we're going to have to disguise ourselves as slaves to get in. The guards won't spend too much time checking slaves when they're focusing on looking for a Concubine."

"A Concubine?" repeated Verna, glancing at Cassandra. "Mie, what the hell have you gotten yourself into this time?"

"Mind your own business, V. But thanks, you did get everything!"

"Hey, I want my money, Mie. Now! Or I'm ratting you two out to the soldiers. I'm not stupid, you know!"

Missandra sighed, took out the little purse, and threw it to her. Verna caught it and started fanatically counting the money. It was a minute, but then her angry expression slowly returned.

"Are you kidding me!? This isn't even a fifth of what you promised! I knew I couldn't trust you!"

"Do you think I'm walking around with gold bars in my purse? You'll get the rest once you get us inside!"

Verna seemed to hesitate for a moment, glancing at Cassandra and Missandra. Her eyes fell on Kassian too, for a couple of minutes. The baby was awake and quietly laying in the fabric tied around his mother, his mouth making a little O. Verna spent a few more seconds observing his features and his mother's skin tone before her eyes went back to Missandra's bag with a suspicious frown.

"A Concubine, you said? You're not going to get me into more trouble, are you?"

"I promise, as soon as we get to my residence safely, I'll make sure you get the rest of your money," said Cassandra.

She was desperate, but if the woman didn't help them now or decided to sell them out to the soldiers, the situation would take a tragic turn. Cassandra only hoped that the people at the residence still had enough money on hand to pay the difference. They didn't want to lose any more time. If Kassian cried or Kian got impatient, the soldiers could notice them, and then they'd all easily be captured. At least once they were past the gates and inside the Capital they would be safer.

Verna clicked her tongue.

"Fuck you, Mie, you better have my money or I swear I'm exposing you to the first guard I see!"

Missandra nodded and gathered everything inside the bag again. Then she grabbed Cassandra's arm, pulling her sister away from the crowd to a spot under some trees where no one would see or disrupt them.

"So, these people are probably going to be looking for girls matching our physical description. Even if we're disguised as slaves, we still couldn't just walk in. That's why I asked Verna to bring all of this." Missandra motioned over all the little pots of make-up.

"Will this really tan our skin enough to blend in with the locals? Is that even possible?"

"Of course! You have no idea how much make-up the girls inside the brothels used. First, this is to dye our hair black. It's rather quick and they use it all the time. There was an uproar every time someone spotted a white hair. Oh, and this is for naturally tanning the skin. I'm not sure how much it'll work on us but at least we won't look as white. Crap, I hope there's enough. Well, we don't need to be completely coated, as long as we keep our arms covered and are careful about our hands."

Cassandra kept nodding, she was truly impressed. Her sister had really become a master at deceiving people. To even think up such a plan so fast was a little bit scary, but still extremely impressive.

"What about Kian and Kassian? They're going to search our bags, and if they find us with a baby..."

"We can have Verna carry him. She doesn't look anything like you and thankfully, he looks more like his dad."

"Excuse me!" said Verna, looking astonished. "I never agreed to smuggle someone else's brat in!"

"Stop fussing, think about the money," retorted Missandra, brushing her aside. "The problem is Kian. It's not going to be that easy to conceal a dragon, he's already almost too big for the bag and they are definitely going to check it."

Cassandra glanced at the sky with a little frown on.

"We can try having him fly over the wall. He probably won't want to follow me through the crowd and might decide to just fly over the wall himself."

"Yeah. That would work. We just need to make sure the baby flying lizard could be mistaken for a bird. A very big bird, but still, a bird nonetheless."

The two sisters spent the next hour dying their hair black and covering their skin with the bronzing powder, making sure nothing was too unnatural. They couldn't hide the color of their eyes, but this was another advantage of posing as slaves; their eyes would be directed at the ground with no one questioning it. It actually didn't take them as long to cover Kian with dust, making sure the silver scales weren't shining anymore and covering its tail with leaves to make them look like feathers. The result was quite strange, leaving Verna, who was still speechless about the Baby Dragon in the first place, with a grin.

"You think people will take that for a bird? Are you insane? He would have a better chance of posing as a cat with wings!"

"Oh, shut up," retorted Missandra. "We're not taking him to be examined up close, he just needs to fly above us for less than a minute and come back down. No one will give a second glance at a bird and there are several sizable falcons living in the area. We just need the illusion to last for as long as it takes us to cross that border."

"You're crazy," concluded Verna. "A crazy genius, but crazy. I'm still holding you to what you owe me even if this doesn't work"

"Stop whining. We just need to set you up with Kassian, cross that stupid checkpoint and you'll get your money."

Cassandra frowned. Aside from Missandra, she was very reluctant to let another woman carry her child. However, she didn't have much of a choice right now, and it would only be for a few minutes. The two girls made sure the baby was comfortably secured against Verna, and Cassandra kissed his forehead gently, making sure he wasn't too perturbed by the new person. He had been carried by Missandra several times before and rarely cried. Kian was usually the one to get fussy.

Cassandra focused on him for the next few minutes while her younger sister checked her hair for her once more and braided it.

"Alright, it doesn't really suit you, but it should at least deceive the guards unless they are make-up experts, which is highly unlikely."

"Can we just go already?" Verna huffed.

"Ready, Hinue?"

"Ready," sighed Cassandra.

The wait in the line was awfully nerve-wracking and there were a lot of people waiting impatiently to get inside the Capital. Cassandra and Missandra did their best to keep their heads low, the younger sister trying her best to mimic her older sister. The big rings of metal around their neck were actually old slavery collars that Verna had retrieved from girls that had bought their freedom. The locks were broken so they could easily be opened, but that wouldn't be visible to the guards, as they were also wearing shawls and covering their napes with their hair.

Verna was the worst actress of the three. She kept glancing down at Kassian, looking very awkward. The baby didn't seem to care much about who carried him as his eyes were constantly following his mother. Meanwhile, the one who was supposed to be pretending to be his mother looked like she was horribly embarrassed to be carrying a baby at all. Thankfully, Kian was quietly staying in the forest. Cassandra was worried, though. After several attempts, she thought she managed to lull the Baby Dragon enough to stay put and hopefully take a nap while they made their way inside, but she was still afraid it would come out at any moment and give them away. She was counting on the crowd though - Kian had never been around so many people at once and tended to stay away from strangers. Hopefully, the little dragon would find something in the forest to distract itself with for long enough before she called for it to fly over.

When they were only a few people away from the entrance, both sisters tried to pay extra close attention to the guards. The men were obviously bored with the job and not paying much attention. People were getting angry about the wait and several officials didn't even hold back and were complaining and scolding them. Therefore, the soldiers were doing their best to check the people quickly and move on to the next one. This was good news for the girls, they probably wouldn't be checked too long either.

"You, with the baby," one of them called when Verna stepped forward. "Is that yours?"

"It's my niece, I'm bringing her back to my brother. His wife couldn't take it anymore and left him alone with the kid. Can you believe that?"

"What a bitch. Your niece is cute though! My wife just had twins and all they do is cry. You look lucky, she's quite behaved. Can I see your bag?"

"Sure, here," she stated as she handed over her bag, "So far so good, but it's almost her milk time. Gotta get her back to her dad soon."

"Oh, sure. Wait, are those slaves with you?"

Missandra and Cassandra, kept their heads down and stepped closer to Verna. They could barely breathe, but everything had been going well so far.

"Yeah. Is there something wrong?"

"You have two slaves? You don't look that wealthy."

Missandra felt a pearl of sweat glide down her spine. Stupid guard, couldn't he just mind his own business!

"Hey, I might not have the looks but I work hard. The Red District pays well, hun. I actually got those two from their Masters, and at a good price, too. Just check the bag, you'll see I have plenty left."

"Oh, I see. Be careful though, they're getting stricter on the laws about slaves. Well, those two look pretty fat, probably not too bad, eh?"

Cassandra went red. This was her first time being called fat! She had just given birth, but still! Missandra, making sure to keep her head down, couldn't keep herself from rolling her eyes - stupid soldier.

"Alright, you're free to go. Come on people, let's keep it moving!"

Finally, they made it in, making sure to get away from the crowd as quickly as possible and slide into one of the narrower side streets. Cassandra let out a long sigh of relief.

"I can't believe that worked."

"Me neither," said Verna. "Here, just take back your kid."

Cassandra happily opened her arms. She was glad to finally have her son back and the baby immediately gripped a strand of her hair. She checked him over, but Kassian really didn't look upset in any way, his eyes stayed riveted on the strand of black hair with his familiar little frown on.

"Good one, making him pass for a girl," chuckled Missandra. "Guess you're smarter than you look."

Verna glared at her while snatching the bag from her hands, furiously rummaging through its contents.

"Oh, shut up. Now, where the fuck is my money! You better..."

Before Verna could finish her sentence, a sudden ruckus was heard behind them. Cassandra went white. People near the gate were screaming and pointing fingers towards the sky while someone yelled something about a horrible, flying monster. Missandra grimaced.

"I guess the other baby decided not to wait for the cue."

Sure enough, they soon spotted Kian quickly flying their way. The little flapping wings were causing the fake feathers to fall off and the dust was blowing away with the wind. Not far below the little dragon, the girls could hear soldiers screaming as they tried to follow it. They would have no problem spotting them now!

"Oh, crap!"

Missandra reacted quickly, grabbing her sister's hand and dragging them down several different streets. Verna didn't follow, opting to grab their bag and take off in the opposite direction. The two girls didn't have any time to think about the loss. They started running through various alleys trying to hide from the soldiers. Behind them, Kian thought it was so fun to be flying overhead, but still following closely. Missandra quickly snatched the Baby Dragon from the air. They couldn't risk it flying above their heads and giving away their position.

Cassandra held Kassian tightly, completely panicked. She had no idea where they were headed as she blindly followed her younger sister, praying they wouldn't be followed. They ran for a while until Missandra suddenly grabbed Cassandra's hand and pulled her into a hideout. The door looked locked from the outside but, to those who knew, it only needed a slight push to allow entrance into a small, abandoned garden. And it was very small indeed as Krai wouldn't have even been able to squeeze its head into it. The sisters scrambled in and Missandra quickly closed the door behind them. With their backs to it now, they tried to quiet their breathing so they could listen for the soldiers' steps - they were already hard enough to hear over the constant yelling of orders. Once they finally heard the footsteps run past the door, both girls finally let out a breath of relief as they held onto the babies.

Kassian was wiggling around in Cassandra's arms looking uncomfortable, probably unhappy about the excitement from earlier. Kian too, didn't like being held. The dragon struggled in Missandra's arms, wagging its tail in protest. Thankfully, she had quickly picked up how to handle the Baby Dragon and kept her hand tight around its snout to avoid getting bitten.

The sisters waited like that for a few more minutes, standing with their backs against the door, holding their breath... They were both terrified. Those men had definitely seen Kian and would probably realize Cassandra was back in the Capital now too. Once it calmed back down outside, Cassandra slid down the door, her bottom hitting the ground with a small thud and releasing a sigh from her lips. She couldn't believe they had really made it in with her sister's crazy plan. She took off the fake collar, tossing it to the side, and rubbed Kassian's little hands to help calm herself.

"I'm exhausted," sighed Missandra. "I hope your people have got some good beds for us."

"Me too. But that woman took our money."

"Verna? No, she didn't. I have it here."

Missandra suddenly pulled out a little purse from under her shawl. Cassandra had lost hers while they were running, but apparently that didn't matter.

Cassandra frowned.

"But she had it when we were checked. How did you...?"

"Funny enough, when she grabbed the bag away from me."

Cassandra sighed.

"Mie..."

"What? We need the money, just in case. Plus, she doesn't even know where we're going, so it's fine."

Cassandra kept shaking her head. Missandra was truly another level of mischievous. But at least they had some money for now, so they wouldn't have to worry in case something went wrong at the residence. Cassandra didn't know what to expect there, but she hoped her friends would be able to help them out. They had been sleeping in the woods for a week now with a baby and a dragon baby and they could really use a good night's rest.

"How did you know that door wasn't locked?"

"I know several good hideouts like these throughout the City. It's kind of useful when you need to run away."

"Missandra..."

"What? I already told you I pissed off a lot of people!"

"We need to talk about your debts once this is all over," sighed Cassandra.

Missandra shrugged.

"Anyway... Do you know how far we are from your residence?"

Cassandra took a deep breath as she tried to recall which part of the Capital they were in. It was such a large city and they had run through several streets too. Cassandra wasn't so familiar with all the districts, but she could remember the way from the gate. Judging by how much they had run earlier, they probably weren't too far.

"Maybe about ten minutes away."

"Alright, then let's wait a bit more to be sure those soldiers are gone and then go."

Cassandra nodded. She got up and looked around for a water source, as all gardens had one, and went to wash away the tan from her hands and face. With her shawl and their spare clothing gone, there was no point walking

484

around with her hands and face being darker than her arms. She quickly washed all of the dye from her hair as well and Missandra did the same after her. They both still had some black in their hair, but their skin was back to its original porcelain color.

Meanwhile, the young Prince and Dragon had been playing next to them on the shawl Missandra had laid out. The human baby was still too young to move around much, but he'd grab Kian's tail and hold on despite the young dragon's attempts to shake him off. Cassandra chuckled while catching the scene, and took Kassian in her arms, gently kissing his plump, little cheeks. The baby grabbed at her dress with a pout.

"Alright, let's go," she sighed.

They couldn't put Kian in the bag anymore, as Verna had run away with it. So, Missandra tightly wrapped the little dragon in her shawl, covering its head as much as she could so it would look like it was just an oddly shaped package. Thankfully, it was dusk now and with the sky getting darker, it would hopefully decrease their chances of being spotted. Both sisters carefully stepped out of the hideout.

Missandra walked a bit ahead to check each street first. They were being extremely careful, and luckily didn't run into any soldiers. Following Missandra's instincts, they took the most crowded streets, hiding among the people and acting as if they were just passing through. Cassandra was the most afraid of being spotted. Holding Kassian against her chest, she desperately tried not to look up at the sky. If only the Black Dragon could appear now.

After waiting in a narrow street for a bunch of soldiers doing their patrol to leave, they finally arrived at the street of Cassandra's residence. She was nervous. What if Vrehan knew about this place? What if something had happened while she was away? What if they were locked out, without any help and with only the little bit of money they had left?

Cassandra took a deep breath and knocked on the door while her younger sister kept a lookout, but thankfully, the street was deserted. At first, no one answered. Desperate, she tried again. She hadn't been here in ages.

"This is a private residence!" yelled a voice from behind the door. "State your name and your business!"

Despite the rude answer, Cassandra immediately smiled.

"Yasora! It's me, Cassandra. Open the door please!"

"Don't yell that!" Missandra said, looking worried.

"Oh, by the Gods! Finally!"

The woman opened the door and grabbed Cassandra's wrist, yanking her in. Yasora was wearing a green dress with her hair braided down her back and some streaks of white showing through. She seemed to have aged a bit, but she still looked much healthier than the last time Cassandra had seen her.

As Missandra and Cassandra walked in, they were surprised to see several lights on in the residence. Yasora wouldn't let go of Cassandra's hand, almost shaking.

"We've been waiting for you two!" the older woman exclaimed, her eyes looking as if she was about to cry. "I was starting to fear something had happened! Now, come on!"

After one last glance around to make sure they hadn't been followed, both sisters were pulled inside, the door closing tightly behind them. Kian, who apparently had enough of being carried by Missandra, let out a little high-pitched chirp as it jumped out of the shawl she had been trying to keep him wrapped in. The Baby Dragon landed on the ground, more of a little tumble than gracefully, but quickly got back on its feet to start sniffing and looking around.

Meanwhile, the exhausted sisters finally let out a long sigh of relief. Cassandra turned to Yasora, confused.

"You were expecting us? Why?"

Next to her, she knew Missandra already had her hand on her little dagger, just in case this turned out to be a trap of some sort. However, it was very unlikely. Officially, there was nothing tying Cassandra to this residence. Kairen had just gotten rid of its owner and freed all the slaves. More than likely, no one had stopped to take care of the paperwork.

With the exception of her tired eyes, the middle-aged servant lady looked the best that Cassandra had ever seen. Yasora took her hand, nodding.

"We've been so worried! Two days ago, out of the blue, a man showed up at the door saying he had come under the orders of Imperial Concubine Kareen! He told us you would likely arrive here soon, with your younger sister and a newborn. He told us to be ready to help you! He said we had to do anything we could to assist you as soon as you arrived, and make sure no one found you. He gave us plenty of money and food to fill our storage cupboard too! Oh, and we also have a letter that came for you, carried by a messenger bird, from an Imperial Servant named Evin."

"Evin!" exclaimed Cassandra, surprised to hear about him.

"Someone you know, Hinue?" asked Missandra, confused.

"Prince Kairen appointed him as my... attendant back when we stayed in the North Camp. He accompanied me everywhere all day, he's a good man."

Just then, Kassian started getting agitated in his mother's arms. A bit unhappy, the baby started moving his closed fists and cried, visibly upset.

"Oh, come in! Let's take care of you first, you must be exhausted! Don't worry, we have everything ready!"

Yasora guided them inside the residence. Cassandra had lived several years in this place, and she could see the changes since the last time she had come here. First, the roof that Krai had torn apart had been repaired, though the place seemed to have been renovated as some storage place. Furthermore, leaving all the servants in charge without a direct Master had made the house appear livelier than ever before. Plants were happily growing in the gardens, with some cats playing around. Also, a lot of doors were left open, allowing the

486

young servants to rush from one place to another without worry.

However, as Yasora had promised, everyone had been waiting for them. As soon as they walked in, Cassandra was surrounded by many familiar faces. The young servants and former slaves she had worked with years prior circled around her, greeting her and vocalizing amazement and awe for her baby. However, Kassian wasn't in the mood for the introductions. The young little Prince continued his crying and fussing until Yasora yelled for the young ones to clear the area and get to work. She was apparently appointed the natural head of the house until Cassandra returned.

First, both girls got to take a bath in one of the large indoor bathtubs of the residence. As if they were some valued guests, the two sisters and Kassian were given complete attention by the servants. After almost a week of surviving in the wilderness, Cassandra and Missandra enjoyed being able to properly relax in some hot water with fancy soaps. They let Kassian play in the water a bit. Just like Kian, they had already noticed that the baby enjoyed water a lot. As soon as he was laid in, he naturally tried to paddle and splash with his feet, wiggling around. Kian was swimming around them in the bathtub too. The dragon's wings were still not fully developed, but it could make short little flights and jump out of the water before diving again.

Once they were done bathing, the sisters were given some large bathrobes. They noticed someone had even gone to purchase new diapers for the baby. The dragon was a bit harder to persuade out of the bath, though. Cassandra attempted to call Kian out many times, her pleas falling uselessly on deaf ears. Eventually, Missandra had to wrestle the mischievous Baby Dragon out, it was having too much fun making her chase it around, until she was finally able to grab the silver tail.

"Come, while you were bathing we got some dinner ready for you," said Yasora. "I imagine you have much to tell us!"

Indeed, a large table had been prepared with food, making them immediately hungry despite their current fatigue. Missandra almost jumped to get a steamed bun. Meanwhile, Cassandra carefully laid Kassian down in a little basket containing a blanket that the young servant girl Mira had prepared for him. As soon as he was on his back, the baby yawned, and Kian jumped next to him to curl up for a nap, too.

"So?" said Yasora. "I'm very confused, Cassandra. Last time we saw you was at the slave market, and after that we barely heard anything."

"I'm sorry, things got...hectic."

Cassandra went on to explain everything that had happened to her since the last time she had come here to free the slaves, and Kairen had killed her previous mistress. It was a lot from when she had left the Palace, and Missandra helped her fill some blanks as well. Both sisters were also trying to eat while talking, as the sight of cooked food made them realize just how hungry they really were. With all the stress, Cassandra hadn't realized how tired she felt, either.

Once she was done, both for explanations and eating, she turned to Yasora, worried.

"What about the letter?"

"Oh, right. Give me a minute."

She left and came back, handing to Cassandra the letter she had mentioned earlier.

"I didn't open it, as it was addressed to you. Just like I said, this letter arrived the next morning after that man had come by, delivered by a messenger bird. The previous man warned us we'd better...welcome you properly, and also make sure you stay safe. "

Missandra and Cassandra exchanged a glance.

"Definitely one of Lady Kareen's spies," said Missandra.

"Probably," agreed her older sister, opening the letter right away.

Cassandra read the lines so fast that she had to go over a second time before handing them to Missandra.

In this letter, Evin was true to himself, hoping Cassandra was alright as well as giving her a detailed report on the situation in the Northern Army Camp. He wrote how he had persuaded Shareen to bring him back with her to the Diamond Castle, and described their current situation up to the time he had sent this letter. Which was written and sent in a hurry. She let out a sigh of relief, though she wished it contained some better news.

"So, Lady Shareen is at least back at the Diamond Palace with Prince Anour," reiterated Missandra.

"However, they still had no news of my Lord when that letter was sent. What is going on?"

Cassandra couldn't hide how worried she was for Kairen.

She was indeed happy about Shareen's return to the Diamond Palace, thankful for Lady Kareen to have an extra ally by her side. The Mother-Daughter duo was so strong, they had actually chased away the Second Prince. She didn't care much about Phetra's fate, but Cassandra was worried to know where that treacherous Brother of hers had gone. Did he follow the fake leads to the North? They hadn't heard anything about the Second Prince's army on the way here, but this could have been because moving his army was a slow process. Maybe he was only a couple of days behind.

Missandra gently put a hand on her older sister's leg, feeling her worry. She then turned to Yasora.

"How is the situation here? We heard some bad rumors about the Emperor on our way here."

The middle-aged woman sighed and nodded, grabbing one layer of her dress with a sour expression.

"I fear it is all true. The rumors have been all over the streets for a couple of days now. The Old Emperor has become very sick. We don't know what's going on in the Palace, the security was increased so suddenly and there was a

488

big ruckus. They tried to prevent people from coming in or out, which made people even more suspicious. Some Ministers and Scholars were even executed publicly, people are terrified!"

Cassandra was livid. How could so much happen in a single week? Just because Sephir had died. Now, the Emperor was supposedly near death as well... people being executed... that sounded like someone was purging. Her heart sank. What if Kairen didn't come back in time to stop his brother? She exchanged a look with Missandra. Her younger sister didn't look worried, but angry.

"That rat face probably put his plan in motion as soon as your man was sent to war," Missandra said. "What a snake."

"So no one has been able to enter the Palace since then?" asked Cassandra. "What about the Fourth and Fifth Princes?"

"I haven't heard anything about those two."

Cassandra bit her lower lip. That meant the Fifth Prince Lephys and Fourth Prince Opheus were probably still inside the Imperial Palace. The problem was, she had no idea if they would side with their Second Brother or Kairen. Cassandra had only met the two of them very briefly. Lephys didn't give her a good impression at all, and she couldn't even remember seeing Opheus aside from his presence during the Red Moon Festival. He was known to be very secretive and avoided his father's banquets almost as much as Kairen and Shareen. Could he be a potential ally? She couldn't approach either of them without being sure.

"What about the battlefront?" she asked, her throat a bit tight. "Tell me you have news?"

Yasora seemed to hesitate for a few seconds and nodded.

"I do, but... it is not much better. The last thing we heard came from some soldiers, yesterday. Ethen went to buy some groceries and heard them. Apparently, they said the War God was ambushed in the last city, and the fight isn't going too well. I honestly don't know if that's true, but...the Eastern Empire had dragons."

Cassandra was shocked. Dragons? How could the Eastern Empire have dragons when none of their people had Dragon Blood! Were those dragons captured? Or conveniently given to them by a certain Prince. Cassandra tried to remember.

"Vrehan has two sons, but he wouldn't send his own sons' dragons to war," she muttered.

"Maybe he took some of his brothers?" said Missandra. "Didn't the First Prince have sons, too?"

"Sephir had one son, and other than Vrehan's sons, I think the Fifth Prince Lephys had sons as well... Oh God, the First Prince's Concubines, and their children!"

Cassandra had almost completely forgotten about those two. What had happened to them after Sephir's death? She clearly remembered the two

Concubines who had tried to befriend her, back at the Imperial Palace. Kareen had stated those women and their children would be in danger as soon as their Lord died. What had Vrehan done with them, and with the children? Would he use his nephew's dragon?

She remembered those women, Berissa and Chiara, when they had come to her. Cassandra hadn't thought too much about it since then... She hoped they were fine. Did they manage to leave the Imperial Palace? Maybe they were fine for now, as the Old Emperor was still alive.

"I hope they are doing all right... You said the man brought gold and food. Did he say anything else?"

"No. He was very discreet, probably a spy."

It made sense. Cassandra wished Lady Kareen had left more information. At least she had found a way to provide them some assistance.

"Lady Kareen probably didn't want you to move from here until they arrived," said Missandra. "Without the Third Prince, you're a target for them. Especially with those two."

She was pointing at Kassian and Kian, both peacefully sleeping already. Cassandra sighed. The last thing she wanted to do was put her baby and his dragon in any danger. This house was probably safe for now, but the word that she was hiding in the Capital would definitely spread around now that Kian had been spotted at the gate. Now more than ever, she couldn't stop worrying about everything going on. The Concubines and their children, and the Old Emperor... The battlefront, as well. What was that story about dragons! This was supposed to be an easy victory, but now, her dear War God could really be in trouble.

"Shareen will probably go to help him if she's gone back to the Diamond Palace," said Cassandra. "However, I think this sounds too much like a giant trap."

"Definitely," sighed her sister. "I told you from the beginning. What do we do though? We should stay still until they arrive, right?"

Cassandra hesitated a bit. Could she stay put, though? Time was against them. If that letter had arrived two days ago through a bird. If everything Evin had said was right, and Shareen had to go help her brother on the battlefront before they could come back here, her Prince most likely wouldn't be able to return to the Capital for at least a couple more days. That was only an optimistic estimate, too.

Meanwhile, his father was dying in the Imperial Palace, only a few paces away from Cassandra. She bit her lip, making Missandra frown.

"Oh, no, no, Hinue."

"This might be our only chance to save the Emperor," she said.

"Or our one chance to get killed! Why would you go to the Imperial Palace when that would be the obvious place we could get ourselves killed!"

"The Second Prince isn't in the Capital at the moment, right?" asked Cassandra, turning to Yasora.

"No."

"See? Missandra, if the Emperor dies, we will be in much more trouble than we are now. We are losing time, the Old Emperor could die any minute from whatever they did to him!"

"Yes, and maybe that old man is already dead and done for, Cassandra! In any case, I'm pretty sure Lady Kareen didn't want you to go there and expose yourself! They freaking closed the Imperial Palace for a reason, they don't want you in!"

"Maybe we can find a way around that," whispered Cassandra.

Missandra was about to retort something, but before she did, Yasora raised her hands, putting an end to their dispute.

"Ladies, I think you are both very tired and in need of some decent sleep. So, even if you want to come up with a plan, I suggest you wait until tomorrow."

Chapter 30

Despite all the worries and thoughts she had, the exhaustion from the journey allowed Cassandra a long, deep sleep. She and Missandra were finally able to sleep in a real bed, after a long bath and a hot meal. It was the first time they didn't get up to tend to the babies since their arrival. Kassian and Kian were carefully watched by Yasora, and the young Mira and Ethen, who made sure the two young babies didn't miss a thing. Cassandra wouldn't have entrusted them to anyone else, but she really needed one night of uninterrupted sleep.

When she woke up the next morning, she felt refreshed and her mind felt clearer. However, Cassandra's desire to help hadn't changed. She was simply determined to convince Missandra to participate. It wasn't just about having her sister agree, Cassandra realized her younger sister's wit may be a life-saving skill. It could be necessary, if she had to infiltrate the heavily guarded Imperial Palace. Missandra had demonstrated that she had her own resources over the past week. The difference in abilities between Cassandra and her sister could be crucial to completing the task at hand.

Hence, when she walked into the little room that had breakfast waiting for them, Cassandra tried to think about how to approach her sister. Carrying Kassian, who was a bit grouchy from having just woken up, she sat next to her.

"Good morning."

"Morning," yawned Missandra, her hair still all over the place.

Somehow, Yasora seemed to have understood that the two sisters would have important topics to discuss. None of the younger servants were around. Everyone that was around them was simply busy with their tasks, not staring or asking any questions. They began eating in silence, only Kian and Kassian making little noises. While the baby was being breastfed, Kian was devouring a full plate of meat buns, apparently a new favorite food.

Cassandra waited a bit before opening her mouth, trying to gauge her sister's mood, but Missandra was being a bit too quiet.

"Missandra..."

"If this is about last night, Hinue, my answer is still no."

Cassandra sighed. She knew how stubborn her sister was. This wasn't going to be an easy one.

"Missandra, we cannot stay passive."

"Yes, we can. We are not going to get ourselves killed by infiltrating a Palace guarded by hundreds of guards under that maniac's control, just to save an old man who, if we're that unlucky, might even be dead already."

"The Emperor isn't dead yet," retorted Cassandra. "Missandra, I cannot stay hidden here while he might be dying. Not when I could possibly save him."

"You don't know if he's really dying, if he's fine, or already dead! You don't know if you'll be able to save him either, Cassandra, and that could actually cost you your life! The only thing we do know for sure right now is that the crazy Second Prince wants to kill you, and Kassian. That's about it. We don't even know if your own Prince is well and alive!"

"I know Kairen is fine," retorted Cassandra, almost angry now.

Missandra shook her head. She didn't like to be scolding her older sister, but she was terrified that Cassandra was about to put herself in danger once more, and she wouldn't be able to stop her. Missandra put down her plate and turned to Cassandra, looking very serious.

"You barely escaped him once, Cassandra," she said. "You barely did. If it wasn't for the Diamond People, or for Lady Kareen buying us some time, we would already be dead, or worse, dead in his Dragon's stomach. This psychopath might even have taken his sweet time and tortured you, just to piss off the War God. In any case, I will not abide by anything that might put you and I anywhere near that guy. Not until we are sure to be safe."

Cassandra sighed. She understood Missandra's reasons and in many ways, her younger sister was actually right. It was a miracle they had been able to travel here to safety and remain unharmed. Cassandra had gotten a new scar on her arm, but it was healed already. Given the circumstances, it wasn't the worst thing that could have happened.

However, something was telling her to go to the Imperial Palace. Not only for the Old Emperor, but she felt like something much bigger was going on, and they had to stop it before it was too late. If her Prince was still caught up in a war, how could she stay here and drink tea?

"Missandra, I can't. I can't stay hidden here. We already did the hardest part, the journey. Our goal was to arrive in the Capital."

"Yes, because we thought the Old Emperor could save us. We had no idea he wasn't doing well! If we go there, we can't be sure he will protect you or Kassian!"

"What if he can? What if we can save the Emperor and end this? Missandra, another thing we know almost for sure is that the Second Prince isn't there, right?"

The younger sister frowned, but before she answered, Yasora cleared her throat.

"Actually, he is not. News came in very early this morning. Two of our people who were in the market said the Second Prince was on his way here, but is still a couple of cities away."

"See?" said Cassandra. "We will know right away if Prince Vrehan comes here, Missandra, his..."

"He is on his way back!" yelled Missandra, getting on her feet. "Cassandra, this cold-blooded murderer, and his crazy bitch sister might be only a few hours away from here!"

"That is exactly why we have to move now! The longer we hesitate, the more time we will lose! What if this is our chance to beat him, heal the Emperor, and punish Vrehan and Phetra for what they did?"

Missandra stayed silent for a few seconds. This was really too crazy. She was the one trying to hold Cassandra back, and her sister the one who wanted to take action? This was truly too much! This was a life and death kind of decision, and she was scared they were running into a trap.

"What if they expect us? What if we run into a trap? Have you thought about Kassian? And Kian?"

Cassandra looked down at her son and took a deep breath.

"I'm thinking about him. If his Grandfather dies, what do you think will happen? Maybe something will happen to his father, maybe Kairen won't be able to keep Vrehan from becoming Emperor. I am done letting Kairen fight every battle for me. I am good at one thing, Missandra, that's healing people. If the Emperor is sick, this is my call. It is up to me to do what I can. I will let Kairen deal with Vrehan, but the Emperor's health became my responsibility the moment I heard about it. Doing nothing is the worst thing. I'd rather die attempting to do something than stay here and close my eyes, hoping someone else will solve the problem for me."

Missandra opened her mouth, but she found no words to respond to that. She was annoyed. Annoyed, as her older sister was probably right. Nobody could save the Emperor better than Cassandra. The Second Prince wasn't expecting them to be there. He wouldn't know until he returned to the Capitol, and they still were a little bit ahead. They still had a chance that the War God would return too, but they didn't have any more information on his whereabouts. Actually, the information they did have was that neither of the Princes were there. The old Emperor, however, was there, and was very sick. She let out a long sigh of frustration.

"What about Kassian?"

"We can watch him here," immediately replied Yasora.

"What makes you think I trust you?" retorted Missandra, a bit too coldly.

The middle-aged woman put her fists on her waist. She knew that the young lady was Cassandra's younger sister, but she could use some manners!

"Well, you're still alive, aren't you? Also, there isn't a single human being in this place that doesn't owe their life to Cassandra. She freed us from slavery or servitude, which was just as bad. Everyone here would die for her."

Missandra pouted. Why was it that Cassandra always had that kind of effect on people? The North people, the Diamond people, and now these servants, everyone loved her. Was it okay to trust them? If it was up to Missandra, she wouldn't even have entrusted them with a single hair of her nephew! She let out a long sigh, turning to her sister once again.

"I suppose we don't have any better option?" she asked, totally ignoring Yasora's glare.

"I'm afraid not," said Cassandra. "No one knows where I came from, or that I'm in any way related to this place, aside from the Prince. At least Vrehan won't be able to find them here, even if something happens to us."

This way, even if something happened to Cassandra, Kairen would immediately know where to look for their son. She didn't say that out loud, though, as Missandra was already rather upset.

"Fine, say that I do agree to all of this, what's the plan? How do we get into the Imperial Palace? Because the heavily guarded situation is still pretty much a problem there."

Cassandra took a minute to think about it. Unfortunately, there was no way the dragon could fly them into the Palace. This was the way she had most used, recently. The only exception had been with Shareen, when she had gone downtown. But then they had used the main gates, and that was out of the question.

"You could use the servants' entrance?"

They turned around. The young Mara had just come back, carrying a big bowl of meat buns since Kian had happily emptied the previous one. She carefully put the new bowl close to the young dragon, making sure to keep her fingers away from it, and sat on her knees, close to Cassandra.

"The servants' entrance?" asked Cassandra.

The young girl nodded.

"Do you remember when you came back and the dragon ate the Master? A lot of the other servants left, but some are still my friends, and now they work at the Imperial Palace. They said the servants' entrance is not well-guarded, there are only two guards!"

Cassandra and Missandra exchanged looks, a bit doubtful. Only two guards? That almost seemed a bit too good to be true. She actually had no idea there was a different entry for the servants, but remembering her days at the Imperial Palace, Cassandra had indeed noticed that they would appear to come out of literally nowhere. They had to stay out of sight, so as to not annoy the many members of the Imperial Family. The Imperial Servants were often invisible to most people, walking quickly and keeping their heads lowered. In a strange way, it almost made sense. So many scholars, ministers, Imperial Advisors, and soldiers were circulating through the main door, who would bother with the lower-class people? The servants entrance should actually be much less guarded.

"We are still pale," Missandra reminded her.

"Well, we have already proven to be good at disguising ourselves, haven't we? If you managed to fool them once, when we only had a bit of make-up and a few trees to hide behind, you should be able to do it again, right?"

Missandra was bitterly starting to regret her display of make-up skills now. She sighed and turned to Yasora and Mira.

"Do you think you could get us some servant outfits and make-up?"

"Anything you need! We have servants going to the market and shops every day, no one will suspect a thing."

Just like that, Missandra and Cassandra started reviewing each step of their plan, with Yasora and Mira's help. The more she heard her sister, the more Cassandra knew she was going to accept this. Missandra was making sure every detail of their plan to infiltrate the Palace would work, and there was no end to her questions. Just from hearing her talk, she could tell her younger sister had much experience in dealing with all kinds of people. She was talking about the guards' rounds and breaks, the servants' schedules, the rotations and tasks inside the Palace.

However, they didn't have that much time to spend talking. No matter how well they tried to plan this, they wouldn't be able to prevent anything bad happening. With that in mind, Yasora sent a couple of servants to go grab the things Missandra asked her. While they waited for their return, the sisters agreed to go to the Palace early that afternoon. Cassandra didn't want to lose any more time. She knew that right after lunch the activity inside the Palace would be much calmer, as it would be time for court. Cassandra only had a glimpse of the Emperor's activities, but with his illness, she expected the Ministers and Generals to have even more work to make up for his absence. They had a rough idea on which areas to avoid, thanks to Mira's servant friends, and they agreed that neither the Fourth or Fifth Princes were to be trusted. Cassandra wasn't too sure about Opheus, but she definitely didn't want to run into Lephys. Missandra's plan was simple; avoid anyone wearing purple and get to the Emperor's quarters as quickly as possible.

When the servants came back with all the make-up, they ate a quick lunch and started getting ready, being more cautious about the tan and returning their locks to a solid black color. This felt all too familiar, but the preparation was necessary. Once the sisters were ready, Yasora nodded.

"You do look like our people now... except for your eyes, of course."

"We'll have to remember to look down," said Missandra.

Meanwhile, Cassandra was hugging Kassian. The baby hadn't been very noisy during their preparations, but as if he knew what was going on, he was now starting to cry and get upset. This broke Cassandra's heart. She had been with her son for a full week. If this wasn't so important, she wouldn't separate from him, even for a short while. She hugged him closely, kissing his forehead and whispering to calm him down. At her feet, Kian too seemed nervous, walking in circles and emitting quick, little, high-pitched sounds, trying to get her attention.

496

"It's going to be fine, my love," she whispered. "Your mom will be right back, I promise."

Kassian started crying even louder, and she had to take a deep breath before hugging him, and the Baby Dragon, one last time. It was difficult to feel their warmth and part with it. She gave her baby to Yasora, and made a promise to herself. This wasn't going to take long. She'd definitely be back soon for her son.

Cassandra had the urge to cry when they left the residence, but tried her hardest not to. Even Missandra had her little good-bye moment with her nephew and his small dragon, but she didn't say anything. She knew she couldn't afford to be emotional now, they had to focus on this plan and ensure their survival. Even if she had agreed to it, Missandra was still not feeling anywhere near confident enough. Anything could get them killed, even the slightest mistake could end their lives in a split second.

At least they looked different now. With green dresses on, their skin darkened to match those of the people, and their hair black as ink, they would be hard to spot by any soldiers who were looking for them. Not having a baby or a young dragon definitely made it easier to move around, too. They also had an extra asset, as Mira had rallied a few of the former servants of the house. They quickly met the three girls in the middle of the market, where no one would be suspicious. They were all familiar with Cassandra, as they had worked under the same roof, briefly. These three had been there the day she had freed the residence, and even if they were now working at the Imperial Palace, they were happy to look out for her and help the sisters as repayment.

This was also a good omen in Missandra's eyes. The two sisters would be less likely to be noticed if they walked into the Palace as a group of five servants instead of a duo. They had no idea if the Second Prince was looking only for Cassandra, or for the both of them. In any case, this was still working in their favor.

They walked towards the Imperial Palace, and seeing the high walls from up close gave Cassandra an inexplicable feeling of nostalgia. She hadn't been there in weeks, and this time, she wasn't with Kairen. She had never liked this place, but this feeling of dislike was much stronger now. To Cassandra's surprise, the soldiers weren't very familiar with the servants going in and out all day. They checked their belongings in detail, but they didn't find the hidden daggers on either of the sisters. She realized there were truly too many servants for the soldiers to bother recognizing all of them. The Imperial Palace was gigantic, and with all of the Imperial Concubines, Princes and Princesses, the servants probably changed a lot every week. It was probably the same for the soldiers as well. Unless the same soldiers would be assigned to the same doors every single day for weeks and weeks, it seemed hard to think they'd remember the faces, unless they were memorable.

Ironically, one of the soldiers even smiled at Missandra, though his eyes were focused a bit lower. Cassandra had a little fright, but to her surprise, her younger sister even had the guts to wink at the soldier! She kept her head low, trying to pray silently until they were inside and away from the soldiers. All the girls smiled at each other.

"I can't believe we got in that easily," whispered Cassandra.

"That's because the Imperial Family isn't actually in danger all of the time," sighed one of the girls. "You know, the danger usually comes from the inside. They poison each other and find excuses to murder each other more efficiently than any assassin out there. Aside from that, they have dragons! Like, those creatures are terrifying!"

Cassandra and Missandra exchanged glances. The dragon they had been living with over the past few days wasn't exactly terrifying, though they did understand the girls' concern. They probably didn't picture Kian eating meat buns while saying that.

"I don't even think they ever bother to hire assassins," added the other with a nod. "You know, sometimes those women scare me more than the dragons themselves. A single tantrum and they can have you tortured or killed!"

As the girls kept nodding and agreeing, Cassandra realized this was the reality for them. She had always been protected by Kairen, his dragon, and his family. But for any servant working in the Imperial Palace, they were risking their lives every day. This should never be considered normal. It does explain the large turnover and high salaries, though.

After reaching one of the servants' resting rooms, Missandra and Cassandra parted from the girls, thanking them for their help in getting to this point. Somehow, Cassandra felt like they were entering the part of their plan where everything could go downhill very fast.

Walking with trays of food, as if they had been asked to deliver them somewhere, they tried to find their way through the corridors. The sisters had previously agreed to not go anywhere near Lady Kareen's apartments, or Kairen's, or Shareen's, as they would be very likely watched. Those would be the first places Vrehan would expect her to hide, so they had to avoid those aisles at all costs. Another thing Cassandra was worried about were the Concubines.

Though there weren't a lot of Princesses hanging around, the Concubines were often going from one place to another, chatting with each other in the gardens and wandering around. Cassandra was afraid one of them would recognize her if they crossed paths, and this was bound to happen. She made sure to keep her head down, hoping her appearance and green dress would do the trick. Moreover, as Missandra had reminded her, even Cassandra's body shape had changed a lot over the past few weeks. The only thing that may give her away was her green eyes, and she kept them down while they walked.

It worked. Despite a few frights on the way, Cassandra made sure to walk behind her sister and thankfully none of the Concubines they crossed paths with had recognized her. Most of the women didn't even spare them a glance, they were used to the servants getting out of their way.

The Imperial Palace was so vast, it took some time to get to their first destination. Prince Sephir's apartments.

Despite Missandra's warnings, Cassandra just couldn't come here without checking what had happened to the First Prince or his Concubines and children. Besides, if she had any allies left between these walls, it would most likely be those women. She vaguely remembered the configuration of the First Prince's apartments, and the sisters moved quickly.

The atmosphere was heart-wrenching in there. Some of the women were still silently crying and mourning the death of the Prince, but at least, most of them seemed safe, the children also. Cassandra was extremely careful while moving around. She wasn't sure where the two Concubines she was looking for resided exactly, so Missandra eventually asked another servant they met, pretending she was new in the Imperial Palace.

Once they found their rooms, Cassandra knocked, a bit afraid. To their surprise, a little girl in a purple dress came to open the door. She was four or five years old at best.

"Silena, don't just... Oh, by the Great Dragon!"

The young Concubine ran to them and pulled the sisters inside before hurriedly closing the door. Then, she turned around, completely stunned.

"What are you doing here?" she whispered.

She had obviously recognized Cassandra, so she put down the tray on a table. They were alone, too, and the room was now closed, despite Missandra sending regular glances towards the other openings.

Lady Chiara walked to Cassandra, staring at her as if she had seen a ghost, looking on the verge of tears.

"By the Great Dragon, Lady Cassandra, I can't believe you're here," she whispered.

"Are you alright?" asked Cassandra, as the young woman seemed completely in shock.

The young Concubine immediately shook her head, looking horrified, and about to cry.

"You shouldn't have come here! The Second Prince wants to kill you."

"Noted," said Missandra, rolling her eyes.

"No, no, this is serious!" insisted Chiara. "He... he said you poisoned my Lord."

"What happened?" asked Cassandra, hoping she would calm down a little bit to explain.

The young Concubine shook her head and fell onto her knees. Her daughter immediately ran into her arms to hug her, and she held her child, crying silently.

"I'm not sure. It all happened so fast! Everything was just as usual, and one evening, I heard people yelling, screaming... The other Concubines kept saying our Lord had died. Prince Vrehan came out of his room, all of sudden, dragging

Lady Berissa by her hair, calling her a murderer! He yelled to everyone that he had caught her poisoning his brother with something the white witch had given her! Everyone started screaming, we knew Lady Berissa was innocent, but...his dragon...he killed her there, and... They said my Lord was dead."

The poor Concubine was bawling her eyes out in front of them. Cassandra exchanged a look with Missandra, horrified. What had Vrehan done? How could he push all the blame on Berissa and kill her without a proper trial, or even any decent proof!

"How could the Emperor let that happen?" said Cassandra, shocked.

"It happened so fast," cried Lady Chiara. "When his Highness the Emperor came, he was devastated about my Lord's passing, and he was furious at Prince Vrehan, but the Second Prince said he had acted impulsively out of anger."

"That's the most bullshit excuse I've heard, even coming from that dickhead," hissed Missandra.

Cassandra was in complete shock. She hadn't thought things had become so tragic! The poor Lady Berissa, she had been the cruel victim of Vrehan's schemes to get rid of her and his brother. Cassandra was completely revolted. This was so unfair! These people were innocent, Prince Sephir had never even been a threat to him! Vrehan's cupidity was absolutely disgusting! Had Kassian's birth really made him panic and kill his own brother? Did the news of her pregnancy accelerate the Second Prince's agenda?

"Lady Cassandra, you shouldn't be here. They all think you're a murderer, the soldiers will arrest you."

"What about Prince Sephir's Son?" asked Cassandra, ignoring the Concubine's plea.

"I don't know..." cried Chiara. "We haven't seen him since our Prince's death. By the Great Dragon, if something happened to Prince Seban too..."

The poor Concubine hugged her daughter closer and cried even more. Cassandra and Missandra exchanged a silent glance. They wouldn't say it in front of this poor woman, but they feared the young Prince's fate was, unfortunately, already sealed. Vrehan may have taken the young dragon, too.

After all this, no wonder this whole aisle of the Imperial Palace felt so abandoned and at a loss. The Second Prince had wreaked havoc in his brother's entourage. Cassandra felt like it was a miracle that the little girl in the Concubine's arms was still alive. If she had been born a boy, her uncle would have gotten rid of her, most likely.

"What about Prince Sephir's Dragon?" asked Missandra, frowning.

"He's here, but...he hasn't been able to fly," said Chiara, her voice hoarse. "Prince Vrehan had Sire locked down in the dungeons, saying he could be dangerous for everyone in the palace without his Master to guide him. I'm not sure. He didn't even try to free himself when they took him!"

The cells! Cassandra remembered seeing some of the dragons behind bars, the first time she had been in the Imperial Palace. Those who were too unruly had to be chained or placed in cages for their sizes. However, she clearly remembered that the Pale Blue Dragon wasn't among those who had to be put in an actual cage! That was definitely another one of the second Prince's horrible lies.

"So the Prince is dead for real, and his dragon is grounded," sighed Missandra. "Anything else we need to know?"

"What about the Emperor?" asked Cassandra. "Have any of you seen him lately?"

"No...most of us haven't dared to leave these apartments! Everyone is just so scared since our Prince died! However, some of the other Concubines came and said he's ill. The Emperor fell sick soon after my Prince. They say he was so depressed with my Lord's death that the Emperor fell sick too. We haven't seen him in days."

"How convenient," muttered Missandra.

Cassandra didn't believe this lie at all either. For something to happen to the old Emperor so soon after his First Son's death, was nothing but the result of some vile plan. He wasn't such a weak man, even if his son's death was depressing . Whatever sickness had fallen upon the old Emperor was definitely not the result of sadness, or even an accident. Missandra shook her head, disgusted once again.

"Hinue," she said using their native tongue. "I'm pretty sure he won't be as stupid as to leave his old man without any sort of security around him. What if this is a trap? I can't believe no one was able to see the Emperor. This guy definitely has something up, and I'm not sure we should run into this mess. We can still go back!"

"We can't, Missandra. We haven't learned anything we didn't already suspect, but the Second Prince still isn't here. I'm still sure this is our only chance to save the Emperor, if that is still possible. If the Second Prince comes back and is somehow crowned before my Prince comes back, the situation will be even worse than this! Not only Sephir, but he will also get rid of all of his brothers and their Concubines! This will be a slaughter!"

"He can't just..."

"Missandra, he killed Sephir! He killed the First Prince and his Favorite, and probably their son, too. Unless he's captured him instead, but I'm pretty sure he doesn't care about anything except that boy's dragon! If we go back now, Vrehan might be able to kill his father even faster, and then what? He'll just do what he did here to all the Concubines! The only people left will be the ones who didn't oppose him, his Concubines, and his sisters!"

"This is too dangerous! That psycho had no problem killing his own brother, right under the Emperor's nose. If the Emperor is too ill to protect you, what do you think will happen to you? He's capable of feeding you to his dragon and claiming his damn lizard mistook you for a beefsteak once the Third Prince comes here! There is no one here who can help you!"

"Actually, we might have another ally," sighed Cassandra.

"Who?" asked Missandra with a frown.

"Glahad, the Golden Dragon."

Missandra stayed quiet for a while, looking more and more livid. After a while, she glanced down at the Concubine that was still in the room with them and took a deep breath.

"I knew the situation was dire," she said in their native tongue. "But I didn't think it would be so bad that our best hope would rely on the Emperor's freaking Dragon! Hinue, we are talking about an actual dragon. Not a cat-sized one like Kian! I know the Third Prince's black Dragon is basically your pet, but this is another Dragon we're talking about, the Emperor's! I'm pretty sure the most dangerous creature in the Empire hasn't been trained to do paw tricks!"

"Dragons only mimic their owners' feelings. Krai is like that because of Kairen's feelings for me. The Emperor liked me too, you've seen it. He's been nothing but nice and..."

"He is an Emperor! Who knows what that old man was thinking! Gifting you a tiara and some stupid nickname doesn't mean you're his favorite daughter-in-law! I trust you, but I don't trust a pervert that has taken dozens of Concubines, has kids left and right, all while his favorite woman has to live in a different castle to ensure her childrens survival!"

Cassandra sighed.

"I know this is the same refrain coming back again and again," added Missandra. "But I stand by my words, I don't trust the old man's dragon! We can't just walk in there and hope he's going to become our bodyguard! That's a rather big bet and I'm pretty sure we're running out of extra lives just by standing here!"

"Do you have a better idea, perhaps? We were going to see if the Emperor can be saved anyway, Missandra. Perhaps Glahad won't move a...claw to help us. At least it's better than nothing, right?"

"This is us reducing our chances of getting killed by a dragon's hair! And I know they don't have any!"

Next to them, the young Concubine stood back up again, shaking her head. She grabbed Cassandra's hand, as she was trembling herself, whilst looking her right in her eyes.

"Did you just say the Imperial Dragon's name? Are you going to see the Emperor? Please, Lady Cassandra, you have to save him!"

Both sisters were flustered to see the young woman suddenly begging, but neither of them could react to her new burst of tears, as she held on desperately to Cassandra, her lower lips trembling. She didn't look anything like the elegant young woman Cassandra had met only a few weeks ago. This was just a desperate girl, a mother begging for help to save her and her child.

"Please, you're the Imperial Physician. You have to save his Highness! If the Emperor dies, I know he will kill us! The Second Prince will have us all exterminated, our children too!"

Against her leg, the young girl started crying too, echoing her poor

502

mother's distress. Cassandra's heart broke. This little girl was so young, and she had just lost her father. How many of those children would have to grow up without their father now? They were all so terrorized already, but they were now living with the fear of their uncle finishing the job. Cassandra turned to her sister again, a determined expression in her eyes. Missandra couldn't say anything, not anymore, not when they were so frantically being begged like so. The younger sister kept shaking her head in disbelief, but she didn't voice her opinion anymore.

"I... I'll go see the Emperor, Lady Chiara. Stay here with your daughter, it will be safer. Do not tell anyone you've seen us, please?"

"Of course, Lady Cassandra. Please, be careful. Some of my Prince's Concubines are desperate. We are not stupid, none of us think Lady Berissa would have ever tried to harm our Prince! Even some of the Princesses are afraid!"

"What about the other Princes, by the way?" asked Missandra.

"We don't know."

Cassandra frowned. This was one thing she wished she could have resolved now. Not only were they in a den of wolves, but they couldn't even be sure who was their enemy or not. She nodded, and gently retrieving her hand, she turned to Missandra.

"We should go, now."

After checking their appearance, making sure nothing had been undone, the sisters left Lady Chiara, their hearts a bit heavier than before. Cassandra couldn't get that little girl's face out of her mind. She realized that somehow, she vaguely looked like her own son. Maybe it was because they were young, but those two children still had the same grandfather. That child was Kairen's niece. So many innocent young lives were trapped here! The Concubines were more or less circled in the Second Prince's residence. None of them had the means to leave, and they had no dragon to defend them either! With Sire locked in the cells underground, those women were nothing but prey for Vrehan to play with!

"We need to stop this," muttered Cassandra, as they walked alone in a corridor.

"Let's stay focused, we cannot make a mistake now," whispered Missandra. "We're lucky no one has recognized you yet, and that psycho isn't here. Now, where is the old man?"

"The Emperor's quarters were behind the room used for the banquets."

"Why is this place so damn big!"

As they were about to turn left on a corridor, the sisters heard a ruckus, and stopped their steps at the exact same time, both frowning. They listened for a few seconds, but the situation was rather heated.

"You damn little bitches! I'm so fed up with this crap! You sluts! Get the fuck out of my way, go back to my pervert brother before I ruin my nails on your ugly faces! Uglies!"

Cassandra and Missandra absolutely froze. Though they had their doubts, this masculine voice and the mention of a pervert brother were enough clues to guess they had almost run into the fourth brother. They waited to see if he was coming this way, but it didn't seem so, the sound of the man's steps and whoever was following him were getting further away. Cassandra let out a silent sigh, while Missandra raised an eyebrow.

"Well, that explains why that one doesn't have kids," she muttered.

"Why?" asked Cassandra, confused.

Missandra rolled her eyes.

"That guy is definitely not into women. Trust me, I've seen a lot of guys like that in the Red District. This one is definitely a man-player. Plus, the only person I've heard being sassier than that guy is Lady Shareen, and that alone says a lot."

"Oh..."

That did solve one mystery about the lack of descendants from Opheus, the Fourth Prince. However, that didn't give any insight into his position towards his brothers. Was he affected by Sephir's death? On Vrehan's side, or uninterested? What of Prince Lephys? After what they had just heard, Cassandra crossed out any thought she ever had of asking for help from one of the other Princes. The relationships between all the siblings were too complicated and she had no idea who could be trusted or not at this point. Neither the Fourth or Fifth Prince had seemed close to Kairen, or even Sephir, from her experience. Nothing said they would agree with Vrehan becoming the Emperor either, though.

Waiting a bit for the path to clear, the sisters kept walking, until they finally arrived in the Banquet Hall. It was deserted at that time, and most importantly, the area was completely unused at the moment. It would have been suspicious for two servants to walk into a room not in use, with food trays, so the two sisters had to act quickly and not linger.

Cassandra remembered that whenever one of the Banquets she attended in the past was over, the Emperor left through a door behind his Golden Throne. The Emperor's seat was so large and impressive, it seemed like a wall behind him, but Cassandra clearly remembered seeing Glahad curled up in that space, between the actual wall and his owner's seat. No one wanted to go anywhere near the Imperial Dragon's favorite spot, but she knew the doors to the Emperor's apartments had to be behind that throne.

However, as soon as the sisters pretended to walk through the Banquet room, both noticed the men guarding that door. They pretended to chat and leave the room, but as soon as the door was closed behind them, Missandra shook her head.

"So, no big dragon, but two guards. I wouldn't have been surprised if that psycho had put more men than that. How are we supposed to get to the Old Man now?"

However, Cassandra wasn't listening to her. She was already staring away at one of the windows. She walked to the opening and stuck her head out to look down. Missandra frowned in confusion.

"Hinue, what are you doing?"

"When my Prince had...Well, when he injured Princess Phetra, he threw her out of one of the banquet room's windows. Lady Kareen had mentioned there were only three or so floors below, and she was right, there's actually a roof. I can see it from here. The building below goes all the way down to the Emperor's apartments."

Her sister shook her head in disbelief. That was it. Her older sister had officially gone crazy!

"I'm not breaking my ankles to go and save a dying old man," said Missandra, coming to stand next to her at the window, to check what was below.

Cassandra chuckled and pointed her finger.

"We don't have to fall if we can climb. Just like I thought, the stones in the walls are very uneven. Which means we could possibly climb laterally until we reach it. We would use the outside instead of walking inside and past the guards."

Missandra was astonished. This idea was easily taking first place for the most dangerous idea her sister had that day, and that was saying a lot! Sure, they were exceptional swimmers, but swimming was nothing like climbing up and down walls! Missandra was about to protest, but for the first time, she decided against it. Instead, she scrutinized the wall Cassandra was thinking of climbing.

Indeed those were the typical rock constructions of the Dragon Empire. It was mostly uneven, however, from the many years of dragons attempting to climb on the buildings. Large, sharp claws had clearly scratched deeply into the wall, taking off some of the stones and helpfully given the duo even more spots to safely put their hands and feet on. Technically speaking, this wasn't impossible. Both girls were in pretty good shape, physically speaking. Missandra hesitated a moment, sending a backwards glance towards the other room. Those guards didn't look to be the pleasant type at all. That damn Second Prince had probably chosen men that would guard his father's room very carefully. She quickly tried coming up with another strategy to get rid of them, but Missandra was nervous someone would recognize her; she resembled Cassandra too much.

Missandra decided the climb, in comparison, didn't look as dangerous or as crazy to try. They had the physical condition for it, a stable and hidden path, and they even had the luxury of a rooftop below them to fall on, in case of failure. Of course, they'd probably suffer major injuries like Phetra if they did fall. But at least, the chances of survival were decent, given the situation.

Checking that the corridor was empty, Cassandra climbed out of the window, carefully hanging onto the window's rail. She moved to the first target, a larger hole in the wall. She had never liked the Imperial Palace, but the place was old enough to have had many, many dragons' claws leave their imprints on the walls. The indents in the stones gave her some easy spots to grab onto and move around. Sure enough, Cassandra made her way to the external walls of the previous corridor. Biting her lower lip, Missandra watched her sister's progress.

Every imprint that she placed her foot or hand into seemed stable. Not even a speck of dust moved. Checking her surroundings, Missandra climbed out of the window to follow her.

Quickly and silently, the sisters moved around the external walls, keeping their heads below the windows. The main danger would be that someone spotted them from another window. However, from what they had seen so far, not many people were hanging around the premises. So they continued moving, climbing the wall sideways until their position was past the guards they had seen inside. There were some problems, though. Cassandra had no idea how many rooms there were inside, their configuration, or who might be inside. They would have to take a guess on which window to climb back in through, but they had to decide quickly. Climbing was a difficult exercise, and neither of them were very experienced at it. Their arms were starting to get painful and their muscles were aching. A pearl of sweat was growing on Missandra's forehead, threatening to take away some of the fake tan that was covering her. When she finally found a position right under one of the windows she could stay in without too much strain, Cassandra stopped, trying to listen to what was going on inside. Seemingly, nothing. The other side seemed strangely quiet, though she couldn't tell if this was a good sign or not. She exchanged looks with Missandra, who nodded. In any case, the longer they stayed there, the more risk they were taking of being found by someone. They had to climb back inside.

Carefully, Cassandra climbed up, glancing inside. It looked like she had actually picked a bathroom window! Luckily, that room was small, and with the door facing the window, she could immediately tell the place was empty. With a sigh of relief, both sisters climbed inside to finally rest their aching muscles.

Missandra stretched with a grimace and even went to the little basin of water to drink. Their arms were sore, but at least they had made it inside the Emperor's apartments. Cassandra walked as quietly as she could and put her ear against the door. It was complete silence on the other side.

Very carefully, the sisters came out of the bathroom. This was truly a strange atmosphere, almost like the inside of a church. The aisle was beautiful, all made of marble and white stones, but it was as silent and intimidating as a mausoleum. In such an environment, each step or breath the sisters took seemed too noisy.

"All right, now to find the Old Man," whispered Missandra.

Cassandra nodded, and they started walking down the corridor. They had no idea which door to push, and were terrified to run into someone that would give away their position. However, after a while, it looked like this place was truly abandoned. They pushed open many doors, each time to find an empty room.

"Are you sure these are the Emperor's apartments?" asked Missandra, frowning. "There's nothing going on here!"

"I don't understand," muttered Cassandra. "If he's sick, the Emperor should definitely be kept in his apartments!"

"That's the rule of the Imperial Palace? Well, someone needs to learn them again, because the Old Man isn't here! Cassandra, this place is completely empty! There's not even a single servant, those two idiots outside are guarding nothing but air!"

Cassandra shook her head in disbelief. Where was the Old Emperor then? If he was sick, the Emperor should be resting here, in his quarters! The sisters turned to each other.

"That damn Second Prince expected someone would come and he probably hid the Old Man elsewhere!" Missandra decided.

"But where? It's the Emperor, he can't simply vanish this way!"

"We..."

A sudden movement was felt from somewhere behind Missandra. Both sisters froze. Something was moving just outside of the room they were in. They slowly turned around, and it was there at the window. One reptilian blue eye, surrounded by white scales. Staring right at them.

Both sisters almost stopped breathing. A drop of cold sweat ran down Cassandra's spine. She had been hoping to find the Emperor and his Gold Dragon, but this was definitely not Glahad. Where did this white one come from? The sisters hadn't even heard anything until then. Missandra didn't dare move either, but she sent a glance towards her sister. No words were exchanged, but her expression was clear. Which dragon was that?

Cassandra tried hard to remember. She couldn't remember if the White Dragon was the Fourth or the Fifth Prince's, she had only seen it once! She couldn't even see its size, as only a little portion of its head was stuck against the window. The only thing that was a little bit reassuring was that it didn't seem to be unhappy at all. The white creature wasn't growling, and its eye just seemed... curious. Was it simply observing them? Either way, if it was there, its master definitely knew where they were. She didn't want to wait to see which Prince was about to show up!

"Let's go back," she whispered.

Missandra nodded slightly, but neither of them could take their eyes off the gigantic beast staring at them. Both sisters started stepping back, very carefully. The big blue eye was following their every move. They hesitated. They definitely couldn't go back the way they came in, with the White Dragon climbing along the tower as well. It would put them one arm away from the dragon, and its maw was definitely longer than that. Also, they had already struggled to get this far, Cassandra wasn't sure she would have the strength to go back the same way without making a mistake this time.

The main entrance then? It didn't solve the problem of the guards on the other side. The Dragon or the Prince could warn them at any time. Cassandra was trying to gauge their options quickly, but no good idea came to mind, and Missandra was terribly quiet too.

"What the hell are you doing here, you two idiots?!"

Cassandra sighed internally. It was too late.

Both sisters turned around, to find the Fourth Prince standing there. Opheus was very much like his brothers. Tall, with long black hair and fine musculature under his open shirt. His only marking trait was his strikingly blue eyes, both delicately circled by black ink. He was probably the most handsome of all the Imperial Brothers, but he was making a sour face at the moment with his arms crossed. The long gold earring on his left ear kept dangling as he shook his head.

"Sorry, Your Highness," said Cassandra, bowing instinctively. "We will leave and..."

"Oh, don't you dare act like that! I recognized you, White Witch!" retorted Opheus.

Cassandra went white under her make-up. She had the feeble hope that he wouldn't recognize her, as she didn't recognize him either, until two seconds ago. It seemed impossible to pretend to be two clueless maids now.

The Prince let out a dramatic sigh.

"You are all driving me nuts here! Darling, I have a good memory for faces, and even if you were as skinny and bleached as a skeleton back then, I still vividly remember the unfashionable slave girl Kairen went nuts about! Lephys may have hundreds of his little whores, I don't care. But the one lady that proved my older brother wasn't just a monk with a sword, despite his questionable tastes, that one I remember!"

Cassandra was utterly speechless. She hadn't expected the Prince to have such a... colorful personality. Until then, he had only been described as someone with a lazy and easily bored personality. It was apparently more about his attitude. At least, it didn't seem like he had given any alerts yet.

Unsure of what to say, Cassandra glanced Missandra's way. However, to her surprise, Missandra was nervously chuckling, focused on the Fourth Prince's face. He noticed it too, and clicked his tongue, pouting his lips.

"You can stop staring like that, darling. We are not playing on the same level."

"I know you," suddenly said Missandra with a snicker. "You're the Minstrel in Gold!"

"Oh," said Opheus, raising an eyebrow.

Cassandra was completely lost. What was her younger sister talking about? The Prince himself didn't seem very surprised, but his expression had completely changed after Missandra had said that. Cassandra turned to her, trying to understand what the hell she was talking about.

"Linue?" she called her.

"This Prince was a regular in the Red District!" exclaimed Missandra. "He was only known as the Minstrel in Gold, because his name was unknown and he always came dressed with lots of gold jewelry, and would always write stupid poems to his lovers."

"Stupid poems? Watch your mouth, you little bitch! I'm a lyricist, and everyone always says I have a lot of talent!"

508

"Yeah, let me guess, Your Highness, they're the same people to whom you generously give your gold to whenever they say that?" retorted Missandra with a snicker.

"Wait," said Cassandra. "You know him from the Red District?"

"Well, not all the workers are female," explained Missandra with a shrug.

"Oh..."

Cassandra hadn't thought of that. It did make sense though. The Fourth Prince probably wasn't given the kind of entertainment he wanted in the Imperial Palace. She clearly remembered his siblings talking about his lack of interest for his Concubines, despite his mother's desperate attempts to have him give birth to an heir. Well, now that explained a lot.

Cassandra gave a little glance, but the dragon outside was still there, patiently watching. So they weren't in danger with it so far. Opheus flipped his hair over his shoulder.

"I was wondering what my darling had found here, but it turns out, it's just you two. You are quite stupid for coming back here, though. Do you have any idea what Vrehan wants to do to you? That psycho seriously went crazy this time."

"What about you?" asked Missandra. "You don't look like you're about to report us."

"Oh, please, do you think I care about my brothers' stupid games?"

"This isn't a game," retorted Cassandra, almost shocked. "They are killing each other! Prince Sephir died!"

Opheus rolled his eyes.

"He was unfortunate to have been born first, yes. But me? I'm the one that nobody gives a shit about. Honestly, I'm quite content with that."

Cassandra understood that he was the one nobody would see as a threat, but that doesn't mean his brother's crimes are any less horrible! His older brother had been murdered only a few days ago, he couldn't be that insensitive as to not care at all!

However, he did look like he didn't care. Opheus put a hand on his hip, gauging the two of them.

"I honestly don't give a damn about reporting you, I don't even care enough to yell," he said. "However, I am curious why the hell Kairen's favorite and her sister are in my father's chambers."

"We hope to save the Emperor," explained Cassandra. "I know he is sick, I want to see him."

"We can heal him," added her younger sister. "If you tell us where the old man is, we can..."

Opheus scoffed, interrupting her. He used one of his long nails to point at Missandra.

"First, no offense, darling, but I wouldn't entrust you with a spoon."

Missandra looked put off by his words, but the Fourth Prince ignored her to turn to Cassandra.

"Secondly, why do you two care what happens to my father? Shouldn't you be somewhere taking care of the brat you were pregnant with? Waiting patiently somewhere for your man to slice Vrehan's head off? Because I'll be honest, I know I am."

Cassandra was a bit surprised to hear that.

"You don't like Vrehan? You support Kairen?"

Opheus dramatically rolled his eyes once again.

"You may be a physician, or whatever, but you're quite slow, darling, aren't you? Vrehan is a freaking sicko, his sister Phetra is the Empress of the bitches, and trust me, I know much more than they all think I do. Comparatively, Kairen is at least not bouncing about, murdering our family members in some sick attempt to become Emperor."

"So you can help us?" asked Cassandra, getting her hopes up again. "You can tell us where the Emperor actually is?"

"Why would I? I told you, I'm fine as long as neither of them thinks I'm against them. I am already being quite generous by not giving you little rats away to the guards. I hope you're taking notes about that."

Cassandra's hopes melted immediately. So he wasn't going to help them at all? Were the sisters condemned already? There was no way they were going to be able to walk out of here while the two guards were still standing outside the apartments! They couldn't stay hidden here forever either!

Next to her, Missandra took a deep breath and crossed her arms, looking surprisingly confident.

"Well, it's a bit too late for that, isn't it? You're already an accomplice."

"What?"

"You've seen us. Like you said, you didn't denounce us right away and you have no intention to. So, that means you're on our side."

Opheus narrowed his eyes, looking a bit confused.

"Didn't you listen to anything I just said, you little pest? I am not on anyone's side! Unless I go into the throne's room and walk around naked, I won't be considered a target by Vrehan either! I am the invisible Prince and I like that!"

"Oh, but you have seen us already. So now, you're technically hiding our existence from the Second Prince. If we get caught and say you had actually found us first, it would be bad for you, wouldn't it? You wouldn't be so invisible anymore."

Cassandra couldn't understand. What was Missandra thinking by provoking him like that?! Despite her doubts, she remained quiet to let her younger sister talk. After those few weeks together, Cassandra knew that Missandra was better than her for those kinds of things. Missandra was what you'd call street-smart; she was better at getting out of a situation when she was cornered.

"What are you talking about?!" screeched the Fourth Prince. "I am not helping you, I'm just keeping my mouth shut!"

510

"Oh, I bet the Second Prince will think the same when he learns that you had us right under your nose and did not let his soldiers know. He'll probably overlook this and think you just didn't care."

Opheus opened and closed his mouth twice, completely taken aback. Finally, he scoffed, outraged by Missandra's words and her confident smirk. Putting his hands on his hips, he was now glaring at her.

"Why shouldn't I give you up right now then, you little pests? I am extremely generous already to let you go without saying a word! Why the hell are you threatening me?!"

"I am not threatening you," replied Missandra with an innocent smile. "Of course, you're very free to rat us out to the psychopath's men if you prefer. However, I cannot guarantee that the War God won't be back first."

Once again, the Fourth Prince was rendered speechless and blinked several times.

"Kairen? He's coming back here? Seriously?"

Missandra nodded. Whether she was truly convinced or lying through her teeth, her older sister couldn't tell. However, they clearly weren't sure that the War God was really on his way back, or even how far away he was at the moment. This was a heavy bet her sister was putting on the table right now.

"Yes. His Favorite Concubine is here, after all," she said. "The War God will be back in the Capital at any time. I mean, you could give us up, but it would truly be bad timing if the Third Prince came back meanwhile. If the War God learns that you sold out his Favorite Concubine... If my older sister dies, just like that, I wonder who he will get mad at? I mean, obviously, the Second Prince is the first choice, but I wonder who he will get angry at then? It tends to get pretty bloody when the War God gets mad, you know."

Cassandra was once again stunned speechless. Her younger sister was truly shameless! She was putting the Fourth Prince in a horrible position, torn between the fear of the Second or Third Brother's wrath. It was too late for him to pretend he hadn't seen them, not after everything Missandra had just said. The poor man looked like he was about to vomit, he was completely trapped by the teenage girl.

"You... You... By the Great Dragon, you're the worst little swine!" He yelled. "That was me being nice!"

"Oh, it's nice of you to not rat us out, but now we would like to know where the Emperor is. So now, you can pick a side. Because either you help us and we can get out of here without making any waves, and potentially getting a chance to save the old man. Or my sister and I will get caught as soon as we try to get out of here, by your sicko brother's men, tortured, and will most likely die in a horrible way. Your choice, Your Highness."

Chapter 31

The man stood up, letting out an exhausted sigh.

He was drenched in blood. His blood and that of the two dragons he had just fought. The dragons weren't dead. One was lying down on the ground, a sword pinning his wing, and the other was cornered, growling furiously while trying to hide his injured leg. The War God's body was covered in black scales, struggling to heal the many cuts on his body. All of his armor had been torn away, leaving him with only his pants on. He put his hand on his neck, checking the fresh injury. His own blood tainted his fingers as he snickered.

They had really given it their all at trying to kill him. However, those two young dragons were mostly afraid, trapped in a tight room with him. In a more open ground, they probably would have had more chances to succeed in killing him. However, in here, they were as trapped as he was and unable to use their wings. They even hindered each other quite a few times, mistakenly biting or scratching their skins. Without that, maybe they would have had a better chance.

"Kairen!"

He heard a long bang on the door behind him and turned around. His sister violently burst in, sending the locked doors flying. Shareen's hair was all over her face, and she seemed angry. She had her sword out, too, for the minute it took her to assess the situation. Kairen, standing alone in the vast room, with a young Dragon cornered at each end of it. She clicked her tongue, shaking her head, and putting her sword back away.

"So, this was his great trap. Using young dragons," she growled, approaching the two beasts. "I fucking knew it."

"You know those?" asked Kairen.

Shareen rolled her eyes, pointing at the two dragons.

"Make an effort, Brother. You can't even recognize your own nephews' dragons? I know we haven't seen them more than a couple of times, but still. This one is from Vrehan's second son, and this one is Sephir's son's. Damn it, that asshole really used the kids."

Kairen frowned.

"Shareen, what are you doing here?"

"You could at least pretend you're happy to see me!"

"You should be in the North," he insisted, frowning.

Shareen nodded, putting her hands on her hips. His sister had come wearing her armor, and seeing how stained it already was, she had probably fought her way there. She didn't have a scratch on her, though. Only a few pearls of sweat and her ruined outfit.

"I would still be in the North if it wasn't for that dead ass Vrehan making a fucking ruckus at the Diamond Palace."

"What?"

The War God's anger rose immediately, scaring the two dragons in the room into retreating even further away from him with whimpers. Kairen didn't give a damn about those two. However, the Diamond Palace was where he had left his mother and his concubine. The mere mention of his half-brother anyway near them was not something he wanted to hear. Shareen didn't make the suspense last, either.

"Yeah, it is bad. That rat face walked into Mother's Palace, claiming to be under our Father's orders to arrest Cassie."

The vein at his temple was violently thumping as his eyes darkened in anger. Kairen's murderous intent had never, ever been anywhere near that bad before.

"He took Cassandra?" he hissed.

"No, thank the Gods. She and her sister managed to run away, but Vrehan is definitely after them. That's why I came to get you back as soon as I could. Anour stayed back with Mother. I didn't want to leave her alone."

Kairen was absolutely furious, even if his concubine hadn't been caught yet, he loathed the idea of anyone near her. Let alone those who wanted to harm her. His blood went cold, thinking about something else.

"What of our son?"

"Apparently, he's been born and is well, from the last news we got of them. Congrats, I guess."

Kairen was furious. He had broken his promise to Cassandra. She had given birth alone, and he had missed their child's birth. For now, he didn't want any congratulations until his concubine and son would be with him to receive them. Furious, he turned around and walked towards the two terrorized dragons. They tried to growl, to warn him not to approach, but he ignored them and came closer.

"Which one?" he asked.

"This one is Seban's," said Shareen, pointing at the dark blue dragon with its wing half-ripped.

Without adding another word, the War God walked to the other dragon. The tall brown beast growled furiously, trying to retreat as much as he could in his corner and show his fangs. When Kairen got close enough, the dragon jumped forward, trying to attack in a desperate attempt. The War God sliced its head off.

The dragon's head rolled away from its body, while the other dragon whimpered in fear from the scene before him. Shareen didn't react much. This was legitimate, in their world. She was even surprised that he had apparently decided to spare Seban's dragon, despite the already poor state of the creature. She glanced down, but the indigo creature was pitifully shivering, its eyes fixated on Kairen in sheer fear.

"You poor one," she sighed.

However, the War God didn't have time for another glance at the young dragon. Kairen walked out of the building, walking back into the battle. Despite his absence, his men were not at a loss.

The Imperial Army was well-trained and perfectly capable by itself. The absence of their Commander-in-Chief for a few hours had not stopped them at all, as they finished the fight against the invader. There were a lot of victims and bodies, but few from the Dragon Empire's people. On her way there, Shareen had been surprised to see how many common people were actually helping the soldiers, using those strange little boxes to tend their injuries. It was even more obvious now that the battle had died down, and the last of the enemies that remained alive were brought together.

The War God had no time to waste. Ignoring all the men that tried to inquire about his situation or rejoice about their victory, he walked straight into the building where his generals had been put together.

"Your Highness! How come you're..."

"Where is their leader?" growled Kairen, ignoring all of them.

One man was dragged forward, and his fancy uniform clearly gave away his high ranking among his army. Despite the large, ugly open injury on his head, he still had a defiant look while facing Kairen.

"Long live the Eastern Republic! We shall not obey the barbaric..."

Shareen gave a violent kick to his jaw before he could finish that sentence. The sound of his teeth breaking against one another made several men grimace. The man coughed up some blood, looking horrified.

"A w-woman! How dare you?! A woman cannot hit a man!"

"Sorry, darling, wrong Empire for your fucking chauvinism. Now, talk before I break however many teeth and bones you've got left, one by one."

"I won't talk! I will die for my country!" shouted the man, despite his mouth full of blood and his missing teeth. "I will never..."

"Oh, fuck you. Just die like an idiot then."

Just like that, Shareen took out her weapon and killed the man right there. No one around was really surprised, as the Generals had witnessed this kind of thing countless times from the Imperial Family within the Palace where all their meetings were held. Kairen turned to them.

"Who else did we get?"

"No one that will talk, Your Highness," sighed one of the Generals, shaking his head. "All the leaders we caught either committed suicide or swore they'd never surrender any of their country's military secrets. We are still interrogating them at the moment."

"This is annoying," hissed Shareen. "We need proof of that rat face's involvement in the war."

"We have no proof that the Second Prince..."

"We have one already," interrupted Kairen.

The men turned to him, a bit flustered.

"W-we do, Your Highness?"

"There are two dragons left inside a building in the southwest," he said. "Get them and make sure they make the trip back to the Capital with us."

He turned around to leave the building, while the Generals and Shareen followed after him.

"You want to use those two as proof?" she said. "Vrehan will pretend his son acted by himself!"

"Then we'll just have to make his son and Sephir's talk."

"Kairen, Sephir is dead."

Kairen stopped and turned around to face his sister. Around her, the high-ranked soldiers that had just heard that news looked shocked, all of them exchanging glances with their eyes wide open. Kairen was focused on his sister. Shareen's expression was cold and serious, making him realize this was the truth.

The War God was shocked, more than he let on. Though they weren't particularly close, he had always considered Sephir a real older brother. Maybe the one he was the closest to, after Anour. His fists clenched. Kairen resumed walking, not saying a word on what he thought about that news. That was just another crime added to the already large debt of what Vrehan would have to pay for.

"I need to go back to the Capital right away," he hissed.

"Your Highness, you can't!" pleaded one of the Generals, running after him. "I'm most sorry about the First Prince's passing, but we need to officially end this war, fortify the border, and have the Eastern Army acknowledge they attacked us! We need to make their leaders pay for the damages, and sign a treaty at least!"

The War God suddenly turned around, grabbing the man by the collar under everyone else's astonished eyes.

"My Concubine and my child are in danger. My older brother just got murdered and you're fucking talking to me about damn paperwork. You don't need me for that," he growled.

"Your Highness!"

He threw the man away, ignored the rest, and kept walking, followed by his sister. No one else dared to follow him.

"Kairen, we have to stop by the Diamond Palace to get Mother," declared Shareen.

"She can wait. I need to find Cassandra."

"Kairen, stop a second and listen!" urged his sister. "Kairen, I know you just want to find them, but things are bad. There are rumors that Father has fallen ill, and Vrehan is acting in his stead. That little rat shit can have himself named Emperor the minute Father dies if he wants. Now that Sephir is gone and you're away on a battlefield, he'll give no choice to the ministers. No one knows your son is born, and Vrehan will definitely try to kill him and Cassie before it is known. We need to get Anour and Mother to help us deal with all this crap. We caught Phetra at the Diamond Palace. That bitch can still spill the beans about Vrehan."

"Where is Cassandra?"

They were hurrying outside of the City, Kairen's eyes on Krai, who was flying a few paces away. His dragon was not done hunting and killing the few survivors trying to flee the battle. Some of them were desperately trying to get to the frontier, but the Dragon wouldn't even let them anywhere close to it.

Shareen sighed.

"According to Mother, Cassie and Missandra decided to head to the Capital. Thank the Gods, they managed to win some time by making that idiot Vrehan think they were headed North to the Onyx Castle instead. They are on their own with your son and his dragon, though, and we don't even know if they are there yet. Dahlia was killed by Vrehan, too."

"Dahlia?"

"That servant girl Mother placed by her side, the one that was always around Cassandra, remember? She died trying to protect your woman... Poor girl."

Kairen nodded vaguely. He did remember a young servant girl that was always around Cassandra. He didn't know she was one of his mother's many spies, though. Not that he cared about that fact at all. His mother was definitely the type to do that kind of thing. All he could think about right now was finding Cassandra and their son, and making sure they were both safe. Anywhere far from Vrehan would be enough.

Roun, who had been waiting at the entrance of the City, stood up as soon as it saw them. Shareen had come on its back, so the Green Dragon had been expecting her to return. Meanwhile, Kairen waited for Krai to arrive, and jumped on the black dragon's back for their trip to the Diamond Palace. By the time they arrived there, Shareen had just finished telling him in detail everything that had happened on her side.

When they landed in their mother's garden, Kareen ran out to greet them. She hugged Kairen with a sad and angry look, and he noticed that she was holding something.

"That..."

"Oh, Cassie was working on it before all this happened," said his mother. "She wanted to give it to your son after his birth."

Kairen had recognized the little dragon plushie, despite the pretty embroideries his concubine had added to mend it. Even Krai, curious, sniffed the toy a bit before running to another aisle of the Diamond Palace. Kairen ran inside after the dragon. They were both headed exactly to the same place.

In the remote garden, everything had been left as it was. Krai was growling, looking at the scene, its back arched furiously. Kairen, too, squeezed the little plushie in his hand. They were both staring at the scattered remains of a dragon's egg. The War God's thoughts at that moment were unfit for words. He was just boiling inside, his eyes dark as obsidian.

Krai, too, kept sniffing the remains of the egg, restless. The dragon had felt the birth, yet the dragon wasn't there for its offspring. It felt just as defeated as its master. To Kairen, this was a bitter defeat. Though Cassandra had survived and managed to flee his brother's clutches, she was still on her own and unsafe. He hated not being with his concubine. He wanted her here, right by his side, where he could hold her and protect her. Cassandra was many things, but she was not a fighter, and she would never be. His blood was boiling when he dared to imagine his brother or any other man near her. He couldn't stand the idea of a single scratch on her soft, fragile white skin. She already had so many scars he could never do anything about. What did she have to go through again because he wasn't there?

She had been reluctant to send him, yet she knew it was his duty. Kairen had never loathed his title as War God as much as right now. He should have been there. With her, with their child. He didn't even know what his son looked like!

"Son, come," gently called Lady Kareen, appearing behind him. "We need to talk."

He nodded, and though his eyes had a hard time losing the horrible vision of the destroyed egg, he stepped back and joined her back inside. Krai was left there.

They reunited in one of Kareen's salons, but he just wanted to hurry to the Capital. He had followed his sister, only because Shareen had insisted on the best strategy to attack Vrehan and help Cassandra. Otherwise, he'd be miles away already. Their mother was seated on one of her throne-like chairs, but at her feet, Phetra was on her knees. As soon as she had seen Shareen and Kairen, her eyes had widened in absolute horror. She was a cunning woman, but outside of the Imperial Palace and without her brother to protect her, she was pitifully defenseless...although none of them felt an ounce of pity for her.

Anour and Evin were standing a few steps away, too. Kairen recognized the Imperial Servant, but only frowned a little and did not ask. He could easily imagine his sister had dragged him here from the North Army Camp. He was most interested in Phetra, that treacherous snake that had, according to what his sister had told him on the way there, injured Cassandra. Though she was already in a pitiful state, the War God slapped the woman.

The sound made by that slap was terrifying. The strength of those hands shook Phetra's whole head, and she was thrown on the floor once again, half of her face burning. She had felt several bones cracking, and the scream that resonated left no doubt about the amount of pain she was in.

Anour and Evin couldn't bear to look. Despite their education in this cruel environment, they couldn't help but feel bad witnessing the difference of strength between the War God and a woman. Kareen clicked her tongue.

"Kairen, we need that little rat alive."

"She's alive," said Shareen, her arms crossed.

She was staring at Phetra with a disdainful look. In Shareen's eyes, Phetra was already very lucky to be alive after angering their family and harming Cassandra. If it wasn't for Kareen, her brother would have most likely not stopped until she was slapped flat as a rug. Phetra's wailing was the only sound heard around, as all the Diamond Palace servants had scattered away.

Kareen put her chin on her fist.

"Anyway. While you were gone, I got some annoying news from my spies in the Capital."

"News from Cassie and Missandra?" asked Shareen.

"Sadly, no. They hadn't arrived yet, but my men informed the residence that guy told us about," said the Imperial Concubine while pointing at Evin. "In any case, they will be ready for their arrival, and of course, I appointed some men to watch the house and let me know as soon as they finally arrive."

"I'm going to the Capital."

"Kairen, I know you want to hurry there, my son, but wait a minute. There is more. First, my spies confirmed your father is ill. No one has seen the Emperor in days. The last councils have all been held without him or Sephir."

"Those damn Ministers," growled Shareen. "They are probably dancing around our treasury and doing whatever shit they want while no one is there."

"Those your brother has corrupted, you mean," said her mother. "Vrehan has always been very smart in politics, he probably has half of those greedy men ready to bow for him, and the other half scared to have him get some spring cleaning done while his father's not there to stop him. In other words, he has the whole Imperial Palace working for him."

"Is that going to be a problem?" asked Shareen.

"A dragon alone can't solve everything, Shareen. If he has the Imperial Palace working for him, he'll kill your father as soon as he returns there and be named Emperor. Then, he'll raise both his army and the Imperial Army against you two. I know how strong my children are, but against two armies, even you won't be able to get inside the Imperial Palace that easily!"

"We can just fly inside," shrugged Shareen. "Who cares about the armies on the ground, if we come from above."

"You think that snake, Vrehan, won't have thought about that? Either he will have a trap ready or hide himself somewhere you can't get to him so easily. He's just the type to let others do the dirty work for him while never getting a speck of dirt on himself."

Shareen rolled her eyes, annoyed.

"Let's get to it, Mother, what do you suggest?"

Kareen pushed Phetra with her foot, making her wail again. The Princess was gagged though, and unable to speak. Her jaw was probably broken anyway, with those two trails of blood that were now rushing out her mouth. She was almost curling up against the throne, like a terrorized animal.

"While you children were gone, Miss Phetra, here, and I, had an interesting talk. Your older brother is expecting you to come flying. That useless little swine didn't know the details, but her brother will have all of the skies filled with traps, most likely with catapults, giant crossbows, and so on. He is expecting Kairen to show up by himself with Krai. He will focus all of his men into stopping you, my son, no matter how much he'll sacrifice. He is already days ahead of us, he will get to the Capital first, anyway, and I bet everything is all ready to welcome you there, on his orders. We have to think he will kill your father as soon as he can and have the Imperial Army return to do his bidding."

"Then..."

"Get the Eastern Army to the Capital. He knows Kairen is not one to bother waiting and summoning his army, he won't expect the Eastern Army to show up and fight Vrehan's militia or the Imperial Army with him."

"True... He would expect Kairen and I to show up alone without the army."

"Exactly. Vrehan may be a coward, but he's annoyingly smart. He will do whatever he can to delay Kairen's return to the Imperial Palace, even throw a whole army at him. Make sure that little rat is distracted enough with what goes on outside, that he won't have time to get to Cassandra. She is our best chance from the inside. If that smart girl manages to heal your old man or at least win us some time, we can even hope to get rid of Vrehan without too many issues. Though, if your father passes first, it will be much more difficult to get to Vrehan and Cassandra."

Shareen wouldn't say it out loud, but they all knew. The next victim in this conflict would most likely be their father. He had to be Vrehan's first target upon coming back. They didn't know why he wasn't already dead, but since Cassandra and her son had escaped, the Second Prince would have no choice but to get rid of the old Emperor as fast as he could. Then he could be named Emperor, and get full control of the Imperial Army.

"But the Imperial Army went with Brother to the battlefront in the East," said Anour. "Brother just returned, they can't go back to the Capital faster than a Dragon."

"Not all of the Army was sent here. The Emperor wouldn't have left the Capital with no defense."

"Father probably sent at least half of it from what I saw," said Shareen.

"Then let's assume half of the Imperial Army is still in the Imperial Palace with that little rat. Vrehan may have acted impulsively but he definitely knows Krai and Kairen will be his biggest problem. If you get there, expect a trap."

"Mother, you can't ask us to wait for the Eastern Army to get here!"

"They are already on the way," retorted Kareen. "Who do you think I am? I sent a message as soon as you left to get your brother! They will meet you in the Capital."

The brother and sister exchanged a glance and a nod.

"So we are good to go, right? The army will meet us there."

"Yes, but do you children even know what to do once we get there?"

"We? Mother, you're coming?" asked Shareen, shocked.

"Of course! What, you think this old lady will stand on the sidelines while your old man is in danger? You're taking me for being more heartless than I am!"

She honestly had nothing to answer to that. So, instead, she pointed at Phetra.

"What about her? Do we kill her now? Has she said everything she had to?"

"Well, probably not," said Kareen, standing up. "At least, I know how Vrehan managed to come here without your father's approval. That little snake. He left the Palace with this annoying sister of his under the pretense of accompanying her to her wedding! Of course, they changed their course to come here and pretend they were arresting Cassandra under the Emperor's order. I can't believe I got fooled by those two. I bet they scattered information back at the Imperial Palace that they were already half-way there!"

She grabbed Phetra's hair, dragging her mercilessly.

"The little bitch..." hissed Kareen. "She spilled all the names of the people Vrehan corrupted in the Imperial Palace, so I will have to do a thorough cleaning once we get there. She's also the one who smuggled the poison that killed Sephir, though she didn't know it was going to be used on her father as well."

"So she knows the remedy?"

"That idiot? She can't even tell the difference between blood and wine! She just did Vrehan's dirty work, as always. Probably ordered from some market."

"What about that abortion potion?"

"She kept saying it wasn't intended for Cassie. Pretty sure she's lying about that, but... In any case, she may be more useful once we get to the Imperial Palace and argue with her brother. She probably knows more dirt on him than she'll say for now. She will talk once he abandons her for real. Who knows..."

Shareen shook her head. She had enough of all that. Kairen was the first to step out, calling his dragon to come. Krai was just as impatient and kept growling furiously. Both the Black Dragon and its Master wanted to hurry back into the Capital, as there was no time to lose. Cassandra was in danger, especially if she had decided to try and go save the Emperor from Vrehan's clutches.

Kairen helped his Mother get on the Black Dragon, forcefully pulling Phetra on, too. Truth was, both Roun and Krai attempted to kill her until their Masters had them stop and keep their fangs away. The Black Dragon was unhappy about carrying that woman, but Kairen put her like a sandbag at the rear, on her stomach, the most uncomfortable position possible. She could still see Roun growling at her, as Shareen, Anour, and Evin were mounting the Green Dragon. Then, both dragons took off.

With each dragon carrying more people than usual, the flight took a little longer. As Kareen had predicted, the two big dragons' appearance in the sky caused quite a commotion. Many soldiers pointed at them, and just like the information spilled by Phetra, catapults and giant crossbows appeared all over the Imperial Palace's roof. Both dragons growled, but before they were within reach, they dove towards the south of the Capital. Evin's directions were only necessary for Roun, Krai and Kairen knew exactly where to go. By mere luck, the residence was far enough from the Imperial Palace, and both dragons landed in the garden under the servants' shocked eyes. They could already hear the yells of soldiers outside, ordering the men to gather, most likely Vrehan's militia.

Shareen and Kairen each jumped down from the dragons first and ran in opposite directions. While the sister took her swords out to go and guard the entrance of the residence, the Prince ran inside.

Kairen couldn't tell if he was imagining it, but the cries of a baby were guiding him inside the residence. His heart was thumping like crazy in his chest, as he could only focus on that sound. He finally found a door, and stopped in front of it, almost out of breath. He was suddenly scared to open that door. He listened to the voices inside, almost covered by the baby's screams.

"By the Gods, won't he stop crying. He's been at it for hours and hours, no one has slept a wink since..."

"His mother left! Poor thing... He probably doesn't understand."

Kairen opened the door wide with a bang. The two women turned to face him, scared by the noise and the sudden appearance of that tall man at the door. However, it was hard not to know who that man was. Tall, with his tanned skin, black hair, and black eyes. And that strange hair.

Kairen barely noticed the two women. His eyes fell right on the baby that was there, his eyes all teary and his little fists clenched. He stepped forward, a bit at a loss. This was not how he had imagined their first meeting. None of this was what he wanted, not when his mother wasn't there. The baby had a little hiccup from all his crying earlier. However, his wailing had stopped, and he was only making an upset pout, his eyes riveted on the big man that was coming towards him.

That baby felt ridiculously small compared to Kairen. However, there was no doubt. He had a little patch of dark hair, and skin barely one tone lighter than his own. Kairen hesitated. Then, he slowly took out the little dragon plushie he had on him all this time. The baby's eyes went right for the toy. He opened his hands and stretched a bit to grasp it, holding on tightly to the little plushie his mother had sewn back in shape.

It was a strange situation, but the beginning of a smile appeared on the War God's lips. He gently took his son into his arms, though one hand would have been enough to carry all of him. The baby whined a little bit, squeezing the toy with an upset expression.

"Let's go get your mother back."

Chapter 32

The Fourth Prince glared at them, annoyed. He kept shaking his head, already sulking.

"You're really one hell of a little pest!" he hissed. "Oh, fine! I never liked that dumbass anyway."

Missandra gave a triumphant smile to her sister, but it was way too early to rejoice, in Cassandra's opinion. Could they really trust this Prince? So far, Opheus hadn't been the most cooperative, and Missandra was basically forcing him to help them now. However, the Sisters were short on options. Moreover, the threat of the War God's wrath was probably their best weapon at the moment.

The Fourth Prince rolled his eyes, ignoring Missandra to turn to Cassandra with a frown, his fingers twiddling with his long earring.

"Can you really heal Father?"

"I hope so," said Cassandra with a little nod. "I can't say before I've actually seen him, though. Do you know where he is?"

"Well, Vrehan wasn't extraordinarily discreet about it. Father was moved to his Chambers, under the pretense of guarding him against any more assassins."

"They let him do that?"

"Sweetie, in case you haven't been following, there is no one left to oppose that douche here. Sephir died, Kairen is gone to play with his toys on some faraway battlefield. Who else do you think will show up to tell him what he can and cannot do? He's the Second Prince!"

"You could have stopped him," stated Missandra, upset. "You could have saved your own damn father if you had said something."

Opheus sighed.

"Just you try growing up in a family where everyone happily serves each other poison for breakfast, while the adults watch, darling. I have nothing against my father, but I'm far from being his favorite son. If he remembers me at all, and I have a long list of siblings who'd only be too happy to stab my back with a sword if they remembered I exist. So sorry about Daddy, but I value my life a tad more."

Though Missandra made a disgusted face, Cassandra couldn't really say she didn't understand his point of view, for she had witnessed it herself many times. All the siblings were in danger, since even before their birth, especially the Princes. Some had to grow with strong personalities, while some like Anour and Opheus, remained quiet and unnoticed. It was one way, just like any other, to try and survive in such an environment. Cassandra stepped forward to address Opheus, speaking softly.

"I understand your position, and I know that what we are asking is putting you in danger, too. But you can't ignore that Vrehan will not stop there. He won't have enough of killing his father and only one or two of his brothers."

Opheus shrugged after a hesitation.

"Why should I care? It's not like I'm a threat to him, I have no children and no will to have any!"

"Do you have no one you care about in this Palace at all?" retorted Cassandra.

This time, her words silenced him. He looked baffled for a few seconds and lost in his thoughts. Opheus had grown up in this Palace. There's no way there was no one here that he didn't hold dear. Maybe he had younger sisters, or lovers that Vrehan could potentially harm. Moreover, heirs or not, his own safety wouldn't be guaranteed either. He couldn't ignore what usually happened to the new Emperor's siblings. After a long while, he sighed.

"Oh, fuck it, we are all going to die anyway."

The Prince walked past them, shaking his head, and actually walked towards the window his dragon was peeping at them from. He scratched his dragon's chin, making the white beast growl softly, and turned to them.

"Come on, I'll give you a ride. Unless you want to walk out into the two idiots my brother has planted there?"

Cassandra and Missandra exchanged a quick concerned look. They weren't exactly fond of the idea of hopping onto a dragon they didn't know and had never seen behave at all before, but it was still better than climbing their way back or risking it in front of the guards. Besides, the White Dragon hadn't been very menacing since the two of them had seen it. It hadn't even growled once at them, only peeking on their every move without showing animosity.

Cassandra walked his way first, and to her surprise, Opheus actually held out his hand to help her get on his dragon's back. She took it after hesitating for a brief moment, and exchanging a glance with him. Somehow, she hadn't noticed before, but he had some features in common with Kairen, though his face was leaner and his forehead more prominent. It was strange to meet all of Kairen's brothers, and all she was concerned about was which ones did not want her dead.

Somehow, Opheus decided not to extend the courtesy to Missandra, and got on his dragon's back right after her, leaving the younger sister to climb on however she could. His White Dragon was smaller than Krai, but its build was about the same, and it was among the biggest of those Cassandra had seen, roughly the same size as Vrehan's dragon. The dragon seemed of a quiet nature, as it took off quietly as soon as all three of them were seated.

It felt strange for Cassandra to fly again after such a long time, and on a different Dragon's back at that. She had never flown on any other dragon than Krai. The White Dragon didn't need any directions. It quietly circled the large Imperial Palace, leaving the girls to see what was going on on all the roofs. Catapults, giant crossbows, and iron nets extended over some of the gardens. The Imperial Palace was clearly preparing for an attack coming from the sky. Opheus, too, had his eyes on there and shook his head.

"What a moron," he sighed. "Come on, Phe, let's get away."

His dragon growled softly in response, but its big blue eyes were also riveted on all the weapons below. They headed down to one of the halls of the Imperial Palace, one Cassandra had never been to before. She had no idea where they were, but Phe, the White Dragon, landed quietly in a large garden filled with purple flowers. It was extremely quiet around.

Opheus jumped down, and once again, helped Cassandra get off his dragon. Whether he hadn't liked Missandra's attitude earlier or was just acting petty, the younger sister had to get down herself.

"Where are we?" asked Cassandra.

"My chambers. Luckily for you, I happen to be living not far from Vrehan's apartments. I don't know where exactly our father was taken, but at least from here, you shouldn't have any trouble accessing his place. If you can get past all the guards, that is."

Cassandra's throat tightened a little. It would have been stupid to think the Second Prince would have left his Father completely unguarded. Not only the Imperial Soldiers, but it was very likely that his own militia would be keeping the Emperor locked in there. She sighed. They had found where the Emperor was and got closer to his position, but the hardest part was still to come.

Opheus walked back inside, and the girls naturally followed, as they were completely lost on their position within the Palace. After walking past a few rooms, Cassandra couldn't help but notice a strange detail.

"It's very... quiet here," she said. "You don't have any Imperial Servants in here?"

"No. I hate noise and noisy people. I don't trust any of those little rats either, they are all working for someone in there. I'd rather take care of myself."

Cassandra was impressed. Besides his excessive attitude they had witnessed earlier, he actually seemed like quite a sensible being. Everything inside the rooms and corridors they walked across seemed strangely bare. Actually, it reminded Cassandra of her first days in Kairen's apartments in the Imperial Palace. Just like his older brother, Opheus didn't seem to spend much on decorations or filling his apartments with luxurious items. The bit of furniture they saw was in pastel colors, adding to the quiet atmosphere around. Cassandra spotted a couple of instruments, too, meaning he probably liked music more than noise.

"Opheus? What's going on?"

Two women suddenly emerged from a room on their left. Both looked around their thirties, and were very pretty. The first had short brown hair, almond eyes, and thin lips, and was wearing a long purple dress. Behind her was a younger girl, in purple too, who was almost hiding behind her.

Opheus frowned.

"We have guests," he sighed.

"Guests? Are you kidding? Aside from your crazy mother, you never..."

She stopped talking, frowning at Cassandra.

"I know you. Aren't you the Third Prince's Favorite? The White Lily. Why do you look like that?"

Cassandra wasn't sure what to say. Should she confirm her words, was there a danger in unveiling her identity to that woman? It seemed a bit late, though, she had clearly recognized her. As she hesitated, Opheus sighed.

"Relax, darling. This is my wife, Mariana, and my younger sister is hiding behind her. They won't talk. Yes, Mari, that's Kairen's woman."

Cassandra was a bit surprised to hear Opheus actually had a wife. He was probably the only one among the Princes, and she had forgotten that one of the actual princes had a wife at all. Was it recent? Before she could wonder more, that woman, Mariana, glared at her husband, looking shocked.

"Are you kidding, Ophe? Didn't you say we should lay low? With the Emperor being sick and all? And now you bring that woman here? Are you crazy!"

To Cassandra's surprise, before the Fourth Prince could even answer, Mariana turned to her.

"No offense to you, really, but the situation is freaking tense here, and that idiot said it himself!"

Opheus rolled his eyes.

"I know what I said, but I found those two in Father's apartments! The little one basically threatened me into helping them, mind you!"

Mariana glanced towards Missandra, and put her hands on her hips.

"Awesome, so now you get bullied around by teenagers? Really, Opheus? I already have to handle your crazy bitch mother, give me some slack!"

"We are not staying," declared Cassandra, stepping up. "His Highness just helped us not get caught, but we only want to get to the Emperor. We won't bother you any longer, we don't want to put you in danger."

Hearing her actually speak seemed to calm that woman a bit. After one more glare at her husband, Mariana turned to Cassandra, crossing her arms.

"Sorry for the yelling, I have nothing against you, Lady Cassandra. I'm just worried about that crazy Vrehan. He's fucking lost it. He killed Prince Sephir, no one here is blind enough to think you're guilty. I remember seeing you with the other concubines, I thought you were a smart but harmless woman. We also heard about the Lady of the Mountain, all the concubines talk.

Cassandra was somewhat touched to hear that most people didn't believe in her being an assassin. That woman, Mariana, seemed to have a lot of common sense and nothing in common with the other Concubines Cassandra had met. After scratching her head, Mariana turned towards the Prince again.

"So, what was the idea here?"

"They get out of here and try to find and help my dad, that's it! Nothing I'm going to concern myself with... hey!"

Before he could end his sentence, Mariana had slapped his shoulder with an angry look.

"Stop being such a baby! You can't let them go in there alone, are you crazy?"

"You're the one who said you were fine with us laying low!" he protested, rubbing his painful shoulder.

"That was before I knew there was someone in this crazy Imperial Palace capable of helping the old man! Stop being a coward, or are you going to let your father die? And your brother's woman, too? What do you think the War God will do to your skinny ass once he finds out?!"

Once again, Opheus let out a long groan of exasperation. Behind Cassandra, Missandra had a hard time not laughing. However, Mariana was not done with him.

"I'm so fed up with you! Do you want Vrehan to get on the throne, perhaps? Because I know I don't! He's going to have us all line up and fucking slaughter us!"

"Fine, fine! Stop hitting me, you crazy woman, I get it!"

If the situation hadn't been so dramatic in itself, it would have been quite funny to witness the Prince being bossed around by his wife... Mariana stopped, though she did threaten him with another slap, making Opheus take one step away from her. She then turned to Cassandra, taking back a serious and gentle expression scaringly fast.

"Sorry about that. Anyway, of course, we will help you, especially if there's a chance you can help the Emperor. We don't know much, though, except for the fact that he's in Vrehan's apartments. No one opposed it when they moved him, so I guess he already had most of the people in the Palace working for him. There are guards, too. Don't worry, though, we can find a way."

"Are you serious?" whispered Opheus, though everyone there could hear him.

Mariana nodded and smiled at him.

"They just need to be able to get in, right? All we need is a distraction. Looks like your crazy mother is going to be useful for once."

The six men guarding the door to the Second Prince's apartments were bored.

They didn't quite understand why a simple entrance door within the Palace was so heavily guarded, as absolutely nothing was going on in that area of the Imperial Palace. Of course, the death of the First Prince had caused quite a stir, but since the funeral had been held in a hurry, and the Second Prince had left, it had been rather quiet. The men actually had no idea what was going on behind those doors, or who they were truly guarding. They were aware of some rumors that the Emperor had been placed in the Second Prince's apartments, but they had no confirmation of it. The servants always talked a lot between themselves, while the soldiers were supposed to keep their tongues tied, unless they wanted to lose their position.

Becoming an Imperial Guard was such a prestigious position, with a heavy salary, yet not much actual work to do, that many envied their position. It took either a lot of work, a lot of money, or good connections to get there. Sometimes a bit of all three, but in any case, they had done the hardest part. Unless they were aiming for a higher position, those men could spend their days guarding doors and simply wait for their paychecks to come. They didn't need to guard the inside of the Princes' or Princesses' apartments, either. Most of them had their own militia, and the others hated any intrusion on their privacy. Plus, there was a long history of Concubines getting into some bad fights over rumors of one another sleeping with the personnel. Since the latest scandal that had the Emperor see red, all of the Imperial Guards had been strictly banned from entering the private chambers of the Imperial Family, unless explicitly being told otherwise.

Those men didn't have much to entertain themselves with. They would lurk at the pretty young servant girls going by, but that was pretty much their only entertainment all day long.

Hence, when the two women appeared at one end of the corridor, they turned heads as soon as they heard the first screaming. Those among the soldiers who recognized them frowned or chuckled nervously, already aware of what was going on.

"You useless little bitch!" the middle-aged woman yelled. "You can't even give me one heir, one! What did you marry my son for if it's for just standing here like a decorative vase?! You're useless! Useless!"

"Take it down a notch, you old harpy! Fucking get a grip! Because Ophe agreed to marry me doesn't mean I'm gonna pop out a child within the year!"

"Don't call him so familiarly before you even get pregnant! I don't know why my son was so adamant about marrying you, but you better give me a grandson quickly, or I'll have your head!"

"My head? And what are you going to do with it? Did you forget that I am his wife? He can't get another woman, now. I'm never allowing it, so you better be happy with who you got and suck it up!"

The soldiers were trying hard not to laugh at the scene. Aside from the Imperial Concubine, no one was blind as to why the Fourth Prince had agreed to marry Lady Mariana. Certainly not to produce any heirs, for one. It was even quite surprising that his mother was still holding on to the pitiful illusion that Prince Opheus could ever produce any children, given his tastes. Lady Mariana was actually doing a good job of acting as his fence against his delusional mother, but even the Emperor had completely given up on his Fourth Son...and his hysterical mother.

"I should have never agreed to that! You're just a useless, little, scheming swine! You did it all for the money! And to kill me! You're going to kill me!"

"Yes, yes... Aren't we getting a little big on the drama, mother-in-law?" said Mariana, ignoring her to keep going towards the soldiers.

"You're useless! Useless!" Kept screaming the woman behind her.

"Old hag," sighed Mariana, approaching the men with a smile. "Sorry about the ruckus, soldiers. Can I go in? I was supposed to have tea with Concubine Gloriata, but I can't find her."

The men felt a bit flustered at one of the Princesses addressing them so politely and gently. They were more used to the rude and mighty attitude of the concubines. Moreover, Mariana was a very pretty woman, and she was standing a bit closer than normal in her flattering purple dress.

"S-Sorry, Princess Mariana, we are not supposed to let anyone in."

"What? Really?" she said, looking surprised. "Is everything alright in there? I..."

"You swine! I'm not done talking!" yelled the woman behind her.

"Oh, shut up!" roared Mariana, turning to her. "Can't you see that I'm talking to these gentlemen? Do you have to make a fuss all the time? I don't know how Ophe's put up with you all these years!"

"He is my son, you little bitch! I am his mother, he's nothing without me!"

"Isn't it the other way around?" sighed Mariana.

The Imperial Soldiers chuckled, some blushing a little bit too. As soon as she saw that, the Imperial Concubine glared at them, and became even more hysterical, agitating her cane all around.

"How dare you laugh! You punks! You useless men! You good-for-nothing!"

With each word, she was dangerously swinging her cane around, making the Imperial Guards dodge it or experience painful hits. She was one of the only Concubines about as old as the Emperor, and though she had lost his favor long ago, the Imperial Guards were completely flustered at how to deal with her.

"Imperial Concubine, please, calm down."

"Calm down? You're telling me to calm down?" yelled the Imperial Concubine. "I'll have you hung! Or beheaded! And then drowned!"

"Oh, really..." sighed Mariana.

While the men were flustered and trying to control the old lady, behind them, they didn't notice the trio that were walking on their toes to get to the door. Opheus' mother was so awfully noisy and agitated that even she didn't see her own son sneaking behind the Imperial Guards and into the Second Prince's apartments. Mariana smiled, seeing that they had succeeded, but she got hit by the cane right after, making her remember that she had inherited the worst part of the plan.

As soon as they were inside, Opheus guided Cassandra and Missandra towards a quiet room, apparently familiar with their surroundings. He checked inside to verify it was empty before letting the girls in. All three of them released a long sigh of relief.

"That's one crazy old woman," said Missandra, immediately getting a glare from her older sister.

"You have no idea," sighed Opheus. "If it wasn't for Mari, she'd be still sneaking girls into my bedroom every night. A nightmare, I swear. Oh, anyway, we are in. Now we need to find Father."

"Do you have an idea where he could be?"

The Fourth Prince shook his head with a frown.

"Not really... I've only been here a few times when I was younger. My mother and his were close a long time ago, though it might just have been to try to get rid of each other. They did end up trying to kill each other until Lady Kareen became the favorite and they changed objectives. Lovely ladies. Anyway, I think the bedrooms were that way, but it is definitely going to be guarded by Vrehan's personal militia."

"Any way around?"

Opheus took a few seconds to think, fidgeting with his earring again.

"There are some rooms that were only used for storage back in the day," he said. "Mari and I used to sneak in there when the Imperial Concubines were having tea, to be alone."

"Mariana is a childhood friend?" asked Cassandra, surprised.

"She's been an Imperial Servant here since she was young, and my best friend. If my Mother wanted to punish me, she'd take it out on her."

Cassandra was surprised. She hadn't thought some friendships could actually occur between members of the Imperial Family and the servants, since the gap between the two was so large. However, seeing how Opheus had always gone against his family's usual patterns, it wasn't too surprising. He had probably married Mariana so they could protect each other. It was a rather touching story, not something she would have suspected to occur inside the Imperial Palace.

Once again making sure there was no one ahead of them, Opheus and the two young women walked out of the room, cautious. They could actually still hear the screams of the Imperial Concubine from time to time, and Opheus made a grimace every time. They carefully took one corridor after another, but if there were any servants around, they had probably gone to see what was going on at the entrance. After a while, though, Opheus started frowning a lot.

"It's strange. I don't remember this place being so deserted when I was young."

That sentence made the girls worry, but it was too late to turn back. Indeed, the atmosphere in this area was a bit unusual. Most of the doors were locked, and it felt like no one had ventured here in a very long time. Cassandra realized that she was getting the same feeling from when she had seen Kairen's childhood bedroom. It felt sad and desolate around here, but she couldn't tell why. It was rather clean, but there wasn't a soul around. The further they walked in, the more that uneasy feeling grew.

All the doors they walked by on their left side were locked, and there were barely a couple of windows on their right, for the light to get in. They had slowed down their pace, since their steps resonated in the silence. Even Opheus kept a sour face on.

"It's weird," said Missandra. "We haven't come across a single servant or guard since we came into the area. If that crazy prince is so on guard, why is there absolutely no one here?"

Cassandra didn't have an answer, but she felt just the same. Something was strange. It was as if no one was allowed here at all. Even if that area was completely deserted, there should at least have been a couple of guards or a servant sweeping the dust.

However, they had no time to stop and check what was going on behind those closed doors. In a tacit agreement, they kept going, following Opheus' lead.

Suddenly, an old maid appeared out of the blue at one of the intersections. She was carrying a tray with food, and she froze upon seeing them, looking shocked. Opheus moved immediately to stand between the sisters and the maid, preventing her from seeing their faces.

However, the old woman looked more shocked to see him, her hands shaking on the tray of food.

"W... What are you doing here... That... This area is forbidden."

"Sorry, I was coming to see my brother," Opheus lied. "Who is that food for?"

The maid went even paler, stepping back as he was stepping closer.

"Ah... No... no one, Sir..."

"No one? This is a large detour for someone going to the main area. You're carrying a lot of food too."

Opheus was stepping closer and closer to the old maid, but she kept stepping back, visibly terrified. She had the face of someone who didn't want to get caught, and from the direction of her feet, was probably considering running away. Yet, before she could take another step, the Fourth Prince suddenly grabbed her, and the tray of food fell loudly.

"Who was that food for?" he insisted.

"I...I'm sorry, Your Highness, I can't tell," whimpered the old woman.

"Is it for my father?" he asked.

"N-no..."

Opheus asked her again, insisting, but Cassandra had her eyes on the food she had left on the ground. This didn't look like a meal that would have been given to a sick old man... but to a pregnant woman. She recognized some of the food Kareen had been insistent on having her eat while she was pregnant with Kassian, at the Diamond Palace.

"P-please let me go," said the old woman. "If Her Highness k-knows..."

"Her Highness? Who?"

Either she had talked too much or not enough, the old woman was now bitterly regretting it. Moreover, Opheus was tightening his grip on her wrist and threatening her with a glare. Just like the rest of his family, the Imperial Prince was well aware of his power, and he kept going until the old woman got teary and talked.

"L-Lady... Madeen..."

Cassandra frowned. She knew that name, it was the name of Vrehan's Favorite, the mother of his first son. If there was someone else that they should fear crossing paths with in that place, while Vrehan and Phetra were gone, it had to be that woman.

Opheus wasn't done interrogating the maid, however.

"Who was that food for, then? Madeen isn't pregnant!"

This time, the old maid stayed resolutely mute. However, her eyes slipped to one of the doors for a second, and Missandra caught that. She ran to the said door, trying to open it, but it wouldn't.

"She must have a key!" said Missandra.

"Ah, no!" screamed the old woman.

Before she could yell anymore, Opheus grabbed her chin, and brutally flipped her head around, killing her immediately. Cassandra let out a shocked cry, while Missandra frowned.

"Did you really have to kill that poor old lady?"

"She would have been killed by Madeen anyway," retorted Opheus, crouching down to search her. "If you want to cry, find a corner, darling, but do it later."

Missandra sighed, but he probably wasn't wrong. He suddenly found a key and walked up to her with a sigh.

"Why are we doing this, anyway?" he said.

"Because whatever that sicko wants to hide is good for us to know," retorted Missandra, opening the door.

The door gave in with a creaking, despite Missandra's attempt to open it quietly. Inside, it was awfully dark. There was no window, and the only light came from behind them, the corridor they were standing in already rather dark itself. Cassandra frowned, and stepped forward, past her sister to venture inside, while Opheus stayed behind them with a frown.

Though they could barely see anything, she could feel a presence. She waited a few seconds for her eyes to get used to the dark and looked for the source of the faint breathing she could hear. This was a room with nothing but a bed. On the bed, was a young woman, curled up against the wall, staring at her with a frightened expression. She had long black hair, black eyes, tanned skin, and was heavily pregnant.

Cassandra was rendered speechless. What was that young woman doing locked up here? She had a chain around her ankle, too. She looked absolutely terrorized. Her eyes were opened wide while staring at Cassandra, and she was curling up the furthest away from her she could get, shivering like an injured animal.

Cassandra gently stepped closer, while Missandra and Opheus were left in awe at the doorstep. The young woman curled up even more, obviously afraid of her. In her appearance, she was somewhat reminding Cassandra of herself, months ago. She was very skinny except for her womb, and her lower lip was cut. Her body bore traces of old bruises, scars, and everything in her attitude screamed fear. Her long black hair was strangely short in some places as if someone had randomly cut it, and some of those strands were still lying on the ground. She was wearing a worn-out green dress, too.

"Who is that?" muttered Missandra, turning to Opheus.

The Prince shook his head. He had no idea, or wasn't sure, but all three of them could see that the young woman had features of the Imperial Family. It was very unsettling to notice that, with her current state. Cassandra took a deep breath, and got closer, being careful not to scare her. The woman was obviously traumatized, not used to seeing strangers, and she didn't want to scare her.

"Hinue, what are you doing?" whispered Missandra, a bit worried.

"We can't leave that poor woman here," replied Cassandra.

She looked for the chain, but it was closed with a lock on the woman's ankle.

"Mie, give me the key from earlier."

Gently, Cassandra approached the key from that woman's ankle. Each of her movements was extremely gentle, clearly letting that poor girl see what she was about to do. That unknown woman hadn't uttered a single word so far, and Cassandra suspected that she wouldn't. Her quiet wailing was the only sound they had heard from her, and she was shivering non-stop, unable to avert her eyes for one second. It was as if they had locked eyes and neither of them could look away.

Cassandra tried the key on the lock, but it didn't match. She frowned, upset.

"This isn't going to work..."

"Let me see," said Missandra, walking up to her with a sigh.

Her younger sister stared at the lock for a while, and turned to Opheus after a minute.

"Can I borrow your earring?"

The Prince seemed confused at her request, but handed it to her. Under their eyes, Missandra started fidgeting and trying to force the lock with it. Cassandra didn't know if she should have been surprised at her younger sister's skill, but she was scared to ask how in the world she had picked that one up.

After a few seconds, they heard a click, and the iron ring fell on the bed.

"You little thief," chuckled Opheus.

As soon as he had talked, though, the young woman suddenly whimpered, staring at him like he was absolutely terrifying, and curled up even more on one end of her bed. Cassandra's heart broke a little witnessing this, and she turned to Opheus.

"Your Highness, would you mind... stepping outside a little? You're... scaring her."

For a few seconds, Prince Opheus made an offended look, but that woman's pitiful attitude was not something he could ignore. He eventually rolled his eyes over and backed away a little. Cassandra waited until he was completely out of sight, and gently rubbed the poor woman's ankle.

"It's alright... We won't hurt you," she whispered.

"Hinue, what do we do?"

Cassandra hesitated. She could never leave that woman here in her state. She was obviously malnourished and mistreated by whoever had locked her up in here. Cassandra had a faint idea of her identity, too, but whether it would be confirmed later or not wasn't her priority for now. She took a deep breath and turned to Missandra.

"Take her to Lady Mariana, she will know what to do."

"What? But you..."

"I will keep going with Prince Opheus to find the Emperor. Missandra, we can't leave that poor woman here. Moreover, she is already dressed as a servant, and chances are high the Imperial Guards will have no idea who she is either. Grab the tray outside, and you can walk out with her and pretend you two were just bringing out some food for one of the Concubines here. They won't worry about someone going out if they never saw you coming in, and if anything happens, Lady Mariana will be around to vouch for you."

Missandra hesitated, glancing at the woman. Would that plan work? That poor woman looked barely able to understand what was going on. Cassandra insisted.

"Missandra, please. We can't leave her like that. It might be her only chance to ever escape this place and whatever they did to her. You know I can't leave someone in need, and she is pregnant, too."

Missandra sighed.

"Fine, fine. Don't worry, I'll find a way to take her out of here, and to Lady Mariana... God, Hinue, I hope we are not going to get ourselves killed for being too nice, once again. Be careful, please. Even that Prince just killed a grandma without feeling the slightest regret about it."

Cassandra smiled faintly to her. She had a heavy heart about letting Missandra leave here with that woman, but on the other hand, she would probably be safer out of Prince Vrehan's apartments, with Lady Mariana. If anything happened here, at least Missandra would have higher chances to survive. She had the wits to make it out by herself, and Cassandra highly doubted many people in here would even recognize her as her younger sister.

"So?" asked Prince Opheus as soon as she stepped out of that room. "I already hid the body in another one of the rooms, which actually was a storage room this time."

"Missandra will take care of... whoever this is. We should find the Emperor quickly. Someone will notice that old servant's disappearance sooner or later."

Opheus frowned for a second, surprised by her decision to part ways with her younger sister, but he eventually nodded. With one last look at the room where Missandra was left with the pregnant woman, they both got on their way, still trying to be as discreet as possible.

"Do you really have no idea who that woman was?" whispered Cassandra.

"No... I mean, maybe, but... to be honest, I might not like the answer."

She nodded. No matter how they looked at it, if Prince Opheus couldn't recognize a young woman that looked so much like him and his siblings, something was definitely off and wrong about it. Moreover, if that young woman really was a member of the Imperial Family, for her to be locked up like this couldn't mean anything good. The fact that she was locked up in Vrehan's apartments was a big clue, and Cassandra clearly remembered the story about that missing sister of his, but... that pregnancy was a heavy mystery, too. She hadn't said a word, but Cassandra had immediately thought about that abortion potion Phetra had asked for, and she was sure Missandra had caught onto that too.

Cassandra's thoughts couldn't spend too much time on that matter, though. She and the Fourth Prince were still looking for his father, and they had no idea how far or close he could be. They finally arrived at the end of the forbidden area, Opheus putting an arm out to stop her before they turned a corner.

"Guards," he whispered.

Cassandra could hear them. The private militia of the Second Prince was most likely guarding the area, just as they had suspected. She frowned. How to get past them? They wouldn't be fooled as easily as the Imperial Guards, and they were out of decoys.

Next to her, Opheus took a deep breath in, shaking his head.

"This is the moment where I know I'm going to regret this," he sighed.

Glancing at Cassandra, he brought his index to his lips, indicating for her to remain there and quiet, and suddenly stepped out, his hands on his hips.

Cassandra gasped, but covered her mouth and waited, listening to what was happening just a few steps away.

"You!" exclaimed the Prince. "Go and get me some eighteen-month refined jujubes!"

"Ju... Your Highness, no one is supposed to enter the Second Prince's residence while he is..."

"How dare you talk back!" yelled Opheus, his voice going a little higher-pitched. "I gave you an order! Or do you think you can disobey an Imperial Prince!"

"That's not it, Your Highness, but His Highness the Second Prince ordered us to..."

"Oh, so now you think I'm not worth the trouble? Because I'm only the fourth? Is that what you are saying? I am not a real Prince, perhaps? I don't deserve obedience? You think anyone in my brother's household is allowed to disrespect me? Are you talking for Vrehan when you ignore me? Is that what your master told you? The second is better than the fourth, so you can just ignore him? Hm? What do I do to get some respect around here! Ah, poor me! I don't even deserve to be obeyed by my older brother's men! All of this because I was the fourth born? Is that how my brothers are showing their consideration? Shall I go tell this dear Mother of mine how her beloved son is disrespected? Huh?"

Despite the current situation, Cassandra had to repress a chuckle. The Fourth Prince might deserve a prize for his acting skill. Opheus was talking non-stop, pressuring them relentlessly and she could hear all the men getting flustered by the sudden threat. The poor guards started talking all at once as soon as Opheus gave them a chance to, making a little ruckus. She mostly heard them begging Opheus to keep his mother out of this. She waited a bit more, but he wasn't done.

"Really? Aren't you just standing there for nothing then! What is there even to guard when he isn't here! You are so busy you can't even obey me? This Prince is hungry and you are all letting me starve! Where is it? There is no damn servant in this Palace, and all I can find is you useless people!"

"W-we have to guard, though, Y-Your Highness..."

"Guard what? Walls, perhaps? Three concubines sipping tea? What do you think I'm going to do with those women anyway?!"

The flustered guards seemed at a loss for words, mumbling something Cassandra couldn't understand again. Opheus wasn't giving them much space left to protest, as they probably couldn't talk about the Emperor either. The guards were obviously at a loss on what to do without risking offending an Imperial Prince. They most likely feared there would be retribution later if they didn't obey him.

"We... we will send someone, Your Highness..."

"You better hurry! I want eighteen month-dried jujubes, a full bottle of wine, three red apples..."

The list went on and on, and Cassandra did not even know what half of his requests were about. Was he making up some of those on purpose? With the list being so long, the guards would have no choice but to send a lot of people to gather up all the items. Did that mean Vrehan had really left no servant in his aisle? That made it easier for them, but also didn't mean anything good for the Emperor.

After a while, she heard some of the men leaving. She had no idea how many there were initially, but Opheus' long list was obviously meant to reduce their number. He kept scolding for a while, and Cassandra was getting nervous. He was never going to be able to get rid of all of those men, there were at least half a dozen.

"You two," said the Prince.

Cassandra froze. There were only two men left?

"What are you doing?"

"We will wait with you for the others to return, Your Highness. We have to stay behind to follow the Second Prince's orders to guard this place."

"I see... I didn't know my brother was so adamant about guarding this place. Why are you two here instead of patrolling around, anyway?"

"We were given orders to stay here specifically."

"I see..."

She suddenly heard a loud noise, and closed her eyes by reflex. Cassandra recognized the sounds of a fight and, for a few seconds, she pondered about checking if Opheus was alright. However, if she came out too soon, she risked getting them both killed. Not knowing what was happening just a few steps away was frightening. For the next few seconds, Cassandra stood there and listened. Then, she clearly heard two weights hitting the floor.

"You can come out."

She let out a little sigh of relief. When Cassandra stepped out of her hiding, the two guards were dead at Opheus' feet, their throats sliced open in a little puddle of blood that was growing. She was disgusted but impressed. Those two men were Imperial Guards, but he had gotten rid of both of them within a minute. The Prince didn't drop a pearl of sweat either, while the two men were obviously in a bad shape.

"Let's hurry," said Opheus, not commenting on what had just happened. "We probably don't have long until the others come back."

Cassandra nodded. She carefully walked past both bodies, but they had nowhere to actually hide them. They had no time to find a good hiding place either.

Opheus pushed a door that was on their left, letting her walk in first. It was a very large bedroom, with what was most likely a large bed hidden by curtains at one end. Cassandra almost ran there, but Opheus caught her wrist before she lifted the curtain. Gently pushing her behind him, he lifted it first. A wave of relief appeared on his face.

The old Emperor was lying there, looking very pale, but his eyes were open and staring at the two of them.

"Your Highness!"

"Father..." whispered Opheus.

Cassandra was astonished. How could he have lost so much weight in such a short time!

"White Lily..." whispered the Emperor.

For the first time, his appearance matched his age, but he looked very sick. Cassandra could tell he had a high fever without even touching him, and the bony hand he raised was even thinner than hers. He grabbed her hand, shaking his head.

"Your Highness, what happened?"

"Vrehan did this to you?"

"You... Your son..."

Cassandra was astonished. He was asking about Kassian now? What was going on?

"He is born, Your Highness, he is fine. But please, tell me what they did to you? Did they make you eat something?"

"Good..." whispered the Emperor with a smile.

Cassandra was devastated. He couldn't even seem to hear her questions, the poor man looked so weakened. He was nothing like the mighty Emperor she had seen just a few weeks ago. All this time, she had prayed for him to be alive. She had hoped to be able to save the Emperor, but he was already on the brink of death!

Aside from the erratic, raspy breathing of the Emperor, there was a horrible silence weighing on them. Cassandra had no idea what to do. His lips were somewhat swollen and purple, his mouth was dry, and the old Emperor was obviously running an agonizing fever. He had lost a lot of weight, too. She wondered if there was even anything she could do when he was already this bad? She looked around for something to help, but there was only a small basin of water - it couldn't be that the poor old man had simply been left to die here! This was the Emperor, for goodness sake!

Next to her, Opheus looked just as shocked and lost as she was. He hadn't given much thought about his father's reported illness, but seeing the powerful figure now lying in bed as a sickly, dying old man was too much for him. He stumbled back, lost for words.

Cassandra couldn't just sit on the sidelines. She looked around again, trying to find something, anything that could help. She ran to the little basin of water, tearing some of her dress's fabric to make a compress. The water was barely lukewarm, which made her even angrier. How was it possible that the Emperor wasn't receiving proper care? She walked back to him and wiped the sweat from his brow. He was no longer the Emperor to her, now, he was a patient. A patient in critical condition, who she couldn't allow to die like this, especially not before she had tried everything she could to save him.

"White Lily..."

"Your Highness, what did they do to you?" she asked, desperate for an answer. "Did you eat or drink something? Do you remember what it tasted like?"

Cassandra was struggling to hold back her tears. If she had been in a proper medical space with all of her plants, she may have been able to do something. If only she had a clue about what had been done to the Emperor, any indication towards what he may have been given. She might have had a chance of figuring something out, but it seemed to be that his state was far too desperate now. She had been too hopeful in thinking she would get here in time, to find a cure for whatever ailed him. She never imagined that it would be too late already.

Her fingers were trembling on the little piece of wet cloth, as she kept questioning in utter despair. Opheus remained silent, slowly coming to the understanding of how bad this really was.

"We have to move him."

He turned to her, staring at Cassandra as if she was crazy.

"Move him? We will be lucky if we get out of here alive! We can't move him too!"

"But we have no choice!" she retorted, almost crying. "I can't heal him here, I can't. I...I have nothing, and he is..."

Opheus sighed, and knelt down, grabbing Cassandra's shoulder. He couldn't look at his father as he tried to contain his own emotions.

"Cassandra, you can't. I am no physician, but I am not blind either. There is nothing you can do to save my father, dear, not here or anywhere else. It's just... too late."

She refused to hear it.

Cassandra wasn't an unreasonable woman, but this truth was just too bitter for her to swallow. Their entire journey here, she had been looking forward to the moment she could heal the Emperor. She needed his help and to have him set things straight - to make sure Kairen was named as his successor, to make sure her family would be safe from his brother's madness... to finally put an end to all this. She really thought they had a chance as long as Vrehan wasn't there.

She hadn't thought things here would have been so bad so soon. How many people inside this Imperial Palace had rallied to Vrehan's side already? How long had he been planning this? Maybe she couldn't see the truth, or just didn't want to, but there had been clues - like how poorly guarded this place was. There were far fewer soldiers than she had thought there would be because there wasn't any way left to save the Emperor. Vrehan had deserted the Palace, confident that he had already won this battle. His father was going to die.

What had he used? Poison? The purple lips of the Emperor suggested as much. She wished she could have gotten at least one answer. Maybe then she wouldn't have felt so powerless.

"Your Highness..."

"White Lily, don't... worry," muttered the old man. "Just... the lake..."

Cassandra frowned. The lake? What about the lake? Was he delusional? She tried to get more from him, but the old Emperor was weakening by the minute. Her heart was so heavy, seeing life leave his eyes with no way to help him. She leaned over his bed, trying to make sense of his fractured whispers. Opheus had his hands on her shoulders, but he didn't dare to get any closer. Though they had never been close, he was somehow affected by the death of his father more than he thought he would be.

"Your Highness, what are you talking about?" she asked, clumsily wiping away her tears.

"What lake?"

Was this a dying man's wish? Or something he had to confess? Cassandra was at a loss once again.

"And... Kareen... I'm sorry... I'm sorry..."

"Your Highness, you have to hold on, please," she begged. "Kairen will be here soon. I promise that he is on his way back, with the Imperial Army. We can..."

"Kareen... And the dress..."

None of what he was saying was making any sense to her. Was he reminiscing about old memories of Lady Kareen? She couldn't tell. Why was he talking about a lake and a dress? Cassandra had no idea. Could she comfort him, or at least find a way to ease his pain? He didn't look to be in pain, just...

"Father?"

To her surprise, Opheus finally stepped forward, grabbing his father's hand. He seemed like he was about to say something, but then just his lower lip quivered, and he stayed mute. A veil of emotions covered his face, and Cassandra's heart broke a little more at witnessing it.

This was the reality of being an Emperor's child. They hadn't had a real bond, not the one that should have existed between a Father and his Son. Yet, the bond was present now, manifesting itself at the cruelest moment possible. Cassandra felt his pain resonate through her whole body and she felt even more sad, even more defeated.

Opheus simply held his father's hand in a long, painful silence. The Emperor turned his head to him and faintly smiled, closing his eyes to help mask some of the pain. Cassandra couldn't take it anymore. Tears escaped from her eyes, and she bit her lower lip, devastated. He was truly dying, and she was there, powerless.

"How touching."

Cassandra and Opheus turned around in the same movement, surprised to hear a third voice.

To their left, coming from another door was Prince Lephys, standing in the doorway with an annoyed expression. The Fifth Prince was draped in his purple robe, leaning against the wall with an evil smirk plastered on his face. He was staring at both of them, shaking his head.

"You really had to make a dumb mistake now, Opheus."

The Fourth Prince placed himself between Lephys and their father, looking furious.

"You fucking knew."

Lephys rolled his eyes, shrugged, and then stepped closer.

"Of course I knew, you idiot. Vrehan was always going to need an ally inside the Imperial Palace, and who else but me would have gone along with it?"

"Why?" asked Cassandra, shocked. "This is your father!"

"My father?" scoffed Lephys. "You call that man a father? Do you have any idea what kind of father he is? He might be nice towards Kairen and Shareen, but do you think anyone else in this Imperial Palace holds any fond memories of our dear daddy? Really? What do you say, Opheus?"

Cassandra glanced at the Fourth Prince, but he obviously had nothing to answer to that. Lephys was right in many ways, and even Cassandra couldn't say otherwise. The Fifth Prince took another step closer. He was acting arrogant

540

and totally unaffected by the dying old man behind them.

"A father," he spat. "What kind of father doesn't give a damn about his children dying? How many of our siblings do you think died over the years? Father had so many concubines, they all gave birth to his children... when they didn't lose them or die first."

"His Highness was not responsible for those murders," retorted Cassandra. "The concubines..."

"Oh, I know. The concubines are the ones who always dirtied their hands. One of their rivals was pregnant? Let's kill her. The baby was born safely? Let's kill it! Who needs more children, anyway? The Emperor already has so many!"

Cassandra glanced at the Emperor, unable to contest that. She knew all too well how nefarious this family was. She would never forget the horror stories of how Lady Kareen had lost three of her children. That was one fear that had been growing in Cassandra's mind ever since Lady Kareen had shared her story - that one day, sooner or later, Kassian would become a target, that he already was. She couldn't stand the idea of a child being injured or killed, let alone one of her own!

None of his children had done anything to warrant that kind of life. Their only crime was being born. They were conceived with no say in the matter and then used as political pawns, killed or maimed before they were even able to understand the cruel world they had been born into. Even those who survived beyond birth and into childhood, had to endure the scheming and rivalries. No one made it out without countless scars, both physical and emotional - the pain of losing siblings, enduring hateful step-mothers, and half-siblings. They all had to face too many monstrosities.

"Do you know how many brothers and sisters I've lost through the years? I saw five of them die, but there were many more. My own mother died, poisoned, and yet he didn't bat an eyelid. See, to the Emperor, no one but his precious Favorite and her children ever mattered. All the other women and children were only there for his own pleasure. He's the kind of man who didn't even shed a tear as his own children died, and yet you're crying for him? You are wasting your tears on a narcissistic bastard"

Cassandra felt horribly perturbed listening to this.

She understood where Lephys' hatred came from. Even his hatred towards Kareen and her children could be somewhat justified, as he had suffered from their mere existence. Yet, Cassandra couldn't agree with any of this. She shifted slightly, placing herself between the Emperor and Lephys.

"You can't trust Vrehan either," she said. "Your Second Brother will try to get rid of you, too, as soon as he gets the throne."

"I really don't think so. I am his ally after all. Do you honestly think Vrehan would have taken control of our father's council so easily, if it wasn't for my help?"

"You son of a... What the hell did you do?" growled Opheus.

Lephys chuckled.

"Oh, I was rather involved. Do you know how many concubines I have, Opheus? How many of those women are the daughters of ministers, scholars, generals? It wasn't easy, but if you look carefully, all those women are nothing but pawns to their families. If I merely hinted to one that they might stand a chance at becoming my wife, the desperate whore would run back to her father and arrange any form of support I needed! It's like having my own little army! A bunch of little sluts, all ready to do anything I want, just for a little hope I'd make her my wife."

Cassandra was disgusted. This man was completely rotten to the core, to use his concubines like mere tools, just to get what he wanted! Was that why Vrehan had decided to include him in his plan? It explained so many things! She hadn't understood how he could have taken control of the Imperial Palace so easily by himself. However, with three of the Princes absent, and one of the remaining two on his side, all Vrehan had needed to do was get rid of the Emperor, and then all of his associates would have no choice but to fall in line!

"And you call our father scum?" retorted Opheus, disgusted. "Would you call yourself a saint, perhaps? You're worse than our father ever was!"

"Am I?" asked Lephys, tilting his head. "I am not doing anything our father hasn't done before. Actually, I'm probably nicer since I don't single out any favorites. He used my mother and sisters like pawns for his own entertainment, for nothing but to make his Favorite jealous. What am I doing that's the same?"

"You're wrong," snapped Cassandra. "It's true that His Highness loves Lady Kareen, but he never wanted your siblings' deaths!"

"Oh, are you trying to make me cry for the old man, princess?" chuckled Lephys. "Don't bother, I truly don't care about his death. As soon as he passes, I will have Vrehan officially named as the new Emperor."

"Just you wait until Kairen comes back and wipes the floor with your blood..." hissed Opheus.

Lephys chuckled once more.

"Kairen? Oh, you are sorely mistaken if you think our precious War God could simply fly in here. We have the whole roof trapped, and every single wall. As soon as we spot his Black Dragon, our entire army will attack. He will be taken down as easily as a fly!"

Opheus laughed.

"Is that why you hid Father's Dragon? You and Vrehan are such cowards. You're too scared to face Kairen on your own, so you've had to resort to underhanded tactics! Did that coward also leave you alone to defend the Imperial Palace, Lephys?"

Saying that, Opheus took out a little dagger that he had hidden up his sleeve. Lephys' eyes suddenly went cold as ice upon seeing this, drawing out a long whip in response.

"You dare oppose me, Brother? You are many things, Opheus, but you are not a fighter. Are you really willing to die for this woman? For Kairen's woman?"

Cassandra feared where this was headed. She didn't know how strong either brother was, but a fight in such a tight space, a dagger against a whip, did not leave her with a good feeling. She kept glancing at the Fourth Prince, but his expression spoke volumes. This fight would not be an easy win.

She glanced over her shoulder at the Emperor. He wasn't dead yet, but his breathing was definitely slowing down, maybe a few hours or a few minutes, but it wouldn't be getting any better. Cassandra had no idea how far out Kairen was, but she couldn't afford to wait for him any longer.

"Don't," she suddenly interrupted.

Lephys looked at her, as if he was amused.

"What is it? You don't want to see me kill my brother? Trust me, it will be over quickly."

"Don't fight," she repeated. "I want to make a deal with you."

Chapter 33

This was obviously a desperate attempt on her part, but she was desperate. The brothers were about to fight and Cassandra could see very few ways that they might get out of there alive or unharmed, but she was determined to make it happen. While she felt cornered, she wanted to at least make sure Opheus and his father could make it out to somewhere safe. Anywhere out of the Fifth and Second's Princes reach would be perfect, as the revelation of their alliance came at the worst possible time - Cassandra hadn't seen it coming at all. But the Fourth Prince hadn't asked to be involved in the first place, and if there was the tiniest chance that he could walk out unharmed, she at least owed him that. He had risked so much for her until now, though sometimes reluctantly, and she couldn't allow him to get killed if it was avoidable. It would be entirely her fault.

Meanwhile, the Fifth Prince raised an eyebrow, visibly surprised by her sudden proposal. He still had that annoying smirk on, something that reminded her of his other family members. She wasn't particularly happy about making a deal with the man and, strangely, she wished Missandra was here. Her younger sister was much better at thinking on her feet in situations like this and would surely have been able to come up with a plan, but she wasn't here and Cassandra would have to face this on her own.

"What kind of deal did you have in mind?" laughed the Fifth Prince. "Do you really think you have anything to offer that I don't already have?"

"You can have me," she said.

Glancing at Cassandra, Lephys and Opheus both looked confused. She took a deep breath, trying to think like Missandra would.

"I am not bargaining with you," he hissed.

Cassandra wasn't going to let it go so easily. She saw him twitch when she first suggested it.

"You don't want to fight your brother," she coerced. "It is a waste of precious time and unnecessary injuries. Regardless of who'd win, you have nothing to gain by battling each other. So, instead of... fighting him, I'll follow you without resisting. You can have me, if you leave this place without fighting Prince Opheus."

This time, Lephys pinched his lips, looking doubtful.

"Why would you do that?"

"I will let you take me without resisting, on the condition that you leave the Emperor and Opheus out of this. You leave them here, and I will follow you to your residence, or the cells, or wherever you want me to go."

The Fifth Prince laughed, staring at her like she was crazy.

"Why would I want you? What kind of value do you have? You are nothing, just Kairen's whore!"

"I am his favorite," she retorted. "Unlike your concubines, I am the only one he cares deeply about. We both know he will come for me, no matter what trap you have set."

This time, Lephys seemed to hesitate, staring at her suspiciously.

Cassandra wasn't sure of anything, so she was making it up as she went along. The reality was, she wasn't sure of when or how her Prince would get back here, but she had faith that he would come for her. Something in her heart told her that he was coming back for her. He would never leave the Imperial Palace, or her, in Vrehan's hands. Maybe he was dealing with his brother elsewhere, but if Vrehan was still chasing after her and Missandra, they would both be coming here.

The fact that Kareen had already placed spies around her residence indicated that the Imperial Concubine was betting that the final battle would take place in the Capital, too. Even if he had been left behind by his brother, Lephys couldn't ignore the fact that his brothers would end up back here sooner or later.

"So you're offering yourself as a hostage?" he asked.

Cassandra nodded bravely. Next to her, Opheus was utterly shocked by her sudden change in attitude.

"Are you crazy, woman!?" he yelled.

"It's alright," she said.

"Nothing is alright! You can't do this!"

Cassandra turned to him, though she made sure to keep the Fifth Prince in her field of vision as well. She took a deep breath, trying to convey her words in the best way possible for him to understand.

"I'm sorry, Prince Opheus. If there is anyone else in this Palace who can do something for the Emperor, I don't think it's me anymore. If I had the proper equipment to help, I would try anything, but I'm no longer in that position. It would only buy him a bit more time, perhaps. But, I can't."

She was very careful about her tone of voice and what she tried to convey through her eyes, hoping he would understand what she really meant by it all. Opheus was completely focused on her, but with his brother listening too, she had to be extremely careful.

"The only thing I can do is give you more time with your father before he... before the Emperor passes. I do not want you to get injured or your father to be left to die alone."

Opheus opened his mouth to speak, but nothing came out, looking unsure and terribly confused, but Cassandra knew he would be smart enough to understand.

In their current situation, Cassandra couldn't do anything for the Emperor. She was trapped with no medicine and no supplies. If she had any chance to bring something to help, she would have. She didn't think the Emperor would have been imprisoned in Vrehan's apartments or that he would be in such bad shape by the time she arrived. But she had to face reality, she couldn't save him in their current situation, even if she did her best. If Lephys hadn't shown up, she may have been able to buy some time, if only a little, but not now, not anymore.

Yet, there still might be hope. There was someone else in the Palace with knowledge similar to hers who could help. Lephys did not know that her younger sister was in the Palace too, but Opheus did. If he could bring Missandra back here with some proper medicine once she and Lephys were gone, maybe they could buy some time.

Missandra was not as good with medicine, but she knew about poisons, and she had learned quite a bit from Cassandra over the last several weeks. It wasn't much, but it might be enough to save the Emperor, or at least win him some time - it was the one thing they needed the most right now.

Time. All the time they could possibly get, if they could just save the Emperor before his sons returned.

"What's the catch?" asked Lephys, squinting his eyes in suspicion.

"There is no catch, Your Highness," said Cassandra, turning to him. "You already know I am not a fighter. I won't resist. All I wish is for Prince Opheus and His Highness to be left alone. We already know the Emperor is condemned. I only want to give him a chance to die peacefully, and for Prince Opheus to leave here unscathed."

"What tells me my brother won't come and kill me as soon as I turn my back?"

Cassandra glanced towards Opheus, who was still glaring at his younger brother. She could understand why there was absolutely no trust between them. It was hard to believe they even shared a drop of blood.

"You have me as a hostage. His Highness won't risk hurting me and losing his chance to be left out of all of this. I...coerced him into helping me in the first place. He has nothing to gain in this."

Lephys looked doubtful. Opheus was indeed not a good fighter and he was the one Prince who probably didn't care much about either side winning over the other. He wasn't close to any of his brothers, but seeing that he had helped Cassandra was already troubling him. It confirmed that he cared enough about her.

The Fifth Prince hesitated. There had to be a catch somewhere. He didn't consider Kairen's favorite to be a cunning woman, but he couldn't process her sacrificing herself for his father and brother without getting anything in return. None of it made any sense, especially not Opheus helping her out in the first place.

"Why did you help this woman?" he asked his brother.

"Why indeed?" sighed Opheus, putting his hand on his neck as if to massage it. "Women are such mysterious creatures."

"Answer me!"

Opheus glared back.

"Don't start ordering me around. I helped her because I wanted to. Satisfied?"

Lephys wasn't buying it. He looked even more annoyed, his fingers fidgeting on his whip.

"You're lying."

"What do you know? Maybe Kairen and I have more in common than you think?"

"Don't take me for a fool, I'm well aware of your tastes!"

Opheus scoffed, covering his mouth in a mocking expression and raising an eyebrow.

"You think you know me, Lephys? Do you really think I'm more like you than Kairen, perhaps? You idiot."

Suddenly, Opheus turned to Cassandra and before she could make a move, he grabbed her chin between his fingers and kissed her. That action shocked her just as much as the Fifth Prince. She couldn't react, her whole body froze. Opheus' kiss was deep, using his tongue, and aggressively playing with her mouth. Watching the scene unfold, Lephys's eyes were wide open and his jaw on the floor. Cassandra realized half-way through that this wasn't just a little kiss and, coming back to her senses, she pushed the Prince away, blushing. She had never been kissed by another man before!

But this wasn't her main concern. She was completely flustered by the kiss, barely realizing Opheus had grabbed her hand during the moment and put something between her fingers. Everything had happened so fast that she had to focus to hide it quickly.

"You're disgusting," said Lephys, still in shock.

"Oh, dear, you're not going to tell us you're a virgin, are you?" retorted Opheus with a smirk.

Lephys was not amused. He suddenly raised his whip and cracked it through the air. Though it may have seemed like a mere outburst of anger, the whipping actually left a large dent in the nearest wall. Cassandra couldn't help but shudder. If he could cut that deep into wood with just a little whip, she didn't want to imagine what damage he could inflict if he used that on a human body.

"Fine! I'm taking the woman with me, but don't you dare attempt to move our father anywhere, Opheus. You won't succeed. I have my guards and our brother's men surrounding the Palace, no one can come in or out!"

That was more than disputable considering that Cassandra and Missandra had managed to walk in despite the security, but surely, the Emperor's health wouldn't allow them to move him anywhere anyway.

Lephys walked over, and though Opheus still had his weapon in hand, both brothers only glared at each other. It was like two beasts in a room, ready to jump at each other's throat. If there had been even a shred of brotherly love between these two, it was definitely gone now. Cassandra stepped forward and placed herself between the two men, fiercely hoping her plan would work.

"You take care of yourself," Opheus whispered to her as he held his glare on his younger brother.

"Thank you."

Lephys brutally grabbed Cassandra's wrist, pulling her to his side and away from Opheus.

"You better not go anywhere, Opheus."

"And where would I go?" retorted his older brother, pissed.

Lephys made a sour face, but he had nothing to answer to that. Working with his whip once more, he wrapped it around Cassandra's wrists, pulling them together tightly and trapping her. She grimaced as the fibers painfully cut through her skin a bit. Opheus saw it too, but did not say a thing.

"Fine," hissed Lephys.

Finally breaking their staring contest, Lephys pulled Cassandra to leave the room with him. She glanced back once more at Opheus. Maybe she dreamt it, but she saw him nod very slightly with a determined expression. Had he understood her silent plea? Was he going to send someone for Missandra, find a way to have her come to help the Emperor? She could only hope so.

It was too late now. Lephys was dragging Cassandra away, walking confidently across Vrehan's apartments. He was obviously in charge with his brother gone. None of the guards they crossed paths with said a thing, and the servants didn't dare raise their heads either. They knew, thought Cassandra. All the people working there were already obeying the Second and Fifth Princes, as if they were already in power.

Cassandra was utterly disgusted. The Emperor had probably taken years to establish himself as a force within his empire, working for years to keep it afloat, and yet the powerful man was overthrown so easily. Fear and envy were getting the best of all these people. They didn't care which Master they served, as long as they could keep their positions and money. She thought about Lephys' speech earlier, about his concubines. It was always the same. People killed and threw their lives away for greed.

"How did you get inside the Palace to begin with?" Lephys suddenly asked as they continued walking.

"I paid a servant to help me," she lied.

She deliberately made it sound like she had used someone she hadn't known before, so Lephys wouldn't try to find and kill the culprit. He wouldn't want to lose his time over simple corruption.

"Tsk...Those little rats cannot be trusted."

Cassandra didn't add anything else. Lephys wasn't Opheus. He would have no compassion for her, and the only reason she was alive at that moment was her relationship with Kairen.

She had to think of her next move. How was she going to get out of this situation, now? She had been captured so easily, it was almost laughable. She continued following Lephys. He didn't seem to fear that she might escape with his whip tightly binding her wrists. Cassandra tried to remain calm.

"Where are you taking me?" she asked. "To the cells?"

"Oh no, darling, that would be too obvious and boring. No...I have other plans for you."

He suddenly turned around to face her, grabbing Cassandra's throat in his hand. She almost choked, barely able to breathe as he tightened his grip. He had a dark, sadistic gleam in his eyes, something that reminded her of his vicious older brother.

"I don't often get the chance to make my annoying older brother suffer, but when the opportunity arrives, I will take it. I wonder what Kairen will do when he learns I had my way with his precious woman? I've found you interesting from the day we met and, though I find you rather ugly, you will still be a nice toy for me to play with before they come back."

Cassandra's blood left her face. She could barely breathe with his fingers tight around her throat and all the blood draining from her face. Her limbs were tingling as she was fighting to stay conscious. Watching her, Lephys was enjoying her panicked state, his grip tightening as a vicious smirk spread across his lips. This time, he really did resemble Vrehan, with a crazy glint in his eyes. Cassandra tried to think, to grab his wrist, when he suddenly let go.

Cassandra fell to her knees, coughing and gasping for air. She could already see the bruises forming on her skin, but for now, she was focused on recovering as fast as she could. She had to stay alert.

"I don't trust Opheus enough to stay here," he said.

He grabbed her by her wrists, still tightly bound by his whip, and yanked her forward causing her to fall and hurt her shoulder. Cassandra grimaced as her mind flashed back to the day of the Celebrations when she had been similarly dragged across the Palace. This time though, she fought to get up before he could drag her any further. Lephys had just started walking without a care as to whether she was following or not, his whip was a leash that hauled her along. Painfully, Cassandra managed to find her balance and get back on her feet right away. With her hands so tightly tied, she had no choice but to follow him through the corridors.

She couldn't recognize where they were headed, but she didn't like that they were going deeper inside the Palace and further away from the Emperor. Cassandra prayed that the Fourth Brother would find a way to get Missandra to the Emperor, and somehow find a way to save the old man.

Lephys looked absolutely sure of himself as he walked through the corridors. Had his apartments always been this far? Cassandra was completely lost, but then, she suddenly recognized the area they were in.

The lake! They were close to the large garden, the one where the New Year Celebrations had been held only a few weeks prior. She recognized the corridor they were walking through, the same one that she and Kairen had isolated themselves in. The memory had her blushing slightly, in spite of the situation she was in. If only she could go back to those days, to Kairen's strong arms. However, she had more pressing matters to think about. The Emperor had tried to tell her something about the lake, what was it? She could now see it through the windows, but no matter how many times she tried to glance at it, there was nothing special happening there. There weren't even any concubines chatting or taking their tea, or servants walking by! The Imperial Palace seemed strangely empty now.

Suddenly, two horn blows resonated throughout the Palace's walls. Lephys, still walking ahead of her, suddenly stopped and grimaced, turning his head.

"Damn it! That bastard is back sooner than I expected!"

"What? Who?" asked Cassandra, a cold shiver running down her spine.

"Vrehan! Anyway, let's do this quickly, before he gets here."

As he started dragging her faster, Cassandra's body shivered. The Second Prince was back already? What about Kairen then? How far away was he with the Imperial Army? If Vrehan was back now, he would go straight to the Emperor, perhaps even kill him right away! Opheus and Missandra were now in more danger than before!

While she panicked, Cassandra didn't realize that they had finally arrived at the Fifth Prince's apartments. Before she could fight back, he threw open the door to a bedroom, where two women were laying, both naked except for some very heavy jewelry around their necks, arms, and ankles. The Fifth Prince glared at them.

"Out!" he yelled.

Both women left hurriedly with looks of disappointment on their faces. Once they were gone, Lephys flicked his whip, throwing Cassandra on to the now vacant bed. Falling to her side, she moved her wrists immediately, desperately trying to free herself as she heard a chuckle.

"That's a bit too late, woman. Or do you think you can escape an Imperial Prince? A man with the Dragon Blood?"

Cassandra glared at him, not even bothering to answer. Lephys was not worthy of the Dragon Blood that flowed through his veins. He was just a horrible, disgusting monster that she was starting to hate even more than the Second Prince, if that was possible.

She kept wriggling her wrists, trying to loosen the knot despite the fibers cutting into her skin. It was painful, and she could feel her flesh being ripped apart, but she had no choice. She had to hurry before it was too late.

Before her, Lephys watched her struggle, visibly amused. A snicker on his face, he started undressing, taking off his outfit slowly. When he put one knee on the bed, Cassandra froze and glared at him.

"Don't touch me," she hissed.

"Oh, I'm planning to do much more than touch you. I bet you'll even like it. Women just can't deny their pleasure. Those whores just want sex and, just like you, they like to refuse me just for the fun of it. You are all like that. You act like a prude and innocent, but you just want to be fucked by a strong man. Don't pretend you're all about my brother. Once I'm done with you, you'll be begging me to keep you, they all do."

"I'd rather die," she retorted.

His words made her want to throw up. She didn't care what his concubines felt about him, she was nothing but disgusted by him. This man was a monster, a sick pervert - she found it incredulous that he even shared some of the same blood as Kairen. But she was steady in her resolve, she wouldn't let him touch her, not a chance in hell.

As he slowly moved towards her, she tried to retreat, wiggling her way back on the bed, trying to crawl away as far as she could. As her hands were still tied, she readied her free legs to kick him if he got too close. Lephys' smile got even wider as she kept furiously glaring at him.

"I like them feisty. I can't wait to tame you and show my brother that his little slut has become mine. Kairen thinks he is so much better than all of us. I can't wait to see the look on his face once he learns I fucked his woman, his beloved witch."

"You won't touch me," hissed Cassandra, furiously.

She was ready to fight with all she had. She had learned from Kairen. Never before had she had such a fiery, murderous look in her green eyes.

The Fifth Prince laughed and, with a quick movement from his hands, undid his whip from around her wrists. Cassandra looked at her free hands in shock, the red marks buried deep on her skin. Suddenly, the Prince moved closer and before she could even react, half of his body was above hers. She tried to kick him, but his hand reacted immediately, catching her ankle mid-air with a grin.

"You can't escape me. Do you think you can even try to fight me? I am a Prince, and you're nothing but a weak woman. You'd better learn to lie down and obey because I intend to have my way with you until Vrehan gets here."

Cassandra wasn't even listening anymore. She didn't care what horrible plans he intended for her or how long it would take his brother to get there. None of this was going to happen. She struggled to turn around on her stomach, despite her ankle still trapped in his hand. She heard him laugh from behind her, but she was busy retrieving what she had hidden in her sleeve earlier.

"What are you doing, witch? You think that's it? Oh, or is that an invitation to your..."

"I said don't touch me!" Cassandra shouted.

Before the young Prince could react, she had turned around and sat up as her arm flew in his direction. This time, he was a second too late. With one hand holding himself up on the mattress and the other still occupied with her leg, he wasn't quick enough to block Cassandra's hand. His eye caught a glimpse of silver as he saw it coming, but he barely had a chance to comprehend the threat until a sharp pain pierced his neck.

The Fifth Prince let out a horrible screech as his blood splattered both of them, his eyes wide open in shock. Lephys suddenly let go of her ankle, his fingers shaking, as they came up to touch the weapon that had just stabbed him. He could feel the warm blood running down his neck, and the sharp piece of metal stuck there. He spasmed for several seconds, completely shaken by the waves of pain. His eyes were trained on Cassandra as she jumped out of the bed. It was clear he was having a hard time coming to terms with what had just happened. She was shivering in fear as she stepped away from him, but she had done it. Opheus' long earring was embedded deep inside his flesh, planted there and not moving. She saw Lephys' eyes following her moves as he gagged several times, trying to get words out.

"Y... You... witch..."

"I'm not a witch," she retorted, out of breath. "I'm a physician!"

With those last words, Cassandra turned around and ran out of the bedroom as fast as she could. She knew she didn't have a second to lose. She had aimed right for his carotid artery and stabbed as hard as she could, but she had no idea how fast he'd recover. She had seen Kairen heal some deep cuts in a matter of seconds, but she had never seen what his younger brother's healing abilities were. If it was a normal man she had stabbed, he would have been dead in minutes, but she wasn't so naive as to think the Fifth Prince would die from this though.

So, Cassandra kept running down the corridors, desperate to find her way back. The reality of what had just happened was hitting her slowly, but she didn't have time to stop and think. She had just tried to murder an Imperial Prince but, strangely enough, she had more pressing concerns right now. She was worried about the Emperor, Opheus, Missandra, and more importantly, she was terrified to face Vrehan or his sister, alone.

Cassandra wasn't familiar with this part of the Palace, and she was afraid to go the wrong way, or run into someone unfavorable. However, she needed to get back, and fast. As soon as Lephys recovered, he'd come after her and if he didn't, someone, like his concubines from before, would be quick to let the guards know the White Witch had assassinated the Fifth Prince!

Suddenly, she heard it. Footsteps, running behind her.

"Come back, you whore!"

A cold shiver ran down her spine. How could he be back on his feet and running already? Cassandra accelerated, but it was too much on her body for one day. The climbing had been easier than she thought, but sneaking by a window, riding a Dragon, fighting off a rapist Prince, and running through the

Palace probably wasn't recommended for a woman who had given birth not ten days ago!

She was frantic. There was no sign of Kairen's return and with Vrehan back, he would soon know she was here. All she had managed to do was win a bit of time for the Emperor, but it may have all been for nothing.

Finally, Cassandra ran into a familiar corridor - the one with its windows open to the garden with the lake! At least she knew where she was now, but the furious footsteps were growing loud behind her. Tears grew in Cassandra's eyes. She wasn't going to make it. She knew the way back to where the Emperor was, but even if Opheus was still there, she wouldn't get there in time. The Fifth Prince was catching up to her, and from the sound of his steps compared to her speed, it would be all over in a couple of minutes.

Cassandra felt like breaking down. What had she even accomplished? She was either going to die or be captured again! She cried without stopping. Kassian, her baby, her little boy, she needed to see him, to hold him one last time. And Kairen - her man, her War God. She didn't want to die before getting to see him one last time, just one last time.

"You wench, stop!"

Cassandra heard a snap and then felt a sharp pain pierce her back. Lephys' whip. She felt like screaming out. He had cut her deeply! She stumbled forward, almost falling, but something kept her going. She managed to keep her feet steady and continued running.

She couldn't stop now, she couldn't give in. No matter what.

Suddenly, a loud horn resonated through the air. Cassandra heard Lephys' steps stop, and she couldn't help but glance behind her shoulder. The Prince had stopped running, his eyes wide open towards one of the windows.

"The Eastern Army?" he whispered.

Cassandra's heart jumped in her chest. Kairen's Army! They were in the Capital! She felt an incredible wave of adrenaline and her feet carried her before Lephys started chasing her again. She still had a chance! Just a slim chance. If the Eastern Army was here, then either Kairen or Shareen was too.

"Come back, you damn witch! I will kill you before his eyes!"

The voice behind her couldn't hold her back. Cassandra took a sharp turn, entering another corridor before she abruptly stopped.

At the end of the corridor stood Vrehan right in the middle of her way, glaring at her. Cassandra's lips trembled. She stepped back without thinking, despite the running that wasn't stopping behind her. For a second, she wondered if she was hallucinating, if she was having some daytime nightmare. It couldn't be. Not now, of all times. However, the Second Prince was standing still, in his military outfit, his eyes on her like a snake about to kill its prey. Her blood turned cold as she noticed the long sword by his side.

"Finally," he hissed. "We meet again, White Witch."

Cassandra felt like the ground was falling from under her feet. She was falling into some hellish nightmare that wouldn't end. Her mind went blank for a couple of seconds.

The Second Prince Vrehan was standing in front of her. The one man she loathed the most, the one person she had tried to avoid at all costs, and now...Cassandra tried hard to repress her fear. She couldn't give up now, not just because he had appeared. She had heard the horn, Kairen had to be close and with his army in tow. Now that she had stopped running, Cassandra could hear the noise outside. It was still far, because of how vast the Imperial Palace was, but she could tell something was happening. Probably a war between the Eastern and the Imperial Armies, but whatever was going on outside, she silently prayed it was coming their way.

Vrehan was hearing it too. He frowned, looking at the window with a sour expression.

"Kairen, that bastard. He was fast."

Just hearing his name gave Cassandra a new wave of strength. She took a deep breath, her eyes still on Vrehan as she thought about her next move. She couldn't stay here, Lephys would catch up at any second, and going forward was now out of the question. She glanced sideways. She had hoped to find a real exit earlier, but it seemed like she had no other choice but to climb out one of the windows.

"Oh, well... At least now I've got a valuable hostage," Vrehan suddenly whispered, his eyes going back to her.

Cassandra took a step back as a reflex. She was not going to let him near her. She had made that mistake once, and the cost was Dahlia's life. She had learned her lesson.

Before he could add another word, Cassandra suddenly jumped to the side and did her best to climb out of the window as fast as she could. She heard him yell something incomprehensible behind her, but she had no time to wonder what it was. She was absolutely desperate and she couldn't stay in that corridor. Plus, the words of the Emperor had been circling in her mind the entire time. The lake. Did he mean this lake? Why this lake?

Cassandra's feet landed in the deep grass of the garden, and started running right away towards the lake. She knew she only had a few seconds at best before both brothers would catch her. She was running as fast as she could. She had no idea what was going to happen or if that lake could save her life, but she had no other option. Diving into the lake seemed like the craziest idea, but it was her last resort.

"Come back here!"

The Fifth Prince had just jumped out of the window too, but Cassandra was several meters ahead of him and had no intention of slowing down. The only thing that interested her right now was the lake, but something caught her attention as she was rushing towards it. On the ground were several shadows of lines crossing over each other. She raised her head to find where they were coming from. A grid!

That crazy Second Prince had laid out a grid of thick, long, silver chains running between the roofs, covering the open area. Was it meant to keep the dragons from entering there? She didn't remember seeing anything like this during her flight earlier with Opheus, but then again it would have been impossible for him to cover the whole Imperial Palace. Had he just laid these in the areas where he had hidden the Emperor? This was insane! It also explained Glahad's absence. Where had the Golden Dragon gone if he wasn't by his Master's side? Had he been trapped in some way?

Cassandra didn't have time to wonder any more, as she heard the crack of the whip dangerously close behind her. She accelerated despite the pain in her back and legs. The strain from all the running and climbing was starting to take its toll on her body, but she ignored it, only focusing on the lake, and running faster than the two princes.

"What are you doing!?"

She ignored them. Her feet were already in the water as she tried to scrutinize the surface of the lake. She walked in, but she couldn't see much. With the sunlight reflecting on the surface, it was too deep and too dark to see anything past a couple of meters beneath the surface. How deep was the lake? While singing her song those weeks ago she had stayed where she could just sit with the water at her waist. Now, she had to go as far as she could.

The familiar feeling of water enveloping her legs gave her some more strength and she tore the edges of her dress so she could walk and then swim more comfortably. The whip cracked again, just breaking the surface of the water next to her. He had just barely missed, but he was close enough to hit her.

"Don't kill her!" shouted Vrehan. "We need her alive!"

Ironically, the Second Prince may have saved her life. Lephys kept trying to get a hold of her, but the Prince apparently wasn't good at gauging his own strength. Either he was too heavy with it and violently slashed the water, or too light and he missed her completely. Cassandra kept going, half-swimming now. She knew the Dragon Princes wouldn't follow her into the water, but everything was going to depend on how long she could stay beneath the surface.

She took several deep breaths, and when her lungs felt full, she finally dove in. As she hurried deeper in the lake, she heard the echo of the whip breaking the surface above her. Cassandra needed to get far enough away so they couldn't reach her.

She had no idea where she was going. It took her eyes a long minute to adjust to the water before she was finally able to see clearly. As she had suspected, it was indeed significantly deeper than it looked from the surface. She couldn't tell how much exactly, but she kept going deeper. As she dove, Cassandra couldn't help but silently pray the air she had stored would last as long as she needed. As she swam past various fish, she thought how eerie it was - being submerged in this underwater world with everything going on above. It was likely no one from the Imperial Family had ever bothered to try swimming in the lake as none of the fish looked bothered by her presence, like she posed no real threat.

Cassandra kept going deeper. Her composition was different from the Dragon Empire's people. Her legs could paddle for a long time without becoming too tired, and her eyes weren't troubled by the water. Her body could handle the pressure, and her lungs could retain air for a long time.

Hence, she continued past what any other person around could withstand. What had the Emperor hoped she would find in that lake? Was this even the right lake he had mentioned? It was too late to wonder and worry about it now. As she got farther away from the surface, she was soon surrounded by darkness. As she soon realized, the light wasn't the only thing that was slowly disappearing. There were less and less fish too. Why? She would have thought all those underwater creatures would enjoy the calmness in the lower levels of the lake, but instead, all the little fish stayed closer to the surface, as if they were too scared to go further and the few that dared venture lower didn't stay long, quickly turning around. Cassandra hesitated. Should she still go down after witnessing that? What were the depths of the lake hiding.

She glanced upwards. It felt strangely calm down here compared to what was waiting for her on the surface, though she had no choice anyway. The danger was surely much more grave up there.

The young concubine kept going down, her eyes now struggling to see anything. She had a strange feeling. As if something was looking at her, lurking in the darkness. Something dangerous.

Cassandra was starting to feel a little unwell. The air in her lungs was slowly running out, and she was becoming tired. Her body was resenting all the vigorous exercise from the day, and the water pressure was compounding her discomfort. She couldn't give-up yet. She had to spend as much time as she could searching underwater and, even if she couldn't find anything down there, she needed to delay her return to the surface as long as possible.

Suddenly, something quickly swam past her. She froze. It was big. Very big. It had what seemed like a long body, something much longer than any underwater creature she had ever heard of. A giant snake, maybe?

Fear was starting to claw at the back of her mind, and not being able to see anything was making it even more terrifying. If a beast did decide to attack her, she was completely defenseless. She had left Opheus' earring in his brother's neck to delay his healing process, and she had given her dagger to Missandra before they left for the Palace. As her younger sister was a better fighter, she was the better choice to hold the weapon, in case they found themselves in such a situation, but she hadn't even thought of taking it back when they parted ways. Though she probably wouldn't have anyway, she was now regretting that. She had nothing to defend herself with.

The creature moved next to her again, and a loud sound resonated like an echo in the water. Cassandra's eyes grew larger. Was that...a growl? It was higher-pitched than a dragon's, but it was still so similar to Krai's! It couldn't be, could it? Suddenly, the strange growl echoed out again as she turned towards its origin, squinting her eyes to try and locate the creature's exact position. If it could see her, why hadn't it attacked yet? Was that thing what the fish were afraid of? Cassandra focused on the water's movements around her, trying to figure out where the creature would swim to next. It ought to be massive judging by the growl it made. A crazy theory was growing in the back of her mind, but it seemed absolutely impossible.

Two big white lights suddenly appeared in the darkness. Cassandra had to cover her mouth so as not to scream and lose more of her precious air. The lights were big, like diamonds, and they were... eyes. A pair of reptilian eyes. The two eyes grew closer, and Cassandra tried to swim away by reflex. Judging from the size of them, whatever creature they belonged to had to be enormous! If that thing decided it wanted to hunt her, she was already dead.

However, the eyes didn't appear menacing. In fact, as they slowly grew closer, there was no animosity in them at all. Cassandra froze, though her heart was beating like crazy. What was that thing? She decided to stop and let it approach. She couldn't go far or fast enough to flee it anyway. If she was going to die, better make it quick.

A giant snout gradually appeared below the white eyes. It was covered in scales and Cassandra thought they might be dark grey, but they really could have been any color. In this darkness, she couldn't tell. A large snout protruded out and sniffed her, the creature's head slowly coming into view as it continued approaching her. Cassandra was speechless! It was impossible, but she couldn't make this up - it was definitely a dragon's head.

The head was a bit leaner than any dragon she had seen, and there were no little horns on the side of its face or on its head, only two long ones, cascading back down from the top of its head, though one of them was broken. The cheeks were a bit rounder too, and Cassandra noticed the wide and long holes along the neck as the creature turned its head slightly. Could those be gills?

The creature circled around her, clearly assessing her. Cassandra wondered if she could even call it a dragon, but regardless, she was fascinated by the creature. The face was clearly that of a dragon, but its body was different from those she knew. It was leaner, with shorter limbs and, more importantly, the joints of those limbs had large fans. The creature was slithering it's body slowly and meticulously to move itself. Cassandra was amazed. From what she observed of them, those had to be like fins. There were several on its back too, and the tail of the dragon had a similar shape, as well. This seemed so impossible, she wondered if she hadn't lost consciousness already and was perhaps hallucinating it all. But, the creature next to her was very real. It kept swimming in circles around her, never taking its eyes off her and growled again. Cassandra wondered if this was it. If she was going to be killed by such an unbelievable creature. Was this what the King wanted her to find?

Cassandra didn't have much air left in her lungs. She was slowly suffocating and her head was starting to spin a bit. She glanced towards the surface. What should she do? It was already a miracle that this dragon-like being hadn't attacked her by now! Such a magnificent creature...

Cassandra had no more oxygen left, she opened her mouth slightly, feeling too tired to fight anymore. The creature slowly swam closer to her, and she somehow managed some strength to extend her arm. The dragon, if it even was one, slid past her, letting her fingers slide across its skin. It was incredibly cold.. contrary to Krai's warmth. Cassandra chuckled, her brain finding that information funny.

She couldn't hold on anymore. She wanted to close her eyes. One last growl resonated through the waters before she lost consciousness.

Chapter 34

As if Kassian had understood his father, the little baby had a very serious frown on and was holding on to the little plushie's tail fiercely. Despite the overall situation, Kairen's heart warmed up a little at that sight. The child was indeed his son...brave and strong, like his parents. He held him for a while as if trying to learn all of his son's features by heart. Kairen had never been interested in children, but Kassian was different. He was truly a part of both of his parents.

Kairen remembered how impatient Cassandra had been to finally see their son and hold him. She only had one week with her baby, while Kairen had lost the entire first week of his newborn's life. Fate truly was too horrible sometimes. He hugged his baby gently. He had never been trained to carry a baby, but somehow, all the right movements came to him naturally, as if his instincts were guiding him. Kassian didn't seem upset being carried in his father's strong and sturdy arms. The baby was actually engrossed with his plushie, though he was barely able to hold on to it. With his little mouth forming O's, he looked like he was sizing up the plushie. His expression was quite amusing.

Kairen couldn't help but recognize some of Cassandra's features there - his little nose, the shape of his eyes. Even his irises had hints of green in them, and his skin was just a shade lighter than his fathers, but not nearly as light as his mother's.

"Oh by the Gods!"

Lady Kareen had just arrived behind him and was staring at the baby, her eyes filled with emotions. The Imperial Concubine's heart melted at the sight of the newborn in Kairen's arms. She seemed at a loss for words, and just gently caressed the baby's hands for a few seconds. From Kairen's arms, the baby squealed in excitement upon seeing a new face. She kept smiling gently at him, but Kairen's mind was elsewhere.

"Mother, take him."

He carefully passed Kassian to his mother, gave him a little kiss on his head in doing so, and then took out his weapon. It was unfortunate that things were so dire already, as they had very little time for a meaningful reunion. Shareen was guarding the door for now, but Vrehan's men knew where they were. Kairen could hear them outside, banging against every door. It would only be a matter of minutes before they barged in, unless his sister lost patience and went to them first.

"Kyun!"

Kairen almost jumped at the little squeal and looked down. Against his leg, a small, silver-scaled dragon was rubbing it's back against him and looking up with big green eyes. The War God smiled once again and leaned down to pick the little dragon up. Kian immediately jumped onto his shoulder, which was broad enough for him to perch on comfortably.

"Oh, by the Great Dragon, he is.. perfect!" exclaimed Lady Kareen on the verge of tears.

Though she wasn't wrong, the new grandmother was already blinded by love. With her knowledge of dragons, she could clearly see Kian was a bit different from all the other dragons she had ever encountered before. He had a longer and leaner body, and his wings were thinner and shorter, too. It was most likely that unless they grew bigger sometime soon, he probably wouldn't be able to manage long flights or heavy weights, like Krai could.

Kairen didn't have time for this, however. Keeping the young dragon on his shoulder, he turned towards the women from before. They might have both been scared of the War God, but at least they did not run away. They were already aware of his tender relationship with Cassandra and Kassian, but he was still an impressive man to see in the flesh.

"Where is Cassandra?" he asked.

"L-Lady Cassandra went to the Imperial Palace," explained one of the women, who was actually Yasora. "She wanted to find and heal the Emperor."

"She went alone?" protested Kareen.

"She went with young Lady Missandra!" added Yasora. "They wanted to find one of the herbal gardens or medicines there, as we didn't have time to procure any here."

"She's not wrong," sighed Kareen. "That rat, Vrehan, must have had all the Capital's apothecaries watched the second he knew Cassie was back. And then?"

"We...we don't know, Your Highness. The girls left hours ago, and we haven't heard any news since."

"Hours ago?" exclaimed Kareen, shocked.

She turned to Kairen, livid. Hours ago could mean bad or good news at this point. At least they hadn't found their bodies strung up on the Palace's walls. But in a few hours, they could very well have been caught, tortured, or killed. There might still be a chance the girls were alive, but there was no leaning towards one option over the other.

"Let's go," said Kairen, determined.

Kareen nodded and followed him, still carrying Kassian. There was no way the War God was going to part with his son for a single minute, and the Imperial Concubine could very well protect him herself. They left the room and found Shareen and Anour in the garden, both of them watching the gate, which was still holding against their assailants, though it was obviously having quite a bad day.

"Oh, here's my nephew," said Shareen with a smirk, staring at the baby. "Wow, you're lucky he took after his mom. Even for a baby, he's cute."

"That dragon is amazing," added Anour, his eyes on little Kian. "His tail is so long. He's even leaner than Roun!"

Actually, all three dragons present were quite intrigued by the Baby Dragon. Kian jumped down from Kairen's shoulder and ran to Krai. Though the Black Dragon looked a bit surprised, it carefully walked closer, the big red eyes wide open with curiosity.

To the side, Roun wasn't as patient. The Green Dragon growled, almost jumping on the Baby Dragon, but Krai reacted immediately, growling louder as a warning. The Green Dragon retreated with its head low. Between them, Kian seemed to have not even noticed Roun; The Baby Dragon kept running up to Krai, all excited. The Black Dragon clearly didn't know how to react, especially as the Baby Dragon easily disappeared under its big body. Krai kept trying to look down and around, but the excited Kian kept scuttling over and under, jumping on its paws playfully, making cute squeaks, and chasing Krai's big black tail.

Finally, the big Black Dragon growled and, when Kian made another move close enough, caught the Baby Dragon under its paw. Surprised, Kian squealed a bit, but Krai tilted its head, and carefully grabbed the baby in its mouth. The Baby Dragon swung its little paws, unhappy with this new position, but Krai ignored it as it walked up to Kairen. The dragon looked like a cat with its pissed off kitten, making everyone smile.

"Don't you hurt him, Krai," warned Kareen with a frown.

It was unlikely Krai would harm the Baby Dragon voluntarily, but keeping the baby in its mouth without biting with those sharp fangs must have been quite difficult for Krai, especially as Kian was particularly unruly. However, the Black Dragon looked like it was controlling the situation, and its offspring, perfectly.

They didn't have much time to keep observing these intimate interactions though. The shouts were getting louder behind the door. Kairen cracked his neck, and his sister looked even more impatient. All the servants had run back inside the mansion to hide. A small army was surely waiting for them out there, but these people had Dragon's Blood and actual dragons with them!

"This is going to take all day."

The Princess took a deep breath, taking in as much air as she could into her lungs and, after a couple of seconds, she exhaled a massive fireball towards the door, sending it and everyone behind it flying. The Imperial Princess smirked.

"Now we can actually get to it."

With a demonic smile on her face, she ran into the crowd of soldiers who were still standing or trying to get back up on their feet. Kairen glanced back towards him, but Kassian was perfectly safe in his grandmother's arms. She had even shielded him from the smoke by raising her sleeve, though the baby only seemed to care about his plushie.

The Imperial Prince ran to support his sister. Shareen didn't need much help though, but the faster they dealt with these soldiers, the faster they'd get to the Imperial Palace and to Cassandra. There wasn't a single second to lose.

Behind them, Roun and Krai began jumping to attack the soldiers, too. When Kian started growling at them angrily, Krai finally let go and, though it was too small to attack, the Baby Dragon jumped from its head to its back, sending growls left and right as if it was the one fighting.

The Imperial Siblings fought their way to the Imperial Palace. It was a long, long fight to get there as they couldn't use the dragons with the roofs being trapped. The residence was quite far from the Imperial Palace, and it seemed like the number of men sent by Vrehan was endless. More importantly, they soon realized the Imperial Army was already there. The colors of the soldiers were codified, and Shareen and Kairen didn't even need to talk to each other to know who they were fighting against. They just exchanged glances, and kept going.

Fighting the Imperial Army was not easy inside the Capital, especially not with two dragons by their side. It was the same as the fight against the Eastern Republic's Army. They had to be cautious of the locals, so the dragons couldn't even use their fire. However, Kairen, Shareen, and the two dragons alone were enough to fight their way through the whole Imperial Army, no matter how much slower the progress. The soldiers were obviously afraid of them, though they were trained not to retreat. Kairen and Shareen fought one man after another, slaughtering everyone in their way without stopping.

It was a dance of death. Blood flying through the air and violence dispersing terrified citizens that dared to venture outside at the wrong time. The siblings and the dragons only occupied a couple of streets, but they were a horror scene. They had no mercy and no time to care about doing a clean job of this.

"Your Highness!"

Kairen turned to the left, taking his sword out of a man's chest, soon realizing they weren't alone anymore. Many soldiers of a different outfit were now standing or running in the same direction as them, opposing the Imperial Army. One of the Generals ran to Kairen's side, bowing with a military salute.

"Your East Army!" exclaimed Shareen, surprised. "Already?"

"We came as soon as we got Lady Kareen's message, Your Highness! We couldn't stay put, especially with Your Highness and Lady Cassandra in danger!"

Indeed, they soon heard the sounds of the two armies fighting resonating from all the nearby streets. The fight had now been taken much farther into the Capital's streets. Screams and sounds of weapons striking filled the air. It was a war scene everywhere the eye could see.

Kairen and Shareen exchanged a smile in spite of their tiredness and the sweat and blood soaking their armor. With the East Army here, they could finally cut through the smaller fights and make it to the Imperial Palace quicker.

The fighting resumed, more violent than before. Throughout the city, hundreds of men fought to get to the Imperial Palace or keep others from it. The fighting going into the night, long past sunset. When the sun had touched the ground, they finally presented themselves at the Palace's doors. The fight wasn't over, but the siblings had finally reached their destination. Both Shareen and Kairen were a bit tired after all of that, but neither of them wanted to stop. They sent people to get Phetra, their hostage, and cleared the area around them, making sure no one would try to stop them from entering. In the streets, the East Army was clearly winning, establishing a clear perimeter around the Palace. Unlike the East Army, none of the Imperial Army had been trained in first aid, and they had to watch as Kairen's men helped their own people, while theirs suffered.

What was happening in the streets was no longer Kairen's concern. He was glaring at the doors, impatient to finally wrap his hands around Vrehan's neck. He glanced at his sister, who nodded. Just like before, Shareen took a deep breath, and used her fire on the large doors. It was the most efficient way and, after that, both siblings only had to use a bit of strength on the doors for them to finally collapse.

Leaving the armies to fight each other outside, they walked in. Kareen followed a few steps behind with Evin and Anour as bodyguards, even though she probably didn't need them.

"Where to, Mother?" asked Kairen, unsure.

"I don't know... Let's just head for the rat's apartments first."

As they walked through the corridors, everything felt quiet. Strangely quiet. They'd had to leave the dragons outside, as both Roun and Krai were too big to squeeze through the front doors, but it was still too quiet. dragons or not. They didn't spot a single servant for a long while. The Imperial Palace had certainly changed a lot since their last visit here, and none of them were particularly fond of this new atmosphere.

"Brother?"

Kairen followed her glare. They were still on their way, but something strange was happening to the side. Several Imperial Soldiers were guarding the lake, their weapons in hand. The siblings exchanged a glance. Men guarding the lake? They decided to ignore it and, instead, continued rushing inside when a loud sound resonated. A long, long blow. Kareen froze.

"The Emperor," she whispered.

They all knew that sound. It was only used in the event of an Imperial Death. Their blood froze in their veins, and without thinking, Shareen and Kairen started running towards the Emperor's Hall.

When they barged in, they were welcomed with a hundred soldiers pointing their weapons at them. The Hall was filled with Imperial soldiers and at the very end, facing them, Vrehan sat on the Golden Throne, his dragon sitting behind him. Both of the red beast's eyes were completely destroyed, they were just two big black holes now. It was obviously blind.

However, the dragon wasn't their main worry at the moment and neither were the soldiers. In front of them, Vrehan was holding Missandra by her hair, a knife threateningly held against her throat.

A strange silence followed their arrival into the room. Kairen and Vrehan were fiercely glaring at each other from across the dozens of soldiers between them. Even if they had been alone, the atmosphere wouldn't have gotten an inch colder. The poor men stuck between the two Imperial Princes even felt a bit out of place, exchanging worried glances at each other. After all, none of them had signed up to be standing up against the Empire's War God himself! Those men were Imperial Guards, trained to obey the Emperor only, and they would do so until their death, but this situation just didn't feel right for any of them. Princess Shareen, who was known for her own military merits, was glaring at them like she was looking at a crowd of vermin. She couldn't believe the nerve of those idiots to side with Vrehan.

The Imperial Princess had a sour expression on her face. She had abandoned her swords to steal a spear from one of the Imperial Generals she had defeated. That weapon was heavy and meant for a man, but she had no problem carrying it nonchalantly on her shoulders. Her stare went to Missandra with a sigh. So things had turned that bad here. Anour, too, was staring at Missandra non-stop, unable to say a word, only feeling scared for her.

"You're a bit late, Brother," said Vrehan, speaking first. "You missed my coronation."

Kairen didn't bother to answer, but Shareen stood forward, furious.

"What coronation?! You're no more worthy of the title of Emperor than you are worthy of putting your dirty ass on that throne, Vrehan!"

Her words angered him, and he suddenly pulled more on Missandra's hair, making her groan in pain. She was keeping herself from crying, but the young woman was teary-eyed, as he was keeping her neck bent in a weird position, and the blade was held against her skin. Shareen clenched her teeth, annoyed. If he had captured Missandra, it didn't mean anything good for her sister either. Anour almost stepped forward, but Shareen quickly held his arm and pushed him back towards her mother.

"What happened to the old man?" suddenly asked Kareen.

For the first time, her voice was cold as ice, but she was strangely calm and composed. The Second Prince answered with an annoyed expression.

"He is dead. I am the Emperor now. You're no longer the favorite!"

This was such a weak insult, it wouldn't make the proud Imperial Concubine flinch. Kareen's glare was much fiercer, and it looked like nothing could make her waiver, not even the news of her past lover's death. Either she didn't believe it, she hid her emotions perfectly, or she wasn't affected, one couldn't tell. She was just standing there, an empty look in her eyes.

From glaring at the concubine, Vrehan's eyes went down to the baby she was holding. His black eyes opened wider, in a horrified, disgusted expression as he discovered Kassian. Kairen moved right away to stand between Vrehan's line of sight and his son, glaring right back at him.

"That little bastard," hissed Vrehan.

Kian who had followed them jumped on Kairen's shoulder at that moment, and growled at him, arching its back.

"Where is Cassandra?" asked Kairen, impatient.

This time, the Second Prince's face broke into a nasty smile, looking quite happy. He chuckled, but it soon turned into a crazy laugh. His voice echoed along the walls, making everyone but him rather uneasy.

"You crazy ass," hissed Shareen.

"She's dead!" yelled the Second Prince.

Kairen didn't move, but his fingers tightened around his weapon.

"Your damn, precious witch is dead! That bitch killed herself to escape me!"

"You're lying," muttered Shareen.

She couldn't help but send worried glances at Kairen. If Cassandra was really dead, her brother was really going to lose it. Facing them, Vrehan kept laughing like crazy, amused by the War God's furious expression.

"You were a War God, Kairen, but now you're so affected by that bitch's death? Well, your woman is dead. She dove into the lake and she never came back."

"It's Cassandra, Kairen," whispered Kareen behind him. "She can stay underwater for a long time."

"Oh, you think she could still be alive? I will break it to you, she is not coming back, you idiot. Your women dove into that lake hours ago. Even that witch can't survive hours under the surface! It's a pity. I would have loved to show you her dead body, just for the pleasure of seeing your face."

Whatever he had hoped to see, Kairen wasn't going to give him that pleasure. Whether he believed it or not, and despite his sister's worried glances, all of his rage was contained inside. However, they did hear the furious growls of a dragon coming from the outside. Unlike Kairen, Krai was going rogue outside the Palace's walls. Yet here, its Master was only clenching his jaw and his fists and glaring like a tiger at Vrehan.

He slowly raised his sword.

"You're going to die," he whispered.

That simple sentence erased all smiles from Vrehan's lips. The Second Prince stood up, and directed their attention towards Missandra. His blade against her throat was tracing a thin red line on her skin. Shareen clicked her tongue.

"Oh, no, I don't think so. You are going to throw your weapons, or I'll slice this woman like a pig in front of you. Both of you," he added, glaring at Shareen as well.

"You scum. And what happens if we refuse? You only have one hostage, once she's dead we would have no problem killing you!"

"Oh, I don't need to kill her straight away," chuckled Vrehan. "I can slice her pretty skin, little by little, until you obey. Her skin is way too neat, compared to her older sister's, isn't it? I could even chop off a few limbs."

"We have Phetra," declared Shareen. "How about we do the same thing to your precious younger sister?"

Vrehan laughed loudly again, his horrible laugh making Shareen roll her eyes.

"Do you think I care about my sister? She was only useful for some time! Princesses aren't as watched as the Princes, you see. She was very helpful in making more allies within the Senate."

"I knew that bitch opened her legs," hissed Shareen.

"You two are such idiots," continued Vrehan. "All you can do is fight, you are not fit to be the Emperor!"

"Oh, right, we are not some vile scheming rat like you!"

Just as she said that Vrehan got even madder, and his dragon growled furiously, too, taking one step forward. They couldn't have missed his eyes, both completely covered in a dry dark liquid that ought to be blood.

"Your dragon doesn't look in top shape, Vrehan," snickered Shareen.

That sentence didn't help make him any calmer, and without warning, he suddenly raised his weapon and carved a long, deep line down Missandra's arm. The young woman screamed in pain, closing her eyes and crying out.

"You bastard!" screamed Shareen

"Keep making me mad, Shareen. I still have plenty of surfaces to keep going on this little bitch's body!"

That's when Kairen recognized the weapon Vrehan was holding. It was Cassandra's dagger, the one that formerly belonged to Phetra. This time, the War God saw red and stepped forward. However, Vrehan was quick to react and put his knife back against Missandra's throat.

"Uh-uh, no, Kairen. If you take another step, I swear I'll butcher that little bitch!"

The Third Prince stood there for a second, his eyes on the young girl. Missandra was crying in pain, her blood dripping from her injury. That bastard had cut her deep on purpose, to make her injury more painful and impressive. He didn't want to give him any victory, but she was still Cassandra's younger sister. He glanced at the blind dragon and snickered. He threw his weapons.

The two swords resonated on the marble floor, and even the soldiers in front of him looked confused. The War God was giving up on his weapons, to save a woman? Behind him, Shareen was just as annoyed, but after hesitating, she was about to throw her spear when Missandra spoke.

"Don't! Please don't care about me! I'd rather die than let this scum survive!"

"Missandra!" called out Anour, horrified, a second too late.

"Shut up, little vermin! Or I shall cut you some more!"

Vrehan put his threat to execution right away, stabbing Missandra's shoulder. She screamed again, and fell down on her knees, in a horrible state of pain. Her voice resonated throughout the Palace's walls, making even the soldiers uncomfortable. This situation was really not one they wanted to be in.

Meanwhile, Shareen's hands were almost turning white from holding her spear so tightly. In her head, she was already going over the scenarios of what she'd do to that scum once he was dead. Next to her, Anour was the most horrified. The young boy looked like he was about to faint, his eyes on Missandra, completely shocked. He couldn't do anything but watch the horrible display of violence against her.

"Vrehan, enough!" yelled Kareen.

"Shareen still has her weapon," he retorted, staring at his half-sister.

"Don't!"

To everyone's surprise, despite her tears, Missandra still looked fierce and determined. Down on her knees, holding her bleeding shoulder, her lips trembling, she was still able to look at Shareen from across the hall. The girl ought to be in an excruciating state of pain, but she still acted as if she wasn't.

"D-don't," she begged. "Don't let that bastard win."

"Shut up, I said!" he yelled.

Vrehan kicked her injury and pressed his shoe on it, forcing Missandra to bow lower and lower, in a horrible position. His shoe sole was soon completely red, but the girl did not avert her eyes from the little group across the room. Never had she looked so much like her older sister.

"That bastard murdered my sister and raped his own sister!"

"Shut the fuck up!"

"He did what?"

This time, even Kareen looked utterly shocked and baffled.

"You rotten rat. What did you do?" muttered Shareen.

"I said shut up! Shut up, shut up, shut up!" yelled Vrehan, absolutely furious.

He kicked Missandra relentlessly until the girl was completely lying underneath him, half-conscious.

A heavy silence followed that horrible scene. Even if he hadn't said a thing, Vrehan's anger at the girl's words made the truth obvious. Everyone in that hall could understand that.

Suddenly, Kian squealed, and jumped down Kairen's arm, running in the opposite direction, leaving the room.

"Kian, no!"

"Lady Kareen!"

The Baby Dragon disappeared into the corridors, while Lady Kareen ran after it, still holding Kassian. Evin immediately ran after her, too. He didn't have his place in a fight against so many soldiers anyway, and the Imperial Servant was concerned about Cassandra's baby. Anour glanced at them leaving, hesitant.

"Go with them," said Kairen, his eyes still glaring in Vrehan's way.

His younger brother hesitated. He wasn't comfortable letting their mother and the babies run away, but War God or not, Kairen was in an unfavorable position there. Moreover, he had already thrown his weapon, and Anour knew he and Shareen wouldn't risk Missandra getting killed either. Vrehan was a poor fighter, but he still had his dragon. Yet, he had trouble leaving. When Missandra was like that.

"Are you sure?" he whispered.

Kairen didn't answer, which was the equivalent of a definite answer from him. Shareen gave him a nod, too. Anour swallowed his saliva, a bit bitter to have to leave them. However, he wasn't stupid. He wasn't on his older siblings' level, he would have been no more than a hindrance here. After one last glare towards Vrehan, trying not to look at the injured Missandra, Anour finally ran out, to catch up to Lady Kareen. Once he was gone, the War God and his sister were suddenly left alone with an army of Imperial Soldiers, Vrehan, and his dragon.

Shareen sighed.

"About two hundred men? Really, Vrehan, you're such a coward."

"Drop your weapon, Shareen, and recognize me as the Emperor," hissed the Second Prince. "Or I swear I'll finish this girl and you'll have to watch her bleed out!"

Shareen glanced down at Missandra. The young girl was still not moving, one couldn't tell if she was still breathing. Only her eyes were still teary, turned towards them. After a few seconds of staring at each other, she very distinctly saw Missandra nod.

Shareen sighed.

"You're not too rusty yet, Brother?" she said, her eyes on Vrehan, making her spear turn between her hands.

"Stop playing."

She snickered. Suddenly, her eyes went up on the Red Dragon.

"Enough!" yelled Vrehan, feeling what was going to happen. "I am the new Emperor! The council already agreed! You can't kill me, I am the Emperor!"

Shareen laughed.

"Oh, Vrehan, you're really the Emperor of rats. The Council you said? You convinced a bunch of scum like you to sign some paperwork, and just like that, you think we should leave you Father's throne? Don't worry about the council. I think it will be time for some serious spring cleaning once we are done with you!"

Vrehan's eyes opened wide, and he stepped back. Shareen was still smiling like a cat about to eat a bird.

"You know what? I think we need fresh blood on the Council's seat. How about we start with yours?!"

Just like that, she suddenly threw her spear across the room. Her weapon flew far above the head of the soldiers and, with a horrible sound, dug deep in the Red Dragon's shoulder.

The gigantic beast growled furiously in pain and anger and jumped to attack, coming their way. The first ranks of soldiers, distracted by the dragon, turned their heads back a second too late. They met Kairen's furious glare from extremely up close, and a second later, the War God's fist began wreaking havoc around him.

Chapter 35

Cassandra slowly woke up to the sound of something dripping next to her. She suddenly felt a horrible sensation in her throat and started coughing out some water, almost suffocating as she was trying to get some air back. She felt exhausted, and a bit dizzy, though she was lying down. Underneath her was something cold... and wet. It wasn't very comfortable either. She struggled to move her body, pushing on her numb arms to help herself sit up. Her hands met with the cold rocky ground. Cassandra coughed a little, spitting some water again. She felt exhausted, but her instincts quickly reminded her of the dangerous situation.

She sat up, looking around anxiously. She had no idea where she was, but somehow, the presence of light disturbed her. Her memories were slowly coming back, and she was almost sure she had lost consciousness in the deep, dark waters of the lake in the Imperial Palace. So the question was, where was she now? Against all expectations, she was alive, but with no idea where she had ended up.

As her eyes got used to the blinding light coming from above, Cassandra slowly realized she was surrounded by rock walls. In all shades of grey, sometimes silverish, the undefined walls of this cave were making a semi-sphere above her head. She could still hear water clearly dripping all around her. How far was she under the surface level? If there was this much light, she couldn't be too deep.

She barely had any strength left and wished to remain seated, but somehow, she couldn't just stay still either. How had she even gotten here? A few meters away from her, there was what looked like a large pond, or a little lake. It was completely still and quiet, and everything else was echoing inside the cave. She could almost hear her own heartbeat echoing. Cassandra realized her body was cold, but not as wet as someone who had just gotten out of the water. How long had she been here? She was completely at a loss and even more panicked due to that. What happened to Opheus and Missandra? What about the Old Emperor?

Her head was aching a little bit. She touched her forehead and felt a vivid pain. It was a bit swollen. So she had bumped her head in something, causing the headache. Cassandra sighed. What had she gotten herself into this time? She looked around, trying to look for the creature from before, just in case, but she was obviously completely alone. After much effort, she finally got back on her feet. She was in a poor state. Her legs and arms were covered in bruises as if she had been dragged around on that same rocky ground. Cassandra looked at the water again. Had she been taken out of there and how? By whom? She was obviously alone here.

She tried to walk to the walls, checking if there wasn't some opening she may have missed. It was all stones, ground, ceiling and walls alike... thousands of little stones, and she couldn't see all of the different levels of the wall. It was sharp too, but some had iridescent reflections, like pink or blue. They almost looked like dark gemstones.

Cassandra's eyes were attracted to the light above again. What she had taken for a bright light was actually some long slit in the ceiling, letting in what was most likely natural light. Cassandra squinted her eyes, trying to see anything. She was almost sure she had seen some movement up there. Was she actually that close to the ground surface?

Suddenly, something moved in the water. She retreated towards the wall as a reflex, but there was nowhere to run. Slowly, scales started appearing at the surface. Cassandra felt her blood go cold again. She could see parts of the body undulate in the water and surface at some places like a snake swimming around. How big was it really? She had been unable to see the whole body in the water, but now, she could see it move in so many places, she was only starting to get the reality of this creature's real size. Then, the head slowly merged out of the water. First, the two horns she had seen, one of them broken at half its length. Then, the silver eyes appeared. They were so clear. If it wasn't clearly staring at her, Cassandra would have wondered if it wasn't actually blind. Then, the nose and maw came out of the water, dripping. She tried to keep breathing normally, but no matter how she looked at it, this creature was part dragon.

A very, very large and strange dragon. With an elongated head and neck, there was plenty of space for the many gills moving with each breath the creature took. Cassandra didn't even know if she should have been surprised, scared, or amazed, but she was all of that at the same time. The dragon let out a long, high-pitched growl that echoed along the cave's walls, and more of its body came out.

The front limbs weren't anything like what she had seen before. She had thought they were short, but unlike the dragons' short paws, those were longer and more retractable.They were obviously half-way between arms and fins. Even the "fingers" of the creature had curved claws and were tied together with webbing. It didn't actually use it's limbs to move around, his body was crawling almost like a snake. Cassandra retreated further, not even daring to blink for one second. She felt like her own breathing was way too loud.

The creature didn't lose her for a second. It was completely focused on her as it was coming out of the water, more and more of its body crawling out. Cassandra had wrongly judged it's size. If she had to compare it with the dragons she had seen before, it's head was about as big as Glahad's, but there was no real comparison in terms of its body. It would have been like comparing a cat to a snake. While it's neck was very thick, the rest of its body didn't grow in size at all. It was all the same width, but very, very long. It felt like the end was never coming, and the body almost had to spiral onto itself to find enough space, as Cassandra kept retreating further and further away.

She was grateful the cave was so vast, because there were few rooms inside the Imperial Palace that could have welcomed this creature comfortably. How old was this creature to have gotten so big? Its body was meters and meters long! When she finally spotted the little legs, she realized those were in no way meant to walk either, but just to stabilize the end of the body. They were thinner and shorter than the front paws.

Finally, the tail came out, almost ridiculously little and simple compared to the rest of that majestic creature. Cassandra was at a loss for words as they were just staring at each other. This thing was not a dragon as the Dragon Empire knew them. It was something similar, maybe a related species. Cassandra exhaled, realizing she had been holding her breath for a while now. Thank the Gods, this creature wasn't menacing at all. It only stared, and had only growled once, if it was a growl.

Cassandra had seen much scarier dragons, so she wasn't exactly afraid... more cautious. She could tell when a beast was angry or menacing, and that creature wasn't either of those. She highly suspected it had actually saved her life by bringing her here, which showed a high form of intelligence.

She decided to take a slow step forward, to see how the creature would react. It didn't seem panicked in any way, and actually, came gently to her. She could see it's thin nostrils moving a bit, smelling her. Cassandra suddenly realized what the shimmering on its scales was, it had been disturbing her for a while now. Salt! Was that water salty? Could it be linked to the actual sea? The creature kept moving its iridescent scales and, just like it's size, Cassandra had been wrong about its color as well. It wasn't dark, but actually more of a shimmery grey. There were some other colors shimmering in the light, making her think those scales were opal-like. Just like the stones of that cave. Was this the Creature's lair?

An idea was beginning to grow in Cassandra's mind, and somehow, she started to really believe in it. She remembered what she had been taught when she was much, much younger. She hesitated, putting an arm out and extending her hand, though she was a bit scared and probably crazy to do so.

The Creature didn't try to sniff it as Krai would have. Instead, it slid it's long body past it, making Cassandra touch it's strange, polished scales. She chuckled, impressed. The Creature began circling around her, making one, then two rings with its body, keeping Cassandra inside. It still wasn't menacing, but she felt like it was establishing some sort of protection around her. Cassandra smiled.

"I think I know who you are," she whispered, amazed.

The Creature didn't react to her words, but after taking a deep breath, the young woman started singing.

She used her native tongue, careful about her voice and her words, and sang the Mermaid's Requiem. After listening to her for a few seconds, the Creature started singing a high-pitched song too. It sounded like a wind blowing against some glass, a high-pitched but gentle sound. When she was done, the creature put its head closer to her, and after a slight hesitation, Cassandra gently caressed its head. Her heart was beating like crazy, almost certain she was right. All the legends from her childhood were taking form in this amazing creature in front of her.

"You're really... the Water God," she whispered.

She was overwhelmed with emotion, almost to the point of crying. She had never questioned its existence, but having the deity-like being right next to her was an amazing sensation. The creature sang softly again, making Cassandra chuckle, a tear escaping her eye. She took a deep breath.

Though it was a beautiful moment, she didn't have much time for that. She couldn't forget the crisis that was going on outside this cave, and how her family needed her. She extended her arm to caress the scales again.

"I need your help," she whispered in her native tongue. "I really need to get back to the others... to my family."

She wasn't sure he would understand her, but just then, the creature looked up, at the long slit in the ceiling. Just as she thought, there was something up there. The exact moment when Cassandra looked up, she very clearly saw a shadow for a second. What was that?

"Kyun!"

Cassandra jumped, as the Baby Dragon suddenly jumped out of the water, flapping it's little wings and chasing the water.

"Kian? How did you get here?"

She ran to the Baby Dragon, who happily jumped in her arms with many little squeaks. Kian kept rubbing its head against her chest while Cassandra looked at the pond again. This was definitely connected to the lake somehow! If so, how deep and wide was the lake under the surface, and beneath which room could it have spread?

"Kyuuuu..."

Kian seemed to have just noticed the gigantic Creature, and very boldly jumped from Cassandra's arm to run to it. Without any fear, the little dragon hopped onto the first ring of the body, under the Creature's eyes. Its white eyes were on Kian with a bit of interest, watching the Baby Dragon's moves. Kian jumped higher, onto the second and higher ring, and glanced at Cassandra. Was he showing off? She tried to call Kian, but the little dragon ignored her and turned to the head of the body it had just climbed.

The Water God seemed interested in the Baby Dragon and brought it's head closer, sniffing it. However, a sniff from such a big creature was like a gust of wind to Kian, and the tiny dragon was pushed away. Just as Cassandra feared it might fall, the dragon started flapping its little wings and looked up. Now that she saw them together, there was a bit of resemblance in their body shape, though Kian was still more like Krai.

"Kyun!"

The Baby Dragon started flying higher, looking suddenly attracted to that slit in the ceiling. The Water God, looking curious about the Baby Dragon, followed its flight up, extending its body to raise it. Cassandra immediately saw her chance. With a silent apology, she climbed on the creature's body just like Kian had done before. She was bigger than the Baby Dragon, but still no bigger than a kitten compared to the gigantic water creature. If it felt her climbing on its scales, it didn't show any discomfort at all. Cassandra struggled to keep going, with her aching muscles, overall exhaustion, and the climb that was becoming more and more vertical and abrupt. Whatever was above them, she silently prayed it wasn't going to be another terrible place to fall into.

Just when she had finally climbed past the second ring, she realized she wouldn't be able to climb up the "neck" of the creature. Just then, it seemed to finally spot her, and before she could do anything, it pushed her up onto its head. Leaving Cassandra hanging on by its horns! Cassandra couldn't help but let out a little scream in fear, but Kian apparently took it for an excited cry, and made a similar high-pitched noise, all happy and flying around her.

The creature kept going higher, understanding her goal, and Kian's. As they finally reached the breach, Cassandra realized it would be just large enough to let her through, but there was no way the creature could follow her. She bit her lip, and Kian jumped through the crack above her, disappearing between the two edges. She was worried for a few seconds, but then, she heard the dragon happily squeak from somewhere above. With a sigh of relief, she found a grip as soon as she could, ready to climb up. Just then, she looked at the creature, whose eyes were very close. She smiled at it.

"Thank you," she whispered, and then, with a push from the creature's head, she climbed up.

Despite the creature's push, Cassandra struggled to reach the upper level. She was really tired, hurting all over, and not sure about what she should expect next. She just hoped that the crack in the ceiling wasn't going to lead her into another deadly trap. She had almost died too many times today already. The only reason she was feeling a little bit better was Kian. Though she had no idea how it had found her and gotten there, the little dragon being all jumpy and fine meant Kassian ought to be safe and sound somewhere out there as well.

Cassandra had no idea how long she had stayed unconscious when she was with the Water God, but she felt like it had been a few hours at least. She hoped things had progressed up there, and in a good way at that. She was silently dying to see Kairen again. Cassandra didn't want to get her hopes up too soon, but she hoped he was somewhere near. She had that strange conviction in her heart that the War God had returned to the Capital.

"Kyun!"

"I'm coming," she sighed, trying to pull herself up and catch up with the excited Baby Dragon.

She had no idea what to expect once she had climbed out of that breach, but anyway, she wouldn't have been able to imagine it. This looked like another cave, only much, much bigger. It was actually carved to have a roughly square shape. The walls were definitely made of the same material as the one below, though, that shining grey stone. Cassandra had no idea what it was, and she couldn't remember having seen anything similar within the Palace's walls. So, where in the world were they?

She felt a bit too tired to stand, and remained seated to look at her surroundings. Kian was already happily running around and sniffing everything with curious eyes. The much bigger cave continued past her line of sight, as if she had emerged at one end of it. More curiously, she noticed some strange, black spherical shapes. A lot of them were broken open, and looked as if they could crumble and fall into dust at any second. Stones? Their shape was a bit intriguing, and Kian too kept sniffing them with curious eyes.

Everything there was really quiet, but Cassandra could hear some sort of faint wind coming from the other side. The light was coming from a little hole in the ceiling, too. This was definitely sunlight, and this opening was too round to be a natural one. Who would have carved a window in a cave, and why? In any case, it was too high for Kian to carry her up there, and actually, she wasn't even sure it would be wide enough for her to get through. The distance was blurred with all her surroundings looking like the same rocky walls.

She finally stood up, and the Baby Dragon immediately ran back to her to rub its body against her leg, almost like a cat. Kian was apparently determined to stay around her, and though the dragon kept venturing everywhere to have a look, it was coming back to her every ten seconds or so. Since the young dragon looked so fearless and enthusiastic, Cassandra walked further into the cave, intrigued. There was nothing but those countless, countless broken spheres. She couldn't understand what they were. They were not made of the same material as the stones, they were darker, but gave off a similar feeling to the Onyx Castle.

As she kept walking, the echo of her own steps made her slowly realize how big this new cave actually was. Unlike the one from before, this one seemed to continue for miles, like some tube just getting wider and wider. The breach she had come out of was already far behind her when she found another window above her, throwing light on more bigger, broken spheres. She suddenly realized she had been wrong. Those things weren't spheres. They were empty shells.

Now that she could see some more complete ones, the shape wasn't so round and was similar to Kian's dragon egg. She hadn't noticed before because even the material looked different, and none looked alive or illuminated like Krai's egg once was. She was baffled. What were those dragon eggs doing here?

There were hundreds of them! Some looked so old they were almost turning into stones.

The Baby Dragon squealed, sniffing one of the eggs and putting its little front paws on it to look inside, but Cassandra grabbed the dragon and carried it instead. Somehow, she didn't like the idea of Kian playing with empty dragon shells. This whole place felt like... some kind of cemetery. There was a really uneasy feeling growing in her heart from seeing those empty shells. From the looks of those, they must have belonged to dragons that lived years and years ago, maybe centuries.

Cassandra kept walking, and as her arms got tired, Kian jumped out of them to walk ahead. However, this time the Baby Dragon didn't look as curious anymore. It actually had its wings close to its body, and looked more cautious than before. Was Kian feeling something she didn't? Cassandra hoped they wouldn't encounter anything too dangerous in here. She kept trying to understand the Emperor's purpose. Did he know she would find the Water God in the lake and understand what the Creature was? Did he even know about it? Or was he hoping she'd find that breach and get here? She hoped the old man was alright.

"Kyuuu?"

Kian had stopped, looking a bit wary of whatever was ahead. Cassandra caught up to the baby dragon with a frown, and indeed, there was a noticeable change in their surroundings. The eggs around them were considerably bigger, and unlike the previous ones, they still had some color on them. They were getting closer to the end of the strange tunnel, she could feel it.

Cassandra was starting to realize where they were standing. She had forgotten about this place, actually. Suddenly, Kian froze, before running back towards her and hiding behind her leg. Something was scaring the baby dragon? It wasn't growling, but the emerald eyes were focused on something right after the next turn. Cassandra walked towards it. The wind she had heard before was getting louder, and coming in little waves. It wasn't wind, but breathing.

They were finally met with an impressive mountain of golden scales.

"Glahad!" she exclaimed.

What was the Emperor's dragon doing there? Recognizing the magnificent creature, Cassandra ran to it, but the gigantic dragon looked uninterested. The dragon was curled upon itself, its ruby eyes half-open, looking incredibly passive. It didn't even seem to care about them, and barely reacted. Seeing that Cassandra wasn't scared, Kian came out and carefully scurried over to look. The difference in size between the two was impressive. Kian was like a big cat, while Glahad was like a little mountain by itself.

The Baby Dragon kept looking around the giant dragon and poking at it curiously. However, the older one didn't seem to care. Cassandra realized Glahad was in some way Kian's grandfather, but the Golden Dragon looked completely disinterested in anything. It was so calm that Cassandra had no fear approaching it.

"Glahad, what is it?" she asked.

Giving no answer, its ruby eyes shifted to her, without any other kind of reaction. It looked like the Golden Dragon was...depressed. That realization carved a hole in Cassandra's heart, as a scary thought sprouted in her mind. She shook her head, choking up a little, and tried to look around. There was nothing else but empty dragon shells here. This was definitely the Emperor's Dragon Vault, but what was Glahad doing there?

Abandoning the old dragon for a few seconds, Cassandra made the detour around its body, which occupied half of the way, to check what was around the other side. She gasped.

A gigantic door. It was made with the same stones as all the walls there, but the square shape and the gigantic handle on it couldn't be mistaken. Cassandra was amazed. So they really were in the dragon's vault! Didn't Shareen say before that this place was right behind the Throne room? Meaning they were just a few steps away from getting back inside the Imperial Palace! Cassandra hurried over, but she couldn't even understand how to open the door. The handle was way too heavy! She couldn't even move it at all, how was she supposed to pull on it? She suddenly realized this was how the Imperial Family members were the only ones who could get in. It took superhuman strength to get that lock open... or a dragon's help. Lady Kareen was human, yet she had been in here before to retrieve Kian's egg. She couldn't have done it by herself. However, with the help of a dragon, she could have.

Cassandra turned back to the Emperor's dragon. Would Glahad help her? Opening that door would be a matter of seconds for a dragon, but how to convince it to help?

She walked over. Kian, a bit lost by her back-and-forth, decided to sit down and tilt its head, observing her movements. Cassandra didn't have time to worry about what Kian was doing, she just went back to face the Golden Dragon's head. She knew Glahad wasn't going to hurt her, as the Emperor did like her. Would the dragon help her? She wasn't sure of the situation outside, but it was very probable Glahad had somehow been forced in here. This was the Emperor's dragon, though. Even if the dragon was locked in here, it was the only one strong enough to break out. Glahad just needed the will to do so.

"Glahad, please, you have to help me get out of here," she said.

This time, there was no movement. The Golden Dragon looked like it had absolutely no intention of doing anything. Even if it was depressed, Glahad couldn't simply stay here! Cassandra walked closer, desperate.

"Glahad! I don't know what happened to His Highness, but..."

This time, the Golden Dragon growled as a warning, its ruby eyes opening wide. Cassandra jumped back in surprise. She wasn't prepared for the Emperor's dragon to actually get mad at her once she'd mention The Emperor. Kian, upset at Glahad's growling, jumped between her and its dragon ancestor and growled back. Its attempts to growl were once again no more than a kitten's meow compared to the fierce growl of a proper adult dragon. Still, it at least got

Glahad's attention.

"But you can't abandon Kairen," continued Cassandra, careful with her words. "You know he is the... the favorite son, the one that should take the Golden Throne. He and Shareen ought to be out there. You can't let Vrehan and Lephys do this!"

Despite her plea, the Golden Dragon didn't move much. At least, Glahad kept both scarlet eyes on her, looking like it was listening, but not reacting much. Cassandra was desperate. She wasn't even sure how much Glahad understood her words. Krai had always seemed able to understand her, but maybe the Black Dragon was just imitating its Master and reacting to her words. Cassandra wasn't sure of anything anymore, but she glanced down at Kian. Kassian was in danger out there, and so was his father. Maybe convincing the Golden Dragon was the last chance to save them.

"Glahad! You know the Emperor didn't want this!"

The Golden Dragon resumed its furious growling, but despite her fear, Cassandra continued.

"You can't stay here and do nothing. Kairen needs you, Shareen too. The Emperor has a new grandson, Kassian, my son, and you can't let him die!"

This time, the dragon stopped growling, apparently having heard her. Cassandra grabbed Kian off the floor, though the Baby Dragon was still fearlessly growling at Glahad.

"You have to help me get out of here, please. Vrehan will kill them! Kairen, Shareen, even Prince Opheus, Prince Anour, and Lady Kareen, too!"

Having heard about the Imperial Concubine, Glahad finally raised its head, making Cassandra sigh in relief. The Emperor's love for Lady Kareen may save their lives, after all! Her name had definitely made the dragon react.

"I know... I know His Highness wanted Lady Kareen to be safe. He loved her, and wherever she was, he was fine with it because she was safe, right? As long as Vrehan is out there, she won't be safe anymore, Glahad. You can't give up on the one love His Highness wanted to protect."

The dragon suddenly emitted a long higher-pitched sound that sounded like a wailing to Cassandra. She was actually crying. She didn't want to admit the Emperor may be dead, but the thought was making its way in reluctantly. So many things were pushing her towards it, no matter how much she didn't want it to be true. She wasn't ready to hear it, neither was Glahad, and yet the Golden Dragon knew.

"Glahad, please..."

With a growl, the Golden Dragon finally moved. Glahad's humongous body slowly rose up, and Kian made itself very small in Cassandra's arms, obviously impressed and scared. Glahad was incredibly big, and once the dragon was standing, its body occupied more than half of the space there. Cassandra had to retreat against the wall to not risk being crushed. It seemed like Glahad knew exactly what to do. The Golden Dragon turned around, its ruby eyes going to the gigantic door. Cassandra couldn't imagine how Glahad had been made to stay here, but she doubted there was anything that could efficiently contain the most powerful creature in this Empire.

The Golden Dragon growled and raised a paw to grab the giant handle. Due to the size of its claws, only two of them could pull, but still, the dragon had no trouble lifting it, unlike Cassandra had earlier. She felt a wave of hope as the door started making an awful ruckus from the pressure. However, it wasn't moving so easily. After a few seconds, it became obvious Glahad had to use considerable strength to try and open it. Something was blocking it, but the Golden Dragon was not giving up. It started growling furiously, determined.

"Come on, Glahad... Please," whispered Cassandra.

In her arms, Kian started cheering too with excited little growls and squeaks, its eyes riveted on the adult dragon. Glahad struggled more and more. The dragon growled furiously against that door that was not opening, and it kept pulling. Cassandra was worried to see the base of one claw starting to bleed, but Glahad wouldn't stop. The old dragon kept using all of its strength, arching its back and putting all of its body into it. Cassandra felt the tension as if she had been pulling too, and silently cheered, praying that this was going to work. Finally, the door moved.

Strangely, an awful noise was heard. The sound of something massive and heavy resonated in the vault, and Cassandra had to protect her ears. Yet, Glahad growled even more furiously, pulling the handle even more. The Golden Dragon was determined, and the door was still resisting, but it was almost done. Cassandra could finally see the opening. Jumping at her feet, Kian chirped excitedly and ran to jump on the Golden Dragon's back. The little dragon climbed up the body that was at least ten times bigger than its own, peeking at what was going on behind the door.

Kian suddenly made another one of those high-pitched sounds, and in a split second, Cassandra saw the baby dragon jump and fly away into the small space.

"Kian!" she called, too late.

Where had it gone? Cassandra didn't like losing her son's dragon, she was scared something would happen to it. She knew that door had to open up to somewhere behind the Emperor's giant Golden Throne. However, soon enough, she heard another furious growling, and this time, it wasn't coming from Glahad. She froze, but those growls were coming from wherever Kian had gone to, and even scarier, she could tell those weren't Krai's.

She was terrified to go there, but even more terrified that something would have happened to the Baby Dragon. Running to the other side of Glahad, she went to face the open space, but almost immediately she stepped back, terrorized by what she had seen behind it. Red scales.

The thought had crossed her mind while seeing where they were headed. She had heard the horn and seen Glahad's misery. She could only think of one scenario to explain all that, but she had been pushing those dark thoughts to the back of her mind, until now. She just didn't want to think about such a horrible outcome.

The growls of both dragons became louder and louder, and more terrifying. The more Glahad was pushing the door, struggling to open it, the more Vrehan's dragon was trying to prevent the Golden Dragon from getting out. Despite the difference in strength between the two, Glahad was somehow weaker than usual. Cassandra bit her lower lip. The Emperor's state had definitely had an effect on his dragon.

She couldn't stay here though, not when she had lost sight of Kian. The gap was now wide enough for her to slip through. Actually, two men could have fit through, but it was still not large enough for a full-grown dragon. Cassandra tried to position herself around the Golden Dragon, watching both creatures' actions. This was extremely risky. Kian had quickly flown out, but she would have to make a run and pray. It would take only a second for the Red Dragon to notice her and kill her. Hopefully, she could escape it, and even perhaps distract it enough that Glahad could finish opening the door and be free.

Cassandra was starting to become concerned about all the ruckus she could hear on the other side. Cassandra wasn't familiar with the battlefield, but the horrible sounds and screams she could hear coming from behind the wall of red scales looked very much like a war was going on out there. What was happening in the Throne's room? Who was fighting whom? Her heartbeat was accelerating fast. If Kian had flown so confidently, it ought to know who was behind that door. And there weren't many people the Baby Dragon would fly to.

Raising her green eyes on the Red Dragon, Cassandra took a deep breath and prepared herself to make a run for it. Glahad was still struggling and growling furiously, and hopefully, the ruckus would hide her escape even more. The Red Dragon probably hadn't even noticed her. She remembered she and Kian had worked together to make the beast blind, permanently perhaps. She took a deep breath, and started running.

This short distance felt like miles away. Cassandra had no idea what she would find behind the door, but she couldn't stay back and wait to be caught in a fight between two adult dragons. She just ran in a straight line, her eyes riveted on the little space where she could see an actual wall behind Vrehan's dragon. Her heartbeat went even crazier when she ran past the door. Just a bit more! She kept running, even stumbled on something, a rock or a claw, and got back up to keep running again.

Finally, Cassandra jumped over a red paw, and fell on all fours, next to the Emperor's throne. Her eyes tried to grasp a hold of the situation as quickly as possible. Dozens of men were fighting in the Hall, but many of them were down on the ground already. The whole room had its floor covered in blood. It truly was a battlefield, all contained in one room. She looked up, trying to find who the assailants were when she finally saw him. Kairen.

She lost her breath for a second. He was standing there, a few meters away from her. As if he had felt her stare on him, his black eyes rose up to look for her, too. For a couple of precious seconds, they found each other. She was shocked, her heart couldn't even contain this much emotion at once. Tears appeared in her eyes. He really was there. Her War God, her Prince. Kairen was there, standing proudly, his body covered in scales and blood, but alive. She smiled, almost nervously, in such relief her mind couldn't formulate a thought strong enough. Kairen, Kairen, Kairen. She could barely believe it, but it was his obsidian eyes riveted on her.

"Kai-..."

She tried to call him when a wave of pain tore her scalp. Cassandra felt herself being pulled back, as a large hand was holding on by her hair. She suddenly felt the cold metal of a blade held on her throat, and she gasped in horror. She had almost forgotten every dragon ought to have its Master close by. She tried to fight herself, but a sharp pain on her neck prevented her from trying any further.

"Look, look, Kairen. Your precious little witch came right into my arms."

Cassandra's heart went from relief to horror in a split second. After she had tried so hard to fight him, she had ended up in Vrehan's hands! She wanted to scream in despair. She couldn't believe it, all of this for nothing! She could hear the two dragons still struggling behind her. Glahad was still fighting to get out, but this seemed like a minor detail compared to the fight between the brothers.

Kairen's face had gone white as soon as Vrehan touched Cassandra. She heard the Second Prince laugh horribly, catching the attention of not only Kairen but his sister, too. Shareen let go of the dead body she was holding and glared at Vrehan.

"You rat face."

"Oh-oh, be careful, Shareen. I already killed one of them, I'll happily make it last longer for the other one."

Cassandra's blood went cold. Killed who? Who had he killed? She felt like she was missing an important piece of information, and her eyes searched around the room.

Then she saw it. She hadn't even seen it when she was so close. Missandra, laying in a pool of blood right at their feet. Cassandra immediately screamed in horror. No, no, not her younger sister, not Missandra. Not Mie. She couldn't even stand that horrible vision. Her sister was lying, not moving, her body circled and covered in red. She couldn't even see her face, as she was lying on her stomach, her face in the blood and covered by her hair. Cassandra couldn't stop crying. She couldn't even check if Missandra was really dead! She couldn't stand it, she kept shaking her head and struggling against Vrehan.

"Enough!"

On her right, another figure appeared. Cassandra glared as she had never glared at anyone before. Lephys, with his neck perfectly fine. The Fifth Brother chuckled, amused by her glare, and walked over. He pushed Missandra with his feet, looking bored.

In horror, Cassandra saw her younger sister's body roll down the stairs. She gasped and cried, fighting Vrehan to try and go see her. Across the room, Shareen was just as horrified.

"Lephys, you son of a..."

"Shut the fuck up, Shareen," protested the Fifth Brother. "You are not in charge anymore, and if you don't want that bitch of a witch dead yet, shut the fuck up, for once."

The Princess glared at him, but for once, she truly had no choice. Vrehan was holding Cassandra, a blade clearly held against her throat, and they knew he wouldn't have the slightest remorse over killing her.

Kairen was facing his worst nightmare. He was too far to do anything without risking Cassandra being killed. From far away, they heard the furious growls of Krai adding to those of the two dragons already present. Kian, who had flown to Kairen earlier, looked worried too. The Baby Dragon began retreating behind Kairen's legs, but still growling a bit.

This situation was a nightmare. Cassandra knew Kairen would kill his brother if she wasn't there. It may even explain why her sister had been... like this already. She gasped, and struggled again, furious.

"You won't be Emperor," she hissed, her eyes full of tears and her voice hoarse.

"Oh, I already am, little bitch. The council agreed to make me the Emperor just an hour ago."

"You are no Emperor," she protested. "And you won't become one. You'll be dead. This Empire doesn't need an Emperor like you, no one would allow that. Not the Council, not the former Emperor, not your siblings, no one. The Gods themselves will punish you. You have no rights but those of a cheater, a coward!"

"Shut up, damn witch!" yelled Vrehan.

Out of anger, he raised his blade, and cut a long line down Cassandra's back, making the young woman scream in pain. She had tears in her eyes, but compared to everything she had experienced before, this was nothing. She couldn't allow this.

She had come here to make sure Vrehan wouldn't be the Emperor. She knew this would mean her son's death, Kairen's death, and if she was the obstacle to ensure their safety, Cassandra didn't care.

"I am the strongest Emperor! Kairen is nothing but an idiot!"

"You're about to die, you asshole," hissed Shareen.

"You can't be Emperor when your dragon is weak," added Cassandra. "Everyone will know the Emperor had the weakest dragon out of his brothers. You can't fight Krai, and you can't fight Kairen! You even locked up the Emperor's Dragon because you couldn't see that!"

Behind them, a horrible ruckus suddenly rose as Glahad broke free from the Vault. The door exploded behind them, and everyone near the throne lost their ground. Cassandra pushed Vrehan, and instead of trying a run she could never make, she jumped to get down the stairs. Her body violently hit the stairs, one after another, but finally, she found herself above Missandra's body, just in time to protect her.

The exploded door sent rocks raining down on them, and she tried to protect her head. She felt vivid pains assaulting her body, but she tried to withstand it.

It only lasted a few seconds, after which she found herself covered in dust, and more importantly, caught between the fight of two dragons. Glahad, finally free, attacked the Red Dragon furiously, despite the little space. She turned her head around, trying to spot Kairen in this mess. The first one she saw was Lephys, screaming something she couldn't understand. His eyes were riveted on the two dragons fighting.

Cassandra knew she had to make use of every second she had. She touched Missandra, and much to her relief, her sister seemed alive. Barely. The younger sister was still breathing weakly. Cassandra tried to stand up next, but a sharp pain kept her still. She turned her eyes and realized her left leg was stuck under a large piece of rock. She couldn't even move it! How come she hadn't felt the pain earlier? She tried to stop her tears and looked around for help through the cloud of dust.

"Kairen!" she yelled. "Shareen!"

She called, again and again, even coughing when she breathed in too much dust. Cassandra was absolutely desperate. With the stones of the door exploding in all directions, and the dragons fighting, this room had gone from a war zone to complete chaos. She saw Imperial Guards running in all directions, and she couldn't spot Shareen or Kairen. She couldn't move Missandra, but she searched her sister, checking all of her injuries and pockets.

"You damn witch!"

Cassandra reacted as soon as she heard the voice coming from behind her. Had he not yelled, he may have avoided this, but the young woman lifted her sister's dagger at the last second, to protect herself.

Vrehan screamed, covering his face and the blood that was flowing. Cassandra was satisfied she had injured him, but she was still stuck there, in front of the murderer.

Cassandra couldn't see the extent of the injury she had just caused. All she could see was Vrehan, staggering back while holding his face and screaming. His hands were literally covered in blood. Sharpened by Kairen, Phetra's dagger had become a murderous weapon used against her own brother.

Cassandra didn't have much time to contemplate what she had done, though. She kept trying to push the rock from her leg, desperate to move and get out of there. Her throat was painful, she kept coughing and crying, as the dust was making the scene an absolute nightmare. She could hear the furious growls of dragons battling somewhere above her. With Glahad free, the two dragons had just taken the fight into the Throne Room, causing more damage every time they threw each other against the walls. Even the roof was starting to creak dangerously above their heads. Cassandra had briefly seen it had been sealed when she had walked in, but how much longer would that hold? Was that Vrehan's precaution against another dragon's attack?

"Cassandra!"

She heard Shareen scream her name, but she felt horribly far away in this cloud of dust. Cassandra tried to answer back, coughing horribly. She glanced back, and Vrehan was wiping the blood off his face. He was going to get back to her any moment now, and Cassandra was still trapped. With Missandra lying half-dead underneath her, she was desperate to free herself. That rock on her leg was massive, and nowhere near anything she could lift with her current strength. Cassandra coughed, trying to clear her throat again.

"Kairen!" she called.

"He won't save you! I'm going to kill you, and watch him weep in front of your dead body!" yelled Vrehan, from somewhere behind her.

Cassandra glared at him, holding the dagger as her last line of defense. Weak or not, she was not going to let that monster approach her without defending herself. She was ready to fight him off using everything she could and all she had. Vrehan staggered, and as he lowered his hand from his face, she could see the horrible line running across his face. One of his eyes was blocked by the blood. Just like his dragon, Cassandra had also blinded one of his eyes with that same dagger.

Vrehan still had one though, and was coming right at her. She shivered. She couldn't die here, not when Kairen was this close! She kept calling his name and screaming, but all she could hear as an answer were the clamors of men all around fighting, and even louder was the dragons wrestling. Another ruckus imploded from another side of the room, and a wall exploded, throwing more dust and rocks into the mix. This was a complete war scene.

"Cassandra!"

Finally! Cassandra turned her head, and in the middle of the fog, Kairen's familiar silhouette appeared. She could have cried in relief from this sight, if she wasn't already too teary from all the dust. He ran to her, and as soon as he spotted his brother standing behind Cassandra, he threw out his fist. She heard the violent crack of a jaw break above her head, and Vrehan's guttural sound. The Second Brother screamed in pain, and turned around, running away and disappearing into the cloud of dust. If Cassandra hadn't been at his feet, Kairen would have gone to finish him off.

However, the War God didn't hesitate a second and crouched down, grabbing the humongous rock that was sitting on her leg. Frowning, he took a couple of seconds to focus and gather his strength before finally lifting it. Cassandra moved quickly to retrieve her leg, despite the pain. Her ankle was twisted or broken, horribly painful. Right after that, she meant to say something, but Kairen's lips found hers.

This was the oddest time and place for a kiss, but they couldn't stop. In those few long seconds, they just needed it. A wild, passionate, intense kiss to sum up how much they had been dying to see each other again. Cassandra felt her whole body warm up again as if it had been in slumber since they parted, and her heart had stopped. She put a hand on his cheek. She would have hugged his whole body, kissed all of his skin, and caressed his hair for hours if she could. Finally, finally. Her War God was here, her one and only man. Kairen's large hand on her neck was all she needed. This warm, intense touch that told her she was finally safe, even in this wretched place.

However, those seconds were short-lived. As another part of the wall exploded somewhere behind them, they had to part their lips as Kairen moved to shield the two sisters. Cassandra was deafened by a dragon's screech for a few seconds. She couldn't see anything beyond a few steps.

"Glahad," she said, her eyes meeting Kairen.

"He's losing. Vrehan's firstborn's dragon arrived."

Cassandra's face lost its blood. Glahad couldn't fight two dragons by himself! She struggled to get back on her feet, Kairen helping her, but her mind was still preoccupied.

"Krai?"

"Still outside. Fighting Lephys' dragon."

The situation was horrible. With dragons fighting all over the Palace, it was a complete mess all around. Cassandra crouched down to grab her younger sister, but Kairen was faster. Grabbing Missandra, he put her on his shoulder under Cassandra's panicked eyes. Was her younger sister going to survive this? She was barely alive.

"Kairen!"

They both turned around to follow Shareen's voice. Just like them, Shareen was fighting her way more into the dusty mist than battling any soldier now. She had made a few more victims on her way in, but it took them a few more seconds to reunite, as they needed to stop and crouch down regularly to avoid the debris falling and dragon claws.

"Mie! Is she alive?" asked the Princess.

"Barely. We have to get out of here."

Shareen nodded, but her eyes were above, on the two dragons fighting. Her eyes suddenly opened wide in horror, and something red and dark suddenly splattered all around them. It smelled horrible, and was warm, giving Cassandra no doubt about what this thing was. Fresh dragon blood. She panicked and turned around, trying to catch a glimpse of the fight, but all she could spot were shadows of two dragons fighting furiously.

"Glahad..."

"Yeah, the old one is not going to last much longer," sighed Shareen, shaking her head. "Come on, let's get out of here."

Without saying a word, the siblings exchanged Missandra's body, Shareen carrying the young girl effortlessly while Kairen grabbed Cassandra to carry her. She didn't oppose him. With her injured ankle, she would have been the one to slow him down, and the Imperial Prince and Princess could get out much faster than her.

As they struggled to get out of the room, Cassandra tried to look around for Vrehan or Lephys. She was scared one of them was going to come out at any moment and attack them from behind. Moreover, she was worried about Glahad. The Imperial dragon wouldn't have gotten into this fight if it wasn't for her, and it was dying. It was it's blood she had on her dress right now, on top of hers.

"Here!"

Shareen had found some opening in the wall, more like a breach where more rocks had fallen from. They climbed a couple of rocks to finally get themselves into the open air and breathe better. Kairen let Cassandra down, though he wasn't letting go, his arm around her waist, ready to shield her at any given moment. In Shareen's arms, Missandra was still inanimate and looked like death. All of this was too much.

"Kairen!"

Cassandra heard Shareen's scream, but was thrown onto the ground before she understood what had happened. Blood splattered her face, and when she raised her eyes, Kairen was on top of her, making the grimace of someone who's suffering horribly. She heard a dragon's growl, and the Prince suddenly pushed her further away from him.

"Kairen!" she screamed.

The Prince was suddenly pulled back inside, under the two women's horrified eyes. Shareen hesitated a second before putting Missandra down. Kairen had no weapon left, and the gigantic Red Dragon had just dragged him back inside the hellish room like a mere puppet. Her brother was going to die.

Before they even exchanged a word, Cassandra handed Shareen her dagger, and she ran back inside. Cassandra had another objective, and no time to complete it. Getting back on her feet, silently praying for Kairen to be alright, she started dragging Missandra further away. They had to get far enough for her younger sister to be safe.

They had somehow gotten back into the Lake's garden. That part of the Throne room's wall had gotten them right there, which was an unexpected chance for them.

"Cassandra! Missandra!"

Cassandra turned her head and saw Anour running towards them. His eyes were wide open in horror upon the sight of Missandra, and he fell on his knees before them.

"What... what happened?" he muttered.

Cassandra had no time for his questions.

"Get her out of here!" she yelled while trying to run away on her limping leg.

She didn't have time to verify if Anour was going to follow her instructions. Kairen was back inside, his sister too, and both of them were almost unarmed, if not for the small dagger that was no match to face a furious dragon! Plus, she had no idea how bad that injury he had suffered before being dragged back inside was. Cassandra had seen too much blood today, she couldn't allow any more.

She wasn't a fighter, but she could find a way to get them some support. She glanced up, at the chains still blocking the way into this garden for dragons from the outside. She could hear Krai's furious growls from the outside, but the Black Dragon had no way in. Cassandra had to get rid of those damn chains.

"Krai! Krai!" she called, yelling all of her lungs out.

She didn't know how the Black Dragon could always find her, but she just knew it would. She heard the growls and kept running. What was happening on the other side? She was unable to run fast enough with her injured leg, but her steps were getting her to the Lake, as fast as she could endure. More growling came from inside the Throne Room's opening, but she couldn't look back. Cassandra was silently crying, unable to hold it, and breathing erratically. She was tired, in horrible pain, and terrified, but she had to keep going. She needed to do anything she could to help them.

Suddenly, a silver creature flashed in front of her, agitating its little wings. "Kian!"

The Baby Dragon had somehow managed to escape the mess of the Throne Room to fly to her, though its silver scales had much dust on them. Kian flipped his wings and landed next to Cassandra, emitting some little, worried, high-pitched sounds, while looking at her and the throne room. She nodded.

"I know. I know."

She didn't have the strength to say more. The young woman slowly made her way to the lake, fighting the tiredness of her own body. She felt as though she was about to collapse. Finally, she made it to the Lake and fell forward. Down on her knees, she fought against the dizziness and took a deep breath. Kian walked up to her side, tilting its head. Cassandra nodded.

"How about you...help me call your Dad?"

She had no idea if the Baby Dragon had understood her, but it suddenly flipped its wings and took off. Kian was very small compared to any adult dragon, and tiny enough to squeeze through the metallic net above them. Cassandra heard the familiar growling and chirping, probably trying to grab Krai's attention. She had no idea what was going on for the Black Dragon, but she really needed it to come down and help its Master, now. However, the dragon couldn't do that unless it could get past Vrehan's traps first. Cassandra laid down next to the lake, extending her arm into the water. It felt strangely good, the freshwater running on her arm, washing the dirt and the blood away. She closed her eyes for a second, yet still fighting not to give in to the darkness. She had to hold on, a bit longer. The fight was not over.

Above her, she suddenly heard the furious but familiar growl of the Black Dragon. Cassandra opened her eyes back up just as the large shadow flew over her. Krai furiously attacked the fence, but just then, she saw some gigantic metallic arrows flying that way. Probably Vrehan's traps. Krai had to fly away again, dodging them as they kept firing. The Black Dragon growled furiously and started spitting fire too. Cassandra frowned and shielded herself. Though Krai was meters and meters above her, she could feel the scorching heat of the fire where she was. This was terrifying. No wonder no dragon ever did that within the Imperial Palace. They would have decimated the whole building and everyone around in seconds.

However, right after that, Cassandra froze, her eyes stuck looking to the other end of the Lake. Another dragon had just appeared, growling at her and coming towards her, slowly. It was smaller than Krai, but this one was under the net, unrestrained, and menacing. Just from the size and purple color, she knew which one it was.

"You damn bitch," hissed Lephys' voice from behind her. "This time, I'm going to finish you off!"

Chapter 36

Cassandra had seen enough horrors for one day, and yet it seemed like this whole nightmare was far from over. Just when an adult, Purple Dragon was slowly walking her way, she heard its Master's voice coming from right behind her. Cassandra rolled in the grass, just in time to avoid the sword that stabbed the soil next to her cheek. She glared at Lephys. She hated that man perhaps even more than Vrehan, if that was possible. His face was deformed by anger, and he had blood running from his temple to his chin. Cassandra had no idea if he had been injured in the explosion of the wall by one of the dragons, or because of the siblings, but she thought he deserved more suffering than that. The sight of that monster pushing her sister's defenseless body down the stairs was something she wasn't going to forget.

"You damn bitch. No more Kairen or dragons to protect you," he hissed. "I'm going to get rid of you once and for all."

Strangely, Cassandra answered his words with a chuckle.

Maybe she was too tired of all of this, but she laughed nervously at his words. Cassandra knew she might be about to die, but after everything she had already gone through in the last few hours, it was at the very back of her mind. She had just seen her lover being dragged back inside the Throne Room by a furious dragon, she had no idea if her baby was safe, and this Empire was about to be overthrown by a mad man. She had just witnessed too much for one day. Having Lephys appear now was like a nightmare's new twist.

"Stop laughing, you crazy woman!"

Cassandra's nervous laugh wasn't that long, but she had no strength to get back up. She was beyond exhausted. Lephys' furious expression was what kept her upright, though. He was another monster that needed to disappear. When he lifted his sword again, she got ready, and using all of her strength, she raised her arm to splatter him with water, and some mud and small rocks she had grabbed. That attack took him by surprise, and he groaned, having gotten some in his eyes. Cassandra's reflexes came back the second she realized she had a chance. Ignoring the pain, she actually grabbed his sword by its blade and kicked him in the flank.

The Fifth Prince wasn't a fighter. That kind of move wouldn't have worked with Kairen or Vrehan, but Lephys was surprised by her sudden kick and made the mistake of lessening his grip on his weapon for a second. Cassandra took that opportunity, and sent the weapon flying, having it fall into the Lake. She knew she hadn't time to turn it around and use it herself, but at least she could get rid of it.

His eyes were red with all the dirt he had gotten in them, and as Lephys fell on his flank, he quickly got on all fours to wrestle Cassandra. He was even more furious that she had even managed to pull this kind of trick on him, and made him lose his sword so easily. He raised his hand and slapped her furiously. Cassandra felt the pain resonate through her whole body, and her cheek burned. Lephys chuckled from hearing her in pain, and quickly got back on his knees to pin her down, and slap her some more. It wasn't just about killing her now. He wanted this woman to suffer, for the humiliation she had just caused him. His eyes hurt, she had just made a fool of him, and he hadn't forgotten she had stabbed him either. He kept slapping her furiously, yet ensuring not to put as much strength behind them so that it would have her pass out. He wanted her to suffer some more before he killed her.

"You damn bitch. You're nothing but a useless woman! You think you can hurt me! You think you can touch me! You slut! You're just a damn, wicked bitch! A witch! A rotten slave!"

With each sentence came a new slap, and Cassandra couldn't even pass out to escape. Her whole face was burning, and she could feel the taste of her own blood in her mouth. She tried to struggle, push him away, but no matter what, Lephys was a healthy, young man who was a lot stronger than her. She could only raise her arms to try and protect herself, but even so, he was having fun hitting her wherever he could. She felt his slaps turn into fists when he started hitting her arms, yet she endured it. She held onto the thought that she had gone through worse, that she had to make it through for her baby. For Kassian.

"You're so weak! You think you can play strong? Do you think you can survive this? You're just weak, useless!"

Cassandra's eyes turned towards the Lake, and the Purple Dragon that was coming their way. She could hear Krai's furious growls above, still wrestling with the chains on the roof, and the soldiers trying to injure the black dragon with whatever weapons Vrehan had gotten ready. Cassandra had to do something. No one was coming to save her, she had to move and help Krai herself. If the dragon could access the Palace, Kairen would have a better chance. That's all she needed to focus on right now.

She purposely let Lephys have his fun beating her some more, but she was thinking. She knew what to do, she hadn't gotten closer to the Lake by mistake. Protecting her face as much as she could, she took a deep breath.

"Sometimes it's not about strength," she whispered in her native tongue. "It's about courage."

"What are you saying, woman?!"

Just when he had stopped to try and understand her words, Cassandra used both of her hands, with her joined fingers, to punch him in his jaw. It wasn't that strong, but it was surprising. Lephys let out another painful groan, holding his jaw with a shocked expression.

Cassandra then quickly turned towards the Lake, and started chanting, as loud as she could, in her native tongue.

"What are you..."

He had expected her to try and run away, to crawl maybe, but this woman was singing loudly. Singing something he couldn't understand, in a different language. For a few seconds, the Fifth Prince got worried, but then, he understood. She was just crazy. He laughed, finding this way too pathetic.

"What are you trying to do, witch? Ask the fish for help? Is that all you can do?"

Yet, Cassandra ignored him, and kept chanting, loudly, as her eyes remained closed. Lephys stopped laughing and frowned. What was this, anyway? It looked like her song from the Celebrations, with that same strange language, but this one had... something scary about it. It didn't sound like a prayer, more like a... battle cry. A chill went down his spine, and for a full minute, he wasn't so sure. Her singing had him worried, yet he couldn't understand why. He couldn't possibly be afraid of a weak woman's singing!

Cassandra stubbornly kept going, her arms still protecting her face, her voice getting deeper and louder. The Fifth Prince was torn. While he didn't want to be afraid of that woman, he still couldn't ignore this very uneasy feeling that was growing, as if something dangerous was about to happen.

"Stop," he muttered. "Stop that!"

"Hisiren da altere, bato. Ya men guerra, ten guerra. Alra mien shin da, almere, li shin, li shin. Oh, God of Water, rise for your daughters, rise for those they murdered, rise for your daughters' blood."

Cassandra kept going, uttering her words loudly and fast, her song echoing all around them. Lephys found himself staring at the surface of the lake with that worried feeling that was nagging and wouldn't go away. There was something wrong, something was about to happen. However, the surface of the Lake was very quiet and calm, and he couldn't understand why he was finding himself so worried about some stupid woman's singing.

"You foolish woman. You're going to die, this time! I'll..."

Lephys raised his hand, but just as he did, something suddenly flew out of the water. A large shadow covered them, and for a second, the Prince thought a bridge had appeared above. However, it wasn't a bridge. It was a humongous, reptilian body. It was just so big that it easily overshadowed them before touching the ground on the other side. Like a gigantic snake, it came out of the water, very slowly. More and more of the reptilian body came out, seeming endless. Lephys was completely frozen, thinking he might be hallucinating. Yet, what he first took for a giant snake, kept coming out of the water, and it's long body crawled on the grass, circling them in its rings. It's small but palmed front paws landed in the grass very close, making him realize this wasn't a giant snake.

Suddenly, a head bigger than any dragon's head he had seen turned to him. The young man didn't even dare to lower his arm, completely frozen. He was just shaking, horrified. Not even Glahad was this big, and this Creature's head was awfully close. It seemed trapped with them under the grid on the roof, with just enough space. The Creature looked very calm, but even the Purple Dragon looked worried and retreated slowly. Everything except for what was going on in the Throne Room seemed to get horribly silent around them. Lephys was still holding his arm high up, ready to hit Cassandra, but with that thing watching him, he didn't dare move a finger. He could tell those white eyes were fixated right on him.

Under him, Cassandra had stopped chanting, but unlike the Fifth Prince, she wasn't scared to move. She pushed him away from her, and crawled away, laying her body down into the water. It had a terribly good cooling effect on her painful cheeks, and she let the water wash away all the dirt and blood on her arms for a few seconds. Above her, she heard Krai growl again, and it made her re-open her eyes. Cassandra knew she still had to move. She turned around, got back on all fours, and slowly stood up.

Just when she staggered and thought she was about to fall, a sturdy, scaled body appeared in front of her. She chuckled and leaned against the Water God's body to stand up properly. She turned towards the Creature's head and smiled. It was strange how calm the Creature was, and how it made Cassandra feel so much calmer, too. Yet, this fight wasn't over. Next to her, Lephys still had his arm held up, he hadn't dared to move. He looked funny like this, but he was glaring at her.

"You damn witch," he hissed.

Cassandra ignored him, turning her head up. Krai was still blocked up there. She took a deep breath, and turned towards the Water God, addressing the creature in her native tongue.

Lephys couldn't understand any of the words she uttered, but he was speechless when it actually made the gigantic Creature move. Under his eyes, the water dragon slowly extended its body up, until it reached the chains. With its little claws and fangs, the creature started pulling on the grid. While they had barely moved under Krai's attacks, the long metallic chains couldn't resist the Water God's strength for long. They heard the stones they had been fixated on creaking horribly, and a portion of the roof crumbled, leaving one side of the roof open.

Krai flew in immediately, with a furious growl. The Black Dragon was injured, two arrows having pierced under its left-wing, but that didn't even seem to slow Krai one bit. Compared to the calm Water dragon, the black one came in like a big raging hurricane. Krai jumped on Lephys' dragon, all fangs out, and the two of them started fighting furiously. While the Purple Dragon had stood still in front of the Water God, it couldn't lay down while being attacked, and the two dragons started fighting furiously.

That battle scene seemed to wake Lephys up.

"No!" he screamed.

The difference in strength was obvious between the two. While his dragon had been safe under the chained roof, it was now completely at the mercy of Krai, despite the attempts to fight the Black Dragon off. For a few seconds, it looked like an easy win for the Black Dragon, who was so much bigger than its younger brother.

However, Lephys' furious eyes turned elsewhere.

"Come out, you cowards!" he yelled.

Cassandra turned towards the shadows he was yelling at, from one of the Palace's corridors. What was he planning now? One after another, she saw multiple pairs of little eyes lighting up. She shivered, understanding slowly what was going on. Young dragons lined up in the shadows.

Lephys was calling out for his sons' dragons to help him. Rather than scared, Cassandra immediately found herself furious. That coward was forcing his children's dragons to fight for him! She turned to him, just when the little dragons started appearing in the garden, one after another.

"Stop that," she said.

Lephys laughed, but it was a crazy laugh.

"Oh no, you damn witch. Just you wait until they rip you apart!"

"They are all going to die," Cassandra retorted. "They are too young! They can't win and you already know that. You're sending those dragons to their deaths!"

"I don't care, as long as I make it!" he yelled.

Lephys suddenly got back on his feet and started running in another direction, away from the fight. Cassandra's anger rose again. That man was the vilest creature, and a coward at that. Not only was he running from this battle to save himself, but he was also basically sacrificing his sons' dragons, allowing them to be killed for him and his fight!

Cassandra exchanged a glance with the Creature, but just like the Rain Tribe's people, the Water God was not a fighter. It had answered her call as she begged, but what now? She couldn't ask the creature to kill young dragons either. She hated the idea of having to sacrifice innocent lives. Cassandra may be angry, but she kept a clear mind about the situation. Those poor little ones were following Lephys' orders, maybe not even of their own will. Some of them were probably barely older than Kian. Half a dozen of the little dragons appeared on the grass, all coming in different sizes and shapes. She could tell how young they ought to be, and it just made it all worse.

Just then, Kian flew back to her too. Landing on the grass in front of Cassandra, the little silver dragon was growling furiously at its peers, warning them to leave her alone. The difference in size didn't impress the Baby Dragon one bit. The young dragons weren't afraid of Kian either, but they were hesitating on coming closer, with Cassandra standing against a portion of the Water God's body. Each of them kept growling and sending glances towards the Water God. They were all taller than Kian, but most were not even half an adult's size.

"Stay away," she warned them, using her mother tongue.

Either they had understood or were scared, as the little dragons stopped coming closer or just started growling more furiously. Strangely, the smaller ones seemed to be the most eager to fight. Was it because they were influenced to follow their father's orders even more than the older ones? Cassandra glanced across the lake, where Krai and the Purple Dragon were still actively fighting and growling at each other.

She turned her eyes towards Lephys. He had barely made it half-way towards the corridors, but he wasn't too far away yet. Cassandra tried to think quickly, and soon found a solution. She ran towards the net of chains that had fallen from the roof. A large portion of it had been ripped down, from where Krai had gotten it, but one of its ends was still hanging above the walls, stretched above Lephys' head. Cassandra's eyes followed his steps.

The Prince was running like crazy in the garden and didn't hear anything of her struggle. Cassandra grabbed some of the heavy chains a few steps away from her and started pulling on it. It was very heavy, they were chains made to keep a dragon away after all, not for a woman alone to pull down. Glancing over his shoulder, Lephys saw her pulling like crazy, and looked up at the chains that weren't even moving. He slowed down to see her struggle, thinking he was far enough away, and started laughing again.

"You crazy woman! Those chains were put up there with the strength of several men! Do you really think you can do anything? You're weak, useless!"

Right at this moment, Cassandra stopped pulling, glaring at the Prince. He realized his mistake a second too late. Had he kept running, he may have made it. Yet, he had stopped while he was still underneath the chains, giving Cassandra time to turn towards the Water God.

"Alteske," she said.

Lephys' eyes opened wide in horror, as the Water God raised its claw and brutally pulled on the chains. This time, the walls above him crumbled right away. With a horrible scream, the chains fell all over the top of the Prince, followed by big chunks of the wall. His scream died under all the rocks that buried him alive. Cassandra heard him scream long after the rocks had stopped falling, telling her he was still alive, but suffering miserably.

On the other side of the Lake, the Purple Dragon felt its Master's demise, as it started screeching horribly. Krai took the chance to jump on the screeching dragon. They had fought fiercely, and despite the difference in size, the Black Dragon had some worrying injuries on it. Cassandra was worried about Krai and even more so about its Master, but it looked like Krai would get rid of its opponent soon.

Her attention was grabbed elsewhere. When she wasn't looking, some of the young dragons had run to the pile of rocks covering Lephys, but two of them were still growling at Kian. The little Silver Dragon was growling just as fiercely as its dad, set on defending Cassandra. Though they were still small and young for dragons, those two could bite off her hand at once, and Cassandra didn't want to risk it.

"Kian!"

The Baby Dragon retreated slowly to her as she called its name, but Cassandra still couldn't leave Kian to be injured. The two younger dragons started running after the baby, and Cassandra was scared something would happen to it.

"Kian, in the water!" she said, while retreating towards the Water God.

The little dragon, running like a silver bolt in the grass, suddenly jumped in the air, using its little wings to go and fly above the Lake. The two bigger dragons followed easily, especially as it was flying away from the Water God they feared. However, they were not done with the little dragon. One of them suddenly threw fire its way, and though Kian dodged it, Cassandra's heart went cold.

Kian wasn't injured. The silver dragon glanced back at its peers, and suddenly disappeared in the water. The two young dragons were confused for a minute, flying above the Lake and trying to spot the silver scales in the water. They couldn't follow Kian inside. They were not made to go underwater, unlike the Water God or Kian. Hence, when the Silver Dragon reappeared, jumping out of the water, it completely took them by surprise, and furiously bit one of their wings before diving back in. Cassandra couldn't keep herself from smiling proudly. The Baby Dragon was learning fast how to use its unique abilities

On the other side of the Lake, though, Krai wasn't done with that fight. Maybe its Master's state had brought despair over the Purple Dragon, but it wasn't giving up. It didn't let the Black Dragon win, and instead, the two of them exchanged injury after injury.

It couldn't last this way. The more Krai was injured, the less the black dragon could help Kairen, and the War God was still trapped inside. The image of Kairen being furiously grabbed and pulled back inside the Throne Room just minutes ago was still printed in Cassandra's mind. She had to do something. She turned to the Water God, but it was here to help her, not injure the other dragons!

Their eyes met, and for several long seconds, she didn't dare say anything. It was a horrible feeling. The Water God was not one to fight. The mythic creature from all her tribe's songs, they had talked about it being a God of love, not war. It was obvious the creature's whole body wasn't even made for a fight, and it probably couldn't even breathe fire.Somehow, they were alike. Not fighters and not ones that would kill either. Her kind wasn't like that. Once again, Cassandra felt utterly powerless. What could she do? Her eyes went to the opening in which Kairen had disappeared, and she could still hear ruckus inside. There was no proof her lover was even surviving the battle.

"Lys, you bastard of a snake!" suddenly yelled a voice behind her.

Cassandra turned around, and with shock, saw Opheus running across the garden, his weapon in hand. The Fourth Prince! She had almost forgotten about him, with everything that had happened. Right as he ran towards her, another giant shadow appeared above them. Phe, the White Dragon! Without waiting for a second longer, the Fourth Prince's dragon flew inside through the opening she had created earlier and started attacking the Purple Dragon too, relieving a bit of Krai's burden. The Black Dragon stumbled aside, blood flowing on its flank. Krai was still furious and growling, but obviously in need of that little break too. After a few seconds of rest, the two of them jumped on Lys, the Purple Dragon again, with the clear intent to finish him off. They were both bigger and stronger, and this time, the Purple Dragon was completely defeated. Bitten furiously at the throat by Krai, dragged on his back, the Purple Dragon died in a horrible screech of pain. That sound was unbearable to hear. Cassandra shuddered, unable to look that way.

Meanwhile, Opheus finally reached her, just when Cassandra fell on her knees. Though the Fourth Prince gently held her shoulder as she almost collapsed, Opheus had his eyes riveted on the Water God, in shock. The peaceful Creature was looking down at him, strangely calm compared to everything going on around them.

"What the... What is that... thing?"

"I don't have time to explain!" exclaimed Cassandra, grabbing his clothing, panicked. "Have you seen my sister?"

"Y-Yes. I met Anour on the way, he was carrying her out, he told me what happened. Lady Kareen, she went to hide with your child. But Cassandra, we have a bigger problem."

"What?"

"Phemera," he said. "The girl...That woman we took out of the cell, it really is Vrehan's younger sister. Your sister made her talk, she told us everything. That bastard had been impregnating his younger sister like a cow to try and breed more powerful dragons!"

"W...what?"

More dragons? Cassandra went horribly pale. She suddenly remembered Phetra's words. Vrehan's secret, why he couldn't kill Phetra yet.

"Vrehan doesn't only have two sons. He's got more dragons stashed away somewhere!"

Cassandra's heart went cold. More dragons? Her eyes went to Krai, still staggering and trying to lick the injuries. Next to it, Phe wasn't too bad, but the white dragon had gotten an injury on its shoulder too. Meanwhile, Kian just jumped out of the water, running on the grass as the other two young dragons that had targeted the baby dragon were struggling to swim their way out of the water. Their wings had been completely destroyed by the silver dragon's repeated attacks.

Cassandra couldn't rejoice in the slightest. They only had three to help them, including a baby one that had hatched only a week ago. How could they fight more? How could Vrehan have even gathered more dragons without anyone knowing? She turned to Opheus, her energy ignited by panic alone.

"How many? Where?"

"She didn't know where her sons and their dragons had been taken! Vrehan hid the sons and their dragons from her. He killed the girls before they were even born!"

That explained the abortion potion they had caught the young Princess buying at the market. As soon as there was no egg to hatch, they knew it was a girl, and Vrehan ensured they ended the pregnancy. Cassandra felt like throwing up. Vrehan was even more of a monster than she had fathomed, and she was even more hell bent on defeating him. If a man like him got on the throne, it was truly going to be the end of this Empire.

"We need to find him or where he hides his sons and their dragons," she whispered.

"I thought he was fighting Kairen inside!" exclaimed Opheus, pointing at the opening.

Cassandra shook her head, getting back on her feet.

"No... No, Vrehan fled in the confusion. Only his men and his dragon are still there. He probably went to get his sons' dragons, then... Who knows how big they are."

"We have to find them then!"

Cassandra nodded, but how? She saw Krai and Phe running towards them from the other side of the Lake, joined by Kian. She had to think quickly. How could she find the young dragons inside this wretched Palace? It was so big! She looked around, and her eyes fell on the Lake. She turned towards the Water God, who seemed to be patiently waiting for her to ask. She let out a long sigh.

"Cassandra?" called Opheus, confusion lacing his words..

"I know what to do, but... You may want to take cover," she whispered.

The Fourth Prince was utterly confused. He had only truly known Cassandra for a few hours, it seemed, yet that frail-looking woman was shattering all of his expectations, one by one. He couldn't understand. There was a giant half-snake, half-dragon looking creature basically wrapped around her, and he had no idea what that creature was. Or more importantly, why it seemed to obey the young concubine. He glanced towards the side, as Krai and Phe were walking around the lake to come to them. He was also in awe of the fact Caassandra had basically almost managed to kill Lephys by herself!

Cassandra turned to the Water God and spoke to it in that strange foreign tongue of hers. Meanwhile, the screams of pain coming from Lephys could still be heard, and Opheus kept his hand on his sword. If he was still alive, he could still heal. He was ready for his Fifth Brother to come back at any moment.

Strangely, he was actually a bit more concerned about whatever the young concubine was about to do. She looked like she had gone through hell, really.

She was covered in so much blood and dirt, not much of her skin was white anymore. Her hair was all over the place, and her dress had even been ripped in several places. Not to mention her ankle, which had turned a horrid dark purple color.

Krai and Phe finally reached them. Both dragons were covered in their siblings' blood. Krai was limping a bit as it came to Cassandra, and lowered its head to sniff the Baby Dragon that had just jumped out of the water. The young concubine didn't have much time for the Black Dragon, as she struggled to get to the Lake. A bit at a loss on what to do, Opheus helped her, though he was frowning.

"What are you going to do?"

"Look for them. The Water God will help me."

He still had no idea what she was actually about to do, but seeing how sure she was, he didn't dare protest and just nodded. Cassandra slowly got into the water, followed by the Baby Dragon, who looked excited about going back into the Lake. For Opheus, it was also his first time seeing a dragon actually enjoy itself in the water.

Once Cassandra had half of her body immersed in the water, to Opheus' surprise, the gigantic creature decided to follow her back inside the Lake. The Fourth Prince stumbled back, almost falling on his own dragon, as the snake-like creature rolled it's long body back inside the water. It was a strangely silent and imposing creature. Only Kian was overexcited, swimming and jumping around in the water like a pond fish. Even Krai looked confused. The Black Dragon had its front paws in the water, looking at the young concubine and its offspring, yet not following them as they went in deeper.

They got into the water in seconds, but it felt like long minutes to Opheus. He had hidden Phemera with Anour and the younger sister, after Anour had found his way around the Palace to protect them. But Opheus wasn't feeling good about any of this. No one could ignore the horrible sounds of the battle still raging inside the Hall. It wasn't a good sign at all.

His attention was caught closer to them, as Lephys kept blaring under all of his rocks. His sons' dragons were struggling to get him out of there, but it was only a matter of minutes before they succeeded. The Fourth Prince frowned. Those damn little pests!

"Phe," he called.

The White Dragon immediately turned towards the little ones, growling. It only caught the attention of a few of the young dragons, but Phe started going their way anyway. Opheus was making a dark expression too. Cassandra may be too nice and gentle to kill the young dragons, but he wasn't the same. All the siblings had grown side by side with death. He knew exactly what to do.

Still growling, the White Dragon started climbing on the little mountain of rocks, and suddenly jumped on the first younger dragon, killing it with one bite. Lephys was buried deep underneath, but Opheus had no intention to bother digging his younger brother out to finish him off. The truth was, he'd rather not dirty his own hands. Instead, it was satisfying enough to have the weight of Phe climbing on the rocks add to his suffering. With a bit of luck, that would finally crush him to death.

Meanwhile, Cassandra had finally swum to the middle of the lake. Even if swimming was easier for her, the amount of pain her body had endured already made every muscle ache. Yet, she had to hold on, for Kairen's sake. He was fighting his own fight inside that Hall. She had to fight her own battle.

The young woman took a deep breath and dived. Kian and the Water God followed her under the surface. She actually grabbed one of the Water God's horns as it swam next to her. The Creature didn't seem to mind, and took her deeper under.

Once she felt like she was deep enough, Cassandra closed her eyes, and with her mouth closed, started singing. It was a song she never thought she'd use, one that wasn't made of lyrics. At best, it was only like several long sounds, like a siren of some sort. However, it used the deeper layers of her voice, ones that echoed in the water. Sure enough, the Water God quickly reacted to it. The Creature started making deep sounds, echoing Cassandra's. There was no comparison. Its voice was much deeper and much, much louder. Soon enough, it started resonating all through the lake, sending gigantic sound waves throughout the lake. Her eyes still closed, Cassandra had to stay focused to listen to the echo. She had never done such a thing before, she had only witnessed it, when she was much, much younger.

Years and years ago, she remembered watching the members of her tribe, diving in the water and all together, using their voices to find where the wood of their shacks was getting weaker, where the fish were, or where to dive to hunt. It was a skill she had never practiced herself, but she remembered it well enough, apparently. She could feel her own heartbeat slowing down, as if to let her listen.

She could feel the water around her shaking. Cassandra had suspected the Water God's voice would be louder, much louder. She would even have trouble staying where she was, if it wasn't for her holding on to one of its horns. Next to her, Kian seemed rather amused by the situation, chasing the large air bubbles that left the Creature, and swimming to follow the echo waves.

On the surface, things weren't as calm. To Opheus' surprise, the surroundings of the Lake had started trembling shortly after the young concubine had disappeared underwater. While he wanted to trust her and that Creature she had summoned, Gods know how. It started to worry him a little as the whole ground under him began shaking. One could tell the epicenter of those strange waves that shook the whole area came from the Lake, and Opheus began to worry.

Before he could call her out though, a huge portion of the roof, a few meters away, crumbled down. It was already fragile from the earlier struggle of the iron net being torn down. But now, all the walls around were trembling. Is that what she meant by taking cover? Taking cover looked rather deadly at the moment!

"Phe!"

The White Dragon was still absorbed by its little hunt in the rocks. The smaller dragons had quickly understood that their survival was linked to whichever hole they could squeeze themselves in. While Phe had caught the biggest and killed them already, the smaller ones had managed to crawl under the rocks and hide themselves, though they could still be heard growling and struggling.

However, there wasn't any time to play, as the whole garden was dangerously shaking. After another heavy shake, the White Dragon finally jumped down from its little playground, and went to its Master. Phe extended one of its wings over Opheus' head, growling at the shaky walls around them. Krai, too, was growling, but the Black Dragon wouldn't leave the border of the Lake, its ruby eyes fixated on the surface. Opheus frowned, feeling the whole Palace tremble. What was this crazy girl doing now? How long could she hold her breath underwater anyway? After everything that had happened today, he felt like he owed it to her to help keep her alive, but there was truly nothing he could do when she was going on a swim with some oversized snake!

To his surprise, the little dragon suddenly jumped out of the water, and flew with a long chirp to Krai, happily reuniting with its parent. Right after that, Cassandra suddenly emerged from the water, struggling to swim. Opheus ran to help her get out of there. She was drenched, and though it had helped wash most of the blood and dirt away, her dress was weighing heavy.

"Are you alright?" asked the Fourth Prince, glancing at her, completely confused. "What was that?"

"It's the Echo, a technique used by my people to...locate things. Anyway, I know where they are."

"You do?"

"I located several younger dragons, somewhere south-west of here, in a very large building, something like a round one."

Their eyes lit up at the same moment, as they both realized what that building was.

"The Arena," whispered Cassandra, astonished.

"Of course. He needed somewhere big enough to put all the dragons, along with what he needed to trap them. That damn rat Vrehan went to free all his little bastards from the Arena!"

The question was, how many dragons were they talking about? Cassandra felt a shudder going down her spine. She turned towards the Great Hall, where the fight was still raging. The truth was, her heart was begging her to go there and help Kairen fight off the Red Dragon. However, she knew she'd be useless there. Shareen was already inside to help him, and Cassandra would be nothing but a hindrance.

Suddenly, just as she hesitated, a part of the wall she was watching burst out, and something violently flew their way.

For a second, she thought she was going to die like this, killed by the humongous projectiled object. However, Opheus jumped on her, and a shadow immediately covered them. Cassandra closed her eyes by reflex, and a horrible uproar burst around them. It felt like a bomb had just exploded behind them. The two of them were thrown onto the ground, and Cassandra felt some of her injuries get worse.

"Phe! Glahad!"

Nothing could have awoken her up more efficiently. Cassandra opened her eyes, and some blood dripped on her cheek. A dragon's thick, warm, and dark blood. She struggled to sit up, and realized the large shadow over them was one of Phe's wings. The White Dragon had jumped in at the last minute to protect them, taking most of the hit. Cassandra crawled to get out of there, and finally see what was going on. Opheus had been quicker to get out of there. The Fourth Prince helped her up, but the two of them had to face the horrible scene.

Glahad had been violently ejected from the Great Hall, and the Golden Dragon was covered in blood. Its battered body landed next to the lake. Cassandra felt her heart go horribly cold. Glahad had really been defeated. Had it gotten weaker because of its Master's disappearance? The old dragon was breathing with difficulty, and Kian was the first to run over, with worried little squeaks. Meanwhile, Cassandra turned to Phe. The poor White Dragon had protected them, but had collided violently with Glahad and gotten injured. One of its wings was horribly ripped open, bleeding and broken in several parts. Opheus looked devastated, running to his dragon to comfort the poor Creature.

Meanwhile, Krai growled and ran to Cassandra's side. The Black Dragon's growls were directed at the ruckus that was still going on inside. Cassandra shivered. Glahad defeated, it meant Kairen and Shareen were alone to fight the Red Dragon. Vrehan was really going to win this if she didn't act quickly. She turned to Krai, grabbing one of the dragon's horns.

"Krai, we have to go to the Arena," she said. "Quick."

She hoped Kairen could hold on a bit longer with Shareen's help, but for now, she really needed Krai. Neither Phe nor Glahad were in a state to fly anymore, and she wouldn't make it to the arena by herself.

The Black Dragon growled furiously, and Cassandra climbed on its back. They took off immediately, headed south-west.

"Cassandra!" yelled Opheus as she was already off the ground.

"Stay with them, I'll be back!"

The Fourth Prince watched the concubine go, with a heavy heart. She was really going to do this on her own? He grimaced and turned to Phe, who was already getting back on its feet. The white dragon may have been in no condition to fly, but it could still attack. Opheus, too, grabbed his weapon, and headed for the pile of rocks.

"When you fucking have to, you have to."

Chapter 37

It felt strange, to fly back to the place where everything had changed for her.

Cassandra could feel her nervousness rise as the Black Dragon flew towards the Imperial Arena. Was she scared to go back? Did she hate this place? Surely it's a bit of both. It didn't bring back good memories, except for the moment she met Kairen. However, before that, there was only death. The many, many people whose deaths she had witnessed. She could still remember it all too well. Dozens of slaves, running in all directions, and being violently killed by the six Imperial dragons.

Six dragons, six Princes. Among them, the only one who had sealed her fate, Kairen. She still couldn't really understand the forces that had saved her life that day. Were his feelings for her really something so strong that Krai had felt it before its Master even had set his eyes on Cassandra? It sounded like something out of an ancient tale, and yet it was her life. For Cassandra, that was all it had taken to end years and years of suffering. She had wanted to die in that arena. Not for those people's pleasure, just because being killed by a legendary beast was one way to end an insignificant existence.

"Come on, Krai," she whispered.

She couldn't ignore all the blood covering the black scales. Though it seemed fine flying, the Black Dragon wasn't as strong or as powerful as usual. Krai was tired from the fight with Lephys' dragon and the soldiers outside. How could those dragons, considered as Gods by her people, simply be seen as weapons by the Empire?

Not only was she dreading going to the Arena, Cassandra had also left a part of her heart back inside the Palace. Kairen was still fighting, by the sounds they heard coming from inside the Hall. At least, she hung onto that hope. That the furious dragon growls were proof that neither was dead yet. She had no idea how long a War God could withstand against a dragon, and she was even scared to think about it. At least Princess Shareen was with him.

Krai finally arrived above the Arena. Strangely, maybe because she was seeing it from above, the Arena felt smaller than when she had come here, over a year ago now. Cassandra's nervousness increased again, as Krai started the descent. She was basically unarmed, except for the adult dragon that accompanied her.

They landed softly in the middle of the arena, and Cassandra had to take a deep breath to chase the memories resurfacing. She kept her hand on Krai's warm scales, bringing her some comfort. She truly hated this place, but she was sure the young dragons were here. Why had Vrehan subjected his own sister to this? What justified such a despicable, immoral act, like the rape of his own blood?

A sudden movement caught her attention on the left, and Krai started growling as well. One of the heavy doors that led to the cells opened, revealing two dragons.

Cassandra gasped. Those didn't look like the usual dragons, though. More like creatures that had come out of a mix between a nightmare and a horrible mistake. The first one had half of its head missing, as if it had melted down, and breathed heavily, it's maw open and drooling. It was walking awkwardly, with its front paws having a noticeable difference in size. The neck was a strange shape as well, and it had scales missing in some spots, exposing horrible, brownish flesh. The second one wasn't any better. It was the fattest, yet shortest, dragon Cassandra had ever seen, and its wings were obviously too small to support its weight. It had a strange arched back too, like a hunchback. Both dragons didn't even come close to the beauty of a proper dragon, like Krai or the Water God. Those two looked like they had come out of a children's bad drawing of a dragon.

"What are those?" she whispered.

"Aren't they amazing?" chuckled a voice behind the dragons.

Cassandra stepped back. Vrehan appeared from the shadows, coming out slowly.

His face bore the horrible injury she had inflicted on him earlier, the flesh still ripped open in the middle of his face. It wasn't bleeding anymore, but the reddish scales were obviously struggling to appear on such an irregular surface. The Second Prince looked like a reptile was trying to take over his face, and his left eye was behaving strangely too, as if it couldn't fix itself but was still trying. He was almost as scary and deformed as the monsters he had created.

"You're... crazy," she whispered.

It seemed like he had heard her because he broke into a burst of mad laughter that echoed throughout the Arena. Cassandra frowned, completely lost by his crazy behavior. Next to her, Krai curled up around the young concubine, arching its back and growling in a warning for the two monsters not to approach them. The scary thing was, no matter how horrible they were to look at, those two things were still rather big. The little ones Cassandra had fended off before were nothing compared to these two. These two dragons were between a third to half of the size of Krai, and unlike the Black Dragon, they looked...up for a fight.

She glared at Vrehan. The Second Prince was slowly walking her way, his mouth distorted with what should have been a smile.

"You... the witch of some lost, meaningless tribe...You really should have died in this Arena. Isn't this ironic? We are about to set things straight. You'll finally be dead, as you should have been, and my Brother will go back to being childless."

Cassandra saw red at those words. The mere thought of that man touching one hair of her baby's head was enough to turn this gentle woman into the fiercest of warriors. She was never going to step back, as long as she could stand between him and Kassian.

Meanwhile, the dragons kept growling at each other, and Cassandra couldn't help but glance at them again.

"How could you do such a thing?" she hissed. "To your own sister."

"My sisters?" he laughed. "Do you know what my sisters are? My sisters are nothing but mistakes. They are useless things, unless they serve me. That's right, even slaves are more useful than those things you call my sisters."

"How can you say such things? About your own family."

"My family? The only woman that ever mattered to me was my mother, and even she was a crazy, crazy bitch. The only thing she did good in her life was keeping me alive. She gave birth to five daughters, and she loathed each. But for me? I was her son. Her only boy, the one she had to protect at all costs to ensure her own survival."

Cassandra suddenly remembered Shareen's words. Their mother was a former prostitute. Phetra had gotten furious when Shareen had reminded her of that fact.

The prince kept talking, coming closer and closer to her. He looked like he was strangely calm, or in some sort of trance. He had never been so scary to Cassandra. She wanted to run away, to not be trapped here with him. Yet, she knew she couldn't. There was no one else left to hold him back from going to the Palace, or to Kassian. Opheus' dragon was injured, and Cassandra knew he wouldn't be able to match up to his older brother. He had to take care of Lephys, first. Kairen and Shareen were still stuck with the Red Dragon, and she hoped Anour was protecting Missandra, Lady Kareen, Kassian, and even the poor Phemera. It felt like the end. Finally, this feud was coming to an end. All the hatred that had stayed concealed was coming out into the open, all the brothers picking sides and fighting each other.

"What was it all worth, all this?" said Cassandra, glancing at the monster dragons. "Your sisters, your children, even your father. You've sacrificed everyone, simply to become Emperor?"

The Second Prince laughed.

"To become Emperor? No, I did it to survive! My crazy mother went through hell in order for me to survive! Every single day, I had to see it. She killed servants that tried to harm me. She begged my father for his attention, acting like the whore she was, just in the tiny hope he'd give her another chance to give him a son. My father was the worst of them all. You think I used my sisters? That man used my mother as a pawn, a mere toy between him and his favorite woman."

Cassandra frowned. She had mentioned it... Lady Kareen had talked about something like this. How the Emperor got closer to other women, even got engaged to them to try and get her attention. Cassandra had never thought twice about that.

"She was nothing but a toy he would toss aside whenever he could. My mother was constantly begging, dying for a second of attention, making herself the most pitiable woman. She cried more than any woman can cry, she screamed, she begged endlessly. She was such an annoying thing to see. She was a crazy, crazy bitch... A useless bitch."

Cassandra was shocked. She had never thought being a concubine was easy. She knew how hard some of them fought to get the Emperor's attention. How some killed and got killed. Cassandra was well aware of how lucky she had been, in this nest of snakes, and she had always kept in mind those women were mostly fighting for their survival. She had never thought about how one woman could actually lose her sanity over this... Lose herself.

"Can you believe, she was actually stupid enough to love that man you call my father? She believed his lies, she was ready to do anything for him. She taught me one thing, and one thing only. Survival. I had to survive, I had to become his only son. I had to become the Emperor, and she'd do anything for me. My mother dirtied her hands more than anyone, and she taught me everything I needed to know. It was quite fun, sometimes. When she wasn't completely crazy, she wasn't totally dumb!"

Cassandra wanted to vomit at each sentence he said. Deep in her heart, she understood. How a woman could have lost herself in her attempt to get the Emperor all to herself. How she could have become absolutely insane with jealousy and paranoia... and took her children down with her.

Vrehan wasn't born a monster, he had been purely created by his mother's madness. She could hear it in his voice. He wasn't crazy. He was just a child born out of resentment and hatred.

"It was so easy, once you understand the rules of the Palace, you know. It was a game for me. Kill, but don't get caught. My mother let me kill the servants that displeased me, or she'd do it herself. She hated my sisters so much. She killed two of them, and the others quickly understood if they weren't useful to me, they might as well be dead, too."

Their mother had killed...her own daughters?

"It was such fun. If I ordered it, my sisters killed anyone. I was already the Emperor of my own Palace, and they were my servants. Phetra was the smartest one. She always did whatever I asked, so I kept her around. She even ordered the others, understanding what I wanted before I even knew myself that I wanted it. It was fun, seeing them thrive, just to keep me satisfied."

Vrehan looked at the two horrors next to him, suddenly frowning.

"I thought I'd be father's favorite in no time. Sephir was going to die anyway, and the others were meaningless idiots. I had forgotten about Kairen."

Cassandra suddenly realized. Lady Kareen had kept her children away from the Imperial Palace to keep them safe. After what had happened to her oldest children, and to the young Kairen, it was a wise decision. It meant they had mostly grown away from their siblings... out of Vrehan's sight.

The Second Prince's eyes got darker, reliving some memories he obviously didn't appreciate.

"I knew the one woman my mother hated most was Kareen. The one woman my father truly loved. My mother killed her eldest, but she killed my mother as revenge. I was... at a loss. I couldn't understand why that woman couldn't be killed, like she had done to my mother, killing her so openly. Plus, if that wasn't enough, that bitch still had managed to have more children, and another Son! That was the one woman I couldn't get to kill. If our Father discovered I killed one of Kareen's, I knew I would die. It was the one game I couldn't play without risking my own life."

So the Emperor's love for Kareen had saved them, buying them some time after all. After Vrehan's Mother's death, the young murderer had understood he couldn't kill his siblings and get away with it. Shareen and Kairen were protected, more so than their other siblings. Cassandra couldn't even begin to understand what monstrosities had taken place behind closed doors at that time. The monsters their Mothers had created, all for their survival or greed... for one man.

Suddenly, Vrehan shook his head.

"So, I finally understood. I had to find a way to be better than him. To have the strongest dragon, the most children. I needed to be the best Prince. The one my father would have no choice but to choose!"

Cassandra was torn. Between disgust, horror, and... compassion. A part of her was hearing Vrehan's story and seeing it through her own eyes. Once pulled into the Dragon Empire, she had always thought there was something wrong with it. She had thought even more so when she had met Kairen, his mother, and heard their story. This Imperial Palace was the scariest place in the Empire. Filled with beautiful women, treasures, all the food and gold one could want, and endless rivers of blood. This kind of place wasn't an environment for children to grow up safely. It was a place for them to kill or be killed.

Her people had an expression for that. The river may not taste like the sea, but it doesn't get sweeter. No one could completely be free of its birth condition, and no child born from the Imperial Palace could be born without blood to be shed either. It was an endless circle of vengeance, jealousy and death haunting those golden walls. How could they pave their own way of staying free of all violence in those conditions? Vrehan had been raised under his mother's madness, and therefore became the monster one woman's tortured mind created.

"I have done everything... I became the best in everything!" he yelled. "I was the smartest child, the strongest, even the one with the largest beast, and yet, when that bastard came back, all of it was for nothing. My Father only saw Kairen and his dragon, nothing else. None of us mattered. He gave him the best opportunities, the best chances. Even giving him an army, so he could come back after that victory and be acclaimed by anyone!"

Vrehan's anger shone through in every single word he spat. He had become about as red as his dragon and didn't bother to control himself anymore. Cassandra looked at him, standing a few paces away, but she was also still nervously keeping an eye on the monstrous progeny. Krai was growling in a low tone, but its arched back and visible fangs made it clear the beast was ready to attack as soon as she gave the word.

That jealousy between the siblings was no different from their mothers'. They all longed for their father's attention, and a chance to survive. Yet, Vrehan was the one who had gone too far, who had fallen into this hole without any chance of repair. Cassandra knew this tone of voice, it sounded like despair and madness, molten together.

"It was always about Kairen, the prodigal son, the War God, Kareen's son. Father was blind anytime that woman or her children were in the room. Even his damn sister mattered more than us, his sons!"

Cassandra remembered seeing Shareen stand like an equal amongst her brothers. She was the only princess allowed to do that, but part of it was because she had taken that right for herself. It wasn't Kareen or the Emperor who had given her a chance to talk and dispute her brothers, to stand above her sisters. The princess had chosen to stand her ground and become as strong as she needed to be. She had made her own way in life. Shareen couldn't have gotten that strong, or became able to discuss matters of the Empire on par with her brothers or her father's counsel, simply because she was the favorite daughter. On the contrary, she may have become the favorite daughter because of everything she had worked hard to achieve.

Vrehan was simply blind and deaf to her actions, just like he was to his own sisters. He couldn't see a woman as a whole human being, only as a thing to be subjected to another man. To a father, a brother, or a son. Just like her mother, Shareen had long decided she was more than that. Cassandra didn't think it was simply her education that had molded her, it was her nature.

"He didn't have to do anything, he always came first in every fucking thing! The minute he was born, that damn Kairen became the nemesis of my life!"

"You're wrong."

After all of his screaming and whining , Cassandra's soft voice took him by surprise. The Second Prince looked at her, looking a bit lost for a second. He probably didn't think she'd even dare talk back, but there she was. The young concubine wasn't even afraid. She was standing tall, backed up by the strongest dragon alive, and she was not about to step down. She wasn't impressed or scared by him.

Cassandra had found in herself the very same feelings she had the last time she stood in this arena. She wasn't afraid to die, she wasn't afraid to stand in the face of a man-killing monster. A lot of things had changed, and she was stronger than before. She wanted to survive this time, but she was also ready to give her life to save her loved ones. She wasn't scared in the slightest, a strange halo of quiet was with her.

"You're wrong," she repeated. "You saw what you wanted to see. Kairen never had it easy, none of your siblings did. You're talking as if he had cheated, but you're the one who took this for a game. You nurtured your own jealousy after what your mother had experienced. You could have ended it years ago. You could even have saved your mother and your sisters, but instead, you played this game of death and you had fun until you didn't."

Vrehan's face was getting more and more distorted with rage as she spoke. Cassandra's composure was even more of a slap to his face. He couldn't stand a woman talking back to him, without any fear in her eyes, and he couldn't stand her being Kairen's woman. He wanted to gouge her eyes out. Those eyes that looked at him like he was a pitiful thing, or a crazy animal. Those green eyes that judged him.

"You could have led a good life if you had stopped all this," Cassandra continued. "Your mother was the one who caused the havoc, but you happily followed her into madness, and you even pushed all the blame onto her. You used her. At least she had her love for you and the Emperor as an excuse. But, you? You didn't have any real reason to inflict all the damage you caused. No one forced you to kill people, abuse your sisters, or even fight your brothers. You could have spared many lives, but you just relished in your power until someone overshadowed it. It didn't even have to be Kairen or Shareen. You needed a bone to pick and you found one."

Vrehan clenched his fists and his teeth, so furious he looked like he was about to explode.

"You ignorant witch!" he shouted. "You think you know the ways of the Palace? Do you think you have any idea how cruel that world is? I was merely a child! I only followed the path my mother had..."

"I was a child too when I was captured," said Cassandra in a very soft and low voice. "I suffered. I saw all the people I loved killed, tortured, raped, and sold by men I didn't know. I saw dozens of young girls like me, crying and suffering. I cried and I begged, too. I was whipped so many times, I thought I'd die. I was cut so deep I know the color of my own bones. I also experienced despair and anger, and it did not make me into a monster."

The Second Prince looked at a loss for words for a few seconds. Then, he scoffed.

"You were merely a slave! You were insignificant, you were bound to

608

be killed anyway! You couldn't rebel! However, if you had the chance, just once, to hold the whip and torture the one who had done this to you, tell me you wouldn't have done it?! Tell me you would have remained all pure and innocent! Do you think I am a monster? We are all monsters then!"

"No one held the whip for you," retorted Cassandra.

He blinked, having lost what she meant. This time, Cassandra simply looked disgusted at him, and resolute. The concubine shook her head and put her hand on Krai's neck as she stepped forward.

"No one inflicted you such suffering, you're the one who caused it. You mimicked your mother's craziness. You don't deserve to even compare yourself to any victim. You and I, we are not the same. You only inflicted pain on others, but you never suffered enough to know the full extent of the pain you caused. You just used it as an excuse to justify yourself."

"I am the victim! I wasn't born to be in someone's shadow! It is my throne! No one knows what I went through, I did what I had to! Don't judge me, you damn slave! You know nothing! I am the new Emperor, the only one that matters!"

His madness was beyond saving.

Cassandra realized that as she watched him scream, shout, and empty his lungs dry. This man had already sealed his own fate several times. There was no use in saving a fool running towards his end. Even if it wasn't for all those reasons, Vrehan was not one that could be saved. Cassandra glanced towards the damaged dragons that were still growling at Krai. It was nothing pretty to see. Those things were never supposed to be created, yet they had been born out of one man's madness and a woman's suffering. The vision of Phemera's terrified eyes came back to her mind, giving Cassandra the conviction she needed.

"Enough," she said. "It ends now. All of your madness, your schemes, and all the pain you inflicted on others."

The Prince scoffed.

"Ha! Do you think you can stop me? You, the slave woman? The white witch? I knew you'd be a problem, ever since Kairen saved you from this arena, I should have gotten rid of you faster... It's high time I get rid of you, you're an eyesore!"

Just as he yelled those last words, the dragons suddenly got more agitated, growling loudly and running towards Krai. The Black Dragon didn't move, staying close to Cassandra, but when the young dragons reached them, Krai was ready. The sound of the first attack resonated throughout the arena. Cassandra dived down to cover her ears, as one of the dragons growled even louder, right above her. A dragon's growl could be as soft as a purr, but it could become a deafening siren when they wanted to be heard. She rolled to the side, blinking through the dust clouds the gigantic bodies had stirred.

So it had begun. She could hear Krai's anger unleashing, but she couldn't stand around. She could be crushed at any moment by their weight, or get scratched by a dragon's claw if she wasn't careful. While Krai had done its best to protect her, the Black Dragon couldn't focus on Cassandra when it had to fight two of those dragons. She had to get out of there, as the fight was bound to get messy. She struggled to escape, as she was keeping an eye on the fight between all three dragons, while not making the mistake of finding herself in Vrehan's reach.

She wasn't losing sight of the main enemy. Cassandra knew she couldn't match up to Vrehan in a fight, but she ought not to lose him for a second time either. She had to find a way to end this.

The Second Prince didn't look willing to fight yet. He didn't have a weapon, and his face still bore the horrible scar of the injury she had inflicted upon him earlier. However, his dark eyes were absolutely burning with rage at her, and the deathly aura around him wasn't good either. Vrehan wasn't even bothering to look at how the dragons' fight was going. The gigantic creatures were making a deafening ruckus, yet he wouldn't even glance their way. He was focused on one thing.

He stepped forward, making Cassandra shiver uncontrollably. She had gone out of the dragons' reach, but she was only a few steps away from the enemy, and perhaps she would have wanted to fight the dragons more.

"You... Everything went off-track because of you," he hissed. "If you hadn't pushed those ideas into him. If you hadn't bore his bastard."

Cassandra glared at him, as she tried to get back on her feet. Her leg was horribly painful, and all of her body was sore, but hearing him insult Kassian gave her a new wave of courage. As he came closer, she grabbed some of the dust around her and threw it at him.

"Ah! You bitch!" he shouted, rubbing his eyes and stumbling back.

Cassandra took those precious seconds she had won to get back on her feet and hurry in a different direction, heading towards the cells of the Arena. She didn't even have enough strength left to run. There weren't many doors open in the Arena, but she had remembered enough from her short stay in the Arena cells to remember which to take.

She couldn't fight Vrehan on her own, but she could buy some time if she could at least find a decent weapon. She remembered the shows at the Arena, specifically the warrior fights. Though their participation may not have been voluntary, their choice of weapon was - they had to have been able to pick them from somewhere around here. Maybe some could have been left inside the cells.

Trying to forget the impending death chasing after her, Cassandra rushed to the cells. She knew Vrehan would kill her, slowly and painfully too. Kairen wasn't here to stop him, no one was. Her only ally nearby was a dragon that was already fighting two other horrid creatures. Cassandra knew she had to fend for herself, she'd have to save herself.

As soon as she reached a cell, her memories brutally resurfaced, like a nightmare haunting her. She remembered being dragged there like all the other slaves, thrown on the filthy grounds of the cages with no water, and no hope of survival. She could feel the weight of the chains on her limbs and neck, like a phantom... She took a deep breath and pushed the fear aside.

They were just empty cells now. Cassandra had to squint to find her way inside and around. Prisoners destined to die had no use for light, so there was only the bare minimum here. A few rays were barely able to make it through the miniscule openings between the stones that composed the grounds of the Arena. She tried to remember where to go, but every cell in there seemed like it was the same, only the contents changing.

Putrid smells hit her as she hurried between them. It was like something left there was rotten and decaying, adding on to the long forgotten excrement. She felt like throwing up; it was the absolute worst. Everything was filthy, but she had no choice other than to hold on to the bars to keep herself going without falling. Vrehan was still following her, closing the distance between them. She could hear his footsteps, making her heartbeat accelerate. Cassandra couldn't fathom dying in here, it was a horrible place to die.

"I swear, when I get my hands on you, I'll tear you limb from limb, and hang you from the Palace's gates for all to see! The White Witch of the Mountain will be no more!"

The way he spoke her nickname with such hatred left a bitter taste in her mouth. But Cassandra was trying not to listen to him, she was hellbent on finding a way out of there. Anything to survive this hell. Where were those weapons? She could clearly remember people waiting to fight, receiving their chosen weapons from the jailers. While they were trained fighters and not slaves, they were insistent that they use these sanctioned weapons - something about the Arena and security. But it was all a lie, Cassandra knew. She had overheard the jailers laughing about it. Discussing how the improperly sharpened and dull blades would make the fights last longer and be more bloody. It was horrible that they couldn't even be granted a swift death.

Cassandra didn't necessarily need a properly sharpened weapon though, she didn't have the skills to fight an Imperial Prince. She just needed something that would, at the very least, allow her to defend herself. Anything at all.

"You're so pathetic... You can't even do anything without a man to protect you. You're nothing without him, just a slave. You should have died quietly like the rest of your filthy people!"

Vrehan's words were echoing along the halls, like a shadow threatening to devour her at any moment. His voice was bouncing off every wall, Cassandra couldn't tell where he was or how far behind. She didn't want to even think about it. Fear would only slow her down, but hope made her faster.

Finally, she spotted it - a pile of weapons randomly thrown against a wall. Cassandra ran towards it and started rummaging through. She even cut herself a couple of times in her frantic search, but she needed to find one she could handle. Many of them were too heavy for her to wield, and she really couldn't afford another disadvantage while fighting off the Prince. As she heard his footsteps closing in, she settled on a small sword. It was a different shape than the one a man would normally use, being thinner and lighter than the others, but she had no time to find another weapon.

While Cassandra pretended to look through the pile of weapons, she was really paying close attention to the sound of his steps. He was getting closer, and she was going to be ready for him. Her only chance would be if she could take him by surprise. She tried to calm herself and focus, she couldn't afford to panic now. She couldn't die like this, not here, not now.

"You damn witch, I..."

As he was almost upon her, and she was ready. Cassandra dodged to the side, and in the same movement, swung her weapon towards him. The Prince let out an agonizing scream as she saw something fly away. She had no idea what it was until she noticed Vrehan's hand covered in blood, missing some fingers.

"You... Bitch!" he uttered between his teeth.

She had managed to injure him just enough that he lost focus for a few seconds. Cassandra retreated until her back hit a row of bars. She had hit another cell, and for a second, despite the screaming, she heard something else. She turned her head, and sure enough, there was something there. Something big that was breathing very slowly. What she had taken as some airflow through the long corridors before was actually from something breathing. A dragon's breathing. She felt a drop of sweat run down her spine. More of Vrehan's monstrosities? Or...?

"Sire?" she called out.

She could barely recognize the magnificent creature as it moved forward from the shadows. It had lost so much weight! The Blue Dragon opened its eyes to look at her and she could tell there was so much sadness in them. So this was where the dragon had been. How did Vrehan even get the First Prince's dragon in there? This cell looked so cruelly small for the large beast!

Cassandra extended her arm to try and reach it. Its scales were barely warm under her touch. The dragon looked like it had given up on life, just like Glahad before. They were bound to a life of despair once their Masters were gone.

She had no time to console the blue dragon, though. Vrehan might have lost a few fingers, but the red scales had appeared just as quickly on his skin to seal the injury, and his madness only intensified after that. His face was so deformed by his rage and injuries, he looked more akin to those horrible creations outside, barely human anymore. Seeing him approach, Cassandra tried to move to the other side of the bars, holding on to them to keep herself from falling. She heard Sire growl behind her, as it recognized her assailant too. With its anger rising, the blue dragon had a surge of adrenaline at seeing the Second Prince. Cassandra continued retreating until her shoulder hit a wall, cornered now between it and Sire's cell. She bit her lip, desperate.

"Finally!" the mad man hissed. "Here we are... A perfect place for you to die. In a filthy cell... It suits you, slave!"

They each raised their swords and Cassandra's was abruptly knocked from her hands in one swift movement. Just as she heard the metal clink on the stone floor, she crouched down as his blade violently dug into the wall right above her ear. She was completely cornered and weaponless now, holding her arms up to shield herself even though she couldn't possibly endure another assault. Her resistance was futile.

"You... You're finally going to die, you b...!"

This time, he didn't have the opportunity to finish insulting her. Cassandra raised her head as she felt something warm drip on her hands. Vrehan was paralyzed, his face frozen from shock, as the dragon's claw retracted from his throat. Cassandra was so stunned by the gruesome sight, it took her a few seconds to realize his shoulder was pierced as well. She slowly glanced to the side.

From the cage, Sire had suddenly lunged forward to extend its claws through the bars. Vrehan had been so focused on Cassandra and insulting her, he likely didn't even notice the dragon's presence lurking in the shadows. His body was now amply perforated by Sire's claws. Gasping for air, he began making some horrible sounds and groaning, as if he were about to start coughing up blood.

Cassandra covered her mouth with her hands. Was he going to die...? However, the dragon started getting agitated in its cell and wriggled itself around violently. Cassandra saw the walls behind suddenly start to shudder under the pressure. Could the blue dragon break out of this cage? If she could manage to get Sire out, it could help Krai!

"Sire, keep pushing, please!" she yelled as she ran for her little sword.

As the dragon retracted its claws, Vrehan was left holding the gaping holes in his throat and shoulder with his own hands. The dragon blood was trying to heal him, but the pain was so bad that he couldn't even stand straight and he stumbled trying to get to Cassandra. He was in a nightmarish condition, and his bloodshot eye was clearly giving away what he was about to do next.

The young concubine didn't even have the time to be scared. She had her sword back, and as he approached, she held it up defiantly to defend herself. While Vrehan had dropped his sword, he was still coming for her, his hands bare but he still had a clearly murderous intent. The situation was unconscionable. With Sire going berserk behind them in its cell, the dragon threw itself against the walls, its cries and screeches were deafening. Cassandra slowly retreated, keeping an eye on them. The gusts of dust coming from between the stones left no room for mistake - that wall could easily burst from the angry dragon's fit. It would just take a bit more.

"Uuuugh... You..."

It was all going to depend on the timing. If she could hold him off for just a little bit longer.

Vrehan approached slowly, no longer looking even remotely human.

There was nothing left but a wrathful monster, out for blood and covered in it himself. She tried to control her sword and swung it in his direction when he came too close. She silently begged Sire to hurry up. She had one last crazy idea, and it might be her only chance to survive this.

"You... Die!!!"

He thrust his hand at her, still missing half of his fingers, but Cassandra managed to raise the blade just in time to protect herself. The Second Prince violently snatched the blade from her, cutting his hand in the process, and letting out another guttural screech. A cold shiver ran down her spine and she felt the control over her weapon leave her. Vrehan had torn it from her hands and thrown it out of reach, across the cell.

Cassandra realized she was about to die. Her eyes went towards the wall a final time as the stones started to give way. About to collapse, even the roof above them was now raining dust and little rocks.

She felt his hands brutally wrap around her throat. She gasped for air, fighting the violent pressure of his grip. He was strong, so strong she was sure her throat was about to collapse. Through the haze, she heard a furious growl from somewhere in the distance.

"Finally..." he gasped through his still-damaged throat.

The evil grin painted on his face, with his bulging eyes and ravaged figure, would be the worst sight to die to. Cassandra brought her hands up to grasp his wrists, desperately struggling to loosen his grip. Her lungs were already painful, but now she couldn't even manage a puff of air, she couldn't breathe at all. Her throat was so raw, she felt tears in her eyes.

Suddenly, a horrible ruckus resonated behind them. She saw Vrehan turn his head, panicked, right as the wall behind them started to collapse. Cassandra closed her eyes for a split second that seemed to last forever. As if her life was flashing before her, she saw her son's adorable face frowning like his dad and staring at his little dragon plushie, she saw Kian jumping around in the water and running towards Krai to play. She saw Shareen and Kareen, sitting together in the garden and laughing, and she saw Kairen lying next to her in bed, whispering words she wanted more than anything to hear again.

Cassandra opened her eyes again, resolute, and in a desperate final attempt, she held onto his wrists as tightly as she could and pulled them both under the crumbling walls.

Chapter 38

The Black Dragon and the other creature were surprised by the sudden collapse of part of the Arena, interrupting their fight. The rocks and stones continued to collapse for a long while as more and more of the structure was attracted to the destruction, falling like dominoes. Soon enough, an impressive portion of the Arena was in shambles, the bars of the cells down below now exposed to the sky. Both dragons stared at the massive mountain of rocks, blinking wildly from the dust that had been exhaled into the air. Once it had settled though, a long silence followed. For a while, nothing in the Arena moved.

Krai softly growled, as if calling for someone. Next to it, the creature retreated back, its sibling already lying dead in the dust a few steps away, and its rib cage exposed to the air. The fight had been horrible, the difference in strength was obvious. Not even two of them had been enough to take on the War God's dragon. This little one wasn't sure what to do. It glanced at Krai as it continued to retreat slowly, limping heavily on its injured leg. It seemed like the Black Dragon didn't care for their fight anymore. No, Krai was focused on the pile of rocks. The Black Dragon began to step towards it slowly, limping from the pain in its leg. Krai growled again, pleading. Nothing moved.

Suddenly, the mountain started to grow, as if it had taken a sharp inhale, and the rubble began to shift. Blue scales started to uncover from the mess, as Sire struggled to free itself. The dragon had been injured and stumbled several times before it could fully get its body out. Krai walked over and both dragons briefly sniffed the other. Both of the siblings were in pitiful states. Krai had some sizable injuries from the fights, and was covered in both its own blood and that of the dragons it had fought today. It was so much that the dragon's black scales were actually shining with a lustrous red under the sun. Sire was just covered in dust, but its body had been mauled in several places by the rocks, some of the blue scales had even fallen off or been damaged. Its foreleg couldn't even seem to bear the weight of its body, its paw kept giving way with each step taken.

Sire suddenly turned its head towards the misshapen dragon that was left behind. The Blue Dragon growled, its eyes shining with recognition and malicious intent. As the larger dragon headed its way, the ugly creature tried to retreat, struggling against its injury to step back. It had lost all of its will to fight, the panic could be seen in its eyes as Sire came closer, growling furiously. The Blue Dragon, despite its injuries and damaged scales, was still in much better shape than Krai, and angrier too. This battle was about to end.

Meanwhile, Krai didn't even care to look at the massacre going on behind. Its ears barely twitched, no matter how loud the younger dragon's screeches were. The Black Dragon kept staring at the rubble, frozen in front of the pile of rocks. Krai didn't move, waiting, the ruby eyes looking over as if it was expecting something.

Krai softly growled again. With its snout, pushed at the rocks, sniffing around to find her. The Black Dragon lifted its injured paw to start digging. It was like a dog, sniffing through the rubble, searching desperately. Behind Krai, Sire was done with the bloody work and watched without moving.

"Krai!" A male voice called.

The Black Dragon didn't turn its head. It just kept digging, its movements getting more impatient than the last. Its claws were not made for such tasks, and the dragon growled in frustration every time it moved another rock.

"Krai!"

Kairen was confused. What was his dragon doing?

The War God stepped forward, ignoring his own pain. He was covered in black scales, especially his chest which was bare and covered in them and blood. A large portion of his face was also breaking out in the black scales, where the flesh was slowly recovering from deep burns. One couldn't even distinguish the injuries anymore, his body just looked like it was half-way through some mythical transformation.

A wave of worry started invading his heart. His eyes glanced over to the dead dragons near Sire, but he just took the sight in. He was focused more on Krai, who was digging anxiously through a mountain of debris.

Kairen started running. Panic was overwhelming his senses. He threw down the dragon's head he was carrying, and ran as fast as he could across the Arena. He had a bad feeling. He never had that extra sense, intuition, but Krai's desperation was going to his head, like a horrible, nagging shadow encompassing his mind. He didn't allow himself to think. Kairen ran until he was in front of the pile and then he started digging too.

For a while, the only sound was the two of them, the Prince and his dragon, endlessly digging through a mountain of rocks, searching everywhere they could. They were so frantic, their labored breathing and the ruckus of the stones being tossed was the only thing that could be heard in the stadium. Sire stood a few feet away, watching somberly.

"What are they doing?"

The Blue Dragon turned its head to look at the source of the words. Stumbling in at one of the Arena's entrances, Shareen was frowning and grimaced with each step, as she was in bad shape too. A large and deep gash was running from her left temple down to her jaw, still bleeding a bit from behind the little, dark purple scales. Her left ear was also cut open, and on the other side, she had another cut on her eyebrow causing her to unwillingly blink because of the scales covering it.

The top of her armor was gone, her exposed shoulder bearing another sizable injury, a large and clear bite mark that was still bleeding down her side. Her purple outfit was drenched in the reddish color of drying blood. She was walking slowly, as if taking each step was incredibly painful, and held her wrist against her flank, her hand now gone.

She came closer, still not quite understanding what her brother and his dragon were looking for.

But they just kept digging, looking for a sign. A movement. Anything.

"Cassandra!" Kairen suddenly yelled, unable to hold it in anymore.

His voice echoed throughout the arena, and Shareen's face sank.

"She can't be under... that..." she muttered.

The Princess hurried to her brother's side, and though she didn't want to know what they were going to find, she started to dig as well. It was slow progress. Sire looked on as if they were crazy.

"Cassandra! Cassandra!"

The War God's voice echoed along with his dragon's growls. They kept rummaging through the rocks in a deathly silence. Shareen didn't want to say the words, but she knew there was no way.

Nothing under this rubble could have survived.

"Cassandra!"

She swallowed and kept going. Rock after rock, stone after stone, they kept digging, skinning their fingers and breaking their nails until they bled. Suddenly, after pulling her umpteenth rock, Shareen saw it. A bit of white skin.

"K... Kairen..." she muttered.

Her brother didn't hear her. Shareen took a deep breath, closing her eyes to take it in.

"Kairen!"

This time, he turned around, and seeing her expression, his heart sank. The War God ran down the little hill he was standing on. His eyes opened wide upon seeing what she had found.

"Cassandra!"

Shareen stepped away a bit, letting him uncover his lover. It was an arm that came first. She was buried under so many stones, it took a few more seconds to completely dig her out, even with Krai's help. The dragon was so agitated, the rocks under it threatened to collapse some more. When Kairen finally pulled Cassandra out, it was like all of his breath had left him.

She wasn't moving.

Her eyes were closed, lying in his arms like an inanimate doll. Her white skin was covered in bruises, her left leg was at a horribly unnatural angle, and her feet were dangling freely at the ankle. A layer of dust covered her skin and hair, she looked as if she was part of the stones themselves.

The War God gasped, unable to accept what he was seeing, what he was holding. It was something that he just couldn't fathom was right before his eyes. His hands were shaking under Cassandra's body. They had never shaken before.

"Cassandra," he called. "Cassandra, wake up."

Shareen bit her lip, unable to say anything, not even to tell him to stop.

The young concubine looked beautiful, even in that state. Some of her hair was glued to her temple by the blood on her face. It had run all over, even her lips were tinted with some red. Yet, her skin had never seemed so grey. She had never seemed so petite and fragile in the War God's arms.

"No," he said. "No, Cassandra, no!"

There was anger in his voice. As if he was ordering her not too, as if he was ordering death not to take her. Krai wasn't making a sound. The dragon was crouching down, approaching in very small steps, as if it was...scared. The Black Dragon sniffed Cassandra's hand, laid on the ground, and slowly started retreating, letting out a pitiful wailing sound along the way.

Shareen had to look away, she couldn't take it anymore. It was painful to hear her brother, to hear them call her name, again, and again, and again, like madmen. She couldn't utter a word though. If she did, she would have broken down too. She was a strong woman, and few things could shake her, but this was one of those things. Cassandra like this, and Kairen breaking over it. They were used to death, they always had been. But this was worse. Even more unbearable. It wasn't possible to accept it, not like this.

As she was avoiding the scene, Shareen caught sight of something else - some movement underneath the pile of rocks. She frowned and walked towards it. As she got closer, a sound resonated from it, like the groaning of some injured beast.

"Oh, by the Gods..." she hissed.

She pushed a couple of rocks with her feet and, sure enough, a black eye peered through. It was moving, but they were merely tremors. The Second Prince was groaning, pinned under a mountain of rocks. He didn't look human anymore, his body had been crushed by the weight of the rubble. His dragon blood was just doing whatever it could, inside and out.

Shareen didn't even have enough energy in her to delight at his pitiful situation.

"Even the Gods don't think you deserved an easy death," she muttered.

Slowly, she removed one rock after another, until his head was completely out. His skull had been crushed, his head taking on an odd shape that was nothing close to normal. But the red scales were still appearing here and there. Shareen grabbed a rock that was about half the size of her fist, gauged the weight a bit in her hand, and turned to him again. She brought her face down to his so

618

he could hear her.

"She killed you," she whispered. "You're going to die knowing that a slave woman beat you, and another woman finished the job. You tell the Gods if they dare send you back here again, I'll kill you over and over every time, just like the damn cockroach you are."

Then, she raised the rock and smashed his face. She raised it again and smiled with satisfaction, and smashed him again. Once just wasn't enough. She had chosen a flat, not too heavy one on purpose. Shareen hit him over and over again, looking into his eyes each time she raised it, channeling all the rage she could into each hit. His dragon blood could try as much as it wanted to keep up, but she'd just keep going. There was so much that needed to be thrown in his face. All the suffering he deserved, everything. It came through in each blow from that rock. His blood splattered around them, on her hands, her body, and on her face. Her grip didn't loosen from around that rock, no matter how much it hurt. Each groan of agony he uttered offered a bit of relief, that some justice was being done for those who had suffered.

Shareen wanted to be sure he saw it all, that he died being able to see and know that he had truly lost. She kept smashing his face until nothing but a bloody crater was left. Only then, did her shaking hand let go of the rock. It tumbled down, landing with a lonely sound on the ground.

Just then, the Princess let out a long sigh of relief. She didn't say a word, but for a second, she thought about her siblings, her brother, her nieces and nephews. Then, Shareen grabbed the body and, with her last bit of strength, took it out of that graveyard and threw it on some open ground. Krai and Sire both growled furiously, but before they could react, Shareen took a deep breath in and exhaled her fire. The corpse started burning immediately.

That bastard didn't deserve any physical reminders of him to remain in this world.

Once it was all over, it became quiet in the Arena again. There was a silence hanging over the place, casting a shadow despite the clear sky. It just didn't feel right. Shareen looked around at the deserted Arena. This place was empty most of the year, and when it was in use, it was just to showcase death. Now, it had served its purpose one too many times. The Princess let out a long sigh. Maybe all of this was meant to teach them something. That it was time for change.

Shareen closed her eyes and took a deep breath. She wiped off the blood dripping down her chin, and with a heavy heart, turned to her brother. Next to him, Krai was still waiting there with its head low, not moving.

"Kairen. We have to go," she said.

She was expecting her brother to ignore her, but he stood up slowly, still cradling Cassandra against his chest. Both dragons turned their heads and watched him go ahead, before following in his steps as he slowly left the Arena. Shareen looked on after her brother. She glanced one last time towards the ashes and the pile of rocks before spitting on the black dust and turning to follow her family to leave this place.

They walked slowly back towards the Palace, neither of the dragons looked like they even had enough strength left to fly. Krai was closely following Kairen, and even when the dragon had to switch to the roof of the narrow corridors, its steps were heard clearly right above them. Sire hadn't followed them back inside. The Blue Dragon parted ways with them, heading for a more familiar area of the castle. It was easy to understand the Blue Dragon had other humans to be more concerned about.

Shareen didn't dare say a word while they walked. After such a long and violent battle, it was odd that everything was so quiet inside the Imperial Palace.

"Brother! We..."

Anour stopped talking, his eyes going down to the body in Kairen's arms. The young Prince's eyes widened in shock, and soon overflowed with sorrow.

"No... She..."

No one answered him. He gasped and covered his mouth, not daring to move when Kairen walked past him. The youngest Prince raised his eyes towards Shareen as if to ask, but he couldn't formulate the words. She glanced at him briefly, and then they both followed the War God.

"The...fight outside is over," said Anour, almost in a whisper.

They could hear it. From far above the Imperial Palace's walls, the cheers of soldiers could be lightly heard. Shareen wanted to go out and slap them one by one. There shouldn't be any cheering right now. Not after what happened, the tragedy that had unfolded. She didn't want to hear those idiots.

"Where is Mother? And Missandra?" Asked Shareen.

"They're with Roun," said Anour. "Missandra was badly injured, but Lady Kareen found an Imperial Healer to look over her, and Phemera, too. He said they will both make it. Everything had quietened down here, so I came out to see... Lady Kareen had said we should hide and wait, just in... Just in case."

Shareen nodded. Their mother had probably prioritized Missandra and the baby's safety.

"Can you go get them?" she asked.

Anour glanced towards Kairen, worried, before turning back to her.

"Are you sure?"

"I don't know," she sighed. "Maybe...It's better if they get a chance to say goodbye."

The youngest Prince gulped, looking like he was repressing some tears himself, and nodded somberly before leaving. Shareen sighed, and continued after her brother. She didn't know where he was going with her, she couldn't even tell if he had a destination in mind.

Kairen seemed like he was just wandering aimlessly through the Palace's corridors, while carrying her body in silence. But after a few more turns, she recognized the direction they were going; towards the Lake.

She frowned. They had heard some incredible story from their brother while on their way to the Arena before, but... Why was he thinking of going back there now? That crazy tale Opheus had told them about some gigantic dragon hidden in the Lake, couldn't be true...could it?

Shareen didn't say a thing though, and just followed after him. No matter what he tried, said, or did now, she probably wouldn't be able to find it in herself to stop him anyway. She had never stood against her brother, and she wasn't about to start, certainly not now. They walked up to the Lake, where Opheus was sitting in the grass with his hand on his dragon. Both Lys and Glahad next to him looked exhausted and covered in injuries, yet they all raised their heads as the group walked into the garden.

The Golden Dragon couldn't move, but growled softly. It was clearly exhausted, lying on its flank. It had fought a lot today. They all had. Krai, too, walked heavily on the grass, coming up to Kairen's side. The Black Dragon had never looked so sad as it laid there, its head tilted towards them.

Opheus struggled to get up as his eyes were riveted on Kairen and Cassandra. He didn't say a thing, but his expression was beyond words. The sight had him choked up and tongue tied. He watched his older brother approach the Lake and fall to his knees at the strand. He was holding Cassandra as if she was simply sleeping, her head against his neck, his large hands holding her tenderly.

"Please..."

His voice was so low, Opheus thought he had dreamt it. Yet, Kairen was staring at the Lake, his eyes searching for something he couldn't see. He didn't know what to call or how to do this. This was Cassandra's world, not his. He knew nothing. The War God took a deep breath, and after a moment of hesitation, he uttered the only word he could think of.

"Almien."

He looked at the Lake, but nothing moved, so he took a deep breath and repeated it, over and over, like a prayer. He hugged Cassandra and begged for her God to come save her.

Shareen stood to the back with her arms crossed, skeptical of what her brother was trying to do. Opheus glanced at the surface too, unsure. Would the creature answer their call? After what they had done... Kairen looked down at Cassandra. After they had done this to her? To her people? He exchanged a quick glance with Shareen. The Princess didn't believe in this, but she wouldn't stop him from trying. She knew there was nothing else he could do but try.

"Oh, by the Gods... Cassie..."

They both turned around. Lady Kareen had arrived with baby Kassian in her arms, followed closely by Anour. Somehow, Kian had found its way to the concubine and was trotting at her feet, looking just fine and unaware of what was going on. Missandra had not come with them, she was likely not in a state to move. Perhaps it was better, in a way, Shareen thought. She'd be spared the vision of her older sister lying lifeless in the War God's arms.

From his grandmother's arms, Kassian began crying. Kian retreated, no longer looking joyful and excited. The young dragon was almost hiding behind

Kareen, peeking out from behind her towards the Lake and whimpering in distress. The scene was just heartbreaking. Kareen didn't even try to soothe her grandson. The Imperial Concubine had her eyes fixated on her son, who looked just completely devastated. She sighed and held Kassian a bit tighter, rubbing his back and whispering gently to him. She shook her head, there was nothing else even she could do.

Suddenly, the surface of the lake began to tremble. They all turned their eyes towards the shapes that appeared there. The ripples started spreading throughout the whole Lake, and somehow, the atmosphere around them became humid, which never happened in the dry, hot Dragon Empire.

Shareen and her mother exchanged a look, completely stunned. They had lived in this Palace for years, explored every corner of it and knew every secret of the Emperor, but the biggest secret didn't belong to their human realm. It came in the shape of a magnificent Creature that surfaced out of the lake for a girl.

The Water God emerged from the water, its head coming up to Kairen. It moved like a snake, slowly swimming just under the surface, large arches of its body randomly breaking through the surface before disappearing again. One could only imagine the actual length and size of the Creature. Opheus glanced towards the dragons, but none of them looked surprised or seemed cautious. In fact, they were all lowering their heads, as if the Water dragon in front of them was some venerable deity, a being they were naturally intimidated by. They hadn't reacted the same earlier in the midst of the battle, but now there was a clear line between the Imperial Dragons and this Water God.

Kairen raised his eyes at the Creature that stood tall above him. For once, the War God was the one being looked down upon, but he didn't care the slightest.

His eyes were red with grief. He just couldn't accept it, he didn't want to admit this reality. And yet, as the Water God stood tall in front of him, he remained quiet. There was a very strange atmosphere between the two.

He was holding Cassandra. She looked so light in his arms. The girl from the Rain Tribe. The girl his Empire had taken from her people, from the life she should have had, and turned her into a slave. They should never have met. They were born into two very different worlds; worlds that were not suited for each other. The moment she had been brought to this Empire, she wasn't meant to survive. She was brought here to suffer and then die. To become a slave.

And yet, of all people, the War God had fallen for that woman, and he had been a bit of light for her in the darkness. They had spent a little over a year together, but she had become everything to him. She had flourished despite the obstacles, like a flower that had managed to bloom in the dirt. The Water Lily. The Lady of the Mountain.

Wherever she had ended up, she survived without complaint and grew. Standing brave against everything his people had thrown at her. She had never even become resentful towards them. Cassandra stayed the same sweet girl from the Rain Tribe, and she changed the people around her.

Kairen was sitting there, lost, just looking at the Water God. What had he come here to do? Beg for a second chance? For Cassandra to be returned to him? He was sitting in front of her God, with her body in his arms. What would he dare beg for? The Water God had heard the Requiem of one of his last daughters. No one knew what linked them, but he was presenting her body to that God, and begging for a second chance. To bring her back into this terrible world? How could he ask for a miracle, when he had brought nothing but chaos?

The Water God was towering there, waiting. No one could say how much time had really passed, while those two Gods simply stared at each other. It was like some silent negotiation was happening between them, yet no words were exchanged.

In Kareen's eyes, her son was paying the heavy price for many other people's wrongdoings. He was the one who had to carry his lover's body, the mother of his son lying in his arms. He had to live with the reality that he had been too late to save her, and that he was partially responsible for her death. Because he had fallen in love with her, so many things had happened. No one knew why the Black Dragon had tied their destinies together. Maybe the War God needed to learn about love? Maybe it was to give Cassandra more time to do all the good she could? There was something both beautiful and tragic about the couple's fate.

After a while, the War God closed his eyes. A tear slowly fell down his cheek and, with a deep breath, he held Cassandra in his arms one last time. He held her tightly, burying his face in her hair, his hands wrapped around her body. From behind him, his family could feel the heavy weight on his shoulders, the mountain of pain and grief that overcame him. Only Kassian's cries could be heard, this man himself was beyond tears.

Then, very slowly, he laid Cassandra's body down in the water. Even from afar, everyone could tell how unwilling he was to let her go. When his hands finally left her body, he took a couple of steps back with his eyes still on her. Never have the obsidian eyes been so dark, without so much as a spark of light in them.

He raised his dead eyes to the Water God, and bowed lowly.

Kairen had never bowed to anyone before, but now, this man had bent so low, his face was almost touching the water.

"I'm so sorry."

Those three words were spoken so softly, no one else could hear them. The Water God let out a long, low-pitched sound that resonated within the garden walls and beyond. It was as if it had been waiting for this moment. Then, it leaned down to Cassandra, its head right next to hers, and took a deep breath in. When its mouth opened again, it exhaled a very thin, white mist.

They were confused at first until they realized the white mist was slowly coating Cassandra. The air chilled some more, turning the mist on her skin to ice as the layers grew thicker. Soon, her skin turned whiter than it had ever been. It was like seeing a ghost disappear in the snow. Her lips turned purple and then blue.

Kairen wouldn't take his eyes off her until the Water God stopped the ice forming. Then, with an angrier and louder growl, it suddenly moved closer and wrapped its body around her. One of its paws grabbed her arm to keep her in place, but the Creature's eyes were on Kairen the entire time. The War God didn't seem to notice though, and he didn't dare to retreat from the closeness of the Creature either. He just watched it take her, unmoving.

With a final, long growl, the Water God slowly slinked back into the Lake, taking Cassandra with it and disappearing just like that. After a while, the surface of the water hadn't moved again and went back to being a quiet, peaceful Lake.

Shareen sighed. So it was over. Whatever that thing was...it had taken Cassandra's body down, deep into the lake. Shareen didn't know what to feel anymore, it was all just too much to handle. She took a deep breath and glanced towards her mother. Lady Kareen was looking at her son wearing the saddest expression, but she didn't go to him. She knew there were no words she could say that would console him. Her eyes fell to Kassian then, who was still crying a bit, though it seemed that he had tired himself out too much to keep on wailing.

Anour and Opheus had the same horrified expression on their faces. Everyone was staring at Kairen, left there alone to face the quiet Lake. No one knew what to do next.

Krai was the first to move. The Black Dragon walked to its master's side and curled up around him. It seemed like the dragon and Prince were one being at that moment, facing the quiet Lake, united in their loss.

That sight seemed to sober Shareen up. She shook her head and walked over to her mother.

"I'll go take care of the crap outside and make sure we are done with everything... whatever's left."

The Imperial Concubine let out a long sigh and nodded. Her eyes went down on the baby in her arms. She left a long kiss on his forehead while, at her feet, Kian curled up around her, his eyes turned towards the Lake. It looked like the Baby Dragon was confused about what had happened and didn't dare approach. Instead, it stayed with Kareen who was patiently waiting for her son to come out of this trance. She would wait no matter how long it would take.

Opheus and Anour walked up to Shareen. The Fourth Prince was wiping his tears, clearly shaken up. They hesitated before speaking, almost at a loss for what to say.

"What now?" asked Anour.

"You'll stay with Missandra and Phemera."

The Sixth Prince's expression sank.

"But... if she wakes up..."

Shareen glared at him.

"If she wakes up, you'll tell her the truth, Anour. Stop being such a baby, or we can trade and you can be the one to take care of the fucking mess outside and deal with the politics. Your pick."

He looked down, defeated. Indeed, he was the one closest to Missandra, and he wouldn't be able to help anywhere else... it didn't make his task any easier though. Anour nodded and, with a sigh, the youngest Prince glanced at Opheus and left with a solemn expression.

The Fourth Prince crossed his arms.

"You were a bit harsh on him."

"I'm not in the mood to indulge anyone's sensitivities right now."

Her brother frowned a little, glancing towards Kairen and the Lake.

"I can't blame you... Lephys is dead. What do you need me to do?"

"Gather all those damn ministers, counselors, and whomever. It's high time that things change around here, and it's starting today."

"Do you think they are going to listen though?"

"They listened to that rat. So now, they either have an open ear for us, or those bastards can join him in hell. I'll send them there myself. They should start working on it now if they want us to let them live another day after what happened here. Those damn... tsk. Anyway, you can bring Lephys' body along if they need help being convinced. At least that bastard can be useful for something."

"Got it."

They split up to take care of everything that was left after the battle.

Once those three had left the garden, everything was silent once again. Kareen was left alone to contemplate her son's loneliness. In her arms, Kassian had given in and was sleeping, his little eyes still red and puffy from all the crying. His grandmother sighed. The poor boy had no idea what a hero his mother was. Cassandra had never been a fighter, but she was someone who would sacrifice herself for others to survive, and in the end, she had given her life to save theirs.

"Don't worry," she whispered. "We won't let you forget her."

A long time passed as they stayed like that in the garden. Nothing really moved, except for the wind blowing gently around them. Kareen, tired of standing, walked across the garden and came to sit near poor Glahad. The old Golden Dragon put its head against her lap, its ruby eyes focused on the concubine. She sighed and stroked its golden scales.

"That old man... He even had the guts to go before me... So heartless. Don't worry, Glahad. This old woman will stay with you a bit longer. Just a bit longer... He was ever so selfish, wasn't he? That old man. At least you will stay with me a little bit longer, won't you? To help watch over the children. He's left them with nothing but a mess."

The Golden Dragon growled softly and closed its eyes, gently rubbing its face against her hip. The elder dragon looked incredibly tired. Kian, who had been left behind, now slowly walked up to them and curled up under Glahad's wing. A little ball of silver scales, the Baby Dragon rolled itself up against its flank, lowering its head with a sad look. From the little enclave, its little emerald eyes could watch Krai and Kairen on the other side of the Lake, unchanged in their stillness.

Kairen had been sitting there for a very long time already, yet he was still just staring at the surface of the lake. He wasn't even expecting anything at this point, his expression was just blank and emotionless. Abandoned. Man and Dragon remained there, like statues, until the sun started going down and the sky turned orange. On his knees, he didn't move; it was like time had stopped in this place.

Voices began to echo through the halls from elsewhere in the Palace as the world resumed without them. Somewhere else, Shareen was discussing with the Imperial Generals, giving orders to clear the streets and round up the traitors. Opheus was threatening the council, clearing up dirty money, and deciding who deserved a second chance at redemption. His dragon, Phe, had followed him, limping to go and help him on the other side of the Palace. Anour was trying to console a crying girl, grieving for her older sister. Life was not resuming peacefully, it couldn't after all the chaos that had been spread around the Palace.

Kassian woke up too as the world resumed. The baby didn't know anything about war, but he knew he was hungry. He started to whine a bit in Kareen's arms. Just as she was about to try and soothe him, she was surprised to see that, across the lake, Kairen was finally leaving his trance and standing up.

While his dragon didn't move, the War God silently left the shore and walked around to his mother. A bit surprised, Kareen stood too and waited for him. He didn't look like the same man as before. Something was broken inside him, she could see it in his eyes. It wasn't about the injuries or the exhaustion. When he came to her, his eyes went directly to his Son, and for a second, there was a spark of something there. Kairen gently took Kassian in his arms and the baby stopped his wailing, only a few tears sliding down his cheeks after. He squirmed a bit in his father's arms, but only as if adjusting to a more comfortable position. The black scales still trying to heal Kairen's body probably weren't too agreeable for him either, but his father's warm skin was enough to calm him down.

Kairen spent a long time staring at his son.

"What do you want to do now?" Kareen asked gently.

"She hated this place."

The concubine slowly nodded. It was only right that he wouldn't want to stay here with Kassian, not after all of this.

"I understand. I'll help you the best I can."

He didn't reply. His eyes were still on his son. He gently caressed Kassian's forehead with his thumb. The baby squirmed a bit, pouting. Kian too, went from Kareen's side to Kairen's, staying at his feet quietly. The War God just seemed tired right now. A man who had fought a war and lost more than he had won. It was written in his eyes. It may have been even worse if he didn't have his son to hold on to.

"How about you go to... The Residence, for now?" she suggested. "They have everything needed to take care of Kassian."

He nodded slowly. That was all she needed. Although she was going through her own mourning, Kareen knew it was without comparison to her son's sorrow. After some hesitation, she raised her hand and gently touched his arm.

It was just a light touch on his skin, just for reassurance, for him to feel that she was there. She'd always be there for him.

"Go," she said. "Your sister can handle it. I...I'll join you soon."

And just like that, she watched Kairen go, carrying his son and his grief. Kian sent a glance her way, a bit unsure of what to do. The young dragon eventually followed, scurrying up behind Kairen and sending reassuring glances. Kareen watched them leave until they were out of sight, and then turned her attention back towards the Lake.

Krai was still there, still lying by the water, having not moved at all. The dragon was exactly where its Master's heart had been left. No one could tell if it was waiting, or simply abandoned. The Black Dragon was as frozen as a statue, its ruby eyes reflecting nothing but the Lake. It didn't even seem to care about life anymore. Kareen's heart broke once more for her son's dragon. It would remain here forever, she could see it. The Imperial Concubine repressed the cries in her heart and walked out of the garden.

She hated this place too. Kareen had seen too many children die within these walls. If a new age had finally come, it would happen without her. She was an old woman with no strength left to give. She would no longer be the untouchable Imperial Concubine, if she had ever really been... Nothing was tying her to this place, nothing ever had. Next to her, Glahad growled softly, pushing against her hip a little. She smiled half-heartedly, caressing the golden snout again.

"Do not worry... Wait for me. I still have one last thing to do here. Then I'll take good care of you."

The dragon growled again as Kareen walked away. She took a different direction than the one her son had taken, heading back to the place where they had hidden earlier. As she got closer, she could hear the screams. Missandra's wailing was unbearable, but Kareen took a deep breath and went in. She didn't flinch upon seeing the younger sister's distress, or Anour's attempts to calm her down. No one could blame her after losing her sister in such a horrific way. Missandra was mourning.

Kareen's heart ached for the girl. In a way, they were a lot alike. Though she loved Cassandra dearly, the Imperial Concubine saw a lot of herself in the younger sister. She knew Missandra would move on and become stronger from this. They were the type of women who always grew stronger in order to survive, turning their anger and fear into rage. She only hoped Missandra would be able to open her heart again in spite of all this. That child needed to learn how to love and trust people again.

Kareen hadn't come back here to console Missandra though. She took a deep breath and opened a room that had been locked until now. Inside, Phetra was there, tied to a chair, her face ruined by her tears. Her eyes had grown wide and red from terror. Maybe she knew what had happened to her brother, but as soon as she saw Kareen, her panic increased. Despite being gagged, she started wailing even more loudly and trying to break free from the chair.

The Imperial Concubine was incredibly calm though. She came close and untied the ribbon they had used to cover her mouth and, as soon as she could, Phetra started begging and pleading.

"Please! Please spare me! I didn't want to! Vrehan forced me! He'd kill me if I didn't obey! I had no choice, I had to obey! I didn't want to! I didn't want to!"

"Who else was working for him?" Kareen asked calmly, ignoring her pleas.

"I... I already told Opheus the truth, I swear! I didn't want to help him! He... He made me sleep with all those dirty old men! He forced me to!"

"What about your sisters?"

Phetra seemed scared, but she was unable to stop. She could barely breathe under her loud sobs.

"I... I only taught the young ones to follow orders! We had to! I didn't..."

Kareen let out a long sigh.

"You're just a pathetic little thing, aren't you?"

As she said that, Kareen took a dagger out from the pocket of her dress, causing Phetra to go into absolute hysteria.

"No, no, no! Please! I don't want to die, I don't want to die!"

"No one wants to die," retorted Kareen. "No one wants to kill either, but here we are, you and me. We all have things to protect, things we'd dirty our hands for."

And in one swift movement, she killed Phetra. The Princess and her chair fell to the floor, her throat sliced open. Her eyes were still twitching, her face laying in the growing puddle of blood that would be her final vision. Kareen stepped back to avoid stepping in it, and slowly wiped the splatter from her dress. One final act, so that it could truly be over.

She simply walked out after that, closing the door behind her. Kareen took a deep breath and walked back into the Palace. She could already feel the winds of change that were overtaking this place's filthy air. Her steps took her to another corridor. No one was there yet. Everyone was busy elsewhere, with whatever was going to come next. Kareen opened the door to the Emperor's Chambers.

He was lying in his bed, his eyes closed. From afar, one would have thought he was simply sleeping. Kareen took a deep breath, trying to hold back her tears. She slowly walked up to the bed, looking at him from above.

"You really were selfish to the end," she whispered. "Leaving me and your children with this mess... Was this what you wanted? To die and leave all the trouble you caused, you old man? You could never abandon a single one of them, and yet, look where it got you... Death and jealousy. Was it worth it trying to protect them all? You..."

She stopped. The sadness was growing like a knot of frustration in her throat. Kareen was too proud to cry, but she couldn't simply stand in front of her deceased lover like a statue. She had once loved this man. She had given him many, many nights alone, before she had to put the lives of the children they had created together first.

She stepped back, closing her eyes. She was truly grateful he hadn't died alone, although no one could say the Emperor had died in peace. She simply wished he could find some peace in the Gods' Realm, and could watch what was to become of this Empire. Kareen took a deep breath, and as she averted her gaze elsewhere, her eyes fell on a large door. She frowned and turned to the wardrobe. She couldn't remember what was behind those doors, but something felt nostalgic about it.

The concubine slowly walked up to the wardrobe, and as she came closer, she noticed her name carved into the wood above the handle. Kareen frowned, and slowly opened the door. There was a single piece of clothing inside.

A magnificent golden dress.

Final Chapter

It was a dark and quiet night at the Palace.

The moon was high in the sky, bright and white. The beautiful light was reflected on the surface of the wide, quiet Lake, and nearby, a magnificent Black Dragon lay, its scales shining in the moonlight too. It seemed to be sleeping, its head peacefully resting on its front paws. The dragon had been still there for a very long time, this was only one night of many others that it had been inside that garden. On the surface of the Lake, dozens of flowers were gently floating, as pure and as white as the moon. Water Lilies. A little ripple appeared in the middle of the lake, causing the flowers to drift slowly away.

It could have been a little gust of wind blowing over the surface of the Lake, or a fish tempted by a potential meal. It might have even been one of the delicate fireflies that had made a home there, and yet the Black Dragon raised its head. Its ruby eyes glowing in the dark of night, as it scanned over the surface, looking for something. And for a few seconds, nothing happened. It slowly stood up, moving closer to the water, and gently sniffed, a bit unsure. And then, its tail started swaying through the air gently.

More ripples appeared, over and over, and at the center of those ripples, some brown curls started appearing at the surface. Slowly, a woman emerged from the water, gasping for air, her pink lips shivering. The Black Dragon jumped into the water, throwing its surroundings into chaos as it ran to her. She welcomed it with open arms as soon as it arrived.

"There, there...You missed me, didn't you?"

The Black Dragon growled softly, rubbing its head against her beautiful white skin. She smiled, feeling her heart warming up again as she brushed against its warm scales. She found the dragon's favorite spot underneath its jaw and scratched it. The dragon growled softly, almost like a cat would purr.

"I missed you too... I missed you all."

The Black Dragon kept growling happily and stayed right by her side as she slowly stepped out of the Lake. If it had any colors before, her dress had now lost them all and turned a beautiful white, with all the pink beads shining like little diamonds under the moonlight. With her pale skin and thin body, she almost looked like a ghost, albeit a beautiful one, coming out of the water. Leaning on the Black Dragon for support, she stepped barefoot onto the grass and looked around.

"Everything is so quiet. I wonder how long it has been..."

Even though it couldn't answer, she smiled at the dragon as if it had. It was rubbing its head continuously against her, completely overjoyed, moving and more alive than it had been in months. She chuckled.

"Alright, alright... Shall we go now?"

The dragon growled softly, and she easily climbed up on its back. Krai barely waited until she was properly seated to take off. She felt the familiar thrill in her stomach as they got higher in the sky. It was a clear night, so clear she could see all the streets below. It ought to be late for everything to be so quiet in the Capital.

The time to observe the City was limited though. The dragon was in a hurry and flew high and fast through the sky. The beautiful woman on its back took a deep breath in. She didn't feel the cold anymore, she just felt the fresh air filling her lungs, making her shudder. It was so nice to be able to breathe again. She closed her eyes, letting her senses overtake her. It felt amazing to be able to come back to this. She could feel the wind dancing on her skin and blowing her curls gently.

She didn't even realize how long the trip really was. When Krai started descending, she just smiled happily. She recognized the lonely Shadelands so easily. Few things had changed - a few more trees sprouting and the snow was fresh. Was it winter here already? She could only imagine so. It felt strange to witness this all from above.

Just like the Palace, everything was quiet here under the darkness of night. Even as the Black Dragon gently landed in the snow, nothing else moved. Yet, her heartbeat was going crazy from anticipation. She wanted to run upstairs, to rush to them. Yet, she was feeling a bit shy as she got down from the dragon. Cassandra gently caressed Krai's scales, thanking the dragon silently. The Black Dragon had always been the first to come to her. Krai was reluctant to part from her, but it just growled softly when she walked inside.

It felt like she hadn't been here in years, but everything was just as she remembered. Slowly walking up the stairs, Cassandra slid her fingertips against the cold black stone of the Onyx Castle. She liked this place, so lonely, just a quiet little corner of the world. She felt her heart flutter with delight as she took one step after another.

Suddenly, as she reached another floor, something silver jumped into her arms.

"Kian!"

The little dragon was growling softly, and completely snuggling against her, rolling its long body around her neck and shoulders, rubbing its head against her chin. Cassandra smiled, caressing it as she kept walking. Kian had grown so big already! The young dragon probably had no idea but it was twice the size of what she remembered, and was quite heavy on her shoulders. Cassandra petted it while she kept going. She could hear the giggles now, and sure enough, she found him in the little room.

Her face lit up as her eyes found the little boy standing in his bed, his little hands holding on to the rail and smiling wildly at her. Kassian was giggling and jumping, absolutely excited. Cassandra felt her heart fill upon seeing her son's face again. He had grown so much already! She felt a couple of tears run down her cheeks as she ran to him.

"Oh, my baby...Kassian..."

The baby was excited to see her and kept hopping until she finally got a hold of him. Kian jumped down, leaving her some space to take her son into her arms. Cassandra couldn't believe it. He was already able to stand up, and smile, and even grab her hair in his tiny fingers. He was so small the last time she had seen him. Kassian hadn't forgotten her though, or maybe his dragon's instincts were kicking in. He snuggled into his mother's arms, happily holding on to her. Cassandra was happy to see him looking so well. He was already starting to take on some of his father's features, and some of hers too. He had dark brown hair, but his green eyes were the same as hers. She liked his smell too. Her baby's smell. She hugged him for a very long time, kissing his little face until he squealed from being tickled that way.

"Da... dadaaa..."

"It's Mama, love. Your Mama is back."

"Mama..." repeated Kassian, looking at her curls in his hands with a cute frown that mimicked his father's.

"Your dad took good care of you, didn't he?" She smiled.

"Dada!" exclaimed Kassian.

"That's right, Kassian, your dad..."

Cassandra smiled, but she could see her son was tired. It was the middle of the night after all, and he was too young to be up this late. Kian had probably woken him up as he felt her arrival, but now, the little Silver Dragon was curled up on one end of the toddler's bed, and Kassian was struggling to keep his eyes open, too. She kissed his forehead and put him back down as he started to fall asleep. Her heart couldn't bear to part with him so soon, so she stayed a little while longer to watch him sleep. He did look like a happy boy. She felt relieved. He wasn't too old yet, and had grown beautifully so far. Cassandra glanced around. His bedroom wasn't too big, and it was filled with toys of all kinds. He had a little castle and a big dragon plushie. Cassandra smiled, recognizing the little one in his bed. That forgotten treasure she had clumsily stitched back into shape a long time ago... So this old thing had really made its way to him.

After a while, she just couldn't bear it anymore. She turned to leave the room, letting Kassian sleep and following her heart elsewhere. The few steps to the next bedroom were enough to have her heart racing again. She stayed a second on the doorstep. The door had been removed, surely so he could be closer to Kassian...Cassandra's heart started burning.

The retired War God was sleeping there, alone in the large bed and half-naked, his face tilted towards the window. Seeing Kairen again left her breathless. He was frowning slightly, even in his sleep, as if he was having a bad dream. She wanted to run to him, and yet, some strange shyness was keeping her from it. Cassandra's heart was on the verge of bursting, almost pouring out. It was too much. To see him again, after all this time.

She stepped forward, so nervous she felt dizzy. She wanted to run to him, but her legs suddenly felt heavy. Cassandra walked slowly instead, surprised he wasn't waking up. Or was it because it was her?

"Don't."

Cassandra froze. His eyes were still closed, but he had very clearly spoken, making her heart skip a beat. She opened her lips a bit, unsure of what to say.

"Don't torment me again. Not tonight."

Cassandra's expression relaxed a little. She stepped forward with a little smile on her lips.

"I said, please..."

Her smile grew wider as she reached the bed, her heart so full it might explode. She extended her fingers, gently touching his hand. She saw him flinch, but he finally opened his eyes. The darkness there made her shiver. He glanced at her and frowned.

"You look different tonight," he whispered.

"Do I?" she gently answered.

He frowned again and kept his eyes on her as she came closer. It was like he was observing a dangerous, wild beast; he was almost... scared. Cassandra slid her fingers up his arm until she reached his biceps, and then moved down to his exposed torso. His warm skin... She had missed it and wanted to touch it more. She climbed on the bed, coming over him, and noticed his confused expression. She could see it in his eyes. He was scrutinizing her, a little wrinkle forming between his brows.

She couldn't even express how much she loved this man. How much she had missed him. How much she wanted him... As Kairen remained frozen with a confused expression, she slowly brought one leg over, straddling his waist, and put both her hands on his chest. She could tell he was afraid to trust this vision. His black eyes were fixated on her, looking at the young woman as if she was some illusion.

Cassandra gently leaned over to kiss him. It was a very soft kiss on his lips, but it sent shivers down the depths of his being. He gasped and suddenly sat up, grabbing her face between his hands. His eyes were wide open, completely shocked, his breathing intense. It took a full minute for him to realize, to accept it. It really was her. She was real this time. None of his nightmares or dreams had been able to replicate her face so perfectly, so beautifully, even down to her imperfections. The color of her green eyes, the curves of her lips, the delicacy of her nose.

Just then, she broke down crying. Cassandra couldn't hold it in anymore. She put her hands on his neck too, her tears rolling down her cheeks uncontrollably.

"I missed you..." she cried. "I really missed you..."

Before she could add another word, he suddenly kissed her, taking all of her in. It was a desperate, savage kiss that they both needed. She felt the warmth spread inside like a wildfire, driving her crazy. All of her being was invaded by this hurricane of desire. They had been apart for too long. If this was another treacherous dream, it was the most realistic one he'd had so far, and he was not ready to let it go.

He wanted her, to carve his being into her, to touch and taste her body. They kissed desperately, so eager their lips couldn't bear to part for a second. They just wanted each other, their other halves. It was a reaction that nothing else could provoke but a wild, carnal desire. Something as old as time itself, buried in their flesh.

His hands were wandering all over her, touching and grabbing every inch of Cassandra's skin as if to keep her there, to make every second of it reality. Kairen couldn't understand, but he wanted this. He was like a mad man begging for a dream to last forever. He couldn't stop. Cassandra was just as eager as him. His warmth - that warmth that came from his core was driving her insane. She felt sensations she hadn't felt in a very long time. When he put his hands on her legs, under her skirt, she shivered with desire. Her hands were all over him, caressing his torso, his neck, his back, all of his hot skin. She wanted him.

They didn't have time for anything else, their desire was burning like a hot flame and erasing all restraint. He took off his pants in a matter of seconds and ripped the piece of clothing that was separating them, and after some other clumsy moves, their bodies reunited in one movement.

Cassandra cried out under the brutal invasion. She felt him filling her, completing her in a wave of pleasure. She bit her lower lip, but it only made him want to kiss those lips more. They exchanged a long, gentle kiss. Kairen wanted to lose himself in the taste of her lips. It was gentle, yet a bit savage. They just couldn't express their love and desire enough. He started moving, making her breathe louder. They had their eyes locked on each other, completely lost in the moment, as if they were alone in the world. His movements made her moan and cry for more. The sensations waking up in her were stronger than she had remembered, and he wasn't slowing down to let her catch up.

The War God just couldn't get enough of her. He kept pounding, not stopping, not slowing down. He just wanted all of her. He had craved that skin, that gentle taste, the sound of her voice in his ear, echoing in the room. He needed to make sure she was real, that she was really there with him. He had his arms wrapped around her, keeping her close. Grabbing every inch of her skin that he could, feeling her, confirming this was real. Kairen was so desperate as he kept moving inside her, almost crying at how good it was to have her there. Cassandra kissed his eyes, his tears, repeatedly running her fingers through his hair. Their bodies moving together so perfectly was causing things to burn up, fast and hard. They just needed this, this beastly passion between them. They couldn't hold it in anymore. After just a few minutes, he thrusted with a few wild movements, making her jump and cry out for him. Cassandra couldn't restrain her voice, the pleasure was breaking down walls and making her lose control. All her extremities were burning, sweating from the intensity. She cried out in pleasure when he finished inside her, exhausted.

They were both left panting in the same position they had started in. It had probably been their wildest and shortest love-making ever. She chuckled, still trembling a bit from the pleasure, and came to kiss him gently. He willingly responded to everything her lips desired, caressing her skin restlessly. The previously cold room had gotten very hot in a very short time, their heat melting them together.

As he kept caressing her skin, he finally figured out what had been bothering him from earlier. Cassandra's skin was perfectly white and smooth, not an ounce of imperfection, not even the tiniest scar. He frowned, confused by this new revelation, and raised his eyes towards her once again.

"How?" he whispered, caressing her hair without stopping.

Cassandra smiled gently.

"The Water God," she simply said. "I guess he wanted to save his last daughter... before he passed on."

Kairen let out a long sigh, and buried his face in her neck, closing his eyes and breathing deeply. Whoever he had to thank for this miracle, he was grateful to no end. He didn't care to know how or why. He could only imagine why the Creature had decided to take Cassandra away from him, from their world. But eventually, he sent her back again... That was all he needed to know.

Cassandra felt a bit sad. She still didn't know why the Water God had decided to trade its life for hers... No one could tell what such a magnificent Creature was thinking at a time like that. She took a deep breath and kissed her man again. She changed positions to get off and lie against him. Kairen was unwilling to let go and tightly wrapped her in his arms. She liked being trapped in his embrace.

"It's good to be alive," she whispered. "I'm glad Kassian is fine... Did you decide to raise him here alone?"

He nodded. Cassandra smiled. She would have all the time in the world to catch up with what she had missed... With her sister too. She hoped Missandra was happy. Lady Kareen and Shareen, too. She wondered what they were up to now. Who had taken the Golden Throne? Opheus or Anour? Kairen obviously had no intention of sitting there... For now, she was just happy to be away from all those questions. It was like they were hiding in a private little corner of the world. She chuckled.

"What is it?"

"I think... I'll get to live my dream after all."

The memory of a conversation they had many months ago slowly came back to him. He nodded.

"We'll do it all. Everything you wanted... Change it all."

"What about you?" she asked gently. "You never told me what dream you had in mind."

The War God smiled.

"It's fine. Mine has already come true anyway."

Cassandra was about to ask what it was, but she decided it didn't really matter. This happiness was enough. She was in a good place right now, a place where she was safe and happy... Where she could be free.

In the Onyx Castle, lost in the forgotten lands, the two of them fell asleep, side by side.

The silent War God, and the slave girl who had changed his world. He was born to kill. She was destined to die. As two worlds collided, destiny had changed.

Epilogue

The Last Day of the White Moon Festival.

The streets of the Capital were crowded with people from all over the country, as they all gathered to the festival to celebrate. For the Dragon Empire, the White Moon Festival was one of the biggest celebrations of the year, the one that was held to take their freedom and happiness to the streets. Every citizen in the Country waited for that day to throw off their status, and have fun among the common citizen. Those who weren't as carefree found tactics to pretend to be, just for a day.

Warriors without their shiny armors, Officials walking like common folks in the streets, women showing off their beauty and even children of any household running down the streets laughing. If one had any trouble, they were to forget it that night, for freedom was everything in the Dragon Empire.

It wasn't an old tradition. The Dragon Empire was one that had risen from the ashes of the past and turned each defeat into a lesson. Not so long ago, slavery and poverty had filled those streets. Now, what once was a cold and frightening slave market had been replaced by a joyful large market. A larger one where anyone could buy flowers, potions, fresh products, and wonders from further east. The children running between the stalls had no idea the clatter of chains once filled this place instead of laughter.

The years had passed, and life had gone on. A new Empress had taken the golden throne, bringing a new Era and a lot of changes with her. Those who hadn't complied had regretted it, and those who did follow her lead had found themselves in a lucky sight.

The young girl wandered in the streets, hopping from one stall to another, checking their merchandise, and buying some snacks to eat on her way. After a couple of streets, she had two chicken skewers in her hand, and one little bag full of jujubes.

She kept walking and humming, her long ponytail of brown curls swinging behind her. The bystanders sometimes stared at her, confused by her strange attire and appearance. She had honey skin, and big emerald eyes, and a slender but toned body. Her clothes were a bit strange. She had a mix of purple and green fabrics, with simple embroideries, and her only jewelry was the little anklet that tinkled at each of her steps. Not only was her outfit very strange and completely oblivious of the usual rankings, that girl even daringly wore the Imperial purple!

People were totally confused. Was she supposed to be treated like an Imperial Family member? She was going around barefoot! She only had one piece of jewelry and some wildflowers in her hair... That girl was truly too strange.

"She's there! Catch her!"

As soon as she heard that, the girl ran and hid under one of the stalls, right after turning a corner. However, to her surprise, she wasn't the one the children were chasing after. Another girl, about her age, ran past her, looking panicked. The young girl with honey skin grabbed her and pulled her into her little hiding spot.

"Who are..."

"Hush!"

The girl, dressed in brown, frowned but nodded. They both stayed hidden, listening to the little crowd running past them, confused. The children yelled and began spreading in the nearby streets.

"I think they are gone..."

"Who are you? And why did you hide too?" Asked the dark-haired girl, frowning.

"My name is Kiera. I thought I was the one being chased after! I ran from home. And you?"

"I'm Lorey, and... they think I stole something..."

"Did you?"

"Of course not!"

The girl with the food chuckled and handed her one of her chicken skewers.

"Here. You look hungry."

"Oh... Thanks..."

The two girls chuckled and ate their chicken, hiding there for a while. That little snack was indeed enough to start a friendship, at least if one had an empty stomach. They whispered to talk but were smiling too.

"Are they your siblings?" Asked Kiera.

"No... I mean, sort off. They are other children working in the same house as me..."

"Oh. For me, it's always my siblings who are chasing me around."

"Do you have a lot of siblings?" Asked Lorey, curious.

"So many! I have three sisters and three brothers. And my mom is pregnant again!"

"Wow..."

"I know right? My dad is crazy about our mom. Our house is so crowded with everyone! That's why I ran, it's funnier to play here!"

Lorey nodded. Most families with a lot of children had to live together in tiny houses, it could easily feel cramped. Kiera probably had to share everything with her siblings, too...

"So? What do you want to do?" Asked Kiera, raising her thin eyebrows.

Lorey was about to say anything, but just then, her stomach growled loudly. Kiera laughed.

"Let's buy more food!"

"I don't have any money..." Sighed Lorey.

"It's fine, I have plenty!"

"...Are you sure?"

Kiera nodded, and grabbed her hand to take her out of their little hiding place. For a long while, both girls went from stall to stall, buying the food they found yummy, and running or hiding again when the other kids chased them. At some point though, Kiera pulled her to another hiding, frowning.

"So annoying! Are you sure you didn't steal anything? They are really persistent."

"I really didn't! They just like to pick on me the most..."

Kiera sighed.

"Well, they are not going to stop so easily, then. Come on, let's just go where they won't find us!"

Lorey thought her newfound friend was full of surprises. Kiera grabbed her hand, and the two girls quickly left the market, getting into the hot streets of the Capital. It was full summer, and the heat was scorching unless one found some shadow to hide from the sunlight. Kiera seemed fine, though. Despite her paler skin, the young girl was barely sweating a bit, while Lorey was thirsty in minutes.

Moreover, she was taking the direction to the Palace, making her frown.

"Where are you going?"

"To a place, we can have fun!"

Lorey didn't dare ask, but Kiera was indeed headed straight to the Palace. The strange girl was indeed full of surprises, but Lorey was intrigued to see what else she had in store. They entered the Palace just like that. It was a first for Lorey. She knew they had decided to open the doors to the Palace a few years ago, so anyone could come and go as they wanted, but Kiera was headed deeper inside the Palace, to the area restricted to the Imperial Family.

At some point, she couldn't take it anymore and grabbed her sleeve.

"Kiera, we shouldn't be here. We will get scolded by the guards..."

"Don't worry, my aunty is working here, they won't care!"

Was her aunt one of the servants here? Or one of those new scholars, perhaps? Now that the new system was allowing women to take the higher education test, more and more ladies were entering the Palace as new scholars, with the Empress' support...

Kiera suddenly smiled wide and grabbed her hand to pull her.

"Here! Let's play in the Lake!"

Under Lorey's shocked eyes, Kiera ran to jump into the water. In seconds, the young girls were completely soaked and laughing. She looked a bit crazy, playing by herself in the middle of that lake, but Lorey was terribly tempted to join her.

"Come on!" Kiera encouraged her.

Lorey took a look around, but no one was there to stop them. After a hesitation, she ran to get into the lake too. It was probably the craziest thing she had done in her life, to simply jump into a lake in the middle of the Imperial Palace to play! Kiera was ecstatic with her friend joining her, and the two girls played for a while in the water. Although, Kiera was going further into the water.

"Don't go too far, Kiera," said Lorey. "You'll drown."

"I know how to swim!" Said her friend.

Once again, Lorey was surprised. It was so rare to know how to swim! There were few places to swim in the Capital anyway, but she knew most of the children living in Cities near the river learned how to swim... Did that mean Kiera wasn't from the Capital? She looked like she perfectly knew it, though.

Lorey was about to ask, when something touched her ankle, making her yelp. She looked down into the water and saw something shiny swim away in a swift movement.

"What is it?" Asked Kiera, who was a few steps away.

"Something touched my leg, like a big fish..."

Kiera's face lightened up immediately, and she started looking around in the water, a malicious smile on her lips.

"Something like a fish, huh... Which color was it?"

"I don't know... perhaps grey..."

"Ha... Gotcha!"

She suddenly dived, making Lorey panic a bit. Where had she gone to! For a while, her friend had completely disappeared from the surface, and despite her fear, Lorey took a few steps forward to try and see her.

"...Who are you?"

Lorey froze and turned around, embarrassed to death.

A tall and beautiful man in a blue robe was looking at her. Lorey gasped. He had the outfit of scholars, but he was wearing a lot of jewelry, and his long hair wasn't very orderly for someone working there... He had his arms crossed and was looking at her, a bit surprised but not angry.

"I... I am sorry, I..."

Before she could think of a proper excuse, Kiera suddenly emerged, a bit further away from where she had dived. Not only that, but her friend was obviously playing with some large creature. Lorey's jaw dropped. That wasn't a fish, but a dragon! A proper, grey-scaled dragon! The beautiful creature was wrapping its body around the girl's playing around with her and trying to escape her grip. Kiera was laughing so loudly and so focused on catching it that she didn't realize who else was there.

"So it's you, Kiera," sighed the man.

"Oh, hi uncle!"

"You little stray cat, did you ditch your brothers again to come to play here?"

"Yup!"

To Lorey's surprise, Kiera's uncle smiled, looking a bit proud.

"What about your grandma?"

"They are all at the Diamond Palace at the moment because mom is about to have another baby, it's boring..."

"So that's why you came all the way here to play. Your brother is going to scold you."

Kiera answered with a wry smile.

"He can't scold me if he can't find me!"

Her uncle laughed.

"True. But if I were you, I'd at least great her Highness, or she'll kick you out once your brother comes here."

Kiera nodded, and just with that, her uncle left. Lorey had a lot of questions, but Kiera was still playing with the young dragon, and she didn't dare ask any. After a while though, her friend noticed her confusion.

"Oh, sorry. Come on, Kiki!"

The grey dragon turned its head towards her friend, and finally, ended her little fight with Kiera. Kiki swam swiftly into the water, and Lorey couldn't help but feel a bit scared as she saw the long, snake-like body come towards here. Kiki was as big as her thigh, and probably twice her arm's length too. However, the dragon gently swam around her, until Lorey relaxed a little. She extended her hand, and Kiki swam past her fingers to get caressed.

"It's so smooth..." She couldn't help but whisper.

"Right? My Kiki is so pretty!"

"You're... part of the imperial family?" Lorey finally asked.

"Yep. I only come here to play, though! My aunt is the one doing all the hard work. My dad says he's retired now!"

"I know! And so, your mom is the Lady of the Mountain?"

Kara was the one surprised, for once.

"You even know about my mom?"

"Of course! I want to be a healer, just like her! I like to go to the market to see the new medicines they bring! I'm learning to read so I can read all of her medicinal guides, too!"

Kiera pouted.

"You sound just like my big sister, she's always obsessed with books! But it's fine if you want to do it! Me, I want to be a warrior like my dad!"

Lorey chuckled.

"You mean a soldier! There are no more wars now, the Eastern Empire is an ally and your father defeated the Northern Barbarians..."

"I'll do what I'll do!" Protested Kiera. "I want to see the world with Kiki, beat the bandits in the mountains or whoever is stirring some trouble..."

"You can come with me, then! I'll tour the isolated villages to heal them!"

The two girls kept talking about their plans, excited and playing around in the water with the young dragon with them. They didn't realize a woman was watching them, her shoulder against one of the pillars. She had a little smile on and was drinking a glass of wine. A woman that looked like her was standing a few steps behind, watching them too.

"Those kids... Do you think they like to come here annoy me, or is it that their parents are worried I'll be lonely and bored otherwise?"

"It's nice to see them grow up," whispered the other lady. "They look happy... Aren't we going to say hi?"

"You can go if you want. I probably need to go back to work before Evin throws a fit."

"That's because you always start working last minute..."

"I need my alcohol to get the work done, and he just won't let me drink. When are those two coming back, anyway? My stock is going to go empty!"

"Lady Missandra said she was working on a new alcohol for the summer, she should come by soon."

"If only those two would stop flirting around and get married right here. We have an empty Palace and all they think about is their ridiculous little shop downtown!"

Her half-sister chuckled behind her.

"Aren't you the one who emptied it in the first place..."

"I got rid of the useless ones, not them! ...As if I was going to keep feeding all those annoying mouths! Nah, we are better off without all those leeches. Come on, Mera, let's find another bottle before he comes back."

"You'll get really drunk so early anyway, aren't you?"

The Empress laughed it off, and the two of them went to find the kitchens, ignoring the poor Counselor who would complain later on.

It was just another long, long day of the sun going down in the Dragon Empire. Two girls playing in a lake under the sun, with a dragon, laughter, and lots of promises to come.

A brighter future to come.

The Dragon Empire Saga continues in

The
White King's
Favorite

Bio

Jenny Fox is a French author, born in Paris in 1994.

She reads alone for the first time at 6 years old, Harry Potter and the Philosopher Stone, and writes her very first story at 9 years old. Her teacher reads it in front of the whole class, and from then on, she will never stop writing, from short stories to fanfiction.

In the winter of 2019, while living in Boston, US and confined home by a snowstorm, she starts publishing online novels in English and finds an unexpected success and a fast growing readership. His Blue Moon Princess is her first story to be entirely written in English, inspired by her experience overseas and her love for Fantasy Novels.

Reassured by her first successes and hoping to improve as an exophonic writer, she keeps writing daily until her story The War God's Favorite becomes a new online Best Seller.

Now living in London, UK, Jenny continues to write with the daily support of her readers, self-proclaimed "Foxies".

Follow her at @AuthorJennyFox on her Facebook Page

Novels by Jenny Fox

THE SILVER CITY SERIES
His Blue Moon Princess

His Sunshine Baby

His Blazing Witch

*

THE DRAGON EMPIRE SAGA
The War God's Favorite

The White King's Favorite

*

STAND-ALONE STORIES
Lady Dhampir

The Songbird's Love

A Love Cookie

*

THE FLOWER ROMANCE SERIES
The Fairy & The Thug

The Nymph & the Chef

The Vampire & The Secretary

The Demon & The Student

The Angel & The Soldier

Printed in Great Britain
by Amazon

81562260R10369